THE TONDEAU OF CHARTRES

THE TONDEAU OF CHARTRES

Glen Petrie

ISBN 0 333 31134 5

First published 1981 by
MACMILLAN LONDON LIMITED
*4 Little Essex Street London WC2R 3LF
and Basingstoke
Associated Companies in Delhi, Dublin,
Hong Kong, Johannesburg, Lagos, Melbourne,
New York, Singapore and Tokyo*

Computer assisted phototypesetting by
ELANDERS LIMITED
Corby, Northants NN17 1PB

Printed in Great Britain by
ST EDMUNDSBURY PRESS
Bury St Edmunds, Suffolk

For Pat

Der welcher wandert diese Strasse voll Beschwerden,
wird rein durch Feuer, Wasser, Luft und Erden;
wenn er des Todes Schrecken uberwinden kann,
schwingt er sich aus der Erde himmelan,
Erleuchtet . . .

(He who travels this path with burdens,
is purified by fire, water, air and earth;
if he but conquers the fear of death,
he will ascend from earth to Heaven,
enlightened . . .)

The Magic Flute – act II, sc. 8

PROLOGUE – December 29, 1939.

Bishop Joachim was afraid. He glanced across the room to where Burgomaster Prumers was sitting.

Herr Prumers was quite still, apparently concentrating on the music. His broad hindquarters were buried in the cushions of his chair, his steel-rimmed spectacles were slightly askew on his thick nose, and the wet tip of his cigar pointed at the tiny, scarlet-ringed swastika button which gleamed from his lapel like a beady little eye.

It was impossible to read the expression on his face.

Petra, Bishop Joachim's sixteen-year-old daughter, was accompanying herself on the piano.

'*Ich mich im Krieg auf grüne Haid* . . . ', she sang. 'I must to the wars, to the green meadows . . . '

Behind the raised lid of the piano, through the broad picture-window, the forest trees gleamed in the false twilight of heavy snow. The snow was still falling.

It had been a miscalculation, the Bishop realised, to invite the Burgomaster on the same evening as his old friend Professor Krieck. There had been some nonsense about Frau Krieck befriending a Jewish shopkeeper's wife a little time ago. The Bishop had hoped that by bringing Professor Krieck and the Burgomaster together, the Professor would be restored to favour in certain quarters.

Too late, he realised that he was more likely to have brought about his own fall from grace. Fortunately, the dinner-party had been saved from immediate disaster by the presence of Dieter, Bishop Joachim's only son, who had returned home on leave early that morning from his squadron, posted on the Luxemburg frontier. In the presence of a young war-hero, Burgomaster Prumers was disposed to suppress his dissatisfaction at Professor Krieck's appearance at the table. Instead, he had been fulsome in his attention to Dieter. He had asked him for his opinion as to a spring offensive on the Western Front. He had smiled archly at him, and had tapped his nose with his forefinger.

'Aha!' he had said. 'But we must not tell what we know, eh, Herr Rittmeister!'

He had continued,

'The French are afraid to fight this time. That is why they sulked inside their Maginot Line like schoolgirls, while our brave lads . . .' he nodded to Dieter, 'were winning their spurs – or should I say, their Knight's Crosses? . . . '

He tittered.

' . . . in Poland. The will of the French is sapped by Bolshevism and Rothschild usury,' he concluded.

Bishop Joachim saw an opportunity to draw Professor Krieck into the discussion.

'You paid a visit to France only last June, didn't you, Gerhard?' he asked.

Professor Krieck glanced nervously across the table at the Burgomaster. The poor fellow had grown paunchy over the past few months, not from good-living, but from enforced idleness.

'I'm engaged in a study of the Prince de Turenne's campaign in the Low Countries in 1672,' he explained hurriedly. 'Battles fought long ago. A hobby merely. Quite harmless.'

He smiled wanly at Dieter, as if he expected the boy to understand.

'I did visit one place of interest, actually,' he continued. 'Of great interest. Not, of course, to military men. But to a historian and antiquarian like myself.'

Burgomaster Prumers grunted, and sat back in his chair.

'It was a place near Rethel, in the Aisne valley,' Professor Krieck continued. 'The Château de la Berlière. Turenne had had it built as a hunting-lodge. Or as an advanced military headquarters. Today it is deep inside metropolitan France, but in the seventeenth century it looked across the border into the Spanish Netherlands.

'Perhaps one of our own commanders,' suggested Bishop Joachim, 'will soon have the opportunity to use it once more as an advanced headquarters!'

There was laughter round the table. Even Herr Prumers managed to smile.

'The present owner of the château was extremely courteous,' said Professor Krieck. 'He showed me the points of interest around the place. But it was in the chapel – in the oldest part of the château – that I made my most exciting discovery.'

He glanced at the Burgomaster. Bishop Joachim noticed that Herr Prumers' face was clouding with anger. Dieter, who was sitting at the table beside Herr Prumers, and was unable to see the expression on the Burgomaster's face, urged Professor Krieck to continue.

Professor Krieck shook his head.

'It is of interest only to antiquarians,' he demurred.

'Oh do go on, Herr Doktor Professor!' Petra protested.

'*Liebchen!*' her mother chided her.

'It was standing in a niche, just beside the altar,' said Professor Krieck, looking straight at Petra. 'In a kind of monstrance. A silver medallion, about a hand-span in diameter. A tondo – a solid silver rondel with the figures on it beaten out of the silver. I could hardly believe my eyes! You see, I had only seen it before in a picture: a full-size portrait of the Duc d'Enghien, the victor of Rocroi. He was wearing that same medallion on a ribbon round his neck. And if it is what I believe it to be, then it must be the medallion known as the Tondeau of Chartres: the medallion worn on the breastplates of all

8

the Constables of France – the commanders of the French feudal hosts – since the reign of St. Louis in the thirteenth century. Now, we know that the last Constable of France to have worn it on campaign was the Prince de Turenne. There is no further record of it after his death; it has been assumed that, like so many *objets* in France, it was melted down at the time of the Revolution to finance the Revolutionary Wars.'

'And this was Turenne's house?' Dieter had asked.

Professor Krieck had nodded.

'One of them,' he had replied.

'And is the present owner of this château a descendant of the great Turenne?' Bishop Joachim had asked.

'The present owner's grandfather bought it from an elderly unmarried lady who was descended directly from the Prince de Turenne,' Professor Krieck had replied. 'According to the present owner, the medallion had been acquired with the house.'

'Did you ask the owner whether this was indeed the medallion – the Tondeau of Chartres?' Bishop Joachim had inquired.

'I asked regarding its antiquity,' Professor Krieck had replied. 'He said that the villagers of La Berlière venerate it as a holy relic of St Louis, and have done as far back as anybody can tell.'

'It is all speculation!' the Burgomaster had suddenly snapped.

Everybody had been taken by surprise at the vehemence of his anger.

'That is what academics do!' Herr Prumers had exclaimed. 'While others fight, or labour for the Fatherland, they sit and speculate!'

His cheeks had turned quite red, Bishop Joachim had noticed. Before an embarrassed silence descended round the table like the snow descending outside, the Bishop had managed to introduce a new and anodyne topic of conversation.

There was a clatter of crockery behind the semi-circle of seats. Bishop Joachim glanced quickly across to Maddelena, his wife. She rose instantly. Krystina, the Teschen-Czech maid, had brought in the coffee things; she was standing there stupidly, just outside the circle of lamplight, clutching the tray into the lap of her apron. She was an unintelligent creature who had managed to pick up no more than a handful of German phrases in the seven months since she had been sent to the Bishop's house. Maddelena went and stood beside her in the hope that her proximity would prevent the child from making any more noise until Petra had finished her song.

Petra was touching the keys so gently that, had it not been for the snow-enclosed stillness of the room, the notes would scarcely have been heard.

'*All wo dort die schönen trompeten blasen* ... ' she sang in her untrained treble. 'There, where the shining trumpets are blowing, there waits my home, under the green turf.'

The simple accompaniment died away. At first, nobody moved. It was not until Petra herself closed the lid of the keyboard gently that Herr Prumers stuck the end of his cigar in his mouth, and clapped his pudgy hands.

'Bravo!' he called noisily.

Relieved, the others joined in the applause.

'A charming German song,' Herr Prumers announced, 'sung by a most charming German maiden, eh?'

Petra rose and curtsied slightly. She turned and took the music from the piano and placed it in the stool. Then she sat down again, facing the others.

'Such a sad song!' her mother sighed.

The maid, Krystina, brought the coffee-tray to the table in front of the settee, and put it down, rattling the cups noisily as she did so.

'I'm not sure it was at all suitable, *liebchen*,' Maddelena told Petra. 'There's enough sadness in the world!'

She shooed Krystina away as if she were a farmer's wife shooing away a goose which had strayed into the wrong field. She squatted at the table and began pouring the coffee.

'Sadness in a song, *Frau Bischof*,' Professor Krieck assured her, 'is like the snow outside. One's sense of comfort, one's enjoyment of such excellent hospitality, is positively enhanced by it.'

Maddelena stared at him, wide-eyed and uncomprehending.

'Do you truly think so, *Herr Doktor Professor*?' she asked.

Bishop Joachim took a cup of coffee to Herr Prumers.

'The snow makes everything so peaceful,' he said, 'it is hard to remember that we are at war.'

Herr Prumers reached over and patted Dieter's shoulder.

'Thanks to our brave German lads like the Rittmeister here, we have had a peaceful Christmas,' he said. 'But it will be very different in the spring, eh? Presents from Paris, or London, next year – what do you say, Rittmeister von Leonarte?'

Dieter smiled, but moved slightly so that the Burgomaster had to remove his hand.

'Families should always be together at Christmas,' said Maddelena.

Herr Prumers nodded: 'That is so,' he agreed, as if uttering some profound truth.

Petra was smirking at Dieter, as if sharing some childish secret with him.

'I don't think Dieter was broken-hearted at having to stay with his squadron over Christmas,' she said.

Dieter grinned.

'He was presented to Olga Tschechowa,' Bishop Joachim explained quickly. 'Fräulein Tschechowa visited the north-west sector of the front over Christmas.'

'Aha!' Herr Prumers laughed roguishly.

He waved his cigar at Dieter.

'A beautiful woman, Olga Tschechowa,' he said. 'You must see her latest film – *Befreite Hände*. I saw it a fortnight ago, on my last visit to Berlin. It had opened only a few nights before. It has important things to say about our German art.'

He looked across at Petra who had resumed a demure expression, sitting on the piano-stool with her hands folded in the lap of her dirndl apron.

'It is about a sculptor,' he continued, 'and, of course, the woman he loves. It is about how love and art can find true fulfilment only in a nation which understands its own heart.'

He sucked at his cigar end.

'You would enjoy it, Fräulein von Leonarte,' he said. 'The heart of a maiden like yourself would respond to its message, I'm sure!'

Petra smiled sweetly.

'Olga Tschechowa threw up when she saw Dieter,' she said.

'Petra!' Dieter pretended to be indignant.

'Petra!' Maddelena exclaimed. 'What will the *Herr Burgermeister* think!'

'It is true that Fräulein Tschechowa was sick,' said Dieter. 'It was when she was climbing down from the plane to the landing-strip. There was Colonel Hassler, and Major Thiele – that's our regimental adjutant. And myself. But it was Anton who saved the day,' he said to his father.

'Anton Kirst is a particular friend of Dieter's,' Bishop Joachim explained.

'I don't suppose Fräulein Tschehowa is used to flying in a military Junkers 52. You smell the oil in those things,' Dieter went on. 'And then the freezing weather when she stepped out. When Anton realized what was happening, he shouted to the honour-guard to about face. We all turned our backs to the plane – even Colonel Hassler – until Fräulein Tschechowa could recover her composure.'

'And did Fräulein Tschechowa recover her composure?' asked Herr Prumers.

'Completely,' said Dieter. 'When we'd all turned about once more, she insisted on inspecting the honour-guard. She held onto Colonel Hassler's arm. But she looked as beautiful in her furs as she did in *Der Choral von Leuthen* – a real snow-queen. And we all pretended that nothing whatever had happened.'

'That is the true German way,' said Professor Krieck.

He had been sitting watching the snow through the window.

Bishop Joachim was appalled. 'It would be difficult to imagine the French carrying off a situation of that sort,' he said hastily.

Fortunately, Herr Prumers laughed loudly.

'Or the Poles, eh?' he asked. 'Faced about! That is good! I'll remember that!'

He leaned forward and stubbed out his cigar in the ash-tray.

11

'It is hard to tear oneself away when the *Frau Bischof* makes her guests so comfortable,' he said. 'And on such a night! But duty, you know? Duty!'

He pulled himself out of the chair.

'I must be in my office by first thing tomorrow,' he said.

When they reached the front door, and the Burgomaster had put on his coat and galoshes, they found that his chauffeur had already brought round his car, and was standing by the rear door, a travelling rug folded over his arm.

'Poor man,' sighed Maddelena. 'He must be frozen!'

'Perhaps we should send him somewhere where he can get warmer!' Herr Prumers suggested jovially. 'Like the Western Front, eh, Herr Rittmeister?'

Dieter managed to smile, Bishop Joachim was pleased to note.

'You'll have a cluster of oak leaves to add to your Knight's Cross by next autumn, I daresay,' Herr Prumers added.

'You have to be colonel of a regiment at least,' replied Dieter, 'before you can be awarded a Knight's Cross with Oak Leaves.'

'Promotion comes quickly in battle,' Herr Prumers told him. 'There were colonels no older than yourself in the last war.'

He did not appear to notice the effect his words had on Maddelena.

'You have no children, Professor Krieck?' he called to where the Professor was standing framed in the doorway of the music-room.

'No, alas,' Professor Krieck replied.

'A pity,' said Herr Prumers. 'The *Frau Doktor Professor* might have had more to busy herself with at home if she had had children to bring up for the Fatherland!'

He smiled again, and bowed over Maddelena's hand. As he stepped down onto the snow-covered path, he turned once again and raised his arm.

'*Heil Hitler!*' he called.

Bishop Joachim half-raised his arm in reply. As the Burgomaster's car glided forward through the snow, and the headlights splashed onto the snow-flecked trunks of the trees, he stepped inside, and closed the front doors against the cold.

'Our duty is done for the winter season at least,' he said.

He felt an enormous sense of relief, which he could scarcely hide. He went and put his arm about Professor Krieck's shoulders.

'I should not have inflicted that on you, dear friend,' he said. 'Another cigar? Another glass of schnapps – to show that you forgive my clumsiness?'

Professor Krieck hesitated. Then he nodded.

Dieter excused himself on the grounds that he had had a very long day. Petra retired with her mother to the kitchen.

'Do you know?' said Professor Krieck, as he settled back on the settee. 'I told the editor of the *Nord-Deutsch Historische Blatter* about my find. About the medallion. He told me to write a piece about it for his paper. I wrote the piece exactly as he had specified. It was returned to me a fortnight after I had sent it, with a formal rejection slip – the editor regrets etc.'

'Perhaps it was due to the paper shortage,' Bishop Joachim suggested. 'Our own humble little parish magazines are desperately short of paper.'

'I went to the editor's office, in Lubeck,' said Professor Krieck. 'The editor is an acquaintance of long standing. He was most embarrassed to see me, I can tell you! But he was good enough to take me out to a restaurant for a meal – a quiet place along the shore, where we would not be noticed.'

He paused long enough to light the fresh cigar which Bishop Joachim had given him. He drew on it several times, then examined the tip.

'He told me that he had received instructions via the Gauleiter's Office, here, in Kessim, that no contribution of mine was to be printed. You see? They will never forgive me for my poor Ute's warm-hearted foolishness.'

'And that was why the *Herr Burgermeister* was so displeased by the mention of the medallion over dinner,' said Bishop Joachim.

'I would not have pursued the matter if the children had not seemed interested,' said Professor Krieck. Then, in a slightly querulous tone of voice, he added, 'There is nothing so frustrating as being prevented from making important findings known! It is so unjust!'

Bishop Joachim poured a couple of brandies. He handed a glass to Professor Krieck, then sat down on the settee beside him.

'This medallion, you say, was worn by the Constables of France? It was their special insignia?' he asked.

'From the reign of St Louis,' Professor Krieck confirmed.

'But the owner of the château could not be sure?' asked Bishop Joachim.

'The Baron de Bart-Mendel is Jewish,' replied Professor Krieck. 'I did not dare tell you that in the presence of our honoured Burgomaster.'

Bishop Joachim nodded sympathetically.

'The present Baron's grandfather was Daniel de Bart-Mendel,' said Professor Krieck, 'a prosperous Lyons banker. He was clever enough to lend a considerable sum at a low interest rate to the Bonapartist cause when the future Napoleon III was plain Monsieur Louis Bonaparte. The baronage, and the Château de la Berlière, were his reward. I don't suppose the de Bart-Mendels give a rap for the significance of the Tondeau of Chartres: they placed it in the chapel to please their Roman Catholic peasants.'

For a short while, they sat side by side, smoking their cigars.

'But you, old friend,' said Bishop Joachim, at length, 'you are in no doubt as to its authenticity.'

'None whatever,' Professor Krieck replied. 'The figures on the medallion in the portrait of the Duc d'Enghien are precisely the same as those on the medallion itself. They are quite remarkable. So extraordinarily long – attenuated. They match perfectly the figures of the apostles carved on the west porch of Chartres Cathedral – as if the same master craftsman had designed both. There can be no question of the medallion's authenticity.'

'I know somebody who would be very interested in your discovery,' Bishop Joachim said quietly.

Professor Krieck turned to stare at him. It was as if he hardly dared to speak.

'Who could let me publish . . . ?' he asked.

'Perhaps,' said Bishop Joachim. 'He is a man of some influence in the right quarters. And I am sure he would be most interested to hear from you.'

'Tell me!' said Professor Krieck.

'His name is Alfred Reuther. He is Petra's godfather, so he is a good friend of ours. At present, he is with the *Heerenarchiv*, attached to the Ministry of National Enlightenment – he holds the rank of colonel. His particular concern is to research into and to collect detailed information about art treasures and historic objects belonging to our enemies, and to recommend ways in which they might be put to use – under certain circumstances – in our German cause.'

Professor Krieck stared down at the half-inch of ash on the end of his cigar. Bishop Joachim knew what he was thinking. He put his hand on his friend's sleeve.

'Your discovery will be made known, Gerhard. I'm sure you can see why my friend would consider the insignia of the Constables of France to be important! And you will have demonstrated your loyalty to the Reich quietly, and without ostentation, as becomes a man of learning.'

Professor Krieck nodded.

'Colonel Reuther has the ear of the Reichsminister of National Enlightment,' added Bishop Joachim.

'It would be like the end of a nightmare!' agreed Professor Krieck.

Bishop Joachim thought that his friend was on the edge of tears.

'I shall give you Colonel Reuther's address,' he said. 'And I shall write to him myself, tomorrow.'

'God bless you!' whispered Professor Krieck.

As the Professor's dog-cart creaked through the snow, down the forest path under the white-laden branches, Bishop Joachim watched, disregarding the cold in order to wave a final, encouraging goodnight. He fingered his small pectoral cross as the dog-cart disappeared into the winter stillness. *Heilige Nacht*, he thought, *Stille Nacht*. And he gave thanks to God for having granted him the opportunity and the courage to assist Gerhard Krieck.

Part One: **MONTCORNET**

1

'Darling Ambrose,' Julie began writing. Then she wrote on the opposite side of the sheet, where the address should be, 'Somewhere in France'. She liked that.

On the stage beyond the tarpaulin back-cloth – a platform of trestle tables set up at the open end of the marquee in which Julie and the other members of the concert party were sitting – Vic Walters was singing his opening number with its insistent chorus about how we shall always be friends, 'says the English tommy to the French *poilu*'.

A midge crawled up Julie's arm. She brushed it off before it could crawl under the puffed sleeve of her costume. It fell onto the writing-paper in her lap. The paper was pink and deckle-edged. She had borrowed it from Elaine who was standing beside her. Ambrose would certainly disapprove of it.

There was laughter and applause from the other side of the tarpaulin. Vic Walters had concluded his song. As the applause subsided, his familiar catch-phrase rang out, 'It's all right, mum! I've left me tricycle in the back yard!'

Julie heard the thump of his feet as he crossed the stage. Even without stooping, she noticed that the metal legs of several of the tables forming the platform were sinking into the soft ground.

It would be her turn next. Hers, and Elaine's, and the veteran of Sir Herbert Beerbohm Tree's company who played their mother. She had begun to feel nervous; had begun to mouth the opening line of the playlet about the Scarlet Pimpernel which they were about to perform. She got up and put the writing-paper down on the stool. Elaine was stubbing her cigarette out on the sole of her shoe. The smell of cigarette smoke and trampled grass under canvas recalled to Julie's mind vicarage garden fêtes and agricultural shows at home in Cumberland. And the scented heat inside the marquee was oppressive even though it was only the second week in May.

Vic Walters was leading the audience in singing, 'We're gonna hang out our washing on the Siegfried Line'. Everybody sitting in the field outside was bawling at the top of his voice. Julie followed Elaine and the veteran actress up the steps to wait behind the tarpaulin back-cloth. The tables sank slightly beneath them.

Amidst thunderous applause, Vic Walters came in through the canvas flap. His eyes were glistening.

'Wonderful, those lads!' he said. 'Best in the world!'

He brushed his cheek with his fingers, and went out to receive his second ovation.

Elaine beckoned to Julie. There was a tear in the tarpaulin through which she had been looking. Julie stooped to put her eye to it. Below the improvised platform there was a row of folding chairs. On them were sitting the Commanding Officer, the Adjutant, a dozen other officers and four or five army nursing sisters. All around the row of chairs was a sea of sallow faces, Brylcreemed heads, and limp forage-caps pushed under khaki shoulder-flaps. All were applauding enthusiastically. All save one: a single officer in perfectly tailored riding breeches and jacket, his kepi bearing the four embroidered silver rings of a major in a French cavalry regiment, sat beside the adjutant. He was staring into the sky above the top of the marquee, his features composed into a mask of boredom.

Vic Walters came off again. The audience quietened down. Elaine and the old actress went on. Julie counted five slowly, and followed them through the flap onto the sunlit stage.

'Oh, *maman*!' she began.

Her mouth was as dry as chalk.

She stepped forward toward the mass of upturned faces. The level of the platform had sunk some six inches. She stumbled, managed to regain her balance, but caught her toe in the hem of her costume, ripping the skirt away from the bodice and exposing the peach-coloured silk of her drawers. There was a burst of applause.

'Oh, *maman*!' she repeated through the uproar. 'Is there no news yet from the Conciergerie?'

She dared not put her hand to the gaping hole at her hip. Instead, she clamped her arm against it as Elaine replied, 'Something may still be done ... ', a sentiment which inspired vociferous agreement from some quarters of the audience.

The barracking was good-humoured, however, and the audience anxious to be entertained. The play continued with Julie holding her arm clamped to her side, moving as stiffly as a female Quasimodo. Below the platform the French officer sat with eyes staring, his mouth open in astonishment, as he realised that what he was watching purported to be an episode from his nation's history. There was a steady obligato of clicking cigarette lighters and the scrape of matches. An occasional aircraft droned above, drowning the voices.

At last the moment came for Julie's big speech. The audience was listening intently, and Julie was beginning to enjoy herself, when she saw a figure ploughing his way between the first and second ranks of the audience. He was wearing a crash-helmet, and had a leather jerkin over his battle-dress; he had pulled his goggles down onto his neck, and his face was flecked with oil. As he approached the Commanding Officer, he pulled off his heavy leather gauntlets and slipped them under his arm. Every member of the audience turned his head to watch the man's progress. Julie continued her speech with an ever-increasing sense of futility.

The Commanding Officer and the Adjutant turned in their seats to face the newcomer, who saluted smartly and drew a long envelope from his belt. The Commanding Officer took it, tore it open, and began to read the contents. His face became grim and set. He showed the document to the Adjutant. The other officers leaned forward. As Julie recited her lines, she heard the murmur of voices below the stage as the Commanding Officer held a brief, *sotto voce* conference with his staff.

The Commanding Officer took a note-pad and pencil stub from the Adjutant and scribbled something down. He tore off the page and handed it to the dispatch-rider. The dispatch-rider slipped the note into his belt, jerked up his arm in a parade-ground salute, and ploughed his way back through the expectant audience. There was a ripple of excitement through the ranks, but the Commanding Officer and the Adjutant pointedly turned their attention to the stage, folded their arms and crossed their legs, and appeared to be listening to Julie's words with whole-hearted concentration. For all that, Julie knew that she was battling into a fog of polite inattention.

The applause at the end, however, was gratifying. Julie and Elaine took their bows to a cacophony of wolf-whistling. Julie clutched the ragged edge of her skirt against her hip as she went off through the canvas flap.

'What's up?' she whispered to Elaine who was immediately in front. 'I thought we were going to die the death!'

The actors stood round the foot of the steps as the concert party's operatic duo went out and sang 'Only a Rose' and 'You are My Heart's Delight'. When they were finished, Vic Walters twitched his boater to a rakish angle, and went up for his final appearance. The audience welcomed him with genuine enthusiasm. A few minutes later, he returned to beckon the entire company onto the stage for the final call. They trooped up into the sunlight. Vic Walters stepped out in front of the single rank and held up his hands for silence.

'Thanks a lot, lads . . . '

He paused, and glanced down at the nursing sisters in their khaki uniforms.

' . . . and lasses. Mustn't forget the lasses, eh?'

There were shouts and whistles of approval. Vic Walters cleared his throat and the audience became still.

'You've been marvellous!' he told them. 'Best in the world!'

He paused a second time. With a throb of emotion he said,

'God bless each and every one of you!'

Julie saw that the Commanding Officer and the Adjutant were mounting the stage from the front. A stentorian voice stilled the applause by bawling out,

'Ba . . . ttalion!'

Rank upon rank of men scrambled to their feet on the grass slope overlooking the stage. The Commanding Officer and the Adjutant took their places at the edge of the platform. The Commanding Officer stood with his feet slightly apart, his swagger stick held in both hands as if it were a riding-crop.

'Battalion!' shouted the voice from below the stage. 'Battalion attention! . . . Stand at . . . ease!'

'Stand easy, men,' the Commanding Officer said quietly.

The ranks in front of him relaxed visibly.

'My first duty,' the Commanding Officer began, 'is to say "thank you" to these very talented ladies and gentlemen who have provided us with such a pleasant afternoon's entertainment. We've all heard jokes about ENSA – some of us have invented some, I daresay. But the E in ENSA stands for Entertainment . . . '

He turned to the performers.

' . . . And it's Entertainment with a capital E we have enjoyed this afternoon, Mr Walters – or may I call you Vic? – from you and your friends.'

Vic Walters smiled his diffident smile. He had many other smiles, but this was the one appropriate to the occasion. The Commanding Officer turned to face the front once more.

'My second duty is a weightier one, I'm afraid,' he announced. 'At the same time, it is one which should inspire us all. The weeks and months of waiting are over. You've probably heard by now, most of you, that the balloon's gone up at last. Jerry's decided that Britain, France, and Norway aren't enough enemies for him, so he's attacked Belgium and Holland!'

He paused to let the scattered laughter die.

'We're going to show him that this time he really has bitten off more than he can chew. We've been waiting to have a go at him for too long already! Well, men, I can tell you, because Jerry's going to find out for himself soon enough. I have received orders from General Brooke himself: we are to move up into Belgium tonight, to take up positions along the Dyle River in support of the Belgian army . . . I have replied to General Brooke on your behalf. I've told him that the lads of the 2nd Rutlands and the 1st Fenland Light Infantry can't wait for a chance to give Adolf a bloody nose!'

Julie gathered up her pen and writing-paper, then followed Elaine out of the marquee. Quite suddenly she and her colleagues had become irrelevant. The stage was already being broken up into trestle tables, and men in their shirtsleeves were loosening the guy-ropes of the marquee. A line of Bedford lorries, their canopies leafy with tagged camouflage netting, was drawn up along the track where the concert party's charabanc and small Peugeot props-and-costume van were parked. Men were unfastening and dropping the tail-boards. As

20

Julie hurried across the cinder-covered parade ground, the air rang with shouted commands, while groups of the erstwhile audience scattered at the double in various directions.

A subaltern came strolling out from the lines of huts to meet the small knot of artistes, as Julie was trying to catch up with them. He was wearing brassards on either arm with the letters RTO on them, and he was carrying a business-like clipboard. He spoke to Elaine.

Elaine waited for Julie to catch up with them.

'He says we'll have to stay here tonight,' she said. 'He says all the roads are to be kept free for troops moving up into Belgium.'

'Does he know we're supposed to be giving a show again tonight?' Julie asked.

She pushed forward to speak to the subaltern.

'We're supposed to be giving a show for British troops in the town hall at Bapaume,' she said.

'He knows that, darling,' said Vic Walters, putting her in her place.

The subaltern looked like a rather young public school prefect. He was sweating in the afternoon heat, under the peak of his cap.

'Actually,' he said, 'if you managed to get to Bapaume in time, I don't think you'd find much of an audience. They'll all be as busy as we are, down there . . . Anyway, Colonel Maitland has suggested you should take over our quarters for tonight. We won't be using them – we'll be moving out in stages throughout the next twelve hours . . . And it really would be advisable to keep off the roads for a bit.'

'I'll ring the Paris office first thing tomorrow,' the concert party road-manager told Vic Walters.

He was a weary-looking, failed comedian.

'That'll be best, eh?' he added.

The others murmured their indecisive agreement. As they straggled down the alley between the rows of huts, there were wolf-whistles from the open windows despite the air of preoccupied bustle. Julie could not help recalling an occasion some twelve years earlier. She had been invited to a children's party. She had been certain that it was not a fancy dress party; but her mother had been as certain that it was. Her mother had insisted that she should go as Alice in Wonderland – in those days, Julie had long, beautiful hair. When she had arrived at the party everybody had assured her that it did not matter a bit because she looked so pretty, and the costume suited her so well.

After dinner in the officers' mess, Vic Walters sat down at the piano in the lounge and began strumming the old favourites: 'Just a Song at Twilight', 'Roses are Blooming in Picardy' and 'Red Sails in the Sunset'. The remaining officers were grouped around the piano, singing or humming quietly, even thoughtfully, and drinking. Some of them were already wearing their web-belts and revolver holsters. The members of the concert party were scattered amongst them.

21

Elaine was standing at the curtained window with a glass of Scotch in her hand, and the arm of a subaltern round her waist. Julie was sharing a battered armchair with the captain in the Rutlands who had entertained her at dinner, and whose name she hadn't caught. He had his hand on her thigh, and was stroking the button of her suspender as if it were a surrogate nipple.

The man on whose knee she would like to have sat was standing by the stove. He had arrived just before dinner. The room which she was sharing with Elaine overlooked the officers' car park, and she had seen him get out of his small four-seater Morris. She had remarked on him immediately, not only because of the empty sleeve pinned Nelson-like to his jacket, but also because of the smart jacket, Sam Browne belt and riding-breeches he was wearing instead of battle-dress. She had recognised from her father's Great War decorations the ribbon of the Military Cross on his breast.

He had been introduced to her at the mess bar – Major Hardwicke, Tank Corps, now serving on Lord Gort's staff. He had looked at her with a sort of amusement, as if secretly he had already known her. He had said merely that he was sorry to have missed the show, and hoped that Hitler would not succeed in disrupting their tour altogether. The weathered crows-feet about his eyes made him look older than his years.

He was standing only a few yards from the armchair, talking to Major Rawlings, senior officer present in the mess.

'So what's happening to you now, Hardwicke?' Major Rawlings was asking.

'Gort is sending twelve of us to liaise with the key units of French Army Group One.' He smiled. 'I gather the old man's staff have christened us the Twelve Apostles – you know? "Behold I send you forth as sheep in the midst of wolves"? . . . At any rate, Nigel Milnes and I have been winkled out of the flesh-pots of GQG Vincennes. You know Milnes don't you, Rawlings – 17/21 Lancers? Well, he's off to Sedan or thereabouts to attach himself to Papa Gransard's Xth Corps. And I'm off to Laon to find the 4th Armoured Division.'

'Is there a 4th Armoured Division operational yet?' asked Rawlings. 'I've heard of three Frog Armoured Divisions. I thought the 4th was still on the drawing-board.'

'It's got a CO,' Major Hardwicke replied. 'A colonel suitably named de Gaulle. Whether it's got men and vehicles, I've yet to discover. No doubt I shall have done so by tomorrow morning.'

'But you're permanently detached from GQG Vincennes, are you, Hardwicke?' asked Major Rawlings.

'Absolutely,' Major Hardwicke agreed.

'Vincennes?' asked a lieutenant in the Fenland Light Infantry. 'Isn't that where they shot Mata Hari?'

'You'd better be careful, Miss Armitage,' said the captain on whose knee Julie was sitting. 'Vincennes is a grim sort of place, they say. Like the Bloody Tower, only much worse.'

'It's a good place to escape from,' Major Hardwicke agreed. 'I said flesh-pots. The food is pretty good at GQG *Forces Terrestres*. And there's wine. But no women, and precious little song. Gamelin has scrapped *le week-end* since the invasion of Norway and Denmark.'

'What?' exclaimed an officer in the Royal Signals. '*Pas de week-end dans l'armée* Frog?'

'You've never seen so many scarlet majors struggling to get out of Base,' Major Hardwicke replied. 'Me included. But it is nice to know that Gamelin means business.'

An orderly in a white jacket came into the lounge. He peered through the fug of tobacco smoke and noise.

'What is it, Deakin?' called Major Rawlings.

'CSM, D Company's outside, sir,' the orderly replied.

'Trevor?' Major Rawlings called over the top of the piano. 'Sounds as if you're off.'

Another major picked up his small pack, to which was strapped his helmet.

'Sar'nt Major Hill says as D Company's ready for inspection, sir,' the orderly told him.

'Very good, Deakin,' the major replied.

He slung his web-belt and service revolver in its holster over his shoulder. Julie wondered whether the revolver was loaded.

'See you somewhere in Belgium, chaps!' he called.

He noticed Elaine standing at the window. He went over to her.

'Move off, old chap,' he told the subaltern who had his arm round her waist. 'Need somebody to say goodbye to, don't I?'

The subaltern released her. From outside came the sound of lorry motors turning over.

'I don't suppose I'll be lucky enough to see *you* anywhere in Belgium,' the major told Elaine.

'Oh, I don't know,' Elaine replied. 'Depends on how long you stay there, I expect. Might even see you in Germany!'

There was a cheer at this. Elaine put down her glass of whisky on the window-ledge. She reached up and put her arms round his neck, and kissed him on the mouth. There was a round of applause. Vic Walters banged out a chord on the piano. An elderly comedienne pushed her way to the window. She was carrying a large glass of port in her hand.

'Here!' she cried. 'What about a goodbye kiss for me, then?'

She put her arms round him. Port slopped on the carpet behind him. There was more applause. Voices shouted 'Good luck, Trev!' as the major finally escaped out of the door.

There was a sudden hush in the room.

The concert party road-manager wandered past Julie's outstretched feet with a pint mug of beer in his hand. He looked as though he felt it was his duty to speak to somebody or to tell a joke – anything to break the silence – but was overwhelmed by the responsibility.

Vic Walters played another chord, this time softly. He began to sing:

'There'll always be an England . . . '

Others joined in, at first almost humming, and then letting their voices rise in crescendo so that the men of D Company assembled outside should hear them:

'And England shall be free,
While England means as much to you
As England means to me . . . '

The sound filled the room, with the baritone of the operatic duo thundering,

'Red, white, and blue,
What does it mean to you? . . . '

And everybody else shouting,

'Marching along,
Singing this song . . . '

But not quite everybody. It was false somehow, Julie felt; as if Vic Walters had contrived the emotion, and had manipulated everybody into it. Her eyes met those of Major Hardwicke. He had not been singing either; and he had noticed that she had not been singing. She would like to have spoken to him if she had had the nerve. Instead, she rested her head on her captain's shoulder.

As the final note of the song ceased, Major Rawlings said to the concert party's manager,

'Heard that your van-driver chappie has been in a spot of trouble over at the cook-house. Doesn't speak much English apparently.'

'Jean-Pierre?' asked the road-manager. 'He was wished on us by the Paris office. Quite unsuitable, of course. I mean, he doesn't fit in exactly. Bit of luck, though – Miss Armitage, here . . . '

He pointed down at Julie.

' . . . speaking the lingo like a native.'

One of the younger officers drinking by the piano laughed loudly, put down his mug and raised hands upwards and rolled his eyes.

'Sandi de wise! Sandi de strong!' he chanted in crude imitation of Paul Robeson in 'Sanders of the River'. 'Hater ob lies, righter ob wrongs!'

He glanced about him.

'Native,' he explained. '"Speaks de lingo lahk a native", eh?'

'That,' said Julie, forestalling the laughter, 'is bloody stupid, if you don't mind me saying so!'

The young man was quite taken aback.

'I'm sorry,' he said. 'I didn't mean anything personal. Anybody can

24

see you aren't a darkie. Its just the way our chum here said you talked like a native.'

'It's a stupid song and a stupid film,' Julie replied vehemently.

'Actually,' said Major Hardwicke, 'I thought Leslie Banks's performance was very convincing. Very much the sort of fellow any young British officer might hope to turn out to be.'

'Hear, hear!' one or two voices agreed.

The very last position Julie wished to be in when holding a conversation with Major Hardwicke was sprawled on the captain's knee. It was just her luck, she thought. But she wasn't going to retreat.

'It makes me mad,' she said. 'The thought of getting a bloody marvellous actor like Mr Robeson and putting him in a grass skirt and all that nonsense!'

'I don't think anybody's suggesting Paul Robeson isn't a good actor,' said Major Rawlings. 'For all I know he might be a very bright sort of chap – particularly for a darkie.'

'You must admit, Miss Armitage,' the young officer rallied, 'darkies are a bit like children. Even the best of them.'

In the face of all the sweet reasonableness, Julie felt put to shame.

'I mean to say,' the young officer persisted. 'If Paul Robeson's the intelligent fellow you say he is, he must know that darkies are like that. That's why he was willing to play that Bosambo chappie.'

Julie was saved by the reappearance of the orderly.

'Who's it for this time, Deakin?' called Major Rawlings.

'Mr Graham, sir. Adjutant asks if Mr Graham will report to his office, if you please, sir.'

'Off you go, Mark,' said Major Rawlings.

The young officer smiled regretfully.

'Yes sir,' he said. 'Sorry, ladies and chaps. Just as it was beginning to get interesting, eh?'

He slung his web-belt and revolver over his shoulder.

'See you all soon, I hope,' he called, picking up his equipment.

There were further shouts of goodbye and good luck. Julie got off the captain's knee.

'Haven't done anything I shouldn't have done, have I?' he asked.

Julie shook her head.

'No dear,' she told him. 'I've got to powder my nose, that's all.'

As she made her way to the door, Elaine tugged at her sleeve.

'Are you all right, darling?' she asked solicitously.

'Right as rain,' Julie told her.

She closed the door behind her. In the narrow little washroom, she opened the window. An endless column of pin-prick lights was moving slowly across the darkened fields, the throb of motors sounding on the cold air. An army was on the move, she thought. She was reminded of 'Gone With The Wind': the young men riding from Tara, off to war; the artillery trains galloping through the streets of Atlanta.

Half an hour later, Elaine found her in their room. She was kneeling on her pillow, staring up through the open window at the starlit sky over the empty car park.

'Made a bloody idiot of myself, didn't I?' said Julie.

Elaine didn't deny it.

'We've all had a spot to drink,' she said.

She stood beside Julie in the darkness.

'Trouble is with you,' she said, 'if you don't mind me saying, is that you ought to get married or something. And I don't mean Ambrose.'

'What makes you say that?' asked Julie.

'You need to find a centre. A sort of centre of gravity or something,' Elaine told her.

'Ambrose is my centre. He's the absolute bloody centre,' said Julie.

She drew the curtains across the window, and got off the bed. Elaine switched on the light.

'You could have fooled me,' said Elaine.

'You don't understand at all,' said Julie.

She undressed in silence and got into bed. After Elaine too had undressed, and had switched the light out, Julie heard the sound of a car motor starting and voices on the car park outside. Major Hardwicke was continuing his journey to Laon. She would probably never meet him again.

All night, the sound of transport columns grinding and rumbling penetrated her dreams and drowsy wakenings. Once she awoke to hear boots crunching the cinders outside, and a voice clearly enunciating across the night air,

'Here! You lad! Who's your best bleeding friend when you meet the enemy, eh? Your bleeding mother, eh? Your bleeding father, eh? No, they bleeding well ain't, lad! It's your bleeding rifle, that's what it is! So carry the fucker properly, eh lad?'

Julie heard Elaine giggling. She giggled back just to establish friendly contact, then snuggled down into the warm bed and fell asleep again. As though borne on the wind from a far distance, she seemed to hear two thousand voices singing,

'Whether the weather it be wet or fine
We'll still march on without a care.
We're gonna hang out our washing on the Siegfried Line,
If the Siegfried Line's still there. . . . '

2

The lines of huts seemed strange and disconcerting when Julie and Elaine got up in the morning. The emptiness and near-silence of the camp was made more eerie by the appearance of a single soldier sweeping and tidying up after the departed regiment. The officers' mess, where they had breakfast, had the smell and tawdriness of a nightclub bar in daytime.

After breakfast, Vic Walters rose to his feet and announced to the company that they would remain where they were until midday. He would then decide whether the tour should continue. He was sure that it would be a great disappointment to them all if it had to be called off. There were a few desultory 'Hear! Hear!'s.

They all carried their suitcases through to the lounge, and sat in the armchairs, adding their cigarette smoke to the smell of last night's beer which hung heavy in the air. Vic Walters took his place in front of the black iron stove. He cleared his throat.

'Of course,' he said for everybody's benefit, 'when you think about it, it's hardly surprising the Hun is on the move. The poor buggers haven't any choice. To start with, there's the Big Blockade. Saw a report in *The Telegraph* just before we left – don't know if any of you read *The Telegraph*. Said most Germans are having to live off sauerkraut and potatoes. Haven't got anything else to eat, because of our brave lads in blue ... And then there's the Siegfried Line. Somebody told me the other day – somebody who's in a position to know, I may say – that the Siegfried Line is unfit to live in. They had to build it in a hurry, do you see, before they dared to invade Poland. It's not like the Maginot Line one bit. In fact you could say ... '

He paused momentarily.

'You could say that it's Jerry-built, eh?'

There was laughter and a few groans. Vic Walters waited for the noise to die away. He looked pleased with himself.

'Seriously though,' he continued. 'It's riddled with damp, and the living conditions in it are absolutely bloody frightful. Thousands of their best troops are having to go sick with rheumatism and lumbago. And they didn't have time to put in proper W.C.s; you can imagine what it must be like, living underground with no proper sanitation, eh? So if Hitler didn't get his men out of the Siegfried Line and give them something to do, he'd have a mutiny on his hands. Or a plague.'

He paused again.

27

'That's my theory, at any rate,' he concluded.

One or two of the company said, 'Yes' or 'That's very interesting'. Others crossed and recrossed their legs.

At noon, after consulting with the road-manager, Vic Walters announced that the tour would continue, at least as far as the RAOC depot at Landrecies. They all picked up their cases and filed out to the charabanc. The small Peugeot van which carried the costume hampers and lights was parked behind it. Its driver, Jean-Pierre, observed the artistes with his habitual cynical smile as they passed him.

Julie had just settled into her seat beside Elaine, and had taken her cigarette-case and lighter from her handbag, when the road-manager came down the aisle.

'Hope you don't mind, darling,' he said to her. 'It's Jean-Pierre, you see ... '

Julie saw that Vic Walters had turned in his seat behind the driver to look at her.

' ... Says he'd like somebody to ride in the van with him. And me and Mr Walters ... well, we thought you were just the person, seeing as how you can chat to him in his own language.' There was a strained look of anxiety on his face. 'Sort of liaison, as you might call it,' he added.

Julie turned to Elaine.

'Come with me, darling?' she asked.

'What?' Elaine laughed. 'In that little van? Where would I sit?'

Julie pulled herself to her feet. She slipped her cigarette back into her case. Vic Walters nodded his approval. As Julie pushed her way to the front of the charabanc, he boomed,

'Good girl! See you in Landrecies, eh?'

As she stepped down with her suitcase, and carried it to the van, she had the absurdly gratifying feeling that she had received an accolade.

Jean-Pierre did not move from his driving-seat, but let Julie load her case into the back for herself, among the costume hampers. She shut the rear doors, and came round and sat beside him.

'*Ça va?*' she asked with a pretence at cheerfulness.

She slammed the door. Like so many Frog cars, the van seemed to be made of tin. The charabanc was moving off. Jean-Pierre became aware of Julie's extended hand. He started the van, then gripped her fingers. His own were rough-surfaced and damp.

'*Pas mal,*' he said, answering her question at last.

He set off up the cinder-track in the wake of the charabanc.

The road ran straight as a ribbon across the shining landscape. The metal of the van was hot to the touch, and the sloping bonnet and windscreen were coated with the white dust thrown up by the charabanc. On either side, the fields rolled away in gentle folds of lush

28

green; the winter, the hardest in living memory, had been followed by an unexpectedly warm spring.

Jean-Pierre displayed no desire to make conversation. For this, Julie was grateful. As they drove on through the quivering afternoon heat, she dabbed at her forehead with a handkerchief which still smelt of last night's perfume, and composed letters to Ambrose.

Her mother and father had found out about Ambrose only a few weeks ago. She had gone home for a week before rehearsals had begun for the concert party. She had realised from her father's behaviour on the first night that something was up. He had been curiously awkward in her company, as if he had not known exactly what to say. The following evening, her mother had come to her room while she was changing for dinner, and had handed her the letter she had received from Julie's older cousin, Virginia. It ran, more or less, 'I know it isn't any of my business really, but Julie is still rather young, so I thought I ought to pass on to you something which has been worrying me ever since I was told about it . . . '

Julie read the letter through from beginning to end. She rather wished that some act of God would suddenly occur, or failing Him, Hitler – Gleaston Fell, nearby, bursting into volcanic eruption, or some stray bombs falling on the village of Matterdale down the road.

Her mother took back the letter, tore it up and threw it into the fire.

'Your cousin Ginny never did have much sense of humour,' she said.

How, Julie wondered, do you tell somebody that her daughter is living in sin with a middle-aged man, and make it sound humorous?

Her mother had continued,

'I've no doubt she really believes she was acting for the best. People like Ginny always do.'

She had paused.

'I'm sure you love him,' she had told Julie. 'I know you wouldn't enter into a relationship with somebody you didn't love.'

That had been the worst bit, Julie had felt.

'You'd better put something on, darling,' her mother had concluded briskly. 'You'll catch cold. And so will dinner if we don't go down very soon.'

Julie had wished her mother had put her arms round her to kiss and comfort her. She had felt dreadfully shaken, and very close to tears. But her mother was undemonstrative, even at the best of times.

The charabanc stopped in Cambrai, in a narrow side street off the Place Aristide Briand. Jean-Pierre parked the van behind it. The houses were high-gabled and ancient, tilting forward to overhang the pavements. There was a litter of refuse from the market at the end of the street: broken boxes, dry straw, and packing-cases. Water ran freely down the gutters, spilling over onto the cobbles.

The concert party moved in small groups of two or three out into the market place under the shadow of the great Flemish bell-tower. They filtered like tourists into the noisy crowd thronging between the stalls.

'Din-dins,' said Elaine, taking Julie's arm.

Jean-Pierre had disappeared into a dirty-looking café.

'All right, was it?' asked Elaine. 'I mean, your virtue was safe, was it?'

'Don't be horrid!' Julie replied as they pushed their way through to a stall where cheese was being sold.

On their return, Julie left Elaine with the others, climbing into the charabanc. As she got back into the van, clutching bread, cheese and a bottle of wine to her bosom, Jean-Pierre emerged from the café, and shook hands with a couple of men with whom he had been drinking. He sat down beside Julie.

'Are we going to Paris now, mademoiselle?' he asked.

Julie was taken by surprise. Because of the language barrier, nobody had told him their intended destination.

'We're going to Landrecies,' she replied.

His face turned more than ordinarily sullen.

'Why didn't you say so before?' he muttered.

Julie pretended not to have heard. Jean-Pierre started the van as if he would have preferred to have disembowelled it. He waited for the charabanc to move off. On the other side of the narrow street, a woman was watching from the shadow of a hotel doorway. Her face was relaxed into a careworn weariness under the make-up – it looked older than the blonde hair, which fell loose to her hips, would have led you to expect. Her arms were painfully thin.

They followed the charabanc out into the square. When they had left Cambrai behind, and were driving along the white ribbon of road across the green haze of the landscape, Julie broke off pieces of bread and cheese, and ate them. Jean-Pierre refused the bread, but drank from the wine bottle, putting it skilfully to his mouth while keeping one hand on the wheel.

The heat, and the food and the wine, sent Julie to sleep for a short time. When she awoke, she found that Jean-Pierre was slowing down at a cross-roads in the square of a small town. In front of them, between them and the charabanc, was a herd of cyclists who were stopping and dismounting. The charabanc was on the far side of the cross-roads, and was drawing away. She was about to tell Jean-Pierre to go on after it, when she noticed the French army motorcyclists. There were three of them. They had parked their machines on the

30

pavement, and were standing on the road, holding up the traffic. She saw the white cross-straps on the khaki jackets, and the white gloves. Evidently they were some sort of military police. Behind them, the charabanc was disappearing up a street on the far side of the square.

A column of ambulances began to cross the square, nose to tail, escorted by several more motorcyclists. They seemed enormous to Julie: like cattle-trucks, except for the huge Red Cross rondels painted onto their olive-green canopies. And still they came, more and more of them.

'Are they going up into Belgium, do you think?' Julie asked Jean-Pierre.

Jean-Pierre shrugged. He picked the twisted stub of Caporal from off his lower lip.

'They're coming away from Belgium,' he said.

He sat back in his seat, and sighed noisily as if at her stupidity.

'It's obvious,' he said. 'There's been a battle.'

He thrust a nicotine-stained thumb in the direction the ambulances were taking.

'They're carrying the wounded to Paris,' he said pointedly.

The last of the ambulances crossed the square. The army motorcyclists mounted their machines and wheeled them onto the road. They slammed their heels down onto their kick-starters, and roared off down the road after the ambulances.

As they drove out of the town, Jean-Pierre put on speed in an attempt to catch up with the charabanc. They took the first turning off to the north since Jean-Pierre seemed certain that Landrecies lay to the north of the road along which they had been travelling. Julie felt tired as well as anxious. The road was bumpy, and the springs of the passenger seat were broken. The wine and the heat of the day had made her thirsty, but she dared not ask Jean-Pierre to stop.

Afternoon was turning to evening. The air became cooler, and Julie pulled her cardigan over her shoulders. The landscape too was changing, the green, undulating hills becoming steep chalk escarpments fringed with brambles and heavy undergrowth. They stopped at last at a roadside café which had a petrol pump. They filled up with petrol, and water for the radiator, and Julie retired to the unsavoury little washroom where she managed at least to splash cold water over her hands, face and neck. She went through into the bar, bought a bottle of lemonade for herself, two enormous veal sandwiches, and a bottle of red wine for Jean-Pierre.

As they drove on, the light was beginning to fail and the sunlight to filter very low through the trees. And still they had not caught up with the charabanc. They had travelled some nine or ten kilometres up the road, when Julie saw it. It was drawn up onto the grass verge. There were figures clustered about the radiator.

31

'Look!' she exclaimed in relief to Jean-Pierre.

But Jean-Pierre had already seen. He began to pull up, though they were still some distance away.

'What are you doing?' Julie demanded.

Then she noticed that the roof-rack of the charabanc was empty, and that the people gathered around the radiator and bonnet were in khaki jackets and breeches, and were wearing the forage-caps and helmets of the French army.

'It must have been requisitioned,' she suggested.

Several of the soldiers had turned to look at the van. Even in the failing light, Julie was able to catch an impression of sagging, grit-lined faces, and bright, sunken eyes staring straight into hers. One of the soldiers held up his hand. He started shouting, and running towards the van, followed by one or two others.

'Deserters!' said Jean-Pierre.

He threw the gear-lever into reverse. More of the soldiers began to run towards them. He swung the van about, hitting the rear doors against the grass verge so violently that Julie was thrown forward off her seat. She clutched at the rim of the dashboard locker, and was thrown back into her seat as Jean-Pierre accelerated up the road in the direction from which they had come.

For a moment, Julie sat catching her breath. Jean-Pierre took a crumpled packet of Caporals from his pocket, extracted one and lit it, all with one hand, and without slackening speed. Julie lit one of her own cigarettes.

'Where do you think the others have got to?' she asked.

'Paris perhaps,' Jean-Pierre replied. 'Who knows?'

Julie stared into the darkening hedgerows as they flew past. The van was rattling and shaking as if it would fall to pieces.

'Would they have hurt us?' she asked.

'Who knows?' Jean-Pierre repeated.

He did not want to talk. They drove on, passing through the town where they had first stopped for petrol, and on into the darkness of the countryside. At length, Jean-Pierre pulled over and came to a halt on the gravelled forecourt in front of a plain, two-story, brick building. A dim light over the narrow double doors advertised that it was an *Hôtel de Commerce*, and that its cuisine had won the approval of the *Bureau Social du Pneu Michelin* and of the *Conseil Gastronomique de la Societé Nationale des Routiers*.

'We had better stop for the night, mademoiselle,' said Jean-Pierre. 'Now it's dark.'

There was no need for him to explain further. Tomorrow they would go to Paris, and she would go straight to the ENSA office. The ENSA people would send her back to London, and Ambrose. In the meantime, she was ready to spend what money she had left on the relative comfort and safety of an hotel room.

She got out of the van. The air was cold. She put on her cardigan and her jacket, and buttoned them up. As she went over to the hotel door, Jean-Pierre waited by the van, his cigarette a pin-prick of light in the blackness. There was little sign of life about the establishment; as Julie pulled the bell, she was shivering with cold and nerves. There was no sound from inside. She rang again. Stepping back onto the gravel, she could see chinks of electric light between the window-shutters. She pulled up her jacket-collar about her neck, and, holding it close under her chin against the cold, stepped up to the door. She pulled at the bell several times in succession. This time, footsteps came slapping across the vestibule floor.

'What do you want?' a woman's sharp voice called from behind the locked door.

'Have you any rooms for the night?' Julie called.

'None!' the woman replied.

'None at all, madame?' Julie asked.

'None,' the woman repeated.

'May we eat here?' Julie asked.

The idea had occurred to her that once they were admitted into the hotel, there would be a chance of them staying.

'No,' the woman shouted back.

'Why not?' Julie demanded, hardly able to keep the crossness out of her voice. 'Your sign says you are a hotel!'

'We're not open!' the woman shouted. 'It's the war! You do know there's a war, don't you, mademoiselle?'

'Your sign is lit up!' Julie shouted stubbornly.

'You're not French, mademoiselle!' the woman replied.

'My companion is French!' Julie shouted. 'I'm English!'

'You're both dirty Boches for all I know!' said the woman. 'Parachutists!' she added. '*Allez, mademoiselle! Allez! Allez!*'

Julie heard the slippers on the vestibule floor retreating into the back. She felt inclined to shout after them. Instead, she shivered, and said, 'Fuck!' loudly. As she recrossed the forecourt to where Jean-Pierre was smoking by the van, she repeated, 'Fuck! Fuck! Fuck!' She saw Jean-Pierre smiling behind his pebble-glasses, and realised she had hit on the one English word he knew. She got back into the van, and slammed the door after her. Jean-Pierre got in beside her.

Jean-Pierre suggested that the best thing would be for him to drive on a little way, and turn off the road. They should then spend the night in some hidden spot, with Julie sleeping stretched out in the back of the van, and using what was in the costume baskets to make up a bed, while he sat in the front. He drove on down the road until they came to a track leading off into the blackness of a wood, then turned and followed it, before stopping far enough from the road to ensure that the van was well concealed from it, even in daylight.

Julie got out, and went round to the back. She took a sweater from her suitcase, and put it on over her cardigan. All around, the woods were still except for the occasional scurrying in the undergrowth. She stumbled away into the obscurity of the trees. The thought occurred to her as she crouched in the blackness that Jean-Pierre might drive off and leave her. She tested the fear like somebody who feels the tenderness of a bruise.

When she returned to the van, she said,

'We are on the right road for Paris, aren't we?'

Jean-Pierre had moved from under the wheel, and was sprawling comfortably in the seat which had been hers. He had the thick crusty remains of his veal sandwich in his hand, and the wine bottle between his knees.

'Did you think I would drive you to the Siegfried Line, mademoiselle?' he asked.

She went round and climbed in, closing the doors behind her. Fumbling in the thick, musty darkness, she unbuckled one of the hampers, and arranged the contents into a bed. She lay down, and pulled her mackintosh, which had proved so unnecessary on the tour up till then, over her as a blanket. The costumes provided quite a comfortable mattress, so that her bottom, which ached from the journey, was eased. It would have been pleasant to have changed into clean things, but she did not have the energy. She was beginning to feel warm and drowsy; things didn't seem so bloody awful after all.

As the night progressed, the floor of the van pressed harder through the layer of costumes. She kept stirring as the ache in her hips and arms penetrated through her sleep, and, as she did so, the mackintosh would slip off her. The upper part of her body remained warm, but the draughts which blew in through the cracks in the doors, seeped through her slacks, raising goose-pimples on her thighs. She could hear Jean-Pierre snoring through the partition. Once, he snored so loudly that he woke her up completely. At first, she thought it was already morning; moonlight was streaming in through the rear windows of the van, and the distant sound of traffic on the road filtered through the woods. She thought she heard footsteps cracking through the undergrowth just outside. She held her breath, and heard distinctly and unmistakably the snapping of fallen branches. It occurred to her to wake Jean-Pierre, but, on reflection, she decided that his scorn of her was bad enough already. Despite her fears, she fell asleep again.

She was woken suddenly, her sleep shattered by a rattling and clattering like that of children playing on tin drums. It was daylight. The noise was coming from the rear doors of the van. She sat up. Faces were staring in at her, framed in the small oval windows at the back: grimy, dark-lined faces, with weary, sunken eyes, and unshaven cheeks half buried in greasy khaki collars. The doors were being rattled and wrenched so severely, the whole van was swaying. She scrambled to her knees to look through the partition window. Jean-Pierre was not there; instead, there was a man in khaki greatcoat and flattened forage-cap leaning across the driver's seat inspecting the dashboard. He turned his head to stare at Julie. His face, through the glass, was only a few inches from hers. She drew back quickly and squirmed round.

So this is it, she thought in a sort of calm beneath the panic; it is going to happen, the thing of which one has been most afraid ever since one was first told about such things.

The men were shouting. As they wrenched at the door, Julie could see the slivers of light along the top growing wider and wider with each wrench; any moment and the locks would break. Before she had gone to sleep, she had unfastened her slacks and her brassière. There was no reason why she should make things too easy for her assailants, she decided. She managed to button up the waistband of her slacks, but fumbled in vain with the hooks and eyes against her back. Pulling down her sweater, she crawled over, and unlatched the doors so that they swung open. She scrambled to the ground, blinking in the sunlight.

'*Qu'est-ce que vous faites?*' she demanded, the school-teacher voice masking her terror.

There were five of them, in dirty, ill-fitting military greatcoats, with their packs slung about their shoulders. Two of them were wearing the crested, blue-steel helmets of the French army; none of them was carrying a rifle, though all of them were wearing long, ugly sword-bayonets hanging from their belts. None of them seemed to understand what she had said. They glanced enquiringly from one to another. Nor did they appear to be about to harm her. In fact, they looked so tired they hardly had the energy to stand upright.

One of them, whose helmet had been dented in two places, and who had the frayed chevrons of a sergeant on his sleeve, bowed slightly to her, and saluted. He addressed her as '*mademoiselle*', and spoke to her in an approximation to French of which she could not understand a single word. She looked about her; in the sunlight, the trees and the small clearing in which the van was parked were all new to her. Jean-Pierre was nowhere to be seen. The men pushed past her, and climbed into the back of the van. The sergeant went round to the front, and climbed in. They were all shouting to each other in a language which she did not recognise. She realised at last that they must be Dutch or Flemish.

They threw the hampers and the costumes onto the ground. One of them was about to throw her suitcase away.

'*Non!*' she shouted. '*Non! C'est à moi!*'

The man grinned and handed it to her.

'*Vous n'êtes pas française, mademoiselle?*' he enunciated in a dry, careful accent.

'*Je suis anglaise,*' Julie told him.

'*Les français – mal!*' replied the soldier. '*Les anglais – pas mal!*'

One of his companions pulled Julie's handbag out from the interior of the van, and held it out to her. She had quite forgotten about it. She took it gratefully. The van started to move away down the track towards the road, its doors swinging open. Silence descended over the woods. Julie closed the lid of one of the hampers, and sat on it amidst the litter of eighteenth-century petticoats, gowns and mantles. She took her cigarette case from her handbag. She remembered long ago, looking out of her nursery window at the sloping lawn stretching down to the tennis court, and her nanny standing behind her saying, 'It's no use crying over spilt milk, Juliet dear!' At the time, Julie had never been able to understand why she should not cry if it made her feel better. Now she smoked a cigarette instead.

When she had finished her cigarette, and felt a little less shaken, she picked up the costumes off the ground, folded them, and replaced them in the baskets. Nanny Richards would have approved of her. The sun was warm on her back, so she removed the sweater and cardigan she had been wearing overnight, and put them in her suitcase. Putting on her jacket, she hitched the strap of her handbag over her shoulder, picked up her suitcase, and set off down the tyre-rutted track between the trees to the road.

She consoled herself with the thought that it would be an easy matter, once she was on the highway, to thumb a lift into a town from which she could catch a train to Paris. Two hours later, however, at half-past eight, she was still trudging along the raised verge of the dusty road in the direction they had been travelling the previous evening. Her suitcase had become increasingly heavy; the handle had begun to bite into her fingers, and there was a rim of sweat in her palm and under her breasts. She was wearing sensible brogues, but the balls of her feet were beginning to burn on the stony path.

There was no lack of cars. There had been a steady trickle of them, ever since she had reached the road – prosperous-looking limousines with cabin-trunks and portmanteaux strapped to the boots – all of them travelling in the same direction as herself. On two occasions, she had left her case on the bank and had slithered down to stand on the roadside with her thumb out, hoping that, by offering a better view of herself, at least one driver might be persuaded to stop for her. But almost all the cars were packed tight, with children and old people squeezed into the back seats. They were all intent on making the best speed possible.

On the second of these occasions, she had just managed to scramble back onto the path, when a squadron of large, Panhard armoured cars came grinding up the road in the opposite direction. They forced the cars to pull over. Blue, greasy smoke spilled from their exhausts, billowing from verge to verge. Julie saw the tricolor rondels on the armour-plated slope of the bonnets, and the pet-names painted between the huge rivets on the flanks: *Minette*, *Dalila*, *Princesse*, and *Louisette huit à minuit*. Standing high on the grass verge, Julie was level with the turrets as they roared and clattered past, with the cavalry pennants fluttering from each vehicle, with the black, shining grease on the recoil springs of the cannon, and the two crewmen in khaki overalls, who sat with their legs dangling into the turret-hatches. As each armoured car passed, she saw the faces of the men on the turrets, the mouths under the heavy goggles grinning at her and shouting out to her. She could not make out a word of what was said, above the roar of the motors, but from the cheerful obscenity of the gestures waved to her through the reeking clouds of exhaust, she could imagine the nature of the suggestions being put to her. Instead of being offended as she would have been ordinarily, she felt quite cheered up by them, and smiled and waved back.

She was still standing there, watching the rear of the column disappearing up the road, and the blue exhaust drifting over the grass into extinction, when she became aware that a small, battered Citroën was pulled up at the roadside, a few yards past her. Attached to its rear was an empty, mud-splashed, wooden trailer of the type used by farmers to take sheep or pigs to market. A man was leaning out of the driving-seat window.

'Where are you going, mademoiselle?' he shouted up to her.

Julie grabbed her suitcase, clutched at the shoulder-strap of her bag, and slithered down again into the road. The man was wearing the beret and dirty, blue cotton jacket of a farmer. His face was broad, and deeply lined and creased, and he had the heavy, grey, nicotine-stained moustache made famous by the *grognards* of the old, imperial armies.

Julie ran round to the opposite door.

'I'm on the way to Paris, monsieur,' she told him.

The old farmer smiled, as if the absurdities of his fellow creatures could no longer surprise him.

'I can take you to Marle, if you wish, mademoiselle,' he told her.

Julie had never heard of Marle, but she got in just the same.

'Car broken down?' he asked, as they set off.

'Yes,' she admitted.

'Belgian?' he asked.

'No. English,' she replied.

She explained that she was an actress, and that she had been touring, entertaining the troops; that she would have to report to her headquarters in Paris before she could set out on tour again. The old farmer was pleased with her.

'Ah yes!' he told her. 'I saw you smiling and waving to those young villains just now.'

'They were doing no harm,' Julie replied.

'They're going to war,' the old farmer agreed. 'I'll tell you, mademoiselle – when I saw you standing up there with your suitcase, I said to myself, there's another Belgian soiling herself at the very thought of the Boches. I'd have driven on, I can tell you! Then I saw you smiling and waving to our lads, there. And I remembered what it was like, going up to the line – and a pretty woman catching my eye, and giving me a wave. What a difference it made, eh?'

A large, shining, black Studebaker swung past, overtaking them. Crocodile-skin luggage was strapped on the roof. The old farmer thrust a calloused thumb at the windscreen, in its direction.

'Quelle bêtise!' he continued. 'All this time, they've been telling themselves the Boches won't do the same as before. And now our lads are having to go and help them, just look at them!'

'You were in the Great War, monsieur?' asked Julie. 'Like my father?' she added.

'Four years, mademoiselle,' he replied. 'I was with the old 38th Division at Douaumont – under General de Salins. That was real fighting, mademoiselle!'

His voice was filled with pride and satisfaction.

The market place of the ancient little town was bare and quiet, as they parked and got out of the car. Groups of people in dark suits and dresses were climbing the crumbling grey steps to the west door of a tall, Gothic church which reared its spire into the dazzling sunlight. Julie realised that it was Sunday. She saw the mantillas, and rosaries clutched in women's hands, and the missals which the men held stiffly to their chests. In the quietness, she noticed that everybody going into the cool shadow of the church was either stooped and elderly, or very young.

'Will you take a glass of red with me, mademoiselle?' the old farmer asked.

Julie accepted gratefully. She admitted that she had not eaten breakfast that morning. The farmer led her down a narrow, silent street of tall, steeply-gabled, ancient houses, under the shadow of the church. At the far end, they came out onto a second tree-lined square, crossed at the far end by a road which edged a steep escarpment falling down to a river. Julie was led by the farmer to one of the tables under the trees outside the café. As she sat dunking her brioches in her coffee, she watched the occasional luggage-laden car crossing the end of the square. The old farmer pointed one of them out to the fat patronne who was serving at the table. The patronne shrugged as if it were of no consequence.

'Les flamands,' she said.

Julie then asked her how she might get to Paris.

'Paris!' the woman exclaimed, as if Julie had been asking the way to Timbuktu.

She considered the problem. It became obvious to Julie that Sunday morning was not the time to travel to the capital, not, at any rate, from Marle.

'There's a bus to Montcornet,' the *patronne* said doubtfully. 'If it's running. And certainly there's a bus from Montcornet to Reims – my son-in-law always takes the Reims bus when he goes to Neufchâtel. The Montcornet bus stops on the main road, just round the corner.'

Julie offered to pay the bill, but the old farmer would not let her. As the *patronne* picked up the saucer, she said to Julie,

'There's usually a bus at half-past ten, mademoiselle. But it's war-time again . . . so who knows?'

Julie shook hands with the old farmer, and thanked him with real sincerity; she felt that she was launching herself once more onto an uncharted ocean. Carrying her suitcase, she went round the corner, onto the main road. The bus-stop was a short distance away; there was a seat under the shade of a tree, with its back to the escarpment edge and the river flowing below. She sat down to wait, watching the cars go past, with their Dutch or Belgian registrations. Once or twice, she caught the eye of a child, its face squeezed against a rear window. One little boy stuck out his tongue at her and pressed it against the glass. In the heat and the stillness it seemed as if everybody in the town had gone to Mass.

There was no bus. She waited for an hour or more. Then she began to wonder whether she should return to the café, to ask whether the town of Marle possessed a taxi which might take her to the nearest railway station for Paris. At the same time she wondered whether she could afford a taxi to another town, and the railway fare to Paris, and the taxi fare from the Paris station to the ENSA office, wherever that might be situated. And, all the time, she sat on the seat, with the noonday heat filtering through the leaves, listening to the river splashing against the rocks below, incapable of reaching a decision.

A large Buick sedan came out of the square onto the road. Julie could see two men with frizzy hair and dark suits sitting behind the windscreen. There was no sign of heavy luggage. Feeling like a gambler who decides on one last throw before giving up the game, Julie stood up, and thrust her thumb in the direction the sedan was travelling. To her surprise, the car drove past her, then pulled up against the kerb. One of the frizzy-haired men leaned out from a front seat window, and bawled back at her in a hard, unfamiliar accent,

'*Eh! Dis donc! Là-bas!*'

Julie chose to assume that the rudeness had been unintentional. In any case, she would find out soon enough. With her suitcase banging against her hip, and the shoulder-strap of her bag slipping down her arm, she ran down the pavement to the car. The man leaning out of the window pointed to the rear door. Julie opened it.

'You are in need of some assistance, mademoiselle?' asked a soft, heavily-accented voice.

Julie peered into the gloom of the interior. The spacious rear compartment was curtained off. Even the glass partition set in its lacquered wood, which separated the rear from the front seats, was curtained, all but a few inches, in ruched baize. A man was sprawled against the far corner of the wide, leather-upholstered seat. His milky face and soft cheeks, together with his thick head of yellow-white hair, made it impossible to guess at his age. He was fat, Julie noticed, but his three-piece suit was so tailored that it was slightly too large for him. A large fob hung on a chain from his waistcoat pocket, and there was a heavy red stone on his signet-ring, wider than the plump finger on which he wore it. He was smoking the stub of a cigar, and its smell, together with a sweet scent of eau-de-cologne, seemed to have impregnated the entire interior.

'I'm trying to reach Paris, monsieur,' Julie told him.

'*Tu es anglaise, ma chère?*' he asked.

He patted the leather of the seat beside him. Julie pushed in her suitcase, rested her handbag on top of it, and climbed in. As the car moved off, the man said, in English,

'We are going to Paris, my dear. But not today, alas!'

His eyes took in the shape of her breasts and travelled down to her lap. The inspection was so methodical, that Julie suspected that she was intended to be aware of his interest.

'Tonight,' he continued, 'we shall stay at Rethel ... '

'Will you be going through Montcornet?' Julie asked. 'I know I can get to Paris from Montcornet.'

She noticed that the end of his cigar, between his fat, stubby fingers, shone with damp.

'Montcornet?' he echoed her, vaguely.

Then he pushed himself up, parting his legs to make room for his stomach, leaned over, and knocked at the little glass window in the partition. The driver opened it. In spite of the dark, pin-striped suit and white tie, he had the swarthy, grizzled look of a Mediterranean peasant. Julie's host addressed him in a language unknown to her. The driver spoke rapidly in the same language to his companion.

Julie's host sank back into his seat. The driver closed the small window.

'We shall indeed be passing through Montcornet,' the fat man said. 'All too quickly, I fear, for such attractive company.'

His smooth round face folded into a smile. He reached out his hand for Julie's.

'We have not introduced ourselves, my dear,' he said. 'My name is Papayannis – Chrisostom Papayannis. My English acquaintances call me Mr Chris. But I prefer pretty ladies to call me simply Chris. I am a Greek, naturally. But I come from Alexandria, and so I am a citizen of Egypt. And I live in Paris, where I have my business. I was educated, when I was a boy, at the English School in Alexandria – so I am a Greek who has enjoyed the benefits of an English classical education! What do you say to that, eh? . . . Now it is your turn.'

Her hand rested on the leather surface of the seat, between them. His hand remained covering it.

'My name,' Julie told him, 'is Juliet Armitage.'

'Juliet!' he exclaimed softly.

He gave her hand a squeeze.

'Juliet is a beautiful name!' he told her. '"Romeo and Juliet"! Such a *very* sad story!'

As her eyes became accustomed to the curtained shade, Julie began to notice a certain shabbiness about the interior: the varnish had flaked off the woodwork, and the leather was cracked on the upholstery. And the smell of cologne was so cloying that there was something in it, however faint, which reminded her of the smell of stale vomit. She would have liked to remove her hand from under the man's, but she did not wish to offend him.

The man released her hand of his own accord. He opened a small locker in the woodwork beside him, and took out a box of cigarettes.

'Egyptian,' he said. 'Very good.'

He offered them to her. She shook her head; the smell of cigar and cologne was bad enough without any addition to it.

He replaced the box and reached once more for her hand. This time, she evaded his grasp.

'And what are you doing here, in France?' he asked. 'Not fleeing from the drunken and licentious soldiery? – German, of course!'

Julie explained her predicament as simply as possible.

'You are lucky to be with me, my dear,' the man told her, without a trace of flippancy. 'You see, I am a neutral. Those men . . . '

He pointed to the driver and his companion.

' . . . They are not neutral. One of them is Lebanese. One of them is Tunisian. If they were not employed by me, a neutral, they would be called up – and they wouldn't like that. They wouldn't like that at all. So they do what I say, and they know they are safe from German bullets. And while you are with me, you too are safe, my dear!'

For a moment, he glanced away from her. He tweaked open the curtain and glanced out, so that a narrow ray of sunlight cut across the gloom. He let the curtain fall again.

'I have friends,' he said. 'Important friends. In these times it is good to have important friends.'

It wasn't far to Montcornet, Julie told herself. The way the woman

41

at the café in Marle had spoken about it suggested it wasn't far. Even this dreadful man had suggested that it was only a short distance.

The man reached out once more. This time, Julie felt his hand on her shoulder, his fingers, like a family of thick slugs, creeping under her hair to touch her neck.

'Why don't you travel with me, my dear?' he asked. 'Under my protection, you know.'

'I'm expected in Paris,' she replied. 'When my friends reach Paris, they'll expect to find me there. It's important.'

'Two days?' suggested Papayannis. 'They will be pleased to have two days' holiday, waiting for you in Paris. And I have influence. I can use influence on behalf of you and your friends ... And I shall see that you do not lose by travelling with me, my dear – I can pay in sterling,' he added.

He began to caress the back of her neck. She turned away.

'Please!' she exclaimed.

He dropped his hand.

'You must forgive me, Miss Armitage,' he said. 'I am a very naughty man, aren't I?'

He wagged his finger as if at himself, and giggled.

'But you must admit I am honest,' he continued. 'I do not play tricks. I do not deceive. It is that, in my enthusiasm for pretty ladies, I demonstrate I am common. I apologise for it, my dear.'

He leaned towards her. His breath smelled heavily of cigars. He touched her knee with his fingers.

'Perhaps,' he suggested, 'if I were to tell you that I am a dealer in antiques? If I were to tell you that there are many people selling their most valued *objets* in these dangerous times? If I were to tell you that, if you care to travel with me, my dear, you may come to my place in Paris when we return there, and choose whatever would give you pleasure?'

He waited.

'Please ask your man to stop the car!' Julie told him. 'I want to get out! Now!'

Papayannis twitched open the curtain again.

'We are not yet at Montcornet,' he said.

'I don't care!' Julie replied.

'You are unkind to me, my dear,' said Papayannis. 'If I wanted to harm you, don't you think that I would only have to give the word to those ... '

He pointed to the front of the car.

'Gorillas?' he said.

'Perhaps I just don't like being with you!' said Julie. 'Perhaps I'd rather walk!'

'Very well, my dear,' said Papayannis.

He leaned forward and knocked on the window. He ordered the

driver to stop the car. Julie scrambled out, blinking, into the sunlight. As she dragged her suitcase out after her, Papayannis said,

'Perhaps, my dear, you should think of joining a convent, eh?'

She slammed the door without replying. The Buick had swept away down the long, straight road leaving a hanging trail of dust behind it, before it occurred to her that of all the insults to which she had been subjected, that was the first time she had ever been offered that one. But she was far too frightened to feel in any way amused. She felt as if she had been touched by evil, and should cry 'unclean!' as she stumbled on down the road.

Like Marle, Montcornet was an old, grey market town, but larger and busier. Even so, as Julie limped up the main street to the bus-stops in the centre, she noticed that the people on the pavements were for the most part elderly. She found her way to the pavement-tables of café opposite the *Mairie* and sat down under an awning, where she had a clear view of the bus-stops. Here, at least, there were some young people: a group of adolescents with bicycles, the girls in white blouses, pleated skirts and ankle socks, the boys in diamond-patterned cardigans and plus-fours. They circled about the dusty trees or lounged on their heavy-framed machines, flirting noisily and obviously with one another, and shouting.

Julie watched them, her suitcase beside her, her burning feet propped up on the chair opposite. She was served coffee and a glass of water by a boy so small he seemed almost to have disappeared behind his waiter's apron. Nevertheless, she asked him if he knew whether there would be a bus to Reims that afternoon. At half-past one, he assured her, and with such conviction that she hardly dared believe him. One of the adolescent boys approached her, followed by a pubescent girl. For a short time they tormented her merely by staring at her, and weaving their bicycles round about the tables. The boy halted his bicycle within a few feet of her.

'Are you a refugee?' he demanded.

Julie decided she wouldn't reply until the boy spoke to her more politely.

'Are you Belgian?' the boy demanded. 'Or Dutch?'

The girl giggled.

'I'm English,' Julie replied.

She spoke in English, out of some bloody-mindedness which she could not have explained.

The boy and the girl both giggled.

'My father says,' the boy called to Julie, in French, 'the English are shit! My father says the English are so shitty they have to get French soldiers to do all the fighting for them!'

The girl was watching Julie. She was pretending to laugh

43

uncontrollably. The boy waited for Julie to reply. When he saw that she wasn't going to say anything, he shrugged his shoulders.

'Let's go!' he told the girl. 'There's such a smell of shit round here!'

They pedalled away between the trees.

At half-past one exactly, a large, dirty bus came trundling down the street leaving a trail of black diesel smoke behind it. A chipped wooden sign swung from two hooks above the driver's windscreen. It read, '*A Reims*'. Julie dragged herself to her feet, and gathered her suitcase and bag together. She began limping across to the bus, when she heard the sound of a car horn close by. She was too intent on reaching the bus to look round, but the horn sounded again, more insistently, and an unmistakably English voice called out,

'Hallo there! Miss Armitage!'

She turned. A small, camouflaged, four-seater Morris was drawn up under the trees by a stone fountain. She recognised the driver's face, under the peak of the British army officer's hat. She glanced at the bus, hoping it wouldn't drive away immediately, then put down her suitcase, and ran between the café-tables to the car.

'Hallo, Major Hardwicke!' she said. 'What a nice surprise!'

'You remember my name,' he said, smiling up at her.

'You remember mine,' she replied.

'That isn't very difficult, Miss Armitage,' he told her.

'I think the same could be said of yours, Major Hardwicke,' she replied.

He glanced down at his empty sleeve, and pulled a face. Julie hoped that she hadn't sounded rude.

'*Touche!*' he said, smiling up at her once more. 'Where are you off to, all by yourself?'

She nodded toward the bus. Its motor was clattering impatiently.

'Reims,' she said. 'Well, Paris really.'

'You don't have to go to Reims to get to Paris, do you?' he asked.

'I expect I can catch a *rapide* at Reims,' she explained.

'You could catch a *rapide* at Laon just as easily,' said Major Hardwicke.

With a triple fanfare on its klaxon, and a belch of diesel smoke, the bus moved off down the street.

'As it happens,' he continued, 'I'm on my way to Laon now. So get your case and hop in.'

'That's super!' said Julie. 'Do you know? You're the first nice thing that's happened to me today!'

'Go on!' he told her. 'Grab your case before somebody takes it. Then you can tell me what you've been up to since the other night in the Rutlands' mess.'

Julie ran back between the tables, picked up her case and returned with it.

'My feet are all blisters!' she said as she put her case on the back seat.

She got into the car beside him.

'You don't know how pleased I am to see you!' she said.

'I'm beginning to have an inkling,' he told her. 'I ought to feel very flattered, I daresay.'

'What are *you* doing here?' Julie bubbled on. 'What have *you* been up to? I mean, I'm so *surprised* to see you!'

Major Hardwicke steadied the steering-wheel with the stump of his left arm. With his right hand, he managed the gears and the hand-brake. As they drove off, he said,

'I doubt if you'll believe me, if I tell you.'

'Try me!' she said.

'I've been talking to a German officer,' he said.

'A prisoner?' Julie asked.

'Not at all. A cavalry officer if I'm not mistaken. Well,' he went on, 'to tell the truth, I didn't actually talk to him, but he waved at me.'

'Near here?' asked Julie.

'Not too far,' he told her. 'Now, you tell me what you're doing, wandering about in a God-forsaken place like this, all by yourself.'

3

At the same early hour as Julie had been sitting on the costume basket, recovering from her fright, Vivian Hardwicke had found himself being shaken awake. The previous evening, he had driven over from the headquarters of Colonel de Gaulle's 4th Armoured Division, to visit his old schoolfriend Nigel Milnes, who was at Xth Corps headquarters near Sedan.

'Come on, Viv old chap!' Nigel was saying.

Vivian's reunion with Nigel had been the excuse for a convivial evening; now his head was throbbing and his missing arm ached abominably.

'It's bloody early, isn't it?' he complained.

He saw Nigel's batman standing behind him holding a tray. Nigel was smirking.

'Feeling a bit previous, old chap?' he asked. 'I've got Alphonse here, or whatever his name is, to bring you up some coffee and brioches.'

'Brioches?' Vivian groaned.

'Best to get a spot of food into the old tum when you're feeling fragile,' said Nigel. 'Ballast, you know.'

As the batman put down the tray beside the bed, Vivian sat up. Clear, early morning sunlight was pouring in through the window.

'What's the news?' he asked.

'Some chaps have just come into the mess,' Nigel replied. 'They say you can see Jerry from up on the Marfée heights. Thought we might go and have a recce for ourselves.'

'Are they in force?' asked Vivian.

'Patrols in force, I should think, probing up to the Meuse,' said Nigel. 'The French 71st Division and 58th are digging in on our side of the river. I've seen some of the emplacements: reinforced concrete; pretty formidable, if you ask me. Jerry isn't going to get across in a hurry.'

Vivian got into his riding-breeches, and was struggling with his boots. It didn't make his head feel any better.

'I say, Viv old man: would you object very much if I offered to lend a hand?' asked Nigel.

'Not at all,' Vivian replied.

Nigel held the riding-boot as Vivian thrust his foot into it.

'Bit scared to ask,' he explained. 'Some chaps resent being helped you know.'

'It's silly not to accept kindnesses when they are offered,' Vivian replied.

'I expect Rosemary helped you a lot at first,' said Nigel.

Vivian pushed his foot into his second boot.

'You haven't heard?' he asked. 'No, of course not! Why should you?'

'Haven't heard what?' asked Nigel.

'Rosemary and I have gone our separate ways,' Vivian told him.

'Oh God!' said Nigel. 'I'm sorry.'

'It doesn't matter,' Vivian assured him.

'No, I really am most awfully sorry!' said Nigel.

'Don't think about it,' Vivian told him. 'It happened two years ago. And a lot has happened since then.'

He took a razor from his case, and began to strop it, holding the end of the leather between his teeth. It saved him, for the moment, from having to explain why Rosemary and he had divorced. Explaining it was always an exceptionally dreary business, made no easier by his conviction that it had been entirely his own fault. Not just because he had allowed his brief affair with Kitty Schouvaloff during a week's leave in Beirut to be found out, nor because he had allowed concern for his military duties to impose an unacceptable strain on the marriage.

He let the end of the leather fall from his teeth.

'Actually,' he said, 'I was very fortunate. Audrey Christie invited me to spend my convalescent leave at Glyndebourne, after I was discharged from hospital. She spoilt me to death.'

'Of course, I remember,' said Nigel. 'You always were a bit odd – I mean, keen on opera, and that sort of thing.'

Anything which had kept Rosemary from the inner sanctuary of his mind.

Nigel watched as Vivian lathered his chin.

'You really do manage most awfully well,' he remarked. 'How long has it been, now?'

'Just over a year,' Vivian replied. 'The first day I was allowed out of bed was the day Adolf marched into Prague.'

When he had finished shaving, he drank his coffee. Nigel helped him on with his jacket and Sam Browne belt.

'It was a lucky thing they managed to save the arm from below the elbow,' said Vivian. 'It's surprising what one can do with a decent-sized stump!'

He wished it hadn't sounded so bloody heroic.

A small open Renault was waiting for them in the farm-yard of the manor. Nigel decided to drive it himself.

'I thought we'd go up onto La Marfée above Pont Maugis,' he said, 'One gets a splendid view across the Meuse from there.'

They rattled down the unkept drive and under the gatehouse, between the two sentries. On the sloping meadows leading up to the Marfée woods, they found artillerymen, stripped to the waist, building up sandbagged positions above the concrete emplacements, and digging in batteries of 75's. Nigel stopped the car, and he and Vivian got out. Nigel reached over and picked up his binoculars case from the back seat.

They climbed the slope toward the edge of the woods. Although it was early morning, the artillerymen's hard torsos gleamed with sweat as they heaved the sandbags up onto the earthworks, and dragged the ammunition caissons into position behind the guns. Above the battery, under the trees, a large half-track was drawn up. An awning had been stretched out from its side, on poles. Under it, tables had been set up where groups of men were operating telephones and making calculations on artillery-boards. Nigel and Vivian followed a track up into the tangle of the woods. It was chilly under the thickness of the branches where the sun had not yet penetrated. They came across a telephone cable running along the track. Vivian hooked his toe under it.

'Bit careless,' he suggested. 'Particularly if they propose to stay here for four or five days.'

'Come off it, old chap!' Nigel protested. 'They've only just arrived!'

'They've got their OP's out,' Vivian replied. 'They're operating their RT boards. They should be burying their land-lines.'

'I bet you were a right bastard when you were with your squadron,' said Nigel. 'I bet you gave your men the runs just by looking at them!'

'One learnt to be a bit of a sod with a name like mine,' Vivian replied. 'Had to live down my Christian name, and live up to my surname.'

A crag reared above the trees. They walked round its base, following the telephone cable and the track, until they came to a huge moss-covered boulder which blocked the path. As they made their way downwards again, under the trees, still following the cable, they came across an artillery captain sitting on the slope, his back against a tree-trunk. Below him, there was a natural gap in the trees through which they could see the expanse of the sunlit landscape. The meadowland stretched on downwards until it reached the lip of the gorge through which the Meuse flowed northwards towards Belgium. Beyond the gorge, a further expanse of rolling grassland, speckled with small copses, reached away to where, in a bright haze, a rising wall of woodland marked the edge of the Ardennes.

The artillery captain was in his shirtsleeves, with his braces hanging down at his sides; his jacket was folded up between his back and the tree, as a cushion. He had removed his puttees, his boots and his socks. He was puffing at a thick briar pipe, and was leaning forward slightly, massaging his feet. On a rack close at hand stood an antique field-telephone receiver in its unbuttoned canvas case. Beside it stood a large pair of field glasses. Under the trees, beyond the captain, two men were engaged in screwing an artillery-board onto its tripod.

When he saw Vivian and Nigel approaching, the captain removed the pipe from his lips; Vivian noticed that he had the sort of face he had seen on downland shepherds, or fenmen in his native Norfolk.

'*Bonjour, messieurs*,' said the captain. 'You are a bit far from your own sector, aren't you?'

'I'm on General Gransard's staff,' Nigel explained. 'We've come up from Chaumont.'

'Come to see if the battle's started, eh?' asked the captain. Then, in a friendly voice, he asked, 'Have you had breakfast, *messieurs*?'

A small pack was open at his side. The neck of a bottle was sticking out of it. He reached over and pulled out the bottle.

'A mouthful?' he suggested.

Nigel took it from him, removed the cork, and put it to his lips. He passed it to Vivian. Vivian drank from it, and passed it back to the captain.

'Headquarters don't seem to think there'll be any action here for at least four days,' Vivian said.

'Headquarters can think what they like,' replied the captain.

48

'I noticed you haven't buried your line,' Vivian remarked.

The captain shrugged.

'What's the point?' he asked. 'You'd have to bury it pretty far down to stop it being blown apart by a bomb from a Stuka, eh?'

He put his pipe back in his mouth, puffed twice reflectively, leaned forward, and began to massage his toes once more.

'Ever seen a Stuka in action, *messieurs?*' he asked, his pipe clenched between his teeth.

'No,' Vivian replied.

'An interesting experience,' said the captain. 'Very interesting.'

'Where did you gain this experience, monsieur?' asked Vivian.

'On the Semois, before we were ordered to pull back,' the captain replied.

'So you've already seen action, these past few days?' Nigel asked.

The captain looked up at them both with calm, amused eyes set in a weathered face.

'Why yes,' he replied.

They said goodbye to the artillery captain. Vivian followed Nigel down through the woods, and out onto the open meadow where it sloped away to the Meuse. Across the gorge, over the meadows stretching to the abruptly rising edge of the Ardennes Forest, the early morning haze was beginning to disperse. As Vivian trampled the short-cropped grass, he remembered with nostalgia Sunday mornings at school at Fernyhurst, strolling across the terraced playing-fields below Chapel before matins. He had known a sort of happiness at school, the same comfortable happiness he found in the social life of an officers' mess.

'It's Whit Sunday,' he said to Nigel.

'My God!' Nigel replied. 'So it bloody well is. Beginning to lose track of the days.'

'I expect the Reverend Swinners will be preaching the same old sermon,' said Vivian.

As Nigel laughed, Vivian heard from over on the far side of the river gorge, the familiar grind of powerful motors and the clatter and squeal of tank-tracks. He watched as the tank appeared, rising up from the dead ground behind a smooth, grassy hillock. As it reached the crest of the rise, it paused, the front of its tracks thrust upwards, before lurching forward onto the downward slope. It advanced half way between the crest of the rise and the edge of the river gorge, leaving a trail of torn earth behind it, and stopped. Vivian could see quite clearly the figure of its commander standing in the open cupola of the turret, his hands gripping the sides of the hatch. Nigel opened his binoculars case, and pulled out the glasses. The tank commander lifted himself out of the turret, lowered himself onto the roof of the chassis, and jumped down to the ground.

'The cheeky sod!' Nigel exclaimed, staring at him through the glasses as he came strolling down toward the farther bank of the river. 'Here, you're the professional. See what you make of him.'

He handed the glasses to Vivian, who propped them on the elbow-stump of his left arm, and adjusted the focus. He could see quite clearly the steel helmets hooked over the squadron number painted on the curved sides of the turret; the detail of the filter-holes in the headphones lying discarded on the open lid of the cupola; and the latitudinal and longitudinal lines on the map which was lying in its talc-faced case beside the headphones.

'It's a 38T – Praga, medium-light,' he told Nigel. 'I don't want to worry you too much, but there are two medium machine-guns and a 37.7 mm Skoda all pointing straight at us, just in case we try drawing a bead on our cheeky friend over there.'

He lowered the glasses slightly, taking in the ground in front of the tank until he reached its commander. As he focussed on him, Vivian saw that he too had taken his glasses from the case about his neck. He took in the badge on the German's wide beret, and the yellow insignia on the smart black jacket. He noted the polished leather on the inside legs of his breeches.

'One of your lot, Nigel,' he said. 'Cavalry.'

He saw the German's glasses staring straight into his own. The mouth under the glasses stretched into a grin; the glasses were lowered, and Vivian saw the clear, blue, youthful eyes smiling straight at him. Still smiling, the German raised his black-gauntleted hand and waved across to him.

'My God!' said Vivian. 'He's a cool customer!'

He handed the glasses back to Nigel. The German was strolling back to his tank. He swung himself up onto the chassis, and climbed into the turret once more. The motors revved up noisily, belching greasy blue exhaust across the fresh grass. The tracks rattled and screeched, and bit into the turf as the tank began to lurch backwards up the slope. As it hesitated on the crest, Vivian saw the commander raise his hand again for a final wave, before the tank toppled back and disappeared once more into the dead ground.

They returned to the road, and got back into the car. Along the grass verges, stretching back as far as the eye could see, a battalion of infantry had halted and fallen out. The men appeared to be middle-aged, weary, and out of condition; many of them, Vivian noticed, were over-weight, and pallid-faced under the grime. Some had removed their boots, and were examining their feet for blisters. Others, still in full equipment, with their rifles hugged between their knees, had fallen asleep. Behind the men, in the field, a small group of officers was standing smoking, watching as their orderlies walked their horses up and down.

'I'll tell you something,' Vivian said. 'That Jerry we saw over there was no 'B' reservist. He was wearing the insignia of the Prussian 1st

Cavalry as if he wanted the world to know about it. And he had the Knight's Cross round his neck. A young veteran if you ask me – a real member of the super-race.'

'You might call this lot veterans,' Nigel remarked.

'*Invalides*, I should say,' Vivian replied.

'Oh, I expect it was just a reconnaissance job,' said Nigel. 'I expect Jerry wants everybody to think he's got his élite over there. It's bluff: I mean, he can't afford a major push up north *and* use crack units to hold his flank down here.'

When they reached advanced HQ at Chaumont once more, Vivian refused the offer of a second breakfast.

'I've got to get onto the Vouziers-Rethel road,' he told Nigel, as he threw his grip onto the back seat of his own little Morris, and climbed in. 'Colonel de Gaulle has told me I must call at this Château de la Berlière on my way back. I'm to present his compliments to a friend of his. He was most insistent – and I don't want to blot my copybook with him just yet.'

He started the car.

'Well,' he said. 'At least I can say I've seen a Jerry – which is more than most of the BEF have been able to say these past six months or so!'

For some miles, he encountered long files of dusty, weary infantry, plodding behind their mounted officers towards Sedan and the Meuse. Many of them, he noticed, were colonial troops, Algerian or Senegalese. Once or twice, he was forced to pull up where the road was blocked by heavy carts laden with equipment and supplies, pulled by teams of horses. At one point, he came across a huge dray tilted over into a ditch. The horse which had been drawing it was lying in the road on its flank, and was as dusty as the road itself. It kept trying to lift its head. Its nostrils were covered in foam, and its eyes rolled wildly. Its driver, a North African, was standing over it, screaming imprecations at it in a high falsetto, and lashing its sweating, bleeding side with his whip. A small group of other ranks, with one mounted officer, stood by and watched apathetically as if waiting for some lorry driver to complete a running repair on his motor. Vivian suppressed his futile sense of indignation, and drove on.

He had just driven through a tiny, unmarked hamlet when he was stopped at a level-crossing by the lowering of the boom, though there was no sign of any train approaching. A soldier – a corporal – in a stained and weathered forage-cap, with bloodshot eyes, and two or three days' growth of beard, came over from the crossing-keeper's cottage, and stared into the car.

'Where are you going, monsieur?' he asked.

'Rethel,' Vivian replied.

The man's breath smelt stale with wine. Vivian rested his stump on the steering wheel. The man stared at it.

'Are you able to drive – with that, monsieur?' he asked.

'Evidently,' Vivian replied.

He noticed that the corporal had left his rifle with bayonet fixed leaning against the wall of the cottage.

'The lieutenant wants a word with you,' he said.

He nodded towards the cottage.

'Why?' Vivian asked.

'We have been ordered to stop and question anybody we have reason to suspect might be a saboteur, monsieur,' the corporal replied. 'In case there is an attempt to block the railway track.'

'Do you suspect me of being a saboteur, corporal?' Vivian asked.

'How far do you think you can drive with only one arm, monsieur?' the corporal replied.

'Aren't you being a little foolish?' Vivian asked.

The corporal shrugged.

'They all say something like that,' he replied, pulling open the door of the car.

Vivian got out and followed the corporal into the cottage. Two more soldiers were sitting in the parlour, just inside the door. Empty wine bottles were littered about the legs of their wooden chairs. One of the soldiers was slumped against the back of his chair, his hand hanging limp to the floor, his unshaven mouth fallen open. His whole body was at such a tilt, it seemed as if it might drop onto the floor at any moment. The other soldier offered Vivian a glassy, vacant stare. His pipe lay unnoticed on his knee, spilling dead ash onto his breeches. Their commander, the lieutenant, was sitting behind a table at a telephone, a saucer full of cigarette-ends in front of him, and several dirty coffee cups beside him. His cheeks were mottled and hollow – he was an elderly man, even by the standards of the French army's 'B' reservists.

'We have here a suspected saboteur, lieutenant!' the corporal bellowed in a parade-ground voice from behind Vivian's ear.

The old man stared up at Vivian with rheumy eyes.

'Vivian Stoddard Hardwicke – Major, British Army,' Vivian announced. 'Tank Corps, seconded to British Military Mission GQG *Forces Terrestres*, Vincennes. Attached to the French 4th Armoured Division under the command of Colonel Charles de Gaulle. Travelling to Rethel on Colonel de Gaulle's instructions.'

'There is no 4th Armoured Division, lieutenant!' the corporal barked from behind Vivian. 'There is a 1st, a 2nd, a 3rd, and a 5th. But no 4th!'

'The 4th Armoured Division is based on Laon, monsieur,' Vivian told the lieutenant. 'You may ring Colonel de Gaulle's headquarters at Bruyères, if you wish.'

52

The lieutenant smiled with weary resignation.

'The phone doesn't work, monsieur,' he said. *'Voilà!'*

He lifted the receiver from its cradle, and dropped it back again. It was dead.

'Some men from General Lafontaine's 55th Division came last night,' he went on. 'They carried off the wire – they said they were short of cable up north.'

'How do you know they weren't saboteurs?' Vivian asked.

'They were Tunisians, monsieur. Have you means of identification?' the lieutenant asked.

'Of course,' Vivian replied.

As Vivian took his papers from his breast pocket, the lieutenant sighed, put two fingers to his eye, and tried to pull a fragment of dried rheum from the lashes.

'I deeply regret the inconvenience this is causing you,' said the lieutenant, as he took Vivian's papers.

He fumbled through Vivian's AB 64. It was obvious to Vivian that he could not understand a word of it.

'Monsieur says he is an Englishman,' the corporal remarked. 'But he speaks French without an English accent.'

He clearly regarded this as a matter for the gravest suspicion.

'You do speak French quite well, monsieur,' said the aged lieutenant.

He returned the documents.

'You may go, monsieur,' he said. 'Naturally. You must understand that Corporal Goutard, here, wishes to demonstrate that he takes his duties seriously. It is something to be commended.'

He took a cigarette from the packet on the table, and lit it with a stub which had been lying smoking in the saucer in the midst of a yellow stain.

'It would be even more commendable, monsieur,' Vivian observed, 'if Corporal Goutard had not left his rifle and side-arms unattended outside.'

The lieutenant stared up at him with his sad, watery eyes.

'It is hard, in this world, monsieur,' he said, 'to be perfect.'

Vivian turned off the main Vouziers-Rethel highway into a wooded valley between the gentle hills, and drove on for three kilometres. The road ended in a village consisting of two rows of low, stone cottages facing one another across the wide grass verges of the street.

Beyond it a drive led away across the bright green of the parkland with its sentinel trees breaking the even carpet of grass. Above the trees, Vivian could see the turrets, and the steeply sloping mansard roofs of the Château de la Berlière. As he approached the house, he noticed the curved, branched, balustraded steps leading up to the double-fronted doors, and the high, symmetrical windows.

He drove over a balustraded bridge across the lily-covered moat, through the line of sentinel trees, and out onto the front carriage-drive. There were three large limousines drawn up at the foot of the front steps, black, and gleaming in the sunlight. There were half a dozen women in their hats and coats, and several men in livery jackets and peaked caps, by the cars. There was one man, clearly in authority, with a Burberry raincoat over his arm, and a bowler-hat on his head. Another, a valet in shirtsleeves and striped waistcoat, came bustling down the steps, a suitcase in either hand and suitcases under either arm. The boots of the three cars were stacked with luggage.

As Vivian drew up, the bowler-hatted man came over.

'I appear to have arrived at an inconvenient time,' Vivian said to him, in French.

The man took in Vivian's uniform.

'You are wishing to speak with Monsieur le Baron, sir?' he asked in English.

'I had hoped to do so,' Vivian replied in English. 'But it doesn't matter.'

Had the household servants who were clustered about the cars been wearing their uniforms and aprons, they would have cast only the most discreet glances in his direction. Being in their holiday clothes, they stared at him.

'Monsieur le Baron's household is moving to Paris, sir,' the bowler-hatted man explained. 'Monsieur le Baron will, however, remain here until tomorrow.'

He opened the car door, and held it open. As Vivian got out, the man called across the drive,

'Danielle!'

A girl came forward.

'Yes, Monsieur Severin?' she asked, smiling pertly from under her old-fashioned cloche hat.

'Show Monsieur le Commandant into the house, Danielle,' the man instructed her. 'And inform Monsieur le Baron of his arrival.'

'Of course, Monsieur Severin. Will you come with me, please, monsieur,' she smiled at Vivian.

Her dark eyes encountered his, and held his glance impudently, as if awaiting some hint of self-betrayal on his part. She was the perfect maid for the setting: not Zerlina, and certainly not Susanna, but Blonde, or, even better, Despina. As he followed her up the steps, he noticed, under her coat, her flowered silk dress against her black-stockinged legs. Her clothes, like the high-heeled shoes she was wearing, had been expensive but now they did not quite fit her, and were slightly worn-looking.

She pushed open one of the heavy doors, and let him into the lofty hall.

'What name shall I tell Monsieur le Baron?' she asked.

'Major Hardwicke – Vivian Hardwicke,' he replied. 'You may tell

Mousieur le Baron that I was asked to call here to present the respectful compliments of Colonel de Gaulle to Monsieur le baron.' The thought of Colonel de Gaulle paying respectful compliments to anybody other than Joan of Arc or Louis XIV was laughable, Vivian decided. Still . . .

'Major ardoueek, monsieur?' the girl attempted to pronounce.

'That is very good,' Vivian complimented her.

She giggled, and closed the great door behind her. The noise of it echoed to the high, painted ceiling.

'*Voulez-vous me suivre, s'il vous plaît*, Major 'ardoueek?' she asked, and giggled again.

'*De mieux en mieux*,' he told her, as he followed her to the broad marble staircase.

Their footsteps echoed on the tiled floor.

'Are you off to Paris with the others?' Vivian asked her.

He continued to admire her legs and the slight edge of lace under her skirt-hem brushing the back of her stockings.

'At once, monsieur,' she replied, as she mounted the stairs. 'Monsieur le Baron has said we must all go. He says we shall be safer in Paris.'

She paused, and looked back at Vivian.

'We could hear the guns, monsieur,' she said. 'Yesterday afternoon.'

'I expect you'd be glad to be going to Paris, even if there were no guns,' said Vivian, as they went on up the stairs.

'Naturally, monsieur,' she replied. 'It's so much more gay! There's nothing here but the same old faces – you could die of boredom!'

They were on the curve at the top of the stairs. Vivian could see that she had pouted her lips. There was a young boy of about nine or ten years of age standing at the head of the stairs. He was dressed like an English schoolboy, in a red blazer and grey flannel slacks.

'Tell me, Hugo,' asked the maid, 'is Papa in the library?'

There was a note of sharpness in her voice. When he did not reply immediately, she said as if addressing a tiresome younger brother, 'Come on! Tell me!'

The boy looked at her with unmistakable distaste.

'Perhaps he is,' he replied. He sidled away along the balustrade overlooking the hall. 'You'd better go and see.'

The maid jerked her head in a gesture of impatience. She turned to Vivian, 'Will you wait here, please, monsieur? I'll see if Monsieur le Baron is in the library . . . *Major 'ardoueek, un ami de Colonel de Gaulle?*'

'*Oui, c'est parfait*,' Vivian told her.

Her high heels clicked away across the marbled gallery, and were hushed in the soft carpet of the passage beyond. The boy smiled charmingly at Vivian, and came forward, his hand outstretched.

'Hugo de Bart-Mendel, monsieur,' he said, taking Vivian's hand.
'Vivian Hardwicke,' Vivian replied.

'*Bonjour, monsieur*,' said the boy. 'Welcome to La Berlière. Papa is in the library, monsieur.'

He switched off his smile, scowled in the direction of the passage down which the maid had disappeared, and ran away down the stairs. Vivian leaned against the balustrade, and looked across the hall through the windows at the trees so meticulously placed in the green spread of the parkland. There had been a sexuality about the maid which had disturbed him. It reminded him of the fear which he had relegated to the lumber-room of his mind.

'Major . . . ?' The man came across the gallery. 'I'm afraid I could not quite follow the girl's pronunciation of your name,' he added with a smile.

His English was faultless. He was a slim, dapper man in his early forties. His face had the feminine sensitivity characteristic of fashionable film-actors such as Leslie Howard and Robert Donat.

'Hardwicke,' Vivian said. 'Vivian Hardwicke.'

'Victor de Bart-Mendel,' said the baron. 'Welcome to La Berlière, Major Hardwicke.'

'It is very beautiful,' Vivian told him. 'I particularly admired the approach across the park.'

'It is a pity you could not have seen it under more peaceful circumstances,' said de Bart-Mendel. He waved his hand in the direction of the hall and stairs. 'It isn't usually so bare,' he went on. 'We have sent the tapestries and better pieces of furniture ahead of us to Paris.'

The maid, Danielle, crossed the gallery and went downstairs.

'She informed me that you are a friend of Charles de Gaulle.' said de Bart-Mendel. 'Will you come with me to the library, Major Hardwicke? That, at least, remains tolerably comfortable.'

'I can hardly claim to be on terms of friendship with Colonel de Gaulle,' Vivian said, as he went with de Bart-Mendel down the passage. 'I am attached to his division at Bruyères on the orders of GHQ, British Expeditionary Forces. I suppose our people decided I was suitable because I too used to be a tank man. Knowing that I was coming on a visit to these parts, the Colonel very kindly suggested I should call on you here, and present his compliments to you.'

The library was a long, dark-panelled room. At either end, in cavernous alcoves, bookshelves rose from the floor to the lofty ceiling, lined with the crumbling, leather spines of old books. Between the two alcoves, on the thick rugs, the sofas and armchairs were covered in light-coloured chintz to set off the gloom of the walls and shelves.

'So de Gaulle has his division at last,' de Bart-Mendel said.

'At last, Baron?' Vivian asked.

De Bart-Mendel held out a silver cigarette box. Vivian took a cigarette.

'He had waited a long time,' said de Bart-Mendel, lighting it for him. 'You may have noticed, Major Hardwicke, that Charles de Gaulle is a proud man. He is also a devout Catholic, he is faithful to his wife, and he loves France. These are none of them qualities which find approval in the Third Republic!'

He noticed Vivian's surprise at the vehemence with which he had expressed himself, and smiled.

'I expect Colonel de Gaulle asked you to come here in order to let me know that the Republic has at last seen fit to offer him a command.'

He went over to the heavy table which stood in the shadow of the bookshelves.

'Would you care for a drop of armagnac, Major Hardwicke?' he asked. 'I would offer you coffee, but now that my servants are leaving, there is only Joseph, my chauffeur, to look after us.'

Vivian accepted.

'Do you mean to stay on here?' he asked.

'Twenty-four hours, perhaps,' de Bart-Mendel replied. 'To make certain arrangements. There are also one or two things I prefer to carry to Paris personally.'

De Bart-Mendel brought the brandy over to where Vivian was standing at the window.

'A knot garden,' said Vivian.

'Not as fine as that at Azay, I'm afraid,' said de Bart-Mendel.

'But very fine, nevertheless,' Vivian told him.

'You are seeing it from the point of vantage,' said de Bart-Mendel. 'They are all designed, you know, to be viewed from upper-floor windows. From the ground, the paths are an aimless maze. From above, one may admire their order and composition.'

'Are you a Catholic, Baron?' Vivian asked, thinking of his host's stricture on the Third Republic.

'Certainly not,' de Bart-Mendel replied. 'I am a free-thinker and a Mason, as my father was before me.'

He looked directly at Vivian.

'One does not have to be a devout Catholic to be uncertain, in these days, of one's faith in the Republic, Major Hardwicke.'

He motioned Vivian to sit down in one of the chintz-covered armchairs.

'Were you in the last – er – unpleasantness, Major Hardwicke?' he asked.

Vivian shook his head.

'Of course not,' de Bart-Mendel continued. 'You are still young. Would it be impertinent to ask where you received your injury? In India, perhaps? The North-West Frontier?'

'Palestine,' Vivian told him.

'You were wounded in action?' asked de Bart-Mendel.

'I found myself at the wrong end of a Bedouin flint-lock,' Vivian replied. 'Heaven knows what the fellow had loaded it with. The surgeon at the base hospital in Hebron told me that he extracted metal tacks, bits of stone, and a couple of steel ball-bearings from what was left of my arm. What made the whole thing even more humiliating was that the Arab chap was on a camel, and I was in one of the old Vickers Medium tanks.'

'I've no doubt it helped prove to your War Office,' de Bart-Mendel said, 'that mounted cavalry is still superior to armour.'

'I daresay it convinced some people in the War Office,' Vivian replied.

'I was a prisoner in Germany, in 1917,' said de Bart-Mendel. 'That is how I came to know Charles de Gaulle. We were in the same camp. I cannot say that we were intimate friends – one does not become intimate with de Gaulle. I found that his views were always worth hearing, though I can't remember that he would ever allow anybody to discuss them. Has he expressed his opinion of our present situation?'

'He told me in the mess, the other night,' Vivian replied, 'that he thought we should prepare ourselves for a campaign of rapid movement. He said there would probably be sudden breakthroughs which would call for great agility in defence, and that the action would cover a great deal of ground. He seemed doubtful as to whether we were ready for that sort of fighting.'

De Bart-Mendel nodded.

'It hasn't been the fashionable view to take in either of our countries,' he said.

'I daresay there are plenty of old dug-outs in the O.K.H. in Berlin, as well as in Paris and London,' said Vivian.

There was the sound of cars revving up coming from the far side of the house.

'You must think this hasty evacuation a little cowardly,' he said.

'Not at all, Baron,' replied Vivian. 'I'm sure it's the wisest thing under the circumstances. It must be a dreadful thing to contemplate this beautiful place being set in a theatre of war.'

De Bart-Mendel shrugged. It was a strangely Gallic gesture, Vivian thought, in one whose restraint was as Anglo-Saxon as his appearance.

'La Berlière has witnessed many campaigns, Major Hardwicke,' said de Bart-Mendel. 'The wounded have been brought here from so many battles. One learnt often in school about the Cockpit of Europe, didn't one? Well, La Berlière lies in the very heart of that Cockpit. Somehow it has endured.'

'Colonel de Gaulle told me that you had one or two treasures kept here which he said were part of the heritage of France,' Vivian remarked.

De Bart-Mendel laughed.

'Ah, yes!' he said. 'And one in particular. Another reason why he suggested this very pleasant visit, I think!'

There was a soft clearing of the throat from the library door.

'Danielle!' de Bart-Mendel looked up and smiled. 'All ready to leave now?' he asked in French.

'Monsieur Severin said I was to come and tell you, Monsieur le Baron,' the girl replied.

As Vivian looked round, she smiled at him, then glanced back at de Bart-Mendel.

'You will forgive me, won't you, Major Hardwicke?' asked de Bart-Mendel. 'I shall be gone only a moment.'

'Of course, Baron,' Vivian replied.

'If you should care for a drop more brandy . . . ' de Bart-Mendel suggested.

He left the decanter on the occasional table beside Vivian's chair, and left the room. Vivian heard his voice and that of the maid fading down the passage outside.

A few minutes later, de Bart-Mendel returned.

'So it goes,' he said apologetically.

He went back to the window, and stared down into the knot garden.

'My wife loved this house, Major Hardwicke,' he said suddenly.

Vivian could hear the sound of the cars driving across the park in the direction of the village.

'She died in the 'flu epidemic, four years ago last February,' de Bart-Mendel explained.

'I'm sorry,' said Vivian.

'She would have hated to have seen this happen,' de Bart-Mendel continued. 'I think she would have preferred to have waited for the Germans.'

He paused, then turned to look at Vivian.

'After the experience of marriage,' he said, 'one hungers for companionship . . . You are married, Major Hardwicke?'

'Yes,' Vivian replied.

He had no wish to enter into explanations regarding his divorce. The compulsions which sprung from loneliness were, however, something which he understood well enough.

'Your wife was very dear to you, Baron?' he asked.

'Yes,' de Bart-Mendel replied. 'We loved one another.'

Silence spread through the house. It hung on the air like the still specks of dust in the sunlight.

'A clever author,' said de Bart-Mendel, 'French, of course, wrote about a gentleman who always chose his mistress from among the servants. A friend asked him for what reason he had chosen to share his bed with a housemaid. "For her conversation," the gentleman replied. Of course, the author meant it as a joke; but it is in fact perfectly just. A housemaid's body is – mechanically speaking – no different from that of any other young woman. It is the banality of her conversation which is so comfortable.' He turned away from the window. 'But I was going to show you our most precious relic, Major Hardwicke.'

He went over to a shelf of tall, leather-bound volumes in one of the alcoves. He began to remove the books, placing them on the leather-covered top of the heavy table.

'As you see,' he explained, 'we do not indulge in the convenient vulgarity of false bindings.'

Behind where the books had stood, he opened one of the panels – a sliding door – to reveal the steel door of a small safe. Reaching up, he twisted the knobs clockwise, then anti-clockwise until the combination clicked into place. The thickness of the door swung open, and he reached inside. He drew out a flat, black case with strap-worked monograms in silver at the corners. He placed it reverently on the table.

'In happier times,' he said, 'we have it exposed in the chapel. I do not use the chapel myself, you understand, but we have always maintained it for the convenience of the household – and visitors, of course. For those who attend the chapel to pray, or to hear Mass when Monsieur le Curé comes up from the village, I suppose this is a holy relic.'

Vivian stood immediately behind him, watching over his shoulder as he unlocked and opened the two flaps of the lid. De Bart-Mendel lifted the dark green cloth which was spread inside. Underneath lay a silver medallion, six inches in diameter. De Bart-Mendel lifted it very carefully, holding the edges with his finger-tips, raising it so that the sunlight shone on it.

'You see?' he asked. 'We have Christ presenting the sword to Louis IX – St Louis.'

Vivian gazed at the strange, attenuated figures with their extraordinarily gentle faces; it was like an encounter between lovers, he thought.

'They remind me of the carvings on the west porch of Chartres,' he said.

'It was made by the Master Silversmith at Chartres,' de Bart-Mendel told him. 'It has always been known as the *Tondeau de Chartres*.'

'"Resurgam",' Vivian read the single word inscription. '"I shall arise".'

'It was worn round the necks of the old Constables of France, when they led the king's armies into battle,' de Bart-Mendel told him.

He placed the medallion back in its case.

'It was worn by Bertrand de Guesclin when he overthrew the Captal de Buch at Cocherel and drove the Black Prince from Limoges. It was worn by the Bastard of Orléans when, with Jeanne d'Arc, he destroyed the English in the Tourelles, and raised the siege of Orléans. It was worn by the young Duc d'Enghien when he broke the Spanish power at Rocroi. And it was worn in battle for the last time when the great Turenne defeated the armies of the United Provinces at Maastricht.'

He replaced the green cloth over it.

'Was d'Albret wearing it at the Battle of Agincourt?' asked Vivian.

De Bart-Mendel glanced at him, then laughed.

'No, he wasn't, as it happened,' he replied. 'There was some sort of quarrel at Rouen as to whether he or Marshal Boucicaut should wear it. The king decided to withold it from both of them – fortunately for the English, since it was supposed to endow any wearer worthy of it with certain victory.'

'Shouldn't Gamelin or Georges be wearing it now, Baron?' asked Vivian. 'It sounds a useful acquisition.'

'I don't believe anybody has decided what dreadful penalty awaits anyone who wears it who is *not* worthy of it,' de Bart-Mendel replied. 'Tomorrow, I intend taking it with me to Paris. There are those who believe it should be placed with other relics of King Louis IX, either in Notre Dame or the Panthéon. My family certainly has no historic claim to it. It came to us with this house, when my grandfather bought it from an impoverished descendant of the great Turenne – my grandfather made a fortune in speculation during the Second Empire. Like my father, however, I regard myself as holding the *Tondeau de Chartres*, and the house, in sacred trust.'

He laughed again.

'At least, that is, until an indisputable Constable of France claims it as his due!'

He closed the lid of the case, and locked it.

'I'm very grateful to you, Baron,' said Vivian, 'for letting me see it.'

De Bart-Mendel turned.

'Ah! Come in Hugo,' he said in French.

The boy was standing just inside the library door, beyond the sunlight which poured in through the high window. 'Major Hardwicke, may I present my son, Hugo? My only child, and much indulged, I'm afraid.'

'Hugo and I met on the stairs when I was coming up, Baron,' Vivian said.

The boy turned to his father.

'Everybody is gone now, Papa,' he said.

'Why don't you go down to the kitchens and see whether Joseph needs help with the lunch?' de Bart-Mendel asked. To Vivian, he said, 'You will stay to lunch, won't you, Major Hardwicke?'

'That is very kind of you, Baron,' Vivian replied, 'but I think I should start back to Laon. One can't tell what the roads will be like.'

The boy was staring fixedly at Vivian's sleeve.

'How can one be a soldier with only one arm, Monsieur le Commandant?' he asked.

'Hugo!' exclaimed de Bart Mendel. '*C'est très mal élevé* ... '

'I'm sure Hugo's interest is purely academic,' Vivian interceded. 'Not all soldiers,' he said to the boy, 'actually engage in fighting. Indeed, for every soldier who goes into action, there are nine who never fire a shot. There are engineers, pay-clerks, drivers, cooks – all sorts, in fact. So when you see a soldier, the chances are he won't be a fighting man!'

'What do you do, Monsieur le Commandant?'

The boy stared up at him. Vivian hesitated.

'I don't know really,' he answered. 'I suppose you could say my job is to speak to French people for the British army, because I speak French.'

He smiled.

'In fact, I speak French quite well, don't I?'

'Very well, Monsieur le Commandant,' Hugo replied seriously.

He pointed up at Vivian's breast.

'*C'est une croix militaire, n'est-ce pas?*' He turned to his father.

'*C'est la même chose que la croix de guerre, papa!*' he announced.

'You see, Hugo,' de Bart-Mendel told him, 'Major Hardwicke *is* a real fighting soldier.'

'As was Papa, in the Great War,' Vivian said to the boy.

'You don't mind him drawing attention to the decoration, Major Hardwicke?' de Bart-Mendel asked.

'Not at all!' Vivian replied. 'One likes to have one's virtue recognised.'

De Bart-Mendel laughed. As he was leading Vivian down the stairs to the front entrance, he said, 'I cannot really believe that self-regard is a vice. In fact, it's necessary to happiness ... That is not something one would ever have to preach to Charles de Gaulle, however!'

They stepped out into the dazzling sunlight of the empty drive. When Vivian had got into the car, de Bart-Mendel looked in through the window.

'I'll tell you a story about Colonel de Gaulle,' he said. 'It happened on a day like this – very warm and still. We were together, sitting in the shade of a hut in the *stammlager* compound near Koblenz. De Gaulle was explaining how an army should be organised – the distribution of specialised corps, armaments and so on. I was dozing off in the heat, but either he did not notice or did not care. Suddenly, I realised he had stopped talking. So I said to fill in the silence, and to provoke him a little I must confess, "*Mon cher*, you must not laugh when I tell you this, but I have the strangest feeling that you are pledged to a great destiny!" The Long Asparagus didn't even look at me. He stared away in front of him, calmly and gravely. At last, he said to me, "*Mon cher Baron*, I must tell you that I have the same feeling – very frequently." Now I have another strange feeling: it's that he wants to be quite sure that I am keeping the St Louis *Tondeau* safe until the moment comes when destiny decrees that Charles de Gaulle be appointed Constable of France. That is why he arranged that we should meet here today – a meeting which, I assure you, Major Hardwicke, has given me a great deal of pleasure.'

Vivian felt his spirits lighten as he drove back between the open fields towards Rethel and the main road to Laon. The sun had reached its zenith, and the road was white in the heat, yet all trace of his hangover had gone. It was not merely that he felt a physical improvement; it seemed as if the depression which had hung over him during the hard winter months spent in the grim fortress of Vincennes had at last lifted.

As he entered Montcornet, and was crossing the small square to the Laon road, he was compelled to swerve, pressing his stump on the wheel, to avoid a flurry of youths on their heavy bicycles. It was at that moment he caught sight of her, walking, suitcase in hand, under the shade of the trees toward the bus stop. He recognised her immediately from the evening he had spent in the Rutlands' mess near Arras. She was a very attractive girl in a rangy, pantomime-boyish sort of way.

Now she was quite dishevelled. Much of her thick hair had escaped from the broad bow which was tying it back on her neck. Her slacks looked as if she had slept in them, and a fastener had come apart on her hip so that the hem of her blouse stuck out through the gap. Her blouse was even more creased, and there were circles of damp under her arms. He sounded his horn as he slowed down, but she was too intent on reaching her bus to pay any attention. He could see no sign of any of her colleagues on the square. He sounded the horn a second time, as he drew nearer to her. She paused and turned her head. Vivian leaned out of the open window and shouted, 'Miss Armitage! Hallo there!'

She stopped and recognised him. As she brushed the untidy curls from out of her eyes, he caught the pure delight in her face. She put down her suitcase, and with only a momentary glance in the direction of the bus, came running between the café tables to the car.

'Hallo, Major Hardwicke! What a nice surprise!'

She brushed her hair out of her eyes again.

'You remember my name!' he said, genuinely pleased.

'You remember mine,' she replied.

'That isn't very difficult, Miss Armitage,' he told her.

He had been a fraction too smooth, and got what he deserved. She glanced at his arm.

'I think the same could be said of yours, Major Hardwicke,' she said.

Almost immediately there was a look of remorse on her face. He smiled to soften it. 'Where are you off to, all by yourself?' he asked.

He noticed that the bus she had been about to catch was on the point of moving off. He was delighted to see that she had noticed it too, but was making no effort to get to it. A few minutes later, they were driving together out of Montcornet towards Laon with the breeze blowing through the open roof, and the road stretching away across the sleeping countryside.

4

Dieter von Leonarte jumped down from the engine cowling of his tank. The sun was warm although it was still early in the morning. There was sweat on his forehead under the leather and steel lining of his Panzer beret, and the leather panels of his cavalry breeches were clinging to his inside legs where he had been bracing himself against the open cupola of the turret. He wiped the sweat from his face with his gloves, and stamped loose his breeches.

Senior Driver Helm swung himself up, out of the front hatch.

'We're going to be broiled again today, eh, Herr Rittmeister?' he grinned.

The two other crew members were climbing out: Graser, the gunner co-driver, through the cockpit; the other, wireless-operator Radinski, through the cupola.

'You'd better get some breakfast while you can,' von Leonarte told them.

He sniffed the air. There was a deciduous smell from the wooded slopes on the opposite side of the Meuse. It reminded him of home – of childhood, and his father waking him early in the summer morning to go down with him to the river for a swim before breakfast.

'We'd better not be on the move again today, Herr Rittmeister,' Helm told him. 'The old girl's engine needs tuning. She's been on her tracks for three days now, and they'll need looking after . . . And that goes for all the others, as well.'

He waved his hand at the two lines in which the squadron's tanks had been parked. Von Leonarte patted his shoulder.

'I'll have a word with General Guderian,' he told him, smiling.

'Look out, Herr Rittmeister,' said Helm. 'I think we have visitors!'

Von Leonarte turned to look down the avenue of parked tanks. Major Spiesser, the squadron commander, was strutting towards them. Behind him, ambled the tall figure of the squadron sergeant-major.

'Sergeant-Major Greis has reported to me,' shouted Major Spiesser, before Von Leonarte had had time even to salute, 'that one of our vehicles – a PzKw 38T – has been taken out of picket lines without proper authorisation! Your vehicle, Rittmeister Leonarte – Number 157!'

Von Leonarte stared at the droplets of sweat on the folds of Major Spiesser's cheeks. Major Spiesser reminded him of Burgomaster Prumers, at home in Kessim.

'With the Herr Major's permission,' he replied calmly, '*von* Leonarte, if you please, Herr Major.'

He was standing to attention, but in the relaxed posture permitted to cavalry officers. Behind Major Spiesser, Sergeant-Major Greis stared into the middle distance as if preoccupied with his own thoughts.

'You know I could have you reprimanded for this?' shouted Major Spiesser. 'I could have you placed under arrest, Rittmeister *von* Leonarte!'

'With the Herr Major's permission,' von Leonarte replied in his normal voice, 'may I remind the Herr Major that my command is a cavalry troop *attached* to the Herr Major's squadron; and that it has always been the practice in the cavalry to permit officers in charge of pickets to reconnoitre at will?'

'On horseback!' yelled Major Spiesser. 'On horseback, Rittmeister von Leonarte. Not in an armoured fighting vehicle.'

Von Leonarte saw Sergeant-Major Greis's lips twitching.

'If I have exceeded the limits laid down in current regulations, then I must apologise to the Herr Major,' said Von Leonarte.

Major Spiesser cleared his throat awkwardly, as if uncertain how he might climb down from the peak of his wrath.

'You are required to report to Colonel Hassler's headquarters, Rittmeister,' he said abruptly. 'Immediately.'

He turned on his heel, his cheeks still dangerously purple. Von Leonarte saluted his back, clicking his heels as he did so. He nodded to Senior Driver Helm, then followed Major Spiesser at a discreet distance.

The squadron had established itself round a farmhouse which had been abandoned by its occupants two days before. As von Leonarte went inside, his fellow tank-commanders called on him to join them at breakfast, but he shook his head. Oberleutnant Kirst, who had joined the squadron at the same time as von Leonarte, followed him into the wash-house behind the kitchen.

'What's up, Dieter?' he asked.

'I've got to get over to Bazeilles,' von Leonarte replied.

His pack was lying against the wall where he had left it at dawn. He took out his peaked officer's cap, replacing it with his discarded beret.

'I gather Spiesser has complained about me to Colonel Hassler,' he said. 'I've got to report to Regiment HQ.'

He put his cap on his head, straightening the peak over his forehead.

'The man is a shit,' said Kirst, 'a common or garden Brownshirt. God knows what he's doing in a decent regiment!'

'Appointed by the Bendlerstrasse, I suppose,' von Leonarte replied, 'on Party orders.'

He sighed.

'Still,' he said, 'I don't suppose Hassler's going to come down too hard on me. Not just before we attack across the river. He'll have better things to think about.'

Out in the yard, he commandeered a motorcycle and side-car, and ordered the driver to take him the kilometre and a half to Bazeilles. All down the rough, pitted road there was evidence that Division had decided this Sunday was to be a day of rest. In a field on the outskirts of the small town, a Roman Catholic chaplain was offering Mass, employing the tail-board of a horse-drawn ambulance as his altar. His large congregation was all in the reed-green denim fatigues of Panzer tank crews. Against the roadside hedge, a band of ragged, dirty-faced children under the care of a ten or eleven-year-old girl, was watching intently. They turned round as the motorcycle and side-car roared past.

Regimental headquarters were in the parish church of Bazeilles, overlooking the site of Napoleon III's surrender to Field-Marshal von Moltke in September 1870. The driver parked the motorcycle amongst the other military vehicles assembled round the shattered west front, and Von Leonarte ran up the steps into the nave. Despite the sunlight pouring in through the gaping holes in the roof, and the debris littering the aisles, the interior still smelt of incense, reminding von Leonarte to remove his cap. He stepped over the tangle of telephone cables on the floor, and made his way across the narrow transept. The sanctuary had been untouched by the bombardment of the previous day. A bunch of freshly-cut flowers stood in a vase between the bare feet of the Virgin, in her niche overlooking the altar-rail. Two head-scarved women and an elderly man were kneeling on the sanctuary step, the strings of beads spilling from between their gnarled fingers. They continued to mutter their prayers, ignoring the clatter of jackboots and the rattle of typewriters from the nave behind them.

'Dieter von Leonarte!' exclaimed Major Thiele, the regimental adjutant, as von Leonarte entered the sacristy.

He rested his hand on the map spread in front of him.

'You've been quick,' he added.

'I'm to report to Colonel Hassler,' said von Leonarte.

'The colonel has gone down to have a look at the river,' said Major Thiele. 'You'll have to make do with me, I'm afraid.'

He looked at von Leonarte.

'It's all right, Dieter,' he said. 'It isn't because you've been a bad boy, though you have – careering up and down the countryside, wasting valuable fuel! We're hard-pressed enough to keep all our squadrons operational as it is, without people like you going off on early morning joy-rides.'

'I'm sorry, Herr Major,' said von Leonarte.

He respected Major Thiele. The major gazed at him. His expression was serious.

'That thing round your neck' – he pointed to the Knight's Cross at von Leonarte's throat – 'won't protect you from certain people, you know!'

Von Leonarte nodded.

'Anyway' – Major Thiele relaxed – 'we've got to send you on an even longer joy-ride. Up into Belgium ... Had any breakfast yet?'

Von Leonarte shook his head.

'Schwartz!' Major Thiele called through the sacristy door to one of his orderlies. 'Some coffee and one of those vile sausages for the Rittmeister! ... Grab yourself a lump of bread, Dieter,' he added.

Von Leonarte tore a piece from the loaf on the table.

'Where am I being sent?' he asked.

'There isn't a lot I can tell you,' Major Thiele replied. 'We've received a request from XVth Corps headquarters for you to be detached from 10th Panzers for a day or two. You're to be sent over to their Special Intelligence for some scouting assignment or other. I expect it's the sort of thing they send light cavalry on, you lucky beggars. You are to find General Rommel's HQ with 7th Panzers. At the moment it's supposed to be ... let me see, now' – he looked down at the map – 'yes,' he said, 'here at Rochefort. God alone knows where it will be by the time you've caught up with it. 7th Panzers haven't reached their sector on the Meuse yet, so they'll be advancing in that direction. You'd best go up to Rochefort, and move on from there.'

'Who am I to report to?' von Leonarte asked.

'A Colonel Reuther,' Major Thiele replied. 'A Colonel Alfred Reuther.'

It took a moment for the name to sink in. Then Major Thiele saw the disappointment on his face.

'What's wrong?' he asked. 'Do you know him?'

Von Leonarte nodded. 'An old family friend,' he said.

'Well!' said Major Thiele. 'An old family friend in Special Intelligence, eh? It's no bad thing to have a friend or two in the right places!'

'My mother has probably written to him,' said von Leonarte, 'asking him to make sure I'm wearing dry socks.'

When von Leonarte had eaten, and had drunk his coffee, they went out of the church to where the motorcycle was parked. Half an hour later, he was following the winding road up through the forest to the crest of the ridge overlooking the Semois. The crossing of the fast-running stream had been fiercely contested the morning before; he had not had time to admire the scenery. Now he could look down the steep forest mountainside into the valley. Rags of early morning mist still hung among the trees at the base of the gorge, half concealing the roof-tops of the town of Bouillon where they crept up the lower part of the opposite slope. Straight across the valley, the bright sunlight was catching the mountain-tops and the rock-faces shone like coal against the pale blue of the cloudless sky.

As von Leonarte's driver set off down into the gorge, they saw the burned-out vehicles which had been hauled off the road. Groups of Pioneers were already filling in the craters caused by exploding mines. At the bottom of the valley, they drove along a street of shattered small shops to the pontoon-bridge which had been thrown across the Semois. The driver was forced to pull over as a convoy of horse-drawn trucks came clattering over the newly timbered bridge. A young officer of the Field Gendarmerie came over to them. He was in shirt-sleeves, and a disc-baton was stuck into his belt.

'It's been quite a morning down here!' he said. 'Just as they got the last planks down on the bridge, the English air force arrived. They didn't manage to hit it, thank God, but they've made even more of a mess of the town than we did!'

He pointed to the ruined shops. As the last truck of the convoy rattled off the bridge onto the road, he waved von Leonarte on.

The main street on the other side had been cleared of rubble. Mark IV tanks were parked nose to tail up the hill, with the support vehicles hidden in the side alleys, all waiting for the order to move forward. During the few hours lull in the fighting, the tank-crews had made themselves at home in the ruined houses on either side of the street. They were sprawling in tattered armchairs, which they had dragged onto the pavement, in the sunlight. They were brewing coffee over small bonfires made of broken sticks of furniture. Through a shattered wall von Leonarte caught sight of a tank-crewman lying on a bed, his boots resting on the black iron bed-rail, reading a copy of *Signal*.

They drove on for miles up the steep mountain roads, through the densest part of the Ardennes. In the green dappled darkness under the trees, riderless horses stood cropping the grass, their reins sweeping the ground. Some came ambling towards the road, their stirrups swinging against their sweat-shining flanks. Many of them were lame; others had suffered worse injuries. Von Leonarte saw a mounted trooper, his body in its mud-encrusted greatcoat slumped over the pommel of his saddle, his arms dangling on either side of his horse's neck, his head, still in its dull-blue helmet, lolling against the mane.

His driver slowed down as they came across a small herd of horses standing aimlessly on the road itself. He sounded the klaxon, and swerved between them as they sidled into the ditches or stupidly stood their ground in the centre of the road. Looking up as they drove past, von Leonarte noticed the R.F. monogram stitched in silver on the saddle-cloths. He smelt the familiar scent of sweat-stained leather and of iron shoes on flint, and felt nothing but anger at the military incompetence which pitched horsemen against armour. This contempt and anger was increased as they began to pass the columns of weary, bewildered prisoners who plodded up the road, unarmed, their hands clutched over their helmets or woollen caps, although there was scarcely a German soldier to be seen guarding them. Most of them were Spahis, dark-skinned Moors with the lean, creased faces von Leonarte recognised from pictures of oriental bazaars in school textbooks and travel picture-books. In their ill-fitting uniforms, with their cloaks tied blanket-like about their necks despite the hot weather, they looked dirty beyond the natural grime of combat, an odd sort of negro dirt which would not wash off. He was shocked that the French should employ semi-barbaric troops in a European theatre of war.

They left the forest and began to descend into a valley of broad open meadows. Here the war seemed to have been left behind. The only sign of it they encountered for many kilometres was a convoy of horse-drawn supply carts driven and guarded by supply corps men who were too elderly for front-line combat. Their easy pace was somehow suited to the sunlight and gentle scenery.

As they crossed a small, humped, stone bridge over a stream, von Leonarte caught sight of four or five young girls in cotton frocks and blue aprons, drawing mown hay into stooks with wooden rakes. A white dog was scampering between the stooks, yapping and jumping to catch flies. Further on, beyond the hedgerows and down the long gentle slope of the fields, he could see the Rochefort-Dinant highway. A curtain of dust hung over it. From one end of the valley to the other a seemingly endless column of motorised transport was grinding westwards.

When they reached the highway, and the pounding roar and dust of the column, von Leonarte's driver, with the skill of experience, inserted the motorcycle into the line. High above von Leonarte, pressed against the tailboard of their half-track carrier, the Panzer riflemen were sitting knee to knee – bronzed, dusty young faces grinning down at him from under the lips of their steel helmets. Von Leonarte felt envious. They were heading for battle, while he was about to be assigned a staff job by an old family friend who was anxious to do his mother a favour. At that moment, he felt homesick for his crew and for his troop facing the enemy across the Meuse in front of Bazeilles.

At a crossroads outside the village of Celles, four kilometres from Dinant, the convoy was diverted off the main highway to head north towards Houx and Yvoir. Von Leonarte could see that they were approaching an active battle area, and knew that the 7th Panzer headquarters must have advanced forward. He decided to press on to Dinant. Almost immediately they were flagged down by a Field Gendarme. Von Leonarte was obliged to show his papers. His driver was relegated to riding pillion while a Field Gendarme NCO drove them down through the woods into the town.

The town was built on the steep escarpment overlooking the Meuse. Streets of small stone houses were ranged in terraces, each looking out over the roofs of the street below. Narrow lanes ran behind each row under the cliffs, twisting in steep hairpin bends until they reached the quays and the warehouses on the river-bank. As von Leonarte and the motorcycle descended the escarpment, although there was no sound of gunfire, there was every sign of the town having been recently taken. Roof-timbers were visible where slates had been shattered and knocked off by machine-gun fire. Windows and doors had been smashed in. House walls were crushed at street-corners where tanks had been forced to swivel round abruptly, and although there was little sign of intensive bombardment, the streets were littered with dusty rubble. The inhabitants of the town had disappeared entirely. Files of Panzer infantry crouched behind yard walls, rifles between their knees, cigarettes in their cupped hands, awaiting the order to move down to the river. Here and there tanks had smashed down a yard wall, and lurked up against the houses where they could not be spotted from the far bank of the Meuse. In one of the narrow streets down which von Leonarte passed, the body of a Belgian soldier lay sprawled across the cobbles. His head, and the upper part of his torso, had been crushed to pulp under the tracks of some armoured fighting vehicle, while the lower half of his body appeared to be intact.

The Field Gendarme NCO drove the motorcycle into a small

courtyard surrounding a fountain. The emblem of the 7th Panzer Division, painted on a wooden board, was propped up against some wooden steps. A Panzer infantry lance-sergeant with two men, rifles slung over their shoulders, and regimental police brassards round their wrists, stood at the back door of a modest house. The lance-sergeant came forward as von Leonarte dismounted. He saluted.

'Advanced Headquarters, Field Intelligence?' von Leonarte asked.

'The Captain is correct,' the lance-sergeant replied.

'To see Colonel Reuther,' von Leonarte told him.

He held out his identity papers. The lance-sergeant saluted and opened the door for him. Von Leonarte went into the dark little passage way and up the stone stairs between whitewashed walls. At the turn of the stairs, he stood aside to allow a couple of signallers to pass him; they were backing down the steps, paying out telephone cable from a wooden spool as they went. At the top, daylight spilled from an open door, across the landing. Von Leonarte went in. Four senior officers were standing in the window embrasure, their field-glasses slung, about their necks, staring out into the sunlight. Behind them, the room showed evidence of having been cleared in a hurry. A chest of drawers had been placed under the slope of the roof by the window as a table for the officers' map cases. The delft-tiled washstand had been stripped of its jug and bowl. It now stood under a dark-stained Italian oleograph of Christ's agony in the garden, with three field-telephones mounted on it. The small double-bed had been pushed against the empty iron stove in the corner. The patchwork cover was littered with leather coats and document portfolios. A blue cotton pinafore and a white undergarment had fallen to the floor; they had been trampled over and marked by the officers' boots.

Von Leonarte cleared his throat.

'Gentlemen?' he asked, announcing his presence.

He clicked his heels. The smell of women's cheap scented soap still hung in the air. The officers turned round. It was a moment before von Leonarte recognised the tall, spare frame and the hollow, elderly face. He realised that he had never seen Uncle Alfred in uniform before.

Colonel Reuther's normally severe expression broke into a smile.

'Good heavens, young man,' he said, taking von Leonarte's hand, 'you've made excellent time.'

'I came as soon as the message reached me, Herr Oberst,' von Leonarte replied.

'How did you find us?' asked Colonel Reuther. 'We have advanced so rapidly!'

Von Leonarte explained how he had managed to move up towards

71

Dinant with Colonel Werner's 31st Regiment. Colonel Reuther put his arm round his shoulder affectionately, and brought him into the window embrasure.

'With the Colonel-General's permission,' he said, 'I wish to present to the Herr Colonel-General the Rittmeister of 1st Cavalry, Dieter von Leonarte. Rittmeister von Leonarte is the son of my old and dear friend, Bishop Joachim von Leonarte. Rittmeister von Leonarte has managed to find his way here since daybreak, this morning. From Sedan, was it?'

The most senior of the officers smiled. 'Is Sedan ours, young man?' he asked.

'Not yet, Herr Colonel-General,' von Leonarte replied, 'but it is fully invested. It's only a matter of time, Herr Colonel-General.'

A staff-major who had been peering out of the window through his field-glasses lowered them, and said, 'I expect, Colonel Reuther, your young friend would like some food after his long journey.'

'But of course,' Colonel Reuther agreed. 'There's a kitchen up the street.'

He went to the door, and called down to one of the signallers on the stairs to go and fetch some bread and soup, and to bring it to the parlour below.

The major removed his field-glasses from about his neck, and handed them to von Leonarte.

'Care for a peep at the enemy, Rittmeister?' he asked.

'I saw them on the west bank of the Meuse early this morning,' von Leonarte replied. 'English,' he added, to make himself interesting in such august company.

'English, Rittmeister?' asked the Colonel-General. 'In the Sedan sector?'

'Two officers,' von Leonarte replied. 'Walking about out in the open, examining us with their glasses, as cool as you please.'

He looked out of the window, over the rows of chimney-pots and down to the fast-flowing Meuse. From the narrow streets below reverberated the clatter of armoured vehicles. Immediately under the window, a machine-gun company of motorised infantry was dismounting from its motorcycles. Von Leonarte saw the men carrying the long-barrelled guns and heavy tripods, belts of ammunition trailing off their shoulders, crossing the back yards and disappearing into the houses to take up firing positions. Across the housetops, he could see the while cliffs overlooking a bend in the river, and a bridge with its parapet shot to pieces. On the nearside of the bridge, two large tanks stood lurking in the midst of the rubble, Mark IV's with their guns pointing at the far bank. In the bright sunlight, the Balkan crosses on their flanks stood out as if they had been freshly painted.

Looking directly in front of him through the glasses, von Leonarte could not see the river itself over the roof-tops, where it was buried in its steep gorge, but he could see across to the far bank, and the mass of trees shimmering in the afternoon heat.

'Somewhere in those woods,' said the Colonel-General, 'is General Corap and the French Ninth Army. They are just waiting for us to throw a bridgehead over. God knows how many guns he's got emplaced over there. And we've moved so fast, we've left all our heavy stuff miles behind – it's probably all still back at Rochefort. Corap's got some of the best field artillery in the world sitting there waiting for us.'

He lowered his glasses and rubbed his eyes.

'Too damned quiet over there,' he added. 'They haven't fired a single round since we moved in here. It's not healthy.'

Colonel Reuther was standing behind von Leonarte. He asked the Colonel-General's permission to take von Leonarte downstairs for a briefing.

'Of course,' the Colonel-General replied.

He glanced at the ribbon and cross about von Leonarte's throat.

'Where did you win that, Rittmeister?' he asked.

'Poland, Herr Colonel-General,' von Leonarte replied. 'With General Reinhardt's 4th Panzers at the first battle of Warsaw.'

The Colonel-General smiled.

'One of our young veterans, eh?' he said.

'Thank you, Herr Colonel-General,' von Leonarte replied. He wished that his father could have heard that.

He followed Colonel Reuther downstairs. At the bottom, as he was about to stoop under the low door-lintel into the parlour, he looked across the small, stone hallway straight into the kitchen. At the bare, scrubbed table sat an old man and his wife. The old man's face was creased in misery. His eyes, which stared into von Leonarte's, glistened with tears. The old woman who was all in black, with her hair in plaits just like a farmer's wife at home, was holding the old man's hand in hers. She was speaking to him, trying to console him. It was very strange, von Leonarte thought, that such a woman, in such clothes, should have used the sort of pungently scented soap which he had smelt upstairs. No German peasant woman of her age would have done so.

The parlour was empty except for one of the signallers, who was wiring up yet another field-telephone. A chaise-longue had been pulled under the window, into the light: a map pinned under talc to a board had been stood up on its worn velour covering. Von Leonarte noticed the oil-lamps in their polished brackets on the wall. Then he saw the electric light bulb suspended from a flex which was slung over a hook in the ceiling.

Colonel Reuther put down his cap and gloves by the field telephone.

73

'We may not boast of bringing culture to the Low Countries, this time,' he said, 'but we're introducing some modern amenities.'

He pointed to the electric light.

'The advantages of moving with Divisional Headquarters,' he continued. 'Chemical lavatories, hot water for washing and shaving, electric light – ah, and a hot meal!'

The signaller had entered the parlour. He put down a canteen of soup, and a tin plate bearing a small loaf of white bread.

'With the Herr Oberst's permission,' he said, 'would the gentlemen care for a bottle of wine?'

'I believe the gentlemen would,' replied Colonel Reuther, as the signaller took the bottle of red wine from under his arm and placed it on the table.

The man saluted and went out. Colonel Reuther took out his penknife, and opened the dusty bottle.

'*Vin ordinaire!*' he said. 'You'd think they could manage a decent Moselle in these parts, wouldn't you?'

He filled a cup and passed it to von Leonarte.

'I'm sure you'll have realised that we are about to launch the offensive which will win us the war?' he continued.

'It's obvious something big is happening,' von Leonarte agreed.

'I think I ought to tell you,' Colonel Reuther said, 'that 10th Panzers will form the spearhead of our advance.'

He paused before adding, 'But you, Dieter, will not be with them.'

Von Leonarte was not surprised, but his disappointment was acute. Colonel Reuther smiled kindly; he took two long cigars from his tunic pocket, one of which he put in his mouth, the other he placed in front of von Leonarte.

'Have it when you've finished eating,' he said.

'Supposing,' he continued, 'I were to tell you that you will cross the Meuse tomorrow, at Sedan, *ahead* of your comrades in the 10th Panzers? What of that?'

He lit his cigar.

'I would still prefer to be with my comrades,' von Leonarte replied.

'Of course,' said Colonel Reuther, 'but I have been given my task to perform in this campaign, and I have decided that you are the best man to assist me in it. I know you, you see, Dietl – and I know you are the sort of fellow for the exploit I have in mind.'

'Exploit, Uncle Alfred?' asked von Leonarte.

'I'm too old now,' said Colonel Reuther, 'to be leading cavalry raids deep behind enemy lines and that sort of thing, so they've put me in Special Intelligence. I want you to do the dashing stuff for me!' He went over to the map by the window, and pointed with the damp end of his cigar.

'Tomorrow morning,' he said, 'General Guderian's XIX Corps will attack across the Meuse above and below Sedan. The infantry of the 10th Panzers will be the first to cross, but they won't immediately be able to put a bridge across in their sector, so the 10th Panzers' armour will have to remain round Bazeilles for another twenty-four hours. The first bridge will be constructed here, at Floing, below Sedan. Lieutenant-Colonel Graf Von Schwerin will be leading the Grossdeutschland Regiment as the vanguard of the 1st Panzers, and they'll have a bridge-building Pioneer detachment with them. The 1st Panzers' armour – two hundred and seventy-six fighting vehicles in all – will be waiting here, in the Fond de Givonne. And that's where you'll be. Your own regiment will have provided you with a *kübelwagen*, with machine-gun mounted, and three men including a senior NCO and a proficient driver. You and your men will hit the west bank of the Meuse the moment the last plank of the bridge is laid – even before the tanks start crossing . . . Light your cigar, young man.'

He passed his box of matches over to von Leonarte, and waited until the cigar was alight.

'Your target,' he continued, pointing at the map, 'is here, just south of the Rethel-Vouziers road – the Château de la Berlière. Since the main thrust of the 1st and 10th Panzers will be to the north-west, in the direction of Abbeville, La Berlière will be to the south of our left flank. But the enemy will, no doubt, be expecting us to head straight for Paris, and will be confused by the direction our advance will take – at least for a few hours. A small, fast-moving raiding party such as yours should be able to take advantage of the enemy's confusion; by mid-morning, the day after tomorrow, you should report back to me, safe and sound.'

He leant over and refilled von Leonarte's cup.

'Any questions?' he asked.

'What is the objective?' von Leonarte asked.

'Ah!' said Colonel Reuther. 'Now that requires some explanation. It is a medallion. It was worn in ancient times by the commanders of the French kings' armies in battle. It is quite unique; of the sort known as a tondeau – a relief beaten into solid silver. It was made in the thirteenth century, and represents the figure of Christ giving a sword to St Louis.'

'Forgive me, Uncle, but what is the importance of this medallion?' von Leonarte asked.

Colonel Reuther's face reflected the enthusiasm of a schoolmaster who has been lured by a pupil away from the matter of his lesson onto a pet theme.

'I have proposed a plan by which this medallion should be seized by us, and be put to our own use. It is a plan which has been endorsed by the Ministry of National Enlightenment, and has won the approval of the Reichs Chancellor himself – so your exploit will not go unnoticed!'

The note of enthusiasm in Colonel Reuther's voice took von Leonarte by surprise. In common with most senior members of the Officers Corps, Colonel Reuther had never manifested much liking for the Leader, and had flinched from the vulgarity of his public utterances. He was warming to his theme, however.

'The more people must suffer in war,' he was saying, 'the more they require symbols to reinforce their determination. We Germans will fight for our Führer-oath, I suppose – some of us, at least. Some of us will fight for Schiller, or Kant, or Bach; and some of us for the Black Knight of Bamberg.'

He smiled indulgently.

'The English have their King George – and a class system which makes the tommy ready to die for his officers. But the French are divided. Some would die for the hammer and sickle; some for the lily banner of old. What Frenchman would die for the Republic? So they are left with nothing to unite them but idols so old as to be uncontroversial. My plan is that we should take such an idol and use it to our advantage!'

'Won't it have been moved to Paris for safe keeping?' asked von Leonarte.

'It is possible, of course,' replied Colonel Reuther. 'On the other hand, we have no reason to suppose that the French are expecting to be attacked in that quarter; from their point of view, the major push is here, and further north. I don't suppose the Baron de Bart-Mendel – the owner of the Château de la Berlière – feels any sense of urgency. He keeps the medallion in a monstrance or some such in the Château chapel, but I don't suppose he appreciates its – how shall I put it? – quasi-religious significance. He understands its monetary worth, of course. He's a Jew.'

'But he keeps this medallion in a chapel?' asked von Leonarte. 'A Roman Catholic chapel, I take it?'

'As you know, young man, I'm like your father; I don't hold with all this anti-Jew nonsense. This Baron de Bart-Mendel is probably a very decent fellow who maintains his Christian chapel for the benefit of his servants and his tenants. But we should remember that the case of Alfred Dreyfus has never been allowed to die away entirely in France; there are many Frenchmen who believe that Dreyfus was pardoned only because of the influence of the Jews and the Freemasons. Some of those Frenchmen are men of the highest rank and social eminence. Just think, Dieter, what'll happen when we've defeated the Third Republic. We shall prove that we are the friends of France – the true France. We shall return this medallion, this blessed relic of St Louis, which we shall have taken from its Jewish owner, and we shall present it to some famous French soldier, in a great public ceremony in Notre Dame perhaps, or in the Panthéon. It will be just like the Grand Master Winrich Von Kniprode of the Teutonic Order returning the cross of St Kasimir to King Jagellon of Poland.' He tapped the ash from the end of his cigar. 'Imagine the scene as an illustration in a school history-book of the future. It'll rank with the picture of Prince von Blücher's meeting with the Duke of Wellington at La Belle Alliance, or that of Wilhelm I being acclaimed by the Princes in the Salon des Glaces at Versailles!'

He stopped and smoked his cigar, savouring both it and his mental picture. Von Leonarte listened to the throb of engines and the shouted commands from the street below the house.

'May I take my own tank crew with me?' he asked. 'They have been with me since Poland.'

'That would probably be best,' Colonel Reuther told him. 'I will give you a written order to take back with you.'

Von Leonarte could not help feeling a certain pleasure at the thought of reporting to Major Spiesser that he was to be attached to the Grossdeutschland Regiment.

Through the noise of movement outside came a sudden, ear-blasting shriek. He was thrown to his knees; blood was racing past his eardrums like a shield between the intolerable roar and his brain. Huge lumps of plaster were falling from the ceiling. Colonel Reuther was on the floor beside him, his arms over his head. Von Leonarte looked up through the showering dust. There was another deafening thud nearby, which shook the walls and brought plaster cascading down like white flour. The windows were shattered into tiny slivers of glass spread across the dust-covered floor. He saw a crack down one wall from ceiling to floor. Above his head, he could see the wooden slats where the plaster had fallen. There was another thud, and then another. He tried to call to Reuther but the thick fog of plaster dust choked him. Outside a voice was bawling out, 'Stretchers! Stretchers!'

'Colonel Reuther?' somebody shouted from outside the room. 'Are you all right in there?'

Colonel Reuther put his hands to the floor and lifted up his head. 'We're all right, thank you!' he called back.

He scrambled to his feet. He was as covered with dust as a miller, but he was smiling. Von Leonarte got up.

'Wash the dust from your mouth, young man.'

Colonel Reuther pointed to the white-covered wine bottle. A piece of plaster fell from the ceiling, hitting von Leonarte on the shoulder. He looked about for his cup, but could not find it.

'From the bottle!' croaked Colonel Reuther.

Von Leonarte picked up the bottle, and drank from it. He handed it to Colonel Reuther, who raised it.

'Success to your mission, and to my scheme, eh Dietl?' he said. 'And to General Corap!' he added.

'To General Corap?' asked von Leonarte.

'To General Corap and the French Ninth Army!' said Colonel Reuther. 'They're behaving normally, at last! It's quite a relief. Now our lads can start spotting their guns.'

Von Leonarte blinked as sharp bars of sunlight cut through the cloud of floating rubble.

5

The afternoon shadows were beginning to lengthen as Vivian and Julie reached Laon. Vivian drove the car round the outside of the medieval city wall. Above it, the cathedral stood on its lofty escarpment like some great stone ark stranded by the receding flood.

Julie had dozed off several times during the journey from Montcornet, lulled by the warmth and the steady purr of the car along the main road. She still felt muddied with sleep.

'Is your HQ in the town?' she asked.

'It's at Bruyères, about four kilometres to the south,' Vivian replied, 'a military secret undoubtedly well-known to Jerry.'

They turned down an avenue of plane trees.

'Have you got somewhere to stay in Paris?' he asked.

'I'm sure the ENSA office will fix me up with somewhere,' Julie replied.

The station was at the far end of the avenue.

'You must be very tired after all your adventures,' he said. Julie glanced at him.

'I'm sorry I kept dozing off,' she said. 'I expect I'll get some rest on the train.'

He nodded.

Cars were parked all round the kerbs of the station forecourt. People were sitting against the walls of the buildings, on their upturned suitcases. Others huddled in family groups, their luggage about their feet.

Vivian stopped as close to the entrance as he could. A family trudged past them to take its place in the small crowd round the doors. The young mother was carrying two heavy suitcases; on either side of her, a toddler was trying to reach for her hand. One of them was crying steadily. The father had a third young child, a little girl, riding on his shoulders, its fingers clutching at his hair. Julie reached over to the back seat for her case.

'I think perhaps I'd better come in with you,' said Vivian.

'I'm sure there's no need,' said Julie.

But he got out of the car and took the case from her. She felt the touch of his fingers on the back of her hand.

'I expect you're awfully busy,' she protested.

'I'm going to report back to Bruyères,' he told her. 'But I don't suppose there'll be anything for me to do. They haven't a lot of use for a liaison officer at the moment.'

He led her through the door. The vestibule inside was packed; would-be passengers were squeezed onto the benches, others squatted against the walls, and the floor was crammed with piled luggage and groups of people. Vivian pushed a way for Julie through the throng; they stumbled over cases as they went. Julie slipped her hand under the stump of his missing arm. To her surprise, he pulled it away from her abruptly.

At the opposite side of the vestibule, they found the window of the booking-office shuttered and padlocked. A steel grille was drawn across the entrance to the open spaces of the platforms; it too was locked. An unshaven official was standing in front of it, trying to make himself heard about the noise of fractious children.

'*Mesdames et messieurs!*' he kept on repeating in a hoarse voice. The sweat was trickling down his temples.

'There will be no more trains until tomorrow! No more!' he repeated.

'Why not?' somebody yelled.

The official shrugged with gallic expressiveness.

'Military necessity?' he suggested. 'The War Council?'

He raised his hand, imploring silence.

'*S'il vous plaît, mesdames et messieurs!*' he begged.

Suddenly, he shouted at the top of his voice:

'The next train for Paris. . . .! '

For the first time, the adults made a concerted effort to quieten their exhausted children.

'The next train for Paris will be the *rapide* at 0800, tomorrow morning! There will be the usual *omnibus* at 0715 for Chalons via Reims. And at 0730 to Abbeville via Amiens.'

Even as he was speaking, a porter appeared behind the steel grille. Before anybody could realise what he was up to, he had put a key into the padlock and twisted it round, removed the padlock, and had opened the grille a little way. The official slipped through it onto the empty station. The grille clanged shut once more, and was locked.

'I'm afraid you're going to have to stay the night in Laon,' Vivian told Julie.

They pushed back through the crowd, and stepped out onto the forecourt.

'I'll take you to a hotel,' he said decisively. 'I know a reasonably good one·...'

'Are you sure you should be wasting your time on me?' Julie interrupted anxiously.

She didn't have enough money for an hotel of any kind.

'I really can manage, you know,' she went on. 'I'm quite resourceful when I have to be.'

'I'm sure you are,' he replied. 'But I have to go through Laon to get onto the road for Bruyères. And I expect there'll be quite a few people looking for a hotel tonight, so you might as well give yourself a head start.'

He carried her case back to the car.

'I'll take you up to the old quarter by the cathedral,' he said as he unlocked the door.

'I'm sorry,' she said.

'About what?' he asked.

'To tell you the truth, I don't think I've got much more than my train fare to Paris,' she admitted.

He looked at her. She seemed deeply embarrassed.

'I'd better stay here,' she said. 'I expect a lot of people will be camping out here tonight. And I'll be sure of getting a good seat on the train.'

He went round and got into the driving-seat. He leaned over and opened the door for her.

'Don't you have a kindly old aunt,' he asked, 'to sew gold sovereigns into your stays before you set out on adventures?'

'I've got an aunt,' Julie replied, 'but she wouldn't thank you for calling her "old". And she's not the sort to sew anything into anything!'

'Get in,' he said.

Obediently, she sat in beside him. His leather wallet was open on his knees. He drew out a small wad of vividly coloured French notes, and doubled it up between his finger and thumb.

'Please don't go proud and independent on me,' he said.

'Really, Major Hardwicke! I couldn't!' Julie protested. I'll be all right – truly! You've been terribly kind already!'

'Don't be silly, Miss Armitage!' he told her. 'We've no idea what might happen tomorrow morning. I'll give you the address of my flat in Town, and then you can return it to me whenever you feel like it. All right?'

Julie took the money and put it into her purse.

'I don't know what to say,' she told him. 'I've never done anything like this before.'

'You mean you never borrowed money when you were a student?' Vivian asked. 'When you were at drama school?'

She was taken by surprise. But, of course, he knew she was an actress.

'Oh yes!' she said. 'But never from a man!' They drove back down the approach road. The shadows of the trees had lengthened, spilling like bars across the pavement. They turned up the hill into the medieval town, and out onto the broad *parvis* alongside the cathedral, under the shadows of its five massive towers. They stopped at a low archway leading into a courtyard. A brass sign on the side of the arch read 'Hôtel des Frères le Nain'.

'Here we are,' said Vivian, leaning across her to open the door. 'I don't promise we'll get you a room here, but it's worth a try.'

He took her suitcase once more, and led her into the courtyard. On either side it was overlooked by stone galleries wreathed in vine-leaves. At the end, Vivian pushed open a glass door into the small reception hall, and held it open for her with his shoulder. A woman in steel-rimmed spectacles came out of the back office and took her place at the heavy, leather-bound register.

'*Bonjour, monsieur?*' she inquired. '*Bonjour, mademoiselle?*'

Julie explained that she wanted a single room for one night only. The woman's expression was distinctly frosty.

'*Bien sûr, mademoiselle!*' the woman replied. '*Comme tout le monde, n'est-ce pas?*'

Vivian rested his elbow on the counter.

'Excuse me, madame,' he began in a very earnest voice. 'Miss Armitage came here this morning, from Paris. I am attached to your Fourth Armoured Division over at Bruyères. I had leave of absence for this one day only. Perhaps it may seem a little foolish, madame, but Miss Armitage and I so much wanted to spend today together; things being as they are, when might we have another opportunity? Now we find that we have spent too long looking at your beautiful city – all evening trains back to Paris have been cancelled. I have brought Miss Armitage here to the Hôtel des Frères le Nain because I remember so well spending a few days here in happier times. I have such good memories of the comfort and, if I may so so, of the cuisine . . . '

The woman was smiling somewhat regretfully.

'Alas, monsieur – mademoiselle – the hotel is absolutely full. The Belgians. Unfortunately!'

'I know we may be asking you to put yourself to some trouble, madame,' Vivian pleaded. 'We have had such a happy day to-gether!'

'One moment, monsieur!'

The woman disappeared into the back office.

'I don't know why,' Julie said in a low voice, 'but somehow I would never have expected it of you!'

'What? That I'm an accomplished liar?' he asked.

She nodded. '*Have* you stayed here before?' she asked.

'Of course,' he replied. 'Otherwise I wouldn't have brought you straight here. And the food is really excellent. Substantially, I was telling the truth. I just added an appeal to the natives' incurable romanticism.'

The woman emerged once more from the office. She pushed her spectacles up her nose with her forefinger, and beckoned Vivian to the farthest end of the counter. She glanced at Julie to ensure she was out of earshot, then began speaking to him rapidly in a whisper. When she was finished, Vivian returned to Julie. He was smiling.

'She says there is a single room,' he told her. 'It's little more than a closet. Apparently it's set into the outer wall – at the far end of the first floor, over there . . . ' He pointed to the end of one of the galleries across the courtyard. 'It isn't normally let,' he went on. 'In fact, it's kept for when there's a special function, and they take in extra maids from out of town – so that they can stay overnight. She says they keep it as a chambermaid's pantry: the cupboards are full of brooms and buckets and so on, but it's clean, and the bed's comfortable.'

'It sounds perfect!' said Julie.

'Monsieur will be staying for dinner?' the woman called from behind the counter.

Julie wondered if she dared ask him to stay.

'I must report to Bruyères,' he smiled. 'Perhaps Madame would let me have a scrap of paper?'

He took out a pencil and scribbled down the address of his flat in Belsize Lane.

'You see?' he said to Julie. 'It's a form of blackmail. By expecting you to repay me, I'm ensuring you will get in touch with me at home!'

'I shall certainly get in touch with you,' Julie replied, 'and thank you so very much. If it hadn't been for you, I don't know where I'd have ended up.'

'Paris, I imagine. Via Reims.'

'I'm glad I didn't,' said Julie, surprising herself.

He smiled, and held out his hand to her. She took it and gave it a squeeze.

'Thank you again,' she said.

She watched him cross the courtyard. He turned under the gateway and waved back at her. A middle-aged chambermaid appeared to take her to her room. Julie followed her up the stairs and along the length of the open gallery.

The bedroom was long and narrow, like a very short corridor. There was a four-foot thickness of stone round the window. Walls, ceiling, and even the floor, except where there was a worn rush mat at the bedside, were as dull and grey as those of a dungeon. Several birch-brooms and pails had been placed under the window, with stiff dried floor-cloths draped over the sides of the pails. The room was clean, but the wash-basin with its old-fashioned tap and the bidet were both streaked with rust-coloured stains. From the street below rose the noise of traffic, footsteps, voices calling. Julie thrust a note into the chambermaid's hand; the woman's face registered her surprised delight. As the door closed behind her, and the heavy latch fell, Julie sat back on the bed. It was soft and comfortable. She lay down without bothering even to kick off her shoes.

The noise from the street below kept to-ing and fro-ing through her dreams. Each time she floated upwards into consciousness, she told herself she must not allow herself to fall asleep again. She was woken finally by the chill on her midriff where the edge of her blouse had parted company with the waistband of her slacks. It was getting dark; she realised that she was very hungry as well as cold. She rose stiffly, and undressed, washed, and changed into her pleated skirt and short-sleeved pullover. She brushed her hair, made up and dabbed on a little scent, and felt a little better. Then she set off down the open gallery. Although it was quite dark the evening sky still had a hollow paleness above the hotel roof-tops. As she went down the stairs, she slung the cardigan she was carrying over her shoulders and bare arms.

She crossed the cobbled yard under the vine-leaves to the restaurant. It was crowded and noisy, with tables packed so close that the waitresses were having to squeeze between the chairs and benches. Julie stared across the chattering, clattering haze into the corners, seeking for an empty place. At first she did not see him because of the number of uniforms in the room. He was in the farthest corner, almost an alcove. He was waving to her, not daring to leave the small square table set for two.

'I thought you'd never come down,' he told her as he rose to greet her. 'I was beginning to wonder how long they'd let me stay here.'

'I fell asleep,' she admitted. 'Again.'

He helped her to her chair.

'Am I welcome?' he asked as he sat down opposite to her.

There was just a hint of uncertainty in his voice.

'Don't be silly,' she said to reassure him.

'Our HQ is in a state of organised chaos,' he explained. 'I felt that the best thing for me was to keep out of everybody's way.'

He had put on a freshly laundered shirt; his uniform jacket was newly pressed, and his Sam Browne gleamed with polish.

'I'm glad,' Julie told him. 'It's good to have your company.'

'What's your broom-cupboard like?' he asked.

'A lot better than the back of a van,' she replied. 'It's actually got a bidet – only cold water of course.'

A waitress had come to the table. Julie let Vivian order. When the waitress had gone away, he filled their glasses with wine from the carafe. He raised his glass.

'To your safe return home,' he said. Then he asked, 'What's your Christian name?'

'Julie,' she answered. 'You know that – and yours is Vivian.'

'I meant your real name,' he said.

She pulled a long face.

'Juliet,' she told him.

'It's a very beautiful name,' he said. '"Romeo and Juliet".'

'That's exactly what that awful man said,' Julie replied. 'The one who was giving me a lift into Montcornet before you turned up.'

She shivered and drew her cardigan closer about her shoulders.

'Do you know?' she went on. 'It sounds silly, but he really was one of the nastiest things that has ever happened to me.'

Vivian nodded.

'The scavengers are moving in,' he said. 'They're like vultures. They can smell battle coming.'

'When he touched me,' said Julie, 'it was like being touched by something slimy.'

Vivian laughed.

'It isn't funny!' Julie objected.

'I know,' Vivian agreed. 'But you do make him sound rather like one of John Buchan's "greasy levantines".'

The waitress returned to the table.

'I hope the memory of him hasn't taken your appetite away,' he added.

'Nothing ever does that,' Julie replied. 'It's being on the stage – you always have a good appetite because you never know where the next meal's coming from!'

'What made you decide to go on the stage?' asked Vivian.

'It's wanting attention, I suppose,' she told him. 'You know? All those people out there, looking at me. It's people showing you that you matter. And of course the companionship. It's just that you're never lonely – as long as you're working, of course.'

Vivian nodded.

'Are you afraid of loneliness?' he asked.

'Yes,' she admitted. 'I think I'd go dotty if I had to be by myself for too long.' She checked herself. 'Hey, let's talk about you for a bit,' she said.

'What in particular?' Vivian asked.

'The obvious,' she suggested. 'Why don't you have two arms?'

'Do you really want to know?' he asked.

'Of course. I don't meet one-armed soldiers every day,' she told him.

The pain was the thing he chiefly remembered. He had loosed off two ammunition drums from the lewis-gun before he had been hit. Before his eyes, he had seen the flesh and bone of his arm, and his shirt-sleeve, become one mangled pulp. He'd heard his own screaming as Sergeant-Major Tucker had dragged him down through the turret hatch into the safety of the disabled tank. He had prayed to be allowed to faint, and his prayer had been answered.

'You can never really describe pain, can you?' he told Julie.

'You can talk about it, can't you?' she said. 'I mean, the more horrible a thing, the more it helps to be able to talk about it.'

'You have to be very careful whom you try to talk to,' said Vivian. 'You've the first person I've tried to explain it to.'

'Wasn't there anybody you could trust?' asked Julie.

'Well, it is a bit of an imposition, isn't it?' he asked.

'What you mean is,' she replied, 'if you told your friends in the mess, they'd think you were a cry-baby!'

'I don't think they would put it quite like that,' said Vivian.

'But it would be a bit much?'

'Yes.'

He paused. '*Die Lieb' versüsset jede Plage*', he remembered – the words of Pamina in *Die Zauberflöte: Love soothes the wound all creatures feel.*

'I suppose there are things one feels one can tell a woman,' he said, 'which one can't tell to one's friends.'

'That's ridiculous,' she told him.

'I don't see why.'

She didn't want to engage him in an argument about equality of the sexes. Not at that moment.

'You aren't married?' she asked.

'Was,' he told her. 'I'm divorced.'

He looked at her, waiting for her to be shocked.

'Oh dear,' she said. 'I'm sorry. I always seem to go too far!'

'It's all right,' he told her.

'I really am very sorry,' she said.

'Don't worry,' he said. 'I mean it.'

'Was it? – Was it before you were wounded?' she asked.

He nodded.

'Rosemary would never have asked me for a divorce if I'd been disabled like this,' he said. 'She would have considered it her duty to stand by me.'

He unbuttoned his jacket pocket and took out his cigarette-case. He held it open across the table. She took one, leaned forward to light it from the candle in the centre of the table. She picked up the candle-holder and held the flame for him to light his cigarette.

85

'You're really quite different from the person I thought you were when I first saw you the other evening,' she told him.

'In what way?' he asked.

She put down the candle on the table, between them.

She laughed. 'I mean wounded hero, medals, and that sort of thing. And all those officers were looking up to you.'

'You don't think they should have done?' he was amused.

'No,' she said, 'It wasn't that. Perhaps I was scared of you. You looked the sort of person who would make me feel awful if you disapproved of the way I behaved.'

'And you don't feel that way any more?' he asked.

She laughed. 'Actually, I think I'm getting terribly confused!' she said. 'I do feel that way still. But differently somehow.'

Vivian would have liked to have told her how lovely she was looking. Instead, he said: 'Perhaps I feel the same way about you. You have quite a line in disapproval I seem to remember.'

'That was awful!' she said. 'I was so ashamed!'

'You were standing up for what you believed to be right.'

He paid the bill, and they left the restaurant.

'Would you like to go for a stroll?' he asked. 'Round the Cathedral square for example? Or are you too tired?'

'No, I'm not too tired,' she said.

Vivian clamped his cap under the stump of his arm. Julie slipped her hand under his other arm. They walked side by side out of the hotel courtyard, and up the Rue de Cloître under the lofty shadow of the Hôtel-Dieu.

'I noticed you,' said Vivian, 'the moment you came into the mess that night. I couldn't stop looking at you.'

'I know,' said Julie. 'You were wondering who that silly girl was, sitting on that stupid man's knee.'

'No,' Vivian told her, 'that was later. But I did wonder, actually.'

'Nobody else offered me a knee,' she replied. 'It didn't mean anything.'

They were walking along the path beside the cathedral. On the far side of the square, the severe outline of the Bishop's Palace stood against the starlit sky. They walked to the end of the path.

'They say,' Vivian told her, 'that if you stand here on a clear day, you can see for seventy or eighty miles across Champagne.'

Julie stared out over the roof-tops of the town below.

'I hoped so much we'd meet again, Julie,' Vivian said quietly, so that she knew something was about to happen. 'And then, this afternoon as I was driving across Montcornet of all places, there you were. I could scarcely believe it.'

'I felt the same way when I saw your car,' said Julie.

'Did you?' he asked.

'Yes.'

She looked up, making out the expression on his face in the gloom. He put his arm round her, drew her to him and kissed her. She gave him her lips slightly parted.

'I wanted to meet you again too,' she whispered.

She let him kiss her again.

'Do men fall in love with you?' he asked.

She couldn't read his face in the starlight.

'They say they do sometimes, but you mustn't.'

'Why not?' he asked.

'Because it would be very silly,' she told him, 'and you aren't a silly person.'

'Why would it be silly?' he asked.

'Because men think they have to say it to get what they want,' she replied.

'If I said it, it might be because I actually meant it,' he suggested.

'That would be silly too,' she replied. 'You have to go back to your regiment, and I've got to go home ... I hate letting things get complicated!'

'If we really want to, we can meet again,' he said. 'In Town ... Unless there's somebody else?'

Oh shit! she thought.

'It isn't that,' she replied. 'I just get scared when things start happening. As if I'm losing control.'

One always knew what was going to happen with poor old Ambrose – he'd be there waiting.

'You've chosen a strange profession for one who likes to know what's going to happen to her,' Vivian said.

He sounded amused, which was nice.

They walked slowly back across the square. His arm was still about her, and she kept close to him. At the top of the street leading down to the hotel, he stopped and kissed her again.

'I do trust you,' she told him. 'I think you're a very honest sort of person.'

'You shouldn't tell people things like that,' he said. 'It isn't fair on them.'

He could not tell her of the fear which had stepped out of the shadows.

'I'm immature in many ways,' he said. 'I'm not very good at relationships – I have a divorce to prove it.'

'What happened?' Julie asked. She felt that he had invited the question.

'Our tastes were very different,' he said. 'And service life always imposes strains on a marriage. Mind you, Rosemary was a very good

87

soldier's wife. She remarried recently, bettered herself, in fact; he's a major in the Coldstreams.'

'Was it very hurtful?' Julie asked.

'It was an amicable agreement,' he replied. 'Once it's obvious you'd be better off apart, you can cope with the idea.'

They had reached the archway gate of the hotel. His car was parked against the pavement a few yards away.

'I don't want to let you go,' he said.

She rested her cheek on his shoulder.

'You're not making it easy for me to say goodnight,' he told her.

'You don't have to say goodnight,' she told him quietly.

There had been a night shortly after he had been discharged from the military hospital at Fleet, near Aldershot, and just before Mrs Christie had invited him to stay at Glyndebourne. A vague but uneasy restlessness had compelled him to take the car down to Hyde Park. He had parked it, and had walked along the path between Rotten Row and Knightsbridge Barracks. A plump, young middle-aged woman had got up from the seat she had been sharing, under the lamplight, with three other women. She had approached him, smiling. She had been holding an unlit cigarette between her gloved fingers.

'Got a light, dear?' she had asked.

In her genteel dark-blue two-piece suit, with her close-fitting little velour hat, she had looked like a lady clerk or a shilling store supervisor. She had dipped her head to his lighter-flame, and had then stood up.

'All by yourself, darling?' she had asked. 'Want to keep me company?'

The women on the seat had been watching without real interest in the proceedings. But he had known at that moment why he had gone there. He had paid the woman seven-and-sixpence, and had taken her to the car. They had got into the back together, and she had helped him to unfasten his clothes. As she had paused in her fumbling to expose herself to him, the fear that had lain in wait lurched out of the darkness of his mind. The blankness in his empty sleeve seemed to have spread, so that half his body had become vacancy. Struggling with the fear, and with the woman's assistance, he had fought himself into some shallow state of arousal, but it had ended in premature ejaculation.

The woman had laughed.

'Traitor,' she said.

He had tried to apologise to her.

'No need to say sorry, dear,' she had told him as she got off him in the cramped gloom.

She had taken a handkerchief from her handbag, and had wiped the inside of her leg before pulling up her plain, crêpe-de-chine drawers. She had wiped the leather of the seat, folded the handkerchief carefully, and placed it back in her handbag.

'No harm done, is there, dear?' she had said as she got out of the car. As she turned to go off down the path back to the seat, he had seen the bored sadness in the downward curve of her printed mouth.

It had been a point at which life had seemed all loss.

'What about things getting too complicated?' he asked.

'I won't let them,' Julie replied, her head still on his shoulder.

It would have been easy to have made an excuse. He only had to say that he had to report back to Bruyères. He decided to meet the fear head on.

He disengaged himself from Julie.

'I'll be quite open with you,' he said. 'You might find I'm not a terribly adequate lover.'

Julie was shocked. 'What sort of a person do you take me for?' she asked.

He looked down at the ground.

'I'm sorry,' he said.

For a moment, she stood looking at him. She reached for his hand, and held it.

'Idiot,' she said. 'Come on, you great leader of men!'

She led him through the arch into the hotel courtyard.

The woman at the reception-desk studiedly failed to notice them as they passed up the stairs. Julie led Vivian along the open gallery, unlocked her door and switched on the light.

'There!' she said. 'As a broom-cupboard, it's luxurious. As a bedroom – well, it isn't too bad!'

Vivian looked about him. Now the electric light was glaring, Julie noticed that its flex was encrusted with cobweb up to the discoloured ceiling.

'I'm sorry about the mess,' she said.

She slipped her cardigan off her shoulders. Vivian put his khaki cap down on the chair.

'It's quite homely,' he said.

She pulled loose her ribbon, and shook out her hair over her shoulders. She took off her skirt and pullover, and folded them neatly over the back of the chair. Vivian was struggling with the buckle of his Sam Browne.

'Here!' she said. 'Let me help you with that. Or are you too proud?'

'You're the second person who's asked me that, today,' he said.

She was standing close to him, letting him admire her.

'Not the second woman, I hope,' she said.

'No,' he assured her.

She pulled open the buckle and unbuttoned his jacket.

'Do you think I'd make a good batman?' she asked.

'Certainly a more attractive one than the one I've got,' he replied. 'He has a half-inch of black stubble on his chin. There doesn't seem to be any regulation in the French army which says that a man's got to shave.'

'Then I've got something in common with your batman,' she whispered. 'I don't shave either.'

He kissed her in the curve of her shoulder and neck.

'Wait a minute!' she told him.

She reached down and pulled off her slip over her head. She took his jacket from him, and placed it carefully over the back of the chair.

'There,' she said. 'That's better.'

He had removed his collar and tie. She hung them over the shoulder of his jacket. He began to remove his boots and jodhpurs. This, thought Julie, was the moment which ruined all bedroom scenes. Even the most exciting man in the world was unable to look anything but ridiculous taking off his trousers. She wondered if Scarlett O'Hara could have taken Rhett Butler seriously when he was taking down his trousers.

'You have also got much prettier legs than my batman,' Vivian said.

He hung his jodhpurs carefully over one of the cupboard doors.

'They are nice legs, aren't they?'

She glanced down at them shining in their silk stockings.

'The trouble is,' she said, 'my top part and my lower part don't match. I mean, I've got too much bosom for a dancer, and my legs are too long and skinny for a sweater-girl. It's tragic, really.'

She came up close to him, and tried to unbutton his shirt.

'No!' he said, and backed away.

She was taken by surprise. She told him, 'Now you're here with me, you'll have to trust me a little bit.' And smiled. 'I don't really like men who keep their shirts on.'

He stood still, letting her unbutton him. She drew the shirt off his shoulders and down his arms.

'It wasn't so awful, was it?' she asked.

Looking up into his face, she reached for his elbow, then, before it was too late, she ran her fingers down the inch or two of his arm and cupped the palm of her hand about the stump.

'You do trust me, don't you?' she asked, willing him not to remove the stump from her hand.

'Have I an alternative?' he asked.

'No,' she replied. 'You haven't.'

She unbuttoned her drawers at the waist with her free hand, and let them slither down her legs to the floor. Kicking them off from round her ankles, she sat down on the edge of the bed without leaving go of the stump.

'It's sort of smooth and rounded,' she said. 'Knobbly.'

'What did you expect?' he asked.

'Flat, I suppose,' she said. 'Sawn off, like the branch of a tree.'

'There's the bone and sinew,' he told her. 'It would be asking rather a lot of a surgeon to plane it off!'

He sat down on the bed beside her.

'Julie,' he began, but did not go on. Instead, he pressed the stump into her hand. As she put her arm round his bare waist, feeling the firmness about his ribs and spine, he unfastened her brassière. She fell backwards, parting her legs and pressing her sore feet into the cool softness of the duvet. As he bent over her to cover her, she put her arm round his neck, and reached down to hold his penis. She felt it grow in her hand.

'That's good,' she whispered. 'What's wrong with that?'

She stroked him, playing with him gently, caressing its size and its hardness.

'It's beautiful,' she kept telling him.

She did not come; she was too concerned with giving him confidence. She did not pretend, as she had done with Ambrose from time to time, but she was careful not to allow him to see that she had been left unsatisfied. She lay as still as she could as Vivian covered her with the duvet and lay down beside her. He fell asleep before she too dozed off.

It was not long before she woke up for the first time. There was still the slight ache, the throbbing between her thighs. There was still the sound of traffic in the street below the window, and of voices on the galleries of the hotel yard. In the moonlight, she could see Vivian's face on the pillow, only a few inches from her own. The worried look was gone, the marks of a peaceful, gentle strength left. She wanted very much to kiss him, perhaps to arouse him, but decided to leave him at rest. Very carefully she unfastened her suspender-belt, drawing it out from under the duvet, and dropped it on the floor beside her. Then she tried to roll her stockings down her legs, but found that she could only just push them off her knees without disturbing Vivian's half of the duvet. She fell asleep again with them rolled half way down.

The second time she awoke, there was the faintest hint of daylight from the window. A single bird was chirping its welcome to another spring day. She was very warm and relaxed. But beyond the chirping of the bird, beyond the stillness of the sleeping town, came a steady, dull thudding. At first she thought that there must be an air-raid somewhere nearby. But as she lay listening, she realised that it was too regular, too monotonous. She wondered whether it was artillery-fire. Once again she looked into Vivian's untroubled face. She knew they hadn't much time; she would have liked to have woken him, to have put her arms about him. His face, though weathered and rugged, appeared so much younger when he was asleep. The guns would wake him soon enough, she thought. As the thudding continued and seemed to grow more intensive, she lay watching over him, guarding his rest.

6

Von Leonarte was woken by the dew creeping up from the crushed grass through his greatcoat, and by the sound of the guns round Sedan, four or five kilometres away. Senior Driver Helm was crouched over the primus a few yards off, heating a dixie full of coffee. As soon as he saw von Leonarte sitting up, he filled a mug and brought it over. Then he went back to the primus, borrowed a bayonet from tank-crew-member Graser, and began to cut a side of bacon into rashers. A few minutes later, the fresh dawn air was filled with the smell of bacon frying in its own fat. Von Leonarte had no idea where the bacon had come from, nor did he ask.

From beyond the hedges on either side, came the sound of men stirring; the clatter of dixies, voices calling, and the swish of jackboots trampling through the long grass. It was a relief to know that they had found the 1st Panzers. The previous night, Von Leonarte with his three men had set off northwards across the Fond de Givonne to find them, and had discovered utter confusion as they had driven in the dark, without lights, along the winding country roads. Again and again they had been forced to stop and pull over onto the verge, as some huge, unlit vehicle reared up in the blackness, the driver with his head sticking out of the window, shouting down, 'Hey, comrades, anybody know where we are?'

Von Leonarte had become convinced that the entire Tenth Panzer Group was wandering aimlessly in the night, between the Belgian frontier and the Meuse.

He drank his coffee and ate gratefully the bacon which Helm had fried for him. It would soon be time to move up to join the Grossdeutschland Regiment at the river. He was glad to feel a stirring in his lower bowel; a good shit now would be an excellent preparation for the day's activity. He rolled up his greatcoat, and threw it to Radinski to put in the back of the *kübelwagen*.

'Heat up some more coffee,' he ordered Graser. 'See the thermoses are properly filled. We may need a hot drink before we are through.'

At the far end of the hedgerow against which the *kübelwagen* had been parked, there was a small knoll covered in dark bushes. Von Leonarte trudged over to it and climbed into the privacy of the bushes. When he was finished, he stood up and climbed to the summit of the knoll, onto the top of a large boulder. From this point of vantage, he could see the whole way up the broad, gentle valley of the Givonne – its tightly enclosed fields, farms, and orchards – to the steeply rising woodlands of the Ardennes. And what he saw astonished him. For on every road, lane, or cart-track which led down the valley, there were columns of tanks, trucks, troop-carriers, stretching back into the distant morning haze. In every fold or dip of the ground, there was a mass of field-grey infantry in bivouac, or vehicles parked. He had not seen such a spectacle even in central Poland.

On the far side of the Meuse rose the forbidding heights of La Marfée. The French up there must have been able to see every tank, every carrier, every infantry company from the banks of the Meuse back to Givonne itself. Von Leonarte couldn't understand how the French artillerymen, who were undoubtedly in position up there, could resist such a target. They scarcely needed to adjust their aim; they merely had to open fire to hit a target.

In one sector at least, battle was already joined. Looking due south over the clustered orchards which still carried spring blossom on their branches, he could see the roofs of Sedan, huddled in its bend in the river. The town was burning, the smoke hanging in the still air, uncertain which way to drift. Contained within Vauban's fortifications, houses, shops, and small factories were ablaze, like coals trapped in a brazier. It was difficult to imagine its garrison holding out in the midst of such a holocaust, but the gunfire was fierce and continuous, clearly audible above the steady roar of tanks and half-tracks grinding down the Fond de Givonne.

Von Leonarte returned along the hedgerow to the *kübelwagen*. Helm, Radinski and Graser were already climbing aboard. Graser had mounted the 34MG machine-gun on its stand between the two front seats, and was easing the breech-mechanism as if he were expecting to go into action within the next few minutes. Helm was revving up the engine. Von Leonarte swung himself into the seat beside Helm. He took the road map from its case, and pointed to the village of Floing where it was scattered close to the river bank.

'That's the Grossdeutschland's starting point,' he said.

They jolted over the field, and onto the narrow road. A weathered signpost had collapsed into the grass of the verge. Somebody had propped the bullet-pocked sign against its broken pedestal; it read 'D.967 Floing 1 km: Glaire 2½ km'. On the other side of the hedge, Assault Pioneers were scrambling up onto parked trucks and unloading them. A long column of infantrymen was carrying rubber dinghies away across the fields toward the river bank. The men were bare-headed and stripped to the waist, plunging through the long fresh grass at a jog-trot, straining six to a boat.

A Field Gendarme came over to the jeep and saluted von Leonarte. His eyes were hidden behind his dark glasses.

'14 Company, Grossdeutschland,' said von Leonarte.

The Field Gendarme pointed up the road. A cluster of houses, with their church spire, rose abruptly out of the shimmering fields.

'The Herr Hauptmann will find 14 Company HQ in the centre of the village, by the town hall,' he said.

A single motorcyclist came tearing up the road from the village leaving a trail of dust behind him. As he passed the *kübelwagen* and the Field Gendarme, he gave a friendly wave of his gauntleted hand before bouncing up onto the verge to avoid some oncoming trucks.

The sound of gunfire was growing heavier, but it was still coming from the direction of Sedan. In front of them, the village of Floing was ominously still. As they drove into it, they found that almost every house was a ruined shell. Below torn roofs, blackened rooms still smouldered, and rubble lay in heaps on the street and pavements. Men of the Grossdeutschland Regiment were squatting on either side of the main street. Their tunic sleeves were rolled up, concealing their regimental cuff titles. They were clutching their rifles, but most of them had taken off their helmets and had parked them on doorsteps or window-sills. Many of them had unfastened their T-belts so that their equipment hung loose. One or two were rolling cigarettes. A small group of regimental machine-gunners was sitting on two adjacent doorsteps. They were swathed in ammunition belts, and were stripping and cleaning their weapons.

Von Leonarte told Helm to draw up in front of what had been a bakery. The shelves inside the shattered windows were stripped bare but were still powdered with flour. Four or five grinning *Landsers* were lounging round the door, bareheaded, their helmets hooked onto their T-belts. One of them held up a pair of women's voluminous white bloomers at the jeep. He feigned terror, calling out in a crude approximation of a French accent, 'Soldiers! Comrades! I surrender!'

His comrades laughed loudly and von Leonarte heard Radinski snigger, in the seat behind him.

'Where's your company command-post?' he demanded sharply.

The *Landsers* snapped to attention. The man holding the bloomers tried to crush them in his hand like a handkerchief. He dropped them on the step behind him.

'With the Herr Hauptmann's permission,' said a corporal, 'straight over there. Can't miss it, Herr Hauptmann.'

Von Leonarte permitted himself a slight smile. As Helm drove off, he waved and called, 'Good luck, lads!'

Just inside the entrance to the village square, the wall of a house had collapsed. As Helm negotiated a way round the mountain of rubble, von Leonarte noticed a black stain which had trickled from under the fallen bricks. A dog was licking at it. As it saw the *kübelwagen* it backed away cringing, then slunk off across the square.

The *mairie* was still flying a tattered tricolor; outside it was parked another *kübelwagen*. Two half-track troop-carriers were parked in the alley beside it. Some young officers were standing round a café table, smoking. They had opened the umbrella over it to shade them from the sun; it bore a large, colourful advertisement for Dubonnet. A map was spread out on the table. The officers turned as von Leonarte got out of the *kübelwagen*, and went over to them. They glanced at his Knight's Cross and his cavalry insignia. He returned their salutes.

'Have I the honour, gentlemen,' he asked, 'to be in the presence of the commander, 14 Company, Grossdeutschland?'

A lean young senior-lieutenant, whose scarred cheek made his face severe under the black peak of his cap, bowed slightly, and extended his hand.

'Von Kötze, Berlin Guards,' he introduced himself.

'Von Leonarte, 1st Cavalry,' von Leonarte returned.

Senior-Lieutenant von Kötze introduced the other officers round the table. Von Leonarte explained his presence.

'My orders are to take my vehicle across the river at the earliest possible moment,' he said. 'You, of course, will be crossing in assault-craft. But I have been told that I should move up to the bank with you.'

'The Herr Rittmeister lends distinction to our company,' von Kötze replied.

'Has the Herr Rittmeister had breakfast this morning?' asked another lieutenant.

'My men and I have eaten very well, Lieutenant,' von Leonarte replied, 'thanks to French hospitality.'

The officers laughed.

'It is very quiet here,' Von Leonarte said.

'There wasn't a soul left here, when we arrived,' von Kötze replied. 'The whole place had been evacuated.'

'We've found the bodies of one or two old people killed in the bombardment,' said another officer.

A signaller came down the steps of the *mairie*.

'With the Herr Oberleutnant's permission . . . ' he announced.

Von Kötze nodded.

'Regiment has broken radio silence, Herr Oberleutnant,' said the signaller. 'They're transmitting *en clair*. 7th Company has been ordered to embark. 6th Company has been ordered up to the mill-house to await further orders.'

Von Kötze turned to his officers.

'If Regiment is transmitting *en clair,* we can expect the enemy to pay us some attention,' he said. 'To your platoons, gentlemen, and helmets on, if you please.'

Von Leonarte had returned to the *kübelwagen,* and was standing by the driving-seat talking to Helm when the first shell landed. The ground shuddered. Heavy black smoke came rolling down the street and poured out into the square. Helm, Radinski, and Graser threw themselves out of the *kübelwagen,* and crouched against its side with von Leonarte. Another shell screamed overhead, and plunged into the ruined houses behind them. The square shook as if in an earthquake. For a moment, von Leonarte was deafened. Helm had his goggles pushed up so that they rested on the lip of his helmet. His face was a mask of grey dust. The dust was settling on all four of them. The square was thick with smoke and hanging particles of rubble. Two men came running through it, past the *kübelwagen,* carrying a third man in their arms.

The smoke began to disperse. Von Kötze had climbed into his own vehicle. He turned and waved to von Leonarte to follow on. As Helm started the engine, fragments of rubble vibrated off the cowling. They followed close behind von Kötze, crawling along in bottom gear so as not to overtake the infantrymen who were scrambling in single file over the wreckage on either pavement. They were driving slowly between the orchards, towards the river, when the air above them was split with the shriek of passing shells. Von Leonarte looked back. The village was enveloped in a towering mass of smoke in which explosions flashed, like lightning buried in thunder-clouds.

Immediately ahead of them, a cluster of buildings rose from among the trees along the bank of the Meuse. One of them, a lofty wooden creosoted building, was fiercely ablaze. Beyond it, through the smoke and quivering air, the meadows on the far side of the river sloped upwards to the rim of the woods. And there, von Leonarte told himself, the French were dug into their redoubts. A helmeted officer, covered in dust from head to foot, scrambled up onto the road from a ditch. Dribbles of blood had dried and congealed in the stubble on his cheeks. He raised the palm of his outstretched hand, signalling von Kötze to halt, then waved at him directing him to go through a gap in the hedge into the field. Helm and von Leonarte followed, jolting across the sun-baked turf. Behind them, infantrymen poured through the hedgerows, and fell out to rest under cover of the hedges and in the folds in the ground.

Ten minutes later, as they were standing at ease round the *kubelwagen,* they heard the rapid crump of their own 88mm guns returning the enemy fire from across the river. Von Leonarte saw the men of 14 Company scrambling to their feet, adjusting their T-belts, and picking up their weapons. Von Kötze, his second-in-command, and his headquarters group were standing rigidly to attention. A handful of officers was coming through the hedge onto the field, marching so quickly as to be trotting almost at the double. Striding in front of them was a very tall, distinctive figure, in dark uniform and riding-breeches and close-fitting, mirror-polished, black riding-boots. The Knight's Cross with Oak Leaves hung at his throat, and he was wearing a monocle on a looped gold string. Despite the speed with which he was striding along, he was wielding a silver ferruled walking stick as if he were some elderly Potsdam Guardee strolling down the Unter den Linden on a Sunday afternoon to eye each *süsse mädel* he passed by on the pavement.

'At ease, men!' he called, as he came across the grass.

He paused at a platoon of men lined up against the hedge. He let his monocle fall to his chest.

'Ready for a hot day's work, eh lads?' he called.

'With the Herr Oberst's permission,' replied a sergeant, 'we'll show the French what's coming to them, Your Excellency. If they wait for us to get across, that is!'

'That's the spirit, lads,' the Colonel called back.

He waved his stick at them in salute, and strolled on, screwing his monocle back into his eye as he did so. One platoon had occupied a shallow dip in the centre of the field. As their commander saw the Colonel and his staff approaching, he tried to get his men to their feet. The Colonel let his monocle slip from his eye once more.

He repeated the performance. 'What are you carrying in your flasks, Lieutenant?'

'Coffee, Your Excellency,' the platoon commander replied. 'With Your Excellency's permission, hot coffee.'

'That's good, Lieutenant!' the Colonel told him. 'I'll let you into a military secret, lads.' He raised his voice so that the whole platoon could hear. 'If any of you are parched for want of a cold beer, there's a brewery in Glaire, over on the other side. So go to it, eh lads?'

The men laughed.

He turned and noticed von Leonarte watching him. He made his way through the grass towards him, his staff scuttling along after him. Von Leonarte saluted.

'Dieter von Leonarte, 1st Cavalry,' von Leonarte reported. 'With Your Excellency's permission, Your Excellency's adjutant gave me permission to advance to the river with 14 Company, Grossdeutsch-land.'

A captain with Colonel Graf von Schwerin whispered to his commander. The Colonel nodded.

'None of this "Grossdeutschland" nonsense, please,' the Colonel told von Leonarte. 'I have the honour to command the Berlin Guards

– have done for a number of years now – intend to go on doing so, eh, gentlemen?'

He turned to his staff. They laughed obediently.

'1st Cavalry, eh Rittmeister?' he asked von Leonarte. 'Well, never mind – can't all be in the Guards, eh?'

Von Leonarte bowed slightly.

'So you are the young man who is supposed to be crossing our bridge when we've built it, eh?' asked Colonel Graf von Schwerin. 'We'll have it ready for you sooner than you suppose.'

He put the tip of his black-gloved finger on the centre of von Leonarte's Knight's Cross.

'Where did you win that, Rittmeister?' he asked.

'Warsaw, Your Excellency,' von Leonarte replied. 'With Your Excellency's permission, I was with the advance guard of General Reinhardt's 4th Panzers, during the first attack on Warsaw.'

'A hard-fought action,' the Colonel observed. 'A number of good men lost their lives in that attack. God bless you, Rittmeister, and good luck. Glad to have you with us.'

'Your Excellency is very kind,' von Leonarte told him.

Colonel Graf von Schwerin gave a wave of his stick and went to join Senior-Lieutenant von Kötze. They remained standing in the middle of the field, ignoring the shells falling in the fields about them. They were still standing talking some minutes later when there came a steady drone of engines loud enough to be heard distinctly above the noise of the gunfire and the impact of the falling shells. Everybody turned his head to face the roar. From behind the ridges of the Ardennes, three aircraft soared upwards, apparently vertically into the sky. Three more followed, and three more. Over to the right, yet more were soaring upwards like birds driven by beaters.

'Stukas!' Radinski exclaimed with the excitement of a schoolboy.

They watched, craning their necks to peer up into the dazzling blue. Von Leonarte heard himself exclaim, 'My God!'

Ahead, squadron after squadron was forming into line far, far above them, hovering almost at stalling speed over the broad meadows and orchards of the Fond de Givonne. In line, each squadron droned slowly above the drifting smoke from Sedan until they were hanging, seemingly as motionless as watching hawks, over the heights on the western bank of the Meuse. From each line, single aircraft began to tilt away, falling almost perpendicularly so that they appeared to be dropping out of the sky. As they dropped, each aircraft set up a scream so ear-splitting it drowned out all other noise. Von Leonarte felt it stabbing into his ears, penetrating into his brain so that he felt physically sick; he found it impossible to imagine what it must be like to be a Frenchman up there on La Marfée. Twelve Stukas were falling out of the sky simultaneously. As they banked upwards once more, their bomb-loads – one large bomb and a scatter of smaller ones – continued the descent. Twelve more Stukas followed, and twelve more after that, the whistle of the bombs audible above the scream of the aero-engines. As the bombs landed, it was as if the entire roof of the heights was being lifted off in a mass of fire and smoke. Before the debris could fall back to earth, more bombs landed to blast up more fountains of earth and splinter trees. Squadron after squadron dropped down onto La Marfée until it had become an inferno of flame and smoke. An ammunition dump had been hit. A vast pall of smoke had risen to blot out the sunlight.

The Stukas turned back for home in flights of three. While the bomb-blasts from La Marfée continued to shake the ground, several flights came low over the mill buildings, and dipped their wings to the men of the Grossdeutschland Regiment waiting below. Von Leornarte saw quite clearly the two-man crew of one of them, as it passed overhead, perched high above the crooked wings under their perspex canopy. He waved with an enthusiasm quite unbecoming in a well-bred Prussian officer, and saw the pilot raise his hand in salute. Across the meadow, Colonel Graf von Schwerin, who had been watching the attack through his binoculars, was waving his walking-stick to the pilots with equal enthusiasm.

The last flight of stukas droned away over the forest ridges to the east, and a heavy silence descended, broken only by the occasional chatter of small-arms fire. It was as if the attacking forces were themselves shocked by the ferocity of the bombardment. Men stood still in the open fields waiting for the first sign of renewal of French artillery fire; but it did not come. Colonel von Schwerin began to stride back across the thick grass to the gate in the hedge, his staff half running along behind him. Senior Lieutenant von Kötze was shouting out commands, and his orders were taken up by 14 Company's sergeant-major. The section began to move in the direction of the gate, in file and at the double, their fluted, cylindrical gas-mask containers – filled with clean socks and underwear, cigarettes and bars of chocolate – banging against their hips.

Von Kötze, who had been watching his men's departure from beside his *kübelwagen*, strolled over to von Leonarte.

'We're moving up to embarkation now,' he told him. 'If you care to come with us, we shall be honoured.'

Von Leonarte held out his hand. As von Kötze took it, he said with genuine warmth, 'Good luck, Oberleutnant. Perhaps we may have dinner together in Paris, soon.'

The wooden building was still smouldering, the smoke drifting like a screen between the meadows and the river. On the road, the extent of the losses suffered by the first assault waves became evident. The ditches were lined with half-drowned, blood-soaked, coughing men. Files of stretcher-bearers came trotting out of the smoke, bearing the sodden loads whom they had rescued from the river. Medical orderlies were dressing wounds and loading stretchers onto trucks bound for the advance operating theatres. At the roadside, young officers, who were themselves casualties, were shouting out for medical attention for men whom they had been commanding only a few minutes before. Von Leonarte saw a junior lieutenant of the Grossdeutschland, his uniform drenched to the armpits, and his head swathed in bandages. He was cradling in his lap the head of a grey-haired senior sergeant whose tunic had been ripped open, and whose singlet was an even mass of blood. The sergeant's eyes stared open and fixed. The junior lieutenant was sobbing aloud like a young child.

The stone mill-house reared above them in the smoke. Behind it, a cart-track led down into the dried up bottom of a stream. Von Leonarte ordered Helm to drive down into it. The roof of the mill's main building had been reduced to a few smashed ribs of timber, but in the windows there were still cracked panes of glass held in their frames by the heavy dark-blue paint which had been used to black them out against air-raids. Helm switched off the engine, and they climbed out among the nettles which had sprung up between the smooth pebbles. The long grass and tangle of the banks which hemmed them in had a peaceful smell of vetch and hedgewort.

Von Leonarte told Radinski and Graser to remain with the *kübelwagen*. He led Helm, clambering up through the nettles and briars against the mill-house wall, and worked his way round the building. They had just turned into a gateway leading into a rubble-littered yard, when their ear-drums were blasted and deafened by an explosion of gunfire. Mounted on the concrete ramp used for loading bales of cloth was an unlimbered 88 mm flak gun manned by four gunners, its long barrel pointing out to where, through the smoke, von Leonarte could see the glittering expanse of the Meuse. An empty shell case spilled from the open breech and fell ringing onto the stones below the ramp. Another shell was rammed into the breech, which was slammed shut, the gun was fired again, the breech opened, and the reeking, smoking shell case clanged once again onto the yard floor. Von Leonarte led Helm away as the gunners continued their methodical barrage. Other 88's were firing nearby. Between the explosion from the guns, von Leonarte could hear orders being relayed, and the sound of boots crunching on the paths. He and Helm made their way round the outside of the yard wall. A dense mass of low trees and brambles stretched between the wall and the towpath which formed the river bank. Von Leonarte plunged into the thicket. He was struggling through it with Helm following when there came burst after burst of small-arms fire from across the water. As they struggled and thrust their way through the brambles, the sound of rifle and machine-gun fire became more intense. There was the crump of stick-grenades, and shouting and cheering. Von Leonarte felt excitement clutching at his guts. He did not care about the brambles lacerating his hands and wrists and scratching at his cheeks. In his determination to watch what was going on, he threw himself through the last of the tangle, and crouched in the open, on the edge of the towpath. Kneeling upright in the long, thick couch-grass, he gazed across the shimmering, rippled surface of the river in the bright sunlight. On the slopes of the far bank, where the green hillside met the skirts of La Marfée woods, plummets of white smoke were drifting, where the shells from the 88's were landing. Swarming across the broad, exposed river was an armada of assault dinghies packed with crouching, helmeted men. The shore on the far side was encrusted with empty dinghies, and clusters of empty dinghies were drifting downstream on the current. Grey clad, helmeted figures were pouring up from the bank, through the reeds and long grass; they were running for cover, with the involuntary stoop of men under fire. Von Leonarte raised his glasses and focused them on the pathway leading up from the river bank to the village of Glaire. Already men had spread out into the fields above it, and were taking up positions from which they could attack upwards to La Marfée. Along the pathway to the village, grey-uniformed men were marching openly, in file, and stretchers were being carried down to the boats. The bridgehead was clearly established. Von Leonarte felt an elation he had not felt for seven months or more – the joy of witnessing victory.

'We'll be over there today,' he told Helm. Helm touched his arm. He pointed down into the undergrowth below the towpath, a few yards away. Almost obscured by the branches and the gloom, there was a natural inlet of black, still water where a disused portion of the towpath had collapsed. An assault craft was afloat in the mouth of this inlet, held motionless by the long, emaciated finger-tips of the branches. Four men lay still in the bottom, crouched grotesquely over a heavy-calibre machine-gun. One of them was on his back, his head resting on the inflated bulkhead, his eyes hidden by the lip of his helmet as if he were cat-napping, and wished to shield his eyes from the glare of the sun. Bullets had ripped into the composition rubber of the boat, tearing off fragments as if it had been a rubber ball torn by sharp gravel.

Von Leonarte climbed down through the nettles and brambles into the gloom. Reaching for one of the rope loops on the side of the boat, he drew it further into the gloom of the inlet, the ends of the branches scraping along the rubber surface. He threw the painter across to Helm. Stepping onto the thickness of the bulkhead, and kneeling, he removed the identity disc from the neck of each man, and took the paybooks from their tunic pockets. He was about to step ashore, when he noticed the watch on the wrist of the sergeant-major lying dead at the tiller. It was shock- and water-proofed in a heavy rubber casing; it had both stopwatch and compass mechanism.

He took off his own watch and slipped it into his pocket. He unfastened the watch from the sergeant-major's wrist, and strapped it on his own. Then he reached out his hand so that Helm could pull him back onto the bank. He opened the paybooks he was holding, and removed the folded Reichmarks he found in them. He passed them to Helm, who said, 'Thank you, Herr Rittmeister.'

Helm refolded them and slipped them into his own tunic pocket. He followed von Leonarte up through the bushes to the wall of the mill, and rejoined the others at the *kübelwagen*.

7

When Julie woke up again, two hours had passed. Vivian was standing at the window in a shaft of sunlight; he was in his jodhpurs and singlet, and was quite still, listening to the gunfire. Julie sat up, drawing the duvet around her to cover her breasts.

'It's been going on a long time,' she told him. 'It woke me up earlier.'

'I'm afraid I'd better get back to Bruyères straight away,' he said. 'It's coming from the Sedan sector. Will you forgive me if I don't wait to take you to the station?'

'Don't be stupid,' she said.

She got out from under the duvet, put on her underwear and fastened up the stockings she was still wearing.

'Let me give you a hand,' she told him.

She was fastening his collar when a violent tremor shook the room, rattling the water-jug against the washbasin. From the street outside came the tinkling of broken glass. A man was shouting up from the pavement. Julie fixed Vivian's collar, and leant across the stone thickness of the window-ledge. All she could see, however, were the five massive towers of the cathedral, looming above the roof-tops into the cloudless sky. They seemed very permanent.

'If it's what I think it is,' said Vivian, 'it's damn near incredible!'

He was holding his tie. She took it from him, placed it under his collar, and tied it.

'What is?' she asked.

'I think it's Jerry trying to cross the Meuse,' he told her. 'And if I'm right, it means that everybody has miscalculated. It means that Jerry has sent an army through the Ardennes forest, which – according to the experts – is impossible.'

'How far away is Sedan?' asked Julie.

'About fifty kilometres.' Vivian put his arm round her shoulder and held her to him. She laughed, embarrassed by her own fears.

'It doesn't feel like fifty,' she said.

He didn't reply. Then he said, 'I must be going.' He held onto her for a moment longer. 'You get to Paris as quickly as possible,' he told her.

'Yes.'

He let her go.

'I'm going to see you again, aren't I?' he asked her.

'Of course you are,' she replied. 'I've got your London address now, haven't I?'

'You will get in touch?' he insisted.

'Don't worry about it,' she told him. 'The moment you have a weekend's leave in Paris, go to the ENSA office and ask for me. I might still be there; you never know.'

He picked up his jacket, and lifted it over his shoulder.

'I'm afraid,' he told her, 'that I'll see your name written up in the West End somewhere – the St James's Theatre, perhaps, or Wyndham's. I'll come round to the stage door after the show, and the chappie at the desk will tell me, "I'm sorry, sir, but Miss Armitage can't recall anybody by the name of Vivian Hardwicke."'

'Oh Vivian,' exclaimed Julie, 'don't be so bloody stupid.'

She was within a hair's-breadth of bursting into tears.

'I'm sorry,' he said. 'Truly.'

'So you should be,' she replied.

She helped him to ease his stump into the pinned-up sleeve of his jacket.

'You won't be doing any real fighting this time, will you?' she asked.

'I doubt it,' he replied. 'I don't suppose Colonel de Gaulle would let me. I've no doubt he thinks I'm in the way, but I've still got a job to do, for all that.'

He slung his Sam Browne over his shoulder and buttoned his shoulder-flap down over it. Julie buckled it round his waist.

'Kiss?' he asked.

She nodded. Please God, she thought, don't let him say thank you or anything like that. He didn't.

'Bristles!' she smiled, to conceal the depth of her feelings.

He picked up his cap. He hesitated.

'Julie?' he asked. 'Won't you let me have your address? In London, I mean.'

Oh God, she thought, there was only Ambrose's flat.

'I haven't got anywhere at the moment,' she told him. Why the bloody hell did she have to lie to him at a moment like this? she wondered. 'Look, Vivian, as soon as I get back and I find myself some decent digs, I'll write and let you know, I promise.'

He nodded. He went without further ado, closing the door behind him. As soon as he was gone, Julie looked about her, hoping that he might have left something for which he would have to return. Then she sat down on the bed. Despite the sunlight coming through the window, the small stone room was quite chilly. She wrapped the duvet round her shoulders and lit a cigarette.

When she went downstairs, carrying her suitcase, there was a small crowd gathered round the reception desk. They were jostling one another in their anxiety to pay their bills and be off as quickly as possible. The woman in the steel-rimmed spectacles glanced over their shoulders at Julie.

'Mademoiselle?' she called. 'Eh! Mademoiselle?'

Everybody turned to look at Julie.

'The Englishman has settled the account, mademoiselle!' shouted the woman.

'Thank you, madame,' Julie called back as carelessly as she could.

Bloody Vivian, she thought. Of course, it had been very generous of him; and no doubt the woman didn't give a damn . . . but still. Then, as she crossed the newly-swept cobbles of the courtyard to the restaurant, she thought how marvellous it would be if she were to find him there, sitting over his coffee. She carried her suitcase down the steps and into the restaurant, but he wasn't there.

The gunfire seemed more distant and remote as she sat waiting for her coffee and brioches. Only a few people were sitting at the other tables having breakfast. They were talking to one another in low, eager voices. The girl who brought Julie's breakfast over to her was young – probably, thought Julie, she helped with the breakfasts before going on to school. She looked serious and tired-eyed.

'Are you worried?' Julie asked. 'About the noise, I mean.'

The girl shrugged. 'They won't come here,' she said. 'Papa says they'll go to Paris first.'

She was more likely to be worried about passing her *baccalauréat* than the fate of Paris, Julie decided.

When she had finished breakfast, Julie set off down the winding streets which led out of the old town. Some shops and cafés were opening, but everywhere seemed quiet and subdued. It was still quite early, but that did not entirely explain the emptiness of the streets in the bright sunlight. She passed under an archway through the ancient ramparts, and stepped out onto the grass-bordered pavement of the Rue Gambetta. There was a steady stream of cars travelling in the opposite direction – not the large, Belgian-registered limousines she had seen the day before, but small, popular French models, many of them old, with shabby paintwork. Their roofs and luggage racks were piled not only with cases and baskets, but also with bedding and rolled-up mattresses, tables and chairs, and even pots and pans.

When she reached the station forecourt, Julie found it even more crowded than on the previous afternoon. By sheer determination she pushed her way through the crowd to the vestibule entrance. At this point, she realised she could make no further progress. She put down her suitcase and stood with it between her legs. Behind her, the crowd closed in. She felt a wave of sadness: even if Vivian, on his return to his headquarters at Bruyères, had found that there was nothing for him to do, he would never manage to catch up with her now.

A girl was standing pressed against the doorpost. She had a baby on her arm, its head resting on her shoulder. It had been crying, but was now more than half asleep and whimpering quietly. The girl was still pretty, but blowsy from exhaustion and the cares of motherhood. She was bareheaded: there was sweat streaking her face, and the tangled hair which had spilled over her forehead and cheeks was matted with sweat. Her V-necked jersey was streaked with the baby's dribbling on the shoulder and breast. The limp edge of her satin petticoat hung against her bare legs below the hem of her ill-fitting skirt. Her mouth was petulant with a discontent which had existed longer than her present predicament. Nevertheless, Julie felt pity for her.

'Is he a boy, madame?' she asked.

The girl turned her head, surprised that anybody should have addressed her. She nodded.

'How old is he?' Julie asked.

The baby's clothes were of good quality, but soiled.

'Nearly a year, mademoiselle,' the girl replied.

She sounded friendly, and pleased to be spoken to.

Somebody behind Julie was trying to push his way into the booking office. Julie was thrown forward so that she had to reach out for the wall to prevent herself from stumbling against the girl.

She recovered her balance.

'Are you going to Paris, madame?' she asked.

The young woman nodded.

'The 0800 hour *rapide* has been cancelled, mesdames,' a man's voice said over Julie's shoulder.

Julie turned to see who it was. An elderly gentleman was standing behind her, holding himself very erect. He had a neatly clipped moustache, and in the lapel of his well-worn but sharply pressed suit was the tiny, frayed rosette of the *Légion d'honneur*.

'The Boche is coming, mademoiselle,' he said to Julie. 'So our conscript fathers piss in their trousers and cancel the trains. It was to be expected.'

Julie became aware of the people close about her.

'In England, monsieur,' she replied, 'we have been told that the French army is the finest in the world.'

'It was, mademoiselle,' the elderly man replied. 'It was, in the days of Marshals Foch and Pétain!'

He grunted, and glared about him as if daring somebody to argue with him. There was some laughter, but nobody spoke.

'In England, mademoiselle,' he went on, 'you are fortunate. You have King George – and the Channel,' he added. There was a murmur of agreement at his last remark. 'You cannot be expected to understand these matters, mademoiselle,' he concluded.

The crowd was moving, swaying and pushing through the doors; the pressure carried Julie along. She was just able to pick up her suitcase before the weight of the crowd lifted her off her feet and bore her into the station. As they were swept onto the platform, the elderly gentleman kept a firm hold of her arm; without it, she would have been knocked over by those pressing behind her.

The congestion eased. The crowd still poured through the gates, but spread out over the platform. The elderly gentleman released her arm.

'Fools,' he said.

Across the lines and platforms, in the sunlight beyond the passenger station, a row of flat-cars was drawn up. On them stood the massive steel bulk of heavy tanks. Julie could see the loops of heavy chain draped on the rear of each tank, and the stub-barrelled cannon projecting from the squat, domed turrets.

The elderly gentleman gave a sharp little laugh.

'One must not say so, mademoiselle,' he told her. 'One must certainly not say so, but a little National Socialist discipline wouldn't do any of these people any harm. They have forgotten what it is to be French, alas.'

If Julie had been tempted to argue with him, she was immediately forestalled by events. Soldiers in khaki fatigues had climbed up onto the flat-cars. They were engaged in knocking away the blocks which had been placed under the tracks of the tanks, unfastening the chains, and removing the tarpaulin sheets which had been tied over the engine cowlings. A column of heavy transporter-trucks was drawing up alongside the cars. Suddenly, a woman near to where Julie was standing began to shriek, 'What are they doing? What are they doing? The German aeroplanes will see them. The German aeroplanes will see them and drop bombs on all of us.'

Another woman screamed, 'We shall all be killed.'

Mothers snatched up their children and ran back to the gate in an attempt to get clear of the station before the German bombers arrived. Since others were still trying to get out onto the platform, scuffling and fighting broke out round the entrance. A uniformed member of the station staff strolled past at an easy pace, his bag over his shoulder, from which the metal cup of his thermos-flask projected. He appeared to be oblivious of the pandemonium at the gate.

'Excuse me, monsieur,' the elderly gentleman called, 'is there to be a train to Paris this morning?'

The man shrugged.

'Who can tell, monsieur?' he replied. 'They say there's been bombing up the line, beyond Vervins. They may put on a special *omnibus* from here, I suppose. Who knows?'

'And is there a train to La Fère?' asked the elderly gentleman.

'But of course, monsieur!' the railwayman replied, as if no more stupid a question could have been put to him. 'In a quarter of an hour exactly.'

He pointed to three carriages standing in a bay. He continued up the platform towards the train, blowing his whistle as he went, and calling out, 'Ticket-holders for stations to Amiens only, if you please. Show your tickets for stations to Amiens.'

'You aren't going to Paris, monsieur?' Julie asked the elderly gentleman.

'Alas no, mademoiselle,' he replied. 'I'm going to see my daughter and grandchild at La Fère.' He bowed to Julie.

'Adieu, mademoiselle, et bonne chance!'

'Merci beaucoup,' she replied. *'Vous êtes bien aimable!'*

To her surprise, he simpered with pleasure before marching away down the platform to take his place in one of the wooden carriages. She propped her suitcase up against the wall, in the shade. She was just about to sit on it, when she saw coming through the throng at the platform entrance the bedraggled figure of the girl. She was struggling along with the baby still supported on her arm and shoulder, and was carrying a heavy wicker suitcase in her other hand. Julie waved to her, but the girl did not see her. Instead, she looked about her wearily, as if unsure where to go. Julie hesitated, then leaving her case against the wall, she went over to her. When the girl saw her, she tried to smile.

'Come and sit with me for a little,' Julie said. 'Here, let me take your case.'

She took the heavy wicker suitcase and carried it over to her own.

Julie reached out. The young woman let her take the baby from her. It smelt of sour milk and ammonia. As Julie supported it on her arm, its head on her shoulder, she could feel the dribble from its mouth through her blouse. The girl sat on the ground, her legs stretched out. She held her arms out, and Julie returned the baby. Sitting down on the ground beside her, she said, 'My name is Julie – Julie Armitage. What's yours?'

The girl cradled the baby in her lap. It was fast asleep.

'Marie-Claire,' she replied at length.

She was silent for a moment. Julie glanced at the weary, blowsy face. The girl was still very young – much younger than Julie had at first supposed.

'And the baby's name is Joseph-Marie,' said the girl. 'His papa's name is Joseph, and mine's Marie; it's very suitable, don't you think?'

She fumbled in the pocket of her skirt, under the baby, and pulled out a crumpled blue Caporal packet. She opened it, muttered *'Merde, alors!'*, and screwed it up before throwing it across the platform. Julie took her cigarettes and lighter from her handbag.

'Saved my life,' said Marie-Claire as she took the offered cigarette.

She borrowed Julie's lighter. Julie noticed that she wasn't wearing a ring.

'Is your family in Paris?' she asked, as she took back the lighter.

'I haven't got a family,' Marie-Claire replied. 'I haven't got anybody. And I can't work because of the baby. I was working for Dr Vauthier, here, in Laon. He was very kind, was Dr Vauthier – and Madame wasn't too bad, even if she was strict. When the baby's papa got his papers, I went to see if they'd take me back; but they'd got somebody else. And the baby's papa hasn't sent us any money – the shit knew what he was doing; as long as we haven't been properly married, I can't make him send me an allowance.'

'Where are you going to go?' Julie asked.

'The Convent of the Little Friends of Jesus,' Marie-Claire replied. 'The sisters looked after me when I was a kid. It was them who sent me to work for Dr Vauthier. They were quite good to us if we did what we were told. They'll look after the baby and me. Sisters have to look after people.'

Since all that Julie knew about nuns was what she had seen at the pictures, there was no reason why she shouldn't agree.

They waited sitting on the platform all day. Whenever the baby cried, Marie-Claire attempted to feed it, spilling milk from a medicine bottle onto pellets of bread, and pushing them into his mouth. But it was Julie, when she could stand the smell no longer, who changed the cheesecloth towels which served as nappies.

It was growing dark when a train finally drew in. The engine was smaller than the huge engines Julie had seen previously drawing main-line trains on the French railways. The wooden carriages were decayed and unlit. Sparks showered in the dusk from the engine's funnel, and white smoke billowed about the platform. There was no announcement regarding the destination of the train. But Julie, as soon as she noticed the crowds moving towards the edge of the platform, snatched the baby up from Marie-Claire's lap and, clutching it against her breast, called to her to pick up the suitcases and to follow close behind her.

108

Protecting the baby in her arms as best she could, she elbowed and shouldered her way through the throng. She reached the very edge of the platform only inches from the running-board of the carriage when it pulled up in front of her, bathing both her and the baby in wet steam. The baby awoke and began to writhe and scream against her breast. Ignoring both the din and the wetness dribbling down her blouse, she put the baby over her shoulder, and pushed back from the edge of the platform everybody between herself and the nearest open door. Only half aware of the expostulations ringing from behind her, she reached up, snatched at the rail, and managed to haul herself up the step. Somebody behind her grabbed at the waistband of her slacks. She threw herself forward into the compartment, onto the floor between the passengers' legs, and pulled herself free without losing the buttons on her slacks. The baby had fallen from her shoulder in the struggle, and was lying backwards over her arm, screaming. Hands reached down out of the gloom and took it from her. A woman's voice clucked over it, through the yelling, 'There there, my little one! All safe and sound, eh?'

Julie scrambled to her feet, clutching at a man's corduroy covered knee for support; it smelt of the farmyard. She looked round. Marie-Claire was fighting to climb in after her. She pushed Julie's suitcase in front of her; it was resting on Julie's toes. Julie took it and pushed it between passengers' feet to the far end of the compartment. The woman who had the baby on her lap, a sturdy, matronly shape in the dark, heaved herself up the wooden slats of the seat to make a few inches of space. Disregarding the audible murmurs of protest from the other passengers, she said,

'Here, *maman*, there's room for you and the baby. See?'

'There you are, *maman*,' said Julie to Marie-Claire, with only the slightest hint of irony in her voice. 'You sit down.'

Marie-Claire pushed past Julie, and squeezed down onto the bench. She stared up at Julie.

'I've torn my frock!' she whimpered.

The big matronly woman turned to her, half-offering to return the baby, but observing that Marie-Claire was still in a state of distress, she continued to rock it gently and to cluck over it.

Through the doorway, men were trying to climb up the step, and were struggling to pull one another down onto the platform. The two men who were sitting on either side of the door were now standing, pushing down those who were trying to force their way in.

'We're full up in here,' they shouted. 'No room, I tell you.'

One of them reached for the leather window strap. He pushed the first man on the step backwards, and slammed the door shut. There was much shouting, whistle-blowing, and shrieking of steam from outside. The train began to move. Julie propped her own suitcase up on the floor, and sat on it, her back to the door leading into the corridor.

'Excuse me, *messieurs*, *'dames*, but is this the train for Paris?' asked a woman in the semi-darkness.

'But of course, madame,' a man's voice replied.

'They said at Vervins that this train would go only as far as Soissons!' said another voice.

'My wife and I are travelling all the way to Paris,' said the first man. 'They knew that at St Gobert. Nobody said anything about getting off at Soissons, I assure you!'

'If you and your wife are going to Paris, monsieur,' said the second man, 'you'll have to walk from Soissons!'

He laughed. In case others in the compartment had not fully understood his witticism, he repeated, 'If Madame and Monsieur want to go to Paris, they'll have to walk from Soissons, eh?'

An old man in corduroy trousers who was evidently the husband of the woman holding Marie-Claire's baby, said, 'They told us at St Gobert that the train would be going as far as Meaux.'

'They never said that at Vervins, I assure you, monsieur,' someone else said.

'One can catch a bus into Paris from Meaux,' said the old man in corduroy trousers, ignoring the last speaker.

The carriage jolted abruptly to a halt. Steam hissed and ticked in the silence under the carriage. There was the sound of a train approaching in the opposite direction. There was the shriek of a whistle, and an engine rushed past, rattling the windows, its furnace blazing in the night. The windows of the carriage which followed were dimly lit, so that it was possible to see glimpses of steel helmets and military accoutrement on the men which crowded the compartments.

The carriage began to move forward once again. Julie opened her handbag. She had managed to buy two packs of expensive American cigarettes – the last in the station buffet at Laon. She put two cigarettes into her mouth, cupped her hand close over her lighter, and lit them. She handed one of them over to Marie-Claire. Resting her hand on the girl's knee, she whispered, 'Are you crying?'

'It's my frock,' Marie-Claire whispered back. 'I tore the skirt getting in. I did it with my heel.'

'We can do something about it when we reach Paris,' Julie told her.

'The sisters of the Little Friends of Jesus will be so angry if they see it,' said Marie-Claire.

'Don't be absurd,' said Julie.

'They will,' Marie-Claire persisted. 'They're terribly strict about things like that. They used to make us stand on the window-sill

110

holding the Bible for an hour, if we made a mess of our clothes. They used to say that Our Lady always kept her clothes neat and clean.'

'I've never heard such nonsense,' Julie told her.

She couldn't imagine the gentle nuns in the film version of *Cradle Song* behaving in such a way.

She sat back on her suitcase, resting her head against the door. She wondered what Marie-Claire's nuns would say to her. She was greatly in need of a bath, and her cardigan smelt of the baby's vomit.

After she had stubbed out her cigarette, she began to doze. The train stopped suddenly, carriage jolting against carriage. Marie-Claire's case fell against Julie's knee. There was silence. Then somebody asked,

'Where are we?'

A man opened the window.

'Nowhere,' he said. 'We're in a cutting. The bank is too high to see anything.'

Doors began to slam. Voices called out on the fresh night air. Somebody was walking along the ballast below the carriages, shouting an announcement.

'*Messieurs, 'dames*, the train will be delayed for a short time. Do not show any lights, if you please. It is forbidden to show any lights.'

One of the men by the compartment window opened the door, and dropped down onto the track. One or two more followed his example. Julie stood up. Her bottom ached, and she was very stiff. Marie-Claire asked, 'Where are you going?'

'Just making myself a little more comfortable,' Julie reassured her.

Voices were calling up from outside the door.

'It's bombs,' somebody said.

'It must be Paris,' said somebody else.

'It looks too bright,' said a third voice. 'Paris is too far away. It could be Compiègne.'

'It's certainly bombing,' said the first voice. 'And it's down the line. My God, we could be stuck here forever.'

'How long are we going to be here?' a voice called.

'Who knows, monsieur?' came the reply.

Footsteps crunched away down the ballast.

'Julie,' said Marie-Claire in the stillness. 'I don't want to go back to the sisters of the Little Friends of Jesus. They weren't kind to us. They used to beat us, and lock us up in dark cupboards without any dinner.'

'Excuse me, darling,' the old woman said to Julie, 'would you mind lifting my basket down from the rack?'

'Of course,' Julie replied.

111

She lowered the basket into the old woman's lap; it was heavier than she had expected.

'I imagine you must be hungry,' said the woman. 'You and the little mother here. You must be very far from home. Are you Dutch, by any chance?'

'English, madame,' Julie replied.

'Have some bread and cheese,' the woman offered.

She handed pieces to both Julie and Marie-Claire. There was now an empty space on the bench beside the woman's husband, vacated by one of the men who had jumped down onto the track. Julie was glad to sit down. The old man was pulling a cork from a bottle.

'Cider,' he said. 'What we need, eh? On a night like this.'

The woman turned to Marie-Claire.

'My darling,' she said, 'the time to worry about tomorrow is tomorrow. That's what Our Blessed Saviour told us, isn't it?'

'Yes, madame,' Marie-Claire agreed obediently.

'You have a little milk for the baby?'

'Yes, madame.'

'And we have food and cider. So there's no need to fret, even if we are here all night, eh?'

Julie was fast asleep by the time the real owner of the seat she was on returned. She drifted into consciousness as he climbed back into the compartment, but she kept her eyes tight shut, and continued to breathe heavily. She felt him standing over her for a moment or two, then heard him say, '*Alors! Que faire?*'

He moved away, and she was able to drift off into sleep once more.

8

At one o'clock exactly, von Leonarte told Helm to drive up onto the road. The whole area around the mill was ablaze with light – klieg lamps, unmasked headlamps, and flares. Under the lamplight and stretching back into the darkness for many miles were the stationary lines of tanks which had been clattering up towards the river all afternoon. The Assault Pioneers had launched the first section of the bridge over six hours previously. Now it stretched away from the quay below the mill, out into the blackness of the Meuse. Around the perimeter of the bridgehead, amongst the jumble of supply and communications vehicles, kitchens, and field-ambulances, men strolled about, talking and laughing in the exhilaration of victory. Exhausted though many of them were, there was a reluctance, shared by the men's officers, to let so momentous a day come to an end. Besides which, in only a few hours, the great column of tanks would start rolling across to the west bank. General Guderian, the old man himself, would be arriving at any moment to watch the triumphant spectacle, and nobody wanted to miss him.

The wounded who were being carried on stretchers back across the newly completed bridge, from the slopes of La Marfée, were as elated as everybody else. As they entered the great pool of light, they struggled up on their elbows, anxious to share their experience of the battle with anybody who would listen. Their accounts of fortified bunkers and concrete emplacements overrun without a shot being fired, of redoubts split apart by dive-bombing, were modified by descriptions of pockets where there had been determined resistance, and these were spoken of with a decent, soldierly respect.

Helm drove the *kübelwagen* up to the edge of the bridge. The bridgemaster came over to von Leonarte.

'Good luck, Rittmeister,' he said. 'They're expecting you on the other bank.'

Von Leonarte saluted the bridgemaster. They bumped up onto the planks of the bridge. The bridge swayed slightly on its pontoons. A cold black wind blew off the river. At the far end of the rattling planks, a group of Assault Pioneers signalled them up onto dry land with their torches. In the dim yellow light, von Leonarte caught sight of a major's collar-boards and saluted. His salute was returned. Von Leonarte glanced behind him, and saw, across the blackness of the water, the waterside of Floing blazing in an island of lamps and napthalene flares.

They drove along the path along the west bank between the village of Glaire and Torcy on the outskirts of Sedan. The landward side of the path was covered with prisoners waiting to be led across the bridge. Their guards, no more than four or five ordinary *Landsers*, stood watching them from the opposite side of the path, huddled against the chill, in their greatcoats.

Ahead loomed the silent ruins of Sedan. Naked, roofless gables reached up to the cloud-scattered sky; broken windows gazed in the moonlight, as hollow as the eye-sockets in a skull. The whole west-bank district of the city had been engulfed in flames. As von Leonarte drove through the deserted, cratered streets, he could taste the gritty smoke from the charred and smouldering timber. Bedsteads, chairs, and sideboards reared crazily from the rubble of the fallen walls.

They drove past the church of St Leger whose spire reared up into the moonlit sky like a gigantic broken tooth, and on to the remains of the main railway station. They drove out into the countryside once more, and into the cold, fresh air, away from the smell of smoke, passing the quiet fields which swept up to the edges of La Marfée.

From over on the right, there came the distant sound of rifle fire, where Balck's 1st Rifle Brigade was preventing the retreating French from regrouping. Occasionally there was heavier gunfire, and bowl-shaped flashes silhouetted the sky-line. A mortar flare rose hissing above the trees to hang on its parachute, blazing white, bathing fields and hedgerows in its deep-shadowing light, before being drowned in the comfortable dark. Once a machine-gun opened up close by with a noise like ripping calico, sending a thin stream of tracer-bullets in a graceful arc through the tree-tops.

They were skirting the outskirts of the small town of Bulson when a junior lieutenant of Panzer Grenadiers stepped out onto the road in front of them, and signalled them to stop. As they drew up, von Leonarte saw that the boy's face was aged with dirt and the fatigue of battle. The lieutenant saluted, having taken in von Leonarte's rank by the light of his torch.

'With the Herr Rittmeister's permission,' he said. 'We're the advance picket, Herr Rittmeister. It's enemy-held territory down the road – if they haven't run away.'

'That's what we're going to find out, Lieutenant,' von Leonarte told him. 'My orders are from Army HQ.'

He held out his pass.

'Good luck, Herr Rittmeister,' said the lieutenant.

He took a step back and saluted smartly. As they drove past him, von Leonarte waved cheerfully. In the moonlight, the southern-bound road was strewn with the wreckage of a defeated army. Discarded rifles, packs, bandoliers, and canteens littered the roadside verges. They passed carts with half their loads pulled off, the horses still standing in the shafts unattended, their heads drooped in sleep. Between Bulson and Maisoncelle, the road rose up onto a causeway overlooking a broad spread of fields. The standing hay was cratered at irregular intervals where guns had been positioned. Their long barrels reared up out of the tall grasses, but of the gunners to serve them, there was no sign.

A figure in the képi of a French officer staggered out onto the road with his hand held up. Von Leonarte sensed Graser moving at his shoulder. The barrel of the 34 MG swung round over his head. He told Graser,

'Don't open fire before I give the word!'

God alone knew how many French troops were bivouacked in the fields and copses on either side of the road.

'And take your finger off the trigger,' he snapped.

Helm slowed down. Von Leonarte opened his holster and put his fingers round the grip of his pistol. Helm, with one hand on the wheel and his foot on the brake, was stooping forward, reaching for the Schmeisser machine-pistol on the floor under his legs. Von Leonarte put his hand on his sleeve to restrain him. He had noticed the

114

red-cross brassard on the officer's arm. Nearby, at the road-side, stood two orderlies in flattened forage-caps and white coats. Helm drew up. The French officer came over and saluted.

'Forgive me, monsieur,' he said, 'but do you speak French?'

'Well enough,' replied von Leonarte.

'We had not expected you so far south, monsieur,' said the French officer, 'but since you are here, we're in desperate need of your help. We have a battalion – an entire regiment – suffering from abdominal wounds; there are amputation cases. We have run out of both anaesthetics and morphine, monsieur. Can you tell me how close your medical units are behind you?'

Von Leonarte replied almost without hesitation, 'Not far, monsieur, but it's a question of waiting, I'm afraid.'

The French officer nodded. Von Leonarte motioned Helm to drive on.

'Bonne chance, monsieur,' he called.

He saw the white-coated orderlies staring at him, their mouths hanging open. One of them had a cigarette-end stuck to his lower lip.

They made a detour round the outskirts of Le Chesne. Von Leonarte had the road-map spread on his knees and was examining it by the light of his pocket torch, when Helm said, 'Railway crossing just ahead!'

Once again Graser gripped the handle of the machine-gun. There was a small group of men by the door of the crossing-keeper's cottage. Von Leonarte could make out the shapes of French steel helmets. The barrier, however, was tilted against the sky.

'Put your foot down hard,' he ordered Helm.

The bonnet lid rattled with the acceleration as they tore towards the crossing. The moment before they hit the wooden ramp, Von Leonarte caught a glimpse of the faces under the helmets, and the expressions of sheer astonishment as the soldiers realised who were passing in front of them. The *kübelwagen* jumped, bounced across the tracks, and plunged down the far side. Von Leonarte waited for the crack of rifle-shots, but none came. The remainder of the drive to the Vouziers-Rethel highway, across the flat, deserted countryside, was uneventful. Even the bridge across the Aisne had been left unguarded.

After two kilometres they turned off the highway into a narrow lane, and drove down between the gentle sleeping hills to the parkland which surrounded La Berlière. They passed between the cottages of the village. Away to the east, beyond the end of the valley, there was a ribbon of mother-of pearl in the sky which edged the tops of the low hills. On the far side of the park, the turrets and steep-sloping roofs of the château reared above the ring of trees. The grey light in the east caught the upper windows, so that their carved embrasures were quite distinct.

They travelled up the drive at full speed, crossed the lilypond moat and passed between the tall trees, finally skidding to a halt on the main front carriage-drive in a shower of stone chippings. Von Leonarte already had his pistol in his hand as he jumped down. There was a tang of damp lilac in the air. He glanced up at the windows above the twin flights of steps which led up to the main entrance. There was no sign of life.

'Helm, Radinski – through the back,' he ordered, motioning with his pistol.

They ran towards the side of the house.

'Keep the front covered,' he ordered Graser who had already swivelled the machine-gun round to cover the windows.

He ran across the drive and up the main steps, his boots snapping on the stone. He turned the heavy iron ring on one of the doors, lifted the latch, and swung it open, stepping back as he did so. There was silence. Holding the pistol levelled, he stepped inside, into the echoing gloom. He felt as nervous as a child in a big house who had been ordered to go upstairs at night alone. Taking his torch from his pocket, he switched it on. The beam struck across the spacious emptiness and splashed over the marble balustrade at the foot of the stairs. Sweeping the torch-beam about him, he crossed the hall. He was advertising his presence, trusting that Helm and Radinski would make their way through from the back in time to help him if he found himself in trouble; it was impossible that the ring of his boots on the tiled floor should not have been heard throughout the house.

He lifted the torch-beam, following the balustrade up the broad staircase. At the top it struck full onto the white, melon-shaped face which was staring down at him from the gallery balustrade above. The mouth was thick, the pouched lips slack.

'*Bonjour, monsieur!*'

The voice echoed on the marble and the painted vault of the ceiling. The face smiled with vacuous benevolence. Von Leonarte held him in the torch-beam. He gripped the pistol by his side.

'Have I the honour of addressing Monsieur le Baron de Bart-Mendel?' he asked.

The smile on the milk-white face did not alter by a fraction. Nor did the eyes blink in the torchlight.

'Alas no, monsieur. Monsieur le Baron has gone to Paris.'

'You are a member of Monsieur le Baron's staff?' asked von Leonarte. 'His agent, perhaps?'

'Not exactly, monsieur,' the man replied, his empty smile still unchanged.

'Who are you then, monsieur?' von Leonarte demanded.

'I'm a visitor, monsieur,' the man replied, 'like yourself.'

'You are not one of the baron's people?' von Leonarte asked.

The man hesitated before answering.

'No, monsieur. There are none left.'

The reply left von Leonarte feeling even more uneasy.

'You are an intruder then?' he asked.

The man spread his pudgy hands. Several large rings gleamed on his thick fingers.

'If you wish to put it like that. I came here on business. To see Monsieur le Baron. Unhappily, he had gone before I arrived.'

From deep in the interior of the house, there came a crash of falling crockery, and a sudden cry of pain. The man affected not to notice.

'We did not expect you to arrive here so soon,' he said.

'Helm!' von Leonarte shouted. 'Radinski! Here!'

'Allow me to show you my papers, monsieur,' said the man. 'Identity card, visiting card, passport.'

He put his hand inside his jacket. Von Leonarte pointed his pistol at him.

'In a moment, monsieur,' he said.

The man's hollow smile did not alter.

'Of course,' he said, and put his hand back on the balustrade. 'We must wait.'

A moment later, a door under the stairs crashed open. Two men half-ran, half-stumbled into the grey dusk of the hall. They were followed by Helm and Radinski.

'With permission, Herr Rittmeister,' Helm reported. 'We caught them hiding in the back kitchens. They were trying to get away into the garden. We thought that they might be going to try to reach the French army.'

The man above giggled. Clearly he had understood what Helm had said.

Von Leonarte switched off his torch. There was enough pale morning light for him to see the man.

'They wouldn't want to do a thing like that,' the man giggled.

Von Leonarte looked at the two newcomers. They had the appearance of Sicilian or Spanish peasants, he decided: sallow-faced and grizzle-haired.

'Tell Graser to come inside,' he ordered Radinski. 'Tell him to bring in the MG.'

He started upstairs.

'Now, monsieur. Your papers, if you please.'

He was still pointing the pistol. The man at the top drew a leather wallet from inside his jacket.

'I am a citizen of a neutral power, monsieur,' he said. 'You shall see. I am Greek, monsieur; but I am a citizen of Egypt.'

Von Leonarte took the wallet from him and opened it; the man smelt heavily of eau-de-cologne. The photograph in the wallet was

117

that of a younger looking man. The face was not thin, but it did not have the bloated, albino paleness of the features in front of him. The eyes, however, bore a true resemblance. Startled by the photographer's lights, they protruded from the folds of skin in which they were set, but were as devoid of expression as those of a dead fish.

'Chrisostom Papayannis,' the man explained helpfully. 'My friends call me Monsieur Chris. It is simpler, don't you think?'

'I believe I can manage the name Papayannis, monsieur,' von Leonarte replied coldly.

He heard Graser below, coming in through the main doors, and the scrape of the ammunition belts along the tiles.

Von Leonarte glanced down at the wallet once more.

'Your identity-card is French, Monsieur Papayannis,' he said. 'And you are resident in Paris – Number 6a, Passage de Pantois.'

'That's my place of business, monsieur. Off the steps of La Bonne Becquerel, just below the Rue Lamarck. It has been provided for me by my friend, Monsieur Aris Liassides. Monsieur Aris Liassides is very rich. And a great philanthropist. His business is ships, monsieur, but his pleasure lies in relics of our great classical past.'

'And those men down there?' asked von Leonarte. 'Are they also Egyptian citizens?'

The two men were looking down the barrel of Radinski's rifle, their hands clasped over their heads.

'No, monsieur,' replied Papayannis. 'They are Parisians, also provided for me by Monsieur Aris Liassides.' He lowered his voice. 'They are scum, monsieur. They do what they are told because they are afraid of being drafted into the French army.'

'Show the Herr Rittmeister what we found on them, Radinski,' Helm said.

Radinski slung his rifle over his shoulder. He came up the stairs, pulled a pair of small automatic pistols out of his belt and showed them to von Leonarte.

'With the Herr Rittmeister's permission,' he said, 'they are wearing shoulder-holsters, Herr Rittmeister.'

Von Leonarte nodded.

'Keep your eye on them,' he told Radinski.

Radinski returned downstairs, his rifle still slung on his shoulder. He brandished the two automatics as if he were a gunslinger in a Hollywood Western. Even Helm grinned at him.

'Are you armed, Monsieur Papayannis?' von Leonarte asked.

Papayannis hesitated.

'Search him, Helm,' ordered von Leonarte.

Helm slung his Schmeisser over his arm, came up the stairs, and began to frisk Papayannis. He pulled a heavy, steel-grey Colt automatic from inside Papayannis's jacket, under his arm.

'You know the penalty for carrying arms as a civilian, Monsieur Papayannis?' Helm asked.

'It is for protection, monsieur,' said Papayannis. 'In such times as these, there is a danger that law and order will break down. And one cannot trust even those who are supposed to be one's closest associates.' He smiled down at the hall. 'Of course, monsieur,' he went on, 'now you have come, we shall have no need of such toys.'

'What have you done with your car?' von Leonarte asked.

'My car, monsieur?' asked Papayannis.

'I presume you didn't walk here, Monsieur Papayannis,' von Leonarte told him.

He turned and explained his question in German to Helm who was thrusting the Colt into his belt.

'There is a large American car parked behind the laurel bushes, round the side, Herr Rittmeister,' Helm replied. 'I'd say they were trying to keep it out of sight.'

'There are thieves,' Papayannis explained gently in French, 'and deserters. The countryside is swarming with fugitives – many of them are armed, and would kill to get a car which would take them to the south.'

The smell of the man's cologne on the morning air made von Leonarte feel slightly sick. He stared into the white, puffy features and the blank, meaningless smile.

'I think, Monsieur Papayannis,' he said, his disgust affecting his tone of voice only slightly, 'that you and your associates are *gangsters.*'

He used the English word, pausing to allow the implication of what he had said to sink in.

He glanced up at the vaulted ceiling. The billowing robes of blue and brown worn by the goddesses painted there had become quite distinct now. The plump faces smiled benignly down on him from the cloud thrones.

'My orders regarding this house are quite simple, Monsieur Papayannis. I am to take possession of a certain medallion at present in the ownership of the baron. It is silver, about a hand-span in width. On it is carved the figure of Christ presenting a sword to St Louis of France. I am told it used to be worn by the French Marshals of Nobility.'

'The Constables of France, monsieur,' Papayannis replied. 'Not the Marshals of Nobility.'

'Then you know where it is?' asked von Leonarte.

'Alas, no, monsieur,' Papayannis replied, 'though I did come here in search of the article. What a strange coincidence. Unfortunately, we are both losers. Monsieur le Baron has taken it with him to Paris.'

Von Leonarte levelled his pistol at him once more.

'You are quite certain of that, Monsieur Papayannis?' he asked.
'Oh yes,' Papayannis replied. 'We have searched the chapel, and we have opened the safe in the library. I am quite certain, I do assure you.'
'How can I know you are telling me the truth?' von Leonarte asked.
'Perhaps we had better go to the library. If I must court-martial you, I should prefer to do it in comfort.'
'Shooting me won't help you, monsieur,' Papayannis said equably. 'I am here as agent for Monsieur Aris Liassides, not for myself. Monsieur Aris Liassides wouldn't be at all pleased if I were shot – and he is a good friend to the German government.'
'We shall go to the library nevertheless,' von Leonarte replied.
He glanced at his watch in its heavy rubber casing. It was half-past four.
'Graser,' he called down. 'Mount the MG up at this window here.'
He pointed to the high window at the end of the gallery.
'Let me know the moment you see anyone approaching from the village,' he said.
Graser carried the machine-gun upstairs cradled in his arms. On reaching the end of the gallery, he smashed two of the diamond shaped panes with the butt, then thrust the long barrel through the broken window.
'Keep those two clowns covered,' von Leonarte called down to Radinski. 'Shoot them if they so much as scratch their fleas.'
As Radinski smirked, he repeated the order in French.
'You come with me, Helm,' he ordered.
They followed Papayannis down the corridor away from the gallery.
'Is Monsieur Liassides also a *gangster*?' asked von Leonarte.
'No, no,' Papayannis giggled.
He waddled along, splay legged. The fat on his bottom shook inside the baggy seat of his trousers.
'Monsieur Liassides,' he said, 'wishes to acquire the *Tondeau de Chartres* – that is what the experts call it, monsieur – so that he may present it as a gift to the Department of Antiquities in Cairo. Monsieur Liassides is a philanthropist, as I have told you.'
He sounded slightly impatient. He led them into the library at the end of the passage. The first sunlight of morning was shining onto the stone sill of the great window; it gleamed on the dusty gold tooling on the leather spines which lined the bookshelves. In the distance, beyond the furthest reaches of the wooded valley, gunfire had started with the first birdsong.
'What has the medallion to do with the Department of Antiquities in Cairo?' asked von Leonarte.
'Ah, monsieur, you are unacquainted with its history,' said

Papayannis. 'King Louis IX had it struck by the Guild of Silversmiths in Chartres to commemorate his personal deliverance from Egypt.' He giggled again. 'In the great tradition of French commanders, he returned to Paris, leaving his followers to disease, slavery, and death. One has only to think of the great Napoleon after Aboukir or the Beresina, or Marshal Bazaine at Metz. Or, perhaps, Monsieur le Baron de Bart-Mendel!'

At the far end of the library, above the great table, a number of books had been pulled down from the middle shelves. They lay littering the top of the table and the carpet round about – heavy, calf-bound folios with age-stained pages. For the first time, von Leonarte detected the smell of burnt fuse and gelignite mingling with Papayannis's scent and the stale smell of cigar. Between two of the shelves, the safe was set into the wall. Its door was wide open, its locks twisted, and the stonework framing it was blackened and flaked by the heat of the explosion.

'Herr Rittmeister,' Helm called. 'Look!'

At first von Leonarte thought that he was referring to the safe which had been blown. Then he looked to where Helm was standing. A woman was sitting in a high-backed chair between the table and the window. Her head drooped forward, but von Leonarte could see that the face was that of somebody in her middle years, while the hair which fell over her back and shoulders was flecked with silver. She would have fallen to the floor had she not been tied to the chair by the cord of her dressing-gown.

'The housekeeper,' Papayannis explained. 'There was a man with her, but he escaped. Maybe he was a coward. Maybe he was not her husband – we live in such times, monsieur.'

Von Leonarte went over to her. Helm was standing behind the chair pointing his Schmeisser at Papayannis.

'They tortured her, Herr Ritmeister!' he said.

Von Leonarte raised the woman's head. Her eyes protruded, staring fixedly upwards; one of them was ringed with a swollen yellow and black bruise. Her loose gaping mouth was a black hole between her swollen, cracked and blooded lips. Her dressing-gown and nightdress had been ripped off one shoulder. There was a mass of cigarette-burns in the flesh.

Papayannis had taken out a cigar. Von Leonarte heard the click of his lighter.

'An accident, monsieur,' he said. He puffed his cigar alight. 'On my part, at least,' he added. 'I told you that those men downstairs were scum. They are both of mixed blood, monsieur, the children of whores – raised in the gutter. One would have thought that Monsieur Aris Liassides could have found better, but these days, real men are determined to die on the battlefield, aren't they?'

121

The obese figure stood smiling ingratiatingly. The blue cigar smoke drifted like a transparent veil in front of his face.

'When we questioned the woman, monsieur,' Papayannis explained, 'she became frightened. She told us that the *Tondeau* was hidden in the chapel. It was not in its reliquary, of course, so they ransacked the place. I did not do so, myself; I am a believer, monsieur. Since we did not find it there, we were compelled to question the woman further. The house is a big one, monsieur – we do not have the time to search it thoroughly. She kept saying that Monsieur le Baron had taken the *Tondeau* with him to Paris. I'm sure there was nothing else she could say, that she was speaking the truth. Poor wretch, when I realised what those villains had done, I made the sign of the cross over her and said a prayer for the repose of her soul. You must not imagine that I am without compassion, monsieur.'

'With the Herr Rittmeister's permission,' said Helm, 'we should kill him before we leave. He is a looter and a murderer.'

'That would be a waste of a good opportunity,' Papayannis said immediately, in French.

He glanced across to the window.

'You are far ahead of your own advance guard, I think, monsieur. Those guns we can hear – they are still some distance away. You shouldn't attract attention to your presence here by shooting off your rifles unnecessarily.'

'The penalty laid down for looting under German military law,' said von Leonarte, 'is hanging.'

'A business proposition?' Papayannis suggested. 'May I sit, monsieur? It has been a long night.'

He sat down in the swivel-chair by the table without waiting for permission.

'I can't imagine what business there could be between you and me, Monsieur Papayannis,' von Leonarte told him.

'You will be returning to your lines empty-handed, monsieur,' Papayannis replied. 'Perhaps I can help you by making your visit just that little bit more worthwhile.' He glanced at the body tied to the chair a few yards away. 'You will do worse things before this war is over,' he said.

Von Leonarte was about to deny it, but he stopped himself. 'Not in cold blood,' he replied. 'Not for personal gain.'

'That's lawyers' talk, monsieur,' Papayannis told him. He giggled. 'We've no time for the cut and thrust of debate, eh?' he said. 'I don't know why your superiors should think the *Tondeau de Chartres* to be so important that they send an able young commander like yourself in search of it; but obviously they do think it important and perhaps I can be of use to them.'

He tried to cross his legs, but the sag of his belly in his lap prevented him from doing so. He spread his knees apart.

'It will be a little time before your armies reach Paris,' he went on. 'I have no doubt you will reach Paris, of course. The Republic has no stomach for war, this time. The English, as always, will hide behind their moat. In the meantime, however, I shall be searching for – and obtaining, I hope – the *Tondeau de Chartres*. Supposing, monsieur, I do obtain the *Tondeau*? Supposing, when your generals parade down the Champs-Elysées, I were to come to them, bearing the *Tondeau*? I have my methods, monsieur. It is not beyond the bounds of possibility.'

'I have no authority to strike bargains,' von Leonarte replied, 'and certainly not with murderers and criminals.'

'Monsieur,' Papayannis protested gently, 'your great National Socialist hero, Horst Wessel, lived off the prostitution of his mistress!'

'I am a German officer, Monsieur Papayannis,' said von Leonarte, 'not a politician.'

'Of course, of course. There is a distinction,' Papayannis apologised. 'But I was not seeking to strike any financial bargain. All I am suggesting is that you put it to your superiors that Chrisostom Papayannis, number 6a, Passage de Pantois, off the steps of La Bonne Becquerel, will obtain on their behalf the *Tondeau de Chartres*, and will hold it for them until their arrival in Paris. In return for which, they might of their goodness put a little business in the way of Chrisostom Papayannis – *objets d'art, objets de piété*, in the possession of Jews, socialists and other undesirables.'

'I can make no promises,' von Leonarte replied. But it would be a relief to return to Colonel Reuther not entirely empty-handed, he thought. 'I shall keep your visiting-card,' he added.

He returned Papayannis's wallet. Papayannis slipped it back into his inside breast-pocket.

'Herr Rittmeister!'

Graser's voice rang down the corridor leading out to the gallery.

'French soldiers, Herr Rittmeister, approaching from the village.'

'Time to go, monsieur?' Papayannis suggested calmly.

'Quick, Helm,' von Leonarte ordered.

They ran down the corridor and out onto the gallery. They joined Graser at the window, at the far end.

'Over there, Herr Rittmeister.'

Graser pointed through the broken frame at the drive across the park. Von Leonarte ordered him to carry the machine-gun back to the *kübelwagen*. He told Helm to go out and start the motor. Then he looked out of the window, using his field-glasses. A dozen or so French infantrymen were straggling up the drive, packs drooping half-empty down their backs as if they had thrown away half their marching equipment, rifles dangling carelessly from off their shoulders. None were wearing helmets; one or two were wearing forage caps, the remainder were bareheaded, except for the commander. He was distinguishable by his képi; he was limping, leaning heavily on a walking stick.

Von Leonarte ran back up the gallery and down the stairs. He called Radinski, who was still covering Papayannis's men with their automatics, to follow. The two thugs in their pin-striped suits watched as von Leonarte and Radinski ran to the main door. One of them spat noisily onto the tiles. Von Leonarte was opening one of the doors, when a voice called, 'Monsieur!'

Papayannis was standing on the gallery looking down, his belly pressed to the balustrade.

'He who sups with the Devil, eh?' he called, and giggled again.

Outside, Graser had already mounted the machine-gun on the pedestal between the two front seats, and the motor was turning over. Von Leonarte and Radinski ran across the gravel and climbed up on board. The air, even in the sunlight, was fresh and cold.

'We're going to drive straight through them, lads!' Von Leonarte said. 'They look a very sorry bunch. No shooting unless we have to. Let's go!'

The *kübelwagen* leapt forward, the tyres ripping up the gravel and rattling the stone chippings against the front steps. They swerved between the nodding lilacs and out over the bridge. The file of French soldiers was toiling up the drive immediately in front of them.

'Steady, lads!' von Leonarte shouted above the noise of the engine.

Helm put his foot down. To von Leonarte's astonishment the French lieutenant dropped his walking-stick as soon as he saw them, and put his hands on top of his head. So did most of his men, letting the slings of their rifles slither down their arms to the ground. Von Leonarte told Helm to stop, and the *kübelwagen* skidded to a standstill. The French lieutenant limped over, his hands still resting on his head.

'Captain,' he said in German. 'Comrades. We surrender. Yes?'

He was an elderly man – even an old one. His cheeks were sunken and veined. His hands were mottled. His men, though not as old in appearance as their commander, were older than any reservists in the Wehrmacht. They were grinning broadly. From the way one or two of them were swaying, von Leonarte supposed that they must be at least half drunk.

'You may speak French,' von Leonarte told the lieutenant.

'Of course, Monsieur,' said the old man. 'Thank you, monsieur.'

He too was smiling, but it was a sad, sober smile. Von Leonarte hoped that the old fellow would not embarrass him by weeping. He had probably fought gallantly for his country, twenty-five years earlier.

124

'Please put your hands down, lieutenant,' he told him.

He turned to Radinski.

'Hop down and pick up the old gentleman's stick for him,' he ordered.

As Radinski did so, the lieutenant told von Leonarte, 'They told us in the village that you were up at the château, monsieur, so I thought it best to come and present myself to you.'

He thanked Radinski as he took his walking-stick from him.

'Will you tell your men to drop their rifles to the ground?' asked von Leonarte. 'Those who have not done so already. I hope you will not consider it a discourtesy, monsieur, but I can't spare anyone to guard prisoners. I shall have to ask you to remain here, at La Berlière, until the next unit of the German armed forces arrives here ... Radinski, you will take up the rifles, remove the bolts and firing mechanism, and throw them into the moat. Help him, Graser!'

As a precaution, it was scarcely necessary, he thought. The rifles were long-barrelled Lebels – old-fashioned even in the Great War. He felt an irrational anger at the pathetic old man and his drunken reservists.

'Monsieur,' he said, 'you will please order your men to remove their boots ... '

He paused momentarily.

'And their trousers,' he added.

The lieutenant hesitated.

'Is that really necessary, monsieur?' he asked. 'You can see for yourself my men aren't likely to fight again.'

'That is more than I know, monsieur,' von Leonarte replied coldly.

One of the men, a corporal with sunken, bloodshot eyes, and three or four days' growth of beard, began to protest. The lieutenant smiled wearily at him.

'We have no choice, Corporal Goutard,' he said.

He began to unbuckle his own belt, and to unfasten his trousers.

'Your men, monsieur,' von Leonarte hastened to assure him. 'Of course I would not give such an order to a brother officer.'

The old lieutnant drew himself to attention, the flies of his breeches hanging open.

'Monsieur,' he replied. 'My men shall see that an officer of the army of the Republic is not ashamed to share with them the humiliation imposed on them by their victors.'

'Very well, monsieur,' von Leonarte told him. 'If that is your wish. . . . But it isn't mine,' he added in self-exculpation.

He and Helm sat and waited as Radinski and Graser gathered the boots, trousers, and rifle-bolts, carried them over to the moat and dropped them between the broad lily leaves. The naked legs of the

French reservists were white, shrunken and varicose in the clear, early-morning sunlight.

Graser and Radinski climbed back onto the rear of the *kübelwagen*. As it began to move forward, von Leonarte saluted the old lieutenant. The lieutenant remained stiffly at attention, his eyes staring ahead, his walking-stick held close to his side and slightly at an angle like a parade-ground sword. His thighs were so lean he could scarcely hold them together.

As they drove away toward the village, von Leonarte knew that there was a pale, florid face observing him from an upper window of the château, accusing him with a smile.

9

Julie woke feeling very uncomfortable. She opened her eyes, and sat up. She was almost crippled with stiffness. Looking out of the compartment window, she saw that the train had not moved.

'Julie,' said Marie-Claire, 'what shall I do?' The baby was crying.

'He's such a naughty, dirty little thing,' Marie-Claire added. 'If he had a proper papa, I'd tell him to give him a real thrashing.'

Julie noticed the yellow-brown smear on the baby's leg, under the edge of his pants.

'Have you tried changing him?' she asked sarcastically.

'I don't like to,' Marie-Claire replied, glancing round the compartment at the others. 'Not in here.'

Julie reached out.

'Give him to me,' she said.

Maire-Claire passed the squalling child over to Julie.

'Give me a clean napkin,' Julie said above the shrill uproar.

As Maire-Claire did so, the old woman said very audibly to Julie, 'You're spoiling the young woman, mademoiselle.'

Her husband, who was sitting beside Julie, grunted his agreement. Marie-Claire pouted angrily. For the next few minutes, Julie was peeling the soiled nappy from off the baby's bottom, wiping it as clean as she could with the sodden outer layer. The other people in the compartment averted their eyes, as though that could diminish the smell. Julie used her own precious Nivea cream to soothe the scabby sores on the child's thighs before she put on the clean cheesecloth. She had no sooner completed her task than the baby stopped crying.

'You're not a mother yourself?' the old woman asked her.

Julie shook her head. She managed to smile.

A voice was shouting down the cutting outside. It was too far away to be distinct, but one of the men sitting by the door, who had climbed down onto the ballast, now appeared on the step and called back into the compartment.

'There's been an air-raid at Crouy, down the line. The track has been blown up, and the tunnel's blocked. They're saying there's an engine being sent to pull us back to Laon.'

There was a general murmur of disbelief and indignation. Marie-Claire leant across and said to Julie, in a whining little voice, 'I don't want to go back to Laon.'

Voices were shouting down the length of the train. People were jostling along the corridor, thrusting their luggage against one another. A youngish woman wearing a trench-coat, and with an absurd little trilby hat perched on her Greta Garbo page-boy hair, looked in through the open door.

'You're not going to wait here, are you?' she asked. 'The German planes will see us. They say the Messerschmidts spotted a train outside Crouy station last night and machine-gunned it from end to end.'

'Who says?' asked a middle-aged woman. 'People like you are no better than fifth-columnists.'

But the woman had been pushed away down the corridor by those pressing behind her.

The older peasant pulled himself up from beside Julie. He looked down at her.

'It isn't far to Soissons, mademoiselle,' he told her.

Julie nodded. The old man's wife leant over and patted Julie's hand.

'Come on, darling,' she said. 'We'll go across the fields together, eh?'

Julie smiled. She offered the baby to Marie-Claire, but Marie-Claire shook her head.

'You're so much more clever with him than I am,' she said sweetly. 'The little one loves being held by you. See? He's laughing.'

The old peasant took Julie by the arm and helped her to her feet. He and his wife lowered themselves with difficulty down onto the ballast outside. His wife lifted up her arms and took the baby from Julie.

'You bring the cases,' Julie told Marie-Claire, and jumped down.

It was further than she had thought. Her feet smarted where they had landed on the loose chippings. Marie-Claire dragged the cases across the floor to the step. She climbed over them awkwardly, and lowered herself down. Her skirt was creased and dirty, and her drooping petticoat soiled with the grime of the compartment. Nevertheless, the young man who had been sitting at the window, smiled at her.

127

'Madame will permit me to assist her with the luggage?' he asked.

Julie held the baby to her. It was whimpering quietly.

'Thank you, monsieur,' Marie-Claire enthused, ignoring Julie and the baby. 'You are very kind.'

The man climbed down and drew the cases after him.

'Madame will allow me to carry them for her?' he asked.

The old man and old woman each slipped a hand under Julie's arms to help her up the steep slope of the embankment.

'You can tell who should be a mother, and who shouldn't,' said the old woman pointedly.

'That's true,' the old man agreed.

But Marie-Claire, who was walking empty-handed behind them, was too preoccupied with smiling up into her escort's face to pay any attention.

They reached the top with some difficulty, Julie cradling the baby in her arm, while clutching tufts of grass with her free hand. The dew was still hanging in drops on each blade; she could feel the damp soaking through the knees of her slacks. Behind them, most of the other passengers had started the ascent, slithering and slipping, half-crawling to the top. One man in a dark city suit had almost reached the summit, when his attaché-case fell tumbling and somersaulting onto the track below, spilling shirts and pyjamas onto the cinders.

At the top was a broad, open field with a green haze of shoots over the dark tillage. Beyond stretched a line of trees.

'There'll be a road, just beyond the trees,' said the old man confidently.

They set off across the fields, keeping to the side of the ditch where boots had already beaten down a path. At the far side, they plunged into the ribbon of woodland, and emerged out of a low hedge on the far side. The old woman stopped.

'Heaven preserve us,' she whispered, and made the sign of the cross.

A quarter of a mile of rough pasture sloped gently down to the road. Beyond it was a vast expanse of tilled fields and woodland haze. On the road, a single, dense mass of people stretched in both directions as far as the eye could see. Locked into the flood of those plodding along on foot, were horse-drawn carts piled high with furniture, bedding, kettles, and pots and pans. Some farm-carts were carrying livestock – pigs and calves under nets. There were small family cars, their roofs heaped with luggage, and small vans and trailers piled with household goods on which were perched children and the old and infirm. All were reduced by the crowds to moving at walking speed. Everybody on foot was carrying battered suitcases tied with string, or had huge packs tied to their backs. Many were pushing handcarts or wheelbarrows. Old people hobbled on sticks, helped along by younger members of their families. Children walked in fatalistic obedience beside parents or grandparents. Many of them were wearing their shabby, fur-tippeted winter coats, and had a spare pair of boots tied about their necks.

'It's impossible,' said a man who had caught up with Julie and the old couple.

More people from the train emerged from the line of trees and stopped to stare in astonishment at the spectacle in front of them. The old woman began to weep.

'The filthy Boches!' she cried. 'The filthy, filthy Boches!'

Julie hugged the baby. She felt helpless. She looked up at the old man. His eyes were full of tears.

'They came when we were very little,' he said, 'in 1870. They burned down our homes. And they came again in 1914, when I was with the army in the Vosges. They forced her to wash and clean for them, the pigs. And now, in our old age, they're coming again.'

The tears were flowing down the old woman's face. 'Who would have believed it?' she whispered. 'Who would ever have believed it?'

Julie put her hand on the old woman's sleeve. For a moment, she could only stare into the misery on her face.

'Madame,' she said at last, looking at the old woman's tears, 'they'll never be able to find the real heart of France.'

She spoke softly because she was embarrassed by the theatrical quality of her little speech. But the old woman smiled at her through her tears.

'Thank you, my darling,' she said.

And Julie felt ashamed at her own embarrassment.

10

Vivian was walking up the drive to the ancient, substantial manor which was the headquarters of the 4th Armoured Division. He was deliberately recalling Julie to mind, as he had done many times during the past couple of days. He wished with adolescent regret that he had asked her for a photograph. Being an actress, she was bound to carry photographs of herself about with her. He wished there was somebody to whom he could talk about her without creating an entirely false impression.

A small Renault car drew up. The driver stuck his head out of the window. It was Captain André de Bernac, commander of the 2nd

Independent Company of the new Somua S 35 tanks attached to 4th Armoured.

'Want a ride back to the house, old chap?'

De Bernac spoke English with the same exactness as the English suits he wore off duty.

Vivian climbed into the seat beside him.

'What brings you here,' he asked, 'if that isn't top secret?'

'We've all been summoned to HQ for a briefing. *Le grand asperge* has just returned from a conference with General Georges. I imagine you are not excluded.'

The house was empty except for the orderlies, when they arrived. The senior divisional officers and battalion commanders were assembled in the orchard, and were already settling down onto stools in a wide semi-circle under the shade of the trees, when Vivian and de Bernac joined them. A map-board had been set up on two chairs. De Gaulle was standing beside it. He had removed his képi, and had unbuttoned his leather tankman's jacket. A cigarette was, as usual, smoking between his fingers. He stared with lofty impatience as Vivian and de Bernac found their places. Richard Lebrun, a major of Cuirassiers, and a cousin of the President of the Republic, gave Vivian a cheerful smile, as he sat down beside him.

De Gaulle removed his disapproving stare from the late-comers.

'As you are no doubt aware,' he began. 'I was speaking with the Commander, North East Front, earlier this morning. He said to me – his exact words, messieurs! – "De Gaulle," he said, "for a long time you have proposed to us the very tactics which the enemy is now employing against us. The time has come, therefore, for you to act."'

He paused to clear his throat.

De Gaulle was too disdainful, thought Vivian, too self-absorbed, too angular and awkward in manner to make a dashing Cuirassier commander in the style of Murat or de Gallifet. Even the uniform he adopted deliberately to give the impression of 'a warrior for the working day' was faintly ridiculous. The leather jacket was like the helmet and overalls the Prince of Wales used to wear when he had visited the coal-mines in the Rhondda or the West Riding. And there was the pathos inherent in the situation of a fifty-year-old colonel who had been passed over for promotion so often now that there was scarcely the remotest chance of his ever obtaining it.

'In effect, he went on to instruct me,' de Gaulle continued, 'that we are to employ the full weight of our armour in counter-attacking the enemy, not in penny packets, but at divisional and brigade strength.'

There was a ripple of approval amongst his audience.

'Since dawn, it has become clear that the Boche is attempting to follow his customary path south-westwards, towards Paris.' He smiled faintly. 'It is a relief to discover, after the anxieties of the past few days, that the Teuton imagination is as limited as it always has been.'

This was greeted with some laughter.

'The battle, my friends, has not yet truly begun. Our arms have suffered reverses, it is true. The enemy has succeeded in crossing the Meuse at Sedan and below Dinant. This may well prove his downfall. For he must supply his army this side of the Meuse, and General Georges has assured me that our forces are already exerting pressure on his bridgeheads, and that the brave squadrons of the English Royal Air Force' – he nodded in Vivian's direction – 'have destroyed most of the enemy's bridges. You have heard the reports, I am sure, that enemy infantry crossed the Bar last night. There is nothing grave about the news. The Bar offers no greater obstacle than *le pipi du chat*. Today, however, a new force faces the enemy offensive. XXI Corps, commanded by General Flavigny, consists of General Brocard's 3rd Armoured Division, the 3rd Motorised Division, the 5th Cavalry Division, and the 1st Cavalry Brigade. Thus, for the first time, the enemy will be faced with a concentration of armour as great as his own. Should General Flavigny's XXI Corps be compelled to give ground southwards, then a major attack is to be launched on the exposed right flank of the enemy. General Bruneau's 1st Armoured Division is being pulled back from Charleroi, across the Belgian frontier, to take up an offensive position south of Rocroi, while General Bruché's 2nd Armoured Division is already assembled at Vervins, and is ready to strike eastwards.'

'It's the Marne all over again,' exclaimed Major Lebrun from his place beside Vivian.

'Naturally,' de Gaulle replied. He smiled again. 'But without the English.' He spread his hands, and glanced at Vivian. 'Alas!'

Vivian remembered the first evening he had spent in the mess – it seemed so long ago now, but in fact it was less than a week. With only the slightest pretence at self-deprecation, Colonel de Gaulle had recalled, from his presidential seat at the dinner-table, how, as a young officer in 1914, he had been present at a military review held by Generals Joffre and Kitchener, and how, during the course of the parade, Joffre had introduced Kitchener to General Marchand, that same General Marchand whom, sixteen years before, Kitchener had so deeply humiliated at Fashoda, in the Sudan. General Marchand had opened his arms to Kitchener there, in front of the assembled French troops, in a gesture of reconciliation.

'I swear to you, gentlemen,' de Gaulle had recalled, 'I wept tears of bitterness at the spectacle. You must remember of course that I was young then.'

Vivian had concealed his anger. He had been compelled to reconcile dislike for de Gaulle's more than fair share of weary Gallic arrogance, with admiration for his swaggering energy and faith in attempting to pull together into a fighting force a division which, a few days previously, had existed solely as a flag pinned on a map at Vincennes. There was also the respect in which de Gaulle was held by anglophils like de Bernac, who had gone out of their way to make Vivian feel at home in the mess.

'Since we, the 4th Armoured, are not yet at full strength,' de Gaulle was saying, 'we are to remain here in our lines for a further two days. Two more battalions have been alloted to us – of Renault D 2's.'

There was a groan from the audience at the news that they were to be reinforced with obsolescent tanks. De Gaulle ignored the noise of disapproval.

'The first two squadrons are already arriving,' he said. 'We are to receive also the 4th (Motorised) Chasseurs, and the 3rd Cavalry Brigade. The 3rd Cavalry has been in action, but has been withdrawn from General Petiet's command for regrouping. As soon as these units have arrived, we shall be moving our advance parties to Neuchâtel, to reconnoitre up the Aisne, and to prepare our forward positions on the east bank of the Ardennes Canal.'

The calm recital of troop dispositions, and their indication by de Gaulle's adjutant on the map-board was very reassuring, so that Vivian was able to feel that there was nothing illusory about the peace of the orchard and the sunlight dappling through the leaves. An aircraft droned high overhead. The assembled officers stared up between the boughs. The engines coughed, spluttered, then picked up again.

'It's a Breguet,' said one of the battalion majors. 'Heading due west – for Chauny, I suppose.'

'*Mon Colonel*,' the commander of the 46th 'B' tank Battalion asked de Gaulle, as the noise of the aircraft died away, 'you have made no mention of anti-aircraft attachments.'

'Because, Major Delaherche, no mention of them has been made to me,' replied de Gaulle.

'But, Colonel,' protested Captain Idée, commander, 1st Independent Company, 'we are being made increasingly aware of the enemy's tactical use of aerial bombardment. . . . '

'I am perfectly aware of the need for protection from air attack, Captain Idée,' de Gaulle responded coldly.

A brigade-captain raised his hand. De Gaulle surveyed him with mild curiosity.

'*Mon Colonel*,' asked the brigade-captain, 'will there be air cover provided when we move into the zone of operations?'

'My information is, Captain Sabathier, that we cannot rely on aerial support from *Zone d'Opérations Aériennes Nord*,' de Gaulle replied. 'General Georges has consulted with General Swayne, senior English liaison officer at GQG, La Ferté. General Swayne suggests that our own excellent Major Hardwicke should make contact with the Royal Air Force Advanced Air Striking Force at Chauny when we require air cover.'

'So we are to depend entirely on the goodwill of the English air force to provide us with cover?'

It was the redoubtable Captain Idée returning to the attack.

De Gaulle appeared to ignore him.

'Gentlemen,' he began, 'when the Commander-in-Chief, Allied Land Forces, instructed me to take this command, I expressed my deepest anxieties. I told him that though he had fulfilled my wishes by appointing me to command an armoured division, in fact no such division effectively existed. I told him that it was my deeply felt conviction that we had learnt none of the lessons of Poland, clear though such lessons were. I told him that none of our generals were willing to understand that what had happened at the gates of Warsaw could as easily happen at the gates of Paris. I told him that everything remained to be done on our side, and that if we did not do it in time, we should lose as miserably as we lost the war in 1871 – and that, once again, it would be entirely our own fault. Today, however, when I spoke to General Georges, I was able to tell him that, whatever my feelings about the irremediable lateness in organising our mechanised forces, I felt proud that, as a colonel, I should have been appointed to command this division. I told him that if men of courage and spirit could overcome deficiencies in *materiel*, then I had the utmost confidence that the officers and men under my command would do it. General Georges placed his hand on my shoulder. "*Mon cher de Gaulle*," he exclaimed, "I understand perfectly the satisfaction a commander feels when he has men under his command whom he can trust implicitly. As for your misgivings, *mon cher*, I give you my word, they are entirely unjustified."'

The officers on either side of Vivian sat perfectly still. It was like being in Covent Garden, he thought, as the closing notes of *Parsifal* died away, and the audience was too wrapped in awe to applaud.

As they returned from the orchard back to the house, he joined the group of senior officers about de Gaulle.

'*Mon Colonel*,' he asked, 'would you prefer me to get in touch immediately with Advanced Air Striking Force?'

De Gaulle stared distantly over his head.

'Of course, Major 'ardwicke!' he replied. 'Naturally. That's your job, isn't it?'

He stalked on up the path of the neglected garden, and stooped under the lintel of the door. Vivian felt disconcerted, but made his way through the house and across the walled yard to the dairy-shed which had been converted into the Operations Room. There he managed to find himself a telephone and an ash-tray, as far away from the clatter of typewriters and ancient army tape-machines as possible.

He knew that he should obtain clearance from GHQ, Arras, before attempting to make contact with the operational HQ of Advanced Air Striking Force at Chauny. Since, however, Chauny was no great distance away, and remembering the difficulties he had encountered when trying to make contact with Lord Gort's HQ, he decided to use the ordinary civilian line to speak to Air Vice Marshal Playfair's office. After twenty minutes of confused negotiation with a series of elderly French telephone operators, the phone was answered by a male voice with a North London accent.

'Adjutant's office, A.A.S.F.H.Q., Chauny. Staff Wilkins speakin'.'

'Staff-*Sergeant* Wilkins?' Vivian asked severely.

''s right, sir,' Staff-Sergeant Wilkins replied.

'Would you put me through to the adjutant, Staff-Sergeant,' said Vivian.

'Not 'ere at present, sir,' came the reply.

'Can you put me through direct to the Air Vice Marshal's office?' Vivian asked.

There was a long pause accompanied by breathing at the other end.

'Dunno, sir,' came the reply at last. 'Bit of a flap on, see. Who's speakin', sir?'

'My name is Hardwicke,' Vivian replied, 'Major Hardwicke. I'm British liaison with the French 4th Armoured Division, Laon . . . '

He was interrupted by a series of clicks at the other end of the line.

'Major Hardwicke?' asked a cool, upper-class voice.

'Liaison officer with the French 4th Armoured Division.'

'Knatchbull speaking, Group-Captain. Temporary Station Commander, unpaid and unwanted,' said the voice at the other end. 'What can I do you for, eh?'

'I'm phoning on orders from the divisional commander here,' said Vivian.

There was a rustle of papers at the other end.

'What division did you say?' asked the voice.

'4th Armoured. Stationed at Laon district. HQ at Bruyères. Div. Commander has asked me to enquire as to what extent A.A.S.F. can provide effective air cover. 4th Armoured has been ordered to move up the Aisne in forty-eight hours' time, to take up start position on the line of the Ardennes Canal, Rethel area.'

'Difficult to say, old chap,' said Group-Captain Knatchbull. 'I mean it's nothing to do with me, really. But there's a hell of a flap going on here, and forty-eight hours is bloody close to eternity, isn't it?'

134

'Can you put me through to a member of Air Vice Marshal Playfair's staff, please?' asked Vivian.

'No point, old chap,' came the reply. 'Everybody's in it up to the neck at the moment. It's no bloody secret – every squadron is out, operating round-the-clock sorties against Jerry on the Meuse.'

There was a further rustling of papers.

'Look here, old chap,' said Group-Captain Knatchbull. 'Can't seem to find any reference to a 4th Armoured Division in our bumph here! One, two, and three, but no fourth. Are you sure you mean 4th Armoured Division?'

'4th Armoured is based on Laon. For God's sake,' Vivian said angrily, 'you're almost near enough to see us with a pair of field-glasses. If you don't believe me, why don't you ring General Swayne's office at La Ferté?'

'Haven't got time, old chap,' came the reply.

There was a violent click at the other end, so that Vivian thought that Group-Captain Knatchbull had slammed down the receiver. Then another voice said, 'Wing Commander Connell here. Look here, who are you? What do you want?'

Vivian explained his business with exemplary patience, then spoiled it by adding aggressively, 'And if you don't believe me, ring up General Swayne's office at GQG, La Ferté. General Swayne is my superior officer, and I am ringing you on his instructions.'

'All right, old boy,' came the reply, 'keep your hair on! I believe you. Look here, we are in a bit of a shambles here, just now. To be absolutely frank with you, old boy, our losses this morning have been bloody appalling. We couldn't possibly predict our capability over the next forty-eight hours. Now be a decent chap will you, and ring off? We need every bloody line we've got.'

The note of disaster was clear through the cool, upper-class accent. Vivian put down the receiver. He sat staring at the clerks and signallers in front of him, across the stone-topped dairy slabs. Now it was his responsibility to go across the yard to Colonel de Gaulle's office, to inform him that there was little likelihood of the RAF being in a position to provide air cover.

He decided to go immediately rather than to suffer the discomfort of waiting. To his surprise, he was admitted immediately into the small parlour which de Gaulle had appropriated as his office.

'Major Hardwicke?' de Gaulle asked, staring directly at him.

At that moment, Vivian realised the importance placed by de Gaulle on his phone-call to Chauny.

'I'm sorry, *mon colonel*,' he began.

He tried to explain the little he knew about the predicament of the Advanced Air Striking Force. He said he would try again later, to see if the situation had changed. De Gaulle listened impassively. He raised his fingers, interrupting Vivian.

'It is a pity, Major Hardwicke,' he said, 'that you did not bring back the *Tondeau de Chartres* from the Château de la Berlière.'

Vivian was taken by surprise. He had not supposed that de Gaulle should have thought such a thing worth remembering. It was impossible to understand what it was de Gaulle was implying; the remark had proceeded from some thought buried deep within his mind.

'Why, *mon colonel?*' asked Vivian.

'Didn't my friend de Bart-Mendel tell you?' de Gaulle asked. 'The *Tondeau* is supposed to have miraculous properties.' He regarded Vivian with cold amusement. 'A virtue,' he said, 'clearly denied to the English Royal Air Force.'

11

As the *kübelwagen* travelled along the green depths of the Meuse Valley once more, heading towards Sedan, von Leonarte and his crew met the tanks of his own regiment, the 10th Panzers, ripping up the sweating asphalt, and cutting broad swathes in the long grass of the meadows. There were more tanks spread, parked, over the grassy incline of La Marfée, below the trees, lurking menacingly, only half-visible in the bleached, dusty green. Here and there reared the barrel of an abandoned French gun, like a blackened, ineffective scarecrow.

Von Leonarte had found it hard to keep himself from falling asleep ever since they had passed the last French outpost, a few miles south of Maisoncelle – a weary detachment of Algerian infantry. Now he pulled himself into full wakefulness. Senior Driver Helm halted the *kübelwagen*. Immediately in front of them, a squadron of 38T's were swivelling off the road, and clattering over the splintered debris of a gate into the upward-sloping field. Von Leonarte recognised the numbers painted under the turrets.

'We'll report direct to Regiment,' he decreed.

There would be a chance of coffee and something to eat at regimental headquarters. They bumped uphill across the fields to the edge of the woods. Now and then, von Leonarte recognised a familiar face by one of the parked tanks, and waved a greeting.

The regimental headquarters consisted of three Hanomag half-tracks parked under the cover of the heavy boughs of the trees. As they drove up towards them, a lieutenant and a sergeant came from between the vehicles to see what they wanted. Von Leonarte jumped down even before Helm had stopped.

'Any coffee going?' he asked.

He took off his cap.

'Von Leonarte,' he introduced himself to the lieutenant. 'We've just returned from a scouting party behind enemy lines. We are very thirsty and very hungry. And we need petrol – I have the requisition form.'

The lieutenant was taken aback. He was very young, and unsure of himself.

'Colonel Hassler isn't here, Herr Rittmeister,' he said.

Major Thiele, the regimental adjutant, appeared from inside one of the half-tracks. He jumped down.

'Dieter von Leonarte,' he exclaimed, 'you are a disgrace to the uniform. Every time you come reporting to Regiment, you try to scrounge food and coffee from us.' He came over to von Leonarte and shook his hand enthusiastically. 'How did it go, Dieter?' he asked.

'Wild goose chase, of course,' von Leonarte told him.

Major Thiele listened sympathetically as von Leonarte explained the nature of his mission.

'And now,' he concluded, 'I suppose I've got to trail up into Belgium, to find Special Intelligence, wherever it's got to by this time.'

'Propaganda, I suppose,' Major Thiele said.

'I was told that this medallion was worn by the old Constables of France,' von Leonarte said.

'Perhaps it's round Gamelin's neck at the moment,' Major Thiele suggested.

'If it is,' Von Leonarte told him, 'it doesn't appear to be doing him much good.'

'Schwartz,' Major Thiele bawled across to his orderly, 'fetch some coffee and a drop of schnapps for the Rittmeister. And something to eat. Perhaps your lads would go to the kitchen, Dieter. We fixed it up through the trees there, by the stream.'

'I'll tell them,' said the young lieutenant.

'There's a good fellow,' said Major Thiele. 'Actually, we had such an early start, and such an easy crossing, that we've managed to send out hot meals to virtually the entire regiment.'

'Seen any action?' von Leonarte asked.

'Not really,' Major Thiele replied. 'Lot of sorties by low-flying enemy aircraft. It's been a bit worrying. They're trying to take out the bridge, of course, so they haven't been bothering us up here. You've just missed the boring part – the hanging about, and so on. You'll be back here for the real action, don't you worry.'

'Any idea of what's going to happen?' von Leonarte asked.

'The Colonel's down at Glaire,' Major Thiele told him. 'Colonel-General von Runstedt turned up there just after dawn, and there's the old man, of course, so there's some sort of Group conference or briefing going on.'

'From what we could see,' said von Leonarte, 'the enemy is fairly demoralised. It was simple driving through his lines – if you could call it a line. And then enemy units kept trying to surrender to us. One lot asked us when the main force was going to turn up – thought we were an advance-guard. And then another – a company of infantry under their captain – actually tried to surrender to us when we were south of a line Vouziers-Rethel. They actually marched *south* to try to make contact with us so as to lay down their arms!'

A group of headquarters staff, officers and NCO's, had gathered round to hear von Leonarte's tale.

'Obviously you couldn't bring them back,' said Major Thiele, 'so what did you do?'

'We disarmed them. Made their weapons unserviceable . . . '

Von Leonarte paused, and smiled.

'I ordered them to make their way to their homes,' he continued, 'but first I told them to remove their trousers.'

Some of his audience laughed heartily.

The orderly, Schwartz, returned carrying a tray on which was a metal cup of coffee, a small medicine-bottle containing schnapps, a French loaf, and some sausage. As von Leonarte poured some of the schnapps into his coffee, a captain of signals said quietly, 'Isn't it a little unbecoming in a German officer to humiliate a defeated enemy, Rittmeister?'

'These men, my dear captain,' von Leonarte replied, 'were in no sense a defeated enemy. They were cowards who had never fired a shot in anger, and who had deserted their own comrades. I think you will agree, captain, that such men bring shame on the profession of arms.'

'Dieter is right, Captain Wentzel,' said Major Thiele, in his role as adjudicator. 'Such shit deserves no better treatment.'

Captain Wentzel nodded.

'Here they come,' Major Thiele announced.

Some of the headquarters staff reached for their helmets, but nobody seemed disposed to take cover. Von Leonarte heard the droning pulse of approaching aircraft. He squatted down in the long grass, and stared down into the valley whose meadows were studded with the dark-grey, steely shapes of the motionless, waiting tanks. Here and there, black dots moved through the corn, where tank crews ran to take cover away from their vehicles.

The air throbbed with the noise of the approaching bombers, but the actual sight of the aircraft took von Leonarte by surprise. They appeared from behind a steep fold in the meadows, flying along the valley at the same level as where he was sitting. They were lumbering, old-fashioned, single-engined monoplanes, three of them; from where he was sitting, he could see quite easily the Royal Air Force rondels and flight numbers painted on the camouflaged fusilages. Through the pounding of the propeller engines, he could hear the tearing noise of the 88mm flak guns on the ground, where they were massed around either end of the 10th Panzers' pontoon-bridge. The air above the bottom of the valley was filled with vivid flashes and puffs of drifting smoke. The aircraft disappeared behind the slope of La Marfée. There was a deafening explosion. Seconds later, a thick column of black smoke rose above the tops of the trees.

Major Thiele stood up beside von Leonarte.

'There's another one gone,' he said.

He sounded quite regretful.

'That'll make the score fourteen down at the bridge,' he added. 'A couple of hours ago, they were having to pull the wrecked planes away to make room for the vehicles waiting to cross. . . . The old man made us halt to let the 88's through to defend the bridge. They're positioned wheel to wheel down there – an incredible sight. And still the English pilots keep coming in those big, slow machines. Our lads can't help knocking them out of the air. The French are wiser; they stay up there.'

He pointed to the sky.

'They don't hit us, and we don't hit them. The English, on the other hand – it makes you wonder what their commanders can be like to throw away the lives of brave men like that.'

Half-an-hour later, an open car came bouncing up the hill through the grass.

'Here he is,' said Major Thiele.

Von Leonarte had been resting, his head propped against the thick front tyre of the Hanomag. He scrambled to his feet. Colonel Hassler was getting out of the car, map-case and portfolio under his arm. His aide got out after him.

'We have our orders, Kurt,' he called cheerfully to Major Thiele. 'We move at eleven-thirty hours.'

Von Leonarte saluted. Colonel Hassler noticed him, and came over to shake hands.

'Restored to us, are you, Rittmeister?' he asked. 'We can use an experienced point-troop commander now.'

'I'm afraid my orders are to report back to Army Group Special Intelligence up in Belgium, Herr Oberst,' von Leonarte told him.

'Just paying a call on old friends, eh?' asked Colonel Hassler.

'I'll be back as soon as I can, Herr Oberst, I promise you,' von Leonarte assured him.

'That's the spirit, Rittmeister,' said Colonel Hassler.

He took his map-case from under his arm, and pulled out one of the maps.

'Gentlemen?' he called to his staff, as he spread out the map over

139

the steel guard on the Hanomag's track. 'I hope you've all remembered to bring your towels and bathing suits with you.'

Somebody said, 'Can one swim in the Seine?'

'The Seine, lieutenant?' asked Colonel Hassler. 'Who said anything about the Seine? We're going to the seaside.'

He put his finger down on the map.

'In the words of General Guderian to us this morning, "Road-map Rethel, gentlemen! Road-map Rethel!" Here we are. Our advance will take us along the north bank of the Ardennes Canal, north of Rethel, through Montcornet – that's the road-junction here – then on to the north-west – Amiens, and Abbeville, till we reach the sea here, at St Valéry.'

'And then we take the cross-Channel ferry to England,' suggested the irrepressible lieutenant.

His seniors laughed indulgently.

'Not quite, lieutenant,' Colonel Hassler told him. 'I expect we'll be sent to have a look at Paris first.'

He turned to von Leonarte.

'You see, Rittmeister? If you want a breath of sea air, you'd better get back here quickly. But you can do a job for us, if you will.'

'Herr Oberst?' von Leonarte asked.

'Field Intelligence down by the bridge are holding a couple of English Air Force officers,' said Colonel Hassler. 'They crash-landed their aircraft between the bridge and Bazeilles. Field Intelligence want 10th Panzers to get them back to Group for interrogation. Since that is where you are bound, Rittmeister, perhaps you will take them for us. You can leave two of your men here, and carry on with your driver. You won't find guarding the Englishmen an arduous responsibility. One of them has his leg in splints, and the other will not desert his comrade. ... Now, gentlemen,' he said, returning to the map, 'if you would check your watches – the time is ... 1038 hours precisely.'

As von Leonarte and Senior Driver Helm drove down the road to the bridge, they saw that the descriptions of the English bombing attacks had not been exaggerated. The 88mm flak guns were mounted in heavy clusters around the ends of the bridge. The gun teams were stripped to the waist, as they stood to their guns awaiting the next onslaught of the bombers. The extent of their success was evident all about them. Von Leonarte had seen nothing like it, even in Poland. The wreckage of huge tail-planes, twisted propellers, blackened fusilages, and shattered frames of perspex lay scattered across the hillsides immediately above the bridge. One of the bombers had crashed nose first into the river bank, its great wing lay crumpled among the bushes, its tip touching the edge of the road; its engine was still burning. Flames licked upwards round the cockpit over the side of which the limp body of the pilot was draped – his head, shoulders, and torso were already blackened by the fire, but the sleeve of his uniform was still visible under the charred leather of the flying jacket, with the two silver rings on the airforce blue. The black evil-smelling smoke billowed across the torn road.

One of the bridge-master's field gendarmes stood on the running board of the *kübelwagen*, and guided it across the gently swaying bridge, past the line of waiting PzKw III's whose crews squatted, smoking, in the shade of their vehicles.

'Your fellows are round behind the tent, Herr Hauptmann,' a field-intelligence officer reported to von Leonarte.

He pointed the way. The two Englishmen were sitting with their backs to the canvas. They were unguarded. Both were in their shirt-sleeves, with their light blue jackets draped over their shoulders. One of them had two rings on his sleeves, the other, one. The one with two rings had the right leg of his trousers ripped open from his boot to his hip. The full length of his leg was bound in splints and fresh bandages. He was smoking his pipe. The other one appeared to be unhurt.

'Come,' von Leonarte said, in English.

The man in splints stared up without removing his pipe. He stretched out his hand for assistance. Von Leonarte looked at the other man. With difficulty von Leonarte said, 'You ... help ... friend?. . . . Yes?'

Then he noticed that the man was weeping. He was shocked, but he understood what the man must have been through, and felt no contempt. He called to Helm, who was waiting by the driving-seat of the *kübelwagen*, to come over.

'Help this one up, will you?' he said, indicating the man in splints.

Helm put the man's arm about his own shoulder, and raised him bodily onto his one good leg. The man hopped a few paces, clutching Helm's shoulder, the unfastened buckles of his flying-boots jingling as he moved. His leather flying-jacket lay on the grass beside the dint where he had been sitting. Von Leonarte picked it up and handed it to him, placing it over his arm. He crouched beside the other man.

'Now, you come,' he said in English. 'With you ... war finish – yes? All finish!'

The man wiped his eyes with his knuckles like a child; von Leonarte noticed that his hand had been encrusted with oil. He took out his cigarettes and offered them to the man. The man tried to take one from the case, but his hand trembled to such an extent that he could not manage it. Von Leonarte drew one out for him, placed it between his cracked, grimy lips, and lit it for him.

'*Danke,*' the man said, still shuddering. '*Danke schön.*'

Von Leonarte picked up his flying-jacket, and helped him to his feet. They made their way after the others to the *kübelwagen*. The two Englishmen sat in the back. The injured man placed his leg between the two front seats in the space from which the machine-gun had been removed.

They set off up the road through the ruins of Bazeilles.

The shocked man had begun to whimper. The *kübelwagen* jolted violently. Every time it did so, the Englishman's whimpering became a grunt.

'I say, old chap,' the injured man protested, 'steady on now. Not in front of the Gestapo!'

Von Leonarte turned in his seat.

'Not Gestapo,' he said.

'All right, old boy,' said the injured man. 'No offence meant.'

They drove on out of Bazeilles, up the winding road towards the peaks of the Ardennes. After a while, the uninjured man calmed down.

'Did I tell you about that bint, the other day?' the injured man asked his companion, who didn't reply. 'Don't suppose we'll see another bint for the whole bloody duration,' he added.

They were silent for a moment.

'Tell you what scares me,' said the man who had been weeping. 'Do you think – after we've been in a POW camp for a bit – we'll end up as queer as bloody coots? I couldn't stand being queer. I mean, I suppose if you've been to a bloody public school it doesn't matter so much; but if you're just an ordinary red-blooded, heterosexual oik like me, it's just too horrible to contemplate.'

He coughed.

A convoy of heavy lorries was coming down the winding road out of the forest, billowing clouds of dust above the trees. An entire motorised reserve regiment was moving down to the bridge. Von Leonarte told Helm to pull over onto the verge, and stop. He jumped down from the *kübelwagen*.

The injured Englishman tried to catch his sleeve.

'Hey, Fritz!' he called.

His companion had managed to light a second cigarette. He had it stuck between his lips while hugging himself with both arms to keep himself from trembling, like a Berlin cabbie in winter.

'Heinrich!' the injured Englishman tried again. 'Franz!'

'Von Leonarte,' von Leonarte told him. 'Dieter von Leonarte.'

The injured Englishman beckoned to him to move in closer so that Helm should not hear what he was about to say.

'Here, Franz!' he said. 'We prisoners, ja? Inside offiziers lager, ja? Nein fräuleins in offiziers lager! Nein! What about being a really decent chap, eh? Ein gut kamarade, ja? Tell you what. When we get to the next town. Die ... er ... nachst stadt, vous comprennez? ... You take us to' – he paused for serious thought – 'ein rote licht haus, ja? Mit fräuleins! Before we're locked up and never – er – einsehen

142

eine andere fräulein encore. Not until this fucking krieg ist finito, at any rate.'

Von Leonarte stared down at the Englishman sprawling back on his seat with his broken leg stretched before him, as if waiting for some wretched coolie or native bearer to bring him *chota-peg*. Some residue of Prussian chivalry prevented him from striking the man for his arrogance. He tried to smile. He said slowly, in English, 'I must obey orders, gentlemen.'

He swung himself up, back into the seat beside Helm. As they watched the long convoy of lorries grinding past, he heard the injured Englishman say to his companion,

'They're all bloody Gestapo, old chap. Make no mistake.'

12

Julie had been walking all day, trying to keep up with the old couple. She could feel every sharp piece of grit under her shoes. Every now and then she passed groups of people who had fallen out exhausted onto the verge; families with elderly people and young children sitting in the midst of their pathetic belongings.

By mid-afternoon it had become clear to her that Marie-Claire was prepared to let her carry the baby indefinitely. It was damp again, and smelly; it had begun to cry again, and Julie's arms were aching past endurance. Finally she made up her mind. She stopped, letting the flood of refugees pour on round her until Marie-Claire and her gentleman escort caught up with her.

She placed the baby in Marie-Claire's arms, then reached to take her suitcase from the man. The man refused to let her have it.

'If mademoiselle wishes, I should be happy to carry it for her,' he told her with what he assumed to be suave charm.

'The baby's wet,' Marie-Claire wailed. 'And he's hungry.'

Julie tore the suitcase out of the man's grasp, and shouted in English, 'Piss off, you!' She then hurried away, pushing through the throng to catch up once more with the two old peasants.

She could see no sign of them. The crowd had begun to move more slowly, and to become even thicker than before. Julie could recognise none of the faces about her, neither from the train, nor from the long day's walk. It was as if she had moved into strange territory. Cars and carts had ground to a standstill. A short distance away, there was the grinding of powerful motors, and men's voices shouting.

'Can you see the soldiers?' a man's voice said in Julie's ear.

A fat little priest, no taller than herself, was standing beside her.

He had lifted a small boy of about five onto his shoulders, his round face damp with the effort. Sweat was running down from the brim of his clerical shovel hat. The crowd was as dense as on the London tubes in the rush-hour.

'Soldiers!' the little boy shouted out, smiling.

'He pointed over the priest's hat..

'Soldiers in tanks!'

'Louis? Can you see *Maman* and *Papa*?'

Julie looked down. The voice was that of a pretty, fair-haired girl, eight or nine years old. She was wearing a slate-grey school overall buttoned over her cotton frock, and was pressed against Julie, though Julie had not noticed her in the general crush.

'There are too many people,' the priest replied gently. 'We'll start looking again when there aren't so many.'

'I can see soldiers,' the little boy shouted excitedly, as if soldiers provided an acceptable alternative to *Maman* and *Papa*. 'I can see lots and lots of soldiers.'

The crowd had started to ease forward again, very slowly. Julie put her free hand about the little girl's shoulder, afraid that she might stumble and be trampled on in the press.

'What's your name?' she asked.

The little girl looked up. In the evening light, and in the shadow of people about them, Julie could see the long-dried tear stains on the girl's face.

'Antoinette, mademoiselle,' the little girl replied.

She even managed a slight curtsey.

'That's a very pretty name,' Julie told her.

'Me and Louis – that's my brother – have lost our *Maman* and *Papa*,' the girl explained.

'And Monsieur le Curé found us,' said Louis from up on the priest's shoulders. 'Didn't you, Monsieur le Curé?'

'I met Louis and Antoinette this morning,' said the priest.

'You aren't their priest, monsieur?' asked Julie.

'No, mademoiselle. I'm merely helping them to find their parents,' the priest replied.

'Some thieves stole our car,' said the little boy. 'And *Maman* and *Papa* tried to chase after them. Only there were so many people, we couldn't find them again.'

'Or they couldn't find us,' said Antoinette sensibly.

'Where are they from, monsieur?' Julie asked.

'Namur, mademoiselle,' the priest replied. 'And you – are you Belgian too?'

'No. I'm English.'

'You speak French very well, mademoiselle,' said the priest.

'Where's my supper, Toinette?' Louis called from the priest's shoulders.

The shouting was growing louder all round them. Julie peered between the heads and shoulders of those to one side of her. A heavy truck loomed up only a few yards away. It was pointing up the road, in the opposite direction. Soldiers wearing the berets of the Chasseurs, their helmets strapped to their packs, and rifles between their knees, were sitting up on wooden benches. An officer in a képi had climbed out onto the running board of the cabin. He was shouting and gesticulating at the crowd. 'Don't you want us to stop the Boches?' His voice cracked into a falsetto screech.

As they were pushed on by those behind, Julie saw that an entire column of troop-carrying lorries was stretching away down the road, with the civilian crowd milling around them, preventing them from moving as surely as though they had been caught in a flood.

The little priest gasped.

'Mademoiselle!'

'Hold on to me, Antoinette,' Julie told the little girl.

By main force, bracing her back against those behind her, she made a little space. The priest lifted down the child. Julie could see where the sweat had drenched his soutane, under his arms.

'I must take the children out into the field for a rest, mademoiselle,' he panted. 'Will you go on, or will you stay with us?'

'I'll stay with you, monsieur,' Julie told him.

'Thank you, mademoiselle,' he said.

Julie took Antoinette's hand, and followed the little priest as he forced his way toward the hedgrow, away from the column of lorries. The road was mounted on a low causeway. They slipped through the thin hedge and down the bank on the other side. Ahead of them, a few people were running across the broken earth, pushing bicycles and handcarts, in an attempt to by-pass the crowded road above.

'I don't think the little one can go any further tonight,' the priest said to Julie. 'The ground here is dry. If we stay in the grass, we'll be quite comfortable.'

'What about *Maman* and *Papa*?' asked Antoinette.

The priest glanced at Julie. Then he said, 'If they're in front of us, they'll probably wait in the next village,' he said. 'If they're behind us, they might see us here, from the road. So it's a good idea to stop here, isn't it?'

Antoinette thought for a moment, then nodded.

'What about my supper?' asked Louis.

Antoinette said, 'Be quiet, Louis. I don't expect we're going to have any supper.'

Louis was sitting in the grass. He pondered what his sister had just said, and began to cry.

The priest scrambled to his feet once more. He brushed the grass from his soutane.

'I'll find you a bite of supper,' he told Louis.

145

He adjusted the sash at his waist.

'Are you Catholic, mademoiselle?' he asked.

Julie shook her head.

'Of course not,' said the priest. 'You're English. . . . Most French people nowadays would rather die than give food to a priest, but the Flemish and the south Hollanders are different. They still have respect.'

He hopped back across the ditch, and scrambled up the bank on to the road.

'Will Monsieur le Curé come back with my supper?' asked Louis, recovering somewhat.

'I expect so,' said Julie. 'What's your name? Family name, I mean,' she asked Antoinette.

'Van Scheik,' Antoinette replied. 'I'm Antoinette van Scheik. And he's Louis van Scheik.'

'We're going to France,' said Louis, 'because of the Germans.'

'We're in France,' said Antoinette.

'We're going to France,' said Louis ignoring his sister, 'because it's nice there. *Maman* and *Papa* say there aren't any Germans there . . . . The Germans stole our car,' he added.

'He doesn't know what he's talking about,' Antoinette told Julie. 'He's too young.'

'I'm not,' exclaimed Louis. '*You* don't know what *you're* talking about.'

'We were having a picnic, you see,' Antoinette told Julie. 'And *Maman* and *Papa* saw these men getting into the car. They told us to wait where we were, and not to move. Only they didn't come back.'

'Not for hours and hours,' said Louis.

'Then Louis began to cry,' said Antoinette.

'So did you,' said Louis.

'No, I didn't,' said Antoinette.

'You didn't make a noise like I did,' said Louis, 'but I saw you.'

'I'm sure it was a very terrible thing, *Maman* and *Papa* not coming back,' said Julie, 'whether you cried or not.'

'Yes, mademoiselle,' Antoinette admitted, 'it was terrible.'

The priest came slithering down the bank. He had a single long baton of bread, a small brown paper bag, and a bottle of Perrier water.

'I told you so,' he said to Julie. 'A Dutch family from Geldrop, near Eindhoven.'

Inside the paper bag was a greasy fragment of pâté, and a couple of wizened apples.

'Good Catholics,' the priest explained. 'They gave what they had.'

146

'You don't have to be a Catholic to do that,' Julie said, rather shortly.

'It helps,' said the priest with a faintly patronising smile.

Julie felt too exhausted to argue. After they had eaten, she opened her suitcase, and took out her sweater, and her Burberry. She rolled the sweater up as a pillow and spread the Burberry on the ground for Louis to lie on.

The priest sat a little way apart. He had opened a small black prayer-book; he was holding it up to the fading light. In the dusk over the eastern horizon, there was a glow in the sky, such as Julie had seen when travelling on an evening train through the industrial regions of South Lancashire.

'Are you going to stay with us, mademoiselle?' asked Antoinette.

'Do you want me to?' Julie asked.

'Yes, mademoiselle,' said Antoinette.

'Will you take us to England with you, mademoiselle?' asked Louis.

Julie hedged. 'I'm not going to England just yet,' she told him.

'Are you going to France?' asked Louis.

'We're in France already,' said Antoinette.

'I'm going to Paris,' Julie told him. 'That's in France.'

'I expect it'll be nice in France,' said Louis.

13

Marie-Claire awoke just before dawn. The sound of the baby crying had penetrated her sleep. The damp from his dress was soaking cold through her jumper. For a few minutes, she tried to persuade herself that the smell of dung came from the field in which they were lying. But that too was the baby.

Because of the baby, everything had gone wrong with her life. But for it, she would have been working for the Vauthiers – or Joseph would have returned home and married her. And last night, when the lovely gentleman who had been carrying the cases for her had seen the shitty Englishwoman return the baby to her, he had disappeared.

It wasn't even as if the baby was at all loving towards her. When she was pregnant, although she had realised that God was punishing her for being wicked with Joseph, she had consoled herself with the idea of the baby lifting its fat little arms to her, and gurgling and smiling at her. But it never did. It just screamed, and screwed up its ugly red face, and dirtied itself. And mostly it dirtied itself to win attention. The good sisters in Paris had told her how people often did nasty things just to win attention, and how the only response was either to ignore them completely or, if they were children, to punish them severely. She had tried punishing the baby, but it wouldn't learn. It had been wicked from the moment it was born.

She sat up on the damp earth. There was a hint of light in the sky, but all around were the black, still shapes of handcarts, prams, and huddled figures sleeping on the ground, spreading from the dark shadow of the causeway embankment. There was nothing she could do while the baby went on crying. Worse still, the noise he was making was waking up other young children. She picked up the sodden little bundle and began to rock it and to croon over it, tricking it into believing that its silly, wicked tantrums were being indulged. Finally, she succeeded in lulling it back to sleep. Cautiously, hoping that none of the people nearby would see her, she clutched it in her arms and got up onto her feet. She reached for her wicker suitcase, and picked her way over the broken lumps of earth, following parallel with the road until she came to a grassy ramp leading up the causeway bank to a gate. Once up on the road, she moved more quickly and more stealthily. Glancing behind her, she saw a ribbon of pale, grey light cracking the darkness of the sky on the flat, eastern horizon. She would have to do it now, while the road was empty save for the stalled cars, and the people sprawled on the grass verges were still fast asleep.

There was a cart standing high on its heavy, metal-rimmed wheels. The horse in the shafts was asleep, its head drooping to the ground. The backboard of the cart was pinned up. The family to which it belonged was crouched, huddled together, a little way down the bank. Nobody was stirring nearby. She put down her case, and, standing up on her toes, managed to place him inside the cart, concealed behind the backboard.

Picking up her suitcase, she walked on as fast as she could, down the road to the point where the causeway ended and a long avenue of poplars, black against the still-dark sky, began. Occasionally, she glanced at the people sleeping at the roadside in the hope of catching sight of the gentleman who had abandoned her when the English-woman had returned the baby to her. She even felt, in the silence, a sort of sweet sadness at having had to leave it behind.

As the pale, grey ribbon in the eastern sky widened and shredded into several ever-widening, pale, grey ribbons, the birds began to sing and to chirrup. As more birds began to join the dawn chorus from the hedgerows and the fields, the sound of gunfire began to reverberate in the north-east.

Julie woke up finally with the fresh sunlight in her eyes.

'Monsieur le Curé says you've still got some bread,' Antoinette told her.

The fat little priest was buttoning his soutane over his round belly. Louis was sitting a little way up the bank, digging a hole in the grass with his fingers. Above him, on the road, the exodus had begun again – the trudging crowds with their packs and ancient suitcases, the bicycles and prams, the creaking carts drawn by the weary, hungry horses, and small cars grinding along in bottom gear.

'Louis,' Julie exclaimed, 'you'll get so dirty.'

She heard herself sounding exactly as she had done when she had been an au pair, near Rennes; it seemed an age ago.

'That's what I told him, mademoiselle,' said Antoinette.

Louis looked round. His small fingers were encrusted with earth.

'It's a house,' he explained, 'like Jesus lived in.'

'Only when he was dead,' said Antoinette.

'And when he was born,' Louis replied.

'Exactly so,' said the priest. 'The fault is mine, mademoiselle. I was explaining how the stable at Bethlehem was really a cave in a hillside.'

'Monsieur le Curé says that Jesus was living in a cave *both* times he was born,' said Louis.

'I don't know how he's going to eat his bread with hands like that,' protested Julie.

'The child is happy, mademoiselle,' the priest rebuked her.

Suddenly Julie wanted to cry. She nodded at the priest. She took the remnant of bread from her suitcase, and broke it into four pieces. The remainder of the pâté, she divided between the children – she could not have eaten it anyway.

The people who were still in the field were picking up their belongings, and scrambling back up onto the road. Julie and the priest helped the children up the grass.

'Will we find *Maman* and *Papa* today?' asked Louis.

'Perhaps,' said the priest. 'We must say a little prayer for them, and keep a good look-out.'

'And I'll be the look-out,' exclaimed Louis.

'You can't be,' said Antoinette, 'you're too small. You can't see anything.'

'Some small things can see very well indeed,' said Julie. 'Just think of field-mice, for instance.'

For all she really knew, field-mice might have been near-blind.

'And bats!' said Louis.

'Bats are disgusting,' said Antoinette. 'Anyway, they can't see at all.'

'Bats are nice,' Louis replied, 'and they can see like anything. I like bats – they stick in your hair!'

They walked on into the heat of the day. Once or twice, Julie

149

thought of turning away from the road and crossing the fields. The priest dissuaded her.

'It wouldn't be any use, mademoiselle,' he told her. 'All the roads to Paris and to the south will be in the same state. And we must think of the little ones and their parents. There is always a chance.'

After a few hours, the children grew tired. Julie tried to think of all the songs she had learned when she had been in France. She had just begun to teach them,

'Le Roi s'en va-t' en chasse,
Dans le bois des Bourbons,
Dans le bois des Bourbons,
Mon aimable bergère . . . '

when she first heard the droning in the summer sky behind them. She turned round, as did everybody near them. The road stretched back across to the flat, shimmering plain, and as far as it stretched, the black procession of people, of carts and loaded cars, stretched also.

The aircraft was a single speck in the bright sky, away across the fields, above the long avenue of poplars. It was wheeling, dipping its wing, to point in the direction of the road. At first nobody seemed to know what to do; everybody stood, staring up at it. Then it appeared to be hanging motionless above the road, except that it seemed to grow larger with every moment. The noise of its twin motors was growing louder. People began to spill off the road, dropping their bicycles, deserting their carts and vehicles, and throwing themselves over the verges into the fields on either side. Those who were in cars and vans jumped out of them, leaving them with their doors hanging open, and throwing themselves face down into the grass. The aircraft came roaring up the newly deserted road. Julie found herself irresistibly reminded of the 'big black crow, as black as a tar barrel'. She dropped her case, and grabbed the hands of the children, dragging them to the verge. As she did so, she felt Antoinette's fingers slip from her grasp. She did not dare look up. The throb of the motors bored into her ears like the sound of pneumatic drills. The shadow of the wings blotted out the sun. Through the pounding engines, she could hear the crescendo of the scream, and knew what it was. She covered the little boy with her arms as best she could, trying to draw him under her. The noise hit her ear-drums like an aching, leaden blanket. The entire road seemed to lurch upwards like the deck of a ship struck by an immense wave. The breath was so squeezed out of her, she thought she might never breathe again. As the noise began to recede, she heard the grit, pieces of asphalt, earth, pattering down on the ground all around her. Louis began to whimper, his face buried into her side, under her arm.

'It's all right, darling,' she told him. 'It's over now. They've gone!'

150

Her mouth and throat were dry with dust, her voice was a hoarse, cracked whisper. She looked up as the drone of the aircraft receded. She couldn't see Antoinette or the priest on the grass of the bank alongside her. It was difficult to see anything ahead. A dense cloud of smoke was hanging over the width of the road, spilling out across the grass on either side. Julie scrambled to her feet with Louis clutching at the hem of her blouse where it had come loose out of the waist-band of her slacks, and whimpering with fear.

The surface of the road under the drifting pall of smoke was littered with debris – sharp rocks, spattered fragments of earth, and lumps of asphalt which wept black tar. There were the crumpled remains of a pram. A charred mattress had fallen from the back of a cart, one wheel of which was smashed to pieces. The horse had fallen in the broken shafts. Its leg was moving, lifting slowly in the beast's feeble struggle to get up. Julie noticed that, between its slowly moving legs, its entrails and bowels had spilled out onto the road. They were steaming. She saw Antoinette wandering alone, aimlessly, down the centre of the road out of the drifting grey fog. She had her fists pressed against her eyes. Julie would have run to her instantly, but she had her arms round the shuddering little body of Louis, and for a second, did not know whether to let him go.

Behind the smoke and the hanging dust there came the roar of the returning aircraft. Julie screamed, 'Antoinette! Here!'

The noise of aero-engines grew deafening once again. Julie dragged Louis forward towards Antoinette who had begun to run down the centre of the road. Then she heard the high-pitched chatter of the machine-guns, and saw the pattering fountains of dust where the bullets were striking into the road surface in front of her – exactly as she had seen it happen at the pictures. Louis tore himself from her side and ran towards his sister. Julie ran forward and managed to catch him. She heard the thud and whine of bullets ricocheting around her. She saw the fat little priest, bareheaded, saw his plus-fours and chequered stockings under the open skirt of his soutane, as he ran out into the road to Antoinette. Then she threw herself down onto the surface of the road, pulling Louis down with her. The aircraft roared overhead, so low that the road seemed to shake with the vibration of the motors.

She lay there on the hard surface, holding Louis down with her, until all the noise had gone out of the sky. She could feel the prick of stones under the tenderness of her breasts; there was grit in her mouth, there was grit against her nose and cheeks. She lay there with the stones and grit digging into her, after everywhere had become silent save for the distant rumble of the guns. She heard voices in the fields. People were on the move again, climbing back on to the road. She got up on her knees. Louis hung on her arm. Her hair had come loose and had fallen all about her face. She pushed it back out of her eyes and tossed it over her shoulders. She wiped the dirt from her mouth. All round her, people were beginning to move up the road once more. Three people were standing by the shattered cart, a husband, wife and grown up daughter. The wife was at the head of the now still, disembowelled horse. She was wailing noisily. Her husband and daughter were dragging their belongings down off the tilted back of the cart. People were skirting the edges of the smoking crater in the middle of the road. Nearby, lay the bodies of the little girl and the priest. All around, bullet holes had pocked miniature craters in the broken surface. They were lying on their backs, their eyes staring, wide open. The priest's mouth hung open, giving him a look of astonishment at what had happened to him. The little girl's skirt was rucked up above her waist. The white cotton of her drawers was dirtied with the grime from the road. A black pool had formed under them, in the dust. It was crawling out from under their shoulders in a slow rivulet.

Julie had never seen anyone dead before. She began to tremble. Those who were passing by, looked on her with pity, or pretended to notice neither her nor the two bodies. Nobody stopped.

Louis tugged at her arm, as she finally stood up.

'Why aren't they getting up, mademoiselle?' he asked.

Julie couldn't answer.

'Are they dead, mademoiselle?'

It was a relief that he had asked the question so directly. She heard herself whisper,

'Yes, Louis.'

She put her arm round his shoulder.

'What does "dead" mean, mademoiselle?' he asked.

'Oh Louis,' she whispered.

She cleared her throat.

'It means,' she said, 'that they are asleep, and ... '

Her voice choked up. Louis looked up at her face, questioningly.

'Are they with Jesus, in heaven?' he asked.

She nodded and whispered, 'Yes.'

'I wish they weren't,' said Louis.

He went on staring up at her. The people coming up behind them, began to jostle them.

'Don't you wish they weren't?' asked Louis. His face began to pucker up again, and he began to cry.

'Yes,' Julie told him.

It was indecent to leave their bodies lying there, in the middle of the road. She elbowed a way for herself and Louis to the side of the road. She could hardly see through the mist of her tears. She held on to Louis' hand while reaching down for the handle of her suitcase – as much for her own comfort, as for his.

14

The previous evening, Colonel de Gaulle had driven into Laon to discover where his armoured reinforcements had got to. He had returned to the mess for dinner, his face adorned with its customary expression of loftily detached gloom. After a prolonged and unhappy silence, he had begun to speak of what he had seen in Laon: the procession of refugees trailing down the street under the shadow of the cathedral escarpment; and the soldiers, most of whom had left their weapons and equipment somewhere on the road behind them. From his car, he had noticed that many of the soldiers were wearing the insignia of General Petiet's 3rd Cavalry – the same regiment that was supposed to be reforming at Bruyères under the standard of the 4th Armoured Division.

De Gaulle had got out of his car, and had gone across the street to intercept a column of these men who were accompanied by a captain. Vivian could well picture the scene as he listened to the recital – the long, lean figure with his strange, awkward stride, his dignity impaired by the inevitable ragged cigarette between his lips, accosting the bowed, slouching, defeated men.

'I told them that I was now their commander,' de Gaulle had said. 'I ordered them to take the road south, and to report to Lebrun, here. The captain looked at me – straight in the eyes, *messieurs*, without a hint of shame. "*Mon Colonel*," he said to me, "we are prisoners of the Germans!" I looked back at him. I do not believe that I could have hidden my astonishment. "The Germans!" I exclaimed. "I cannot see any Germans." "Ah, *mon Colonel*," this captain replied to me, "the Germans told us that they had no time to take us to the cages. Instead, they made us give them our word that we would regard ourselves as prisoners of war, and let us go free. I have given my word, *mon Colonel*. Therefore I cannot report to your headquarters without breaking my word as an officer of the army of the Republic."'

De Gaulle had spread his hands upwards and had shrugged his shoulders, as if only Heaven could comment on such contemptible folly. Nobody at table in the mess had said anything. At last, de Gaulle himself had broken the silence.

'Messieurs,' he had said, 'when I was a small child, my dear father took me to the military cemetery at Le Bourget. We stood before the monument to the dead of 1870-71. I remember it very well. I had just learnt to read. My dear father told me to read aloud the inscription – "The sword of France, shattered in their valiant hands, will, by their descendants, be once more reforged." This evening, messieurs, I remembered that moment, and was near to weeping.'

In the morning, Vivian went straight to the Operations Room. He was determined to do all in his power to obtain air cover from Advanced Air Striking Force. He decided to phone General Swayne at General Georges' headquarters, to impress on him the necessity for co-operation from the RAF. All the telephones were, however, in full use, and likely to remain so. He was about to go outside for a breath of fresh air, when Captain de Bernac joined him.

'No good, old chap,' de Bernac said in his slightly pompous English. 'You'll just – er – eat your heart out, eh? Even if they let you use a telephone, you will never find an exchange.'

Vivian was about to explain the importance of his business, when de Bernac suggested a drive out into the country.

'The old Asparagus wants us to reconnoitre beyond Montcornet, along the Serre towards Rocroi. Come along, there's a good chap.'

Vivian noticed that he was carrying his revolver in its polished cavalry holster, slung over his arm. They went together out of the yard, and across the paddock beyond. De Bernac glanced in the direction from which the distant sound of gunfire was coming.

'Somebody is fighting a battle,' he remarked.

They jumped across a narrow brook and crossed a second field.

'Who knows,' said de Bernac, 'You might see something you can report to your seniors when we get back.'

In the lane on the far side of the field were parked two Panhard armoured cars, and a small camouflaged supply-truck with a Hotchkis *mitrailleuse* mounted in the rear. De Bernac walked round to the driving seat of the truck.

'I'll take the wheel,' he told the driver. 'Get in the back and man the Hotchkis. You might have a chance to knock down a Stuka and become a hero.'

The driver grinned, and jumped down. Vivian climbed into the seat beside de Bernac.

'I always drive on these occasions,' de Bernac explained. 'Why waste time explaining to somebody where one is supposed to be going?'

Behind the truck, the two large Panhards were revving up. He turned to face the rear.

'Ready, Morel?' he called to his driver.

Morel was demonstrating that he had been taken off his proper duty by lighting a cigarette.

'Yes, sir,' he replied.

He began to feed an ammunition belt into the Hotchkis.

'Sergeant Narjac,' de Bernac shouted above the noise of the motors.

The sergeant was standing in the open turret of the first Panhard. He raised his thumb in acknowledgement.

They skirted round Laon, and turned onto the main road leading to Montcornet. The windscreen of the truck had been removed; both he and de Bernac had put on goggles. With the breeze about their ears and the steady, loud hum of the motors, there was little chance of conversation, so that Vivian lapsed deeper into his own thoughts. He had travelled the straight, dusty ribbon across the chalky, undulating downland on several occasions. But now it had become entirely associated in his mind with his driving beside Julie. From the fondness of his memory, he recalled in detail everything that had occurred that afternoon, evening and night in Laon.

His day-dreaming was interrupted by de Bernac placing his hand on his arm. Vivian saw the tightening of de Bernac's mouth under the leather frame of his goggles as he raised his hand to signal to the armoured cars behind the truck. He slowed down and halted. Vivian pulled his goggles up from his eyes and rested them on the peak of his cap. In the middle of the road ahead, was a group of soldiers, unarmed, bareheaded, and without their equipment. Three of them had bicycles; two of them were up in the saddle, the third was running alongside his, trying to put one foot on the pedal and to lift his other foot over the saddle. They were being pursued by the remainder. Vivian was reminded of his school days, and the way the skivvies at Fernyhurst used to play boisterously on bicycles in the kitchen yards during their hours off in the afternoons, between lunch and high tea. But this was no game. One of the soldiers on foot caught up with one of the cyclists, and kicked the front wheel from under him so that he fell headlong across the road and lay there. Immediately, three more men set on the man who was trying to grab the bicycle. More men, unarmed, dusty, bedraggled with sweat, came pouring up the road.

A large black sedan came driving through the crowd of soldiers, spilling exhaust, with steam hissing out of the radiator cap. It was packed with soldiers. Those on foot crowded round it, wrenching at the door-handles, throwing themselves across the bonnet. Several of the men inside still had their rifles. They thrust the butts through the windows to beat off their assailants.

De Bernac swung himself out from behind the wheel, and stood up on the running board. The Panhards had drawn up behind the truck. Sergeant Narjac was sitting up on the open hatch-cover of the first. The men fighting over the bicycles stopped. Behind them, the oncoming flood of dirty, khaki-clad figures jostled and pushed forward, trampling over the body of the man lying in the road. De Bernac had taken his whistle from out of his breast-pocket. He blew it, and the shrill noise cut through the hubbub. He drew his revolver from his holster. Under cover of the dashboard, Vivian had already unbuttoned the canvas flap of his own holster, and had tucked it behind the grip of his pistol.

'Corporal!' de Bernac shouted. One of the men engaged in the struggle round the black sedan looked round. 'Come here,' de Bernac shouted.

The corporal pushed his way between the men who had been fighting over the bicycles. Vivian glanced back quickly, over his shoulder. Sergeant Narjac was sitting with his legs dangling over the side of the turret. He had a rifle across his knees.

'What regiment do you belong to?' de Bernac asked the corporal.

Men were crowding round the stationary sedan from which the steam was still pouring. Still more were coming up the road, packing into a solid mass in front of the truck. Those in front had a dangerously surly look in their hollow, worn faces. There was a brightness in the dark-ringed eyes.

'102nd Infantry, Captain,' the corporal replied.

Immediately behind Vivian, in the back of the truck, the driver, Morel, had one hand on the grip of the *mitrailleuse*. Vivian beckoned to him, and the man leant over.

'Morel?' said Vivian as quietly as he could. 'Don't point it ahead unless Captain de Bernac gives the word.'

'Yes, monsieur,' replied Morel.

'Where is the 102nd Infantry supposed to be?' asked De Bernac.

A large, thick-set warrant officer wearing a week's growth of beard pushed forward.

'We *are* the 102nd Infantry, Captain,' he announced.

'Where is your commander?' asked de Bernac.

'General Portzer is dead,' the warrant officer replied. 'Regimental HQ was overrun by enemy armour early this morning. Our officers have gone.'

'They took all the transport with them, the pigs,' shouted a voice from the densely-packed crowd on the road.

'German tanks are everywhere,' exclaimed the corporal. 'You don't know whether they're behind you, in front of you, or where.'

'Monsieur,' said the warrant officer, 'the 102nd are brave men. Our machine-gunners held back the German tanks for two whole days. It's the bombing, monsieur. They bomb, and bomb, and bomb – Stukas and Junkers 88's. And where is our air force? We have had no food; our canteens are empty. And then their tanks appear all round us. You can't expect infantrymen to fight against tanks and bombers for ever, monsieur!'

There was a murmur of agreement from the front ranks of the crowd.

'Very well, Sergeant Major,' said de Bernac. '4th Armoured Division is grouping south and south-east of Laon. Take what remains of your regiment, and report to divisional HQ at Bruyères.

I am sure you will all welcome a second opportunity to demonstrate the courage of the 102nd Regiment in the face of the enemy.'

He stared into the face of the warrant officer, challenging him to refuse the order. A voice from the crowd shouted, 'We aren't fighting for the English shit any longer.'

The noise of agreement was louder than a murmur. Somebody else bawled out, 'It's the English officer who's giving the orders.'

'The English major here is a brave soldier!' de Bernac shouted back. '*Mutilé de la guerre!*'

The cat-calling grew louder and more threatening. The front ranks were beginning to edge forward, pushed by the mass of men behind them. Somebody howled out, 'Pity they didn't finish the English major off. It was the English who started this war.'

Amidst the rising hubbub, the warrant officer came closer to de Bernac.

'Captain,' he said, and there was no mistaking the anxiety in his face, 'these men have already shot two of their officers.'

'You may tell them, Sergeant Major,' de Bernac replied calmly, 'that if they will not let us pass, we shall shoot our way through them.'

He swung himself back behind the wheel, and revved up the motor. He turned and signalled to Morel. Morel swung the *mitrailleuse* round, and depressed the long barrel over the heads of de Bernac and Vivian. Vivian heard the click as Morel drew back the cocking lever. He heard the roar of the Panhards' motors behind them. As the truck rolled forward, the sullen soldiers filling the road stepped aside to let them pass.

'I'm afraid I appear to be something of a liability,' said Vivian. 'Like Jonah.'

'Bolshevik rabble,' said de Bernac, in English.

As they drove on eastwards, through the quiet, dusty centre of Montcornet and beyond, following the banks of the Serre, the numbers of fugitives thinned out. Those that there were, were mostly troops, unarmed, weary, and without an officer to be seen, often sitting at the roadside, resting their heads in their hands, staring fatalistically in front of them, or huddled under the shade of the trees. Later on, as they drew nearer to Rozoy-sur-Serre, they found the roads empty and silent under the afternoon sun. There were several farm-workers labouring in the fields as if there were no war.

De Bernac turned off the main road, and led the Panhards down a dirt-track between two wide fields of barley, and onto a path along the river bank. Under cover of a line of trees, they halted to allow the motors to cool, and the crews of the Panhards to rest from the burning heat inside their vehicles. The number two driver of the second Panhard was complaining of feeling unwell. De Bernac examined him under the eye of Sergeant Narjac, showing a consideration towards the man which Vivian had not previously observed in French officers towards the men under their command. He told the man to change places with Morel for the return journey. The men were allowed to stand down, and de Bernac and Vivian sat in the grass, in the cool of the river bank, to share the food and wine which de Bernac had brought with him.

They finished their meal, and were smoking, when one of the sentinels posted by Sergeant Narjac, came running up, followed by the sergeant himself.

'Tanks, Captain, coming up the road from the east.'

De Bernac glanced at Sergeant Narjac. Sure enough, from across the river and the barley fields beyond came the familiar noise of squealing and clanking armour tracks. They scrambled to their feet.

'They must be withdrawing from Signy l'Abbaye,' said Vivian.

Through the screech of the armour came the phut-phutting of motor-cycles. De Bernac gave Narjac the orders to get the men back to the vehicles and to have the guns manned. Vivian followed de Bernac as he ran to take up a position crouching in the long grass between the tailboard of the truck and the front of the first Panhard. The branches of the trees hung low over them, forming a roof of leaves.

'My God!' exclaimed de Bernac.

On the other side of the barley fields, moving along the road back towards Montcornet, was a procession of grey steel half-tracks with white outlined Balkan crosses on their armoured sides. All were packed with steel-helmeted troops, and were escorted by motorcycle combinations with machine-guns mounted on the side-cars. The column seemed unending. The noise of engines and the squeal of tracks increased. A squadron of tanks was moving across the fields between the column on the road and the river, the wireless antennae and pennants swaying. Vivian recognised the Czech-built 38 T's. The turrets of the two Panhard armoured cars had traversed to cover the tanks, but their 25 mm guns could never penetrate the armour of the 38 T's, whereas the 37 mm cannon of the tanks could blow the Panhards apart.

For twenty minutes, de Bernac and Vivian crouched in the long grass, watching, not daring to move, as half-tracks and open trucks moved up the road, all packed with field-grey Panzer infantry, Panzer Mark 3 tanks, and lorries towing 88 mm flak guns, while escorting 38 T's chattered across the field parallel with the road, showering clods of loose, dry earth behind them. They moved with the precision of a field exercise.

When finally they had passed, and the fields, now torn by the tank-tracks, were silent once more, de Bernac got up. His face was grim.

'That rabble from the 102nd was telling the truth,' he said. 'My God! They must have broken through everywhere.'

'They'll be in Montcornet by this time,' said Vivian.

He knew, and was aware that de Bernac was thinking the same, that nothing now stood between the advancing Germans and the line of the Somme in the west except the still unprepared 4th Armoured Division.

Sergeant Narjac and the corporal-driver of the second Panhard came over to join them.

'We must return to base as quickly as possible,' de Bernac said. He managed a smile. 'But not, I think, by the way we came.'

He took his Michelin road map from the dashboard locker of the truck.

'Vigneux,' he pointed, 'Ebouleau, and Pierrepont. We'll just have to hope that the Germans haven't had time to fan out.'

As they returned to their vehicles, Vivian noticed that everywhere was quite still; there wasn't even the sound of distant gunfire.

The Battle of the Meuse was over.

15

Julie and Louis had stumbled along hand in hand all day. Sometimes Louis had cried; sometimes he had trotted along at her heels saying nothing. Sometimes he seemed to understand the meaning of death; then he would ask, 'Will Toinette come back, mademoiselle?', as if he needed Julie to explain, and comfort him, all over again. His small hand became hot and sticky; she tried to let it go, pushing it away with an impatience caused by her own utter weariness. But he would reach to find her hand again, and when she snatched it away from him, he burst into tears. Then she felt her whole heart spilling out to him, and to all children who had been caught up in the nightmare. She put down her case and cuddled him until he stopped crying.

The evening was come. Louis was whimpering and stumbling as he walked. The road went on and on like the endless procession of refugees who plodded down it. Louis stumbled against her in his sleep. She gathered him up, holding him on one arm while carrying the suitcase with the other. He rested his hot cheek against hers; she felt his steady breathing against her neck.

There was no point in going on. A line of trees ran at an angle away from the road towards a small wood. It would provide some shelter for the night.

She left the road and followed a cart-track between the avenue of

159

trees. The track ran straight as a die into the cavernous darkness of the wood. A few yards inside the wood, she came to an open space, sparsely carpeted with grass and the dead leaves of the previous autumn. On the far side of the space, inappropriately, was a large black limousine. Three people were sitting in the grass in front of it and playing a board-game in the dwindling light. The most elderly of the three was grey-haired, and moustached like an old soldier; he was wearing the grey livery of a chauffeur. Beside him was a slight, slim-faced man with straight, dark hair, dressed in a well-cut Norfolk jacket and English plus-fours. The third person was a boy about nine or ten years old, wearing grey flannel shorts and blazer like those of an English prep-school boy.

As Julie entered the glade clutching Louis and her suitcase, none of the trio seemed to notice their presence. The boy and the man in the Norfolk jacket were too engrossed in their game, while the elderly chauffeur looked on with a sort of paternal indulgence. Julie, as she approached across the grass, recognised, from her nursery days, the square gridded board with its blue and green map, and the pasteboard rectangles on their tin base-clips. The boy and his father were playing l'Attaque.

She put down her suitcase. She knew she would fall if she did not sit down. Still holding Louis to her, she gently lowered herself on to the grass, and sat there, too tired to make her presence known. The man in the Norfolk jacket said to the boy.

'You've lost your brigade, I'm afraid. You've just attacked my mine.'

As he removed the boy's piece from the board, the boy exclaimed, 'That isn't fair!'

'It's absolutely fair,' the elderly chauffeur told him.

'But Joseph,' the boy protested, 'a brigade would have sappers to clear away mines – lots of sappers.'

'Of course,' the chauffeur agreed, 'but not in the game of l'Attaque.'

'We have to keep to the rules,' said the man in the Norfolk jacket.

'That's a stupid rule,' said the boy.

'Rules are frequently stupid,' said the man in the Norfolk jacket, 'but we must stick to them; otherwise everybody would make their own rules, and there wouldn't be any game at all.' Before the boy could argue any more, he went on without turning his head, 'Why don't you join us, madame?'

'Because I'm too tired, monsieur,' Julie replied.

The gentleman and the chauffeur both rose to their feet. Julie had thought that her voice had sounded remarkably calm, but they must have detected the note of desperation in it. The chauffeur took Louis from her, very gently, and cradled him in his arms. The gentleman put his hand under Julie's arm and lifted her to her feet. He picked up her case.

'Mademoiselle,' she said.

For a moment he did not understand what she meant. Then he smiled.

'I'm sorry, mademoiselle. But the child, you see.'

'I met him on the road, monsieur,' Julie explained. 'He has lost his parents – and his sister. We were bombed and shot at, monsieur. His sister and the man who was looking after them – a priest – were both killed.' He helped her over to the car. 'There wasn't anybody else,' she explained.

'With Monsieur le Baron's permission,' said the elderly chauffeur, 'the little one would sleep more comfortably on the back seat, inside.'

'Of course, Joseph,' the gentleman agreed.

The chauffeur laid Louis gently down on the leather seat, and placed a small cushion under his head. The gentleman introduced himself to Julie, indicating that she should sit down again.

'Victor de Bart-Mendel,' he said.

Julie rested her back against the white painted rear tyre of the car.

'This,' de Bart-Mendel continued, 'is my old and very dear friend, Joseph. Joseph has looked after me and been my good counsellor since I was very young.'

Julie managed to smile at the old man.

'And this young reprobate,' said de Bart-Mendel, 'is my son Hugo, who, as I'm sure you have already perceived, is exceedingly spoilt.'

He had introduced his son in English. Julie was taken aback.

'You speak French with a very good accent, mademoiselle,' de Bart-Mendel assured her. 'You speak French almost as well as I speak English.'

He laughed at his own immodesty.

'Now, mademoiselle,' he continued, 'I hope you're not too tired to tell me who you are.'

'Julie Armitage,' she replied. 'Juliet really.'

'Have you eaten?' he asked. 'I'm afraid we've only some chocolate with us. But we can share it, and leave a little for the child to have for his breakfast. I'm sure a child of his age would enjoy that.'

Julie felt a little better for the chocolate. She told de Bart-Mendel her adventures. In his turn, de Bart-Mendel told her that he had been journeying to Paris on business when he had found the road choked by refugees. He had decided that they should park off the road to wait until the way was clear.

'Perhaps you would care to travel with us, Juliet?' he concluded. 'Tomorrow we should be all right. The northern frontiers have been closed; that ought to stem the flow of refugees. And when our people

161

realise that our armies are holding back the invaders, they will remain in their homes.'

Julie noticed that the boy, Hugo, was observing them as they talked, watching his father with an amused, knowing smile. Through her fatigue, she was aware that de Bart-Mendel would not have welcomed her so warmly, and have taken such an interest in her, had she not been, for all her grime and dishevelment, an attractive young woman. The realisation made no difference to her relief at having met him.

16

Some two hours later, Vivian, having returned safely to Bruyères, was sitting in the Operations Room, leaning wearily over a telephone. The hurricane lamps cast angular shadows against the distempered walls. Now and then, officers would push past him to examine and assess on the map-boards the news which de Bernac had brought back from their patrol. Vivian was too busy to pay much attention to them. He had succeeded in getting through to BEF Headquarters at Arras, and had persuaded a reluctant duty officer to ask Colonel Lord Bridgeman to leave the mess to come to the phone to speak to him.

'I know that Montcornet isn't in our sector, sir,' he was explaining, 'but the fact that Jerry has captured it means that the entire corridor to the west, between the Aisne and the Serre, lies open. The forces who were supposed to be holding the sector are in complete rout – totally demoralised. The reconnaissance I was on today has established that Jerry isn't striking in the direction of Laon and Soissons, towards Paris. He's heading towards St Quentin and Peronne. In twenty-four hours he'll have reached St Quentin, and begun to threaten the BEF from the rear.'

His eyes burned with dust and exhaustion; it was only with difficulty that he managed to speak coherently. He heard Lord Bridgeman at the other end grunt acknowledgement.

'Sir,' he continued, 'the 4th Armoured, here, is the only effective strike force in the area, but we have no anti-aircraft cover whatever. If it is to be deployed effectively, Advanced Air Striking Force must provide us with cover.'

Tiredness had made his voice more strident than he had intended.

'Major Hardwicke,' Lord Bridgeman replied coldly, 'it is none of my concern to ask favours of Air Chief Marshal Barratt on behalf of individual detachments, French or English. Such a request must be made through, and be endorsed by, North East Command, as well you know. As for the alleged German occupation of Montcornet...'

He paused. Vivian presumed that he was searching for it on the map.

'...We have been informed by General Georges' headquarters that everything is going according to plan. Generals Giraud and Touchon are in command of your sector. We may assume that they know what they are about, and are in control of the situation. It may very well be that they are encouraging the Germans to expose their flank by engaging in a planned withdrawal.'

Vivian put down the receiver. He sighed. Quoting a French saying, he declared, 'Death to all fools!'

He felt a hand resting lightly on his shoulder.

'That might prove to be a task so enormous as to be beyond our capabilities, my friend.'

He looked up. Colonel de Gaulle was standing behind him.

'Thank you for your efforts, Major Hardwicke,' de Gaulle added. 'Sleep well.'

He patted Vivian's shoulder, went across to the door, his shadow leaping up and down on the wall, and stepped down into the yard.

One of the two officers who remained with Vivian and the duty-sergeant in the Operations Room, switched on a wireless. There was a squealing of oscillation as he tuned it, followed by the final verse of a song advertising Byrrh. The call-signal of Radio Normandie followed, announcing the news bulletin. Vivian pushed back his chair. The voice of the newsreader was as reassuring as it was bland. It announced that the German advance into the Low Countries was being held by the French 1st Army and the British Expeditionary Force along the Scheldt and the Dyle. The French 9th Army had withdrawn to prepared positions on a line between the Sambre and Rethel, according to plan. In the Ardennes sector, the newsreader continued, the 9th Army had thrown back wave after wave of German assault troops and tanks, inflicting very heavy losses on the enemy. Here and there, it was true, small groups of German armour had penetrated the French defences, but always in insufficient strength to make any significant difference to the outcome of the battle.

'They are operating like lost children,' the newsreader announced. 'Soon they will be without either petrol or ammunition.'

Vivian could only bury his face wearily in his hands.

163

17

'There's been one phone call for you, Monsieur Chris. Early yesterday evening,' said Mademoiselle Roche.

'Only one?' asked Papayannis.

He hung his unnecessary, camel-hair overcoat on the stand under the stuffed owl. The owl had lost an eye; there was a patch of dried, matted sawdust on the cheek feathers.

'Only one of any importance, Monsieur Chris,' Mademoiselle Roche told him.

There was a self-satisfied smirk on her face. Footsteps clattered on the pavement below the window, hurrying along the passage to the steps of La Bonne Becquerel.

'From Alexandria, Monsieur Chris. Monsieur Liassides.'

She paused. Papayannis had no intention of gratifying her by any display of reaction. He lowered his girth into the swivel chair by his roll-top desk. Above the desk was a large, framed pen-and-ink study by Felicien Rops of a girl still in her late teens, seated on an upright chair. She was wearing the costume of the mid-1880's: the dress close-fitting, with a high collar, and utterly plain save for the single deep flounce about the hem of the skirt, the shading suggesting that it was probably black; certainly her gloves, stockings, narrow, high-heeled shoes, and wide-brimmed hat with the black lace veil lifted, seemed suited to a funeral. Her face contrasted with her dress. Her mouth was full, almost slack with sensual greed. Her eyes were rimmed with the fatigue of scarlet nights. A book lay open in her lap; one gloved finger rested between the pages. Her other gloved hand rested under her chin, with one finger on the drooping lower lip of her slightly open mouth. She was staring out invitingly at the beholder, despite her evident fatigue. Below the figure, the artist had pencilled the words, *'Celle qui fait "celle qui lit Musset"'*. The picture had had the most powerful effect on Papayannis ever since he had acquired it. It provoked feelings of pity in him which brought him close to tears. At the same time, there had been afternoons when it had caused him to have erections so hard as to be painful.

'Did you have a successful trip, Monsieur Chris?' Mademoiselle Roche persisted.

He turned to face her.

'In many ways, Lina,' he replied, 'I think I may say yes.'

He had to lower his voice. Rahman and El Chamoun were lounging against the banisters on the stairs outside.

But, of course, he *had* been astonishingly successful in disentangling both himself and them from the attentions of the young German officer at La Berlière. Considering their brutal clumsiness in dealing with that obstinate housekeeper, he could probably go so far as to say that he had saved their lives. Not that they would be the slightest bit grateful. They were all spies, Rahman and El Chamoun – the sweepings of the Belleville gutters – and Mademoiselle Lina Roche who was so neat and respectable in her pince-nez and her two-piece suits and jabots. They had all been personally selected by Aris Liassides to keep an eye on him.

'But you did not succeed in bringing back the *Tondeau de Chartres*, did you, Monsieur Chris?' she asked.

'It is in Paris,' he replied evasively.

'But not with you,' she said.

He declined to answer. Mademoiselle Roche shrugged, signalling that she was prepared to indulge his mood. She reached over her table, and picked up the telephone receiver by its mother-of-pearl handle.

'Shall I book a call through to Alexandria for you, Monsieur Chris?' she asked.

'No,' Papayannis replied. The thought of it made him feel quite ill. 'Not yet.'

He swivelled his chair round, took the receiver from her. Laying it on his shoulder, he took the Paris telephone directory, opened it, and, running his plump finger down the page, found a number. Mademoiselle Roche sat watching him, tapping the india-rubber end of her pencil on the keys of her typewriter. He dialled, and listened.

'Monsieur le Baron de Bart-Mendel's residence? ... Ah! Would you be so kind as to inform Monsieur le Baron that Marcel Lecuyer ...'

He paused.

'Yes. Marcel Lecuyer of the Galerie Lecuyer, Rue des Pyramides ... would be greatly obliged if Monsieur le Baron would permit him to speak with him. Monsieur le Baron is expecting to hear from us.'

'Alas, monsieur!' came the reply. 'Monsieur le Baron has not yet arrived in Paris.'

'Do you have any idea when he is expected?' asked Papayannis.

'Who can tell, monsieur,' came the reply. 'The condition of the roads – you understand.'

'Of course. Of course,' said Papayannis soothingly.

He had, himself, been too cunning to have been caught up in the exodus from the Low Countries. He had done what few others would have had the ingenuity to do. He had made Rahman drive northwards to Amiens, and had returned to Paris via Beauvais.

'It is merely that Monsieur le Baron has requested us to make certain arrangements about some valuations we had the honour to be asked to undertake for the Baron,' he said. 'Perhaps I may be permitted to ring again tomorrow?'

'Of course, monsieur,' came the reply. 'And I shall inform Monsieur le Baron that you have rung, should he arrive.'

Papayannis hung up. Mademoiselle Roche thrust the pencil into her hair, behind her ear.

'Monsieur Chris, as a friend,' she said, 'might I suggest that you speak to Monsieur Liassides as soon as possible. It would be better in the long run.'

He must control his rising anger, he told himself.

'When I have something to tell him, Lina,' he replied with exaggerated patience, 'I shall get in touch with him immediately.'

Mademoiselle Roche shrugged her padded shoulders.

'As you wish, Monsieur Chris,' she told him.

She took her pencil out of her hair, and reached for her note-pad.

He must never betray his nervousness in front of these people. They existed only to help him in working for his old friend and patron. But if only God would allow him the means of setting up in business for himself – perhaps when the Germans came. And then he would never again feel the nausea of apprehension in his throat. He might even take serious steps to diet and lose weight.

Mademoiselle Roche flicked over a page of her notebook.

'Marius Grimaud rang two days ago,' she said. 'He says that he has several pieces of silver which might interest you. Spanish silver, he says.'

'Grimaud wouldn't know the difference between Spanish and English silver,' Papayannis replied. 'Why didn't you tell him to bring it over? Do you think I'm going to trail across Paris for that pimp?'

'Like Monsieur le Baron,' said Mademosielle Roche primly, 'you were not in Paris, Monsieur Chris.'

Papayannis sat and thought for a few moments. He finished his cigar. Reaching across his desk, he opened a drawer, took out a small, black automatic pistol, and slipped it into the holster under his arm. With some effort, he pulled himself up out of his swivel chair.

'I'm going out,' he announced, buttoning up his jacket.

'Where to, Monsieur Chris?' asked Mademoiselle Roche.

'That is my business!' he retorted shrilly.

It was the tone of voice of a fat man, he realised.

'Just in case Monsieur Liassides rings again,' said Mademoiselle Roche.

One day, when he had his own business, he would pay somebody – a big buck nigger – to force Lina Roche, drag her down, and thrust and squeeze into that purse-lipped, smirking, Gallic-superior Sapphist until she lay gasping and throbbing and moaning in utter indignity. It would have to be done by some animal: someone who had none of his own sensitivity and fastidiousness. But he would take the greatest pleasure in watching.

'The car, Monsieur Chris?' asked Rahman, as he started down the stairs.

Rahman was leaning against the wall at the top, his hands buried in his pockets. Papayannis shook his head.

He passed El Chamoun at the door, went off down the passage outside, to the steps, and descended to the Rue Custine. There, he stopped on the pavement, waiting for an empty taxi to come down from the Buttes de Montmartre. As he hailed one, he had no doubt that either El Chamoun or Rahman would be watching from the top of the steps. He squeezed through the door into the back seat, fell into the upholstery, and sighed deeply.

'Rue Quincampoix,' he gasped to the driver.

Papayannis's destination lay in a narrow crumbling street of five storey dwellings connecting the Boulevard de Sébastopol with the Rue Quincampoix. The tall buildings had long since been converted into grimy little shops and dusty, ill-lit *cabarets*, or one-night hotels. At this hour of the morning, when the markets of Les Halles were at their least busy, there were only a few of the fat "bed-bugs", in their shapeless frocks, and with their thick, grotesque make-up, loitering on the pavements. They knew him, and they knew better than to approach him unasked. One or two of them said '*Bonjour, Monsieur Chris,*' without entirely managing to keep the surliness out of their voices. They knew that he liked to be recognised.

The place he was visiting was a hotel half way up the street. The unlit lamp over the door had '*Hôtel*' painted on the glass, but otherwise it bore no name. Instead, over the window of the manager's office facing the street, was a large sign which read '*Changement de Propriétaire*'. The painted lettering was flaking with age, and the wood was weathered and split. Inside the door, immediately behind the dirty windows, a child in a faded pinafore, with her blue woollen stockings tumbled below her knees, was mopping the floor in front of the reception-desk.

'*Bonjour, Cecile,*' Papayannis called, as he entered.

The child scowled. '*Bonjour, Monsieur Chris,*' she muttered because she had to.

He patted her cheek with his pudgy hand. She tried to turn away her face.

'Is your Papa in?' he asked.

She nodded, and concentrated her attention on making damp arcs with her dripping mop on the tiled floor. Papayannis went to the counter and struck the bell which stood beside the small pile of towels.

'Why has the sun hidden its face behind a cloud, *ma petite?*' he asked. 'Smile for me, eh?'

He took a ragged, faded five franc note from his pocket, and held it between his fingers.

'Eh?' he repeated.

She saw it, stopped mopping the floor, and smiled without looking at his face.

'That's better,' he told her.

He put his cigar between his teeth, patted her cheek again, and gave her the note. The bead curtain across the door behind the counter rattled.

'*Eh, bonjour Monsieur Chris! Comment ça va, eh?*' Papayannis turned round, and shook the proprietor by the hand.

'*Ça va, Marius?*' he replied.

The proprietor was a thick-set man, brawny rather than fat, who had been a market porter until a few years ago. He was short-sighted, with horn-rimmed spectacles that did not suit the rest of his appearance. He was wearing a moth-holed woollen sports shirt over a filthy singlet. His chin, like his fist, was as grimy as a collier's.

'You wish us to do a little business, eh?' said Papayannis.

The proprietor shrugged, as if it were a matter of little importance. But Papayannis was not taken in. As far as people round here were concerned, Monsieur Chris was a *boss*, whereas Aris Liassides was not even a name. The proprietor pushed aside the bead curtain and held it back over his wrist.

'See to the towels, Cecile,' he called.

As Papayannis went in behind the counter, the proprietor said, 'Some silver, Monsieur Chris. Candlesticks, a cigarette-case.'

Papayannis waited for him to lead him into the shabby office. He lowered himself into one of the chairs behind the oilcloth-covered table.

'How is my little Yvette?' he asked.

The proprietor shrugged with eloquent fatalism. 'The *perdrices* took her and put her on the camel. She's in La Roquette. Raguet will kill her when she gets out. She's given him a dose.'

'She should go back home to Orléans,' said Papayannis. He took out his wallet. 'Give her this, for her fare.'

'You're too soft-hearted, Monsieur Chris,' replied the proprietor. But he took the roll of notes Papayannis offered him.

'For my soul's sake,' Papayannis explained.

'Ah, Monsieur Chris,' said the proprietor, taking two glasses from the battered roll-top desk against the wall, 'what it is to be religious!'

He put one of the glasses in front of Papayannis and the other in front of himself, uncorked a bottle of brandy, and poured out two large tots. Papayannis relit his cigar.

'Business, Monsieur Chris?' the proprietor asked.

He replaced the cork in the bottle, and wiped his fingers on his shirt. Papayannis raised his glass.

'Your health, Marius,' he said.

Marius grunted as disagreeably as he dared. From a drawer in the desk, he took out a small bundle wrapped in a green baize cloth.

'Spanish Republicans,' he commented, 'held in the prison camp at Hendaye. They give such things to the guards in return for medicine, extra rations, tobacco. Good quality, Monsieur Chris.'

'My friend, before we discuss your goods,' said Papayannis, 'there is a more important matter I must put to you.'

The proprietor turned to face him. His expression was one of apprehension. Papayannis had to smile.

'A favour, Marius, that is all. Because you are my good friend – and a man of experience and discretion.'

He turned the brandy-glass in his hand, and drew on his cigar. The proprietor sat down opposite him, still looking warily at him. Papayannis was beginning to enjoy himself.

'I'm acting for a good friend,' Papayannis explained, 'who is not in a position to act for himself. He is anxious to obtain a certain *objet d'art* – a certain piece of silver, a medallion – at present in the possession of the Baron de Bart-Mendel. The piece in question is a silver *tondeau* – figures carved in relief on a circular base – representing Our Blessed Saviour and St Louis. It is a hand-span in diameter . . .'

'What is this to do with me, Monsieur Chris?' asked the proprietor.

'My friend lives abroad,' explained Papayannis. 'It is difficult for him to obtain certain sorts of information – it is only information he seeks, for the moment. For example, the Baron's Paris residence is off the Avenue de Wagram, in the Hôtel de Brey. Does he keep the medallion there? Or has he placed it in some safe deposit – in a bank, perhaps? Or in some national shrine? And if perhaps the Baron *does* keep it in his house, how easily might he be persuaded to part with it? These are the things my friend, who lives abroad, is anxious to know. And you, my dear Marius, are a man of some resources. You have – contacts, shall we say? – denied to me, for instance.'

The proprietor scowled into his brandy. He drank it, poured himself a second glass, and pushed the bottle in Papayannis's direction. Papayannis pretended not to notice it.

'My friend who is far richer than I am – yes, Marius, it is true! – will pay in gold.'

The proprietor looked up.

'You wish to know where Monsieur le Baron keeps this object?' he asked. 'If he does indeed keep it at the Hôtel de Brey?'

'My friend wishes to know – yes,' Papayannis confirmed.

The proprietor nodded. Papayannis sighed as if a burden had been removed from off his back.

'And now, my dear Marius,' he said, 'let us have a look at your Spanish silver, eh?'

A quarter of an hour later, he stepped out into the street once more. The fat woman who had been loitering outside the hotel approached him and put her hand on his sleeve.

"allo, Monsieur Chris!' she said. 'Something you like? Something special for you? And no hurry?'

The smile on her face creased the white, scented powder which lay like flour on her cheeks and forehead. He brushed her painted nails from his arm.

'Another time perhaps, Monsieur Chris?' the woman wheedled.

She did not spit, or toss her head, or even turn her shoulder on him. She respected him. All the girls round the Rue Quincampoix respected him, he told himself, as he waddled into the bright sunlight of the Boulevard de Sébastopol.

18

It was still dark when Louis found his way out of the limousine. He stood in the early morning twilight, his small fists pressed against his eyes, crying '*Maman*! *Maman*!' Julie sat up, tousled and bleary. She was cold, with raised goosepimples under the sleeves of her blouse.

'Louis!' she called softly.

The dark heaps in the grass, about the car, did not stir.

'Louis!' she called again.

The little boy lowered his fists, and stared about him. He saw her where she was sitting up, and came running over to her, holding out his arms. She cuddled him to her.

'We're going in the car, this morning,' she said. 'Isn't that good?'

'This car?' he asked, pointing.

'The very one,' she replied.

'Where are we going?' he asked.

The question took her aback.

'We must talk quietly,' she told him, 'so that these kind people can have a little more sleep. They didn't go to sleep nearly as early as you did.'

'Where are we going?' he repeated in a whisper.

'Oh,' she replied, 'quite a long way, I expect.'

'Will you be going with me?' he asked, frowning.

170

'Of course,' she replied.

De Bart-Mendel stirred and sat up. When she attempted to apologise to him for disturbing him so early, he replied, 'It's too cold, and the ground is too uncomfortable, to lie just dozing. It's more comfortable sitting up.'

He reached into the pocket of the coat which had covered him.

'Would you like some breakfast, *mon petit?*' he asked in French.

Louis stared at him, not knowing what to make of him; he had not seen de Bart-Mendel before.

'This is the kind gentleman who is going to take us in his car,' Julie told him.

Louis turned his face away, shyly.

'I'm afraid we only have chocolate,' said de Bart-Mendel. 'Do you have chocolate for breakfast, Louis?'

Louis shook his head. But he went over to de Bart-Mendel.

'In parts of the Low Countries,' de Bart-Mendel explained, 'they actually do have chocolate for breakfast. On bread.'

'Not in Namur,' suggested Julie.

'Ah, so you are from Namur,' de Bart-Mendel said directly to Louis.

Louis nodded, taking the piece of chocolate from him.

'If we make a start now,' said de Bart-Mendel, 'before it's properly light, we could reach Paris in a matter of hours.'

He woke up Joseph and Hugo. As they set off, driving through the awakening streets of Soissons and out onto the Meaux-Paris road, the sunlight was bright but still cool. It seemed that the flood of refugees had been stemmed. The woods and meadows about Villers-Cotterets glistened in the sun, and were peaceful. Under the shadow of the piers of an ancient stone bridge, women in caps and aprons were pounding at their washing as they had done for centuries.

De Bart-Mendel glanced to where Louis was sitting close to Hugo, looking out at the passing landscape. He spoke in English, in a low voice.

'I don't know whether or not you have any plans for the child,' he said.

Julie shook her head. For the past two days, she had had no vision beyond the next few hours. Even now, riding in comfort, she was too tired, too stale, too leaden in mind, to have any real idea of what she intended to do once she arrived in Paris. She would have to phone Ambrose, she supposed, to tell him she was safe.

'There must be places,' she said, 'where lost children can wait for their parents to find them. The Salvation Army, I mean. Or the Red Cross.'

'There is a place near here,' he said.

'Is that why we are driving this way?' she asked.

He nodded.

171

'Partly,' he replied. 'And partly because, as you can see for yourself, the traffic is not heavy on this road.'

'I learnt to mistrust the word "partly" a long time ago,' she said.

'The place is a convent – the Sisters of *Sainte Marie Auxiliatrice*. They are very kind, and they are used to looking after young children.'

'What sort of a place is it?' Julie asked. 'An orphanage?'

De Bart-Mendel smiled.

'No,' he replied. 'It is a boarding school for young ladies, actually; though they do look after very young boys as well.'

'It's a place where you have to pay fees?' asked Julie.

'It's the sort of place to which young children are sent,' said de Bart-Mendel, 'by wealthy parents who do not wish their social round to be disturbed by family responsibilities. The good sisters make up for the parents' neglect by their own kindness.'

'And who will pay for this one?' Julie asked.

'It won't be for long,' de Bart-Mendel replied. 'When we arrive in Paris, we shall get in touch with the Belgian agencies immediately and inform them of the child's whereabouts. No doubt his parents will be in touch with their own people ... You aren't happy with my suggestion?'

'I promised him I wouldn't leave him,' said Julie.

'You won't be able to take him with you to England,' de Bart-Mendel reminded her.

Julie didn't listen to him.

'His parents vanish,' she said. 'His sister is killed before his very eyes. And now I'm going to desert him. I don't see why a child should have to put up with so much.'

Even as she heard herself saying it, she wasn't quite sure whether she was addressing de Bart-Mendel or God.

'You know, Julie,' he told her, 'his feelings of being deserted might be a lot worse if you leave it till later.'

'I'm sorry,' she told him.

'The sisters will be kind to him, I promise you,' he said. 'He is very young; they'll all spoil him ... The convent is at Brissy-Frenoy, about three kilometres off to the right.'

He leaned forward and directed Joseph, who turned into a side road leading through the woods.

They went up a long avenue of trees. At the end, was a high wall into which were let two great doors set in an arch, like the entrance to a castle or prison. A crucifix supported by fat cherubs was set in a niche above the pediment. On either side of the gateway, grit paths stretched away under the shadow of the wall. Joseph stopped the car, and got out. He pulled at the black iron bell-chain beside the gate.

Louis turned from the window.

'Why are we stopping?' he asked.

172

Julie reached out for him. He hesitated, then came to her.

'We're going to a big house,' she told him, 'where some nice ladies live. They'll look after you until Maman and Papa come to fetch you.'

She felt instantly that she had miscalculated.

'I expect there will be lots of other children to play with,' she said.

De Bart-Mendel was watching sadly. Hugo looked as if he were trying to think of something sensible to say. One of the great wooden doors was opened, and a large, elderly nun, wearing a blue apron over her habit, came out. She was about to ask Joseph his business when, stooping to the car window, she saw de Bart-Mendel sitting in the rear seat. She smiled in recognition, returned to the gateway immediately, and opened both doors. They drove under the arch. Lawns stretched away from either side of the drive, to clumps of black-branched yew-trees. The grey stone house was high, and severely fronted, with circular turrets. The ground-floor windows had black iron grilles over them, and the front door was shut. Joseph drew the car up level with the door-steps. Even the eye-level window set in the thick wood of the door had an iron grille over it.

Hugo jumped down from the car, and held the door open.

'I thought they only let ladies into convents,' he said. 'Do you think they'll let you in, Papa?'

'I think they'll let me in a little way,' de Bart-Mendel replied.

He helped out Julie who lifted down Louis.

'Are you coming in, mademoiselle?' asked Louis.

Julie stroked the hair out of his eyes. His face was very dirty; the nuns would probably be shocked.

'Of course I am,' she whispered.

They left Joseph with the car, and walked across the gravel to the front door. From behind the house came the sound of young girls laughing. Julie felt a sense of relief, even though Louis was clinging to her hand apprehensively. De Bart-Mendel pulled at the bell. Inside, there was the clatter of pattens on stone. The lock turned with a metallic clatter. The door opened inwards.

'*Bonjour, ma soeur*,' said de Bart-Mendel.

The polite smile on the face of the young nun grew taut at the edges when she saw the dishevelled little group on the top step.

'We should like to speak to Reverend Mother if that would not be inconvenient,' de Bart-Mendel continued.

The young nun saw the limousine and the uniformed chauffeur in the drive.

'We've come from the wars, I'm afraid,' de Bart-Mendel explained, smiling. 'In the case of two of us, quite literally.'

The young nun's face relaxed slightly.

'I don't know, monsieur, if . . . ' She broke off. 'Will you come in, monsieur? Madame?' she asked.

The cloister passage shone with scrubbing. The wooden table by the door of the portress's office, and the chair, gave off a smell of wax.

'Who should I tell Reverend Mother you are, monsieur?' asked the young nun.

'Tell her that Victor de Bart-Mendel would regard it as a favour if she could spare him two or three minutes of her time.'

'Oh, Monsieur le Baron,' exclaimed the young nun, 'please forgive me.'

'For what, *ma soeur*?' asked de Bart-Mendel.

'For not recognising you, monsieur,' said the nun. 'You have been a frequent visitor here. Reverend Mother speaks of you often.'

A tall statue of the Virgin stood in a niche in the scrubbed wall. Hugo read out the inscription on the rim of the arch above the statue's head.

'"I am the Immaculate Conception",' he announced in a clear, penetrating treble. 'What does that mean, Papa?'

'Oh, what a good little fellow!' simpered the nun. 'Excuse me, monsieur, madame. I'm sure Reverend Mother will be delighted to see you.'

She clattered away in her wooden pattens, her hands tucked sedately under her scapular. The expression on Hugo's face was one of disgust.

'She's just pretending to be nice,' he said.

'*Trying* to be nice might be a more charitable way of putting it,' de Bart-Mendel suggested.

'She wasn't trying at all,' said Hugo. 'She'd have turned us away if she had thought we were real refugees. She's pretending to be nice because she knows you're important, Papa.'

The nun returned. She led them round the cloister to the far end, and across a low stone threshold through which they passed into the Mother Superior's guest parlour.

A small black crucifix hung over the mantleshelf. There was a large, garishly tinted print of Jesus the Good Shepherd, his gaze turned dewily to the sky rather than on the sheep about his feet. Slender, fragile-looking wooden armchairs with straw seats were placed along the walls. The Mother Superior stood with her back to one of them, reserving it for her own use. She motioned Julie and de Bart-Mendel to sit down. As a parlour, thought Julie, as she tried to settle in the chair indicated to her, the place had no reality. It offered only the appurtenances of hospitality, and none of the substance.

'It is most kind of you, Monsieur le Baron, to think to call on us again,' said the Mother Superior.

'I have come to seek a favour of you, madame,' de Bart-Mendel replied.

The Mother Superior inclined her head.

'I'm sure we owe you many favours, Monsieur le Baron,' she told him. 'How may we be of service?'

De Bart-Mendel began to tell her what he knew about Louis. Hugo twisted round in his chair to look through the window into the garden. Louis pulled at Julie's hand.

'Mademoiselle? Are *Maman* and *Papa* here?' he asked.

'No, *mon petit*. Not yet,' Julie whispered.

She tried to smile at him.

'Are you going to stay here with me?' he asked again.

'No, *mon petit*,' she whispered. 'The ladies will look after you. Do you know, they are called sisters?'

'Is my real sister dead?' he asked.

'Yes,' Julie nodded.

'*Please* will you stay with me?' said Louis.

Before she could reply, Julie heard the Mother Superior ask, 'Does the young English lady speak any French?'

'She speaks French very well, madame,' de Bart-Mendel replied.

'I do speak French, madame,' Julie answered for herself. 'Though Monsieur le Baron is perhaps a little too kind.'

'Not at all,' smiled the Mother Superior. 'You have a very good accent, mademoiselle.'

'I had an excellent teacher,' said Julie.

'In England?' asked the Mother Superior.

'In England,' Julie replied. 'But my teacher was French.'

'*Mais naturellement!*' the Mother Superior exclaimed.

As Julie went on to explain how she had met Louis, the child kept on tugging at her arm and pleading, 'Will you, mademoiselle? will you?'

'The little man doesn't want to be parted from you, mademoiselle,' the Mother Superior smiled indulgently.

'I can't stay here with you,' Julie told Louis. 'If I don't go home, my *maman* and *papa* will be very worried about me.'

'I don't want to stay here,' Louis protested. 'I don't like it here. Let me stay with you.'

De Bart-Mendel had taken out his cheque book. He wrote in it, tore off the cheque, and handed it over to the Mother Superior. Julie noticed the expression of surprise on her face.

'The fees for the child,' de Bart-Mendel explained, 'and enough for whatever maintenance in the way of clothing, books – extras you understand – which you may consider to be to the child's advantage.'

'But, Monsieur le Baron,' said the Mother Superior, 'would it not be better to pay by the quarter, as other guardians do ... '

175

'Permit me to give you a little worldly advice, madame,' de Bart-Mendel interrupted her. 'Clear the cheque as quickly as you can. Make sure it is cleared before the Germans arrive.'

'The Germans, Monsieur le Baron?' she asked.

'Yes, madame,' he replied. 'They have an unfortunate habit of closing all bank accounts belonging to Jews.'

'Monsieur le Baron is joking!' she exclaimed.

'Alas no, madame,' de Bart-Mendel replied. 'And I would urge you not to wait to find out the truth of what I am saying.'

'But the Germans will never reach here,' the Mother Superior protested.

'They did last time, madame,' de Bart-Mendel replied. 'Only just – but they did.'

The Mother Superior rang a bell. Another nun appeared.

'Sister Charles Borromeo will take the little one to the younger children's schoolroom,' Mother Superior explained.

Julie kissed Louis.

'Be good and brave,' she whispered.

As the second nun pulled him away from her, she said to the Mother Superior, 'Madame, I think I must leave immediately. I'm sure you will be kind to him, and love him.'

The Mother Superior said, 'Of course, mademoiselle! I understand perfectly.'

Julie had already risen to her feet. She ran from the room, across the small stone threshold, and back into the sunlit cloister. She swallowed hard and tried desperately to relax. De Bart-Mendel and Hugo joined her almost immediately. De Bart-Mendel took her arm and led her away. They had almost reached the front door when she heard Louis' voice crying out, 'Julie! Julie!'

He had never addressed her by her name before. Unable to help herself, she looked back. He had torn himself free and was running, stumbling, up the cloister after her. She turned abruptly, and walked on to the front door. No footsteps followed; he must have realised that she had rejected him.

The nun who had admitted them opened the front door for them. Julie heard herself say, *'Au revoir, ma soeur'*, as she stepped out into the heat of the drive. As the front door thudded shut behind them, she let herself go, and sobbed, letting the tears stream down her cheeks. In her tears, she felt she could hide from the knowledge of her own treachery to the child. De Bart-Mendel put his arm round her, to comfort her. She buried her damp face in the sleeve of his jacket.

'They make children stand on mantlepieces,' she mumbled, 'to punish them. They make them stand there for hours and hours, holding big Church bibles.'

'Whatever makes you think that?' asked de Bart-Mendel.

'I just know about it,' Julie sobbed.

'And I know they don't,' he replied. 'That is typical anti-clerical propaganda.'

She lifted up her face.

'You're Jewish, not Catholic. You don't know what goes on in convents,' she told him.

'I know what goes on in this one,' de Bart-Mendel replied. 'My late wife went to school here.'

He paused to allow Julie to dry her eyes on his handkerchief.

'Are *you* a Catholic, Julie,' he asked.

'No,' she replied.

'The worst thing that happens here, my dear,' he told her, 'is that the good sisters tell you off if you whistle in the cloisters because, they say, the Blessed Virgin would not approve.'

Joseph held the car door open for them. As they settled into the plush seats, de Bart-Mendel continued, 'Your Louis is a very lucky little boy.'

'I didn't mean to give you the idea that I don't think you are very generous, monsieur,' Julie told him.

'I wasn't thinking of that,' de Bart-Mendel replied. 'What I'm saying is that he'll cry today, and maybe tomorrow, and think himself the unhappiest boy in all the world. And then he will begin to find new people to love him, and spoil him. When the Germans come, he will be as safe within these walls as though nothing has happened. The war will sweep round him like a sea-tide round an island. He may even be luckier than we are. And he'll certainly be luckier than thousands and thousands of other children.'

Joseph started the car. They returned down the drive between the lawns and the yew-trees, towards the main gate.

'All the same, Papa,' Hugo said thoughtfully, 'I'd rather be out here with you, than locked up in there.

19

'Don't start taking life too easily, gentlemen,' called Major Spiesser as he strutted up the main square of Montcornet.

He was heading for the *Mairie*, accompanied by the corporal whom he had designated official squadron photographer. Von Leonarte, Anton Kirst, and several other squadron officers, groaned audibly. They had arrived in Montcornet two hours before, as spearhead of the Panzers' advance. Now they found that they had an hour or two of leisure, waiting for their fuel-tankers and armourers to catch up.

They were sitting at a café table in the shade of a striped awning, drinking glasses of iced water with their coffees and cognac, and watching two or three NCOs herding French prisoners into tidy groups, to await the arrival of a Field Gendarmerie detachment. Mounted up in the open cupolas of their 38 T tanks, they had sweated in the noon sunlight. It seemed as though the sweating would never stop: von Leonarte had brought with him to the table a field-grey towel he wore round his throat when he was inside his tank with the hatch down. He was mopping his forehead and bared chest.

'We'll be moving off almost immediately, gentlemen,' called Major Spiesser, cheerily. 'We've just heard that General Kempff is coming up behind us – the 6th, 2nd, and 1st Panzers are all converging on us. We don't want to be caught in the traffic jam, do we?'

'Speak for yourself, shit-hound,' murmured Senior Lieutenant Kirst.

Von Leonarte could see Helm and Radinski, with other crewmen, lounging round the fountain in the centre of the square, trying to keep cool. Curiosity had drawn a small knot of adolescents and younger children out of the cellars where they had been taking cover, to look at the tanks. The tank crewmen were trying to attract the attention of one or two of the older girls.

Up on the steps of the *mairie*, two good-humoured *landsers* who had been dispatched by Major Spiesser to fetch out the mayor, were guarding their prisoner. Major Spiesser was determined to receive a formal surrender of the town, and in the absence of a French army officer of any rank, the mayor would do as well. Now, the mayor, in his tricolor sash, stood facing the gallant major. As the photographer crouched to take his pictures, Major Spiesser ordered the mayor to remove his sash and hand it over.

A girl appeared from out of the knot of adolescents huddled under the trees round the fountain. Her light brown hair was pulled back from off her freckled face, and was tied in a broad satin bow. She was wearing navy-blue slacks rolled up her plump calves, and was astride a heavy, boy's bicycle. Despite her rounded figure, she could not have been more than fifteen years old. Von Leonarte was reminded of girls he had met at the seaside at Rugen, during family holidays so long ago.

A junior lieutenant of the squadron, Erich Schneider, took his own Leica from its case, to snap a photograph of the officers sitting under the café-awning. Two of the officers put their arms affectionately about one another's neck. Von Leonarte called out to the girl, '*Hey, chérie, viens ici!*'

She glanced across the street at him.

'*Viens ici!*' he repeated.

She turned the bicycle towards him, and propelled herself towards the table by pushing herself along with her outstretched toes. She came to a halt at the edge of the pavement, a few yards from the table. Helm and Radinski were watching from beside the fountain, grinning broadly.

Von Leonarte patted his knee. The girl shook her head. She hesitated. Then she propped up her bicycle against the standard of a street lamp, and came over.

'What's your name?' asked von Leonarte.

'Jacqueline,' she whispered hoarsely.

'Mine is Dieter – Dieter,' he repeated. 'Will you sit on my knee while my friend takes a picture?'

She did not reply, but she settled on his knee and put a freckled arm round his neck. She stared into the camera.

'Smile please, gentlemen,' Erich Schneider called. '*Souriez, s'il vous plaît, mademoiselle.*'

The shutter clicked, and the officers applauded, jumping down from the chairs. Helm and Radinski were grinning even more broadly from the fountain. Von Leonarte felt that the incident would do his reputation no harm with his men.

The girl got off his knee.

'Where are you all going?' she asked.

'To the sea-side,' Anton Kirst replied, from beside von Leonarte.

'We're going for a bathe,' said von Leonarte.

The camera-shutter clicked again. The girl glanced round.

'*Tiens!*' she called.

The camera clicked a third time, amidst more laughter.

'*Comme tu es belle!*' Erich Schneider called.

He put finger and thumb together in a gesture of approval.

Two elderly women were walking along the pavement under the trees. They glared in the direction of the girl, and muttered to each other. The girl shrugged her shoulders pointedly at them.

Major Spiesser came strutting back across the square. He held his arm extended in front of him: it was draped with the broad sash of red, white, and blue silk. As he approached, von Leonarte could see the sweat gleaming under the rim of the steel helmet he had insisted on wearing for the ceremony.

'Excellent! Excellent!' Major Spiesser shouted to them. 'It will make a perfect picture, gentlemen.'

He beamed at von Leonarte. The girl edged away.

'Lieutenant Schneider,' said Major Spiesser. 'You must send the negative to Doctor Paul Leverkuehn. The *Herr Doktor* may wish to publish it in *Signal.*'

He laughed noisily, in an attempt to participate in the cheerfulness of the officers under his command.

'We can suggest a caption for it, eh gentlemen? "The Tribute of Conquered Beauty to the Conquerers".'

179

The girl had returned to her bicycle. Von Leonarte saw that she had a half-scared, half-defiant look about her.

'It will have a splendid effect on morale,' Major Spiesser said.

20

Marie-Claire watched out of the compartment window the crowds pouring down the platform, clutching their bulging, broken, cardboard suitcases, trailing their bewildered children behind them. It was impossible to imagine how so many people could have travelled on one train.

The young man beside her stood up and reached down her suitcase from the rack.

'There's no need to hurry,' he told her. 'We'll wait until the forecourt is a bit clearer. It'll be easier to find a taxi.'

He gave her suitcase a teasing little shake, then said, smiling, 'There! All's safe!'

He put it down on the seat opposite. He knew exactly what to do, she thought. She felt entirely safe with him beside her. On the journey from Soissons, tiredness had overwhelmed her. She had fallen asleep with her head resting on his shoulder, although he was a complete stranger. She had not woken until the train had been clattering over the points outside the marshalling yards of the Gare de l'Est. As they had drawn into the station, the young man had asked her if she had slept well. He had then asked, with the most charming hesitancy, if she would spare the time to dine with him that night.

At first, she had refused. She had pointed out the state she was in and had added, deliberately, that though she had intended to stay with relatives, they were not expecting her arrival. He had suggested that she went with him to his hotel to wash and change. As for having somewhere to stay the night, it need not be an insuperable problem.

The idea excited her. After a proper display of hesitancy, she had agreed.

An elderly couple with their two grandchildren hurried past beneath the compartment window. The lid of the big, battered suitcase which the old man was carrying, fell open, the metal locks scraping the pavement. Clothes and wooden toys tumbled out in a heap. One of the toys, a red, wooden engine, trundled away on its wheels across the platform. A railway fireman, his face, hands, and cotton overalls still smeared with soot and grease, bent down, picked it up, and offered it to the child. The child stared wide-eyed at him, refusing to take it from the man, clearly terrified. Marie-Claire would have liked to have jumped down and to have run to the little one, and given him a great big cuddle.

'I think we might leave,' said the young man. 'We'll find a taxi now.'

He picked up his attaché-case and her suitcase. He put the attaché-case under his arm as he opened the doors. Once out on the platform, he put them down, and held up his arms to help her. She let him lift her down from the top step. Carrying the luggage once more, he set off up the platform towards the barrier at such a smart pace that she had to run along behind him. She wondered at it, but he kept looking back to make sure she was with him, and smiling to her, encouragingly. Of course, she thought, she must look very shabby and dirty.

When they were through the barrier, he turned to her.

'Now I'll go and find a taxi,' he told her, pointing to the main exit. 'I'll take our things. I suggest you go and wait in the Rue du Faubourg St Martin entrance, and I'll bring the cases round, eh?' He smiled. 'And don't you go wandering off, whatever you do. You're not to go leaving me when I've only just met you.'

The way he said it made her feel even more excited. It was lovely to be looked after, and not to have to make decisions.

She watched him striding away under the signs indicating the ticket-offices and the taxi-rank. She turned away, and went across the concourse, making her way between the pavement vendors' barrows and the baggage-trolleys.

The sun beat hot off the steps under the main arches overlooking the Rue du Faubourg St Martin. Clusters of people who had just arrived in Paris stood in the midst of their baggage wondering what to do next. An old woman, grey-haired and dressed in black, was sitting on a suitcase, her back against a sooty brick column, while her husband fanned her face with a newspaper. A few, more confident than the others, stepped down into the glare of the road, looking about them for a taxi. Plenty of taxis drove past, but none of them stopped. It was just as well, thought Marie-Claire, that the young man had gone off to find one.

For ten minutes or more, she stood under the arches, with the sun pricking the sweat onto her forehead, but the young man did not come. One or two taxis drew up below the steps. With each one, she stopped to see if he was sitting in the back, but they were empty, and other waiting passengers went down the steps, clutching their luggage, to negotiate with the drivers. Then for a time there were no more taxis, and a sort of quiet descended on the space between the station concourse and the traffic on the main street. Marie-Claire began to feel panic. The young man had lulled her into feeling that there was no need for her to make any immediate plans, that he would be looking after her, tonight at least, and after that anything might turn up.

A single taxi drew up below the steps. A young man's head appeared through the rear window.

'*Eh, chérie, viens!*' he called.

For a moment only, she thought it was her escort. Then she was jostled from behind. A voice said threateningly in her ear, '*Va, sale morue!*'

A young woman with a handbag under her arm, and a cigarette between her fingers, clicked on high heels down the steps, and, after haggling for a few seconds with the young man, got into the rear of the taxi beside him.

'You'll be in trouble if you stay here, my darling,' a voice said quietly.

Marie-Claire turned round. Standing at her shoulder was a very tall, slender young woman.

'Time to move along, darling,' she said.

'I don't understand,' Marie-Claire began.

The very appearance of the woman was frightening: the bright, hollow-set eyes, the gaunt cheeks, ash pale but with a hectic flush of rouge on the bones; the arched, pencilled eyebrows, and the thin, scarlet lips; and all framed in a mass of glistening titian-red hair.

'If the chickens don't pick you up,' the woman said, 'the *Nanas* will get you. You've been warned off their patch already.'

She spoke as if she wasn't one of them.

'I've only just arrived,' Marie-Claire explained. 'I'm waiting for my friend. He's coming with a taxi.'

'Where's your luggage?' asked the woman.

'My friend's got it,' said Marie-Claire.

The woman stood staring down at her. She was all in black, like one of those official ladies who interviewed you in the St Lago's when the police pushed you in for examination: black suit, black silk stockings, black shoes. But she wasn't one of those either. You could tell that from the beret pinned at a tilt on the red mass of her hair; from the high heels of the satin shoes; from the scarlet fingernails clutching the black satin purse.

'My sisters were quite worried about you, darling,' said the woman.

Marie-Claire glanced about her, wondering whom she meant. There were eyes watching her from the clusters of people gathered under the arches. Quite close by, to the left, there was a girl who would have been pretty but for the livid acne spots on her chin. Behind her was another girl whose face was half-concealed by the curtain of hair which fell over her cheek. One eye was hidden by her hair; the other was bright and unblinking as a rodent's.

182

'Florence was worried about you,' said the tall young woman, as if she knew exactly which girl Marie-Claire had noticed.

Marie-Claire turned to look up at her.

'Smoke?' asked the woman.

She had taken a slim, gold-plated cigarette-case from her purse. In it was a row of gold-tipped cigarettes.

'I had better look for my friend,' said Marie-Claire.

'He won't come,' smiled the woman. 'Don't worry, my darling. We'll look after you if we think you are a deserving case.'

She raised the cigarette-case to Marie-Claire. Marie-Claire took one of the cigarettes. As the woman lit it for her, and she drew on it, she found the gold tip shiny and tasteless between her lips.

'Where did you come from?' asked the woman.

Marie-Claire looked about her again. Other faces were staring from out of the shadows: a swarthy, gipsy-girl's face; a fat, blotched face under close cropped curls; a sweetly open, young girl's face, with light brown hair drawn back under a tortoise-shell band.

'I've come from Laon,' said Marie-Claire.

'Where are you going?' asked the woman.

The girl with the sweet, innocent face was smiling directly at her, as if to encourage her.

'Don't know,' Marie-Claire shrugged.

The tall woman reached out to stroke Marie-Claire's cheek.

'You could be quite pretty, *ma petite*,' she observed. 'I can understand Florence's point of view.'

Marie-Claire could feel the edge of the scarlet nails against her skin.

'You don't have to be pretty, of course,' said the woman. 'My sisters and I came together for companionship as well as love.'

She laughed as if she had said something which had surprised even herself, then stopped very suddenly.

'Where's your card?' she asked, gazing down directly into Marie-Claire's eyes.

'I don't know what you mean,' Marie-Claire replied.

'Give me your card, my darling,' the woman said, the mask of her face smiling at Marie-Claire's pathetic attempt at evasion. 'One of my sisters needs a fresh card.'

She stroked Marie-Claire's cheek gently with the points of her nails.

'I haven't got one,' said Marie-Claire. 'The *Commissaire* at Laon tore it up.'

'Is that true?' asked the woman.

The points of her nails pricked into Marie-Claire's cheeks.

'I swear it,' Maire-Claire replied desperately. Fear grabbed her. 'I wouldn't have come to Paris otherwise,' she said.

183

The tall woman took the cigarette from between Marie-Claire's fingers, and dropped it to the ground and trod it out.

'Do you have nobody to look after you, my darling?' she asked.

Marie-Claire shook her head.

'No one at all?' asked the woman in an exaggerated tone of sympathy.

'No one,' said Marie-Claire. 'They even took my baby from me,' she said. 'They said I wasn't a fit person to have control over it. That's what they said! "You are not a fit person to have control over it!" Those are the exact words.'

'Who said that?'

'*Monsieur le Commissaire des Moeurs,*' Marie-Claire replied.

'Where is your baby?' the tall woman asked almost sympathetically.

'With the good Sisters of the Little Friends of Jesus,' Marie-Claire replied. 'I'm not sure where.'

She sniffed, and rubbed the end of her nose with her hand.

'You must hate them all very much, my darling,' said the tall woman in a soft voice.

Marie-Claire nodded.

'You might become one of our sisters, if you wished,' said the tall woman. 'Our stories are all remarkably similar – and we look after one another.'

A gentle warmth had come into her voice.

'We are the Rats of Venus. I call myself Cybele. . . . Would you like to stay with us for a little?'

'Would you like me to?' Marie-Claire asked.

'Florence wants you to,' said Cybele. 'She wants you to very much!'

She glanced across the column behind which was lurking the girl who wore her hair so that it fell hiding half her face.

'You will find us,' she continued, 'in the Passage Serniers. You must cross the Rue du Faubourg St Martin, here. Go up there . . . '

She pointed across the street to an alleyway between two tall, derelict-looking warehouses.

'Only, my darling,' she said. 'You must bring your luggage with you.'

'I haven't any luggage,' said Marie-Claire. 'My friend – this man – has taken it.'

The gaunt, hectic face stared down at her.

'Either a card or some luggage,' said Cybele. 'My sisters will expect it, you see? And there is so much luggage here.'

She paused for a moment, then patted Marie-Claire's cheek once more.

'*A bientôt, ma petite!*' she said. 'When you have found some luggage, we shall be waiting for you in the Passage Serniers.'

She walked away briskly into the shadow of the station. Below the arrogant tilt of her beret, the thick mane of red hair shook imperiously about her shoulders. And, in spite of her tallness, she was wearing high-heels, carrying herself as though proud of being taller than those about her. The other girls were all gone as suddenly as if the earth had swallowed them up.

Marie-Claire paused for a second, wondering if it were not yet too late for the young man to appear in a taxi.

She ran back into the station. Another train had just come in, its engine hissing jets of steam behind the buffers. Cybele's tall figure was making for the main exit, through the stream of passengers. Marie-Claire began to run after her. A trio of well-dressed foreigners was standing under the sign 'Bureau de Renseignements': mother and father fussing over their daughter, a thick-set young woman with her hair in braids, who was bent over, vomiting onto the platform. Their baggage was heaped behind them, disregarded. On top of the pile was a vanity case and a purse-handbag. Without hesitating, Marie-Claire snatched up the vanity case and the handbag, and ran towards the exit. The vanity case was heavier than she had expected; it bumped against the side of her knee, bruising her through her skirt. She heard men's voices shouting behind her, but with the reverberant clangour of the station all about her, there was no way of knowing if it were directed at her, nor did she pause to find out.

She ran down the steps. Suddenly, as if she had plunged into warm water, she was bathed in the dazzling, hot sunlight. The taxis were grinding and honking their horns on the cobbles on either side of her. She dashed for the corner, the vanity case banging against her legs. Without daring to look about her, she ran straight into the busy street. A bus swept down immediately in front of her, its bulk looming over her, its bell ringing loudly. Its driver shot his head out of the window and shouted abuse at her. There was a military lorry with a high, canvas, camouflaged canopy drawn over the back, parked against the opposite pavement. Four or five men in baggy khaki uniforms and thin, greasy forage-caps, were lounging around it. As she reached the pavement and pushed past them towards the entrance to the alley, they called out to her in English. One of them grabbed at her arm. She told him to shit himself, and tore herself free. They called after her, mocking her, as she turned the corner into the alley.

She stopped to take breath. Strands of hair clung to her face; her heart was thumping under her breast as if it would never stop. For a few moments, she hid in the shade of a doorway, amongst a litter of dirty straw and boxes filled with empty, dusty bottles. She was afraid that she might be pursued, and that the English soldiers might be telling her pursuers where she had gone, but the alley remained deserted and quiet save for the sound of traffic out in the street.

After waiting a minute or two, she picked up the leaden weight of the vanity case, slipped the purse-handbag up her arm and went on up the gritty cobbles. She found that she was in a cul-de-sac. For a moment she thought that the tall young woman had been playing a trick on her. Then, as she reached the high warehouse wall which blocked off the end, she saw the narrow entry, and the dented blue plate which read 'Pge Serniers'. The buildings on either side reared up five stories, and seemed quite derelict. Most of the windows were smashed, and from some hung rags of sacking. The narrow space between the buildings was piled with rubbish: crates of wine-bottles once stacked carefully, but now tumbling down on one another, heaps of waste paper which had become sodden over the winter months but was now drying out again, and the last shreds of decaying vegetation and butchers' carcasses. As Marie-Claire picked her way through the rubbish, a girl's voice called from high above, 'Hey! You, down there!'·

Marie-Claire looked up. The girl she had seen at the station, with the hair over her face and down her back, was sitting astride the window ledge up on the fifth floor, under the gutter of the roof, with one leg, bare almost to the hip, dangling against the wall. Her hair hung like a shawl, covering her arm and waist.

'Where did you get to, eh?' she called. The vanity case was grabbed from out of Marie-Claire's hand.

'In there, darling.'

Another girl had come up behind her, out of some hiding-place, as Marie-Claire had been staring upwards. It was the swarthy, gipsy-girl; her black hair had a greasy look about it, and there were pock-marks on her olive-complexioned face. Her figure was concealed by the blue boiler-suit she was wearing. The top buttons were undone to display the small silver crucifix which hung on its chain in the deep valley of her breasts. Inside one of the capacious trouser-pockets, Marie-Claire could see the black handle of a heavy clasp-knife. As she stepped across the rubbish to the broken door indicated to her, the purse-handbag was snatched from off her wrist.

'Upstairs, darling,' said the girl.

Her accent was foreign. Marie-Claire started up the broken wooden stairs, picking her way carefully. The rooms on either side had long been deserted. The furniture stood broken and stripped amidst the litter. The wallpaper had peeled away in many places to show the faded newspapers underneath. There was a smell of decay and excrement everywhere.

Climbing up from the third landing, one of the treads gave way under her. She grabbed for the wooden rail, but it snapped under her hand, and she fell forward.

'One has to be careful,' the girl behind her told her, disapprovingly, as she picked herself up.

186

A third girl was waiting on the landing at the top, as swarthy as the girl behind Marie-Claire, and with similarly greasy black hair. Her cheeks, like those of the other, were deeply pitted.

'So you've arrived,' she said, as if Marie-Claire had kept her waiting.

She was bare-legged, in dirty plimsolls, with a creased black crepe-de-chine petticoat, and over it, an old-fashioned French infantryman's jacket, horizon-blue, with the side-lapels looped up and buttoned at the back. She took the vanity case and the purse from the girl who had brought Marie-Claire upstairs, and led them through the only door leading off the landing.

The room inside was a long attic with the roof sloping sharply down on either side from a lofty central beam. Four windows were set in bays on one side of the roof. There were three low iron bedsteads with bare mattresses and tick pillows. Other mattresses with blankets and pillows littered the grimy floorboards. Washing hung from strings stretched from the central beam to the low walls. There was a smell of damp linen, body-sweat, and stale perfume. Other garments were draped over or heaped on the battered chairs and the sofa, which stood out like islands amidst the debris on the floor.

'Welcome, *ma petite!*'

Cybele was standing in the centre of the room. The girl in the infantryman's jacket put down the vanity case and the purse-handbag at her feet. Cybele ignored both her and them. She reached out to Marie-Claire who went over to her. The brilliance of the eyes in the pallid face compelled attention.

'Florence is so pleased, my darling,' she whispered. She kissed Marie-Claire on the mouth. 'That is to make her jealous a little, eh?'

Her breath smelt of disinfectant. She took Marie-Claire to look into the nearest alcove, where Florence was still sitting astride the window-ledge, bare-legged, her frock rucked up to show her blue cotton drawers. She had thrown her long tresses back from off her face. On one side, translucent scar-tissue covered her cheek from the corner of her eye to the side of her mouth.

'What is your name, my darling?' whispered Cybele.

'Marie-Claire . . . '

Before she could add her surname, Cybele interrupted her.

'None of us have more than one name,' she said, her varnished lips caressing Marie-Claire's ear.

'Florence so longs to have a dear friend of her very own,' whispered Cybele. She raised her voice slightly. 'But she will have to wait.'

Marie-Claire felt sick. She was trembling slightly.

Florence scowled in disappointment. The side of her mouth embedded in scar-tissue could not register expression.

The other girls stood or sat silent, watching.

'We have all come here because we have nowhere else,' said Cybele. 'Like all good sisters, we learn to love one another.' She put her arm round Marie-Claire's shoulders. 'Pauline here called us the Rats of Venus ... '

She indicated the girl with the black fringed bob and the mouth and chin studded with acne, whom Marie-Claire had first noticed at the station.

'It's a good name,' she continued, 'because we, like the little Rats at the Opera School, have nobody to depend on except each other. Pauline and I came here first. We met at the Gard du Nord. Pauline had just been dismissed from a soldiers' brothel behind the Maginot Line. She was an old hand – pre-war – been there two years, working three weeks on, two weeks off. Then some shit of a sergeant says she's rolled him, and just because he's got a couple of medals they kick her out without even letting her pack her things. And when she tries to complain, they tear up her card, and threaten to send her to La Roquette for two years. Then Ginette arrived.'

She pointed to the innocent-looking, childlike girl whose hair was pulled back under a tortoise-shell band. The girl smiled sweetly. She opened her mouth to speak, and uttered a series of soft, grunting sounds.

'Severine brought her to Paris,' Cybele continued, pointing to the girl with the close-cropped curls, whose figure bulged gross through her creased satin frock, and whose calves were swollen and blotched above her dirty white ankle socks and little-girl strap sandals.

'We met them at the Gare de l'Est. Severine was hustling for Ginette; they were both half-dead. Severine had lost her card after some soldier or other had given her a dose. And Ginette – they didn't tell her, when she was working at Le Cateau, she was entitled to a fortnight off for every three weeks in the house. They worked her every night for seven weeks. When they'd shagged her out so she couldn't manage her twenty-a-night, they told her to get back where she'd come from – didn't even give her the fare home.'

Ginette smiled radiantly. Severine was beside her, holding her hand.

'She's been like that ever since,' said Cybele.

There was a heavy smell on the air which was coming in through the open windows, like that of burnt rubber. Cybele sniffed.

'The Germans are on their way,' she remarked. She said it with satisfaction.

'And this is Ines,' she went on, pointing to the gipsy-looking girl in the man's boiler-suit. 'And Manuela.'

She pointed to the second pock-faced, dark-haired girl, in the black petticoat and infantryman's blue jacket.

'They look like twins, don't they, my darling?' said Cybele.

'Yes,' whispered Marie-Claire.

'They are lovers,' said Cybele. 'Of course, they may be sisters as well. They are very jealous of one another, so it's best not to make friends with them singly.'

Marie-Claire glanced past Florence at the window. Beyond the roof-tops on the other side of the passage, a dense, oily column of smoke was spilling upwards into the glittering afternoon sky. Cybele gripped her arm.

'You must pay attention, *ma petite*,' she said. 'You have to know your new sisters. They expect it of you. Ines and Manuela are Spanish of course. They learned to kill on the Ebro, fighting the Fascists.'

The two Spanish girls smiled.

'When they fled over the Pyrenees to escape the Fascists, our lot put them into a concentration camp. They fucked their way out of it, six weeks ago, and fucked their way to Paris. They say they are Anarchists, but they hate the men they fucked just as if they were good Catholics.'

Marie-Claire knew that Dagoes were no different from Corsicans. Dago girls carried knives and knew how to use them. All the girls she had worked with since she had left Dr Vauthier's employ had spoken of Corsicans and Dagoes with respect.

'And finally, Florence!' said Cybele, turning Marie-Claire to face the window again. 'You must learn to love her, my darling. She wants so much to love you.'

Florence swung her leg back over the sill. She drew the skirt of her frock down over her knees. Then she put her fingertips against the scar-tissue of her cheek.

'It isn't pretty,' she said to Marie-Claire.

She thrust her hand under the fall of her hair, and drew it over to cover once more the damaged half of her face.

'There,' she said.

'The brothel she was working in at Charleville was set on fire by a man who thought he caught the clap there. It was a house for officers – a nice place to work. When she got out of hospital, she came back to Paris and tried to work the pavements behind the Rue St Vincent. She had to have her tricks in the doorways because she could not go into the light. Then a man saw her face one night and beat her.'

Florence reached out her hand.

'Take it,' said Cybele to Marie-Claire.

Marie-Claire took it. Florence drew her beside her.

'You don't have to look, *chérie*,' she smiled from under the gleaming curtain of hair.

The hand was warm and affectionate. Marie-Claire felt less afraid.

Cybele squatted down and snapped open the vanity case. She took out one or two of the black jewelry cases, opened them, and glanced at the contents. She returned them to the case, and snapped it shut

189

once more. Standing up, she pushed the case with her foot towards the Spanish girls.

'Take this junk down to the Rue Quincampoix, to Marius Grimaud,' she ordered. 'If he doesn't treat you right, knock his shitty glasses off his nose and tread on them.'

The girls smiled.

'Marie-Claire?' she asked, staring at her where she stood with Florence, her back to the window. 'Why did they take your card?'

'I told you,' stammered Marie-Claire. 'Out there.'

'You told me a lie, my darling,' said Cybele. Her mask of a face smiled.

'We are all liars here, my darling.'

Marie-Claire felt Florence's hand squeeze hers in encouragement.

'The truth?' asked Cybele. 'Did they send you to a St Lago?'

'They took my card,' Marie-Claire replied. Her mouth was so dry it was difficult to speak. 'Only, I didn't go. I ran away instead.'

They had taken her card so that she could not work until after she had been to the hospital for treatment. She had had no previous experience of a St Lazare hospital, but she had heard about the 'camel', and what girls were put through as they squatted astride it. She had run to her room, gathered up a few things into her suitcase, had taken the baby and had hidden in the crowds about Laon station.

'Do you know who Cybele was?' asked the woman who called herself Cybele.

Marie-Claire shook her head.

'Do you know why I call myself Cybele?'

Marie-Claire shook her head again.

'Florence, my darling, tell your dear friend why I am called Cybele!'

'Cybele was a goddess,' Florence replied.

Marie-Claire stared up at the livid, hectic mask haloed in the mass of red hair.

'Cybele,' said the mask, returning her stare, 'was goddess of the Phrygians. She suffered from an insatiable appetite for mortal men. But whenever she took a man, she destroyed his sexual parts so that no other woman should ever enjoy him.' She stared at Marie-Claire, then laughed suddenly. 'You see, my darling? We are all the children of St Lago.'

That evening Ines and Manuela set off to Les Halles, to sell the vanity case and its contents to Marius Grimaud at his hotel. Fat Severine and Ginette went with them. Only Pauline and Cybele remained in the attic with Marie-Claire and Florence. Florence had taken Marie-Claire to one of the beds, and had drawn her down on

190

the mattress with her. She had made her stroke her disfigured cheek.

'You will get used to it, *chérie*,' Florence had said coaxingly.

The scar-tissue was as hard as celluloid, but Marie-Claire had managed to touch it without revulsion after only a few minutes.

'Have you nothing of your own?' Florence had whispered.

'Nothing,' Marie-Claire had replied.

Florence's hand had moved up into Marie-Claire's lap. The fingers had begun to coax it very gently, until Marie-Claire had begun to sigh with pleasure.

'You see, *chérie*,' Florence had whispered, 'if you really love me, I shall look after you.'

Cybele stood at the window, silhouetted against the dusky light. She had been drinking steadily from a wine bottle since the others had gone. Occasionally she had sung softly to herself, or held muttered conversations – one-sided conversations as if she had been speaking to somebody on the other end of a telephone. She was standing unsteadily. The bottle rested on the sill. Pauline was sitting in a chair nearby, the glow from her cigarette lighting dimly the broken plaster of the well beside her. Cybele reached for the wine bottle. She knocked it with the back of her hand so that it fell out of the open window and, a few seconds later, smashed on the cobbles beneath.

'Shit!' she said. 'Fetch another, Pauline.'

Pauline looked at her, shrugged, and got out of her chair. She went over to a row of bottles of red wine by the opposite wall. 'The Boche is coming,' chanted Cybele out of the open window. 'And they're all going to run away – all the rich, fat, *good* people. And the police. And all the miserable, pettifogging officials. And the police-court doctors. And we shall go down to the Rue de Rivoli and the Rue des Pyramides, *mes petites*, and take whatever we want, because there'll be nobody to stop us, and the Germans won't give a fuck – not for a day or two. And we'll piss over everything we don't want!'

Florence put her arm round Marie-Claire's neck, and drew her head down to kiss her mouth.

'Don't pay any attention, *chérie*,' she whispered. 'She is quite mad. It's the infection. It's eating up into her head.'

Her hand was still caressing Marie-Claire's lap. Marie-Claire was wrapped in contentment. Through her drowsiness, above the soft warmth of Florence's embrace, she saw Pauline carrying the bottle over to the window. From the alcove, Cybele was crooning to herself,

'We'll leave our shit in the confessionals, and on the doorsteps of all the doctors and lawyers. We'll shit all over the Palais de Justice. We'll cover the Panthéon in shit. All Paris will stink of our shit. We'll leave such a stinking mess, even the Prussians won't be able to clean it up.'

In the comfort of her half-sleep, Marie-Claire knew that Cybele was speaking for her, as well as all the others. She could have laughed out loud with pleasure and relief.

21

'Mademoiselle's bath is ready now.'

Danielle came into the bedroom holding out a wrap of yellow towelling. Julie slipped it on. It was warm against her skin.

'Lovely,' she exclaimed.

She had felt quite overawed by the house when they had finally arrived. It had been like entering a small palace. There had been the hall with its marble, echoing floor and high, plaster-moulded ceiling; the tall double-doors leading into reception chambers large enough to house a small army; the curved marble staircase, with its watered marble balustrades supported by caryatids clutching electric lamps disguised as torches.

'My grandfather needed to convince himself of his own success,' de Bart-Mendel explained, 'a Jewish trait, I suspect. It's frighteningly vulgar, I know. Like the Second Empire itself. But, actually, one can come to think of it as home.'

A young man with a limp had come out into the hall to greet them, walking with the aid of a stick. He was introduced to Julie as Alain, de Bart-Mendel's secretary. He had told de Bart-Mendel that somebody from the Galerie Lecuyer in the Rue des Pyramides had rung twice to ask if Monsieur le Baron had returned to Paris. The man at the other end had said that the Baron had asked him to ring. De Bart-Mendel shook his head, and said that he had had no dealings with the Galerie Lecuyer, and that Alain should ring the Gallery back to find out whether the call was authentic.

De Bart-Mendel had already persuaded Julie to stay the night, to give herself a chance to recover from the rigours of her journey. Hugo had disappeared through a green baize door under the curve of the stairs, to say hallo to Maryvonne, the housekeeper. Julie had been put into the care of Danielle, a chambermaid, who had taken her up to a bedroom suite on the second floor. The bedroom was thickly carpeted, and Julie had felt her tired feet sink into the soft pile. But the room was still on a grand scale. The deep armchairs and sofa would have furnished a large drawing room, while leaving a small desert of floor-space. The bed was in proportion with the room, so that it was difficult to decide whether it was designed to be a double

192

bed, or simply a single one suited to its palatial surroundings. And there was Danielle herself, in afternoon black, with spotless white apron and cap, smelling discreetly of perfume.

Danielle had made Julie feel ashamed as she had unpacked Julie's few belongings from the now shabby suitcase. She had gathered up the soiled garments as Julie had undressed. Nor had Julie ever bathed in a sunken bath before. It was strange, as she climbed down into the hot water, to look out over the green tiles of the surround, into the pile of the carpet.

'Is Mademoiselle quite comfortable?' Danielle asked. 'I mean the water?'

Julie nodded through the steam.

'Have you been with Monsieur le Baron long?' she asked.

'It was Madame who gave me my first position, mademoiselle, the same year she fell ill and died,' Danielle replied.

She squatted down at the side of the bath, and began to wash Julie, commenting on her arms and shoulders. Julie noticed that Danielle's high-heeled shoes, though scuffed with age, had once been expensive, as had been the lace which edged her white petticoat.

'How long ago was that?' she asked.

'It was in '36, mademoiselle. The 'flu was dreadfully bad that year. Monsieur went down with it – very badly. Nobody dared tell him about Madame – the doctor, Monsieur Alain, nobody. In the end, Joseph had to come upstairs to tell him. You know Joseph, mademoiselle?'

'The chauffeur?' asked Julie.

'Yes, mademoiselle. And such a good man!'

'I expect Monsieur was very upset,' said Julie.

'He was terribly unhappy, mademoiselle – inconsolable for weeks. He would speak to nobody except Joseph. And then he became himself again – except that there has been nobody else. Not really.'

Julie lay back, letting her hair float about her. When she had got out, and was dressed again, she must ring London to let Ambrose know that she was safe. The poor thing would be half out of his mind with worry. He seemed so very far away, as if at the end of a very long tunnel. Her mother and father weren't the worrying sort. She could send them a postcard of the Eiffel Tower with lots of kisses along the bottom . . . She ought to get in touch with Elaine, of course: Elaine was her real pal . . . And she ought to send something to little Louis – something to let the poor little thing know that she had really cared about him . . .

'Mademoiselle? . . . Eh! Mademoiselle?'

Danielle was crouching beside her, the smell of her perfume mingling with the warm smell of the soap. The bath water was still hot, but Julie felt that she had been asleep for hours and hours.

'You looked so happy, mademoiselle,' Danielle smiled, 'I did not know whether to wake you.'

'How long have I been asleep?' Julie asked.

'Five minutes, mademoiselle. No longer.'

Julie pulled herself up into a sitting position. Danielle reached over, gathered her hair up into a towel, patted all over it and tied it over her forehead. She reached down and helped Julie to climb out onto the carpeted floor. She held out the warmed towelling wrap once again. Julie slipped it on.

'Would you care to have a little rest on the bed, mademoiselle?' she asked, as she escorted Julie back into the bedroom. 'I will wake you in plenty of time to dress for dinner.'

Julie shook her head.

'I have so much to do,' she said. 'Letters to write. Phone calls to make.'

She felt no inclination to do either. She felt so completely relaxed and clean that she wanted to remain awake to enjoy the sensation.

'Do you know?' she asked. 'I have never been to Paris before?'

The bedroom windows led onto a balcony. She opened them.

'Perhaps mademoiselle will be able to stay for a few days?' asked Danielle. 'Except they say that the Germans are coming.'

'Even if they weren't,' Julie replied, 'Monsieur le Baron has been so very kind to me, I wouldn't wish to impose on his hospitality.'

She walked out onto the balcony. Before her, rising above the tops of the trees in the courtyard, were high terraces of steep, narrow roofs, and wrought-iron railings running parallel with the street below, down to the Avenue de Wagram. Above the roof-tops, she could see against the sky, and quite close, the gleaming bulk of the parapet surrounding the top of the Arc de Triomphe. Although she had never set eyes on them before, the shape of the roofs – the small dormer windows set in the steep grey leads, and the rim of the Arc de Triomphe, white in the pure sunlight – were as familiar as if she had known them all her life. Tired and saddened as she had been towards the end of their journey, she had experienced the same feeling as they had driven into the city, through the Porte de la Villette, and along the boulevards below the steps of Sacré-Coeur and Pigalle. It was impossible to sense any feeling of crisis: everything she had seen – buildings and the way people were dressed or behaved, even the noise of the taxis – was so precisely what she had come to expect from having watched René Clair or Carné movies at the Academy and Studio One in Oxford Street. The only thing she had missed had been an accordionist playing *Sous les toits de Paris*.

She leaned against the rail, enjoying the light, fresh breeze, the afternoon sunlight, and the noise of the traffic circling the Étoile.

'Julie?'

Hugo was standing across the bedroom, in the doorway. He had

194

washed and changed. He was wearing a striped sailor-shirt, white duck trousers, and his hair had been slicked with water.

'May I speak to you, Julie?' he called.

'Why not?' Julie asked. 'As long as you come out here. It's ever so nice.'

He glanced across the wide bed at Danielle. He looked older than his years – and terribly serious.

'Has nobody ever told you to knock before you come into a lady's room, Hugo?' Danielle asked.

'The door was open,' Hugo answered back. 'And I didn't come in until I was invited.'

'It's perfectly all right, Danielle,' Julie intervened. 'He can come and talk to me if he wishes.'

'Will you wish me to help you with your *toilette*, mademoiselle?' asked Danielle.

'No, thank you very much,' Julie replied. 'You have been very kind.'

'Thank you, mademoiselle.'

The maid picked up Julie's soiled clothes.

'Mademoiselle has only to ring if she requires anything,' she said. 'The bell-pull is here, just by the bed.'

She went out onto the landing, and closed the door behind her. Hugo crossed the carpet and joined Julie on the balcony. Julie untied the towel about her head, and shook out her hair to let it dry in the sunlight. She draped the towel over the balcony rail.

'Why don't you like Danielle?' she asked.

'She's a female pig,' said Hugo.

'That's a very strong expression to use about somebody,' said Julie.

'She's always telling me what to do,' said Hugo. 'Papa has never told her she has a right to tell me what to do. Nor has Monsieur Severin. She's only one of the maids.'

It was true Danielle had spoken to him as if she were his bossy elder sister. Nevertheless.

'*Quelle morgue*, Hugo!' she warned him. 'Nobody is ever "only one of the maids"!'

He fumbled in the pockets of his white trousers.

'Papa told me to come up and give you this,' he said, ignoring her rebuke.

He drew out a crumpled white envelope bearing on the back a small embossed crest, and on the front, the words, in copperplate handwriting, '*Mlle Armitage*'. Julie tore it open clumsily.

'My dear Julie,' it read, 'if you are not too fatigued, it would give me the greatest pleasure to be allowed to take you out to dinner tonight. I have instructed Joseph to have the car ready for seven o'clock. Alain has telephoned Chez Gringoire, where a table is reserved – the Île de la Cité is quite beautiful when there are so few visitors to Paris. Everything is prepared. Only your consent is wanted by your devoted friend, Victor de Bart-Mendel.'

'I didn't want to give it to you while she was here,' Hugo told her.

'Why ever not?' she asked.

'You know how maids talk,' said Hugo.

'You're a real snob,' Julie told him. 'Besides, she wouldn't have known what was in it.'

'Yes she would,' Hugo replied. 'She'd have guessed. I've guessed.'

'Have you?' asked Julie.

'Papa is inviting you to go out to dinner with him,' Hugo told her. 'It's probably somewhere close to the Seine, on the Île de la Cité. Papa is *crazy* about the Île de la Cité – just like a tourist.' He used the English word 'crazy'. 'He's always taking ladies there,' he added. 'Attractive ladies, that is. Are you going to accept?'

Julie laughed. 'It sounds as if I should be flattered,' she said, 'but I don't know. I've nothing to wear. And for once, I really mean it! Danielle's taken almost everything I brought with me down to the laundry-room. In any case, I haven't brought the sort of clothes for going to your Papa's kind of restaurant, I'm sure.'

'Would you like Papa to take you out to dinner?' asked Hugo. 'I mean, if you did have something to wear?'

'Oh Hugo,' she laughed again, 'I haven't had time to think. And I'm a bit too tired to make sudden decisions.'

He stared up at her.

'Wait here,' he said. 'I'll be back in a minute.'

He ran back into the room. Julie followed soon after. She went over to the dressing-table and sat down on the stool. There was a silver cigarette-box by the mother-of-pearl-handled hair brushes. It contained English Craven 'A's. She took one and lit it. After drawing on it once or twice, she put it down on the edge of the small china ash-tray. Picking up one of the brushes, she started to brush out her hair. Then she noticed in the three-fold mirror, that Hugo was still in the doorway, watching her.

'What is it?' she asked without turning round.

'Julie,' he asked, 'are you going to sleep with Papa?'

Resolutely she declined to show any surprise at the question. What was it, she wondered, that made French children of a certain class so much more wordly-wise than their English counterparts? Was it possible that the French really were less hypocritical about such things?

'I don't suppose so for a moment,' she replied. 'I haven't been asked. And I expect I shall be leaving for home very soon.'

She put down her hair brush, and picked up the cigarette. The skirts of her bathrobe had fallen apart, off her knees. She had her back to Hugo, and he couldn't see her legs. Even so, she rose from the stool for a second, and adjusted the robe over her knees.

'What makes you ask such a question?' she said.

'You are an actress, mademoiselle,' he replied.

'Oh dear, you really do have old-fashioned ideas about actresses, don't you?'

She wondered if she was being entirely honest with him.

'Papa says that all the government ministers have mistresses from the Comédie Française. Even the best of them, like Monsieur Georges Mandel. Monsieur Reynaud's mistress isn't from the Comédie Française, of course. Papa says it would be better for the Republic if she were!'

'Well, I'm not even at our Old Vic,' Julie replied. 'In fact, I haven't really done any acting in the London West End. So I don't suppose I'm qualified to become Papa's mistress!'

She began to brush out her hair again, holding her cigarette away with her other hand, to prevent the smoke getting in her eyes. She had surprised herself.

Hugo stood watching for a moment.

'Papa is very lonely,' he said. 'He's good at not showing it, but he is. He's been lonely since *Maman* died, I think.'

Julie ran the brush down the length of her hair twice, twisting her head to look at the ceiling as she did so. She straightened up again.

'Really?' she asked.

The coldness sounded in her voice. Hugo was not to be put off.

'Also,' he said, 'he is very afraid.'

'Do you know?' Julie replied, 'I find that hard to believe.'

'He is Jewish, you see,' Hugo explained. 'Well, half-Jewish, at any rate. And if the Germans are coming, he hasn't much time left. Monsieur Maurois – the writer, you know? – is going to England. And Monsieur Milhaud is going to America.'

Julie put down the brush. Hugo wasn't playing, she realised. He wasn't being precociously offensive, or even impertinent. He was pleading. She remembered articles she had read in the *Manchester Guardian* and, more particularly, a single, half-page photograph in the *Picture Post* which had shocked her deeply. It had shown a group of respectably dressed men and women, the men still wearing their business suits and stiff Homburg hats, kneeling on the ground as they scrubbed the pavement. About them, grinning between the shoulders of black-uniformed Nazi SS officers, were a crowd of equally respectably dressed men and women, and even children. The caption beneath the photograph had quoted the Reich Minister of Public Enlightenment as saying that it was an example of 'the venting of justified and understandable anger on the part of the people of Vienna at the cowardly Jews.'

'Why doesn't your papa go to England or America with Monsieur Maurois and Monsieur Milhaud?' she asked. 'Somebody like your papa must have friends everywhere.'

'Papa won't leave Paris now,' Hugo replied.

'Why not?' Julie asked, though she could guess at several reasons which made it seem impertinent or insensitive to ask.

'He's not at all religious,' said Hugo, 'but he says he won't go as long as the *Grand Rabbin* and the members of the *Consistoire Juif* remain.' He paused. 'So will you stay with him for a few days, Julie?' he asked.

Julie swivelled round on the stool to face him.

'My dear,' she said, smiling, 'I haven't been invited. I don't think I can start to make up my mind until I've been invited, can I?'

Hugo nodded. He went out, closing the door behind him. Julie noticed that her robe had fallen apart once more. She turned back to the mirror, stubbed out her cigarette, and began to brush her hair with serious concentration.

Twenty minutes later, just as she was finishing pinning it up, there came a firm knock on the door. She took a kirby-grip out of her mouth and put it in her hair, adjusted her robe again, and called, '*Entrez!*'

There was a fumbling at the door handle; it twisted around several times. Julie got up and went and opened it. Hugo was standing there. Over his arms cascaded a sleeveless gown of shimmering, pleated green silk. He passed her, and laid it out on the bed-cover.

'Papa says you are to wear this,' he told her.

He corrected himself just in time.

'No he doesn't. It was my idea. I asked him, and he said to tell you, it would give him the greatest pleasure if you were to wear it to go out to dinner with him tonight.'

Julie caught her breath. She was sure she had never seen a more beautiful garment. She felt the silk between her fingers. It was so light, it could indeed have been passed through a wedding-ring.

'I know where this came from,' she said.

'Papa bought it in the Rue Pierre Charron,' said Hugo.

'That's what I thought,' Julie told him. 'It's so beautiful I'd feel scared to wear it!'

She looked at it again with secret envy.

'It belonged to your *Maman*, I expect,' she said.

'Of course,' Hugo replied. 'But I don't suppose she ever wore it. Papa bought her hundreds of dresses. And the colour will suit you so well, Julie. Your eyes especially. And there is a seal-skin cape which goes with it, only I couldn't bring that at the same time.'

Julie looked at him across the bed.

'Hugo,' she told him, 'you're too much for me. Very well, go and tell your Papa that I shall be delighted to be taken out to dinner tonight.'

'That's good,' Hugo replied seriously.

He ran out of the room leaving the door open. It was as if Julie, by accepting the invitation, had turned him back into a little boy.

22

The blue of the sky was deepening into night when Vivian finally caught up with Colonel de Gaulle. He had driven his own car the three kilometres from Bruyères to Parfondu, where Captain Idée's 1st Independent Company was parked in the woods. The Somua tanks were already prepared for the move up to the morning's start-line; engines were turning, and the thick smell of high-octane exhaust mingled with the fresh night-smell of the grass under the trees. Camouflage nets were being rolled back; armourers were filing between the thick, black tree-trunks, carrying ammunition boxes and shells on heavy stretchers. Pioneers were pouring cans of white disinfectant into latrine pits before filling them with earth.

Vivian went on foot down the grit path through the Company's lines until he saw Idée's command-tank parked between two large oaks. A large-scale map had been draped over the armoured shield of the rear track. Vivian recognised Captain Idée, three of his troop commanders, and the senior sergeant-major of the Independent Company grouped around it in the lamp-light, and, towering over the others, the beak-nosed figure of de Gaulle. Even in the semi-darkness under the trees, Vivian thought he could detect the fixed expression of disdain on his face. For one moment, he felt an inclination to turn about and return to divisional headquarters.

The afternoon peace at Bruyères had been shattered by the roar of motorcycles and two-chord fanfares from a limousine's double klaxon. Four motorcycle outriders and a huge black Cadillac with white-painted tyres had swept into the yard of the manor farm. The horns were mounted, carousel-like, on the roof above the windscreen. As their noise expired like the drone of a subsiding bagpipe, a corporal in khaki and a horizon-blue forage cap, and with dazzlingly white cross-belts, had jumped from the seat beside the driver and opened one of the rear doors. A young lieutenant in horizon-blue, and glassily polished boots, his left shoulder a tassled shower of silver lanyard, had climbed out, put his braided képi on his head, and run across to the adjutant's office by the Operations Room. A few moments later, orderlies, in various states of undress, had doubled off in every direction, searching for the Divisional Commander. The *aide-de-camp* in his parade-ground uniform had returned to the car, and assisted its chief passenger to dismount. Those who had been watching instantly recognised the C.-in-C., North East Front, General Alphonse Georges. Though less magnificent in appearance than his *aide*, or his limousine – he was in workaday khaki – he had presented an impressive figure. Almost as tall as de Gaulle, he was broad in proportion, and his face had the look of one accustomed to exercising authority. But the greatcoat draped about his shoulders despite the heat of early summer, the woollen glove encasing one hand, and the ill-concealed limp, had reminded the spectators of the wounds General Georges had sustained when, six years before, in Marseilles, he had thrown himself between King Alexander of Yugoslavia and the king's assassins.

General Georges had stood out in the centre of the yard until Colonel de Gaulle had appeared. He had ignored de Gaulle's salute. Instead he had warmly embraced him.

'My boy,' he had said, loud enough for those who had been watching from the windows to have heard him, 'at last the hopes of France are pinned on you. I am sure you will bear so great an honour worthily.'

One or two of the divisional officers who had been watching the scene had been entranced by the spectacle of their commander attempting to look humble. Others had clearly been moved.

An hour later, after the Cadillac had swept General Georges back in the direction of his headquarters at La Ferté, de Gaulle had summoned his commanders. They were to prepare for immediate offensive action to allow General Touchon time to regroup his Sixth Army for the defence of Reims, and therefore of Paris. They were to move up to their start-lines under cover of darkness, and to move forward at first light to attack the flank of the German advance. The first aim of the attack would be the recovery of the road junction at Montcornet. Idée's 1st Independent Company of Somuas was to lead the thrust, supported by the 2nd Independent Company of de Bernac, since it was believed that the German Panzers had no armour to match the Somua tanks. The two battalions of heavy Char B (bis) tanks were to form the weight of the strike, with the three battalions of obsolescent Renault D 2's in reserve, to act as mopping-up components in conjunction with the 7th Chasseurs who had been compelled to abandon most of their half-tracks on the journey to Bruyères, and had turned up the previous night in commandeered civilian buses.

After the briefing de Bernac, who knew that Vivian would not wish to be left in the rear with the non-combatants, had invited him to ride with him in his command vehicle. Vivian had readily accepted. He had decided, however, that he should maintain the old tradition of English cavalry regiments, by requesting permission from the general officer commanding that he might ride with a regiment not his own against the enemy. It was for this reason he had followed de Gaulle to Parfondu. As he made his way down the grit path towards Captain Idée's command tank, he was seized with a feeling of trepidation. Partly it was the fear of disturbing de Gaulle at such a time with what was little more than a frivolous request; partly it was the nervousness which affects all soldiers on the eve of battle. The preparation in the woods all around him, served to remind him that, though he had been a tank-man throughout his active service with the Colours, he had never been engaged in a major tank action. In fact, he doubted whether the denizens of the War House in Whitehall had ever seriously supposed that such a form of military action could occur. The thought of it clenched his stomach with excitement. He would have liked to have made some mark, some positive contribution to the event. As he approached de Gaulle, stepping into the lamp-light and saluting, he altered his request.

'Colonel,' he began.

De Gaulle turned to regard him from under almost gothically arched eyebrows.

'What?' he demanded rudely. 'What do you want?'

He looked entirely ridiculous, Vivian decided angrily, with his absurd black leather tank-crewman's helmet strapped under his chin, framing his creased face that was twenty years older than those standing similarly clad in the lamplight about him. And with the usual damp, half-smoked cigarette dangling from his lip.

'Colonel,' Vivian repeated, 'with your permission, I shall drive myself over to Chauny tonight, to see if I can speak, myself, to Air Vice Marshal Playfair. I shall try to impress upon him the importance of tomorrow's action. I shall ask him if it is at all possible for A.A.S.F. to provide this division with air support tomorrow at dawn. I can't hold out any great hopes, Colonel, but I believe it's worth the attempt.'

De Gaulle picked the cigarette stub from his lower lip.

'Thank you,' he replied. 'I'm sure that we can trust you to do all that is in your power.'

He was quite serious. Vivian felt a sort of loyalty to the man which he could not have explained, particularly since de Gaulle immediately stuck his cigarette back onto his lip, and turned his back on him dismissively.

He returned between the trees to his car. He would have to hurry on his newly-decided mission. De Bernac would be moving the 2nd Independent Company up to his start-line at Coucy-les-Eppés, some ten or eleven kilometres to the east of Bruyères, and Vivian would have to try to catch up with him before dawn.

The drive towards Chauny was an easy one. For thirty kilometres the road was deserted. Even the villages through which he passed were dark, abandoned by their inhabitants. The narrow strips of light from his car's headlamps caught the hedgerows and the litter of discarded suitcases, baskets, broken handcarts, and upturned, overloaded prams, which lay like some straggling rubbish tip in the ditches. It was desolate enough, he thought, for him to have been driving on the moon.

He saw no sign of life until he reached the ancient stone bridge across the Oise, two kilometres from Chauny. He was driving up to it, when a steel-helmeted RAF police-corporal in a sleeveless, cracked leather jacket signalled him down. An RAF police-sergeant, similarly dressed, tapped a heavy torch against the driving-seat window. Vivian wound it down as the sergeant flashed his torch at the dashboard.

'Bit out of your way, aren't you, sir?' he asked. 'Could've shot you to pieces, you know. We're expecting Jerry to come up the way you've come, any moment.'

Over the man's shoulder, Vivian could see a sandbagged emplacement covering the approach to the bridge. Several steel-helmeted heads were peering over the top. The squat barrel of a Vickers medium machine-gun was trained up the road.

'Trouble you for your papers, sir?' asked the sergeant. 'Don't suppose you're a fifth columnist, but we can't be too careful, eh?'

Vivian reached into his breast pocket and pulled out his documents. The sergeant switched his torch onto them.

'That's the ticket, sir,' he said in gentle approval. He folded the papers and handed them back. 'Destination, sir?' he asked. 'If you don't mind.'

'Air Vice Marshal Playfair's HQ,' Vivian replied, slipping his papers back in his pocket. 'And if *you* don't mind, sergeant, I'm in a bit of a hurry.'

'Expect you are, sir, if you've come down that road,' said the sergeant. 'With your permission, where *have* you come from?'

'I'm attached to 4th Armoured Division, Laon,' Vivian replied. 'And I wish to reach HQ Advanced Air Strike Force as quickly as possible.'

'What is it, sar'nt?' asked an upper-class voice, as if it were inquiring as to the identity of some zoological species.

An extraordinarily young major of Sappers appeared in the light of the RAF Sergeant's torch. He was wearing full webbing equipment, with his service Colt revolver on his hip.

'I'm trying to get across this bridge, Major,' Vivian told him through the open window. The night air was quite chill, despite the heat of the previous day. 'I've a message for Air Vice Marshal Playfair from the general officer commanding 4th Armoured Division.'

'I'm afraid you're too late, old boy,' said the major of Sappers.

There was a note of respect in his voice, as if he were speaking to his housemaster. He had seen his empty sleeve and his Military Cross and had put the two together.

'Too late for what?' Vivian asked.

'Air Vice Marshal Playfair left Chauny this morning.'

'Who's in charge?' asked Vivian.

'Advanced Air Strike Force HQ has been moved south of the Marne somewhere,' the major of Sappers replied. 'Actually, we've heard unofficially that most of the fighter component is being withdrawn to Kent. There's a Wing-Commander Connell at Chauny, but he's only in charge of the rear party. I mean, when last reported, Jerry was only fifteen miles from here, you know. We're expecting him any minute. Our orders are to hold him off until the rear party have finished destroying the fuel and ammo dumps. Then we're blowing the bridge here, and scarpering off, quick as we can. So, Major, if you're going to cross, you can cross; but we can't let you back again. Sorry.'

One became accustomed to bad news in the end. Nevertheless, Vivian found himself asking, 'Do you really know how far west Jerry's got?'

The major shrugged. 'Not precisely, old chap,' he replied, 'but his tanks were crossing the river up at La Fère at tea-time this afternoon. And that's less than twenty miles away. . . . Tell you what. If you want to get back to your lot at Laon, I'd turn around pretty sharpish, and beetle off before Jerry cuts across the road behind you.'

Vivian sighed.

'Thank you, Major,' he said.

'Not at all, old chap,' the major of Sappers replied. 'Only sorry you found your journey wasn't really necessary.'

Vivian backed the car up against the machine-gun emplacement, and turned. He swung back onto the road, then stopped and stuck his head through the window. The major of Sappers and the RAF police-sergeant had been joined by the stooping, bespectacled, shabby-looking figure of a French army interpreter. Standing at the roadside he was the very picture of Captain Dreyfus after having had his regimentals ripped from him, and his sword broken.

'Good luck!' Vivian shouted. '*Bonne chance!*' he added, for the benefit of the French army interpreter.

The interpreter smiled disconsolately into the headlamps.

'Thanks,' called the major of Sappers. 'We're going to need it.' He paused. As Vivian was about to wind up the window, he called, 'I don't know what Jerry means to throw at us, but that's all we've been given to throw at him.' He pointed up at the Vickers mounted behind the sandbags.

'How old is it?' Vivian called back.

'1925 model?' the major of Sappers suggested.

'Bloody good year for Vickers machine-guns, 1925,' Vivian called back.

He waved and drove off. As the desolate road with its sad relics littering its verges stretched before him, he longed to be with de Bernac's company, and to sense once again the quickening excitement of preparing for action.

23

Joseph dropped de Bart-Mendel and Julie at the end of the Pont d'Arcole, so that they could walk across the bridge to the Île de la Cité. Despite the attempts which were being made by the authorities to enforce a blackout over Paris, there had been enough light shining in the streets for de Bart-Mendel to be able to point out to Julie the sights, as they had driven down the Champs-Elysées and the Rue de Rivoli. Accustomed as she had been to a winter of London blackout, Julie had been astonished at the amount of light which had been shown, and the traffic on the main thoroughfares. As they crossed the Pont d'Arcole, however, the Cité reared up before them black and forbidding. The front of the Hôtel Dieu, and the steep terraces behind the Quai aux Fleurs with the towers and the single, needle spire of Notre Dame hanging against the sky, was a huge, black cliff face above the star-reflecting blackness of the river. On the centre of the bridge, a chilly breeze off the water caused Julie to shudder, reminding her of how tired she was. She clutched her seal-skin cape about her arms and shoulders. The skirt of her gown was fractionally too long, and she held it with one gloved hand above her ankles. The silk was gorgeous to wear, and the feel of it against her body quite luxurious, but it was so fine, she was afraid that it would slip through her fingers where she was holding it up.

De Bart-Mendel held her arm.

'There aren't many tourists who could say they've seen Notre Dame looking like that,' he told her.

There were goosepimples standing on her arms under her cape, and inside the sleeves of her evening gloves. There was no doubt the spectacle was awe-inspiring. The Cité must have looked like this after curfew during the *ancien régime*, when the gates had been locked. A sense of loneliness entered into her with the damp chill from the Seine.

As they reached the Rue Colombe, still holding her arm, the Baron guided her off the downward flight of steps and onto a second flight of steps between a pair of stone posts. In the blackness, the vast buttresses of Notre Dame reared above the cramped medieval roof-tops, as if threatening to cascade down over them like the culmination of a tidal wave. They reached the entrance to Chez

Gringoire, a square, carved stone doorway with a heavy, nail-studded door.

'Not only are we in the oldest part of Paris,' de Bart-Mendel told her, 'but also the safest from bombardment. The restaurant is a cellar built into the living rock of the Île de la Cité. I don't suppose even a direct hit from a bomb would do much damage.'

He opened the door for her. The scented warmth of wine and cooking spilled around her. The heavy curtain in front of them was pulled aside by a squat, dark ringletted head waiter. Behind him, the restaurant opened up in the shape of a two-tiered horseshoe. In the centre stood a small fountain surrounded by a circular floor of coloured glass tiles lit from below. On the walls behind both tiers of seats and tables, candles burned in gilt sconces, glowing against the red velvet flock. Prosperous diners sat at the tables, many of them in uniform. Conversation was loud and cheerful; even the waiters gliding between the tables were smiling. It was as if there were neither darkness nor the threat of invasion beyond the walls. The head waiter's face had broken into a welcoming smile.

'*Ça va, Lucien?*' de Bart-Mendel asked.

'Why, Monsieur le Baron!' the head waiter exclaimed. 'We had no idea you had returned to Paris!'

A girl in a white lace pinafore appeared from the shadows behind a turkish screen, and took from de Bart-Mendel his coat, hat and gloves. She glanced at Julie.

'I'll keep my cape for the moment,' Julie told de Bart-Mendel.

It was the very slightest declaration of independence. De Bart-Mendel nodded to the girl, and she withdrew. As Julie went with him, following the head waiter, she wondered whether retaining the cape had not been a clumsy gesture. None of the other women glittering in the flickering light of the candles had their arms and shoulders covered, nor were there any signs of furs draped over the backs of chairs or seats.

'*Bonsoir, Victor!*'

They were crossing the glass tiled floor by the fountain, passing a table on the edge of the coloured light. A portly, greyhaired man, with his elegant, middle-aged wife and his young daughter, had just completed his entrée. As the waiter removed the dishes, he had pulled the napkin from his throat, and had lit a cigar. Wife and daughter would have to wait for their dessert until he had finished smoking.

'*Ça va, mon vieux?*' asked de Bart-Mendel as he shook the portly gentleman's hand.

The wife offered Julie a sad, enquiring smile. The daughter was looking around her in a bored, listless fashion. De Bart-Mendel introduced Julie as an English friend on her first visit to Paris. The couple presented all the assurance of wealth. Julie felt certain that she must be giving the appearance of a newly-acquired kept woman, and that she was being assessed as such.

'So you have decided to keep the family in Paris?' de Bart-Mendel remarked.

'*Pourquoi pas, Victor?*' the gentleman inquired with an expansive gesture.

'And Nicolette here?' asked de Bart-Mendel.

The face of the daughter was transformed as soon as her name was mentioned. She could not have been more than fourteen years old, yet she had the sort of beauty which would never know the stodgy awkwardness of mid-adolescence.

'Nikki is returning to school at Maison Laffitte, tomorrow afternoon,' the child's father replied. 'While things were looking bad, naturally Martine and I preferred to have her at home with us. But now – well, she's so bored – misses her friends.' He smiled up at Julie. 'You know how it is with young girls, mademoiselle.'

Julie smiled back. She found the man quite odious. The head waiter stood by, patiently waiting for the conversation to end. The girl started to look about her once again.

'And Madame Clerand is so good with her,' said the mother. 'She is so much better with her than I am. I don't have the patience!'

De Bart-Mendel led Julie on to a plush, semi-circular settee round a small table. The back of the settee was higher than their heads, so that, while they could watch the rise and fall of the fountain, and the ever-changing patterns of the lights in the water, they remained almost entirely unobserved by the other guests. As they were drinking their aperitifs, de Bart-Mendel told her, 'You surprised me, Julie.'

'How?' she asked.

'You were shy. I did not expect you to be shy.'

She thought of denying it, but only for a moment.

'Yes,' she said. Then she added, 'They are very wealthy people.'

'Your family is not poor, I think,' de Bart-Mendel told her.

'No,' she agreed, 'but they aren't so very rich either. I mean, they did have to make sacrifices to send me away to school.'

De Bart-Mendel's friends had reminded her of the rich elderly people who had filled the small residential hotels at home after the declaration of war – the Matterdale Arms and the Lowther Arms – and how the women in particular made the lounges horrid with their endless complaints and self-pitying. Her father had once remarked after he had taken her for a drink at the Lowther Arms, 'Mustn't tell your mother, darling, but there are times when one feels old Adolf isn't all that wrong about "the chosen race", eh?'

Julie said, 'I found them embarrassing. I suppose I shouldn't say so, because they're your friends. But I did.'

'I find them embarrassing too,' he replied.

'Hugo says that you're not going to leave Paris either,' she remarked.

'Not for the moment, at any rate,' he replied. 'I have matters of business to attend to.' He looked directly into her face. 'I hope you will stay here for a few days,' he said. 'As my guest.'

'I don't know,' she replied. 'I ought to go back as soon as possible.'

A postcard might do, she thought; sent to Ambrose by first post tomorrow. A phone call might prove too awkward.

'I enjoy your company very much,' said de Bart-Mendel, still looking at her intently. 'I've enjoyed it ever since you came out of the trees with the little boy – and with twigs in your hair.'

Had he forgotten the child's name so soon, she wondered. Or would mention of his name dilute the singleminded attention he was paying to her.

'And I have to tell you that the candlelight suits you very well.'

'You mean it suits my dress,' she said. 'The dress I'm wearing,' she corrected herself.

'And Hugo was perfectly right,' he persisted. 'You suit the dress.'

'I think I ought to tell you something,' she replied. 'I'm not very good at accepting compliments.'

'But you are an actress,' he said.

'Perhaps that's why I think pretence should be confined to the stage,' she answered.

A waiter brought the drinks to the table. The head waiter waited in the background to take the order, pad concealed in the palm of his hand, silver pencil poised.

'I did not expect to find you so busy tonight, Lucien,' de Bart-Mendel called to him.

'It is the news, Monsieur le Baron,' the little man replied. 'People feel the need to celebrate good news after so much anxiety. I'm not ashamed to admit to Monsieur le Baron that Chef and I have shared a bottle, this evening.'

'What is this news?' de Bart-Mendel asked.

'Monsieur returned to Paris only this afternoon, of course,' the man said, 'so he has not had the opportunity. . . . I myself was told by Monsieur Delerue – Monsieur Marc Delerue. He came straight over here from the Rue St Dominique.'

He rested his hands on the edge of the table. Candlelight flickered on the shining folds of his jaws.

'The German advance has been checked, monsieur,' he said. 'Our armies between the Serre and Reims have proved too strong for them. The threat to Paris is over, Monsieur Delerue told me so himself. The Germans have been forced to turn north-east, towards the coast. There, they will be caught between our armies on the Somme, and the Belgians and the English to the north of them. They have fallen into our trap, monsieur. Victory is assured.'

There was a burst of laughter from beyond the back of Julie's seat. The head waiter leaned further over the table. Julie could smell the wine on his breath.

'And something else, monsieur,' he said in a low voice. He glanced over his shoulder to ensure that there was no enemy within earshot. 'I have been informed by somebody who moves in the highest circles, that Monsieur Churchill has promised that the Royal Air Force will place every one of its fighter-planes to defend Paris from attack by German bombers.'

As he went away past the fountain, Julie asked, 'Do you believe him?'

'Why not?' de Bart-Mendel asked. 'Head waiters have always been regarded as the best informed men in Paris. It was the head waiter at Maxim's who told my father about the death of President Faure – how the late President was found in the Elysée, in the Presidential Office after lunch, lying on top of his mistress, in a state of *rigor mortis*.'

Julie giggled into her aperitif.

'I don't believe it,' she said.

'Neither did my papa,' said de Bart-Mendel, 'but it didn't make it any the less true.'

After they had finished their meal, de Bart-Mendel took Julie out into the cold darkness, to walk across the Parvis under the great cliff-face of the west front of Notre Dame. Looking up at its shape against the starlight, Julie could make out the statues of the Virgin and Child with their supporting angels, against the huge halo of the Rose Window. Julie shuddered, though it had been she who suggested the walk in the fresh air before they should return to Joseph and the car, waiting for them on the Quai de Gesvres.

'It was designed to represent Paradise,' de Bart-Mendel told her. 'Cherubim and Seraphim, Angels and Archangels, supporting Christ the King enthroned in judgement. Religious plays were put on here, on the Parvis, before the front was completed. The doors of the cathedral were designed to represent the doors of Heaven. And the whole thing was designed to be the greatest stage-set in the world!'

'And you love it,' said Julie.

'And I love it,' he confirmed.

He took off his overcoat. As she peered at the statues in the darkness which supported the arches, she felt him draping the coat round her shoulders.

'You'll catch cold,' she protested.

'I've got more clothes on than you,' he told her. 'And I was very warm in there.'

She drew the coat about her.

They walked on across the vast, deserted pavement, and stood looking down at the black waters of the Seine, under the great statue of Charlemagne.

'I suppose I must admit to preferring the river without the *bâteaux-mouches*,' he said.

He put his arm round her, feeling in the pocket of his coat, and drawing out his cigarette case. Julie let herself rest on his arm for a moment; she would not have done so had she not felt slightly tipsy. As she took a cigarette from him and let him light it for her, she said.

'Hugo told me, you were afraid. Are you afraid?'

'Hugo seems to have taken you remarkably into his confidence. Did he suggest why I should be afraid?'

'Because of being Jewish,' she said. 'I'm sorry. I shouldn't have told you.'

She was about to ask him not to blame the boy, when he said, 'I suppose that at some point in his life, every Jew asks himself whether it is the turn of his generation to face the pogrom. I am too young to remember the riots over *l'Affaire Dreyfus*, but I was told all about the Black Hundreds in Russia and Poland. As a child, I lay awake many times, thinking about such things – wondering whether I could possibly be brave if such terrible things happened to me. Then I lay terrified at the thought of being killed – being burned or whipped to death by Cossacks. Now, I am not afraid of death itself, but of other things. The answer is yes, I am afraid. Very afraid.'

'You don't show it at all,' Julie told him. 'Nobody would ever guess it – except Hugo.'

'It is a question of style,' he said.

'Why don't you go with Hugo to London or New York?' asked Julie.

'That too is a question of style. Everybody who knows me thinks of me as Parisian.'

'Style doesn't mean a thing,' said Julie. 'It's empty. Just like what Falstaff says about honour – you know? In Shakespeare.'

'You are quite wrong, Julie,' replied de Bart-Mendel. 'So was Falstaff. Style – honour – is what people see of you. It's what makes a great leader, a great commander. And a great actor too. Style can be a service one can render to other people. In my case, perhaps it's the only one.'

'So Hugo is right when he says you're going to stay here because you won't desert the other Jewish people in Paris – those who can't leave?' asked Julie.

'Sons often like to make their fathers out to be heroes,' de Bart-Mendel replied.

209

'But you aren't really Jewish at all,' Julie pressed on, 'and Hugo's only a quarter Jewish.'

'Perhaps Hitler has made me Jewish,' he said. 'I bear a Jewish name, proudly, I hope. Do you know about Mendelssohn? Mendelssohn was a Christian – a second-generation Christian. He was wholly German in education, culture, and in his habits of life. He was a convinced, practising Christian. In order to save him from the petty humiliations which he might have had to suffer on account of his Jewish name, his father urged him to take the name of his gentile godfather – the name of Bartholdy. Mendelssohn refused. It was not merely out of respect for his father's name, but because he did not believe that anybody could be wholly true to himself while denying his own name.'

'Women do it all the time,' said Julie, 'when they marry.'

'Or his race,' added de Bart-Mendel.

'Hugo told me that I ought to stay with you for a few days,' said Julie.

'And why did my son tell you that?' asked de Bart-Mendel.

'I've never had a holiday in Paris,' Julie went on. 'We were going to have one, from school. Only there was a lot of trouble apparently; rioting, shooting, that sort of thing. There was supposed to have been fighting in the Place de la Concorde.'

'1934?' asked de Bart-Mendel.

'That's right. I was just fifteen, I remember.'

'The Fascists – the Croix de Feu, the Action Française, Maurras's lot – tried to storm the National Assembly buildings,' said de Bart-Mendel.

'I don't know about that,' said Julie. 'I know we had to go to Cornwall instead, and the weather was dreadful. I'd like a holiday in Paris, I think. Very much!'

She was not at all sure how he would reply. Despite the wine she had drunk, she felt nervous.

She felt his hands resting on her shoulders, through his coat. He turned her to him.

She knew that he was about to kiss her. She found him sexually attractive. He would be a good lover, she had no doubt of it. But there was also the child who lay awake, terrified of the coming pogrom – so terrified that his young son had noticed it.

He kissed beautifully. They walked back, over the Pont d'Arcole to the car. As Joseph held the car-door open for her, she gave him a warm smile. She let de Bart-Mendel hold her hand as they drove back to the Avenue de Wagram. Poor old Ambrose, she thought. And her parents. And the ENSA company – dear Elaine, Vic Walters, and the others. For the time being, they would have to wait. For the coming of the darkness, perhaps. This was a different planet, with different obligations.

He came to her room, that night, after she was in bed. Sometime, in the darkness, with the distanced noise of the traffic circling the Étoile penetrating through the open window, he raised himself, resting on his elbow.

'Hello,' she said, to tell him she was awake.

'I have a question to ask, Julie,' he said.

He sounded quite formal.

'What?' she asked.

'Hugo didn't ask you to sleep with me, did he?'

'No, of course not,' Julie replied.

'Thank God for that,' said de Bart-Mendel.

'Not precisely, that is,' Julie was already saying, too late to check herself. 'What he did ask was, was I going to sleep with you?'

'Heavens,' exclaimed de Bart-Mendel.

He lay back on the pillows.

'What did you say to that?' he asked.

'I told him the truth,' Julie replied. 'I said, I hadn't been asked.'

He lay silent, but she knew that he was staring up at the ceiling. She said, 'Hugo loves you very much.'

'I know.'

'You must see that he is safe, if the worst should happen,' she said.

She sounded very matter-of-fact.

'Yes, but you can't imagine what a temptation it is to keep him with me to the very end.'

'Perhaps there won't be a very end,' she said. 'Not that sort of an end, at any rate.'

He reached out for her, and she moved up against him.

'Perhaps there won't,' he whispered.

He raised his head again, bent over, and kissed her to end the conversation.

24

In the small hours of the morning of 17 May 1940, the night before battle, Charles de Gaulle knelt in prayer. No doubt he prayed as, a few miles distant and five hundred years earlier, a great English captain had prayed – that the God of Battle might steel his soldiers' hearts. Unlike Shakespeare's Henry V, however, he saw no need to beg the Almighty to 'remember not the days' when he had offended against the Lord. It would have been irrelevant; for he knew that God intended him as a man of power, to be matched against events. He prayed only that he should prove worthy of the day which was presented to him. Nor did he suffer any illusion that God intended to deliver the enemy into his hand. God had never allowed his men of power the certainty of physical victory; often the victory was the moral one of martyrdom. He could be certain only of his own rectitude. With that he had to be content.

After his orderly had brought him coffee, and he had smoked the first cigarette of the day – the only cigarette which he was ever aware of smoking – he joined his staff in the yard. They exchanged few words as they walked through the soaking grass, through the hanging damp under the trees, to his command truck. He was perfectly aware of the inadequacies of his command: of the disparate quality of the various components which had been brought together, some untrained in the use of their vehicles and weapons, many already disheartened by defeat; of the absence of any form of radio or telephone communication either between the individual units which comprised the division, or between himself and the High Command, and above all of the absence of air-cover. For all that, there was the possibility that the Germans might be so taken by surprise that the strike would succeed, at least to the extent of obtaining lodgement in Montcornet, thus cutting the extended supply line of Guderian's Panzer Corps, and putting heart into the incompetent and defeatist 'white-breeches' who inhabited the gloomy châteaux of Vincennes and La Ferté. As he mounted the step of his command truck, he glanced at his watch. It was 0610 hours. There were precisely five minutes to go. He pointed his long, eager spaniel-nose upwards, smelling the damp air. Above him, the sun was beginning to filter through the morning fog, and already there were traces of blue in the drifting grey. He made the sign of the cross deliberately – forehead to chest, shoulder to shoulder.

'Holy Mary, pray for us now, and in the hour of our death,' he said silently. 'St Barbara, patroness of gunners, help us.'

A short distance from the village of Coucy-les-Eppés, Captain Idée climbed into the turret of his Somua. He rolled the cuff of his leather glove from off his wrist, and kissed the bracelet medallion of St Thérèse of Lisieux which he had worn ever since his confirmation, sixteen years before. He raised his hand, and waved it, giving the fourteen tanks under his command the signal to advance.

Perched beside de Bernac, on the turret of the command tank of the 2nd Independant Company, Vivian was reminded of the words of Robert E. Lee at Chancellorsville: that it was as well that God made war so terrible lest it should seem beautiful. It was not until that morning, as the curtains of mist rose from the tanks which had been grinding and clattering on either side of them, that he understood what the old Confederate commander had meant. A host of

212

cumbersome armoured vehicles was swarming forward across the open fields like ancient chivalry, and with the same relentless, inexorable purpose, ever increasing in numbers as more appeared from behind the undulations of low hills and out of copses, swaying, screeching, hurling up clumps of damp turf, gathering speed and power with every yard they moved. And with the increase in speed came the stomach-gripping tension of excitement.

In front of him, the two-man crew sat sweltering in the oil-reeking interior, jarring in the noise and vibration of the motors. Though the Somua was the most modern tank in the world, Vivian found the situation as cramped as it had ever been in the old Vickers Medium Mark I; he could have done with both his arms to prevent his banging his shoulder against the edges of armour plating.

They had been heading due north from Coucy-les-Eppés. As they mounted the main Laon-Montcornet road, they swivelled east. A single kilometre further on, and they encountered the enemy for the first time. A motorcycle battalion of the 1st Panzers was emerging out of Gizy. It was taken completely by surprise. As de Bernac led his sixteen tanks after Idée's advance guard of fourteen down the main street, the scene was one of carnage. Field-grey, steel-helmeted motorcycle infantry hung dead and bleeding over their handlebars, or were twisted, half-fallen from their sidecars. An armoured car marked with the Panzer Balkan Cross was smashed into the wall of a cottage. It had been blown by a Somua's 47 mm gun into a weird, sculpted tangle of grey metal. De Bernac's vehicle plunged forward through the pool of burning petrol which had flooded from its engine.

As they came through the smoke at the far end of the village, the two independent companies collided into a column of German motorised infantry. Many of the German soldiers, as they jumped down from their lorries, ran in amongst the French tanks, their hands clasped over their helmets in a gesture of surrender. They were cut down by machine-gun fire, and were crushed under the tracks of the Somuas, which advanced headlong, thrusting and smashing the wreckage of the German lorries into the sides of the road.

A few miles further on, just as they had passed through Chivres-en-Laonnais, they ran into another Panzer infantry battalion. It had fallen out, and was resting in the grass verges along the roadside dikes. As the long column of tanks appeared, the Germans spread across the open fields, attempting to form defensive positions round their machine-guns. They were cut down in swathes as the tanks traversed their turrets, so that the young crops were stippled with their bodies. From the tiny hamlet of Machicourt, a squadron of armoured cars – SdKfz 231's – splayed out in an attempt to rescue the survivors of the infantry battalion. The 47 mm fire from the turrets of the Somuas ripped through their armour, tearing their turrets upwards like the lids of meat-tins. Two of the German armoured cars were slewed across the road to form a barricade. One of them was pushed, burning, aside; the other, trapped against the butt of a broken telegraph-pole, was crushed under the Somua's tracks.

They were approaching another village. De Bernac tapped Vivian on the shoulder, and thrust the folded map in front of him, pointing with grease-blackened fingers. Bucy-les-Pierrepont, Vivian read. He had been through the village on a number of occasions, but the circumstances of the morning had altered it entirely. De Bernac patted his shoulder again, and pointed downwards. Vivian slipped under the hatch, and de Bernac scrambled in after him, closing the cupola-lid after him. The driver glanced back; his face under its mask of oil split into a grin. He raised his hand in its tattered glove in salute. The noise within the tank clamped over Vivian's ears, but through it, he could hear the muffled crump of guns. Suddenly the whole vehicle shuddered and jarred. The vibration seemed to stretch his skull as though his head would burst. He realised the armour immediately above his head had sustained a direct hit. De Bernac was traversing the turret. Red hot shell-cases were spilling past Vivian's sleeve, and clattering into the container on the turret's central column. The tank lurched upwards then subsided. Through his periscope, Vivian saw that they were plunging through yard walls, crossing a back garden, smashing fences and wooden sheds into splinters. On their flank, another Somua smashed through the side of a house. The wall swayed before collapsing, showering the tank with all the pathetic debris of a home. As they broke out onto the main street, it was obvious that Captain Idée's Company was ahead of them. Two German Mark III tanks were blazing in the little square. One of them exploded as they roared past, belching flame from under the turret, and blasting off the hatch-lids. Further on, wrecked German vehicles littered the length of the street, and bodies oozed blood into the dust and rubble of the pavements.

Once out in the open fields again, de Bernac reached up and pushed back the turret-hatch. Vivian was running with sweat; his shirt and trousers were drenched and clinging to his body, and sweat was standing on the stump of his arm. He had felt hardly able to breathe for the stench of oil and cordite. It had been so long since he had been inside an armoured vehicle under these conditions; one forgot what it was like. Now, fresh air flooded through the reek of the tank, and bright light filtered through the smoke. De Bernac had climbed out. He reached down to help Vivian.

Two men came running down a cart-track across the field toward the stationary tank. They were in grease-stained khaki overalls, and carried French tank-crew leather helmets. All about them, tanks were parked.

'Captain de Bernac?' one of the men called up.

He was wearing the tabs of a full lieutenant.

'Yes?' de Bernac replied.

'Captain Idée's compliments, Captain,' said the lieutenant. 'He has instructed me to inform you that the enemy is defending the approaches to Montcornet in strength. They have Mark IV's positioned in Lislet, to the north-east, and several batteries of 88's positioned on the high ground. Captain Idée suggests that both Independent Companies should halt to allow 46 Battalion to approach and lay down a barrage.'

'Very well, Lieutenant,' replied de Bernac. 'You may report back to Captain Idée, thank him from me, and tell him I am complying with his suggestion.'

The lieutenant clicked his heels, and, with his companion, ran back up the cart-track.

Around de Bernac's vehicle, tank-crews emerged from their hatches, lit cigarettes, drank from their canteens, and shouted delightedly to their comrades across the stubbled grass. Some dropped down to the ground or stood on the edge of their tank-chassis, pissing onto the rutted earth.

Vivian and de Bernac sat together on the lid of the turret. De Bernac gazed up into the peaceful sky.

'No sign of a Stuka,' he said. 'Perhaps they are all too busy further up the line.'

Or perhaps, thought Vivian, the attack had so taken the enemy by surprise that they hadn't had time to arrange an air strike yet. But he did not wish to spoil de Bernac's evident satisfaction with the morning's progress. As if to confirm this attitude, de Bernac turned to him.

'Do you know something, old friend?' he asked. 'It is terrible to say it, but I truly believe that I have never been so happy as I am now.'

They waited in the open for about twenty minutes before the huge Char B's of 46 Battalion came enfilading through the ranks of Somuas, their giant tow-chains looped and clattering against their armoured flanks, the ground shuddering under the weight of their thirty-two tons. Twenty-two of them passed before de Bernac signalled to his men to remount and to follow them. The outskirts of Montcornet lay before them, the grey buildings around the crucial road junction stringing along the low, upward slope against the near horizon. And before it, like a forlorn hope, the cluster of dwellings which comprised the village of Lislet. From the crest of the slope came flashes of gunfire. Black and grey clouds burst in showers of earth in front of the advancing tanks. Through the smoke drifting across the meadow, French stretcher-bearers came running with their burdens, the wounded on the stretchers still clutching their leather helmets. De

Bernac, who was still sitting on the open cupola-lid, gave the signal for his tanks to halt again. Above the grinding of motors, Vivian could hear the wail of enemy shells. One of them exploded immediately in front of them, hurling tufts of earth and fragments of stone at them. De Bernac waited for the smoke to drift away. He surveyed the landscape with his field-glasses. He turned to Vivian, and pointed.

'They've got 88's up there,' he said. 'But they can't quite manage the range.'

The giant Char B's were still trundling forward, contemptuous of the fire both from the enemy tanks in Lislet, and the 88's up in Montcornet itself. They manoeuvred into a wide crescent, halted, and brought their fixed 75's to bear on the village. As the smoke began to pile up, Vivian could see the houses and cottages disintegrating into rubble. De Bernac gave the signal to advance, and the Somuas moved forward through the rank of Char B's.

1st Independent Company moved into Lislet first. As 2nd Independent Company followed, there was evidence that Captain Idée's advance had been opposed. One Somua, bearing the marking of 1st Independent Company, had lost a track on the outskirts of the village. It had swivelled round in its own length and been abandoned by its crew. One man was lying face downwards on the ground not five yards from it. Another Somua had been stopped amid the rubble in the very entrance to the village. A ribbon of flame was still flickering along the armour shield of the chassis; the bodies of two of the crew, who had attempted to escape out of the cupola-hatch, were sprawled across the rear of the chassis, their heads scored and blackened like over-roasted meat.

Roaring and clattering through the wreckage, de Bernac's Somua came to a halt in the centre of the village. Here were unmistakable tokens of a French victory. One of the much-feared German Mark IV tanks had crashed into the front of a small café. Its turret had been blown clean off, and lay amidst the debris on the road, curiously intact like the top of a boiled egg sheared off with a knife. A few yards further off, leaning against the stump of a tree, was the turret-ring, a hoop of thick steel plate. On the main street, on the further side of the village where the smoke and dust was just settling, members of 1st Independent Company, revolvers in hand, were assembling a crowd of several hundred men in field-grey who had appeared out of the rubble. Some of the Germans were wearing helmets, others were bareheaded. Many of them wore their tunics unfastened, others were in their singlets. Few of them had on their T-belts and proper equipment. For all the resistance they had put up, it was clear that the rapidity of the French advance had caught them unprepared.

To the men of de Bernac's command, as they struggled out of their tanks, the assembling of prisoners was a heartening spectacle. De Bernac himself was smiling and talking to Sergeant Narjac with an animation which belied his normal affectation of detached hauteur. But Vivian, despite his wish to share the holiday mood of his French companions, could not help observing the vigour and erect bearing of the Germans. In their faces, there was none of the resignation of defeat; some of them were actually grinning to one another. They were confident that this was no more than a pause, a temporary embarrassment in their headlong advance through France. Vivian noticed one or two who were actually mocking the gestures of their captors. At that moment, though he had always regarded himself as a civilised man, he could cheerfully have turned a machine-gun onto the crowd of dusty, unarmed men.

Behind the line of tanks, a house which was already no more than a shell was rent apart in an enveloping cloud of smoke. With an ear-splitting crash, the walls subsided to the ground. The tank-crews scrambled back into their vehicles, and the Germans threw themselves to the ground, as scream followed scream, and explosion followed explosion around them. The tanks began to roll forward once more into the narrow strip of upward sloping meadow which divided Lislet from Montcornet. Already eighteen of the twenty-two Char B's of 46th Battalion had smashed through the town to take up positions round the road junction. Dispatch riders came down the road, weaving their way round the still-smoking shell craters, bringing the news that two companies of Panzer infantry had been driven out, and that a field services communication column had been captured intact, and a convoy of tank recovery vehicles, complete with their cargoes of slightly-damaged Mark IV tanks. The dispatch riders were on their way to divisional HQ to report that the counter-attack had achieved its primary objective and to ask for infantry and artillery support to be sent up to consolidate the victory. De Bernac halted his company in the open field, and had his tank commanders report the state of ammunition and fuel. Both were in short supply. He had, moreover, left behind two of his sixteen tanks whose tracks had snapped. He therefore sent back a request on his own account for petrol, ammunition, and the services of a repair unit. He settled down to wait. It was 1500 hours.

At 1700 hours, they were in the same position. The firing had died down. The smoke and dust which had hung over Montcornet had settled; only a few fires continued to burn. Even the German anti-tank batteries, which had been dug in on the slopes behind Montcornet, had ceased firing. Then out of the unnatural stillness came the sound of heavier explosions. Smoke mushroomed over the grey wreckage of the town. The Germans had brought up heavier guns, outranging the Char B's 75 mm guns. And still no support came from the rear. After a few minutes of German bombardment, the news came that the German guns were self-propelled and were positioned on the far bank of the river Serre; any attempt to attack them would merely result in their withdrawal to safety, to open fire from new positions.

The rattle and squeal of tank-tracks was heard. The men of 2nd Independent Company watched, as the big Char B's came reversing out of the rubble of Montcornet, to withdraw out of range of the German guns until supplies and reinforcements arrived. Scarcely had the battalion of Char B's time to park amidst the Somuas scattered across the meadows, when wave after wave of Stukas came screaming up the summer sky to pause momentarily before spilling out of formation, and dropping like hawks on the stationary tanks.

Since midday, when he had reached Clermont les Fermes, two or three kilometres in the rear of the two Independent Companies, de Gaulle had been trying to find some means of contacting General Georges at La Ferté-sous-Jouarre. Everywhere the telephone lines appeared to be down, and an attempt to achieve a link-up by wireless, even speaking *en clair*, was frustrated by the apparent failure on the part of commands in the rear to man their sets. The danger in his situation had always been clear to him. The rapidity of the advance had exceeded his expectations. His tanks were among the most modern in use – and they were being used properly for the first time. But he did not have the infantry he needed to mop up the German infantry who would undoubtedly be reforming and establishing strong-points in his rear. Nor did he have the artillery to match the guns which General Guderian would bring up the moment he understood the nature of the assault made upon his flank.

German resistance was stiffening. Given the speed of the advance and the fierceness of the action, it would only be a matter of time before the tanks ran out of fuel. If they burned up too much fuel, there would be no hope of an orderly withdrawal if such were to prove necessary. Over the past three years, de Gaulle had begged that French armoured vehicles should be equipped, as he knew Guderian and Rommel had insisted their tanks should be, with the means to take on ordinary civilian fuel from roadside service-stations. The 'white breeches' in the Rue St Dominique had, of course, refused to listen to him.

The tanks of 46 Battalion were in the centre of Montcornet. Messages were coming back to him imploring supplies of fuel and ammunition, and he had none to send. His forces were standing on the single life-line which supplied Guderian's 19th Panzer Corps, yet he was completely without the means to exploit the position. In desperation, he sent out every member of his staff from house to house, in the final hope of finding a telephone which was still connected to the main exchange in Laon. Eventually one was found, but all the elderly woman's voice speaking from the exchange would say was that the German army was entering the city, and that the exchange was closing down.

De Gaulle realised that not only would he receive no support, but the enemy were in his rear and in strength. Then came the news of German self-propelled guns opening up on Montcornet from the north bank of the Serre. There was no help for it but to order 46 Battalion to begin the withdrawal out of range of the enemy guns. He sent a dispatch-rider down the main road to the south, to Reims, to inform General Touchon that he was about to withdraw to a defensive position along the Aisne, and to ask for supplies of fuel and ammunition. A few minutes later, he heard the noise of the Stukas mounting to the attack.

It was close on midnight when the main body of 4th Armoured Division, or what remained of it, arrived at the bridge across the Aisne, at Neuchâtel. Until darkness had fallen, it had been harried by wave after wave of Stukas, Junkers 88's, and Dornier 17's. It was as if the enemy high command was determined to punish the one French division which had opposed them for its presumption, and to warn any other French commander who might be tempted to act in the same way of what he could expect. As 4th Armoured Division approached Neuchâtel, the vanguard of the retreat, having spent the day fighting over a depopulated terrain, found every road choked with refugees pouring southwards. When, at last, de Gaulle himself reached the bridge, he found General Touchon's liaison officer, a Major Frey, waiting for him. It had been impossible, Major Frey explained, to send supplies or any assistance because of the flood-tide of refugees. The truth of the statement was evident enough. Enemy night-bombers had already visited Neuchâtel, and warehouses along the river-bank had been set alight. In the lurid glow of the flames, de Gaulle could see the pathetic, dreadful exodus toiling into the burning town.

'There are whole populations of towns on the move,' said Major Frey. 'And they are all coming south, avoiding Paris. They say there have been twelve thousand from Lille alone. General Touchon has been unable to make any disposition of his forces because of them.'

De Gaulle stared ahead of him.

'If the generals were worthy of the confidence of the people of France,' he said grimly, 'we should not be watching such a scene.'

Major Frey was shocked.

'Perhaps the Republic has proved itself unworthy of its generals, Colonel,' he suggested.

'That is too stupid,' de Gaulle finally exploded. 'The generals have begun this war as badly as they could have done. It is plain enough for any private soldier to see.'

'And what do you propose, Colonel?' Major Frey asked.

Without looking at him, de Gaulle replied, 'That we should continue to fight until there are new generals.'

'Meaning yourself, Colonel?' asked Major Frey.

'Whatever our present generals may intend,' de Gaulle answered, 'if I am spared, I shall go on fighting wherever I may until the enemy is defeated. They have put a stain on our country which must be washed clean.'

'You are said to be a Catholic, Colonel,' replied Major Frey. 'Take care you do not find yourself opposing the will of God. I believe this to be God's punishement on the Republic for having permitted atheistic Bolshevism to march unopposed in France. The country is sick with sin.'

De Gaulle allowed himself to stare in lofty if mild surprise. He shrugged. There was no point in further conversation with the imbecile.

'*Tout est dans tout*,' he said.

A cold breeze was blowing across the featureless open country which stretched away into the blackness on either side of the road. Vivian shivered inside his borrowed overalls. There was a slight ache behind his eyes like a sinus condition. His ears were still thick with the head-splitting screech of machine-gun bullets ricocheting across armour-plating, and the din of the tank. His shoulder ached where it had lurched and banged against the sides of the tank. And his legs were sore and stiff.

The column had come to a halt. Of the sixteen tanks with which 2nd Independent Company had set out, ten remained. They were parked along the roadside, straggling back for a quarter of a mile. They had formed the rearguard of the retreat. Now two of them had exhausted their fuel, and it could not be long before the remainder ran dry.

The men had dismounted from their vehicles. De Bernac was standing in the centre of the road, in conference with his two troop commanders and Sergeant Narjac. Vivian, standing a little distance away, watched their sad faces, lined and tired in the glow of the torch-light. He, for his part, felt little sense of disappointment; only thankfulness at having survived the seemingly interminable German bombardment. Perhaps he had realised the true situation after his visit to Chauny the previous night, and had seen his realisation confirmed in the faces of the German prisoners. Perhaps his own recent experience of life – the dissolution of his marriage to Rosemary, the wrecking of his true military career with the loss of his arm – had prepared him for periodic discoveries of fool's gold. He was becoming a philosopher in his old age, and only that one night in the hotel at Laon, which he recalled from time to time as an adolescent recalls his first sexual encounter, served to remind him that the carapace was not wholly grown about him.

The two commanders and Sergeant Narjac marched away into the darkness of the column. De Bernac came over to Vivian.

'It's finished, old chap,' he said in his slightly too-perfect English accent. 'We've lost the battle. And the war, I expect.'

Vivian couldn't make out the expression on his face.

'Not the war,' he said. 'Not by a long chalk.'

De Bernac wasn't listening.

'I've given orders for the vehicles to be destroyed,' he said. 'The Germans can't be more than a few kilometres behind us. We haven't enough ammunition for a proper last ditch stand. It would simply allow the enemy the opportunity of capturing them. When they have been put out of action, Narjac will march the crews through the night to Neuchâtel.'

He stood looking into the windy darkness.

'I am deeply sorry,' Vivian told him.

'I know, old chap,' said de Bernac.

A light flared up, then flickered, dripping flame onto the road surface. Boots rattled on the stone as the crew ran for cover. Light spread across the dykes and the field as the first tank was enveloped in a membrane of flame. Almost immediately there was the crackle of small-arms ammunition exploding. Further down the road, fuel-tanks and cannon-shells exploded simultaneously; there was a loud clatter as some heavy metal object was hurled across the road. As explosion followed explosion, men came running back up the road. They were met at the head of the column by Sergeant Narjac, who had them fall in into ranks.

De Bernac walked off down the road, passing the men who came running up it, to ensure that the job of demolition was being done properly. Shortly afterwards, Vivian, who was still standing by himself at the roadside, decided to follow him. He found him in the burning glow of the fourth tank down the line. He was lying on the verge, his head subsided into the long grass. The barrel of his revolver was still clenched between his jaws.

Part Two: **RESURGAM**

25

Vivian Hardwicke was sitting in an armchair in the hotel lounge, trying to read the continental edition of the *Daily Mail*, but he was finding it difficult to concentrate. A week had passed since he had been transferred from the 4th Armoured Division to the British Military Mission in Paris. He had been informed on arrival that a special representative of the Prime Minister was to be appointed and sent to Paris, and that he should hold himself in readiness to act as aide to the appointee. For five days he had loitered about in the hotel in the Rue d'Aguesseau, about two hundred yards from the British Embassy in the Rue du Faubourg St Honoré. He had walked out and about like a tourist. Paris had recovered its spirits now it was clear that the Germans did not intend an immediate assault on the city. In the evenings, he drank slightly too much Scotch, and demonstrated that his injury did not prevent him from playing a sound game of billiards. Several times, he had called at the ENSA offices to ask after Julie, but they had heard nothing of her, and had suggested that he should inquire at the Swiss Office of the International Red Cross, to see whether she had been caught in the German advance, and been interned.

Thirty-six hours earlier, he had been ordered to go to the airport to await the arrival of General Sir Edward Spears from London. He had driven out to Le Bourget only to find that it had been bombed so severely the previous night, that it was closed to all air traffic. He had telephoned the embassy immediately, but there was no further information regarding General Spears's arrival, and Vivian had returned to the hotel, feeling acutely disappointed.

Now he was waiting and hoping for a phone call giving him further instructions. He held page two of the *Daily Mail* in front of him. There was an account of Ernest Bevin's speech explaining how the United States was helping to stem aggression without actually going to war. Another story, bylined 'Eyewitness', told how a British Infantry Battalion had routed the Germans 'somewhere in N.E. France' by forming a square – 'the formation which helped us to win Waterloo and other famous victories'. The headline story was the news that five hundred thousand Red Army troops were massed in Lithuania opposite the East Prussian frontier. 'Foreign correspondents in Moscow have the impression that an immense diplomatic game is in progress. Further open Soviet moves to upset Germany are expected in diplomatic circles.' Every story on the foreign news page was a sort of whistling in the dark, Vivian decided.

'Hello, there! Major Hardwicke, is it?'

Vivian lowered the paper.

'My name's Spears. Edward Spears. I say, I am sorry to rout you out when you're looking so bloody comfortable, old chap. Still, I don't suppose there's any comfort to be had from the newspapers these days.'

'I'm sorry, sir!' Vivian said, pulling himself out of the chair. 'I had no idea. . . . '

General Sir Edward Spears was not at all as Vivian had expected. He was half-French, and a Member of Parliament, who had long been off the army's active list. Nevertheless, he stood before Vivian, tall and erect in his general's uniform, every inch a British soldier, with his neat little black moustache.

'Landed at Villecoublay just after dawn,' he explained. 'Drove straight over to my place – keep a place in Paris you know, or rather my wife does – and had a shave and a spruce-up.'

'I was expecting the Attaché's office to give me a ring,' Vivian explained.

'Didn't know I'd arrived,' Sir Edward told him. 'Just been over there. H.E. and Malise Graham have gone out somewhere together. Trouble is we've got to be round at the Rue St Dominique by noon. There's a meeting of the War Council. You'd better be with me. Important you should know what's going on. I managed to get a car out of the Attaché's department. It's outside.'

'Should I take anything with me, sir?' Vivian asked.

'Just your head, dear boy. Pay attention to everything that goes on. Best to have two of us to tell the tale.'

He led Vivian from the lounge. Vivian picked up his cap and stick from the vestibule table. Sir Edward held the door for him out of deference to his empty sleeve. As they stepped out into the shadow of the Rue d'Aguesseau, Sir Edward asked, 'What has the mood been like round here?'

'At the Military Mission, sir?' asked Vivian.

'Generally,' Sir Edward replied. 'Just generally.'

'Well, sir,' Vivian told him, 'even a boy scout might have trouble smiling and whistling.'

A large, dark blue Buick sedan was standing a little way down the street. Its French army driver came to attention and opened the rear door. Vivian climbed in after Sir Edward and sat beside him.

'The death of General Billotte hasn't improved matters, of course,' Vivian explained.

'I shouldn't think it has,' said Sir Edward. 'Shocking thing to happen.'

He leant forward and closed the glass partition behind the driver's head.

'Can't imagine what possessed Weygand not to appoint a successor to command Army Group One immediately,' he said.

'Weygand has only just taken over supreme command from Gamelin,' said Vivian. 'Perhaps he didn't quite appreciate the situation. They say Billotte was the only one who really knew the Order of Battle for Army Group One, and they were hoping he'd recover sufficiently to pass on the information.'

Sir Edward shook his head.

'Madness,' he said. 'There's Jerry pouring into north-east France, and the Supreme Commander, Allied Land Forces, sits on his bum for four whole days before appointing somebody to take over.'

They were crossing the Seine, over the Pont Alexandre III.

'Actually, I told Winston he ought to get in touch with General Swayne at GQG La Ferté; but he thought it more tactful to leave the French to manage their own affairs. I pointed out it would leave poor old Gort out on a limb, but I expect Winston knows what he's doing. I only hope the same can be said of Reynaud.'

They had turned left onto the Quai d'Orsay.

'We must be careful not to let H.E. feel that he's being left out of things, by the way,' said Sir Edward. 'He's a stickler for protocol is Ronnie Campbell – as well as being a thoroughly sound chap.'

He had scarcely spoken when, as they were driving past the high railings in front of the National Assembly, Vivian recognised the British Military Attaché, Lord Malise Graham, strolling in the shade of the trees, and with him, the British Ambassador, a slight figure in a Savile Row suit and stiff homburg. Vivian reached over and knocked at the partition window for the driver to stop.

'I rather think we've stumbled on just the people you wish to speak to, sir,' he said to Sir Edward.

Sir Edward looked out of the window.

'So we have, by God,' he said.

They got out of the car. Lord Malise Graham recognised Vivian instantly.

'How are you, Hardwicke?'

But Sir Ronald Campbell had to blink several times before he recognised Sir Edward Spears.

'Spears,' he said at last. 'Good to see you.'

They shook hands.

'Didn't know you'd landed in Paris, old chap,' said Sir Ronald.

The criticism was as smooth as an oyster.

'Arrived at Villecoublay this morning,' said Sir Edward. 'Rang the Embassy. They said you were out.'

Sir Ronald glanced at Lord Malise Graham.

'Been payin' a call at the Rue St Dominique,' he said.

'Just on our way there now,' Sir Edward explained.

Sir Ronald flicked away a fragment of gravel with the end of his stick.

'It's been a bit trying,' he said. 'Gray and I have been on the receivin' end of a pi-jaw from the President of the Council.'

He had a disconcertingly pale, watery stare.

'Usual guff,' said Lord Malise Graham, 'about how English generals are creatures of instinct. They always retreat to harbours in times of emergency.'

'What did you tell him?' asked Sir Edward.

'I just mentioned Wellington at Torres Vedras, and Raglan at Balaclava. I pointed out that they hadn't done too badly by retreating onto their harbours.'

'Was he impressed by your argument?' Sir Edward inquired.

Vivian wondered whether he was speaking ironically.

'He asked whether we knew if Gort was attacking,' Sir Ronald Campbell said. 'Unfortunately, nobody has seen fit to inform me as to what Gort's movements are.'

There they stood, thought Vivian, like a small group of *boulevardiers* gossiping in the leaf-filtered sunlight.

'You know, Spears,' Sir Ronald continued, 'don't mind tellin' you it would be damn helpful if Gort did counter-attack to the south.'

'It would give Blanchard a chance to organise something between Abbeville and Amiens,' Lord Malise Graham added. 'And it would make all the difference to General Frère's push to the north.'

'Not to mention relations between the French War Council and HMG,' said Sir Ronald.

'Are we sure that General Frère *is* pushing northwards?' Sir Edward asked. 'I'm quite sure Gort is doing everything to comply with Weygand's instructions; and under conditions of the utmost difficulty.... To tell you the truth, communications between the War Office and the BEF are getting more and more difficult to maintain. Tell you something else. From London, it's difficult to see any effective French command in the north-east with which Gort would co-operate. I've no doubt Weygand is preparing plans and giving orders, but are any of his chaps in the field actually implementing them?'

'Impossible to judge,' Sir Ronald admitted. 'Billotte's death has buggered everything up, I'm afraid to say.'

Sir Edward glanced at his watch.

'Tell you what, Campbell,' he said. 'I must have a word with Reynaud before the War Council meets, so we'd better cut along to the Rue St Dominique straight away. I'll come round to the embassy afterwards, and give you a sit. rep., eh?'

'We'll keep a little luncheon by, for when you arrive,' Sir Ronald replied. 'Dare say you're goin' to need it. By the by, de Margerie is in there somewhere, so there'll be at least one person who knows how to keep his head when all about are losin' theirs!'

Sir Edward and Vivian returned to the waiting car, while Sir Ronald Campbell and Lord Malise Graham continued on their leisurely way back to the Rue St Honoré and the British Embassy. Vivian gazed out of the car window; it was the Paris of broad thoroughfares, palaces, and green trees; on the far bank of the Seine a haze of green veiled the edge of the Jardin des Tuileries. They swung round the corner of the National Assembly with its mass of grey columns, and entered the Place du Palais Bourbon.

'Didn't care to say it in front of HE,' Sir Edward remarked in a confidential manner, 'but one always gets the impression that the French treat poor old Gort as if he were a junior battalion commander. Trouble is he tends to react as if he were a junior battalion commander. It's all manner, of course. Fellow is as sound as a rock.'

'"A good commander and a most kind gentleman,"' Vivian quoted.

'Quite so,' Sir Edward agreed.

They turned into the Rue St Dominique and, between high, wrought-iron gates, into the courtyard of the Ministry of Defence. The car came to a halt at the foot of the great flight of steps leading up to the pillared front of the building. A *huissier* – one of those formally-dressed, elderly ushers who were to be found, with silver chains of office about their necks, in every major government ministry – descended the steps with all the dignity of an English butler, as Sir Edward and Vivian got out of the car. He inclined his head courteously.

'General Spears,' Sir Edward told him. 'Personal representative of the British Prime Minister.'

'But of course, Monsieur le Général,' said the *huissier*, as if rebuking himself for not having recognised someone so eminent. 'Monsieur le Président du Conseil is expecting Monsieur le Général. If Monsieur would be good enough to follow me . . . '

They went up the great steps and into the shade of the building, the click of their riding boots echoing on the vast marble floor. Young officers, their hair slicked and polished, portfolios under their arms, marched briskly from sign-posted door to sign-posted door. The coolness of the marble, however, and the white statues of scantily-draped dryads and goddesses made it impossible to imagine the human occupants of the place behaving with anything other than median calm.

'This way, General,' the *huissier* bowed, and led them to the broad sweep of the main staircase.

Above it, vivid against the pale wall, hung a Meissonier battlescape – a huge bustle of scarlet and silver, of wide-eyed horses, of dull grey, sharpened sabre blades against the winter sky, of wounded men suffering expressively, and of shot-ragged standards streaming in the wind.

They followed the *huissier* a short distance down a spacious gallery where the sunlight splashed through the lofty windows onto the marble panelling. At the end was a pair of high double doors, in front of which stood a sentry in white cross belts, with a revolver in his polished holster. He stood to attention at the approach of Sir Edward and Vivian, but the *huissier* led them aside, into the open doorway of an office.

'Spears, *cher ami*! Come in! Downing Street telephoned me just two hours ago to tell me that you were on your way.'

The office was much larger than Vivian had expected; similar to one of the smaller state rooms at Windsor or Hampton Court. The great window looked out over the quiet expanse of the Square Rousseau to the high, east windows of the Church of Sainte Clothilde. The occupant of the office however, was, much smaller than Vivian had expected. Monsieur Paul Reynaud held himself very erect as if to make up for the inches he lacked; his eyes were slanted, giving him a Chinese look, and were lined into a permanent expression of ironic amusement. The shoulders of his elegant black jacket had been heavily padded, a fact accentuated by his wearing it draped over his shoulders like a cape.

The girl stenographer who had been with him quietly picked up her shorthand pad and took her leave. Sir Edward introduced Vivian.

'Monsieur le Président du Conseil, may I have the honour to present to you my friend and aide, Major Vivian Hardwicke?'

'A war hero, I perceive, Major 'ardwicke,' said Monsieur Reynaud.

'Not this war, Monsieur le Président du Conseil,' Vivian replied. 'A skirmish in the colonies. Not very heroic.'

'Ah, a colonial warrior,' Mousieur Reynaud remarked. 'We must introduce the major to our Generalissimo, eh Spears? General Weygand was recalled from Syria, you know.'

He motioned Sir Edward and Vivian to sit down at his ugly Second Empire desk. Vivian slid his chair back slightly, so as to be sitting at Sir Edward's shoulder. Reynaud settled into the swivel-chair behind his desk. He hitched his black jacket up onto his shoulders.

'In the matter of disposing of our forces, *cher ami*,' he began, 'at this time . . .' He paused. 'At this terrible time,' he corrected himself, rather like a priest at Mass who has forgotten a crucial word in his recital of the liturgy, ' . . . it is most unfortunate that English generals should have a predisposition to run for the nearest harbour. It is understandable, of course. One remembers the great Duke of

230

Wellington at Torres Vedras, and Lord Raglan at Balaclava. It is part of the English military experience.'

'My dear Prime Minister,' Sir Edward interrupted him, 'I have only just left the Ambassador. He told me something of your opinion on this matter. The whole idea is, of course, entirely ridiculous. No responsible person in England, least of all so dedicated a lover of France as Mr Churchill, would consider for one moment a withdrawal to the Channel ports – except as a last resort, to keep our army intact.'

That saving clause nullified the effect of Sir Edward's assumed indignation. Reynaud lifted his eyebrows above his Chinese eyes, and Sir Edward realised the mistake he had made.

'Did Sir John French retreat to the Channel before the Battle of the Marne?' he demanded.

'No, my friend,' replied Monsieur Reynaud softly, 'but the situation was not precisely similar. This time, the enemy is not threatening Paris for the time being . He is driving to the sea. One might say he is threatening the British Expeditionary Force, our own 1st Army, and the Belgian army with encirclement.'

Sir Edward sat forward in his chair.

'Monsieur le Président, the enemy has left his flank exposed precisely – precisely,' he emphasised, 'as he did at the Marne. Winston has described him as a tortoise with his neck stuck out too far from his shell. Not a bad simile.' He paused. 'If Weygand has given clear instructions to Lord Gort, I can give you an absolute assurance that Lord Gort will do everything in his power to carry out those instructions. If General Frère is launching a genuine offensive northwards, then there is every chance that Frère from the south and Gort from the north will cut off the tortoise's head – somewhere in the Bapaume sector. But it is absolutely essential, Prime Minister, that the British Government should know what are Weygand's orders to Lord Gort.'

'Mr Churchill has spoken to me on the telephone,' said Monsieur Reynaud. The unchanging smile on his face made Vivian feel uneasy. 'On Thursday, to be exact. He was complaining that Lord Gort had received no orders from Army Group One headquarters. He said that, unless Lord Gort received orders from GQG, Vincennes, the British Expeditionary Force would be compelled to retreat onto its harbours.'

'No army can act without instructions, Prime Minister,' Sir Edward protested.

'Mr Churchill spoke to me two days ago, on Thursday,' said Reynaud. 'General Blanchard did not arrive at Army Group One headquarters to take command until late on Wednesday night. He was hardly in a position to communicate orders to Lord Gort there and then ... You see, my friend, all I am saying is that the idea of a retreat by the British Expeditionary Force onto the Channel ports is very much on the minds both of Mr Churchill and of Lord Gort.'

'Listen, Prime Minister,' said Sir Edward. 'I know Winston. I know him as well as anybody does. He is firm. He's a man of his word. And he is not dismayed. The only thing which might distress him is the bandying about of accusations between French and British commanders. . . . He has the utmost confidence in you, Prime Minister – in your clearness of vision, and in your firmness, believe me.'

Reynaud got up from the desk. He went over to the window and looked out over the square below. He put his finger into his collar to ease it about his neck. Without turning to look at Sir Edward Spears, he said, 'Then you can give me your absolute assurance that it is not true that Lord Gort has received instructions from Admiral Ramsey at Dover regarding the withdrawal of the British Expeditionary Force into beachheads at Fécamp, Boulogne, and Dunkirk?'

'I . . . ' Sir Edward began.

He broke off. His embarrassment was palpable, like a schoolboy found out.

'I daresay certain contingency plans have been prepared,' he suggested, somewhat lamely.

Reynaud nodded. He hitched his jacket up onto his shoulders once more.

'I am sure,' he said, 'that General Weygand and the War Council will be waiting in the Grand Study. If you will permit me . . . '

Sir Edward and Vivian rose to their feet. They waited as Monsieur Reynaud left the office by a green baize door behind the desk. It was bad, thought Vivian. The little man was more angry, more mistrustful than when they had come in.

Sir Edward went over to the window.

'There you are, my boy,' he said quietly. 'What do you make of the French Prime Minister, eh?'

'He's very quick on the uptake, sir,' Vivian replied.

The reply appeared to amuse Sir Edward.

'He is also,' he said, 'a very likeable, gallant little man. And a very determined one.' He paused. 'If Madame la Comtesse de Portes would let him be,' he added.

It had been common gossip amongst the more senior officers at the hotel in the Rue d'Aguesseau, that the French Prime Minister's mistress was a confirmed anglophobe.

'Is she defeatist?' Vivian asked.

'Just a very foolish woman,' Sir Edward replied. 'French politicians have this strange predilection for fluffy women. I don't suppose Hélène de Portes has a thought of her own in her head. But she has a number of friends who are only too willing to plant some there.'

'Might I ask, sir,' Vivian said, 'if there isn't a little truth in what the Prime Minister said just now – about Gort having the Channel ports very much on his mind. I mean, he surely must keep in mind his one possible line of retreat, particularly if his instructions from GQG, Vincenenes are none too clear.'

'Of course, my boy, of course,' Sir Edward agreed. 'But nobody wants to know that – not even Winston. If poor old Gort is compelled to retreat into the Fécamp-Boulogne-Dunkirk beachheads, it'll be a decision made on his own initiative. Then Winston can claim that he knew nothing about it when the War Council here in Paris kicks up a fuss. . . . You just watch, everybody here is already setting up Gort as a scapegoat. They'll blame him for every inadequacy in the French High Command. Gort is going to be the great alibi. Even Reynaud is at it, and he's a decent enough little beggar.'

The door which led out to the gallery opened. A slim, young middle-aged man wearing an English suit, and spectacles, came in.

'Sir Edward, how good to see you,' he said in faultless English.

He shook Sir Edward's hand.

'Good to see you, old chap,' said Sir Edward.

The newcomer glanced out at the gallery, in the direction of the Grand Study. He shook his head. Sir Edward nodded his comprehension of the message.

'Allow me to introduce my young colleague here,' he said. 'Hardwicke? This is a very dear friend of mine – and, may I say, of Britain. Roland de Margerie, whom Monsieur Reynaud has wisely, in my view, appointed his *chef du cabinet*.'

'For my sins,' de Margerie replied.

'Major Vivian Hardwicke,' Sir Edward continued, 'who was, until he joined my staff, liaison with your 4th Armoured Division.'

'Ah!' de Margerie's face brightened with interest. 'And how did you find working with Colonel de Gaulle, Major?'

Vivian sifted his thoughts rapidly.

'Not an easy chap,' he replied. 'But a fine commander. He knows how to inspire confidence and spirit in the men he leads.'

De Margerie nodded.

'He is not liked here,' he said in a low voice, 'but I think they'll find it difficult to ignore him much longer. He is a bit of, what we call, *un monstre sacré*. As you say, not an easy fellow to rub shoulders with.'

'I suppose,' Vivian suggested, 'that *un monstre sacré*'s appropriate place must be the centre of the stage.'

'Quite true,' agreed de Margerie, 'and Charles de Gaulle would occupy it with some distinction. He has the *hauteur*, if nothing else. . . . You are waited on, Sir Edward, in the Grand Study.'

They went out to the gallery.

'De Margerie was First Secretary at the London embassy for several years,' remarked Sir Edward. 'He is greatly missed.'

'Did you prefer life in the Corps Diplomatique to life in the Quai d'Orsay?' asked Vivian.

De Margerie laughed. 'One always prefers to lie to foreigners rather than to one's own people,' he replied.

They passed the sentry. De Margerie held open one of the high double doors, and Sir Edward and Vivian went through into the Grand Study. It was a vast and gloomy place, like a disused banqueting chamber. The table in the centre was awash with files, dossiers and calf-bound folios. From the dark, stained walls, huge portraits of pre-Revolutionary Ministers of War – Condé, Saxe, Turenne – stared down, looking strangely young and supercilious in their cuirasses and periwigs. At the far end, the great window looked out over the dank shadows of the Ministry's interior garden, so surrounded by high buildings that sunlight never reached it.

The group about the table was a small one. Monsieur Reynaud, his jacket still slung over his shoulders, occupied the entire length of one side. He had barricaded himself with sheafs of papers and in-trays. Beside him was a telephone connected to an intercom speaker which reminded Vivian of a small harmonium.

'General Spears has been sent here,' Reynaud explained to his colleagues, 'as the special representative of Mr Winston Churchill.'

He pointed across the table to where there were two vacant chairs. Sir Edward took his place, with Vivian seated once more just behind him.

There were only four other men at the table, apart from Reynaud.

'It has been many years, Monsieur le Maréchal,' Sir Edward said to Marshal Pétain, who was occupying the seat on his left.

The hero of Verdun was propped very erect against the back of his chair, but he was very old. His face was a white mask except for the tiny veins on his cheeks and forehead. His moustache was yellowy white, and very soft. It straggled over his lips, as if he could no longer be bothered with trimming it. As Sir Edward and Vivian had taken their places, his face had been devoid of expression, staring blankly across the table past Monsieur Reynaud who was seated opposite. He started slightly as Sir Edward spoke, and looked up.

'You are welcome, monsieur,' he said.

Somewhere in the bleakness of his face there was a glimmer of life, as if he had recognised a familiar figure approaching from afar off.

'Spears,' Sir Edward helped him. 'Edward Spears, Monsieur le Maréchal.'

'Ah!' Marshal Pétain replied. 'Ah!'

There was a faint smile in the winter of his face.

General Weygand, the Commander-in-Chief, Allied Land Forces, who occupied the end of the table nearest to Sir Edward, welcomed him briskly. He resembled an elderly version of Monsieur Reynaud.

He was almost as small, as neat in figure, and had the same strangely Chinese-looking eyes. He was dressed as the military equivalent of a boulevard dandy, in stiffly pressed khaki jacket, kid riding breeches, and with polished brass spurs on the heels of his boots. But his face, as surely as that of the aged Marshal of France, was that of an old man. The skull was visible under the wizened parchment of the skin; his military moustache was sparse and moulting, his complexion yellow and jaundiced. It was inconceivable to Vivian that such a man could bear the responsibilities of overall command.

Beyond Marshal Pétain's seat, there was Admiral Darlan. Like the Marshal, he seemed scarcely in touch with his surroundings. He was a burly, nautical figure, at first sight the very image of a bluff sea-dog. But the puffy cheeks and thick, fleshy nose were those of the habitual drinker. The fourth member of the War Council present was the Secretary to the War Council, Paul Baudouin. Unlike the others, he was youthful-looking, tall, slim, and with dark curly hair setting off his startlingly blue eyes. He had a frank, open, and intelligent face. Vivian was prejudiced in his favour since he alone of those round the table smiled welcomingly at him.

Monsieur Reynaud sat back in his chair. He searched with his fingers between his collar and his neck.

'Since General Spears is with us, as personal envoy of the British Prime Minister,' he began, 'we must assume that Mr Churchill would wish us to state our views frankly and unequivocally.'

'Of course, Monsieur le Président,' Sir Edward acknowledged.

'Then I fear that we must begin,' said Reynaud, 'by pointing out that the difficulties facing General Weygand, and General Blanchard as commander of Army Group One, grave as they are, are made worse – I was about to say insuperably worse . . . '

He leaned forward and pressed his palm down on the table.

' . . . by the reports of Lord Gort's retreat to the coast. We have the strongest impression here that Lord Gort is acting on orders from London in defiance of orders issued by GQG, Vincennes.'

He stopped. Sir Edward turned and glanced back at Vivian. Vivian nodded slightly.

'Monsieur le Président,' Sir Edward began in measured tones. 'Obviously it is necessary for me to stress that Great Britain is prepared to share in every burden and every responsibility which the time lays upon our two nations. It is my duty, however, to tell you very clearly that His Majesty's government does not consider that the British command either at home or in the field is responsible for the present military situation. Lord Gort and his officers have carried out every order issued from Vincennes and from Army Group One, to the letter. Obedience to such orders has placed the British Expeditionary Force in a situation of the gravest peril . . . '

Vivian had noticed the twitching of Sir Edward's neck muscles. Now Sir Edward broke away from his prepared text.

'It is very curious,' he said, 'how ready people are here in Paris to blame Lord Gort and the British Expeditionary Force ... '

Paul Baudouin intervened, smiling gently.

'General Spears has only been in Paris for a matter of hours,' he pointed out aimiably. 'I'm surprised he has managed to find out what people are thinking here, so quickly.'

Sir Edward let him finish, then drove straight on:

' ... how ready they are to blame the British for disobeying orders. It is particularly curious since nobody seems to know what orders have been issued, or what strategy, if any, they are supposed to implement. Perhaps somebody would care to enlighten me. What orders, precisely, have been issued by General Blanchard to Lord Gort? How far has General Frère's attack on the German left flank advanced? Has General Frère's attack actually left its own start-line? Since Lord Gort's offensive south is supposed to be meeting up with the forces under the command of General Frère, it would be interesting to know where General Frère is.'

There was a moment's silence round the table.

'Does nobody know?' asked Sir Edward.

Again there was silence.

'Is GQG, Vincennes out of contact with General Frère?' Sir Edward demanded.

Reynaud tugged at the lapels of his jacket. He was obviously under great stress.

'Communications with the front have become,' he said, 'a little complicated.'

'But General Frère's own headquarters can't be more than three hours' drive from Paris – at the very most,' protested Sir Edward.

General Weygand turned to face Sir Edward.

'*Mon vieux*,' he began, 'don't worry. I have instructed General Blanchard that in the eventuality of Lord Gort finding it necessary to disengage from the Arras sector, the whole of Army Group One should be employed in establishing a defensible beachhead about Dunkirk – as a base through which the British, Belgians, and our own 1st Army, may be supplied. This is a contingency plan, of course, but it may explain why this misunderstanding regarding Lord Gort and his supposed retreat to the coast has arisen. Only this morning,' he continued, 'I have received a telegram from Blanchard, stating ... '

He pulled out a pale blue note from the file in front of him with the air of one drawing a rabbit from a hat.

' ... that he is advancing, in conjunction with the British 5th Division under the command of General Franklyn, with a view to establishing a start-line from which to launch a major offensive in the direction of Bapaume tomorrow morning.'

236

Sir Edward turned on Monsieur Reynaud.

'This refutes utterly, Monsieur le Président, any suggestion that Lord Gort has been disobeying orders on instruction from London or on his own initiative. At no point have the British forces fallen into disarray – the British Expeditionary Force is still an effective fighting machine. If there is to be an offensive launched in the Bapaume area, it will be British troops who will be bearing the brunt of the fighting. And since you seem so ready to doubt Lord Gort's loyalty, I will tell you: in England, we have a saying, "a good man to go tiger-shooting with". Lord Gort is such a man.'

He saw the smiles on the faces both of Paul Baudouin and of Reynaud.

'Mr Churchill,' he said, 'has stated most firmly that the British government stands absolutely with France. I hope nobody wishes to doubt Mr Churchill's word.'

'I'm sure,' General Weygand told him, 'I'm sure nobody doubts Lord Gort's fighting spirit. His courage has long been proven. I'm sure he is the most loyal of comrades!'

Sir Edward took a deep breath.

'I presume, General,' he said to Weygand, 'that Lord Gort has been provided with detailed information regarding General Frère's offensive northwards.'

General Weygand spread his hands palms upwards in an expansive gesture, expressing surprise that Sir Edward should have felt the need to ask such a question.

'General Blanchard,' he replied, 'is keeping Lord Gort fully informed as to General Frère's position. I have every confidence in Blanchard, just as you have confidence in Lord Gort. Blanchard is a true leader of men. We can rely on him – rely on him absolutely – to take the right decisions, and to fight to the last man, if necessary.'

General Weygand's voice had shed its elderly weariness. Now it rang out like a trumpet-call. Vivian could see in him the bastard son of the heroic, tragic Hapsburg Emperor of Mexico, and the commander of the Polish armies which had routed the Bolshevik hordes outside the gates of Warsaw in 1920.

On Sir Edward's right, the aged Marshal remained unmoved. His eyes were open, but his chin had sunk onto his chest, and he was staring fixedly at his polished English brogues under the table. Admiral Darlan was staring at the portrait of Marshal Saxe which hung above Reynaud's seat. He had puffed his cheeks, and was blowing noiselessly between pursed lips. Paul Baudouin had been listening intently. He had the detached, amused expression on his handsome, sensitive face reminiscent, Vivian decided, of the supercilious *fainéance* of a Voltairean aristocrat just before the Revolution.

The intercom speaker beside Reynaud buzzed stridently. He picked up the telephone. A harsh female voice came over the speaker.

'Paulie, I must speak to you.'

A weary look crossed Monsieur Reynaud's face.

'*Chère amie*,' he replied, 'the War Council is in session. You must forgive me . . . .'

'I know, *chéri*,' came the harsh soprano voice, 'Paul told me. The other Paul.'

Monsieur Reynaud gave Baudouin a look of pure loathing. Baudouin avoided his glance.

'Paulie, this is of the utmost importance,' the voice went on. 'Gaby de Noailles has just rung to say that Michel Duvivier has been appointed Superintendant of Air Raid Precautions for the Bourbonnais.'

'*Ma chère*,' replied Monsieur Reynaud, 'I don't believe I know this Monsieur Duvivier.'

'He is a protegé of Georges Mandel,' said the voice on a rising note. 'You can't know how untrustworthy he is.'

'Are you sure that the Princess is right?' Reynaud asked. 'She isn't always the most reliable of informants.'

'I shall see,' said the voice abruptly.

There was the click of a receiver being put down at the other end. Reynaud put his own receiver down. He smiled wearily, as if knowing that everybody about the table would understand why he had to allow such calls to come through. Paul Baudouin continued to smile away from Monsieur Reynaud. Admiral Darlan had begun to whistle softly to himself. Marshal Pétain continued to admire his shoes. Only General Weygand fidgeted uncomfortably in his seat, as if embarrassed. But his embarrassment was not caused by the scene at the table. An army captain – evidently a member of the Generalissimo's staff – had entered softly, and had whispered a message into the Generalissimo's ear. General Weygand had glanced about him as if hoping that something was about to occur which would save him from an intolerable predicament. The captain stood to attention beside his chair.

As Reynaud reached across the table to return the receiver to its cradle, General Weygand announced, 'Monsieur le Président, it is my duty to inform members of the War Council that I have just been told that an officer attached to General Blanchard's staff has arrived here, at the Ministry. He has come directly from the war zone.'

'Is he outside?' asked Reynaud.

Weygand glanced up at the captain.

'He is outside, General,' the captain replied.

'Let's hear what he has to tell us,' Reynaud said.

'Tell Major Fauvelle to come in,' General Weygand ordered the captain.

The captain clicked his heels and marched out of the Grand Study. The members of the War Council waited in silence. General Weygand drummed his fingers on the table.

Major Fauvelle came in. His appearance was reassuring; his jacket was pressed, his riding breeches spotless, his boots shining, and the four silver-embroidered rings on his képi, denoting the rank of a cavalry-major, gleamed. But his face belied his smartness. His eyes were sunken and ringed with shadow, the skin was loose about his chin like that of a man who has lost weight too quickly, and he had cut himself shaving.

He stood to attention at General Weygand's left hand side.

'When did you leave General Blanchard's headquarters, Major Fauvelle?' asked General Weygand.

'At noon yesterday, General.'

'Yesterday!' General Weygand exclaimed.

'The German advance has cut every road, General,' Major Fauvelle replied. 'I tried to find an aircraft at Dunkirk, but all aircraft have been withdrawn by the RAF Component to airfields in England. The Germans have the sky to themselves.'

'How did you get here?' General Weygand asked, firmly keeping the man to the point.

Vivian could feel his heart sinking. Already the note of scarcely-repressed hysteria was evident in the man's voice.

'I had to go by sea, General,' Major Fauvelle continued. 'From Dunkirk to Folkestone. And then by train to London to find an aircraft to Paris. There is no other way.'

Vivian heard Sir Edward sighing. It was like standing on a stricken field, he thought; the ground was littered with the wreckage of General Weygand's assurances regarding Blanchard's fighting spirit, and talk of offensive strikes northwards.

'So General Blanchard is cut off,' said Monsieur Reynaud. It was a statement rather than a question. 'What was the situation of Army Group One when you left General Blanchard's headquarters?'

Major Fauvelle was silent for a moment. Suddenly he burst out, 'There is no alternative, Monsieur le Président. We have to surrender. If we don't surrender immediately, everything will be lost.'

Was he talking about Army Group One, Vivian wondered, or about the Republic as a whole. Everybody round the table had been taken aback by his vehemence. Only Marshal Pétain continued to stare at his feet.

Reynaud snapped back at Major Fauvelle, 'That is not for you to decide, Major.'

General Weygand spoke to him more gently, 'Look, Fauvelle, reports from Postal Control still suggest that the morale of our men in the north-east is bearing up. We received the last report this morning.'

'If morale amongst the troops of Army Group One has not broken down in the most precise sense, General,' Major Fauvelle replied, 'it is because their brains have been stupified by the German bombardment from the air. The Germans are able to carry out their bombing missions hour after hour, day after day, and there is nothing to stop them.'

'This is quite ridiculous,' Sir Edward exclaimed. 'We are talking about soldiers of France. They aren't dead yet, are they?'

Major Fauvelle turned on him.

'Many ... many of them are,' he shouted. Vivian saw that tears were streaming down his cheeks. 'And those who have survived are without bread,' he added.

There was a sharp buzz from the intercom speaker. Reynaud reached over the pile of dossiers and picked up the receiver.

'Paulie?' the corncrake, female voice demanded.

For a moment, Reynaud did not speak.

'Are you there, Paulie?' demanded the voice.

Perhaps it was as well, thought Vivian. The interruption would allow the distressed Major to take a hold of himself.

'I am, *ma chérie*,' Reynaud replied, 'but the Council is engaged in matters of the gravest urgency.'

'This *is* an urgent matter, Paulie,' the voice told him. 'I have spoken to Marcel Delannoy at the Rue Cambacières, and he assures me that Duvivier *has* been appointed Superintendant of Air Raid Precautions in the Bourbonnais. I must tell you, Paulie, that this is the most stupid appointment imaginable.'

'It is a matter which will wait, Hélène,' said Monsieur Reynaud surprisingly firmly.

'It cannot wait,' insisted the harsh female voice over the intercom. 'Marcel says that Duvivier was appointed on the direct instructions of Georges Mandel himself, because Duvivier is a well-known lover of England. And everybody knows that Mandel takes his orders from the English Jews.'

'This is nonsense, dear,' Reynaud replied.

Before he could continue, the voice interrupted him:

'Paulie, it is not nonsense. I know it is an unfortunate necessity that we must placate the English, but you should be firm, Paulie. You must see that Mandel doesn't make it an excuse to fill every vacant government appointment with his odious Jew friends.'

'My dear, I doubt whether this man Duvivier could do any possible harm in the Bourbonnais,' Reynaud told her. 'There's no need to worry about German bombing in the Bourbonnais.'

'You forget, Paulie, my mother lives in the Bourbonnais,' the voice replied in strident reproach.

'Listen, *chérie*,' Reynaud told her, 'I will phone you as soon as this meeting is finished.' He was wheedling. 'I promise I won't be long,' he told her.

He put the receiver down quickly, and sat back, tugging at his shirt collar.

It was a dream, thought Vivian. The faces about the table sagged with age and weariness; only Paul Baudouin smiled as if he understood everything and was surprised by nothing. Sir Edward Spears was sitting erect and motionless. The traffic circling the Place du Palais Bourbon could be heard as from afar off, a reminder of a waking world drifting into the dream. Soon he would awake and find himself lying between the crisp sheets of the military hospital, or sitting in the summer garden at Glyndebourne.

Monsieur Reynaud hitched his jacket up on his shoulders. He turned once more to Major Fauvelle.

'Please continue, Major,' he said.

The Major had pulled himself together in the interval. There were still grit marks on his cheeks where the tears had spilled.

'Army Group One, Monsieur le Président,' he began again, 'is in complete disarray. There is very little meat and wine left – enough to feed the armies for two days, perhaps. We are without transport – all our horses have been killed by enemy shelling and bombing. We have no armoured vehicles left. Our ammunition will have run out very soon. And we cannot hope to supply our front-line troops from what little supplies we have left in store because of the refugees. We couldn't keep the Belgian frontier closed to civilian traffic any longer. There are two million Dutch and Belgian refugees pouring into our territory, and our own people are on the move. Virtually the entire population of Lille is fleeing south; every road is choked with refugees. Monsieur le Président, it is impossible for us to continue the fight. We can't move; we can't take up defensive positions; we can't supply our armies. There is nothing for us but capitulation.'

'Be quiet,' General Weygand told him.

Monsieur Reynaud's mouth had fallen open. There was an expression of horror on his face. Clearly he had been unaware of the full scope of the disaster in the north-east. Weygand began to speak to him, his shrill voice fighting through the phlegm in his throat.

'This war has been sheer madness from the beginning,' he said. 'We have gone into it with our 1918 army against a German army of 1939. It is sheer madness.'

He was talking nonsense, thought Vivian. The Char B's and Somuas which he had seen going into action at Montcornet had been as good and as modern as anything on the ground. The madness had been that there hadn't been more officers like de Bernac and Idée, commanded by a Charles de Gaulle. Echoing his thought, Sir Edward Spears said to General Weygand, 'That is not what you said in July,

241

General.' His voice was tense with controlled anger. 'You said, if I remember rightly, that the armies of the Republic were a more effective fighting force than at any previous time in their history.'

'I spoke from ignorance,' Weygand replied. He turned on Monsieur Reynaud. 'Monsieur le Président, if I had seen the situation reports two weeks ago, I would never have agreed to leave Syria to take command here.' He turned back to Sir Edward. 'What sort of air force have we got? Four hundred obsolete fighters. And thirty bombers, none of which are capable of night-flying. And where is the Royal Air Force? I will tell you, General Spears! It is being kept in England by men who believe, and hope, perhaps, that France is already doomed. I'll tell you who are the defeatists in this war, General Spears. They are not the poor, brave soliders of France. They are the English. Yes, the English who husband their forces while the soldiers of France bleed to death.'

Sir Edward tried to reply, but General Weygand had already selected a new target for his wrath. Leaning across the table, he addressed Marshal Pétain.

'The entire strategy on which our military planning has been based for the last fifteen years is an utter nonsense,' he said.

The eighty-year-old Marshal's head had drooped right down onto his chest. His eyes were closed, his breathing heavy and regular. As if in an attempt to wake him up, General Weygand shrieked at him, 'For the third time in seventy years, our soldiers in the field have been betrayed by the men in white breeches.'

The force of his outburst was spent. He sat erect in his chair, his sparse moustache quivering on his lip. Reynaud turned to Sir Edward and said calmly, 'You appreciate, General Spears, that if Army Group One were to disappear altogether, it would be extremely difficult for the remaining French armies to hold a front extending from the mouth of the Somme to Switzerland.'

For a moment, Vivian could not understand why he had not addressed the remark to Major Fauvelle who had, after all, been the person who had advocated the surrender of Army Group One. Then he realised – the French Prime Minister was explaining why France might have to capitulate.

'There are other, less extended defensible lines to be held in France,' Sir Edward replied. 'In any case, I can promise you this. Whatever happens, the British people would not allow their government to seek terms from the Germans – even if His Majesty's government were to consider such a course. The British will fight on, anywhere, everywhere. The British will continue this war until Germany is defeated.'

Brave words, thought Vivian. He wondered if anybody in the room apart from himself believed them.

General Weygand sighed deeply. 'It goes without saying,' he said wearily, 'I shall fight on too.' With an effort he turned to Sir Edward, reached out and placed his hand on Sir Edward's sleeve. 'To the end,' he said. 'To the very end.'

He looked up to where Major Fauvelle was waiting. 'Are any of General Blanchard's divisions in a position to launch an attack?' he asked.

'There are three divisions which remain intact, General,' Major Fauvelle replied. 'The Fifteenth, the Twenty-fifth, and the Twelfth, but they are without food or ammunition, and movement is paralysed because of the refugees. The Germans are systematically causing panic by bombing and machine-gunning the refugees on the roads, and our own troops are being affected by this panic.'

Once more he turned to Monsieur Reynaud.

'Monsieur le Président, our men are stupified by the bombing. It never stops. We will have to surrender soon.'

Sir Edward turned to Vivian and said in English, 'I wish we could chuck this whingeing fellow out of the window. I expect the blighter's actually being paid by Goebbels, eh?'

Vivian smiled. He caught the eye of Paul Baudouin across the length of the table. Baudouin was smiling back. He knew precisely what Sir Edward had said.

'The only course open to Army Group One,' General Weygand announced briskly, 'is to fall back and to form perimeters round Boulogne and Dunkirk. It is perfectly obvious. We can't afford to lose so large a force. But the roads into metropolitan France are cut. Our armies must secure a supply route, and that route must be by sea. The Royal Navy still holds the Straits securely: it is perfectly feasible. I shall issue the necessary orders to General Blanchard immediately.'

'That would be best, General,' Major Fauvelle agreed. 'That way General Blanchard can at least avoid the disgrace of a surrender *en rase compagne*.'

'I thought,' Sir Edward intervened, 'that we were discussing the survival of Army Group One as an active and aggressive force, not the most agreeable method by which Blanchard might capitulate.'

'Of course, of course,' General Weygand agreed. 'But it is true that if Blanchard's men are doomed, we must see that they are allowed to disappear with honour.'

'I was under the impression,' Reynaud addressed General Weygand, 'that you had absolute faith in Blanchard. You told us that he was a real leader of men, and that he was moving onto the offensive.'

'Monsieur le Président, if I might be permitted ... ' said Major Fauvelle.

Monsieur Reynaud nodded.

'G.Q.G., Vincennes cannot fully understand the position. General Blanchard has had no real opportunity to assume command. After the unfortunate accident which took General Billotte from us, Army Group One Headquarters has been a staff without a commander. The staff have had to operate without orders from above. They are utterly worn out. General Blanchard arrived into a situation of the utmost disorder. His staff are scattered. He scarcely knows them. And he too is utterly worn out.'

Again there was silence, while this news was digested.

'Lord Gort most assuredly received orders to attack south in the Arras sector,' said Sir Edward.

'He could not have received them from Army Group One Headquarters,' said Major Fauvelle. 'No orders have been sent to Lord Gort since Monday.'

'Do you mean to say that the British Expeditionary Force has received no orders for five days?' exclaimed Sir Edward.

He spoke to Reynaud.

'Lord Gort has been under the impression that he is supposed to be launching an offensive southwards from Arras to link up with General Frère's forces somewhere around Bapaume. The entire Army Group with whom he is supposed to be cooperating is in a state of disorder, is contemplating surrender, is at best about to retreat into perimeters round Boulogne and Dunkirk, and Lord Gort has received no instructions whatsoever. The British Expeditionary Force will be left completely isolated in the middle of Flanders, its rear and its flanks completely exposed. It will be totally destroyed.'

There was a loud snort from the venerable hero of Verdun. He stirred, glanced about him from heavy, rheum-encrusted lids, then let his head drop forward once again.

The intercom buzzed again, and Monsieur Reynaud picked up the receiver. A girl's voice came through.

'Excuse me, Monsieur le Président, but Senator Lefebre wishes to speak to you. He says the matter is urgent.'

'Very well,' Monsieur Reynaud replied, 'put him through.'

'Hallo? Paul, *cher ami*?' came the voice of the senator.

'Hallo, Maurice,' Reynaud replied. 'How can I help you?' He took his handkerchief from his breast pocket and dabbed at his forehead.

'It's my daughter, Marie-Chantal,' said the senator. 'I promised I'd speak to you on her behalf. You know the ladies; they never give you a moment's peace, eh? You'll remember she got married three weeks ago?'

'Yes. Yes, of course,' Monsieur Reynaud replied.

Already he was taking out his fountain-pen and unscrewing the cap.

'The boy's name is Étienne – Lieutenant Étienne Bourget,' the senator went on. 'He is serving with the Chasseurs in General Petiet's 3rd Infantry Division at Forges-les-Eaux. My daughter is terribly concerned about him, *cher ami*. It would be a great relief to us all if he could be posted to a place where there are fewer Germans.'

'I have made a note of the name,' Reynaud replied. 'I'll see what can be done.'

'Thank you, *cher ami*. She is our only child, you understand, so we must indulge her terribly.'

'*Au revoir*, Maurice,' said Monsieur Reynaud firmly.

He put down the receiver.

'Major Fauvelle,' said Sir Edward, 'when you return to General Blanchard's headquarters, will you please tell him, and his staff, that the British will continue to wage war, whatever the cost, whatever may befall. Tell him that neither King George VI, nor Mr Churchill, nor the British people, will for a moment contemplate surrender to the forces of barbarism.'

'Would the English government consider bombing French towns?' asked Major Fauvelle.

The whole room seemed lethargic with old age and despair. Even the specks of dust hung motionless.

'If there is to be capitulation here, in France, Major Fauvelle,' Sir Edward told him, 'you may rest assured that His Majesty's armed forces will bomb, shell, or assault any French town which harbours the enemy, regardless of who else may be there, precisely as you have bombed and shelled Dutch and Belgian towns which have admitted the enemy.'

Once again, Monsieur Reynaud intervened.

'I think all has been said that needs to be said at this juncture. It is my opinion that General Weygand should order this officer back to General Blanchard's headquarters. He should inform General Blanchard that the War Council is fully aware of the difficulties which confront him, and that we all appreciate that he alone can be the judge of the decisions that should be taken.'

General Weygand and Admiral Darlan grunted their approval.

'This officer,' Reynaud concluded, 'shall remind General Blanchard that he, General Blanchard, is custodian of the honour of France.'

The old Marshal jerked his head and woke up. General Weygand nodded to Major Fauvelle who clicked his heels and left. Monsieur Reynaud rose to his feet, and the others followed suit. Reynaud came round the table, and shook Sir Edward Spears warmly by the hand. General Weygand did likewise, then Reynaud and the Generalissimo retired to the Prime Minister's study. Admiral Darlan nodded to Sir Edward and went out alone to the gallery. Sir Edward bowed slightly to Marshal Pétain and to Paul Baudouin. Vivian followed him across the Grand Study to the gallery. At the double doors, he turned, wondering whether to close them after him. Paul Baudouin was standing with the Marshal at the table, his hand resting on the old man's arm. They were talking together. Marshal Pétain appeared to be fully awake and in command of his senses.

Vivian followed Sir Edward along the gallery and down the marble stairs. Roland de Margerie was coming up. He noticed the expression on their faces and smiled.

'Cheer up, gentlemen,' he said in English. 'Worse things happen at sea.'

'I doubt it,' Sir Edward replied.

Sir Edward and Vivian went out onto the steps overlooking the forecourt and, beyond the railings and the rampart of sandbags, the Rue St Dominique. Vivian took off his cap, letting the warmth of the sun bathe his head. Sir Edward drew his cigarette-case out of the breast pocket of his uniform.

'Doesn't help, I suppose,' he said, 'but, by God, I need it!'

Vivian took a cigarette. Sir Edward lit it for him.

'Do you know,' said Sir Edward, 'I deliberately refrain from smoking during important meetings? It gives me something to look forward to when things are going badly.'

Vivian smiled though he did not feel like smiling.

A *huissier* came down the steps to join them. With his greying hair, distinguished air, and mayoral chain, he would have made a much more impressive figure as *Président du Conseil* than the actual incumbent of that office.

'There is a car waiting for Monsieur le Général?' he asked Sir Edward gravely. 'Shall I tell Monsieur le Général's driver to bring it round to the front?'

'If you please,' Sir Edward replied.

The *huissier* inclined his head and descended the remaining steps with leisurely dignity.

'I honestly believe,' Sir Edward remarked, 'that if all the Goths, Vandals and Huns were suddenly to erupt into Paris, the government *huissiers* would remain as calm and unruffled as ever. Like Roman senators. . . . Coming back to the Rue St Honoré? Ronnie Campbell will give us a stiff whisky and soda, and a spot of lunch.'

He sensed Vivian's hesitation.

'No hurry, old chap, if you'd prefer a breath of fresh air,' he told him.

'It was a bit overpowering, sir,' Vivian explained.

Sir Edward nodded.

'I'll have to have a confidential chat with H.E. anyway,' he said. 'Mustn't let him get the idea Winston's going over his head. You come along at tea-time, there's a good fellow. About four-thirty, eh?'

'Very good, sir,' Vivian replied.

The big Buick saloon drew up at the bottom of the steps. Vivian put his cap back on his head.

'Can I give you a lift?' asked Sir Edward. 'Drop you off somewhere?'

'Very kind of you, sir,' Vivian replied. 'I thought I'd take a stroll up the Avenue George V.'

Sir Edward ran briskly down the steps to the car. Vivian followed. As they got in, Sir Edward told the driver,

'We'll go over the Pont de l'Alma . . . The Place de l'Alma suit you, Hardwicke?'

'Admirably, sir,' Vivian replied.

He sat back against the cushions in the corner of the seat. He felt more depressed than he had felt since coming over to France, more than at any time since Rosemary had decided – or had pretended to decide – that their marriage should end. There had been a mortal lethargy in the Grand Study, as if the real feelings and emotions of the War Council had emanated and had polluted the physical atmosphere. Even at the very end, at the headquarters of the 4th Armoured Division, there had been a sense of life, and faith, despite the death of de Bernac.

The remnants of the division, worn out by two unsuccessful attempts at offensive action, had been about to move north out of the Aisne sector to join up with the British 51st Highland Division on the Somme, at Abbeville. Vivian had reported to Colonel de Gaulle, to inform him that he had been transferred to the Military Attaché's Department at the Rue St Honoré. De Gaulle had offered him a weary, disdainful smile.

'Ah,' he had said, 'so, precisely when we require, at last, the services of a sound liaison officer, the English decide to withold him from us.'

'Colonel,' Vivian had replied, 'no one regrets it more than I.'

To Vivian's surprise, de Gaulle had said, 'I believe you.'

Having given Vivian time to digest this extraordinary compliment, de Gaulle had continued, 'There will be another battle, *mon brave*. We will be fighting side by side with your Scotsmen. They are fine soldiers, the Scots. You will miss an interesting event.'

'I shall be very disappointed not to be present, Colonel,' Vivian told him.

De Gaulle had offered him his hand.

'We shall hold our heads high, eh, Major 'ardwicke?' he had said. 'The wounded shall smile. The guns will bark joyously.'

Even though de Gaulle had addressed him, as he had done so often, as if to record his statement for posterity – and British posterity in particular – Vivian had felt a flash of light in the gathering darkness. To have been allowed to stay with the 4th Armoured would have been like remaining on an island of courage and high endeavour in a flood of despair.

He said to Sir Edward in the car beside him,

247

'Don't mind admitting, sir, the sort of thing we saw going on today makes one wish one still held a field command.'

'Know exactly what you mean,' Sir Edward replied seriously.

He glanced at the driver to ensure that the glass partition was closed.

'Tell you what I wish, Hardwicke,' he went on. 'I wish the old Tiger was still amongst us. I'd like to have seen that egregious fellow – what's his name? ... '

'Fauvelle?' suggested Vivian.

'Thank you – Fauvelle,' Sir Edward replied. 'I'd like to have seen Fauvelle deliver that report to old Clemenceau. By God! Clemenceau would have had the fellow dragged off to Vincenenes, court-martialled, and shot, before anybody had time to sit down to lunch.'

They were passing the end of the Pont de la Concorde, along the Quai d'Orsay. The warmth of the sun through the open car windows evaporated as they passed under the huge shadow of the Foreign Ministry.

'Monsieur Reynaud isn't altogether unsympathetic as a character,' Vivian observed.

'The Tiger was never sympathetic,' Sir Edward replied. 'That crowd were all terrified of him. That's why they all hate Georges Mandel. Mandel was the Tiger's friend and pupil. You're right, though. Reynaud isn't a bad little chap at all. Plenty of guts, actually. You remember Hamlet though? ... "That this man carrying the stamp of one defect his virtues else, be they as pure as grace, shall take corruption from that particular fault" – or words to that effect.'

'And Monsieur Reynaud's particular fault,' said Vivian, 'is the Comtesse de Portes?'

'Holed in one, old chap,' Sir Edward replied.

They had turned off the Quai d'Orsay, and were crossing over the Pont de l'Alma.

'Hélène de Portes,' said Sir Edward, 'makes, by comparison, our own ex-Mrs Wallis Simpson appear a gracious and regal asset to the body politic. ... '

He leaned forward and knocked on the window behind the driver's seat.

'Pull over here,' he instructed, then closed the window again.

He sat back.

'Paul Baudouin is the Comtesse's favourite. He's on the War Council virtually as her nominee. And it wouldn't surprise me in the least if that dreadful Fauvelle creature hadn't been put up by Baudouin. Apart from poor little Reynaud himself, the whole pack of them are defeatist. Georges Mandel, over at the Ministry of the Interior, is reliable, but they'll none of them let him onto the War Council. Not that it's all loss, so long as Reynaud can play them off against one another. Darlan will run with the herd, but none of the herd trust him. If Hélène de Portes and Baudouin have brought back Pétain from Madrid to set him up as head and ornament of a peace party, Weygand will pursue the war against the Germans with the ferocity of a lion. If there is one person Weygand hates more than any politician of the Third Republic, it's Marshal Pétain.'

The car had pulled up against the pavement. They were in the Place de l'Alma. Vivian got out.

'Tea-time then, Hardwicke?' Sir Edward called through the window.

'Very good, sir,' Vivian replied.

He saluted, and the car drew away up the Avenue Montaigne. He started to walk at a leisurely pace up the Avenue George V, towards the Champs-Elysées. The cafés were as busy as ever on a summer's day, and the tables were crowded under the striped awnings. There was the usual heavy sprinkling of French and British uniforms, and even some Polish military caps, conspicuous by their rectangular shape. But there was also the sound of loud American voices. War or no war, the holiday season was come, even if most of the tourists were in uniform. The fighting in the north-east was important, no doubt, like the Japanese invasion of Manchuria, or the Italian aggression in Abyssinia; but, for the moment, it did not touch the street cafés in the eighth arrondissement.

Vivian paused at the turning up the Rue Christophe Colomb. He had known he was coming here, and he had known why. But in some strange way, the motive had not occupied the forefront of his mind. One evening after a few glasses of wine, de Bernac had insisted he copy down the address in his pocket diary; the best house in Paris, de Bernac had said. Vivian had recorded it out of politeness. He had not wished to tell de Bernac that he did not ordinarily have recourse to prostitutes. In the Grand Study, however, among the masks and dead faces listening to Major Fauvelle as he delivered his report he had longed for some sign of life; and even the crowds chattering under the awnings of the street cafés had seemed dreamlike in their *insouciance*. Now he was on the corner of the Rue Christophe Colomb, and he knew that he was about to call on the address which de Bernac had given him.

He walked the few yards up the street and turned into the shadows of the Rue Magellan. A voice called in a hoarse whisper from an open archway.

'*Veux-tu coucher avec moi, chéri?*'

He caught a glimpse of a marcelle-waved blonde with a fox-fur stole about the shoulders of her frock. He passed on.

He stopped at the number given him by de Bernac. In front of him was an imposing pair of double doors. On either side, the windows were barred on the outside and curtained on the inside. There was no indication of the function of the house, and there was no sound from within. What if he had made a mistake, he wondered; how would he explain his presence on the doorstep? Two or three people passed on up the road, carrying shopping bags with the necks of wine bottles thrust out, and baton loaves tucked under their arms. They did not give him a second glance. Perhaps they were used to seeing callers there in military uniform.

One of the doors opened silently. A small, dark-haired maid stood inside the threshold. She had the puppy-fat figure of a fourteen- or fifteen-year-old, and a round face. She was wearing a black satin dress which did not suit her at all, a small white, heart-shaped cap pinned onto her untidily bunched hair, and a white lace-edged apron which fell far below the hem of her dress, almost to her toes.

'Monsieur?' she asked.

Vivian had supposed that he would be admitted immediately, if only to spare his blushes. Already he had begun to feel embarrassed. The expression on the child's face was that of one who had been sent by her mother to open the front door to a stranger. There was a wariness, as well as the feeble attempt at a smile. He noticed, under the edge of her apron, that she was wearing rubber-soled plimsolls.

'Monsieur ou-ishes?' asked the maid.

The laboured attempt at speaking in English came so unexpectedly that Vivian could not at first understand what she had said. But for the heavy, red velvet curtain which hung from the arch a little way down the dark-tiled vestibule, he would have been certain he had come to the wrong address. As it was, he could think of no way of replying. On one side of the vestibule was an open door; a woman came out.

'That will do, Claudine,' she said.

She had the ample proportions of a concierge, and her accent had the proletarian harshness of the Twentieth Arrondissement. But the hair, piled up on the top of her head, was blue-rinsed, and she appeared to have been sewn into her art-silk dress. A thick cluster of paste jewels glistened against her powdered throat.

'You may return to your duties, *ma petite*,' she said.

'*Merci, madame*,' the maid chanted, and bobbed dutifully.

She vanished behind the heavy velvet curtain.

It was acting, thought Vivian; a costume production in some British Drama League Competition, of the sort his mother was so fond of sponsoring, with the plump wife of one of the Cathedral stonemasons as an Edwardian duchess, and some elementary-school leaver conscripted to play the maid.

'Monsieur requires?' asked the woman.

'Captain de Bernac was kind enough to give me your address, madame, and to recommend the house,' Vivian replied.

It was like jumping in at the deep end. The woman's smile broadened into a condescending sympathy.

'Alas, monsieur,' she told him, 'Bernac is not an uncommon name with or without the preposition.'

'Of course, madame,' said Vivian, freely admitting his foolishness. 'André de Bernac, Captain, 4th Cuirassiers?'

The look of ignorance on her face was momentary, but enough to register with Vivian.

'Of course, monsieur,' she exclaimed immediately. 'Monsieur de Bernac is very kind.'

She held back the curtain for him to enter the black interior of the house.

'We can only accept clients by introduction, you understand, monsieur,' she told him. 'It is so important in such an establishment that one should feel among friends, isn't it? Important for the sensibilities of the girls as well.'

'Madame is entirely right,' Vivian assured her as he passed under the arch.

It was like walking out of a summer's afternoon in the West End into the matinee of a play. Daylight filtered narrowly past the edges of the dark curtains; but the principal lighting was by electricity, glowing a dusky yellow on the flock wallpaper, and on the gilt tassels. Part of the light was reflection cast from the ornately framed mirrors on the wall and at the turn of the stairs. There was a dry smell of scent, as if the heated air had been dusted with talcum-powder.

'Monsieur wishes to meet the girls?' the woman asked.

She indicated an open door by the foot of the stairs. Through it, Vivian could see a large mirror mounted against the velvet flock of the opposite wall. Reflected in the glass were bowls of lamplight, and, in the midst, some half dozen girls. The girls were sitting in a cluster, two in armchairs, one perched on the arm of one of the chairs, two on a chesterfield, and one squatting on a leather pouffe. Several of them were smoking through long cigarette-holders. One or two of them were wearing necklaces with pendants, and bracelets; all were wearing high-heeled shoes with narrow ankle-straps. The girl on the leather pouffe was wearing a tiny chain about one ankle. Otherwise they were entirely naked.

'Your hat and cane, monsieur?'

The woman held out her hand.

'Of course, madame,' said Vivian.

He gave her his cap, took his officer's swagger-stick from under his stump and handed it to her. As she turned to put them down on the side table under the stairs, Vivian caught the reflection of the girl squatting on the pouffe. She was smiling directly at him. As soon as she caught his eye, she deliberately opened her legs. She closed them instantly as Madame turned back from the table. A door slammed beyond the stairs.

'Maddy, this is too bad,' Madame announced.

251

A girl had appeared from under the stairs. She was still wearing her close-fitting hat; her linen summer coat was draped over her arm.

'You're getting more and more naughty,' Madame scolded her. 'Upstairs with you, immediately.'

Maddy looked into the lamplit gloom of the salon.

'What's the hurry?' she asked.

'Don't be impudent,' Madame warned her. 'I've warned you before.'

'Perhaps,' said Vivian, 'I might be introduced to Maddy.'

Madame was taken aback. So was Maddy, who was on the point of drawing off her hat from her black hair.

'Forgive me, monsieur,' she began.

Madame had recovered her professional composure instantly.

'Why not, Maddy?' she demanded. 'Considering you're more than an hour late, you can count yourself extremely fortunate to have the chance of entertaining this gentleman straight away.'

Maddy stood hesitantly on the bottom step.

'But I'm not ready, madame,' she said.

Obviously she regarded herself as being punished. She was still in the role of the girl who had been walking up the street outside.

'I don't mind waiting until Maddy is quite ready, madame,' said Vivian.

'Maddy will take you upstairs,' Madame said firmly.

She lowered her voice, though Maddy was surely able to hear her quite plainly.

'Each girl has her own, individual room, monsieur. Nobody else uses it. It makes matters more personal, you understand.'

'Monsieur is welcome,' said Maddy from the bottom of the stairs.

She had removed her hat, and held it balanced over her fist. Her glossy hair was cut in a short bob. It fitted her head and framed her face like a close-fitting cap, the points of which, covering either cheek, reached almost level with the point of her small chin. Her regard of Vivian was one of cool detachment.

Vivian took out his wallet. Letting it hang open, he put one flap between his teeth, and drew out a thin wad of notes. Madame took them and ran her finger through them as he replaced the wallet in his pocket.

'It is sufficient, monsieur,' she said. 'Thank you. And monsieur,' she added, with her condescendingly maternal smile, 'no tip for the girl if she does not behave herself to monsieur's complete satisfaction, eh?'

'Is monsieur coming?' Maddy asked.

She had started up the stairs. He followed her, watching the movement of her pleated linen skirt over her bottom. She was able

252

to dress expensively, he noticed. As they reached the turn of the stairs, he said, 'I am admiring your costume, mademoiselle.'

She paused, one hand on the bannister. She was wearing a wedding ring.

'Thank you, monsieur. It is my own.'

He suspected that she was rebuking him.

'I would not have tried to compliment you on it,' he told her, 'if I had supposed it to be anything else.'

At the top, she led him along a corridor to an end room. She unlocked the door and let him in.

'Does monsieur enjoy watching a woman undressing?' she asked, as she closed the door.

'Perhaps,' Vivian replied.

'The house provides clothes for us when gentlemen wish to see us undressing,' she said, quite conversationally.

They were enclosed in a curtained gloom. The air, however, was quite fresh, with a slight smell of furniture polish, as if the window and curtains had only recently been shut. There was a walnut wardrobe with a mirror-door. The quilted satin headboard of the bed gleamed in the filtered light. The sheets were of satin.

Maddy put her hand on his shoulder. She had unfastened the jacket of her suit.

'Tell me, *chéri*,' she said coaxingly. 'Do you like to watch a woman making *pi-pi*?'

He was certain that she was mocking him – insulting him.

'Tell me, *petite gosse*,' he replied. 'On such occasions, do you use your own *pi-pi*, or is that also provided by the house?'

She dropped her hand, and went back to the wardrobe. He unfastened his shoulder tab, unbuckled his Sam Browne, drew it off and hung it over the back of the chair under the window. He unbuttoned his uniform jacket.

'I'm sorry, monsieur,' Maddy told him.

She was hanging her linen jacket and skirt in the wardrobe.

'I'm not being polite this afternoon. I have been so rushed.'

'I understand very well,' he told her.

'Monsieur has not had a good day so far?' asked Maddy.

'A thoroughly shitty day,' Vivian replied.

'And that's why you've come here?' she asked.

'I suppose so,' he said. 'Not a good reason.'

'The best,' she replied.

She stepped out of her slip and hung it on a dress hanger.

'Now we can make it better for one another, can't we, monsieur?'

He found himself quite extraordinarily pleased that she should have used the term 'monsieur' rather than one of endearment.

He draped his jacket over the seat of the chair. He reached over to the curtain and drew it back a little way. The shaft of sunlight dazzled his eyes. As he became used to it, he could make out in the glare the steep, leaded Paris roof-tops. The girl came close beside him and took the curtain out of his fingers, letting it fall into place. He felt the warmth coming off her body.

'Madame prefers that the curtains should be kept closed,' she said. 'Out of respect for the neighbours.'

She was naked now, her body pale in the gloom. There was a tiny Miraculous Medal on a chain round her neck. Her silk stockings were rolled just above her knees.

'Shall I help monsieur to finish undressing?' she asked. 'Monsieur isn't offended?'

Always the same question.

She unfastened the buttons down the front of his breeches with the expertise of a pick-pocket. She began exciting him with her fingers. As his penis grew into tumescence, she whispered to him how big, how enormous it was. She paused, helping him to remove his boots, and then his breeches. She led him to the bidet, offering to wash him. She drew the warm, soaked flannel-glove over her hand, and straddled the bidet with him so close that her nipples touched his shirt. She caressed and stroked him with the warm flannel until he knew that there was no help for it: that he must let himself go. Helplessly, he ejaculated.

For one or two awful moments, it was as if Maddy had not realised what had occurred, and she continued to caress his groin with the surface of the flannel. As he fell limp, however, she glanced down between them, and saw the dribble of semen on the swell of her belly, just above the ragged triangle of black hair.

'I'm sorry, monsieur,' she told him. 'I did not mean to do it.'

He knew that she was thinking of her tip, but he was touched all the same.

'My fault,' he told her. 'It's a predisposition.'

She smiled at him, and nodded sympathetically. She wiped her belly, then stepped back and sat on the bed.

'If monsieur would care to wait,' she suggested. 'sometimes it's better the second time.'

She bent down and carefully removed her silk stockings from her feet.

'We could have a cigarette,' she suggested. 'There's no hurry.'

Vivian smiled and shook his head. He went back to the chair by the window.

'I must get back to my duties,' he told her.

'It's a shame, monsieur,' she replied. 'Perhaps monsieur will come another day, and ask for me by name?'

'Perhaps,' he said.

With her stockings draped over her fingers, she went over to the wardrobe. Vivian reached down to take his wallet from his pocket. Close to the chair, under the window, was a shopping basket. A book was lying on the top, its spine sticking upwards. He drew it out and examined the title. It was a French-German grammar and vocabulary, and it was brand new.

He glanced over to the wardrobe as he slipped the book back into the basket. Maddy was bent over, her bottom towards him, fastening the ankle-straps of her high-heeled shoes. He opened his wallet, drew out some notes and held them out for her, folded over his finger. She straightened up and took them, glancing quickly at the denominations before hiding them in the wardrobe. He finished dressing. As he left the little room with Maddy, the maid was at the open doors of the linen press on the opposite side of the corridor. She was arranging a small pile of draw-sheets over her arm. Maddy said, 'It won't be necessary this time, Claudine.'

'Thank you, mademoiselle,' the child replied.

Several minutes later, he stepped out of the shadows of the Rue Magellan into the petrol-smelling glare of the Rue Christophe Colomb and the Avenue George V. There was a comfort, he felt, in the way one's personal inadequacies and distress could be absorbed into the universal misfortune. He wondered whether it would be merely to add to the burdens of his superiors to report to them his private piece of intelligence – that the ladies of the *maisons de tolérance* were learning German.

26

The night had been very unruly. Papayannis had woken or half-woken from dreams in which he had seen the flames of the newly kindled Easter fire in the church of his Alexandrine childhood, flickering on the ceiling of his Paris bedroom. He had heard the reverberate boom of the voices of deacons and archimandrites, and the sharp reports of the maroons out at sea beyond the Royal Navy yards. His mother, a beautiful woman with a dense mane of glistening ebony hair, a white face, and a red satin dress, and immensely tall, had leant over the bed to tell him that the monster, Drakho, had laid a fog over the sea so that nobody should see him step ashore, and that he was coming to peer in at the windows, and would tear out the eyes of any child who was still awake.

When, finally, he had wrenched himself from sleep, and had managed to drag himself upstairs to the attic window, he had seen over the rooftops to where fires had been started over in the direction of Des Buttes Chaumont, and Les Lilas. He had heard the drone of aircraft overhead. It had seemed strange that German pilots could cruise so purposefully over Paris, with only the pop-gun ineffectiveness of the scattered anti-aircraft batteries, and the several searchlight beams, to oppose their leisurely progress. Somehow it had sounded so normal and reassuring after the terrifying visions of the Easter vigil, and his mother's dreadful coaxing.

He woke finally to the sound of the telephone in the office downstairs. Morning light was filtering through the shutters, and he could hear the sound of the traffic down on the Rue Custine, so that he wondered whether, in fact, he had dreamed during the night about the air-raids, and about rising to see the glow over the rooftops to the east. He glanced at his watch. It was nine o'clock. Mademoiselle Roche would not be in the office to answer, and censor, the incoming phone calls; it was Sunday. But Idris Rahman would be round with the car to take him to Notre Dame, any minute now.

He pulled himself up into a sitting position. The telephone continued to ring – whoever was at the other end was determined he should answer it. He felt leaden and aching, worse than he had felt when he had risen during the night. His chest felt taut almost to the point at which he couldn't catch his breath. His mouth was dry and scented with the cigars he had smoked the previous day. His penis was erect: painfully distended and hard; piss-proud, of course; by the time he had reached for the telephone it would be his bladder which would be aching for relief.

As he put his weight on his feet, he gasped for breath, then took it in like a fish, in little gulps so as not to hurt his chest. He tried to cough, but failed. He would have to struggle down to the office to answer the persistent ringing; the fear of not knowing who was at the other end was worse than any trepidation about actually being spoken to. Two days ago, in the afternoon when he had been out at a business luncheon, Aris Liassides had phoned at last, from Alexandria. When Mademoiselle Roche had told him, he had asked, 'What was his message?'

'For you, Monsieur Chris?' she had replied.

'Of course,' he had replied, scarcely able to keep his voice from trembling.

Mademoiselle Roche had glanced down at the florid pleats and frills of her white jabot. She brushed an imaginary speck of powder out of one of the folds with the edge of her thumb. Then she looked up at him almost coquettishly.

'There was no message, Monsieur Chris,' she said. 'Not for you. He wished to speak to Monsieur Rahman or to Monsieur El Chamoun.'

Papayannis had felt sick.

'Did you ask him if he wished to speak to me?' he demanded.

'No, Monsieur Chris,' she replied, adjusting the pince-nez on her nose. 'I am quite sure that if Monsieur Liassides had wished to speak to you, he would have said so.'

She had pressed her lips together, disapprovingly. He had waited a few minutes before leaving the office, going through the house and down the steps to the yard at the back. Both El Chamoun and Rahman had been there, awaiting his instructions as always, lounging against the wall in the sunlight. El Chamoun had merely glanced at him. Rahman had given him his broad, friendly smile, and had said, ''allo, Monsieur Chris.'

Papayannis had realised that he did not dare ask about Liassides' phone call, and had gone back through the house to the office.

He pulled on his embroidered Japanese silk dressing-gown over his pyjamas, and went through into the bathroom to splash himself with cologne before descending the stairs. It made him feel slightly better, but his penis still thrust monstrously against his pyjama trousers. Panting for breath, he descended, clutching the rail, and taking one stair at a time. Before he reached the bottom, the ringing stopped. He heard the voice of Céline from the office – the little girl who came in on a Sunday morning to do the cleaning. Normally, she did not answer the telephone, being only a child, but she must have thought that he was asleep, and that the ringing would not stop until she did so.

She came to the bottom of the stairs.

'It's a gentleman, Monsieur Chris. Says I'm to get you.'

Papayannis felt a twinge of panic.

'Who is it?' he asked, his voice croaking.

'Don't know,' the child shrugged her shoulders. 'A gentleman. He's waiting.'

She glanced below the curve of his belly. There was a smirk on her face. He wondered whether she could observe the swollen thrust under his dressing-gown.

'Does he speak with a foreign accent?' he asked.

'Not as foreign as yours, Monsieur Chris,' Céline replied, still smirking.

'Fetch me some coffee,' he ordered.

'Very well, Monsieur Chris.'

She bobbed a slight curtsey – a relic from her haphazard attendance at school, no doubt – and went off down the passage to the kitchen. As he crossed the hall to the office, he could hear her singing some cheap American song about being down on the Mexican border: you couldn't turn on the wireless, these days, without hearing it.

Sunlight was falling through the slats of the office shutters. It projected shadowy bars across the expensive *objets d'art*, the porcelain and silver, the dark, oil-painted landscapes, which cluttered the floor space and the tables, and across the form of the one-eyed owl over the coat-stand, and the debauched, sensual features of the girl in the Felicien Rops portrait which hung over his desk. Papayannis was still struggling to catch his breath after the effort of coming downstairs, when he picked up the earpiece of the telephone from where Céline had placed it on Mademoiselle Roche's desk.

'Hallo?' he asked.

'Monsieur Chris? Have I called too early?' asked a man's voice at the other end.

There was a coughing. Papayannis waited for it to finish. Since Aris Liassides had spoken to Rahman, his world had seemed to become uncertain. In the solitary darkness of his nights, he had prayed as he had prayed as a child, to the Virgin of Heraklion, and the Virgin of Sardis. Relief and a sense of well-being now poured through him like the coming of water to a parched land.

'*Bonjour, Marius,*' he said.

'Ah, Monsieur Chris!' exclaimed the proprietor from the Rue Quincampoix through his catarrh. 'You recognise my voice at last. I have some news which may interest you.'

Papayannis was careful to sound less than enthusiastic.

'Indeed?'

'You mentioned, Monsieur Chris, something about an *objet* – the property of Monsieur le Baron de Bart-Mendel,' said the proprietor.

'A medallion. Yes,' Papayannis replied with slight impatience. 'What of it?'

He was entirely himself now. Even his penis had softened, leaving him with the need to relieve himself.

'Listen, Monsieur Chris,' the proprietor said.

Papayannis could tell that he had put his mouth close to the mouthpiece.

'I have a friend. He's by way of having a small business – you know how it is – down by the Porte des Lilas. Now my friend has a friend – or rather an associate – who keeps a shop in the Rue des Boers ... '

He broke off.

'Go on, Marius,' Papayannis said.

'This fellow,' said the proprietor, 'my friend's friend – specialises – acts as a broker, you might say. He handles the little gifts which rich employers give to their servants ... You understand? ... little gifts which the servants prefer to sell than to keep?'

'Go on,' Papayannis repeated.

'Monsieur Chris, my friend's friend has come to my friend with a gold pen – a gold pen with an amethyst tip on the cap. Inscribed on the pen are the initials of Monsieur le Baron de Bart-Mendel. It appears it was given to my friend's friend by a chambermaid

258

employed in the Baron's household. She says the Baron gave it to her as a present, but she needs a little money.'

'She couldn't go to the municipal pawnbrokers with it, of course,' said Papayannis.

The proprietor laughed down the phone.

'Exactly,' he replied. 'Anyway, my friend's friend decided it was a bit hot for him. He told the girl she would have to wait until he had had it valued. He gave her a receipt and told her to come back tonight, when she has a couple of hours off. Then he took the pen over to my friend at the Porte des Lilas, and my friend rang me. I'd told him about your interest in Monsieur le Baron's affairs, you see. If it is convenient for you, Monsieur Chris, he will bring the girl over to the Rue Quincampoix tonight. Nine o'clock. It's no distance for him.'

'There was bombing over in that direction last night,' said Papayannis.

'Terrible,' the proprietor agreed. 'Belleville it was ... But it'll take more than a few dirty Boches to finish off my friend, eh? ... Just thought this girl might be in a position to give you the information – you know – about the – er – *objet* of the Baron which interests you.'

'Thank you, Marius,' Papayannis replied. 'You're a good friend ... Now listen. It may be too late.'

It was his turn to speak close to the mouthpiece. He didn't want Céline to overhear him.

'I'm going to High Mass at Notre Dame,' he continued. 'The relics of St Louis and Ste Geneviève are to be displayed for veneration, and their aid invoked. It may be that the Baron, for all he's a Jew, has handed over the *objet* to which you refer, my friend, to the ecclesiastical authorities. If he hasn't, then you may tell your friend to tell his friend that I will buy this pen from him at a generous price. And, of course, you and your friend won't be forgotten – you can trust me for that, eh?'

'Of course, Monsieur Chris,' fawned the proprietor.

Papayannis could almost smell the foulness of the man's breath.

'*À bientôt*, Marius,' he concluded, and hung the earpiece of the phone on its hook.

Céline brought the tray with the coffee and brioches into the office.

'Monsieur wants something else?' she asked.

She was in the shadow, but he could imagine the smile on her face. He had seen it on the face of the girls of her age who had hung about outside the naval dockyards in Alexandria. They had been Greek girls; the Arabs sent their boys to haggle over their sisters' – or their own – bodies.

The behaviour of the Greek girls had caused him bitter shame, and a hatred for the English sailors who had exploited their childish venality. But the hatred had not been unmixed with envy.

'Monsieur wants something else?'

He grunted a laugh. He patted Céline's plump little cheek.

'Monsieur Rahaman will be here to fetch me,' he explained.

He kept a few low-denomination bills folded in his dressing-gown pocket. He took one out. He put his arm around her waist, slipping it under her faded blue apron. His fingers found the pocket in the lap of her chequered gingham frock. She gave a little giggle as he thrust his fingers between the pieces of broken comb and the crumpled handkerchief, and left the money there.

'Be a good girl for Papa, and do your work well,' he whispered down to her, 'and there could be another one, eh?'

27

The previous evening, Julie and Victor had been to the cinema in the Rue des Mathurins, to see Harry Bauer's newly released version of *Volpone*, with Louis Jouvet as Mosca. Afterwards, when they had returned home, they sat up over drinks, in the study. The servants had all gone to bed; the whole, large house seemed to contain only the two of them. The night was misty and quite cold. There was a fire burning in the wide hearth. Julie sat on the floor in front of it. Victor was sunk into his chair. They talked about great acting, and in particular about Jouvet – his performances in *La Kermesse Héroique*, *Carnet du Bal*, and *Drôle de Drame*.

'You are never going to reach the top of your profession, you know,' Victor told her suddenly.

'What makes you think that?' Julie demanded.

'I was going to say that if you were, you wouldn't be here with me,' he replied. 'You'd think every minute spent away from London's West End was a great part lost – Ophelia, Viola, Desdemona! But I see that it is only an effect, not a cause. The real reason you will never be a star is that you are too happy being yourself. The true *tragédienne* is never fulfilled unless she is being somebody else. You've only to look at the private lives of women like Bernhardt, or Duse – or even, according to one or two of my friends, Garbo. They have no capability for real living. But you have the talent to be joyful when you are most yourself.'

'You should see me backstage,' she laughed. 'You'd hate me – you honestly would. I might be a better actress than you think. Perhaps you are not seeing the real me.'

He leaned forward and reached for her.

'I think I can tell sometimes,' he said.

'That,' she whispered, 'is not at all a fair argument.'

But she allowed him to draw her onto his lap.

Afterwards, when they were lying together on cushions in front of the fire, Julie said, 'There's something I've been wanting to ask you. I always thought that Jews were circumcised.'

'So they are,' he told her. 'My father was never a believer. And there was *l'Affaire Dreyfus*.'

'So he decided you should pass for gentile?' Julie asked.

'If I changed my name,' he replied.

'But – like Mendelssohn – you decided not to,' she said.

'Exactly.'

Time passed. Julie was happy where she was; she showed no inclination to go upstairs. Their love-making had been very good; his face was relaxed in the firelight, all trace of anxiety gone. The sound of the traffic on the Étoile was distant and soothing. She fell asleep.

She was woken by the screech of the air-raid alarms. At first she did not know what it was. There hadn't been an attack on Paris before.

'There's an air-raid coming,' Victor told her. 'Better go down quickly.'

He was already on his feet, fastening his trousers. She knelt upright, befuddled with sleep. She picked up the crumpled silk of her underpants where they were lying beside her. She glanced about her; she had the confused idea that if anybody were to come in and catch her with them, she would be for it. She thrust them under the leather cushion of the armchair.

'I wouldn't leave them there,' Victor told her, 'the maid will find them tomorrow morning.'

'Oh God!' Julie murmured as she extricated them.

She couldn't seem to bring her mind into focus.

The house was awake. Voices were calling from above and below. There was the shuffling of feet on the tiled floor of the hall. Hugo was calling, 'Papa! Papa!' From outside, the noise of the alarm continued. Julie squeezed the underpants into a little ball and pushed them into her handbag. Victor grabbed her by the arm and propelled her out of the study. Severin, the butler, had taken charge down in the darkened hall. As Julie and Victor came down the single flight of stairs from the study, Danielle emerged from the shadows, in a woollen dressing gown, her hair tied tightly about her head in a chiffon scarf.

'I went up to your room, mademoiselle,' she said. 'As soon as the warnings started,' she added.

They went down through the kitchen quarters, to the stone steps leading to the cellars, where the rest of the household had assembled. There they sat, and listened to the distant thud of explosions.

'Have we any real Parisians here?' Victor asked.

Nobody answered.

'Do any of you have families in Paris?'

Nobody answered.

'Then you are all from the country?' he asked.

'Not me, monsieur,' growled Joseph, 'but this is all the family I've got.'

He motioned about the dimly lit cellar, amid grunts of approval.

Victor asked them all, one by one, where they came from. One or two of the girls told him, between embarrassed giggles, that they were from the Rethel district, and had entered his service at La Berlière. He asked them about their homes and their families – whether they had had any news of them. He endeavoured to reassure them. Then he suggested that, as they were in the cellar, that they might open a bottle of wine or two to keep out the cold. They did so, and as time passed, the occasion began to assume the license of a servants' hall party. They tried to guess where the bombs were falling – how far off – rather like passengers on a cruise liner guessing at the rate of passage. The cook-housekeeper, Maryvonne, congratulated Julie on her command of the language, adding that she had always been of the opinion that the English couldn't be bothered to learn any language but their own. Julie glanced at Victor. He was sitting at the table, smiling slightly, his face mandarin-like in the weak, dusty lamplight.

There was a distinct reluctance to break up the party after the air-raid was over. Severin went up and opened the door at the top of the steps, while Victor bade everybody a pointed goodnight. Danielle was clearly intending to escort Julie up to her room. Julie was compelled to assure her that it was quite unnecessary. Danielle bade her goodnight with obvious reluctance.

When they were on the landing upstairs, Julie and Victor said goodnight. They shook hands formally. But Julie could not resist saying, 'You were wonderful, Victor. They were all really enjoying themselves down there. They'll be praying for another air-raid.'

He smiled at her.

'I know,' he said. 'I was enjoying it myself. I'm greedy for enjoyment these days.'

'*Bonjour, mademoiselle!*' Danielle's voice rapped out.

She drew back the curtains, letting the sunlight pour in across the balcony.

'It's half-past nine, mademoiselle.'

Julie had surfaced through a jumble of dream impressions: the firelight in the study, lamplight on the stone walls of the cellar,

Jouvet's Mosca lighting a forest of votive candles in a Venetian church; and through all of these, the relaxed, post-coital warmth.

'What happened last night?' she asked. 'I mean, where was the raid?'

'It was over Belleville, mademoiselle,' Danielle replied.

Her pretty face was controlled but tense. It made Julie feel that she must have done something wrong.

'They haven't said anything about it on the wireless,' Danielle told her. 'But naturally, everyone knows it was Belleville.'

'Didn't they say *anything* about the air-raid on the wireless?' asked Julie.

She struggled into a sitting position. Danielle didn't answer. Julie saw that she was looking for her soiled clothes, to take them down to the laundry-room. She had gathered up Julie's stockings, belt, slip, and brassière from the chair. Now she was searching the floor round about it. Julie suddenly remembered the underpants in her handbag.

'Do you know anybody in Belleville?' she asked, to distract her.

Danielle glanced up. To Julie's surprise, she looked confused, as if she had been found out.

'No, mademoiselle,' she replied. 'Nobody at all.'

She moved the chair.

'They do say that hundreds of people have been killed though,' she added hurriedly. 'Nearly a thousand, some people say.'

'It's lucky Monsieur has a deep cellar,' Julie said.

'Oh yes, mademoiselle. It is.'

Julie couldn't stand the girl's fidgeting about any longer.

'What is it you're looking for?' she asked.

Danielle gave a little laugh.

'I can't find Mademoiselle's *culottes* from yesterday,' she explained.

'Oh dear!' sighed Julie. 'You know how late it was when I came up here. They'll be lying about in the bathroom or somewhere. Please don't worry about them now. If I see them, I'll leave them on the chair for when you come to make the bed.'

'Thank you, mademoiselle,' Danielle replied.

As soon as she was gone, Julie got out of bed. She went to the dressing-table, took out the underpants from her handbag, and dropped them on the carpet behind the dressing-table stool. Just like the second Mrs de Winter, she thought. Madame la Baronne de Bart-Mendel would never have left her knickers lying about on the floor. And only tarts shoved their knickers into their handbags.

When she had dressed and done her face, she pinned on her hat, intending to go out to buy some cigarettes and the airmail edition of *The Times*. Then she picked up her handbag and gloves. Heaven alone knew how she was going to explain to Ambrose all the new

263

things, from hats to underwear, she had acquired since arriving in Paris.

Severin, the butler, was carrying the coffee things on a silver tray, across the hall, when she went down.

'Monsieur le Baron is taking breakfast in the lounge, this morning, mademoiselle,' he said. 'Mademoiselle will be joining him?'

'Shortly,' said Julie.

'I'm going to church after breakfast,' Victor announced.

He had appeared in the doorway of the lounge. He looked very dapper, in a close-fitting, grey, Savile Row suit.

'To church?' asked Julie.

'You don't have to sound quite so surprised,' he complained.

She glanced at Severin's impassive face. There was no need to cover up all the time, she decided.

'Well, I am surprised,' she told him.

'It's something a little special,' he said. 'They are parading the relics of St Louis and Ste Geneviève on the Parvis of Notre Dame. They are bringing them from the Panthéon to be venerated by the crowds after High Mass, so that prayers may be offered for their intercession and protection in these dark times. Everybody will be there: the government, the *Corps Diplomatique*. Would you like to come?'

'If I may,' said Julie.

'But of course,' replied Victor.

'Have I time to nip out to buy some cigarettes and a paper, and have breakfast with you before we go?' she asked.

'Du Mauriers?' he asked. 'I should have ordered some, shouldn't I?'

'They had some yesterday at the kiosk just round the corner,' Julie told him. 'I won't be a moment.'

She wanted to get out into the fresh air for a few minutes before breakfast, if only to clear her head.

She stepped out into the bright morning. The air in the garden square was fresh – unpolluted by traffic fumes. She walked round the cobbled roadway, and passed under the high, stone arch which led out on to the Avenue de Wagram. The concierge's wife was scrubbing the stonework round the office door under the arch. She was a formidably large woman, with her black hair pulled back in a bun. Julie called out, *'Bonjour, madame!'*

The woman looked round from her work. When she saw who it was, she didn't smile.

'Bonjour, mademoiselle,' she said half-heartedly, as if she had not had enough time to decide that she wasn't going to speak to Julie.

As she turned out of the archway and went down the pavement to the kiosk which stood at the corner where the Rue Brey joined the Avenue de Wagram, Julie wondered what on earth she could have done to have offended the woman. Perhaps her moral behaviour had offended her: Paris wasn't Matterdale, but Paris concierges were notorious for taking offence.

She was approaching the wooden kiosk with its tarpaulin-covered roof, when she realised that, since it was Sunday, there would be no airmail edition of *The Times*. She saw between the shoulders of the two men standing at the counter, that there were several piles of *France-Dimanche*, and one solitary copy of the London *Observer*. Julie decided she would have the *Observer*. The woman inside the kiosk was witch-like, with lips painted into a crimson Cupid's bow, and untidy grey hair spilling in all directions. Over her shoulders was a woollen shawl so snagged, ragged and unravelled, that it gave her the appearance of an incompetent *tricoteuse*. She was holding forth to her two gentlemen customers:

'... more than a thousand dead, messieurs. Two thousand. Two and a half thousand, perhaps. Who knows? And half of Belleville in flames. You won't hear about it on the wireless, and you won't see it in the newspapers. They only tell us what the dirty politicians want us to know. So everything is fine. Our generals are leading a victorious retreat.... I can tell you, though. My sister-in-law is from Belleville. Lived there all her life till she married for the second time, the fool. She knows the truth. The water, electricity, sewers, have all broken down. The authorities are doing nothing – what a surprise, eh?'

She glanced between the two men, at Julie, who was wondering if she dared to reach between them to pick up the *Observer* before anybody else took it.

'And where was the Royal Air Force,' she continued, 'while the people of Paris were dying in the ruins of their homes?'

She was looking directly at Julie. Julie wondered if she was expected to provide the answer, but the woman went on.

'First it's the dirty Belgians who shit themselves so hard at the thought of the Boches, they can't fight. Then its the dirty English who run away and piss themselves in the sea. If you ask me, we wouldn't be fighting this filthy war at all if it wasn't for the shitty English. There's one good thing, though. The rotten politicians have had to ask Marshal Pétain to help them. He'll know what to do, eh? It's some comfort to know there's a real Frenchman in the Rue St Dominique at last!'

Julie had backed away. The dreadful woman's stare had frightened her in a quite irrational way; it took every ounce of her self-control not to break into a run as she returned to the archway, and the safety of the little square. Even the disapproval of the concierge's wife was preferable to the evil eye of the woman in the kiosk.

In the cool marble of the hallway, she put down her bag, pulled off her gloves, and unpinned her hat. On Sundays, Victor had an English breakfast. As Julie went into the lounge, he put down his fork, reached out and took her hand.

'Did you get your du Mauriers?' he asked.

He spoke in English, pronouncing the name of the cigarettes with an exaggerated French accent.

She sat down in the chair beside him.

'Hey!' he exclaimed, seeing her face. 'What's the matter?'

'I'm being very stupid,' said Julie. 'It was the woman in the kiosk.'

Victor released her hand. He pulled the neatly-folded hankerchief from his breast pocket, and dried her cheeks under her eyes. It was a good thing that Severin or one of the maids wasn't in the room, thought Julie.

'The kiosk by the Rue Brey?' asked Victor.

Julie nodded.

'That one never stops talking,' he said. 'One has to be rude to her. It's the only way to survive.'

'She was carrying on about the English running away and letting French people die,' Julie explained.

She took the handkerchief from him.

'I didn't dare ask her for an English newspaper and English cigarettes. I just ran away as well.' She paused. 'I feel like St Peter!'

'Come,' Victor told her. *Tu exagères*, eh?'

He put his arm round her shoulder. She shook her head.

'I felt it was evil, the way she looked at me,' she said. 'I can't really explain it. And I just ran away from it.'

'Would you like one of the servants to go for you? Or even Hugo – it does him good to run errands.'

'No,' she replied, 'it's all right.'

'Then you are going to punish yourself?' he asked. 'Like a good English Protestant girl – by doing without?'

She smiled.

'Yes,' she replied. 'Well, until we get to the Parvis at Notre Dame.'

He laughed.

'That's better, at any rate,' he told her.

The streets on the right bank of the Seine were almost completely deserted as Joseph drove Victor and Julie to the Ile de la Cité. They reminded Julie of one Christmas morning in the West End. It had been an occasion when she had been forced to stay in London in the hope of getting a part in a Boltons' Revue. There was the same hollow, rather frightening sense of desolation. Joseph drove them over the Pont Alexandre III and down the Quai Anatole France. All along the street, behind the tall, ornamental railings of the National Assembly, the government offices and ministries, *huissiers*, clerks, and secretaries were hurrying down the steps with armfuls of documents, to carry them across the lawns and burn them in the blackened dustbins,

266

braziers, or on the bonfires which stood there. Smoke was drifting across the street and across the river towards the Tuileries Gardens. Shreds and sparks from charred, burning paper drifted in the air, to land as black specks on the pavements; and the air quivered in the bonfire-heat, as in autumn.

As they drew opposite the Ste Chapelle, and crossed over the top of the Boulevard St Michel, groups of people were to be seen hurrying across the bridges towards Notre Dame, some obviously intent on attending the next Mass – the men in white collars and pinstripe suits, the women clutching prayer-books and lace mantillas – while others were going as spectators. Victor and Julie got out of the car. Joseph drove away to park somewhere behind the Place Michel. They could not have proceeded any further by car. On every bridge the groups of people were becoming a dense, jostling crowd.

Victor took Julie by the arm, and navigated her skilfully, and with a certain arrogance, through the sea of pedestrians. The scene as they reached the Parvis reminded Julie yet again of something out of The Hunchback of Notre Dame. The vast mass of spectators and worshippers occupied every inch of the pavement. Not only children, but soberly dressed adults had climbed onto the park walls, and were balancing themselves on the railings, and supporting themselves on the lamp-standards. Their faces, like a pale ocean, were all turned upwards to the great stone tableau of Judgement and Redemption carved on the towering façade of the cathedral's west front. Round the tops of the lamp-standards had been draped loudspeaker trumpets pointing in every direction. Other loudspeakers had been slung about the necks of Viollet-le-Duc's gargoyles at the corners of the gallery buttresses, high above the heads of the crowd. From them came the monotonous incantation of the celebrant at the High Altar inside the cathedral, the responses of the assistants, and short bursts of plainchant sung by men and boys. The sound had the tinny quality of an early talking picture, thought Julie, except that it echoed off the buildings round the Parvis and across the water.

Victor seemed capable of achieving the impossible, at least to the extent of guiding Julie through a crowd standing with shoulders pressed tightly together, until they had reached a spot to the right of the cathedral front. There, under the shade of some trees overlooking the river, they found an open space occupied by several of the cathedral beadles, half a dozen police officers, and three or four distinguished-looking gentlemen in morning-suits, with sashes over their dove-grey waistcoats, and ribbons in their lapels. Julie was presented to a Monsieur Emile du Plessis, a Monsieur Claude Meurisse, both of whom were Members of the Senate, and to Monsieur Roger Langeron, Prefect of Police. Julie found herself standing beside Monsieur Langeron.

'Mass will soon be over,' he explained. 'They have brought the

267

relics of Ste Geneviève from the Panthéon. The Procession and Litany of the Intercession will soon begin.'

'You must be terribly busy today, *Monsieur le Préfet*,' said Julie.

She was determined to make herself agreeable, though she felt in awe of the eminence of these gentlemen and uncertain of how they would view her relationship with Victor – though they showed every indication of being friendly, in the absence of their wives.

'I mean, with the bombing of Belleville, as well as all this,' she added.

'The attack on Belleville was bad enough,' he replied. 'We must be thankful that it was nothing compared to Warsaw or Rotterdam.'

'Or with the problem of Compiègne,' said Monsieur Meurisse.

'Compiègne, *Monsieur le Sénateur?*' asked Monsieur Langeron. 'What's happened at Compiègne?'

'*Mon cher*,' Monsieur Meurisse exclaimed. 'Do you mean to say you don't know?'

He looked at Julie, and the expression on his face changed.

'Or have I spoken out of turn?' he asked.

'I assure you, *Monsieur le Sénateur*,' the Prefect of Police told him, 'I have no idea what is supposed to have happened at Compiègne. My concern is Paris.'

'You're not going to leave us in suspense, Claude?' said Victor, smiling. 'What has happened in Compiègne?'

'It's no laughing matter, Victor,' said Monsieur Meurisse's colleague, Monsieur du Plessis. 'Claude has no wish to alarm this very attractive young Englishwoman.'

'Miss Armitage has experienced German bombing and machine-gunning in the north-east,' said Victor. 'She is something of a veteran, I promise you.'

'Very well,' said Monsieur Meurisse, 'eighteen thousand of our men have mutinied in Compiègne. They've seized the town and have raised the red flag. They're all conscripts of course, from the industrial suburbs – acting on orders from the Kremlin, I daresay. Weygand's had to withdraw almost his entire armour from the Somme, to put them down, and the Paris air defence system has been stripped of pursuit planes. That's how the German bombers got through last night. Proof enough, if you ask me.'

He looked at Victor, then at the Prefect of Police.

'You don't believe me, messieurs?' he asked.

'I believe I would have been informed if it had been true,' Monsieur Langeron replied.

'If the eighteen thousand troops you are talking about,' said Victor, 'had come from the Paris suburbs, we should surely have known about it fast enough. The raid on Belleville hasn't been reported on the wireless or in the papers, but everybody knows about it.'

'Listen, my dear Victor,' said Monsieur du Plessis. 'Do you know why General de Gaulle's – Colonel as he was then – attack on Montcornet failed?'

'Because Touchon's Sixth Army wasn't sufficiently deployed to support him,' Victor said.

'That was what was said,' du Plessis replied. 'The truth was that when de Gaulle gave the order for the Fourth Armoured to advance, only four tanks moved into action. Four! All the rest had crews drawn from the Paris Renault works; every man of them was a member of the Communist Party, obeying orders from Moscow.'

'That is absolute nonsense, Émile,' Victor protested. 'I am acquainted with several officers who were serving with Fourth Armoured, including, may I say, Charles de Gaulle himself. I have heard nothing remotely resembling such a story. De Gaulle has said that every soldier in the division did his duty in that action.'

'Charles de Gaulle is a very ruthless, very ambitious fellow,' said Monsieur du Plessis. 'He would never admit to having lost control over his own command.'

'They do say,' Monsieur Meurisse intervened, 'that Antoine de Bernac's young son was killed by his own men when he tried to compel them to face the enemy.'

'May I ask where you get your information, messieurs?' asked Monsieur Langeron.

'An unimpeachable source, *Monsieur le Préfet*,' replied Monsieur Meurisse. 'Our information both about the events in Compiègne, and the Fourth Armoured's mutiny in front of Montcornet, is contained in dispatches sent by Ambassador Bullitt direct to the White House in Washington.'

A murmur of anticipation ran through the vast crowd. A young priest in a lace surplice had come out of the St Anne door of the cathedral onto the empty space railed off between the West Front and the expectant crowd. Only a few yards from where Julie was standing stood a microphone. The young priest came over to it and adjusted it for height. The clatter, as he moved it, reverberated tinnily through the speakers, round the square. An elderly priest, vested in liturgical violet, led by three boys in embroidered cottas, the one in the centre carrying the processional cross, came out of the St Anne door. He was followed by two deacons swinging censers; blue clouds billowed out from under the copper lids, to drift like a mist into the front ranks of the crowd. The sweet smell of the incense reached Julie, making her cough slightly.

The elderly priest chanted in a surprisingly strong voice:

'Exsurge, Domine, adjuva nos, et libera nos propter nomen tuum.'

The deacons, who had taken their stand on either side of him, responded, *'Deus, auribus nostris audivimus; Patres nostri anuntia-verunt nobis. Gloria!'*

The young priest put his lips close to the microphone. His voice began with an intimacy which embraced the vast throng from one end of the Parvis to the other, and echoed off the walls of buildings on the far sides of the Seine embankments.

"'Arise, O Lord, and for thine honour's sake deliver us . . .'"

The entire crowd took up the prayer, repeating it in a whisper which surged against the cathedral front then swept back to the façade of the Prefecture of Police on the far side of the Parvis. Above the noise, the voice of the officiating priest chanted higher,

'Ne unquam dominentur nobis inimici nostri: libera nos, Deus Israel . . .'

The priest at the microphone murmured into the ears of the crowd,

"'Be it not said that our enemies triumphed over us: O God of Israel, when wilt thou deliver us . . . ? Arise, O Lord . . .'"

And again the multitude took up the prayer,

"'Arise, O Lord, and for thine honour's sake deliver us. . . .'"

'Deus qui conteris bella. . . .' the elderly priest's voice soared above the groaning noise of the crowd.

The young priest murmured into the microphone,

"'O God who bringest wars to naught, and by thy protection routest the assailants who trust in thee, help us thy servants who entreat thy mercy, so that our barbarous enemies may be brought low . . . Arise, O Lord . . .'"

And again, the surging whisper mounted upwards,

"'Arise, O Lord, and for thine honour's sake deliver us . . .'"

Monsieur du Plessis put a heavy hand round Julie's shoulder. She was quite taken aback as he drew her to him. He bent down and whispered to her as if she were a child watching the Lord Mayor's Show, 'They are bringing out the head of Ste Genevieve, *ma chère!*'

There was a movement, a sound, that ran through the crowd like a sudden stiff breeze through a summer cornfield. The senator continued to rest his hand on Julie's shoulder, to her embarrassment.

The officiating priest cried out,

'Sancte Ludovice . . . Rex Francorum . . . Ora pro nobis!'

The deacons rattled the chains from which hung their censers, spilling the incense smoke into the crowd, as the thousands of voices replied unrestrainedly,

'Saint Louis, roi des français, priez pour nous!'

The priest cried out,

'Sancta Joanna . . . Virgo Domremiensis . . . Ora pro nobis!'

270

The crowd roared back in mounting excitement,

'*Sainte Jeanne, vièrge de Domremy, priez pour nous!*'

Julie noticed that many, particularly in the front ranks of the crowd, had fallen on their knees, their rosaries twisted between their fingers, the tiny crucifixes pressed to their lips. A few, where they had room, had prostrated themselves on the pavement. Many hundreds, both men and women, were openly weeping, handkerchiefs pressed to their faces.

The priest called out,

'*Sancta Genovevia . . . Virgo Nanterrae . . . Ora pro nobis!*'

And the cry went up louder than ever,

'*Sainte Genevieve, vièrge de Nanterre, priez pour nous!*'

A new voice, a powerful, high tenor, rang out above the hubbub:

'*Auge in nobis, Domine, qui in Sanctorum tuorum reliquiis mirabilia operaris . . .*'

Through the loudspeakers came the voice of the young priest:

'Lord who workest miracles by the relics of thy saints, increase our faith in the resurrection, and give us fellowship with thee. How wonderful is God in his saints! The God of Israel will give his people strength and courage!'

As he spoke, a new procession was spilling out from the great central Portal of the Last Judgement, onto the front of the Parvis. There were two lines of altar-servers, several of whom were swinging censers, and one of whom was carrying the great Processional Cross of the cathedral, gold, and massively jewelled. They were followed by the canons of the cathedral, all vested for the celebration of the Eucharist; then the Cardinal-Archbishop of Paris with his attendants; finally, borne aloft by the gentlemen-sacristans of the cathedral, came a white silk canopy tassled with gold, forming a roof over the bier on which rested the domed, gold reliquary. To Julie, the latter looked like nothing more than a large, ostentatious, presentation mantlepiece clock – preferable, however, to the withered, shrunken head she had rather expected to see.

As the reliquary was carried from the Portal of the Last Judgement towards the crowd, the deacons and acolytes tossed billowing clouds of incense, piling them into the already drifting smoke until the whole procession and the front of the crowds was veiled in a blue fog. The priest at the microphone was intoning in a voice filled with scarcely repressed excitement,

'Ste Geneviève, by whose purity and devotion our city was made First Handmaid of the Holy Virgin, Mother of God; Ste Genevieve, at whose intercession our city and its people were saved from the fury of the Huns. . . . '

His prayer was drowned in the cries from thousands of voices,

'*Ste Geneviève! Priez pour nous!*'

271

Near to where Julie was standing, women were calling out individually,

'*Ste Geneviève, sauvez votre Paris!*'

Many of them were already on their knees. Many more fell onto them, dipped their foreheads to the pavement, and clutched their stomachs.

Others tried to run forward towards the reliquary, and were held back, struggling in the swirling clouds of incense, by beadles, clergy, and police.

Monsieur du Plessis said loudly into Julie's ear, 'I didn't know there were so many believers left in Paris.'

His tone of amused condescension angered her.

As the police and cathedral officers held back the would-be adorers, the procession wound its solemn way the length of the great façade, then turned back into the Portal of the Last Judgement. For the last time, the strong voice of the officiating priest rang out over the uproar:

'*Exsurge, Domine, adjuva nos. . . . !*'

And again the young priest at the microphone led the crowds,

'"Arise, O Lord, and for thine honour's sake deliver us. . . . !"'

The excitement subsided as the last of the clergy vanished up the central aisle of the nave.

'*Eh bien!*' said Monsieur du Plessis, as if relieved that a spectacle which he had found singularly embarrassing was now over. To Victor, he remarked, 'If one recalls one's history lessons, my dear fellow, one cannot help but remember that when Aetius, Consul of the Franks, defeated Attila and his seven hundred thousand Huns, it was at Chalons. I fear that the descendants of those same Huns are well past Chalons this time.'

Monsieur Meurisse nodded his agreement.

'Nothing will stop them now,' he said. 'Certainly not the Generalissimo's much vaunted counter-offensive on the Somme – that's an old man's joke.'

The crowd had become ragged, frayed at the edges, as people began to drift away towards the bridges. Monsieur du Plessis's hand was round Julie's shoulder again.

'Are you very fond of our friend here?' he asked confidentially.

Julie was about to reply coldly when he continued: 'I ask, my dear, not from an impertinent curiosity, but in the hope of discovering an ally. I wish, if you could do so, you would add your voice to ours in trying to persuade him to leave Paris before it is too late.'

Julie looked for Victor. He had moved a little way off, and was engaged in serious conversation with the Prefect of Police. The congregation was trickling out of the cathedral through the usual entrance, the door of the Blessed Virgin. The great Portal of the Last Judgement and the St Anne door were both closed. The Parvis was returning to normal. The racks of postcards were visible, slung on the railings. Café awnings were being unfurled. Some of the crowd had gathered on the embankment edge to stare into the sunlight glittering on the green water of the Seine.

'For men like Claude Meurisse and myself, it is not such a matter for concern,' Monsieur du Plessis went on. 'The Republic has been in a state of decay for too long. Perhaps a touch of National Socialist discipline is what the people of France need to restore them to greatness. If only it were not for Herr Hitler's *bêtise* concerning Jews. Our friend has so much to lose by staying here. And he owes it to little Hugo to take him to a place of safety . . . '

Suddenly it occured to Julie that Monsieur du Plessis's solicitude towards Victor might be a matter of political expediency rather than the concern for a friend's well-being; that he wanted Victor out of Paris, and even France if possible. Wondering how she should reply, she saw a face she recognised hurrying toward her across the pavement from the cathedral entrance. She recognised the round, milky face, albino-smooth. She recognised the thick, yellow-white hair. She even recognised the suit, baggy and ill-fitting despite the grossness of the body inside it. And she remembered the smell of cologne so cloying that it had reminded her of stale vomit – of death.

He was smiling directly at her. She was certain that he was about to approach her, to speak to her. She turned to Monsieur du Plessis, standing facing him, so close that she was almost asking to be held in an embrace. Her distaste for the Senator was tolerable compared with the frightened loathing inspired in her by that dreadful pudgy white face.

'I'll do what I can, *Monsieur le Sénateur,*' she said. 'I don't think I'll have any effect on him if he's made up his mind, but I'll try.'

'That's good,' said Monsieur du Plessis smiling down at her as if he were about to offer her a half-crown.

Past his arm, she could see the gross shape of the apparition hurrying away across the Pont au Double in the direction of the Left Bank. She could breathe again.

'You look dreadfully worried, *ma chérie,*' Victor told her as they were walking along the Quai St Michel, back to the car.

It was true she felt shaken.

'I saw somebody,' she replied. 'I thought he had seen me.'

'Somebody you dislike, evidently.'

'It was a man who gave me a lift . . . I was on the way to Laon. He was very nasty. A fat Greek. He tried it on – you know?'

'Mediterranean types have to,' Victor replied. 'It's a compulsion.'

Julie shook her head.

'It wasn't like that,' she said. 'I mean, like being goosed in the

273

London tube, or propositioned and pawed by an ordinary Casanova type. That's bad enough, but there was something really evil about this man – leprous. I can't explain it properly.'

She looked at Victor, waiting for him to laugh at her. He didn't.

'He made me feel quite sick,' she went on. 'He said he was going about buying antiques and jewelry from people who wanted to run away from the Germans. He tried to make himself sound as if he were a charity organisation rather than some sort of hyena. He said he'd give me some of his loot if I did what he wanted. I wanted to throw up – and I really am not exaggerating.'

She paused.

'There was a smell about him,' she continued. 'It was the scent he wore. But it was like – well – decomposition.'

She hugged his arm.

'As order cracks, and the old values fail,' he said, 'the demons come crawling out of chaos. I suppose we should expect to meet them now.'

'I'm not sure I know what you mean,' she told him.

He put his arm round her waist and held her close to him.

There was a sabbath emptiness about the house on their return. Alain, Victor's secretary, had not come in, of course, so the study was silent and still. Everything was clean, polished and in its place. Only Hugo's voice echoed up from the kitchen quarters where, no doubt, he was persecuting Maryvonne, the cook-housekeeper.

Victor took Julie into the drawing-room. This surprised her: she had expected to go into the study. As she put her hat and gloves down, he went over to the cabinet, took down a decanter of scotch, and poured himself a drink. She noticed that his hand was shaking slightly.

'What will you have?' he asked. 'A sherry? Dubonnet?'

'Gin and it?' she asked in return.

'Very well.'

As he poured it, she said, 'Did you believe what they were saying – about the mutinies?'

'There are so many such stories, and all so marvellously authenticated,' he replied. 'I'm not surprised they came from United States embassy tapes. Ambassador Bullitt, like Ambassador Kennedy in London, has been convinced that the Western Allies will be defeated ever since the first day of the war. On the other hand, one can't escape the fact that the Communists have, in some measure, become Hitler's allies.'

He dropped a twist of lemon peel into her glass, and handed it to her.

'Whatever is true, my dear,' he said. 'I think it's time you were going.'

He said it so unexpectedly that, at first, she did not understand.

274

'Going where?' she asked.

'Home,' he replied. 'To London.'

She sat down on the arm of the chair by her hat and gloves.

'Why?' she asked.

She stared stupidly across at him. So this was why they weren't in the study. He hadn't wanted to go where they had made love the previous night.

'You've smelled the *débacle*,' he told her. 'You've seen the hyenas moving in, haven't you?'

He carried his whisky over to the fireplace, and stood there with his foot resting on the copper rail round the hearth, and his hand resting on the mantlepiece. It was a very theatrical pose, thought Julie, as in a Noel Coward play.

'I wish I hadn't said anything about that man,' she said.

'It wouldn't have made any difference,' he replied. 'It's time you were off. I've hung onto you too long for your own good.'

What was the proper way for a discarded mistress to behave when she was being discarded? Julie wondered. Was it proper to pretend to believe the gentleman's pleas in justification? Was that the dignified thing to do? Perhaps he was going to write her out a generous cheque. That was customary, wasn't it? – particularly when the mistress was a not very successful actress?

She wasn't going to be dignified, however. There was a tear running down the side of her nose. He saw it, and came over to her.

'Julie,' he said. 'I've made myself responsible for your safety. I need to know that you are safe.'

She shook her head.

'I won't go,' she heard herself say.

'Listen,' he said. 'The English have been beaten in the north. They are escaping, as many as can. The Belgians have surrendered. The whole German army will be advancing towards Paris at any time now. Once they come across the Somme, they'll reach the Seine within a matter of hours, and that'll be the end of Dieppe and Le Havre. It's time you went back to England, while you still can.'

'I'm not going,' she said, exactly like a child.

He took her hands in his.

'Julie,' he told her, 'these last two or three weeks have been wonderful. It's true, I promise you. But do you know the story by Oscar Wilde, "The Happy Prince"? Do you remember how the little swallow stayed with the prince because she loved him, and would not fly south when the winter came? Do you remember how she died of the winter's cold because she waited too long?'

'There's always Cherbourg, and St Malo,' said Julie. 'I don't have to go back via Le Havre.'

'Julie,' he exclaimed, 'you saw what the roads were like in the

275

north. What do you think they'll be like when the Germans advance on Paris?'

Julie couldn't think of any more arguments.

'It would make me happy to know that you are safe,' Victor said.

'I don't want to go away and leave you here,' she replied. '*You're* not going to be safe.'

'That is diferent, I belong here. You know that. You belong in England.' He paused. 'Julie, don't you think I have enough on my plate without having to feel guilty about keeping you away from all those you belong to?'

'You only say that because I'm a woman,' she answered. 'If I were a man, you wouldn't say I belonged to anybody.'

She was determined to have the last word, but the battle, if there had been a battle, was over.

'After lunch, my dear, I shall drive you to St Lazare,' he said calmly. 'Go and pack your things, and afterwards I shall drive you myself. No need to disturb Joseph's Sunday, eh?'

Julie picked up her hat and gloves.

'I don't want Danielle upstairs with me,' she said. 'I'll look after myself.'

'Very well,' he replied.

The stiffness was setting in, thought Julie as she went upstairs; the *rigor mortis* of a love-affair. She had left her drink behind her untouched, and the tears were drying on her cheeks. It was a pity about the drink – she could have done with it.

She thought of leaving behind all the things that Victor had paid for, all the things whose existence she would have to explain to Ambrose. But she knew in her heart of hearts that Victor was entirely sincere; to leave behind what he had given her would add immeasurably to his unhappiness.

She packed with mechanical efficiency, then checked through her handbag to ensure that she had her passport and her ENSA visa. She decided that she would not cry again – not, at least, until the boat-train had left St Lazare. She went to the dressing-table mirror and repaired her face. It was the thought of the comfortable dullness of Ambrose's flat which she couldn't bear to contemplate, and the hollowness of her own spirit. All her life, she decided, she had been digging pits for herself to fall into.

She remained dry-eyed during lunch. She could see how unhappy Victor was, if only in glimpses. Somehow it reassured her. Perhaps it was as well it should all happen so quickly. Hugo chattered, and asked her questions about England, and the Tower of London in particular. She promised to take him there if he should ever go to London. The nearest she came to tears again was after they had finished lunch. Julie had kissed Hugo goodbye. Severin was carrying her cases out to the car which Victor had himself brought round to

276

the garden square. Hugo appeared on the stairs as she was standing in the hall waiting.

'Julie?' he asked.

'Yes?'

'Please, Julie, I want to say thank you very much. I think Papa has been so happy having you here.'

'Oh, Hugo,' she exclaimed.

She was forced to turn away. She went out of the front door as quickly as she could.

28

Von Leonarte scrambled up onto the top of the dune to join Oberleutnant Anton Kirst who was already there, staring out to the sea.

'Beautiful,' he said.

And it was. The sparse clumps of spear-grass stood like lances and pennants on the dry, powdery sand. Below, the noon sun glittered on the tiny waves which broke on the shingle stretching away on either side. Further out there was a gentle swell which alternately lightened and darkened the ocean green. There was enough of an off-shore breeze to dispel the smell of death, and to scent the air with the smell of wet seaweed.

'Marvellous!' von Leonarte exclaimed. 'Like summer holidays.'

There was such immense pleasure in being alive – a pleasure which would not have a fraction of such intensity if it were not for the presence of death. Therefore, 'long live death!' He looked down as he lifted the toe of his jackboot, and let the dry sand dribble out of the welts.

'Where did you go?' asked Kirst. 'For your holidays, I mean.'

He tucked his steel-lined Panzer beret under his arm, and dabbed his forehead with his sleeve.

'The Baltic,' von Leonarte replied. 'Rügen, usually.'

He had been so terribly afraid, that morning. There was no disgrace in being afraid, particularly under such circumstances. Nevertheless, it had taken him by surprise. He had wondered if it had been only the Knight's Cross at his throat which had prevented him from showing his fear.

'Rügen is all pine trees and chalk cliffs, isn't it?' Kirst asked.

'The sea has the same colours,' von Leonarte replied. 'And the smell of the shore is the same.'

As they had clattered up the esplanade, heading eastwards out of

277

Dunkirk, he had noticed the sand and dried seaweed, where they had been blown across the street. As in the village where he used to stay with his sister, Petra, on the Island of Rügen, the sand had gathered in small drifts against the corners of houses, and on the ledges of shop windows. It had represented disorder, a holiday misrule.

For the past two days, the regiment had been advancing across marshland – evil terrain for armour – in the face of an unexpectedly well-prepared and ferocious resistance on the part of the French rearguard. The day before, General Hubicki's 9th Panzers, which had been deployed ahead of them, had been virtually wiped out by the French 75's firing over open sights at point-blank range. At dawn today, it had been the turn of Colonel Hassler's regiment, with Major Spiesser's squadron at the head, and von Leonarte's troop as leading troop. Von Leonarte had commenced the attack for the entire regiment. He had felt nauseous with fear. Helm, he knew, had been sick before they started – he had pretended not to notice. Even Radinski had been unwontedly silent.

They had met with no resistance at all. They had found the 75's in position with their barrels spiked and their breech-block mechanism wrecked. There hadn't been a gunner, or a man of the Zouave infantry, who had been fighting beside the guns, to be seen anywhere. All had been taken off the beaches during the hours of darkness by the English navy. As the 38T tanks had roared on, to clatter into the silent ruins of the town, von Leonarte had felt sick and tearful with anti-climax.

They had driven on, thrusting aside the wreckage which had blocked their path, past the harbour and canal basins, and out onto the esplanade. There, von Leonarte had ordered his troop to halt to await further orders. He had opened his cupola lid, and had pulled himself out onto the turret, to survey the devastation.

The air had been sharp, reminding him that it was still early in the morning, but it was heavy with the smell of smouldering wood. Around him, the continual shelling had reduced the once-smart sea front to a crumbled mass of weirdly shaped rubble. Above his head, against the sky, reared the dome of the Casino, now a blackened metallic skeleton. Over to his left, a British destroyer, which had sunk by the stern, reared its huge blackened prow out of the harbour like some maleficent deity rising out of the sea. Along the esplanade itself were shattered lorries and guns, choking the approaches to the shore. Death was omnipresent: corpses lay everywhere, like the visitation of a medieval pestilence – on the heaps of rubble, stretched out in the gutters, under the burnt-out vehicles, or crouched over their rifles in the doorways.

Then something miraculous occurred. Two girls came walking down the esplanade, arm in arm, picking their way between the dumped, burnt-out trucks, and over the rubble. With their hair brushed in page-boy style, their rayon blouses and pin-striped skirts and handbags, they were like apparitions of normality through the destruction and death. None of the men who had emerged from the oily heat of the tanks called out; they watched as if spellbound while the two girls walked down the line of vehicles looking neither to left nor right. At the far end of the esplanade, they turned in the direction of the canal bridge and disappeared behind the banks of rubble.

Half-an-hour later, the first French soldiers began to appear. They came crawling, blinking, out of cellars, out of gashes in the walls, out of the sewers, out of caves which they had constructed for themselves in the ruins. They appeared from everywhere – every building, no matter how close to utter demolition, produced its quota of those who had been hiding from the battle. They came onto the streets in their thousands, waiting to be herded into some sort of order. Some of them approached von Leonarte's men with hands above their heads, bleating '*Kamerad! Kamerad!*', and displaying the sort of ingratiating leer on their grimy, stubbled faces, that would have better suited the cheap-skate whores who loitered in the shadows of the Berlin tenement blocks. Some were so drunk, they had to be supported by their comrades. These were not the artillerymen and Zouaves who had been holding the beach-head perimeter so gallantly during the past two days, and the tankmen knew it. Von Leonarte's men gave voice to their disapproval with all the indignation of the honest German *landser*. The French scum in front of them, who were staring up at the tanks, did not seem to appreciate even the gist of what was being said to them. They simply stood there, grinning weakly. What sickness was it in a nation, wondered von Leonarte, that could reduce its fighting men to such objects of contempt?

A few hours later, they had driven out of Dunkirk. They had advanced through Malo-les-Bains, heading east, and had halted on the seaward side of the great sanatorium at Zuydcoote, not far from the Belgian frontier, on what had been the extreme eastern edge of the British-held sector of the perimeter. The Zuydcoote Sanatorium was a high, domed building looking out to sea, whose dark brick walls made it resemble a city railway terminus. From either side of the main block, the dark wards, four stories high, reached out like prison-galleries along the edge of the dunes. The patients had all been evacuated three weeks previously. Now it was occupied by the casualties from the English 151 Brigade, and 18th Field Force, the wreckage of whose vehicles and equipment littered the grounds of the hospital.

The beds from the wards had been wheeled into the spacious palm court which formed the vestibule of the building, to convert it into a single ward containing hundreds of wounded English soldiers. The casualties were being looked after by a major from the Royal Army Medical Corps with two of his junior officers, a section of Medical Corps orderlies, and a base hospital unit of army nursing sisters who had been trapped in the beach-head perimeter due to the speed of the German advance. They had all volunteered to remain behind to look after the men who had been wounded too severely to be taken off the beaches with the rest of the rearguard.

From the moment he had arrived to take over from von Leonarte, Major Spiesser had behaved towards the English with what von Leonarte took to be exaggerated courtesy, as if the man had to demonstrate that a Party member was quite as imbued with a sense of chivalry as any Prussian nobleman. He called for Junior Lieutenant Schneider, and arranged for him to take a photograph as he – Major Spiesser – shook the hand of a severely wounded captain and solicitously asked in broken English how he was feeling. The captain, fuddled with morphia, his head swathed in lint and bandages, was only too grateful for sympathy from whatever source. He smiled weakly, just in time to be caught in the flash of Erich Schneider's camera. He looked vaguely surprised, but before the implication of what had occurred could have penetrated the fog of morphia in his brain, Major Spiesser had moved on to have a few words with an English nursing sister.

The major had chosen the object of his attention carefully. The girl was weary, dishevelled; the man's denim battledress she was wearing was several sizes too large for her, and bloodstained. But she was pretty. Major Spiesser clicked his heels and lifted her fingers to his lips in the approved Viennese style. As Erich Schneider's camera-bulb flashed again, the look on the girl's face was one of astonished embarrassment. On the final print, it would no doubt appear as a charming coyness. Major Spiesser strutted away between the beds towards the door stencilled in English, 'O.C.'s Office'. He shouted back to Lieutenant Schneider, 'Negatives to Cologne. To Doctor Paul Leverkuehn, Editorial Office, *Signal*.'

Erich Schneider had snapped to attention.

'Very good, Herr Major,' he had bawled out in parade-ground style.

He had turned abruptly and bumped into von Leonarte. Von Leonarte, who had still been feeling queasy as a result of the tension of the dawn attack, had been wondering whether Major Spiesser's behaviour was sufficient justification for him to be sick into the kidney bowl on the gilt-legged table nearby.

Erich Schneider had apologised. He had glanced back at the figure of Major Spiesser disappearing through the office door, then had looked again at von Leonarte. He had understood the expression on von Leonarte's face. He had glanced down at his camera.

'One has to obey orders,' he had said.

Von Leonarte had nodded and patted the boy's shoulder.

That was the point at which he had gone out through the revolving door of the vestibule, and had strode out across the sand to join Anton Kirst up on his dune watching the sea.

'The lads would like a swim,' said Kirst.

Graser had already asked. The request had been Radinski's in fact; Graser had done the actual asking, but, from the way Radinski had paused from his self-appointed task of painting *'Nach Paris'* on the side of the tank, von Leonarte had recognised the truth.

'I don't blame them,' he replied.

'Any good reason why not?' asked Kirst. 'Come on, Dieter, Regiment is sending up a field-kitchen detachment. That means we'll be here for at least the rest of today. And we can't leave until our own medical people have taken over here.'

The edges of the sea sparkled. And beyond, for once it really did look wine-dark. The silk underwear beneath von Leonarte's uniform clung to his body with the stale sweat of two days entombment in the throbbing bowels of his tank. He could almost feel the cool salt against his chest and arms, and pouring off his hair, down his face.

'Spiesser wouldn't allow it,' he said. 'Spiesser regards the very idea of the lads enjoying themselves as an undermining of his authority.'

'Why didn't he join the Waffen SS?' demanded Kirst. 'That's where he belongs.'

'Because they wouldn't have him,' von Leonarte said. 'He's an old woman.'

'"Do you appreciate, *Herren*,"' Kirst imitated Major Spiesser's high-pitched voice, '"that because of your irresponsibility, half my squadron was unavailable for immediate action?"'

'There won't be any immediate action,' von Leonarte said, more to himself than to Kirst. 'I don't suppose there's a soldier left fighting this side of the Somme.'

Irresponsibility was beginning to affect his judgement. A holiday excitement was replacing the nauseous sense of tension. He jumped down from the crest of the dune, showering the sand about him. He began to plod through the powdery mounds to the edge of the sea. On either hand, smaller dunes sprouting points of grass, and rimmed with dried seaweed, clustered round sandy bunkers. Flies buzzed inside the bunkers. As he moved shoreward, von Leonarte could see the khaki-clad bodies crouching there, where, days before, they had taken cover from the Me.109's and the machine-gun fire. Each hollow had its compliment of khaki-uniformed men, stiff in the attitudes of death, like the sentinels of Pompeii.

Would it be proper, wondered von Leonarte, to allow his men to enjoy themselves under the reproachful stare of so many dead men? He turned and climbed back up the dunes. At the top, Kirst had been joined by the senior NCO of von Leonarte's troop, Stabswachtmeister Neuffer.

'What is it, Helmut?' he gasped, as he managed to slither up the dry sand to the top.

'Neuffer here,' said Kirst with a smile, 'has come to ask the *gnädig* Rittmeister if he will give his permission for the men to have a swim.'

Von Leonarte laughed, and gave Kirst a push in the chest.

'Very well, Helmut,' he told Neuffer. 'In fact, I'll join you. And I expect the Oberleutnant will be with us as well. Only, I suggest that we move quietly down to the shore so as not to attract too much attention.'

'Very good, Herr Rittemeister,' Neuffer saluted.

As soon as they were out of sight of the front of the sanatorium, the men started to whoop like children, and to hop down to the shore, pulling off their reed-green overalls as they went. As he watched them, von Leonarte carefully removed the Knight's Cross from about his neck, and placed it in his breast pocket. He unbuttoned his jacket. The sun was so hot, and the sea so inviting, it was difficult to resist joining the other ranks in their scramble to plunge into the water.

In fact, the sea was bitingly cold, reminding him that the summer was still very young. The ordinary *landsers,* however, were determined to enjoy themselves, and splashed and ducked one another, and shouted and laughed across the swell. To keep warm, von Leonarte raced Kirst, swimming from the point of one breakwater of rotten wood which reached out into the sea to another. At the end of the far breakwater, they noticed a round, dark-green object bobbing gently in the trough of the swell. They approached it carefully, afraid that it was one of the many magnetic mines dropped by the Luftwaffe in an attempt to prevent the English boats from making landfall during the evacuation of the BEF. But it was only the corpse of some poor tommy grotesquely swollen inside his battle-dress.

Von Leonarte was wading out of the sea towards the rock where he had left his clothes, when he noticed a gaunt figure standing on the top of the dunes, black against the skyline, watching him.

'Who in damnation is that?' Kirst asked.

He had noticed the leather overcoat draped over the watcher's shoulders, and had assumed that the wearer was Gestapo.

'Nobody you need worry about, Anton,' von Leonarte replied. 'He's come to speak to me.'

'Do you know who it is?' asked Kirst.

'Very well,' said von Leonarte, 'unfortunately.'

'Trouble?'

'Not in the way you mean. He's an old family friend.'

Von Leonarte dried himself quickly, and began to dress.

'He's wearing a leather coat,' said Kirst. 'In this weather!'

'He's an old man,' von Leonarte told him. 'His blood is thin.'

He dressed, standing by the damp rock which smelt of seaweed. He emptied the dry sand from his boots and pulled them on. Picking up his steel-lined beret, he said to Kirst, 'See that Neuffer takes my lot back to the lines, will you?'

He climbed the dunes to where the tall, ascetic-looking figure waited.

'Good day, young man,' said Colonel Reuther.

'Good day, *Herr Oberst*,' von Leonarte replied.

'You are very formal today, Dietl,' Colonel Reuther said. 'Aren't you pleased to see me? I'm always delighted to see the son of Bishop Joachim – and a son who is such a credit to his father.'

'You know very well I am always happy to see you, Uncle Alfred,' von Leonarte told him, 'particularly if you have come here as a family friend.'

'Ah,' said Colonel Reuther, 'so you expect that I have other motives, do you, young man?'

'Yes, Uncle Alfred.'

'And of course you are quite right,' Colonel Reuther replied.

He took his cigar-case from his coat pocket, and offered it to von Leonarte.

'Does your squadron commander know that you are letting your troop bathe in the sea?' he asked.

'No,' said von Leonarte.

He took a cigar.

'I thought not,' said Colonel Reuther. 'When I asked where I would find you, he told me that you were stationed to repel any attack by the enemy from the east.'

He struck a match, cupped the flame in his palm and offered it to von Leonarte. Von Leonarte drew on his cigar and lit it.

'From Belgium?' he asked.

Colonel pointed a bony finger at von Leonarte's chest.

'Just because you're a cavalryman, and a "von", young man, and you are wearing that cross at your throat, it does not give you the right to question your superior's orders. It's just as well Colonel Hassler holds you in high regard – though even he has suggested that you're a bit of a bolshevik.'

'Nobody can say I shirk my duty, Uncle Alfred,' von Leonarte said.

'Glad to hear it,' Colonel Reuther told him, 'because I've come to give you new orders.'

Von Leonarte closed his eyes as if wincing.

'That damned medallion,' he said.

'The St Louis Tondeau. The *Tondeau de Chartres*,' Colonel Reuther corrected him. 'Special Intelligence was delighted by your raid into the Vouziers-Rethel sector. They say I can borrow you to have another shot at it.'

283

'Why?' von Leonarte protested.

He hesitated for a moment, but Colonel Reuther waited for him to continue.

'Has anybody ever heard of the damned thing?' demanded von Leonarte. 'I don't suppose many French people have ever heard of it.'

'Quite right, young man,' said Colonel Reuther.

'What is so damned important about it?' asked von Leonarte.

'It could be one way in which those who have your interests at heart try to keep you from getting into trouble with Major Spiesser.'

'Uncle Alfred!' protested von Leonarte.

'He may seem a rather stupid, pompous little schoolmaster to you, Dietl,' Colonel Reuther told him, 'but he does have the ear of rather more influential pompous schoolmasters, you know.'

'Is that the reason?' asked von Leonarte.

'No. But it's something for you to think about,' replied Colonel Reuther. 'Come.' He rested his hand in the crook of von Leonarte's elbow. 'Let's go down to the shore. It's been a long time since I had the chance to smell the sea.'

Von Leonarte held him up as he slid through the sand. Colonel Reuther glanced at the khaki-uniformed corpses behind the dunes.

'It's been a quick victory,' he said. 'Brilliant. But there are still a lot of good fellows dead.'

They walked to the sea's edge.

'It's always the best and bravest who die,' he added. 'It's something to remember, even when the battle is won.'

The shore was silent now, except for the splash of wavelets on the shingles. Colonel Reuther watched the ripples of foam-lace touch the toe-caps of his boots. They smoked their cigars.

'Did you ever have to read the *Metamorphoses* of Ovid when you were in High School?' Colonel Reuther asked.

'We had extracts to translate, I remember,' von Leonarte replied.

He remembered also looking out of the long, latticed window of the schoolroom, and the house-martins ducking in and out of the eaves of the houses opposite. For one whole term, he had watched a family of storks who had built their home on the ridge of the high gable. That had been the term, no doubt, when they had read Ovid's *Metamorphoses*.

'It is the new year,' Colonel Reuther was saying. 'The poet is on his way to the Janiculum. The snow is blowing down the street. He wraps his cloak about him to keep himself warm. Suddenly, he sees the god Janus walking in front of him. Janus is the god with two faces, one of which looks ahead, the other behind. Ovid runs after him, and as he does so, he addresses the face which is looking behind. "Why," he asks the god, "do people celebrate the beginning of the year in your

month, January? Why not in spring, when everything is renewed?"
"Fool," replies the god. "Do you not know that under your feet,
beneath the earth, the seeds are already beginning to sprout. Do you
believe that the only things which are, are the things which are visible
to you?"'

'I don't know it,' von Leonarte admitted.

'It is a story which all soldiers in a victorious army should
remember,' Colonel Reuther told him. 'It is winter in France now;
but the seeds may well begin to shoot again. We must do what the
Romans did with Carthage. We must rip out the very seed from the
ground and take it for our own use.'

He stared out to where sea and sky met.

'When Paris falls, the French will seek an armistice – Paris has
always been the tail which wags the French dog. And when the
French ask for an armistice, the English will stop the war. The
English have no real interest in Europe. The French would have
stopped us in the Rhineland; they would have stopped us in
Czechoslovakia. But the English wanted none of it. They are
interested only in their colonial Empire. We are going to occupy
French soil only so long as it takes to make peace with England. And
then it'll be the old *Drang nach Osten* – we shall revive the old
imperial destiny in the east. I'm sure that is something your father
would appreciate, eh, Dietl?'

'I'm sure he would,' von Leonarte agreed.

'There are men in France who would be glad if everything fell out
so – men who are held in high esteem, whom few Frenchmen would
ever consider traitors. It wouldn't be surprising if the old War Horse
himself, the hero of Verdun wasn't one of them. Special Intelligence
knows what it's up to, believe me. I propose we should provide an
authentic symbol, an order valid in French history, with which such
a man may be invested – so that he may be confirmed as leader in the
eyes of his own people. It is a difficult problem, Dietl. We can't use
an order which is already clearly in French hands. We can't invest our
nominee with something we have looted from the French Church, like
the ring of St Louis, or Joan of Arc's sword, the sword of Fierrebois.
But the Tondeau of Chartres – that is another matter! That, you see,
is the property of a Jew. We may see that the leader of our choice is
invested with it, and, at the same time appear to all Frenchmen who
are not contaminated with the Moscow virus to be true friends of
France.'

A junior NCO came slithering down the dunes. He ran at the
double across the strand to where von Leonarte and Colonel Reuther
were standing. Von Leonarte nodded to the man.

'With the Herr Rittmeister's permission,' the man said. 'Stabs-wachtmeister Neuffel presents his compliments to the Herr Rittmeister and requests the Herr Rittmeister's permission to allow the troop to stand down and to report to the kitchen for a hot meal.'

'Very good, Kubis,' von Leonarte told him.

'Are your people usually as smart?' Colonel Reuther asked, as the man clambered back up into the dunes.

'No,' said von Leonarte. 'Only in the presence of an *oberst*.'

Colonel Reuther smiled slightly.

'I expect you've been looking forward to a cooked meal yourself,' he said.

'I won't deny it, Uncle Alfred,' von Leonarte replied. 'Will you join us? It'll be the inevitable bread and soup, with a little sausage in it if we're lucky.'

He assisted Colonel Reuther back towards the sanitorium.

'They are my second family, you know, Uncle Alfred,' he said, 'and you keep tearing me away from them. Isn't it really a job for the SS?'

He had hesitated before uttering the question, so entrenched was his contempt for the men of the SS – an attitude he had learned from older professional soldiers.

'No, Dietl, it is not,' Colonel Reuther replied. 'You are your father's son. In a word, you are a true *herr*. You will go quietly into Paris, as soon as it is possible for you to do so. You will address yourself to the Baron de Bart-Mendel openly, as gentleman to gentleman. There is just a chance that he will hand over the Tondeau to you rather than to the Party hacks who will be coming after you. At least, you may be able to persuade him to show you the Tondeau, where it is kept. The rest should be easy. One look at an SS detachment, or a car-load of mentally defective Gestapo bullies, and the Tondeau will be gone forever. But you will be addressing him as Baron of France, not as "dirty Jew". And you have to have the breeding to make it sound convincing, young man.'

'And when I've persuaded him to show – or give me – the Tondeau thing,' asked von Leonarte, 'what becomes of the Baron de Bart-Mendel.'

'That is no business of yours, Dietl,' Colonel Reuther replied. 'It is the business of a Prussian officer to behave with honour. What the guttersnipes get up to when you are gone, is none of your business.'

Von Leonarte said nothing. They reached the sand-covered drive in front of the sanatorium. A Panzer medical convoy was drawn up along it. The presence of a field-kitchen behind one of the massive wings of the building was marked by the line of tankmen and medical orderlies who were waiting patiently, mess-tins in hand.

'This way, Herr Oberst,' said von Leonarte.

'You see, young man,' said Colonel Reuther, ignoring the fact that there were ordinary soldiers within earshot. 'I'm doing you a great favour. Do you know where your regiment is off to now? I'll tell you. It's off to clean out the Maginot Line. I took you out of it, and let you cross the Meuse with the Grossdeutschland. I'm taking you out of it now, and while it is still in the east of France, you will be entering Paris with our advance guard. There's something to make the Bishop proud of his son. There's something you can tell your children and grandchildren, eh?'

It was true of course, thought von Leonarte. Surely every Prussian child with a box of lead Grenadiers had, in his imagination, paraded them in Von Moltke's victory parade of 1871 down the Champs-Elysées? And then to return home to Kessim, on leave, with presents bought in the Rue de Rivoli, or the Avenue de l'Opéra. He would take Petra a scandalous set of black lingerie. And after she had gone crimson in the face, and their mother had said that under no circumstances was a daughter of hers to wear such things, he would give her her real present – a large bottle of perfume from Grasse. And then there would be tears, and laughter, and all the happiness in the world.

29

The journey from Victor's home to the Gare St Lazare was no great distance. He drove up the Boulevard Haussmann, staring in front of him as though he did not trust himself to look at her. Julie was reminded of her father, at the end of the school holidays, driving her to catch the early morning train from Penrith to Euston. There had been the same sadness, and the same refusal to admit the sadness.

As they approached the station, the crowds began to thicken. There was a sound of blaring, screeching horns which was noisy even by the standards of Paris. Victor swung the car round into the Rue de Laborde, heading up the gentle slope toward the station forecourt, the Cour de Rome. The great, curved roof of St Lazare, dark brick, steel girders, and glass, was already visible, but the way was choked with a single line of traffic crawling at less than walking-pace between the cars which had been parked on the pavements, or had stalled when their drivers had sought to pass the other cars on the inside. People struggling along on foot, including entire families of three generations, burdened with luggage, jostled and fought to push their way between the vehicles towards the station.

It was the forecourt on Laon station all over again, thought Julie, only worse.

The single line of cars ground to a halt. A policeman in his shirtsleeves, his face glistening under the peak of his képi, was standing in the centre of the road. He was blowing his whistle and waving his arms. It was impossible to tell whether he had stopped the traffic, or whether he was attempting to get it moving again. Victor looked in the driving mirror. Already a line of cars had closed in behind them. He leaned out of the window, and called to the policeman above the noise of horns and the shouting of the pedestrians. The policeman came over and stood with one foot resting on the running-board.

'How is it up at the station?' asked Victor.

The policeman glanced at the traffic and crowds ahead. The fact that he had deserted his post did not appear to have made the slightest difference.

'The whole world is trying to go home to the north,' he said. 'There's a lot of English trying to get back – good riddance, monsieur, that's my opinion. Enough to sink the boat with any luck.'

Victor reached for Julie's hand. A woman who was standing only a few feet away had picked up enough of what the policeman had said to have misheard. She struggled her way round to Julie's side of the car, pushed her head in at the window and screamed, 'English, are you, *chérie*? Another English whore running away!'

She removed her head from the window, and started to dance about on the road, flapping her summer coat on her arms like bat's wings, and chanting, 'Shoo! Shoo! Be off with you, English filth! We don't want you! Shoo!'

The crowds on the pavements, burdened and struggling as they were, still had time to pause and to grin at the woman's antics. For a moment Julie felt that the woman had actually known she was English – had recognised her from somewhere. The thought frightened her.

The policeman took the woman by the arm, but she still flapped about like a bird caught by the wing.

'Shoo! Shoo!' she shouted. 'Go back across the sea with all your English tommies. Run before the nasty Boches get you.'

As the policeman bore her away still writhing and shouting, the crowd applauded.

Victor wound up the windows, dimming the sound from outside.

'It's not fair,' said Julie. She caught the petulant sound of her voice. 'Everybody is accusing the English of running away, and the last thing I want to do is to go home. Oh Victor, there must be something useful I can do here. I do speak French reasonably well, and it would show everybody that not all English people are trying to get away from Paris. Please Victor.'

'You're not going to be able to leave tonight, at any rate,' Victor said. 'We should have got in touch with your Consulate, of course. I expect, being ENSA, you count as a special case.'

Julie put her hand on the door handle.

'Look Victor,' she told him, 'if you think I'm going back with you so you can push me out again tomorrow, I'll leave you now, and take my chance.'

There was a narrow side street nearby. Victor edged the car round, negotiating it round two abandoned cars, forcing a knot of pedestrians to separate and make way. As he drove down the alley to emerge once more onto the relative emptiness of the Boulevard Haussmann, Julie asked, 'And what's so funny?'

'I am a very weak fellow,' he replied. 'Morally, I mean.'

'That could be what I like about you,' said Julie.

The sense of relief was going to her head.

Victor parked in the Rue Auber, under the shadow of the Opéra.

'Julie,' he announced. 'We have a reprieve to celebrate.'

He switched off the ignition.

'Champagne,' he said, 'on the pavement, on a beautiful Sunday afternoon. It is vulgar, isn't it? And I don't really care for champagne. But how does one ever celebrate except vulgarly?'

Julie put her arms round him and kissed him.

'Idiot man,' she said. 'Do you know what you are?'

'What?' he asked, looking into her face.

'A puritan,' she told him.

'Me?' he laughed.

'Yes,' she nodded. 'You.'

'Then it's my Jewish blood,' he replied. 'Good Jews are very dutiful and very puritanical. There hasn't been one like that in my family for a hundred years or more.'

She kissed him again.

'I'm dutiful as well,' she told him. 'I really meant it, you know, about doing something. I'm not going to hang about being nothing but a kept woman.'

He nodded.

'I'll ring Marcia Clementi tonight,' he said.

'Marcia . . . ?' Julie asked.

'Clementi. She's American. Married to a French air force lieutenant. She's a trained nurse. She's been working with refugees passing through the Gare Montparnasse for the past couple of weeks. I'm sure she'd be glad of some help. It is hard work though, so I've heard.'

'I'm not afraid of that,' Julie replied.

They got out of the car, and walked round into the Place de l'Opéra. The pavement tables in front of the café, where crowds would gather on a sunny Sunday afternoon, were occupied by only a scattering of

289

people. Julie and Victor chose a table, and sat down having pulled their chairs close together. They sat holding hands, their knees touching, basking in the warmth, the shade, and their own happiness.

30

'This is Mademoiselle Dubois, Monsieur Chris.'

The proprietor coughed and wiped the back of his hand on the cloth he had tied about his waist. He took a bottle of wine from the side, and clutching four glasses between his grimy fingers, put them down under the fringed light which hung low over the table.

'Dubois, eh?' said Papayannis.

He put the cigar back between his teeth.

The man on the far side of the table, whom the proprietor had not introduced, shrugged.

'*Eh bien! Ça m'est égal,*' said Papayannis.

He lowered his bulk onto a chair. The lampshade was suspended so low that while the jaws and cheeks of the man sitting opposite were brightly lit, his eyes were almost entirely hidden in shadow. Papayannis could see that he was a swarthy fellow, with sunken, tubercular cheeks. Papayannis hoped that Marius had had the sense to tell the stranger that he, Papayannis, was a person of some significance, some influence in the world.

The girl coughed.

'Ah, Mademoiselle Dubois,' he said, 'my cigar-smoke is troubling you?'

She was a pretty girl, so far as one could tell in the abominable light. Although her hair was in the same obscuring shadow as the eyes of the man opposite, he could see that it was well coiffured, and that she had made up her face with the care and discretion expected of an upstairs maid in a wealthy household. The coat she was wearing had been expensive when new and fashionable. It was still smart. In the broad V of the coat collar, however, he noticed that she was wearing her black uniform-frock and her starched white apron. From this, he surmised that she was not, properly speaking, off duty.

There was a chatter of female voices outside. The bell on the counter jangled.

'Excuse me,' said the proprietor, 'Madame should be seeing to the towels, but. . . .'

He went out through the rattling bead curtain.

'You need some wine, mademoiselle,' said Papayannis, 'for your cough.'

He reached across the table so far as his belly would allow, poured out a glass of wine, and pushed it across to the girl. He gasped as he sat back, then drew on his cigar. The smoke curled thickly in the low but bright light from the lamp.

'May I see the pen?' he asked.

He reached over and covered the girl's hand with his own, gave it a squeeze of encouragement, then removed his hand again. The girl glanced across the table to the other man. The man raised his finger.

'Marius!' he called.

He waited. Papayannis turned to the girl.

'First name, child?' he asked.

She stared at him like a frightened animal.

'No need to be afraid,' he told her. 'We're only here to do a spot of business, eh?'

The man opposite had brought her here, along pavements crowded with painted 'bed-bugs' anxious to display their florid charms. She had been brought into this shabby little brothel, where the women traipsed up and down the stairs to fetch their towels, and their Corsican boyfriends lounged against the wall outside waiting to collect their earnings. No doubt the poor child thought she was about to be drugged and carried off to Marseille.

The proprietor came back through the bead curtain. He closed and locked the inside door.

'Right,' said the stranger, as the proprietor sat down with them, and poured himself a glass of wine.

He drew the pen from the pocket of his jacket, and held it under the light.

'I have told Mademoiselle Dubois,' he said, 'that it's no deal. An object like this must be on the stolen goods list at the *Préfecture de Police*.'

'It's a lie,' whispered the girl. 'It was given to me. It's a present.'

'Won't you tell me your name, my dear?' asked Papayannis, very gently.

She did not answer. Papayannis took the pen and examined it.

'You must admit,' he said, still very gently, 'that it is a very generous present for a man like Monsieur le Baron to give to one of his maids. It even has his monogram – his initials, my dear – engraved on it.'

He held it out to show her. She tried to take it from him, but he withdrew it.

'You see, my dear,' he went on, 'I can't blame our friend here for having his suspicions. Businessmen have to be careful to maintain their reputation for honesty. Do you understand that?'

The girl nodded.

'What *is* your name, my dear?' he asked. 'I mean, your baptismal name? I expect you were brought up a good Catholic, weren't you?'

'Danielle,' she whispered.

'Thank you, my dear,' Papayannis replied. 'I expect you are feeling like – er – Danielle in the lions' den, eh? But you have nothing to fear from the lions as long as you are a good, honest girl.'

He twirled the pen between his fingers. The ash fell from the tip of his cigar. He brushed it off the swell of his belly and his trouser-legs.

'I have told Mademoiselle Dubois,' said the man across the table, 'that I consider it my duty to take the object you are holding to the police.'

'A proper course of action, monsieur,' Papayannis replied, 'but I would like to make a suggestion. It is none of my business, of course, but if you, and Marius, will permit me . . . '

'Naturally,' the proprietor replied.

He slurped at his wine, then wiped his chin with the back of his hand.

'I'm listening, monsieur,' said the other man.

'We do not wish to frighten the little girl, here,' said Papayannis.

He reached for her hand again. He felt her fingers twitch in his, but she did not dare remove them from his grasp.

'So I will make an alternative suggestion,' he continued. 'I am going to suggest that you leave the matter with me, for the time being. I will take the pen to Monsieur le Baron de Bart-Mendel. I am not unknown to him – I have done business with him and his associates on the Bourse from time to time.'

He felt the girl's hand tightening.

'If the child did not steal it,' he went on, 'we will be sure, as businessmen, that we are safe. If, however, she did steal it, why then, it may be that Monsieur le Baron may be persuaded to show some compassion toward her – he may prefer not to prosecute her. What do you say to that, messieurs?'

He allowed the girl to remove her hand. He ignored the fact that she had begun to cry. The proprietor twisted about in his chair.

'Well, messieurs?' asked Papayannis. 'Will you leave the matter with me?'

The man on the opposite side of the table sat back in his chair. The lampshade obscured his face in deep shadow down to his chin.

'I'm willing, monsieur,' he replied.

The proprietor cleared his throat.

'Seems a good idea, Monsieur Chris,' he said. 'Hey, you!' he called across the table to the weeping girl. 'Know how lucky you are, eh? Good thing we decided to ask Monsieur Papayannis here. He's a man with friends, he is.'

'It is true,' Papayannis assured the girl. 'I am lucky enough to know people in the Prefecture, and in the Ministry of Justice, too. I may be in a position to help you. So dry your eyes.'

The girl looked across at the man.

'Monsieur André said you made a special business of buying things from servants, no questions asked,' she said.

'No, no,' the proprietor protested. 'You must not say such things.'

'Who is this Monsieur André?' asked Papayannis.

The proprietor shrugged. The stranger offered a gesture with his hands.

'Danielle?' Papayannis asked softly.

'He is Monsieur le Baron's chief stable-boy,' said the girl. 'He's out at Longchamps, only he comes into Paris now and then. And he says he does business with Monsieur ... '

'*Méchante*,' Papayannis wagged his fat forefinger. 'This Monsieur André was quite wrong to tell you such a thing – such a wicked thing. And you were a very foolish child to believe him.'

He dragged himself to his feet to forestall her repeating anything else she had heard. He slipped the pen into his pocket.

'I am going to see Mademoiselle Dubois to a taxi,' he said.

He looked down at her.

'Don't worry, my dear,' he told her, 'I'll see to the fare. You don't want to be out any longer than you can help – not when you are supposed to be at your work. You mustn't get into any more trouble, eh?'

Danielle got up from the table. Papayannis shook hands, first with the proprietor, then with his companion. As he shook hands with the latter, he slipped him a bundle of notes.

Once outside the hotel, he escorted Danielle down the pavement towards the Boulevard de Sébastopol. One of the fat, lard-faced women who were huddled under the dimmed street-lamps or by the ground floor windowsills, called out across the alley, "allo, Monsieur Chris!'

'I have been kind to one or two of these poor women,' he explained to Danielle. 'I'm a soft touch.'

He laughed self-deprecatingly.

As they turned out into the main thoroughfare, he took the girl's arm.

'Tell me, *ma chère*,' he asked, 'you are not a thief. Anybody can see that. Why did you steal the pen?'

'Monsieur le Baron deceived me,' she replied immediately.

'Ah yes,' he said, 'the old story.'

They walked on together; Papayannis was breathing heavily.

'It was after Madame died,' said Danielle. 'He was very lonely. I was sorry for him. You know?'

'Indeed yes,' said Papayannis, 'and he took advantage of your compassion!'

'Yes, monsieur. I wanted to pay him back.'

Papayannis threw the butt of his cigar into the gutter. Down the boulevard, the trees and the kiosks were shadows in the dim filtered light from the street-lamps.

'What are you going to do, monsieur?' she asked.

'Do, *ma chère?*'

'With me, monsieur?'

'Ah!' he said.

He paused as if for reflection. A woman came out of the shadows. She was fashionably dressed.

'Monsieur is looking for somebody?' she smiled.

Papayannis waved her aside, and passed her. She came walking along just behind them.

'Mademoiselle might enjoy it also,' she said. 'A new experience perhaps?'

She fell back when Papayannis refused to take any notice of her. To Danielle, he said, 'A terrible thing, child; even in the hour of France's mortal peril, the streets of Paris are filled with these unfortunate women. You should take warning from them. You have a good position – and I don't suppose a man like Monsieur le Baron forced his attentions on you.'

'He told me things I believed,' she replied, 'about how he needed me.'

'So it goes, child,' said Papayannis. 'So it goes.'

'What are you going to do, monsieur? About me?' she asked again.

He stopped, and she stopped with him.

'Danielle?' he asked. 'Will you make me a solemn promise? A promise to a man who is as old, or even older, than your father? Do you promise never again to steal anything from your employer? Do you promise?'

'Yes, monsieur,' she replied. 'I promise.'

'Very well. Then I shall tell you what I shall do. I shall send the pen to Monsieur le Baron. And I shall send a letter with it, saying that I found it on the pavement – oh, somewhere near the Bourse. I know he often goes to the Bourse. What do you think of that, eh?'

'Monsieur, I don't know how to thank you. Thank you so much; you are very kind.'

She had begun to cry again.

'Now, now,' said Papayannis, 'I'll tell you how you can thank me. You can give an old man a kiss. On the cheek.'

'Oh, monsieur!'

She shook her head in disbelief. Then, impulsively, she embraced him, pressed herself against the swell of his belly, and kissed his mouth. He could taste her tears. She let go, and said, looking up at him, 'I know you gave that man money, monsieur.'

'Ah no!' Papayannis replied. 'That wasn't meant for your eyes, *ma petite*.'

'Oh, monsieur!' she exclaimed.

He took her arm, and led her up the dank, misty pavement. After they had walked some way, they came on a taxi which had just let down a passenger.

'Avenue de Wagram,' Papayannis told the driver. 'Hôtel de Brey.'

The driver pushed down his flag. He reached over to open the passenger seat.

'Wait!' said Papayannis.

He led Danielle a few paces up the pavement.

'Here, child,' he said, 'the money for your fare!'

'Monsieur, I can't possibly,' she protested.

'You must,' he told her, pushing the money into her hand. 'And Danielle? There is a small favour you can do me, *ma chère*.'

'Oh yes, monsieur,' she replied eagerly.

'I have a client,' he said. 'A very wealthy client – as wealthy as Monsieur le Baron. I deal in works of art, you understand. My client is particularly interested in something which Monsieur le Baron has in his possession. You may have heard of it. It is a medallion – the sort known as a *tondeau*. The *Tondeau de Chartres*, in fact. You may have heard of it, my dear?'

'But of course, monsieur,' Danielle replied. 'It was kept in the chapel in La Berlière, but Monsieur le Baron would never wish to part with it.'

Papayannis glanced back at the driver, who shrugged his shoulders.

'The customer pays, monsieur,' the driver called, looking at the meter.

'Whether Monsieur le Baron means to part with it or not, does not concern you, my child,' Papayannis told Danielle. 'Or me, if it comes to that. All you need to do is to phone me at this number,' – he handed her a small card of pasteboard – 'and tell me whether he has it at home, in the Avenue de Wagram, or in some other place of safety ... Oh, and if he keeps it at home, whereabouts he keeps it. That is all, *ma chère*.'

He could see the look of anxiety growing on the girl's pretty face. He laughed.

'Cheer up, *ma petite*,' he told her. 'You'll be able to sleep easier tonight than you've done the past few nights, eh? If the Germans allow you to, that is.'

'Why do you want to know about the *Tondeau de Chartres*, monsieur?' asked Danielle.

'You surely don't think I am a thief?' asked Papayannis.

'No, monsieur, of course not,' she replied.

'Then do as I ask. It isn't much, eh? . . . But I'll tell you. My friend – my client, that is – is a devout Catholic. He has a particular devotion to St Louis. He wishes to be sure in his own mind that the *Tondeau de Chartres* is safe in these dangerous times. And if he cannot be made certain, he wishes to suggest means to Monsieur le Baron by which it can be made safe. Perhaps he is very foolish – but one does not question the follies of the very rich, eh? At least, *ma chère*, not this sort of folly. Does that make you feel any easier?'

'Of course, monsieur.'

'Good. Let me know about it quickly, then. Events move so fast these days, who knows where any of us may be in a week's time – Monsieur le Baron, me, or even you, *ma petite*? And as soon as I hear from you, I'll send the pen to Monsieur le Baron together with the letter I promised.'

He held open the taxi door, and Danielle climbed in.

He lifted his hand in farewell. As the taxi passed him, turning out into the street, he saw the girl's face, framed in the window, bewildered and frightened.

The Baron de Bart-Mendel was a fool, he decided. He should have known better than to keep a maid on in his house after having had a little affair with her. Stupidity of that sort deserved what it got. As for the girl, she could have made a small fortune on the pavement, with looks like hers. It would be amusing to see what would happen when the Germans arrived in Paris.

31

'Shit,' Julie muttered to herself, 'and shit again!'

She had to switch the light on in the bathroom; it dazzled her sleepy eyes. Of course it would have to happen very early that same morning she was due to go down to the Gare Montparnasse, to help Marcia Clementi with the refugees. She wondered if Marcia Clementi had ever slept with Victor. Probably she had. Not that Julie really thought it mattered; she wasn't jealous or anything. She hoped she hadn't woken him up. It was ridiculous, but she felt she had cheated him of something that was his right.

She buttoned on a clean pair of drawers, switched out the bathroom light, and went back into her bedroom. He was awake. He reached out for her, felt the silk of her drawers against his hip, and touched the shape of the pad between her legs.

'What is it?' he asked.

Bloody stupid question, thought Julie.

'It's a doormat actually,' she replied, 'only it doesn't have "welcome" written on it.'

There's no joke like an old joke. Since he was foreign, however, he probably hadn't heard it. She lay down beside him.

'Sorry,' she said. She meant, for having made such a stupid, tired joke.

'It's perfectly natural,' he told her. 'Nothing to apologise for.'

Dear God, she thought; *he* was telling *her*. She suppressed her impatience with him.

'It's started very early,' she said. 'I didn't expect it so soon. I'm usually so regular.'

That could be taken as an apology of sorts, she supposed. She could sense him lying there, staring up at the ceiling.

'Perhaps you'd prefer not to go to Montparnasse this morning?' he suggested. 'I'm sure Marcia would understand.'

I'm *sure* Marcia would understand. *Dear* Marcia – we had such a *beautiful* relationship while it lasted. So *civilised*.

'Oh no,' she replied, 'I'm quite lucky really. I mean, I'm not like some people; I don't have to be treated like an invalid or anything.'

In fact, it was just uncomfortable, and the usual rotten nuisance. Particularly since she had brought only one spare s.t. with her. Still, there was bound to be a chemist somewhere close to the Gare Montparnasse where she could buy some new ones.

Victor put his arm round her, and kissed her.

'I think it's time for me to go,' he whispered.

There was a trace of light through the open windows. A breeze stirred the curtains. There was also the occasional thud of heavy guns in the distance.

'I know,' she replied.

And that was bloody stupid as well. Danielle knew – the whole household knew, if it came to that. She wondered if Danielle would pretend to be shocked if she came in to find the master in bed beside her. Probably, Julie decided. It would be a breach of those conventions which were supposed to be the monopoly of the hypocritical English.

She came down to breakfast in good time. She had dressed in a manner designed to suggest seriousness of purpose, in jersey and slacks, with her hair tied up in a cotton scarf. She had put on eyebrows, but otherwise had used only the minimum of make-up.

Victor was already at the table, dunking his croissant into his coffee-bowl. Sitting beside him was a distinguished-looking gentleman with swept-back, greying hair, pince-nez dangling from a cord about his neck, and the frayed ribbon of the Legion of Honour in his lapel buttonhole. He rose as Julie entered the room.

'This is Juliet Armitage, Maurice,' said Victor. 'A friend from England. Julie, this is Maurice Levasseur. Dr Levasseur is Director of the Hospital of St Anne.'

'*Enchanté, mademoiselle,*' said Dr Levasseur, bowing over her hand.

He smiled at her, inspecting her.

'I ought to ask how you are enjoying your stay in our city,' he said, 'but under the circumstances it would scarcely be appropriate.'

'Dr Levasseur's hospital is close to the Porte d'Orléans,' said Victor. 'So perhaps we might persuade him to give you a lift to the Gare Montparnasse.'

'Of course,' Dr Levasseur agreed. 'I shall be delighted.'

Courtesies complete, Julie realised that she had disturbed a serious conversation. She poured out a bowl of coffee, picked up a brioche, and was about to excuse herself, when Dr Levasseur anticipated her.

'There is no need to go, Mademoiselle Armitage,' he told her. He gave a short little laugh. 'I have been saying only what so many of us have said, and to no avail – that our friend Victor should leave Paris immediately. I have pointed out that our old friend André Maurois has left for London, and without any dishonour attaching to his name.'

'Maurois was sent by the government,' Victor replied. 'He is liked by the English. He will be of use to the Republic there.' He paused. Then he added quietly, 'And you, Maurice, will you go into exile when the Germans approach Paris?'

Dr Levasseur thought for a moment.

'No,' he said. 'I shan't wait for the Gestapo to pick me up, but I shall journey a little further than England, I think – beautiful though your country is, Mademoiselle Armitage.'

He smiled. He looked across the table to where Julie had sat down.

'And you, will you stay on in Paris?'

Julie glanced at Victor. His face was turned from her.

'As long as I feel I can be of use, monsieur,' she replied.

'They say the Citroën workers were demonstrating again on the Quai de Javel yesterday,' said Victor. 'They are demanding that the government arm them for a *levée en masse*.'

'Against the government or the Germans?' asked Dr Levasseur.

'Both, I should imagine,' Victor replied, 'in the manner of 1870. Langeron sent in the riot squad.'

Dr Levasseur nodded.

'Communist hard-liners to a man,' he agreed. 'There's no knowing what they'd have done once they were armed.'

'The great mistake Daladier made last autumn,' Victor said, 'was to have *Humanité* and *Ce Soir* banned. At least they told us what the

Reds were up to. Instead, he should have had Messieurs Duclos and Thorez taken to Vincennes and shot.'

He spoke quite calmly, sitting back in his chair, cigarette-case open in his hand.

Julie was shocked. She wasn't really a political person, she had long since decided, but, like all her theatrical friends, she had supported the Republican cause in Spain, had marched in one or two solidarity rallies, had collected money for the homeless refugee children of Madrid and Valencia, and had signed petitions protesting against the German and Italian interventionists. She had regarded the Left in Britain as being the enemies of the dole queue and the Means Test. Of course, she had heard Daddy say that Phil Piratin and Willy Gallagher, and Major Attlee, should all be put against a wall and shot; but that was different. Daddy was silly, and would never have hurt anybody except when he was a soldier in the Great War. Victor meant precisely what he had said.

'You see?' Dr Levasseur was saying to her. 'How confused we all are? We cannot tell who are our friends and who our enemies these days. Perhaps the demonstrators on the Quai de Javel were honest Frenchmen, anxious to defend their city. And perhaps they merely wanted to set up a Soviet under the instructions of Hitler's Russian allies.

He dropped her off opposite the end of the Avenue du Maine, across the street from the Montparnasse Children's Hospital.

'Forgive me,' he said, 'but the station is a difficult place to get away from at the moment, especially for a doctor. You will see for yourself, Mademoiselle Armitage.'

Julie thanked him, and got out of the car. All about her, the shop windows were barred and shuttered. Iron bars were padlocked across the doors. Above the twisted rooftops, the sky was leaden and overcast, but the air in the street was heavy with warmth so that she felt sticky under her clothes, and her period was more than ordinarily uncomfortable. Courtyard gates were closed up, and the steps between the high buildings were deserted. It was like a film-set of Paris for a picture by René Clair or Jean Renoir, after technicians and actors had gone home.

Dr Levasseur stuck his head out of the car window.

'Mademoiselle Armitage,' he asked her, 'will you try to persuade Victor to leave Paris? It's more urgent than he seems to think. It's my belief that the government do not mean to defend the city.'

'I'll do what I can, monsieur,' Julie assured him.

'*Bonne chance*!' he waved, and drove off.

Ahead of her, up the Avenue du Maine, and looming over the crooked rooftops, was the great glass dome of the old station-house, supported on its wrought-iron, soot-stained girders. As she walked up the deserted street, she saw across the square the crowds occupying the pavement and sitting on the steps up to the station entrance. On reaching the square, she realised that the people outside were those who had been pressed out of the throng packing the interior. They were the defeated, who seemed to have acknowledged their defeat, and had sat down or lain down amidst their belongings to wait for whatever might befall. As she picked her way among them, she noticed the dirt and the apathy, the matted weariness on the faces which stared up at her as she passed. Children were whimpering or crying; they made a dry, rasping noise which seemed to go on and on. The smell was appalling, while from inside the station, under the vast, soot-blackened roof with its forest of curved iron fronds and palm-leaves, came a single mass of noise like that of pandemonium.

Under the shadow of the entrance, as she stepped over a pile of baggage, her arm was grasped suddenly, so that she was forced to turn round. A thin-faced man with high, prominent cheekbones and lank, sandy hair, was gripping her tightly so that she could not pull herself away.

'*Laissez-moi, monsieur,*' she snapped.

'*Pardonnez-moi, mademoiselle,*' he said in a thick heavy accent. '*Notre petite fille, mademoiselle. Elle meurt de soif.*'

His eyes were those of a fanatic, frightening. Behind him, his wife was sitting on the pavement, leaning against the wall, staring fixedly in front of her. A little girl with long, flaxen hair, was lying across her lap, her head cushioned on a rolled-up red coat. A fly crawled across the lower lid of one eye, but still she did not blink. Her cracked lips were parted, motionless. As Julie watched, the fly walked out onto the pupil, and still the child did not close her eye.

Julie wrenched her arm away.

'*Laissez-moi!*' she gasped.

She ran as fast as she could, stumbling over suitcases and even people's legs. Inside the station, she found herself sinking into a sea of heat and infernal noise. There was a babel of different languages. The concourse was a seething mass of people. Here and there, above the heads of the crowd and near the platform gates, Julie could spot the white-topped képi of a policeman. The stench hung in the oppressive heat. Her foot slipped; looking down, she saw that the platform where she was standing was slimy with human excrement. Flies were everywhere.

A small dark man in a dirty white coat was fighting his way through the crowds. Struggling along behind him, a couple of men in army uniform with red-cross brassards on their arms were carrying a stretcher.

'Excuse me!' Julie shouted.

The man in the white coat stopped.

'Mademoiselle?' he asked.

300

He had squat features, not unlike Edward G. Robinson. Probably, he was from the south, thought Julie.

'I'm looking for Marcia Clementi,' Julie explained. 'She's a nurse. An American.'

Obviously, the man hadn't heard above the uproar.

'An American nurse,' Julie shouted.

Behind the man in the white coat, the soldiers carrying the stretcher waited. Julie noticed that the arms which hung down on either side of the stretcher, were limp.

'Madame Clementi?' asked the man.

'Yes,' Julie shouted.

The man beckoned to her to follow him. As he set off with his little cortège, Julie was suddenly pushed aside by a large, dumpy woman in a ridiculous chestnut wig. The woman was shouting, in an unrecognisable but Germanic language, abuse at everybody around her. Behind her, her husband was clearly begging her to calm herself. Julie saw the stretcher-bearers being swallowed up in the throng. With a determination worthy of the dumpy woman who had just shoved her, she forced her way into the crowds after it. It required all her energy to keep the little cortège in view. The mass of people stretched from wall to wall of the concourse, with kiosks and shuttered buffet-stalls rearing like islands out of the sea. Nor was there space to avoid treading in the human dung which seemed to lie everywhere, reeking into the exhausted air.

The white coat and the stretcher-bearers disappeared into the main left-luggage office. As Julie pushed her way towards it, she noticed for the first time, that for all the hubbub, there was one thing lacking. There were no carriages, no sign of engines, throughout the station.

She fought her way through to the left-luggage office. The sick were stretched out on lockers. Some were groaning; children were crying. There were one or two nurses, several Sisters of Charity, and one man in a white coat other than the man who had led Julie there. The huge room was dark and grimy. Those attending the sick had to struggle between the rows of lockers.

'Marcia!' shouted the man Julie had been following.

A slight figure in hospital nurse's uniform was standing beside a stretcher mounted on cartwheels. On the stretcher was a waxen-faced old man, covered in a frayed blanket. The nurse was holding his wrist, feeling his pulse. She turned her head.

'Someone to see you,' the man in the white coat called.

'I'm Juliet Armitage,' Julie told her, in English. 'Victor rang to ask if I could come here to help.'

The severe way her black hair was pulled back under her cap, and her extraordinarily small features and petite figure, made Marcia Clementi look like a ballet-dancer.

301

'Of course,' she said, 'Victor's new girl-friend. Hi!'

She placed the old man's hand back on the stretcher, and covered it with the blanket.

'Hey!' she called to the two stretcher-bearers who had just put down their load. 'You can take him out to Bertillon.'

As they wheeled the old man away, Marcia said, 'The morgue. The poor s.o.b. isn't dead yet, but he will be by the time they get him there ... Got any cigarettes with you? I'm just dying for a cigarette.'

Julie took a packet from her bag and offered her one.

Threads of hair were matted to Marcia's face. Her apron was creased and dirty. Her eyes in the small, oval face, were pouched and bloodshot with fatigue.

'Thanks, hon,' she said, as Julie lit her cigarette for her.

She inhaled deeply. She tried to tidy her hair beneath her cap.

'There aren't any trains,' said Julie.

'There haven't been any trains for three days now,' said Marcia, 'but you can't persuade people there won't be any. Some maniac has spread the tale around there's going to be a train at five o'clock this afternoon, or half after seven – or midnight. So they're all excited, killing each other to get on the platforms. By tomorrow, fifty of them – a hundred maybe – will be dead. Tell some of them they need hospital treatment, but they don't listen. They won't even move off the platform to perform their natural functions in case they lose their chance of a place on the next train.'

She shook her head.

'Sweet Jesus,' she said, 'we'll have the plague here, if the authorities don't step in quick.'

'I saw a dead child out there,' said Julie.

Marcia nodded. 'The children go first,' she said.

'Is there anything I can do?' Julie asked.

'Do you speak Dutch?' asked Marcia. 'Or Flemish?'

Julie shook her head.

'Half those people are Dutch ... Do you speak German, or Yiddish?'

Julie shook her head again.

'The other half are Jews – from Germany, Austria, Poland, Czechoslovakia, just about everywhere. And they're scared out of their minds.'

She gave a tug at the bib of her apron. The strap was torn over her shoulder. It came apart.

'For Chris' sakes!' she said.

A medical orderly came pushing his way across the office. He spoke to her in a low voice. She nodded. To Julie, she said, 'There's a woman giving birth over by platform six. Just gone into labour ... Do you have a safety-pin, hon?'

She flipped the torn strap of her apron back over her shoulder.

'I think so,' said Julie.

She rummaged inside her bag, and found one at the bottom.

'I'll do it,' she told Marcia.

Marcia turned her back to her. Julie pinned the torn end of the strap to the waist-band of the apron.

'Someone grabbed at me outside,' Marcia told her, 'and then hung on. He wasn't sick, except in the head, maybe. Wanted to know if it was true the French army had destroyed two Panzer Divisions near Beauvais. I tore myself away from him – literally!'

She stubbed out the cigarette against the wall, and put the butt into her apron pocket.

'Here,' Julie said. She thrust her packet of cigarettes into Marcia's pocket.

'Is there anything I can do?' she asked, following Marcia into the crowd on the concourse. 'To help, I mean?'

'Done any nursing?' asked Marcia. 'I mean, a lot of these people are going to die. They don't need any amateur Lady Bountiful around, huh?'

Julie struggled to keep up with her.

'There must be something,' she said.

Marcia stopped and turned around.

'Honestly,' she said. 'I don't want to sound unkind, but probably the best thing you can do is to go away, and be as kind to Victor as you can, for as long as he needs you.'

She turned away from Julie, and hurried off.

Somebody clutched at Julie's sleeve. A few yards away, another stretcher was being carried to the left-luggage office.

'Mademoiselle! Mademoiselle!'

A fat, raddled, elderly woman sitting on a suitcase, was clutching at her. The hand on Julie's sleeve was wrinkled and mottled. There were half a dozen rings on the fingers, with huge stones in them.

'When is there a train for Bourges, mademoiselle?' asked the woman, in a gutteral accent.

'There are no trains, madame,' Julie replied. 'None.'

'But my cousin is in Bourges, mademoiselle. She is waiting for me there.'

'Madame,' Julie told her, 'there have been no trains from this station for three days. It is foolish to wait here. You should go home.'

'To Rotterdam, mademoiselle?' asked the woman. 'The Germans have burned down Rotterdam!'

Julie saw the tears on the woman's face. They ran crookedly, following the wrinkles.

'I'm deeply sorry, madame,' she told her.

She noticed the little man in the white coat nearby.

'I'm sorry, madame,' she said hurriedly.

She pushed through the crowd to the white coat. She tripped over a pair of out-stretched legs, and stumbled forward but managed to maintain her balance.

'There must be something – something I can do to help,' she said.

The man looked at her impatiently. She was holding him up, of course.

'Yes, mademoiselle,' he told her. 'There is something you can do. You can find some milk. Milk for the young children. They are dying for want of milk.'

'Where shall I go?' Julie asked.

'Go, mademoiselle?' the man asked. 'To the shops, of course! There are grocers' shops by the hundred in the streets round about, all stocked up with powdered milk. They are bolted and padlocked, of course. The owners mean to keep their goods safe while they run off to Nantes, Bordeaux, the Pyrenees. See what you can do, mademoiselle. Knock on their doors. See if you can wake up dead consciences, eh?'

She watched him disappear into the crowd. She felt dazed by the noise, the stench, and his evident anger.

'It shouldn't be impossible to break into a shop, mademoiselle!'

A man got up from the case on which he had been sitting just by her feet. He was a broad, heavily built Dutchman. Sitting beside him was his wife, and two ash-blond young boys.

'Better than letting kids die, mademoiselle,' said his wife.

Clearly, they believed that Julie held some official position. The man called out in Dutch to several men who were standing nearby. There was a certain amount of argument, but thee of them came stumbling over the baggage to join him.

'You take us to the shops, mademoiselle,' said the first man, 'and we'll see you get inside.'

Julie found herself leading them out of the station, two of them having managed to pick up iron bars on the way. As they left the stench and gloom and passed into the humid but relatively fresh air outside, she did not dare tell her companions that she had no idea where to go. She found that they were heading directly for the Montparnasse Cemetery. She turned right abruptly, and with what she hoped was an air of decision. All along the street they now entered were the façades of dance-halls, cafés, small theatres. Behind the locked grille of a decaying cinema, glossy, yellowing publicity stills advertised the showing of *Pepé le Moko*. She looked up at the steep grey eaves of the buildings. A weather-beaten blue and white sign told her that they were in the Rue de la Gaité. This, she knew, was the old nineteenth-century 'Boulevard des Assassins' – the Bohemia of Frédéric le Maître and of Henri Murger, the setting for the story of Trilby and Svengali. But the actors and actresses, the cheapjacks and whores, the starving poets and novelists, the nocturnal visitors from the sixteenth arrondissement and the foreign tourists who had kept the district alive beyond its natural term – all were vanished. Windows were shuttered, doors barred. There was not a sign of life.

She led her small party up into a narrow side street. A cat screeched from a doorway, and padded swiftly across the cobbles.

'Here,' one of the men said.

Above them was a faded sign which read *Épicerie* in large curling letters. The first man slipped his iron bar under the steel bar across the shop door, and attempted to wrench off the padlock. Julie glanced over her shoulder, expecting the police to appear at the end of the street. The first man gave up his attempt on the door. He thrust his bar between the slats of the shutter, and ripped them off, throwing the splintered fragments down the street as the slivers of glass clattered onto the pavement. Two of the men began pulling out the jagged pieces of glass which still adhered to the sides of the window-frame, and threw them into the road.

The self-appointed leader turned to Julie.

'Will you go inside, mademoiselle?' he asked. 'You are not afraid?'

Julie nodded her agreement.

'My three friends,' said the man, 'will go on up the street to find other shops. I will assist you.'

The three men took the iron bars and went on up the street. They disappeared round a corner. The remaining man lifted Julie up through the window. She crawled across the dusty, empty display shelf, reminding herself that if the worst came to the worst, Victor was a personal friend of Monsieur Langeron, the Paris Prefect of Police. She jumped down to the floor. The shelves behind the counter were packed with tins of food, packets, and bottles. Under the counter and behind it were barrels and sacks. There was a heady smell of wine fumes, cheese and settled dust. The drawer of the till was open, and the trays inside, empty; since nothing else had been disturbed, the owners must have taken all the small change with them when they left.

She pressed her back against the edge of the counter, and examined the shelves. There was a small pyramid of tins labelled *Lait Concentré Sucré*. She did not suppose it would be very good for small children, but she decided to take it for want of anything better, and carried it back to the window. There was a noise of smashing glass from up the street.

'They've found another shop,' said the man.

He gathered up the tins of condensed milk. Julie glanced back into the shop. Then she saw, actually on the counter itself, two large blue sugar-paper bags. They were labelled *Lait en Poudre*.

'Wait!' she called to the man, 'that's what we need.'

305

She ran back to the counter, and fetched the two bags.

'There must be more here,' she said. 'There must be. . . .'

She paused, trying to think of the French for 'store-room.'

'*Un espace pour amasser les provisions,*' she tried.

The bags were quite heavy. The man could not manage them with the tins Julie had collected.

'I'll fetch back the others,' said the man.

Julie went back into the shop. She heard the man's footsteps as he ran up the cobbled street. There was a door behind the counter. It was ajar; she pushed it open and went through. She was in a narrow, bare little passage, facing a dusty, grey window, one pane of which had a long crack down it. To her left, a flight of wooden stairs rose steeply upwards; another flight led down to a door. One of the glass panels of the door was broken; she could just glimpse the ground of the basement or yard beyond. There was a door under the stairs to her left. She opened it cautiously, and found herself in a small office or accounting-room. There was a desk under the window, with a high stool. On the desk was spread a broad, calf-bound account-book. On the wall opposite the desk was an antique-looking telephone. Beside it was a calendar, the picture on which was that of a helmeted soldier in the horizon-blue of the Great War leaning forward to kiss the Cupid's bow lips of a fluffy-haired girl who was lifting the hem of her slip above the tops of her black silk stockings.

Julie left the office, and went down the basement stairs. Through the broken glass panel of the back door, she could see out into the cramped little yard – the heap of half-empty sacks, a battered wooden hand-cart, and opposite, an open lavatory cubicle with a wooden seat stretched over a zinc bucket.

There was another door beside her, she found, which must surely be that of the store-room. She turned the handle, and it opened. Daylight from the broken window of the yard door flooded into the blackness of the room as the smell of sweat and excrement met her. She saw the faces peering at her, the hollow eyes and stubble-growth of beard on the leprous, white cheeks, and the dirty uniforms. As she turned and ran back up the strairs, somebody shouted at her, but though the voice seemed very close to her ear, she did not hear what it was. At the top, she threw herself through the doorway in the front shop. Boots were clattering up the stairs behind her. As she twisted round the counter, bruising her hip against it as she did so, she could imagine the feel of their hands on her. They were shouting immediately behind her. She pulled herself up onto the display shelf, and rolled across it. Somebody caught at the cuff of her slacks. She kicked with all her strength. The tins of condensed milk which were lying where the man had left them, rolled and clattered onto the pavement below. Her heel landed on something soft, and a voice close to her exclaimed '*Merde!*' She swivelled round, and jumped down into the street.

She ran as fast as she could in the direction taken by her companions. It was uphill. Almost immediately she heard the sound of soldiers' boots striking the cobbles behind her. She couldn't catch breath. She tried to call out, but no sound would come, and the street ahead was quite deserted. There was a painful griping in her lower bowel, and a damp soreness between her legs. Her lungs began to feel leaden, as if she were suffocating.

She stumbled into a passage-way. The boots clattered behind her, very close, the noise echoing from wall to wall. There was a door-latch. She reached for it; the door swung open, and she fell through it onto some steps leading down into a yard. She recovered enough to slam the door shut behind her, and to lean against it. The very instant she felt the weight on the other side, and felt the door moving inwards, and saw the iron bolt, and slammed it to. Thuds shook the wooden planking. Hoarse voices very close to her said foul words she understood very well, and some words whose meaning she could only guess at. She hardly dared to breath lest they should realise there was only a thin plank between between herself and them.

The blade of a long knife or bayonet was inserted in the gap between doorpost and door. It slid upwards, trying to find the latch or the bolt. Leaning forward, Julie unlaced her shoes and took them off. In her stockinged feet, she crossed the yard noiselessly. The stone flags were littered with dung and rotted straw; it was foul underfoot, but silent. At the far side was a double-gate secured by a wooden beam. As the rattling and scraping at the door behind her became more fierce, and the planks began to splinter, she lifted the beam carefully, pulled it back, and opened the gate. She looked out into the street. It was quite broad. Above the steep, slated roof of the house opposite, reared the mighty glass and steel roof of the station.

She dropped the beam and, clutching her shoes, ran down the gentle slope of the street as fast as she could. Sharp edges of stone bit through the silken soles of her stockings, but she ran on, though there was no sound of pursuit behind her. She ran on until she was in the midst of the crowds under the station portico. There, she sank down, sitting on the ledge of the pedestal which supported one of the brick piers holding the roof. Her whole body was a jangle of pain and nerves. Pain was everywhere – in her head, her chest, her crotch, dragging at her stomach, burning her torn feet inside the ragged mesh of her holed and laddered stockings. None of the crowds around her paid the slightest attention to her.

She began to weep as soon as she had recovered her breath. Through her tears, she saw a column of ambulances; they were like old-fashioned horse-boxes, high and wooden, mounted on what looked like pram-wheels. She fell asleep where she sat.

Marcia Clementi found her still sitting there late that afternoon, as she was leaving the station.

'Hi!' she called out.

Then, despite her own utter weariness, she saw the state Julie was in.

'You look like you've had one hell of a day,' she remarked.

Julie nodded.

'I guess it's time both of us went home, hon,' said Marcia. 'If either of us is going to be of any use tomorrow.'

Julie had neither the energy nor the inclination to deny that she had been working in the station all day. She managed to stand up. Even with her shoes on, her feet were dreadfully sore. Marcia took her elbow to support her.

'I owe you an apology,' Marcia told her, as she helped her to her car. 'I thought you were just another of Victor's attachments come to fart around while people worked.'

'It was much worse than I expected,' Julie said.

'Of course it was,' said Marcia. 'It's worse than anyone could expect. But you stayed, didn't you?'

She helped Julie into her car.

'Still the Hôtel de Brey, isn't it?' she asked.

'Yes,' Julie whispered.

As they drove across Paris Julie felt a fraud. Marcia dropped her at the archway entrance to the Hôtel.

'Shall I pick you up tomorrow?' Marcia asked. 'About eight o'clock?'

Julie nodded.

'That's a girl!'

Julie tested the soles of her feet on the pavement.

'Hey!' Marcia called out from the car. 'Know something? It is the damndest thing, Victor ringing me up about you. Victor is one of the most considerate and sensitive men alive in some respects – a real nice guy! And yet, in some ways he's as dense about other people's feelings as a California smog. It's being so rich, I suppose.'

Julie didn't know what a 'California smog' was. She didn't ask.

'See you, hon,' Marcia smiled, wrinkling her nose.

Julie hobbled past the concierge's window, and crossed the garden square to the main entrance. As she went in, Alain, Victor's secretary, was limping across the hall.

'Are you unwell, mademoiselle?' he asked, hurrying across to her.

'Very tired,' Julie replied.

'Let me assist you,' said Alain.

He took her arm.

'I must go upstairs,' Julie told him.

'Shall I call for your maid, mademoiselle?' asked Alain.

'If you please,' Julie replied.

He led her across the hall to a wooden armchair at the foot of the stairs. She rested her head against the high back, and closed her eyes. Her eyelids were burning. She had been so stupid, going off to try to do a job like that on the first morning of her period. She had wanted to impress Victor, to show him that she had it in her.

'Why, Julie?' Victor's voice broke through her sleep.

He was leaning over her. Alain was standing behind him, and Danielle was waiting at the foot of the stairs.

'I'm all right,' she said, pulling herself together. She found herself talking compulsively. 'They were just sitting there, in the station. Thousands of them. There aren't any trains, but they all stay there just the same. They won't move – not even to save their children's lives.'

She paused to take breath.

'What happens to people?' she asked.

'Perhaps they have nowhere else to go,' Victor suggested. 'If they are Dutch or Belgians, their governments have surrendered. And a lot of French people regard them as traitors. They are in limbo.'

'Even children?' asked Julie.

'I suppose so,' Victor replied.

'That's bloody stupid,' said Julie.

She got to her feet unaided.

'Danielle will look after me,' she said.

Later that evening, her feet still felt sore, but she felt much better after having washed and changed her clothes. She had not, however, acquired any fresh s.t.'s. In making do, she was forced to confide in Danielle. Danielle promptly offered to let her have two of her own.

32

Over dinner, she could not bring herself to tell Victor how she had spent the whole afternoon dozing under the station portico in a state of shock, but she did tell him about the raid on the shop, and the men whom she had found hiding in the store-room.

'Are you going back with Marcia tomorrow?' asked Victor.

'Yes,' she said firmly, not allowing herself time to think.

If she did go back to Montparnasse tomorrow, she decided, God would forgive her for not having been truthful to Marcia and Victor – an extraordinary notion, since she had ceased to believe in God shortly after her Confirmation.

'I'd feel a bit better,' she said, 'if the storm would actually break.'

Victor looked across the table at her. He put down his napkin.

'That isn't thunder, you know,' he said.

How could he be so sure, she wondered? The noise which had been rumbling away in the distance ever since she had returned, was exactly like thunder.

Victor got up. He switched off all the lights. Then he went to the windows, opened them, and stepped out onto the stone platform at the top of the steps leading down into the garden. Julie followed him, carrying her wine-glass. The night air was fresh.

'See?' he asked.

With each individual rumbling noise, light flashed beyond the rooftops skirting the garden. Victor put his arm round her waist. She leant against him.

'Once you've become accustomed to the sound of the guns,' he told her, 'you can never mistake them. I still hear them in my dreams.'

'Were you in the trenches?' asked Julie.

'For two years,' he replied.

It was absurd. Daddy had been in the trenches; her Uncle Toby, whom she had never known, had died in them. The trenches were part of history; Victor, though he was a lot older than she was, wasn't what one would call old.

'Are they coming?' she asked. 'How near are they?'

'It's not in the papers yet,' Victor replied, 'but one German armoured column has reached the Seine just south of Rouen – at Elbeuf. I'm afraid it'll have to be Cherbourg or St Malo now, if you want to go home.'

'Not yet,' Julie said firmly.

He stooped and kissed her cheek.

'Finish your drink,' he told her. 'There's something I want to show you.'

When she had finished her wine, he led her back into the room. He closed the windows and drew the curtains once more. Then he took her across the hall to the study. On the panelling between the bookshelves, hung the portrait of a serene-faced beauty with raven, upswept hair. She was wearing the incredibly pinch-waisted costume of the Belle Époque.

'*Madame ma mère* must excuse us,' said Victor, lifting the picture off its hook.

There was a keyhole in the panelling behind it. He inserted a key from his waistcoat pocket, and a small door, a single panel, swung open. Behind this was a small safe with a combination lock. This he spun quickly, first in one direction, then the other, in ten separate movements. He pulled open the heavy steel door of the safe, reached deep inside, and drew out a wide, flat, black leather, embossed case.

310

This he placed with great care on the sloping top of his desk. He reached up, and switched on the desk-lamp. With a slight pressure of the thumb on the edge of the case, he opened the two flaps of the lid. He lifted the green baize cloth inside. The brightness of the lamplight struck the silver in a white blaze. The medallion looked as if it had been newly minted. Julie gasped in astonishment.

'It's beautiful,' she exclaimed, realising how inadequate the comment was. 'It's the most beautiful thing I have ever seen.'

'It is a tondeau,' Victor explained. 'The silver has not been poured into a mould. The wheel – the solid round of silver has been – how do you say? *forged* – like iron, you know?'

'Wrought?' Julie suggested.

'Exactly.'

'It's miraculous,' Julie said quietly.

Victor laughed. 'So some chroniclers have maintained,' he told her.

Julie looked at the strange attenuated images within the circle. There was a Modigliani quality about the human figures, she thought.

'How old is it?' she asked.

'It was made in 1250,' Victor replied, 'the work of one of the medieval masters.'

They stood side by side, gazing down at it.

'The year before,' he said, 'in 1249, King Louis IX – St Louis – led a crusade into Egypt. He thought that if he could break the power of Turan Shah, Sultan of Egypt, and destroy his regiments of Mamelukes, the Saracen hold on the Holy Land to the north would be fatally weakened. He landed his chivalry on the Egyptian coast, and captured the walled city of Damietta. He then advanced on Cairo, across the Nile delta. In the swamps and marshes of the Nile, his army was stricken with malaria and dysentery; his cavalry could not fight in their traditional fashion in such a terrain, the Saracens had all the time they needed to deploy their forces. At Mansurah, they caught St Louis's army in a trap, and virtually destroyed it. St Louis, with a handful of his knights, fled into the swamps. He tried to struggle back to Damietta, but he too was laid low with fever. The soldiers of Turan Shah were on the point of catching up with St Louis's band, when St Louis believed that he had a vision. He believed that he saw Christ coming to meet him, walking dry-shod across the swamp water. He fell on his knees there, in the reeds, and, wishing to surrender to his Lord rather than to the Saracen, he offered his sword to Christ. Christ took the sword from him, but returned it immediately, saying that St Louis must use it in His service upon earth.

'Shortly afterwards, St Louis was captured; but almost at once, there was a mutiny amongst the Mameluke regiments against Turan

311

Shah, and he was able to reach the coast, and to set sail for France. The following year, when he was preparing his second crusade, he ordered the Master of the Guild of Silversmiths of Chartres to strike this medallion. It was to be worn on a chain round the shoulders of every Constable of France from then on, when he rode out against the enemies of God and France.'

'What are you going to do with it if the Germans come?' Julie asked. 'Isn't there a Constable of France who should be wearing it now?'

'Weygand?' said Victor. 'Or the old Marshal Pétain, perhaps? The sad defeatists at Vincennes? The true enemies of France aren't necessarily to be found only among the Germans. And this is too holy to be placed on the shoulders of anybody who is unworthy of it.'

'What do you mean – holy?' Julie asked. 'You're an unbeliever, aren't you?'

'I'm not a cynic,' Victor told her. 'I believe that people make things holy. I believe that places can be consecrated by people's prayer – like Bethlehem, or Lourdes, let's say. Or objects, like that relic of Ste Geneviève. Or acts between people . . . '

He paused.

'Like making love,' he said. 'It's all a question of love. It is what our poet, Charles Péguy, called *le mystère de la charité de Jeanne d'Arc*. Not cold faith. Or magic. But love. Which is why, if I were to allow this to be worn by somebody like Weygand, it would be sacrilege.'

'Is there going to be anybody you can be sure is worthy of wearing it?' Julie asked.

Victor smiled.

'That,' he said, 'sounds like a reproach.'

There was a quiet knock on the door. They had left it open behind them. Now, Danielle was standing there.

'Mademoiselle?' she called.

Victor drew the green baize cloth quickly over the medallion.

'Excuse me a moment,' Julie said to him.

She went across to Danielle.

'I've brought you these,' Danielle whispered.

She had a white paper bag in her hand. She gave it to Julie.

'It's what you wanted, mademoiselle,' she whispered.

Julie was taken by surprise. She had expected the maid to have taken them up to the bedroom. And Danielle too was behaving with an odd sort of nervousness.

'What is it?' Victor called.

'It's all right,' Julie called back. 'Danielle has brought me something – something I needed in rather a hurry.'

She thanked Danielle, and offered to pay for the towels.

'It's not at all necessary, I assure you, mademoiselle,' Danielle told her.

It was very strange, thought Julie, as Danielle returned across the hall to the door leading to the kitchen quarters; normally the maid brimmed over with self-assurance, but this evening she had behaved as if she had been profoundly embarrassed.

There was a glass partition along the top half of the wall which separated the kitchen passage from the servants' diningroom. Through it, Danielle could see Joseph and Severin at the table, a bottle of wine and a plate of cheese between them. The plump, matronly figure of Maryvonne was carrying the soup tureen away to the kitchen, followed by Claudine, the kitchen-maid, carrying the plates and spoons. Quickly, before anybody should come out into the passage and see her, Danielle took down her coat from its wooden peg, and put it on over her uniform. She tried to find comfort in the thought that it would be such a relief when that terrible, puffy-faced Greek gentleman finally sent the pen to Monsieur le Baron – if he really intended to do so. There was the sound of the guns in the distance that would not go away. Perhaps, if the Germans came, the problem would solve itself – but that was a wicked thought.

She let herself out into the kitchen yard, then through another door into the darkness of the garden. She crossed the lawn to avoid making any noise on the gravel path, and passed under the trees to the door in the wall on the far side. Looking back, she saw the chinks of light round the curtains of the study window. Leaving the garden, she stepped down into the Rue Brey. There was nobody on the pavements, and only one or two cars passing by. She crossed the street, went up the side street opposite, and went into the café at the corner.

'Ça va, Danielle?'

The toad-like *patron* was drying glasses behind the counter with a greasy-looking cloth. He always gave the impression of being pleased to see her. One or two of the regular customers sitting in the swirl of tobacco smoke, greeted her, and she called back to them.

'Telephone?' she asked.

He jerked his thumb in the direction of the alcove behind the coffee urns. The regulars continued to play cards. Danielle placed the paste-board card on the ledge in front of her. She took down the receiver and dialled the number on the card.

'Who's that?' asked the voice at the other end.

It sounded very close, as if she could feel its owner's breath on her neck. She buried her lips into the trumpet of the mouthpiece.

'Monsieur Chris?' she asked softly. 'It's me, Danielle.'

She twisted herself round in the booth, to make sure nobody could overhear her. She waited, but there was no reply from the other end, though she could hear the man breathing into the phone.

'Danielle Dubois. From the de Bart-Mendel household,' she said.

'Ah yes,' said the voice at the other end. 'I've been waiting to hear from you.'

He sounded very distant and cruel, she thought.

'I can tell you something about what you wanted to know,' she said.

She felt weak with nerves from her stomach into her legs.

'That is good, *ma petite*,' came the reply.

She told him what she had just seen in the study. She told him where the safe might be found.

'That is excellent,' the man replied. He sounded rather kinder. 'You have been a good girl, Danielle.'

'Thank you, monsieur,' she whispered.

'But we have to be sure you are telling the truth, don't we, my dear?' the dreadful voice continued. 'You do understand that, don't you?'

'Of course, monsieur,' whispered Danielle.

She heard the click of the receiver being put down at the other end.

As she returned to the noise and smoke of the café, she felt a dreadful hopelessness closing in about her.

33

A group of soldiers were strolling up the narrow street. Two of them were pushing a wooden handcart; it bumped and clattered on the cobbles. Through the grime of the shop window, and in the dark of the street, Marie-Claire could see the rifles slung on their shoulders.

'Those bandits are up to no good,' Florence whispered beside her. 'Better move, quick!'

They grabbed the small sack containing the tinned food they had been collecting, and carried it between them out into the back of the shop. Ines was standing guard at the back entrance, a silhouette against the glass.

'Soldiers,' Marie-Claire whispered.

She saw Ines' hand move from the pocket of her boiler-suit, and heard the click of the switch-blade opening.

'They've got guns,' she whispered.

Ines opened the door and whispered through it. Manuela came in quickly. Ines bolted the door after her. From the street in front of the shop came the crash of broken glass.

'Upstairs!' Cybele's voice called in a whisper from the landing above.

The four girls crept up and joined her. Across the landing, in the parlour immediately above the shop, Ginette, torch in hand, was ransacking drawers and cupboards.

'Put the light out,' Cybele called to her, 'there's nothing worth taking.'

Ginette switched off the torch. Ines and Manuela remained at the head of the stairs, their knives in their hands.

'The shop door is open,' Florence whispered.

'They won't come upstairs,' Cybele told her. 'Not if we're quiet.'

There was a second crash from across the street, and a clatter of splintered glass. The soldiers were shouting to each other. Florence and Marie-Claire went over to the window and peered round the edge of the lace-curtain.

'Where's Pauline? And Severine?' asked Marie-Claire.

'Keep quiet if you don't want to get killed,' Cybele whispered quite coolly.

She stooped to look out of the window over their shoulders.

There was the scream of a police whistle from up the street. A powerful beam of torchlight struck the three soldiers who were still standing at the shattered shop window. One of them unslung his rifle, knelt on the pavement in the midst of the broken glass, and levelled his rifle. He fired; the shot resounded up and down the street. The torchlight spun crazily about the cobbles. Marie-Claire caught a glimpse of a dark uniformed figure writhing on the pavement some distance away. Behind him, another uniformed figure was kneeling, struggling to open the holster at his belt. The soldier who had fired the shot, lowered the butt of his rifle from his shoulder, and drew back the bolt. A spent cartridge spilled out of the breech and clinked on the pavement. The soldier slammed home the bolt, and raised his rifle again. Again the shot cracked and echoed up and down the street. The kneeling policeman tilted over, and tumbled back into the gutter, his fingers clenched round the butt of his drawn revolver.

The soldier stood up, and slung his rifle back onto his shoulder. From the smashed shop front, three soldiers jumped down to join the three on the pavement. They threw the goods they had looted onto the handcart, and began pushing it once more up the street, the others strolling along behind them as if nothing untoward had happened.

Cybele waited for the noise to fade away into the distance. Below the window from which they were watching, the girls saw Pauline and the fat shape of Severine emerging from the deep shadows not far from where the soldiers had been standing.

'Downstairs,' whispered Cybele.

For the first time, there was a trace of excitement in her voice.

As they all stepped out into the street, they found Pauline and Severine standing over the first of the policemen who had been shot. He was still moving, and uttering sobbing sounds like a sick child. Severine prodded him with her toe.

'Ah, *le pauvre gars*!' she said. '*Ah, le pauvre gars*!'

Cybele went over to the second policeman.

'Give us some light, Ginette,' she ordered.

Ginette switched on her torch. The tall figure of Cybele with her pale, hectic face, her customary black suit, black stockings, and black beret tilted on her head, looked like an emissary of Darkness come out of the night.

Manuela kicked aside the képi of the first policeman, and knelt down. She cradled his head in her lap. He groaned and moved, and looked up into her face.

'*Pauvre petit*,' she said gently. '*Veux-tu aller voir Jesus, eh?*'

She grasped him by the hair, and pulled his head back over her knee. Ginette laughed. The man gurgled in his throat and sighed; his foot jerked and fell limp. Manuela got to her feet, letting his head fall to the pavement. She wiped the blade of her knife on the leg of the boy's factory-dungarees she was wearing, snapped shut the knife and dropped it into the bib-pocket, between her breasts. As she did so, Ines squatted down beside the man, took his revolver from its white holster, cut the lanyard, and stood up, dangling the pistol from her hand by the trigger-guard. She stooped, picked up the man's képi, and handed it to Manuela who put it on her head at a roguish tilt. Then she turned to where Cybele was standing over the second policeman.

'Dead?' she asked.

Cybele smiled and nodded. She put her toe under his body and jerked it. He did not move. Ines crouched down once again; she tried to take his revolver from out of his hand, but the fingers were clenched too tightly about it. She took out her knife once again, and prised the fingers open. Cutting the lanyard, she handed the revolver over to Cybele, and slipped the first revolver into the capacious pocket of her boiler-suit. Then she put the képi from the second policeman on her own head. Standing beside Manuela and putting her arm about her, she announced, 'We are joining the Foreign Legion!'

They giggled.

Led by Cybele, and still wearing the policemen's képis, they set off down the street, followed by the others who were carrying between them the sacks of provisions and bottles of wine they had stolen.

The Rats of Venus had moved from the discomfort of the abandoned warehouse near the Gare de l'Est, to a spacious, luxurious apartment amidst the crumbling grandeur of the Marais, which had been abandoned by its owners in the general flight from Paris. They did their shopping at night, not in the fashionable areas about the Opéra and the Rue de Rivoli which were still effectively policed, but across the river, on the Left Bank. They strolled home down the middle of the street, calling noisily to one another, virtually challenging anyone who dared to intercept them. Ines's pocket bulged where the revolver rested against her leg. Cybele had the other revolver sticking out of the open handbag on her arm.

The night was heavy and sticky. There was the steady thud of gunfire in the distance. There were white flashes against the clouds over in the direction of the Bois de Boulogne and Longchamps. As they made their way under the trees of the Rue de Bourgogne towards the Quai Anatole France, the cool air off the Seine smelt of smouldering cardboard and burning paper. Voices were calling from behind the high walls and lofty ornamental railings of the government ministry buildings, distinct in the night air. Motors were revving up and headlamps splashed across the pavements onto the road. Florence pulled Marie-Claire close against the wall. Several lorries came grinding out of a wide gateway, turned and drove off towards the Pont de la Concorde. The gates clanged shut, and there was a rattle of chains and bolts. A moment or two later, the tall figure of Cybele emerged from the shadows of the trees, and signalled the girls on. Florence led Marie-Claire on, pulling her by the sack they were both carrying. As they did so, Marie-Claire could see, through the tall bars of the gates, the bonfires burning in the courtyard and on the lawns of the ministry. Figures silhouetted against the flames, or casting leaping, tall shadows against the white walls of the building, were carrying crates and tin despatch-boxes, and emptying them into the fires. There were several lorries still parked on the drive by the steps leading to the main entrance. Soldiers were hurrying up and down the steps carrying chests between them. The bonfires looked beautiful, Marie-Claire thought: like the autumn bonfires in the convent garden when she was a child, only much, much brighter.

Florence tugged at the sack so hard that it almost pulled Marie-Claire over.

'Stupid bitch,' Florence whispered. 'Want to get us all shot?'

She dragged Marie-Claire along behind her. Marie-Claire let out a sob. She wasn't used to Florence being cross and rough with her. Florence loved her.

Florence heard the sob.

'Shit yourself or something?' she demanded, and tugged her along again.

They followed Cybele, scurrying across the top of the Boulevard St Germain, and diving into the darkness of one of the side-streets behind the ministries which lined the Quai Anatole France. They were half way down it when they saw the figures of two men coming in the opposite direction. The girls spread into the shadows and

317

waited. As the men came close to, Marie-Claire could see that they were both wearing dark, formal suits, and had thin silver chains about their necks; they were *huissiers* from one of the ministries who had left their posts to take some refreshment and were now returning to their official duties. Obviously they were well refreshed. Their coats were unbuttoned, and the chain of one of them was twisted and draped back over his shoulder.

Ginette stepped out of the doorway where she had hidden herself. She pulled the tortoise-shell band from off her head and let her hair fall loose. She giggled, and smiled coquettishly at the men, and raised her skirt between her fingers. One of the men patted her cheek, and Ginette took his arm. The other man protested, but the first simply laughed, and allowed Ginette to draw him away into the darkness. The second man reaffirmed his protest in a low but vehement voice and continued on his way towards the Boulevard St Germain. After a minute or two Cybele emerged from the darkness and whistled softly. Without waiting for Ginette, the other girls proceeded on their way into the Quartier St Germain. Cars had been abandoned along the pavements, and they would stop to see if anything of value had been left inside them. In one car, parked and abandoned in the Rue de Savoie, Marie-Claire saw a large, life-size doll sprawling on the back seat. She called to Florence. Putting down the sack of food, she managed to open the rear door. Florence flashed her pocket torch round the interior. The owners of the car had left inside it everything which was not essential. There was a pair of tennis-rackets in their presses, a boxful of books which were spilling out over the floor, and even two small and unopened suitcases on the seat.

The doll had shoulder-length blonde hair – real hair. Her eyelids with their long lashes, moved up and down. She had on the most beautiful blue satin party frock with a velvet sash, and underneath, a lace-edged petticoat and a pair of sweet little frilly drawers. Her face and mouth had been moulded into a tender, loving smile.

Marie-Claire picked it up and cuddled it.

'*Comme tu es belle*,' she whispered. 'Did *maman* leave you behind, *chérie*? Ah, *ma petite, maman* was so naughty to leave you. Did you cry a lot, *ma petite*, eh?'

'What in God's name do you think you're up to?'

Cybele's voice was sharp as a knife on the night air. Thinking it was she who was being addressed, Marie-Claire clutched the doll to her breasts. At that moment, she would have run away alone into the darkness, just as she was, rather than have surrendered it. It was Ginette, however, who was being talked to; Ginette, who had just caught up with them. She was standing in the light of Florence's torch. She was smiling happily like a pleased child. Her hair was dishevelled. Her blouse was unbuttoned. Her sleeve was sodden with blood, and blood was on her hands and fingers. Around her neck was the thin chain belonging to the *huissier*. She lifted the end with its tiny medallion, and, laughing, showed it to Cybele. Cybele's face was as hectic, as livid, as that of the Queen in the film of *Snow White*.

'Cretin!' she whispered.

She grabbed the chain and tore it from Ginette's neck. Ginette let out a little scream of pain. Cybele threw the chain into the back of the car. Ginette's blood-stained fingers were crooked like the talons of a bird of prey. She was hissing, beads of spittle spreading on her lips.

Florence caught her by the arm. Ginette started to struggle violently to free herself. The strange gasping and whimpering noise she was making terrified Marie-Claire. Then Pauline appeared. She caught Ginette's other arm, but as if in an embrace.

'Ginette! Ginette!' she said. '*Calme-toi!*'

She repeated it softly over and over again, until Ginette quietened down. To Cybele, she said reproachfully, 'She does not understand. You should not be angry with her.'

Ginette reached towards the car for the chain.

'No, darling,' Pauline whispered. 'Mustn't. If the men catch you with it on, they will punish you. They will punish you terribly.'

Ginette stared at her, wide-eyed.

'You see?' Pauline told Cybele.

Suddenly, Cybele stretched out her arms to Pauline. Her face was become a tragic mask. Pauline left Ginette and went to Cybele. She embraced her. Cybele stooped to lay her head on Pauline's shoulder.

'It's the sickness,' Pauline coaxed her. 'Just the sickness. And I'm here. Till the end, my darling. *Tout va bien, chérie! Tout va bien!*'

They continued down the street together. Marie-Claire pressed the cold, hard cheek of the doll against her own.

'You've got a new *maman* now,' she whispered. 'And you're going to be a very good girl for your new *maman*, aren't you?'

With her free hand, she helped Florence to lift the food sack. They hurried after the others.

They had reached the Boulevard St Michel and were in single file, keeping close to the inside of the pavement, when they heard the roar of motorcycles and cars approaching over the Pont St Michel. They ducked round the corner of the Rue Serpente, and watched from the shadows. Half a dozen motorcycle outriders wearing white gauntlets and cross belts, with carbines slung across their shoulders, led the procession which was travelling at high speed. Behind them came a long line of large and expensive black limousines, their tyres painted white, and each of them flying a pennant – Union Jacks, Hammer and Sickles, and many other tricolors, and crosses, and stars and crescents. Each of them carried the letters CD against the number-plates. Each of them had three or four armed militia standing on the running boards. A second detachment of armed motorcyclists brought up the rear.

For a few minutes after they had passed, the girls could hear the sound of the motors fading away to the south. Then silence descended once again over the empty streets, and the cold, still water of the Seine.

Papayannis was sprawling on the velvet and ormolu settee in the spacious salon of the apartment overlooking the Rue des Francs Bourgeois. Rahman and El Chamoun were watching at the windows. The electricity had been cut off, probably after the owners of the apartment had abandoned the place; Rahman had lit candles which they had found standing in empty wine bottles on the tables, mantlepieces, and display-cabinets about the room. Flame-light flickered on the gilt mouldings of the cornices, the oak-leaf decoration on the furniture, and threw fluttering shadows on the scarlet and gold flock on the walls. Papayannis had lit a cigar in the hope that he would fumigate at least one small space in the salon where a man might breathe. The idiot Grimaud had warned him that the so-called Rats of Venus were little better than savages. Papayannis was already amending 'savages' to 'animals'. The place was awash with filth. Every room was littered with the decaying relics of their meals; dirty plates, cups, broken glasses, lay where they had been thrown, and empty cans and bottles lay on the carpets. Unwashed garments were draped all over the place; the most private items of female apparel lay matted and soiled, exposed to view. They had not bothered even to use the lavatory, but had relieved themselves in whatever receptacle had been to hand. He had encountered the smell as he had come up the stairs.

El Chamoun had found a wind-up cabinet gramophone with two records which the women had neglected to smash – one of Dick Powell singing 'You're the Cream in My Coffee', and the other of Abe Goldman and his Schlemihls playing 'Mose Art's Turkey Trot'. Neither of them appealed to Papayannis whose favourite record was one of Amelia Galli-Curci singing on one side 'Lo, Hear the Gentle Lark', and on the other 'Home Sweet Home', the latter invariably bringing tears to his eyes. Nevertheless, Dick Powell was singing 'You're the Cream in My Coffee' for the fifth time when Papayannis heard the clicking of women's heels on the parquet outside, and the voices calling like schoolgirls coming in from play. As the heels came clicking down the apartment corridor outside, he nodded to El Chamoun to take off the record, and slipped his hand into his jacket to clutch the grip of his automatic.

The double doors of the *salon* burst open. The full glare of a heavy police torch blinded him.

320

'Keep your hands inside your jacket pockets, messieurs,' announced a cultivated woman's voice.

Papayannis could see her shape and the pallor of her face behind the glare. She was at least six foot in height. He could also see that she was holding a Smith and Wesson police-issue revolver.

'Marius Grimaud of the Rue Quincampoix suggested we should take the liberty of calling on you, mademoiselle,' he said.

'*Le monsieur grecque?*' the woman asked.

His eyes were becoming accustomed to the glare. He was surprised by her appearance. He could see now that she was dressed like a superior floor-walker from one of the fashionable stores in the Rue de Rivoli or the Rue des Pyramides. The half-dozen or so girls who were with her, however, were more what he had been led to expect. Two of them were in men's overalls, with police képis tilted on their heads; another couple were so dressed that they looked like overripe school-children; and one girl wearing a black sealskin jacket over an expensive but very ill-fitting silk matinee-frock, was carrying a large, life-size baby doll in her arms. One of the girls in overalls was also holding a police revolver.

'Papayannis, mademoiselle,' he replied. 'Chrisostom Papayannis. My friends all call me Monsieur Chris. I hope you will do the same.' He smiled.

The torch was switched off.

'I need a drink,' said Cybele.

Pauline squeezed past from behind her. She went across the salon into a room through a door at the other side.

'Take your hands out of your pockets, messieurs,' said Cybele. 'Slowly – oh so very slowly. That's good!'

Pauline returned with a bottle of red wine. Cybele took it. Still pointing her revolver at Papayannis, she drew the cork from the bottle with her teeth, and spat it onto the floor. She lifted the bottle to her mouth and drank.

'You must excuse me, Monsieur le Grecque,' she said, 'but I need at least two bottles before I go to bed. I can't sleep at all, otherwise.'

'I quite understand, mademoiselle,' Papayannis told her.

'You won't object if my girls take your gorillas' heaters, will you, monsieur?' she asked. 'They will return them – empty, of course.'

'I won't object, mademoiselle,' Papayannis told her.

'And yours, monsieur?'

She took another swallow from the bottle as fat Severine and Manuela went up to El Chamoun and Rahman at the window, and drew their automatics from their pockets. Papayannis was aware of somebody standing behind his settee. He looked round. A girl was smiling at him – a young girl with straight hair falling down her freckled cheeks, and wearing a childish dirndl frock over her blouse.

321

She reached out to take his gun, and he saw in the candlelight, the dry blood encrusting the sleeve of her blouse and spattered over her lap and bosom. It was as if she had come from an abattoir.

Severine and Manuela had taken the automatics from El Chamoun and Rahman, and had handed them back to Ines. Now they were frisking them. Severine cupped her hand over Rahman's groin. She lifted her skirt to her waist. Her barrel thighs and swollen buttocks were naked.

'*Tu veux faire jig-jig avec moi, chéri?*' she offered. 'They say Africans have the biggest, eh?'

'*Va, salette!*' exclaimed Rahman.

He pushed her away so violently that she pitched backwards over a chair, and crashed headlong on the floor. There was a click; the switchblade shone in Manuela's hand. Another sharp click, and Papayannis saw the steel blade in the hand of the child who had just taken his gun. It was so close, he could have touched it against his cheek.

'Let him be,' ordered Cybele.

Pauline helped Severine up from the floor.

'Severine doesn't like to be refused,' said Cybele to Papayannis. 'It isn't flattering. And her friends don't like to see her disappointed. But, no doubt your African gorilla prefers boys, like so many of his race. . . . Now. To business, monsieur,' she continued blandly, affecting to ignore the anger that her last remark had inspired in Rahman.

She handed her revolver to Pauline. The other girl with a revolver still held hers levelled, and the two with the switchblades showed no sign of putting away their weapons.

'I have a client,' Papayannis began, 'who is anxious to obtain an *objet d'art* – de *piété*. This *objet* is a relic – it is a Christian relic – beyond price. It is in the possession of a Jew, a wealthy, influential Jew – but a Jew. . . . '

He paused. Cybele took a long draught from her wine-bottle. She gulped greedily. Papayannis noticed how bright the eyes were in the extraordinarily lean and sallow, almost jaundiced, face. And the crimson on the edges of the hollow cheeks. The woman was dying: slowly, but assuredly dying. And she was afraid. Was the woman afraid of Christ, he wondered? Of Christ Pancreator – all judging?

'Mademoiselle,' he continued, 'my client is a Catholic. He holds it to be a sacrilege that any *objet* so holy, so full of virtue, should be in the possession of a Jewish banker – a usurer. But there is nothing my client and I can do. We are respectable men of affairs, mademoiselle. Marius Grimaud has informed me that you and your young friends might be persuaded to assist us.'

Cybele did not answer. She finished the bottle in her own time, and

322

placed it unsteadily on the papier-maché table beside her. It fell to the floor, and remained there unnoticed.

'And our reward, monsieur?' she asked. 'Is it a heavenly one? Will the *Divin Enfant et Sa Mère Sainte* receive us all into his Heavenly Kingdom?'

She laughed.

Papayannis offered her the sweet smile which he knew he could manage so well.

'That is not impossible, mademoiselle,' he told her. 'We are all sinners hoping that our sins shall be forgiven. But it is not in the gift of my client or myself. We are considering a more material reward. Your little companions here would want gold, I daresay; hard gold, which will keep its value whether the Republic or the Germans rule in Paris, eh? But you, mademoiselle, are different, aren't you?'

His hunch was correct. She came over to the settee, reaching out for the backs of chairs to help her.

'What do you think I should want, fat man?' she asked, looking down at him.

'Something,' he said, 'to take away the pain?'

She stared at him.

'Wine helps sometimes,' she told him. 'If I drink enough, the pain sometimes floats across the room away from me. But often, I'm sick before I can drink enough.'

'You need something you can depend on, mademoiselle,' he told her.

'Can you get me that?' she asked. 'And a little gold for my children here?'

'Heroin isn't easy to obtain, mademoiselle,' Papayannis replied, 'but my friend is a rich and influential man. And I myself am not without influence in certain quarters.'

He drew his wallet from his pocket.

'A substantial sum for your – er – children, mademoiselle,' he told her, handing her a bundle of notes. 'A token merely. The rest in gold. And heroin.'

Down the passage, in what had once been a nursery, Marie-Claire was putting her doll to bed. Florence was standing behind her, watching her as she undressed it.

Marie-Claire rocked the doll in her arms, and sang softly.

"'Berger, berger n'as-tu point vu,
Passer ici celle que j'aime?"

"Elle est là-bas dans ce vallon,
A un oiseau conte ses peines.
Le bel oiseau s'est envolé
Et le chagrin bien loin emmène."'

323

She put down the doll in the cot, and spread the eiderdown over it. She bent down over the cot-rail and kissed its plaster cheek.

'Oh, baby,' she whispered, 'you're so lucky. Your new *maman* loves you so very much.'

A tear ran slowly down the doll's cheek to the little pillow under its head.

34

Vivian was woken by his batman, Thompson, bringing in his uniform trousers newly pressed, and his shoes mirror polished. Once more he experienced the sense of relief – almost joy – at being no longer in Paris; through the half-open window, he could smell the damp leaves and wet grass.

Thompson stood awkwardly at attention against the rail at the foot of the bed, Vivian's trousers slung over his forearm, as the maid, a round, country girl, emptied her hot water jug into the wash-bowl which stood in the window-bay. The maid chanted out, '*Je vous en prie!*' to the 'thank you' which hadn't been said, and went out. She was in a hurry – understandably, since the entire British Embassy Staff had been quartered in the Château de Champchevrier, and Madame de Champchevrier, a dedicated Anglophile, was determined to treat them all, down to the most junior Secretary, as her personal house-guests.

As soon as the door had closed behind the maid, Vivian got out of bed. Thompson hung the trousers over the bedrail and went over to the window-bay to strop Vivian's razor. Vivian joined him. He rinsed his face in the hot water, and looked through the window. The rain was pattering on the lattices, and dribbling heavily down the glass. Leaning over the basin, he could see through the blur to the balustraded terrace below. Two Royal Military Police sentries were patrolling up and down the wet pavement. They were wearing waterproof ponchos which made them look from above like walking tents, and white waterproof coverings over the tops of their caps. Beyond the terrace rolled the rich green of the parkland, and the broad grass ride which descended from the front of the Château cut a swathe through the dense woods on the far side of the park, and stretched on in an avenue in the direction of Tours.

'The farmers'll be glad of a spot o' rain, daresay,' said Thompson.

He couldn't have been a day over twenty, thought Vivian, and his

324

parents kept a village store in Hengrave, not far from Bury St Edmunds, but he always talked with the grave, middle-aged wisdom of the farm worker.

'Glad to be out of Paris, then?' asked Vivian, lathering his chin.

'Nice to breathe a spot o' fresh air, sir,' Thompson agreed.

The last few days in Paris had been a nightmare: the seemingly endless shredding and burning of documents and destruction of cyphers, even of such elementary codes as the slidex and linex manuals, the crating up and packing and despatch of essential equipment, the muddy sea of defeatism all round, and then the organisation of the diplomatic night ride to the Touraine.

The French government had organised the convoy extremely efficiently. As Henry Mack, the First Secretary, had pointed out, they only had to blow the dust off the plans for the evacuation of the *Corps Diplomatique* dating from 1870. The road to Tours was well trodden.

In many ways, the arrival at Champchevrier had been little better. Junior staff – servants, secretaries, and clerks, had had to make their own way to Tours, so that it had been left to the senior staff to unpack and organise themselves in their new home. Paul Baudouin and the Foreign Ministry were about seventeen kilometres away. The Government's Protocol Office was in the Rue Voltaire at Chinon, fifty kilometres away. The Prime Minister's residence, the Château de Chissay, lay east of Tours, beyond Chenonceaux. Communication between the residencies and the ministries scattered over the Touraine, and the official seat of government, the Prefecture in the Rue Buffon, in Tours itself, depended on the manually-operated telephone exchanges of the region. They were manned as usual by elderly ladies whose ferocity was only equalled by their incompetence. As far as the British Embassy staff at the Château de Champchevrier were concerned, there might very well have been no telephone service at all. By the first afternoon of their arrival, it was found that the short wave radio set on which they depended for contact with the Foreign Office in London had been damaged in transit. The operators, as they examined it, talked darkly of sabotage until forbidden to do so by Sir Ronald Campbell. Whatever the truth of the matter, the embassy was entirely dependent for communications on the Provost Marshal's detachment of Royal Military Police motorcyclists who were billeted in the ornate, grandiose stables of the Château.

And yet the arrival at Champchevrier had come as a great relief. There was the willing hospitality of the Champchevrier family; their cooperation had helped Henry Mack to work a miracle in establishing an embassy headquarters in the *grand salon*, so that as clerks and secretaries came dribbling in from their frequently hazardous journeys from Paris, they found tables, desks, and even assignments waiting for them. Above all, outside there was the sort of peace and

325

stillness in which tired minds and troubled souls could recreate themselves. Indeed it seemed entirely appropriate that, even at such a time, Thompson should remark that the farmers would be glad of a spot of rain.

'Never did care for towns, mind,' Thomspon said. 'My sister, Ruby, now – her married last spring – last peacetime spring, that is – her never been to Ipswich even. Cromer, for her honeymoon, is far as her's ever been. Don't reckon as her's missed much, neither.'

It would be easy to think of Thompson's sister as being limited and Thompson himself as voicing the prejudice of the ignorant; but in the end, perhaps they knew where happiness lay, in harmony with each other, and with the world they knew.

The green stillness through the rain-smeared window reminded him of the weeks he had spent as a guest at Glyndebourne during his convalescent leave. He used to sit in the hedged, private garden overlooking the downs, well clear of the bustle of the theatre where cast and orchestra had been putting the final touches to a new production of Verdi's *Macbeth*. Scraps of melody had hung in the motionless summer air like fragments of burnt leaf drifted from a garden bonfire. Lapped in the glorious peacetime weather, the quiet countryside, and the kindness of his hostess, he had felt that he had returned to a land of lost content.

The Sunday night before his return to London and the solitude of his flat, he had been sitting in the library in the gathering dusk. He was dressed for dinner and enjoying the silence of an evening when the opera-house was closed. Audrey Christie had come to him, also dressed for dinner, the hem of her oyster-satin gown spilling on the carpet about her feet. She had been carrying a large gin-and-martini.

'Here you are,' she said, handing him the drink. 'I've been looking for you all over the place.'

She sat down on the arm of the chair opposite him, and arranged her skirt over her knee.

'I've been wanting to say something to you, Vivian,' she told him. 'Only it's very important, so I haven't had the courage.'

Vivian smiled. 'I don't believe that,' he said.

'It's true,' she replied. 'Anyway, you're leaving us, and John's absolutely convinced that there's going to be a war very soon, and I don't know when we shall be seeing you again. So I'm going to say it.'

Vivian turned the glass in his hand, looking into it.

'About Rosemary?' he asked.

'Yes. About Rosemary,' she said. 'I've known the family for some years now – quite well. I can tell you now that I've never thought for one moment that you and Rosemary were suited to each other. I'm sure Rosemary makes the most marvellous officers' mess wife . . .'

326

She broke off.

'Go on,' said Vivian.

'Only, you, as a person, run much too deep for her. I've never thought she could cope. Are you going to let me explain?'

'Do I have much alternative?' Vivian asked.

'You could walk out on me. I would understand,' she told him.

He shook his head.

'Do you remember,' she asked, "'*Der welcher wandert diese Strasse voll Beschweden* ... "?'

'*Zauberflöte* – the Armed Men?' he replied.

'Yes. Tamino is just about to be put through the last stage of his initiation – the three Ordeals. And Pamina finds him at last, and insists on joining him, and sharing his sufferings ... Well, I'm sure you are a Tamino. You have to go through the initiation to find self-knowledge – and you face it willingly. But Rosemary isn't a Pamina. I don't suppose for a moment, she would ever understand the significance of the Ordeals – let alone why she should go through them with you.'

When Vivian didn't reply, Mrs Christie went over to the piano. Standing at the keyboard, she sketched an accompaniment as she sung softly,

'*Wir wollen uns der Liebe freun* –

We must know Love: we live through Love alone ...

Love shows nothing more noble than a man and woman,

A woman and a man, striving together,

And thus entering, hand in hand, the presence of God.'

The light gentle voice had sounded in his ears like an absolution.

Now, as he stared across the rain-soaked parkland stretching away to the Loire valley, he remembered almost with regret. And remembered also that in *Zauberflöte* Tamino is not allowed to be reunited with Pamina until the very last stage of his trials.

There was still a chance.

He picked up his towel and dried his face.

In the dining room, the Champchevrier family – or families, since every sept of the clan seemed to have evacuated itself to the château – sat at one table, under the presidency of Madame de Champchevrier. On the opposite side of the room, the British Embassy staff sat at their own table, under the eye of Sir Ronald Campbell.

'You have slept well, I hope, Major?' asked Madame de Champchevrier, as Vivian passed by the family table.

The entire regiment of Champchevrier womenfolk turned to bestow their smile on him. Vivian bowed slightly.

'Very well, thank you,' he replied. 'And you, I trust, Madame?'

'I always sleep well, Major,' Madame de Champchevrier replied.

The ladies about her laughed, and Madame herself wore the sort of secretive smile with which a certain elegant sort of Frenchwoman proves her superiority over men.

'Mornin', Hardwicke,' said Sir Ronald, as Vivian reached the safety of the embassy table. 'Slept soundly, eh?'

'Very, thank you, sir,' Vivian replied.

'Didn't hear the bombin', eh?'

'Bombing, sir?' Vivian asked.

He sat down, and glanced about for General Sir Edward Spears. But Sir Edward wasn't at table.

'Over towards Tours,' said Sir Ronald. 'Thought you military fellows always woke at the sound of the guns.'

Oliver Harvey, Minister at the embassy, interceded on Vivian's behalf.

'Major Hardwicke's room is at the far end of the west wing,' he said.

A waiter put a plate of scrambled eggs in front of Vivian. He reached for the coffee-pot.

'Anybody seen my boss, this morning?' he asked.

'Spears?' asked Lord Malise Graham who was sitting immediately opposite Vivian. 'He was just dashing off when we came in.'

'Gone for a pow-wow with Reynaud,' said Henry Mack. 'Left a message for you, Hardwicke. Said he didn't want to disturb your beauty sleep, but would you care to follow him to Chissay as soon as you've had your breakfast.'

The Second Secretary, who was sitting beside Vivian, thoughtfully buttered a couple of pieces of toast for him.

'We're a bit short of cars, actually, Hardwicke,' Mack continued. 'I think you'd better go on your knees to the Provost Marshal and see if he'll let you have an R.M.P. car and driver.'

'What on earth have we here?' exclaimed Lord Malise Graham, staring over Vivian's shoulder.

Vivian turned round. A young man in a very damp hacking-jacket, clutching an equally damp flat cap, and with his trousers secured with bicycle-clips, was coming towards the table. The Second Secretary stared at him.

'Been for a pre-breakfast cycle-ride round the estate, have you, Freddy?' he asked.

'Ought to try to get down to breakfast a little earlier, you know, Freddy,' said Lord Malise Graham. 'Not very considerate to the servants, coming in like this.'

The young man's brogues squelched with every step he took.

'Oh, I say,' he protested. 'Came as quick as I could, sir,' he told Sir Ronald. 'Hope my absence hasn't inconvenienced anybody.'

'What absence, Freddy?' asked Mack.

'Haven't noticed anybody absent,' said the Second Secretary.

'Oh come on,' said the young man, 'give a chap a chance.'

There was a burst of laughter round the table.

'Come and sit yourself down,' said Oliver Harvey, indicating a seat at the table. 'When did you last have a meal?'

'Noon, yesterday, Orléans, sir,' the young man replied.

'Go on, Stansfield,' said Sir Ronald. 'Take a pew. You've made jolly good time here.'

'Thank you, sir,' the young man replied gratefully.

He pulled off his bicycle-clips, and put them in his pocket.

'How far did you cycle?' asked Oliver Harvey.

'All the way, sir,' Stansfield replied. 'There wasn't a car or a ride to be had. I think the whole population of Paris is moving out. Couldn't get a bite to eat after I left Orléans. Like a plague of locusts, the refugees.'

'Hardwicke,' Sir Ronald called down the table, 'when you go to Chissay this morning, be a good chap, will you, and take a message for me to General Spears?'

'Yes, sir?' asked Vivian.

'It's a rather delicate matter,' Sir Ronald called down the table. 'De Margerie has sent a message over here during the night. Says he's received a dispatch at Chissay from our Foreign Office. The dispatch is a request asking him to communicate to me the contents of one sent from Downing Street to Reynaud yesterday, via the French Embassy in London. Only trouble is, de Margerie knows nothing about any dispatch sent to Reynaud from Downing Street. He's asked Reynaud who claims to know nothing either.'

'Could the Downing Street message have been lost?' asked Vivian, 'I mean, could it have been dispatched to the d'Orsay?'

Sir Ronald shook his head.

'Its arrival at Chissay was confirmed, as far as London knows.'

'The Comtesse de Portes has taken up residency at Chissay, I hear,' said Henry Mack gloomily.

'Anyway, Hardwicke,' Sir Ronald butted in quickly, 'the point is this – you and General Spears put your heads together with de Margerie. He's a first rate chap is de Margerie. The three of you are bound to come up with something ... Oh, and tell General Spears I'll come over and join him at Chissay, about noon, there's a good fellow.'

'You'll have trouble with the refugee problem,' said Stansfield, who was trying to wring the rain-water out of the sleeves of his hacking-jacket. 'The road out of Amboise was just about choked when I came through. They'll have reached Tours by now, I should think.'

Vivian sat in the back of the small, camouflaged Morris Minor which he had borrowed from the Provost Marshal's embassy guard, together with an RASC driver. There was almost no room for his legs. He felt nostalgic regret for his own little car which had presumably been captured by the enemy after Montcornet; it had been the framework for a moment of happiness – so very far away now.

He stared out of the window. The rain was sweeping across the countryside; the grass had become a lush green overnight; the cattle were sheltering under the heavy, stooping boughs of ancient trees. They drove under the thick, machicolated turrets of the Château de Langeais, with the graceful renaissance spires rising from behind the fortified ramparts.

The whole region was the heartland of the real France, Vivian decided – the part where Joan of Arc appealed to the people of France to save themselves; the place from which sprang the great fairy-tale writers, Charles Perrault and Madame le Prince de Beaumont; the home of Montaigne, Descartes, Rabelais, and Balzac. It was impossible to drive through such a countryside, burgeoning under the rain, and to believe that France could be destroyed.

As they passed through Tours, however, and approached the bridge over the Indres at Montbazon, the feeling of optimism which briefly he had managed to inspire in himself, began to fade. The car became enmeshed in traffic, and was borne along by it. It was an advance guard, Vivian realised, as he watched the cars in front, creeping over the Montbazon bridge under the protective shadow of the ruined keep on its high mound. No doubt, the big limousines had all reached Biarritz, Nice and St Juan-les-Pins by this time. These were shabby, slightly decayed, and all were crowded. Nearly all the cars had bedding roped to the roof; many had bicycles strapped on top of the mattresses. Around the edges of the roofs hung pots, pans, kettles and even bird-cages.

Before they reached the bridge, Vivian instructed his driver to turn onto the Rue de Moulin, and to proceed in an easterly direction. Now they encountered the slow procession of vehicles coming in the opposite direction to themselves. Cars which had broken down, or had run out of petrol, had been pushed into the ditch by those coming on behind. Some stood tilted, with two wheels sunk into the channel at the roadside, their owners' belongings hanging off the roof and sagging into the hedges like dead objects. Others had been turned right over, and had caught fire, while their passengers stood looking on as their means of transport and all their wordly goods were consumed in flames which the rain turned to greasy smoke. Some families who had abandoned their cars were sitting sheltering under trees and hedges, or were holding tarpaulin sheets over the heads of their children. Some fathers of families, whose cars had run out of fuel, were standing out in the road, begging other drivers to let them have petrol from their tanks. A balding, pouchy-faced middle-aged man with an amiable, weak face, attempted to address himself to

Vivian's driver. The driver shouted, 'Get out of the way, yer stupid git.'

He drove on, nudging the man with his mudguard. So Vivian had seen soldiers behaving towards Jews and Arabs impartially in the Mandated Territory.

They were heading now down the Chenonceaux road, approaching the bridge across the Cher, at Blère. The shops in the small villages through which they passed, were all shut, with their windows barred and shuttered.

'Hark, hark! The dogs do bark. The beggars are coming to town,' thought Vivian.

Around the doors of the bakers' shops, and the small grocers, menacing knots of people were gathered. On a bare patch of grass outside one of the village churches, he saw three small children standing in the rain beside an empty car. The smallest child was crying. The other two were holding its hands; their faces were drawn with anxiety.

At the crossroads by the bridge at Blère, they were forced to halt. A solid mass of traffic was moving across their path up to the bridge. Vivian noticed the lack of active desperation, of hysteria. Amongst the drivers and their passengers, there seemed to be a calmness amounting to apathy. As he sat watching, his driver waiting for a gap in the procession through which he could pass, he saw a baker's delivery van moving up the incline towards the bridge, towing a small Renault tourer in which were travelling a woman and two small children. As the tow rope took the strain, it snapped. The driver of the van clearly didn't realise what had happened. As he drove on, the cars moving up behind closed about the van, bearing it on in the tide. The woman scrambled out of the car, and ran up onto the bridge, shouting ineffectually as she did so. The two children sat white-faced in the back of the stationary car as their mother disappeared. A small lorry, its rear packed with household goods and furniture, came up behind the car. Vivian watched helplessly as it pushed the car aside, slewing it up onto the pavement so that its headlamps were smashed against the wall of a house.

Once Vivian's RASC driver had negotiated his way through the traffic crossing the bridge, the going was easy. The Chenonceaux road pointed to the south-east, and was free of refugee traffic. The driver, to make up for lost time, put his foot down on the accelerator. The village of Chissay consisted of a single street, pointing directly up a steep hill to where the château stood on its wooden escarpment high above the river Cher. Vivian's driver tore up the street, under the gatehouse arch, and up the drive under the dark, dripping trees, with Vivian himself bouncing about on the back seat as they lurched over the gravelled pot-holes. They were just about to pass under the gate leading into the inner courtyard of the château, when a French army

Citroën came screeching round the corner inside, through the arch, and would have smashed straight into the Morris Minor, had not Vivian's driver shot straight up onto the grass verge. As it was, the Citroën dented the rear wing almost under Vivian's seat.

The French driver, a corporal of horse by his insignia, got out of his car, swearing obscenely at Vivian's driver as he did so. Vivian's driver was about to reply in kind, when Vivian restrained him. He opened his door, and got out clumsily – he had never learnt the art of getting out of a small car gracefully with the use of only one arm.

'Corporal,' he snapped at the French driver, 'you were driving recklessly. You could have killed us all.'

The French driver was impressed more by the fluent French proceeding from the lips of the English officer, than by Vivian's rank. He stood in an approximation of attention.

'*Oui, mon capitaine, mais* . . .'

'*Commandant!*' barked Vivian. 'Isn't it about time you learned your allies' badges of rank, corporal?'

He was enjoying the French driver's discomfiture. It was almost like the old days, when he had been orderly officer at Bovington.

A car honked loudly from under the gateway, waiting to pass through.

'You'd better move on, Corporal,' said Vivian. 'We'll forget it this time.'

Suddenly, above the noise of the motors, a woman's voice shrieked, 'What's the matter? What's happening?'

It was harsh, strident, echoing from under the archway. A strange apparition appeared from beside the waiting vehicle: a heavily rouged, middle-aged woman, whose dark, tousled hair lay uncombed about her face, wearing the sort of scarlet satin turkish pantaloons, and thigh-length embroidered Chinese jacket, which had been adopted by *poules de luxe* when Bakst's decors for Diaghilev had been all the rage. She stood just inside the archway, out of the rain.

'*Rangez-vous!*' she screamed at the French corporal. '*Allez! Allez!*'

With a look of genuine panic which Vivian felt certain he could not have inspired even in his most martinet, Monday morning mood, the corporal jumped back into the Citroën. Determined to waste not another moment, Vivian told his own driver to drive into the courtyard when he could, and find somewhere to park and wait for him. He then proceeded on foot under the gatehouse. Beyond, lay the sixteenth-century yard with its arcaded façades, and its *escalier d'honneur* leading up to the carved main doors. The woman was waiting for him in the shelter of a doorway just inside the yard. Regardless of the rain, she approached him. She had the same meaningless, vampyric smile as a Shepherd's Market prostitute; her scarlet, Clara Bow lips were parted.

'Why don't you go back to your own country, Major?' she asked.

'If you stand out here, madame,' Vivian replied, 'you will be soaked through.'

'What do you care?' the woman demanded. 'What do you care about any French person?'

Vivian wondered whether she was drunk.

'Excuse me, madame,' he said, 'but I have important business to attend to.'

He touched the peak of his cap in salute. As he made his way across the courtyard, the woman made a noise after him; perhaps she spat at him.

One of the carved main doors opened, and General Sir Edward Spears came out onto the steps.

'Ah, Hardwicke,' he called. 'Been keeping an eye open for you.'

'Sorry if I've kept you waiting, sir,' Vivian replied, 'the roads aren't improving, I'm afraid. They'll soon be impassable.'

'Don't worry, my boy,' Sir Edward replied. 'Absolute chaos, here. Complete shambles.'

He patted Vivian on the shoulder. As they went up the steps into the château, Vivian passed on Sir Ronald Campbell's messages. Sir Edward shook his head.

'Nobody's said anything about a dispatch from Downing Street to me,' he remarked. 'We'd better get over to de Margerie's office straight away.'

Vivian followed him along the main gallery of the château, and down several corridors. The smoking-room belonging to the château's owner, which was where the Chef de Cabinet's office had been situated, was as far from the main entrance as the building allowed. Sir Edward explained that the reason for the choice was that it contained the only telephone in Chissay. When they eventually arrived there, it was to find Roland de Margerie in his shirt-sleeves, attempting to reduce a mass of documents and cardboard portfolios into some sort of order.

The smoking-room itself smelt of ancient, undisturbed mildew, as if the damp from the tree-tops outside the windows had penetrated indoors. Deer heads moulted from wooden shields on the walls. Hunting horns, black with accumulated soot from the open hearth, hung from picture-hooks on the dusty wainscot panelling. There were several large paintings in the style of Courbet, of ladies exposing massive, dimpled buttocks under raised petticoats.

There was a heavy paperweight on a Persian or Indian side-table of a naked man and woman apparently holding one another off at arm's length; it was the colour of plain chocolate. There was also one grimy Egyptian fez standing on the mantlepiece.

De Margerie's shorthand-typist, a cheerful-looking girl, was sitting at the table. She was typing away on an old machine, like a hailstorm

333

beating on a tin roof. Beyond the room, there was a lavatory-wash-room. A few feet in front of the lavatory-pan, and secured on a wooden panel high up on the wall, was the telephone. It was ringing persistently. The girl was ignoring it.

'It's been ringing for the past twenty-four hours,' de Margerie explained. 'If Delphine answered it every time it rang she'd never get anything else done. . . .I think it's time to answer it, Delphine . . . .It gives one such a sense of power,' he added to Sir Edward and Vivian. 'Like the bestowal of God's grace – haphazard!'

Delphine went into the washroom. She pulled an upright chair in front of the lavatory-pan, and climbed up onto it to reach the telephone, displaying her stocking-tops and blue directoire knickers.

'That,' said de Margerie, 'is how the Prime Minister's office keeps in touch with the ministries, military headquarters, and the entire outside world.'

Delphine put her hand over the mouthpiece, and looked down from her chair.

'It's a lady,' she announced. 'She wants to have a talk with little Mademoiselle Catherine de Beauregard.'

'The daughter of the house,' de Margerie explained. 'Tell the lady,' he added to Delphine, 'that she's got the wrong number.' He turned again to Vivian and Sir Edward. 'It'll take her till tomorrow to get through again,' he said.

Delphine scrambled down from the chair. She began clattering on the typewriter once more. Sir Edward broached the matter of the Downing Street dispatch. De Margerie shrugged helplessly.

'To tell you the truth,' he said. 'I don't believe it ever reached Monsieur Reynaud.'

'Perhaps we might speak to the Prime Minister?' Sir Edward suggested.

'Why not?' asked de Margerie.

The telephone began ringing again. Again, Delphine chose to ignore it.

'We are going to Monsieur Reynaud's office,' de Margerie told her. 'You look after Major Hardwicke. Fetch him a cup of coffee while he's waiting.'

As they left, Vivian told Delphine not to put herself to any trouble.

'No trouble at all,' she replied, getting up from the table. She went to the door. 'I'll be back with the coffee in a minute,' she said. 'And don't let the telephone worry you. After a time, you only notice it when it stops ringing.'

Even so the ringing got on Vivian's nerves. He had just lit a cigarette, when the door burst open, and the woman he had encountered at the gatehouse came in. Her tousled, rain-soaked hair clung to her cheeks. Her clothing was soaked through, and her face looked more raddled than it had done outside.

She did not appear to notice him, but went straight to the table and, to his surprise, started opening the box-files and cardboard portfolios, and rummaging through the documents inside them. Then Vivian noticed that she was removing documents from the files, folding them, and thrusting them into an inside pocket of her jacket. He rose.

'Forgive me, madame, . . . ' he began.

The woman turned and stared at him. She recognised him.

'Forgive *me*, Major,' she interrupted him in her strange, harsh voice. 'You may go and shit yourself!' Whereupon, she marched from the room, slamming the door behind her.

A few minutes later, Delphine returned with some freshly percolated coffee. Vivian told her what had happened. She was neither surprised nor concerned.

'Madame de Portes may do exactly as she wishes,' she replied. 'Nobody can stop her.'

So that was the notorious Hélène de Portes. And she wasn't even attractive. He wondered if Madame de Pompadour or Diane de Poitiers, or Nell Gwynn or Mrs Fitzherbert had been equally blowsy.

Delphine, who would have made a much more agreeable mistress, Vivian decided, drank coffee with him. When she had finished, she decided it was time once more to answer the telephone. A puritan delicacy forbade Vivian from watching for the indiscreet lift of her skirt as she scrambled up onto the chair.

The door opened again. This time, an elderly man came into the room.

'Oh, forgive the intrusion, monsieur,' he wheezed at Vivian.

His eyes were so moist he looked as if he was weeping. He started shuffling about the room, peering under the tables, and into the alcoves.

'Minou?' he called. 'Come to papa! Minou? Minou! . . . *A papa! Viens!*'

He coughed bronchially, then cleared his throat. He bent double, patting the knees of his plus-fours.

'Minou! Minou! *Viens!*' he called.

Delphine put her hand over the mouthpiece of the telephone.

'Minou isn't here, Monsieur de Beauregard,' she called down from her chair. 'I've been here all morning, and Minou hasn't come in.'

The old man pulled himself erect with some difficulty.

'Ah,' he said, 'I beg your pardon, mademoiselle. I did not mean to disturb you, mademoiselle.'

He shuffled out of the room. Delphine hung up the earpiece of the telephone, and jumped down from the chair.

'Poor old man,' she said.

'Who is he?' asked Vivian.

'Monsieur Costa de Beauregard? He is the owner of Chissay, but I don't think he understands properly what has happened.'

She sat down at the table and started rattling away on her typewriter once more. The telephone began ringing again. She glanced up at it.

'*Oh – Je m'en fou!*' she declared without too much animosity. She gave Vivian a cheerful grin, and continued typing.

Sir Edward Spears returned half an hour later.

'No luck, I'm afraid,' he announced. 'Even old Reynaud doesn't know anything about it. H.E.'s just come over from Champchevrier. He's in with Reynaud now.' He sat down opposite Vivian who offered him a cigarette. 'Mind you, I'm not sure Winston really appreciates the state of things here. He believes that if the French just "summon the will, stiffen the sinews, and disguise fair nature in hard-seeming rage", they'll win through to victory regardless of the odds. I remember when the French believed that too: in the Vosges in 1914 and 1915. Half a million of them were left to rot on the German wire as a result. They've never forgotten it – old Pétain in particular.'

He paused, tracing his narrow, military moustache with his finger-end.

'Ah well,' he continued more brightly. 'As soon as H.E. has finished jawing with Reynaud, I'm going to take him down into Chenonceaux for a spot of tiffin. There's a damn fine place just off the Rue Briconnet; you can get the best *ris de veau à l'angevin* you'll find anywhere ... De Margerie is still trying to find that damn dispatch. When he comes back here, you can try to persuade him to join us – he knows the place – and get him to bring you along, my boy.'

'Thank you, sir,' Vivian replied.

'Not at all. *A bientôt*, then?' asked Sir Edward.

'*A bientôt, mon Général,*' Vivian agreed.

Sir Edward smiled, and raised his swagger stick in salute.

Roland de Margerie returned to the smoking-room a quarter of an hour later. Delphine had just answered the telephone once again. She clambered down, leaving the ear-piece hanging by its flex.

'*C'est le Ministre de l'Intérieur,*' she told de Margerie.

De Margerie handed Vivian a crumpled sheet of headed and embossed quarto. He hurried through to the lavatory, and climbed up onto the chair.

'*'allo? Georges?*' he began.

Vivian placed the sheet of quarto on the table, and pressed it flat with the edge of his hand. There was no need for him to read through the flourishes required by diplomatic protocol. Its significance was clear from the two carefully isolated, short paragraphs. The Prime

Minister of the United Kingdom of England, Scotland, Wales and Northern Ireland, together with his senior advisers, and members of the War Cabinet, would be landing at the French Air Force Base outside Tours, at 1300 hours that afternoon.

'Oh, my God!' was Vivian's first response.

Delphine looked up from her typewriter. De Margerie hung up the ear-piece of the telephone and jumped down from the chair.

'That,' he told Vivian, 'was found by one of the de Beauregards' chambermaids, this morning.'

'Where was it?' asked Vivian.

De Margerie glanced at Delphine who was also waiting for his answer.

'In the Comtesse de Portes' bed,' he replied.

The ragged clouds swept low over the trees, but the rain had slackened off. Vivian was riding pillion behind a French dispatch rider, his one hand clamped firmly into the back of the man's belt. He had decided that travelling by car to the air-base, which was near Tours St Symphorien, would have been impossible, given the hosts of refugees who were now pouring across the Loire. De Margerie had found the dispatch-rider before going off himself to Chenonceaux to round up General Sir Edward Spears and Sir Ronald Campbell; Delphine was left in the washroom, standing on her chair, trying to get through by telephone to the French Foreign Office, and Ministry of the Interior. Vivian's own task was to meet Mr Churchill and his party, and to transport him to the Rue Buffon in Tours, where Monsieur Reynaud and other members of the French War Council would be waiting for him at the Prefecture. That, at least was what de Margerie and Vivian had decided between them. It was not lost on Vivian that if the plans of mice and men oft gang agley, this plan was likely to gang a good deal more agley than most, given the state of the roads and the telephone system. At any rate, he told himself, as the heavy motorcycle wove through the stream of refugees travelling in the opposite direction, there were no complications – it was either win all or lose all. The astonishment of finding himself responsible for meeting Mr Churchill and half the Cabinet was such that, for the moment at least, his critical faculties were dulled so that he felt no nervousness at all.

The flood of refugees had grown heavier. As well as the small cars and vans, and the battered lorries spilling over with passengers and their household belongings, there was an army of people travelling on foot, trundling prams and the inevitable handcarts. As they rode nearer to the Loire, the road was packed solid with traffic coming in the opposite direction, like molten lava streaming down from a volcanic crater. Vivian ordered his rider to take to the fields alongside the road. They bounced across the country with Vivian sure that he was about to be thrown off at any moment.

When they reached the bridge, it took them twenty minutes to get across it. As they weaved their way through the on-coming horde, forcing people to step aside, they provoked anger amongst the refugees on foot who were forced to jostle each other against the cars. At one point, the refugees on either side of them became so menacing that Vivian released his rider's belt, and felt for the button on the flap of his revolver-holster. Once across, however, the way northwards was easy, and the dispatch-rider tore up the wet country lanes to Tours St Symphorien at full throttle, with Vivian hanging grimly to his belt.

The rain had stopped altogether when they reached the main gate of the air-field. The base had been visited by German bombers the previous night. Two wooden sheds and one of the hangers were still smouldering, the damp causing the thick smoke to hang like a pall over the hedgerows. Close to the perimeter fence, a large Morane 406 fighter stood tilted over on its broken wing. Aircraftsmen were working on two others standing at the end of a runway, patching bullet-holes in the fusilages with aluminium strips.

An amiable pilot-officer in leather flying jacket and white scarf – one of the bright *jeunesse dorée* who would have been racing his own Bugatti down on the Cote d'Azur, had not war provided him with an even more hazardous and exhilarating hobby – volunteered to take Vivian to the base commander. He led Vivian across a quarter of a mile of sodden field. Passing through the screen of evil-smelling smoke from the burning hanger, Vivian noticed the regular line of bomb craters which had erupted across the runways. The far end of the main runway had received a direct hit. The base commander was himself supervising a detail of some twenty or thirty men who were desperately digging at the mounds of wet, claggy earth in an attempt to fill in the crater. Vivian saluted, and briefly explained his errand. The look of stunned surprise on the base commander's face would have done justice to Fernandel. He stretched out his arms, thrust his face forward, mouth wide open.

'Monsieur le Commandant knows how to pull a joke on someone, eh?' he demanded, his hands circling the air eloquently.

'It is no joke,' Vivian assured him. 'I have come straight from the Prime Minister's office at Chissay.'

'But I have had no warning,' exclaimed the commander. 'I've had nothing in writing from the Ministry. It isn't possible.'

He waved at the crater, where his men were resting on their shovels enjoying this fresh display of Anglo-French accord. One or two of them were seizing the opportunity to light up cigarettes.

'Please believe me, Commandant,' Vivian allowed a note of

pleading into his voice, 'Mr Churchill's plane will be arriving at any moment now. It will be short of fuel ... '

His few weeks' experience in General Spears' office had taught him that eating crow, provided it was done with restraint and a certain elegance, had a wonderful effect on his French counterparts. Even now the base commander's long, Provençal face dropped into mournful sympathy. He rubbed his knuckles with his fingers' ends. He spread his palms upwards.

'It isn't possible,' he repeated.

But the expression had undergone a subtle change of emphasis. It now meant, it is impossible, but I might just be able to achieve the impossible.

A sergeant came running towards them across the runway. He was gasping for breath. He managed to sketch a salute, then glanced at Vivian.

'Message from Chinon, Commandant,' he gasped. 'By telephone.'

He passed a scrap of paper to the base commander. The commander glanced down at it. He looked at Vivian, and spread out his arms as if offering his back to Heaven to receive the burden which was about to be placed upon it.

'Oh!' he said, stretching the single vowel as far as it would extend.

He let his hands fall, and began shouting orders abruptly to the men about him.

'This way, Major,' he said to Vivian, and led him and the breathless sergeant back across the rain-washed air-field towards the grey, concrete administration building.

'What escort will Monsieur Churchill have flying with him, Major?' he asked.

'I understand that the Prime Minister's RAF Flamingo is usually accompanied by a squadron of Spitfires,' Vivian replied.

The commander shouted further instructions to a young officer with two NCO's who were crossing the runway. They started running immediately towards the small white control-tower nearby.

'A squadron?' the commander exclaimed, as if the news had only just filtered through to his brain.

Any further comment he might have been about to offer was forestalled by the steady drone of aero-engines coming through the thick, ragged cloud. The forecourt in front of the administration block had come alive with sudden activity. Men carrying small yellow flags were running to take up positions along the verges of the main runway. The commander with Vivian turned and halted, waiting at the end of the runway.

'I have to take the Prime Minister's party back into Tours,' Vivian said. 'Can you provide me with transport, Commandant?'

'Have you no transport, Major?' asked the commander. 'How did you come here from Chissay?'

'Motorcycle,' Vivian replied.

The commander stared at him. Overhead, the aero-engines were throbbing and pulsing above the low cloud.

'Oh!' said the commander, again stretching the single vowel as if to rebuke Vivian for attempting to joke at such a time.

'Can you provide me with transport, Commandant?' Vivian repeated.

'We have no transport here,' said the commander. 'Only the fuel tenders and an ambulance. We have moved the transport to Ste Radegonde because of the bombing.'

Vivian's heart sank. Above the main runway, two heavy, ragged clouds parted. Sunshine splashed across the grass and on the wet, gleaming tarmac. He realised all of a sudden that he was very scared indeed.

The Spitfires came in formation through the torn cloud. They roared overhead, their broad, elliptical wings spread like a roof over the tarmac. Then they turned to circle above the airfield. There was no escape now, thought Vivian. The big, unmistakable shape of a de Havilland Flamingo – its round, twin Perseus engines, its unusual twin tail-fins, and its heavy pregnant-looking fusilage – was sinking down onto the far end of the runway. As its wheels glided up the tarmac in a perfect three-point landing, it struck the crudely filled-in bomb-crater, lurched, and lifted off the ground once more, then bounced and skidded three times on the wet, oily surface, like a flat stone hitting water in a game of ducks and drakes.

Vivian suddenly realised that the commander was shouting into his ear.

'What?' he yelled back.

'My car, Major,' shouted the commander. 'You may borrow my car.'

'That is very kind of you, Commandant,' Vivian shouted back.

'It is only a family car,' shouted the commander. 'It is my own, you understand. Let's hope your Prime Minister hasn't brought with him a large entourage, eh!'

At this point, the commander's voice went hoarse. Nevertheless, he managed to attract the attention of the NCO nearest to him on the tarmac, who, on receiving his orders, ran off round the side of the building.

'He'll bring the car round here,' the commander shouted to Vivian.

'I'm grateful,' Vivian yelled.

The Flamingo was taxiing to a halt. Vivian and the commander clutched at the peaks of their caps as the wind from the propellers buffeted their faces. They advanced up the tarmac. Beyond the

Flamingo, across the spread of the field, the first flight of Spitfires was taxiing in, bouncing across the grass as they were waved on by the French aircraftsmen.

The Flamingo's propellers turned stiffly, jerkily, then stopped. As Vivian and the commander made their way under the aircraft's wing, the fusilage door was pulled aside. A set of retractable steps were lowered to the ground. Both RAF men then took up positions on either side of the steps. Vivian waited at attention. His bowels were beginning to feel liquescent. He noticed that one of the Flamingo's pilots, secure in the privacy of his own flight-deck, had pushed back the perspex panel of his window, and was grinning down at him.

Mr Churchill was the first of the passengers to emerge. The two RAF men reached up to assist him. Vivian snapped into a salute. He noticed immediately the expensive, slightly old-fashioned pinstripe suit, the watch-chain on the spread of the stomach, and the hand which held both stick and cigar with a certain elegance. As Mr Churchill reached the ground, he noticed also that he was a surprisingly short man, and that the famous babyish roundness of the face contained a dangerous look of petulance.

Vivian held his salute as the other passengers emerged from the belly of the Flamingo. As they each reached the ground, they began to make up a group like the group photographs of political figures one saw in the *Illustrated London News*. From press photographs, he was able to recognise Lord Beaverbrook, Sir Alexander Cadogan, and Lord Halifax. General Ismay he had met on a number of previous occasions, and he detected a flicker of recognition in the general's answering salute.

He dropped his arm to his side.

'*Où est la réception officielle?*' Mr Churchill demanded, glaring beadily in the direction of the base commander.

Vivian could imagine the expression on the face of the man beside him. He intervened immediately, astonishing himself at his own boldness.

'I have to report, sir,' he announced, 'that the dispatch informing the French government of your intention to come to Tours only reached the Chef de Cabinet's office two hours ago.'

Mr Churchill stared at him with pouchy eyes. Vivian gazed over the top of his head, as he had gazed over the tops of heads of inspecting officers when he had been an officer-cadet. Mr Churchill turned to General Ismay.

'What's this all about, Hastings?'

'I don't know, Prime Minister,' General Ismay replied. 'The French Embassy informed me that the dispatch had been received at Chissay and acknowledged.'

Sir Alexander Cadogan and Lord Beaverbrook were whispering

between themselves. Lord Halifax, tall and ascetic-faced, stood in self-imposed isolation.

'Who are *you*, sir?' Mr Churchill demanded of Vivian.

'Hardwicke, sir,' Vivian replied. 'Major. Tank Corps. On attachment to Lord Gort's staff, sir. At present acting as personal aide to General Spears.'

'Where is Sir Edward Spears?' Mr Churchill demanded.

Having a first-class meal in the Rue Briconnet at Chenonceaux, thought Vivian. He remained stiffly at attention, staring over the top of Mr Churchill's head.

'The roads between Chissay and Tours are almost impassable, sir,' he said. 'Because of the refugees. It was thought best that General Spears should come with Monsieur Reynaud to meet you at the Prefecture in Tours.'

'How did you get here, Major?' asked Mr Churchill.

'By motorcycle, sir. I wouldn't have managed it with a car.'

'Motorcycle, eh?' said Mr Churchill. 'One-armed major gets here by motorcycle, eh?'

'Yes, sir,' Vivian confirmed.

He noticed that Mr Churchill's face had been transformed into a radiant, puckish smile. The change in mood had affected the others. Even Lord Halifax's thin lips were stretched into a grin.

'Jolly good show, Major,' nodded Sir Alexander Cadogan.

Vivian realised that they believed him to have ridden alone from Chissay. Bathed in the approval of the mighty, he found no inclination to disabuse them of this belief.

'And how does our – ah – galloping major,' asked Mr Churchill, still beaming at those about him, 'intend to – ah – convey us to the Prefecture at Tours? On the back of his motorcycle, perhaps?'

Everybody laughed. Vivian relaxed and allowed himself to smile.

'Commandant Berthelot here has offered the use of his personal car, sir,' he explained. 'I'm afraid it may be a bit of a tight squeeze.'

The car had been drawn up outside the main door of the administration block. As the small procession made its way over to it, General Ismay drew Vivian aside.

'Hardwicke, eh? Remember you from somewhere,' he said. 'Weren't you gazetted in the spring of last year? For a particularly plucky action on the Jerusalem-Jericho highway?'

'I was gazetted, sir,' Vivian agreed.

'Military Cross, eh? Is that when you lost your arm?'

'Yes, sir,' Vivian replied.

'Tell me, Hardwicke,' asked General Ismay in a low voice, 'how *does* one manage a motorcycle with only one arm?'

'One doesn't, sir,' Vivian admitted. 'One rides pillion, and hangs on to the other chap like grim death.'

342

'You were right not to own up to Winston, Hardwicke,' General Ismay told him. 'You're the first person to make him smile, today.'

Mr Churchill was still beaming as he strolled along between Lord Beaverbrook and the base commander. He waved his cigar in the direction of the burning hanger from which the oily smoke was still pouring.

'*Vous avez vu un peu d'action ici, Commandant?*' he enquired gaily.

Commandant Bertholot looked as if he had just bitten into a very sour apple.

'*La situation est difficile, monsieur,*' he replied. '*C'est très grave.*'

'*Bien sûr!*' replied Mr Churchill. '*Bien sûr!*'

There was no noticeable slackening of his good humour. As the party squeezed into the commander's car, he called out to General Ismay, 'You'll have to have – ah – Beaverbrook on your knee, Hastings.'

Vivian, sitting in the front with the driver, was the most comfortably situated. But Mr Churchill was at first disposed to enjoy the circumstances in which he found himself. As they headed into Tours, however, matters changed for the worse. The rain began to fall again, torrentially, streaming down windows and windscreen. The columns of sodden, wretched fugitives choked the roads from east to west. The first barometric reading on the change in Mr Churchill's emotional temperature occurred as the car was crawling along with the tide of refugees down the Rue Jules Simon under the tall, slender front of St Gatien's Cathedral. He suddenly leant forward to Vivian, and said, 'I trust – ah – that some provision has been made for – ah – luncheon, Major?'

'I'm afraid I can't tell you anything about that, sir,' Vivian replied.

He realised that any verbal placebo would have been better than his bald profession of ignorance.

They turned off into the relative quiet of the Rue Emile Zola, but the Rue Buffon at the far end was, once again, crowded with refugees. The last two hundred yards of the journey was taken at a crawl and the car stalled several times, as they were hedged in with carts, bicycles, wheelbarrows, and prams, all loaded and festooned with their owners' belongings. In the driving-mirror Vivian noticed the dismay in Mr Churchill's face.

It was with a sense of relief at a difficult task completed, that Vivian held open the car door to let Mr Churchill and the other dignitaries out, at the entrance to the Prefecture. He led them into the vine-covered cloisters. Mr Churchill's party waited in the vestibule, as Vivian went to look for somebody in authority. The Prefecture was almost deserted. Telephones were ringing in almost every room, but nobody was answering them. Looking into each office as he passed, he found one or two girl-typists, that was all. A harassed-looking clerk came down the stairs clutching an armful of documents.

'Has Monsieur Reynaud arrived here?' Vivian asked him.

'There's nobody called Reynaud works here, monsieur,' the man replied.

'Your Prime Minister,' Vivian told him.

The man appeared utterly bewildered.

'Why should Monsieur Paul Reynaud come here, monsieur?' he asked.

Vivian refrained from saying, because this is supposed to be the seat of the French government.

'Who is the senior person here?' he asked.

'Why, Monsieur le Préfet, of course,' the man replied.

The documents were beginning to slip from his grasp.

'Then I wish to see Monsieur le Préfet,' Vivian said.

'Monsieur le Préfet has gone to lunch,' the man told him.

All round the building, the telephones continued to ring, unanswered.

'What about Monsieur le Sous-Préfet?' Vivian asked.

'Also at lunch, monsieur,' the clerk answered patiently.

Half a dozen papers floated gently to the floor. He looked down in fatalistic despair.

'It *is* lunchtime, monsieur,' he protested gently.

Vivian marched back to the cloisters. He attempted to explain the situation. Mr Churchill's brow lowered dangerously.

'Are we to – er – presume,' he pronounced the word 'presume' as if it were a particular delicacy culled from a dictionary of obscure expressions, 'that we are to find luncheon for ourselves?' he enquired.

'There is the Grand Hotel, opposite the Railway Terminus,' Vivian told him. 'It's only a few yards up the road, sir.'

The Grand Hotel, Torquay, Bournemouth, Southport, or even Grange-over-Sands, was probably Grander than the Grand Hotel, Rue Buffon, Tours. But he couldn't think of anywhere else in the immediate vicinity.

'Very well, gentlemen,' announced Mr Churchill. 'The – ah – gallant major will lead us to the – er – Grand Hotel.'

He clamped his cigar between his lips, and without waiting for Vivian, plodded off down the cloister path.

They squeezed back into the car. It was a mistake. It would have been easier for the entire party to have walked. The street was choked with refugees camping in and around the vehicles which they intended to abandon there, in the middle of the road, as soon as they could fight their way onto a train travelling south. Whole families had rigged bivouacs – crude tents made of travelling-rugs, raincoats, ground-sheets, and blankets. A few were cooking on spirit-stoves and burners. And there were the usual knots of weary children with black rings about their eyes, pinched cheeks, and dry, cracked lips, crying fretfully, or staring apathetically ahead of them.

As soon as they were within sight of the hotel, Vivian got out, and made his way across to it. The foyer, as far as he was concerned, combined the worst features of a railway hotel – sooty gloom and shabby, well-trodden carpets – with wilting potted palms, and flaking wrought-iron arm rests.

The clerk at the desk greeted him with the words.

'Lunch is finished, monsieur. I regret.'

Vivian explained that there was a party of senior British government ministers outside, including the British Prime Minister, who had just flown over from London to meet Monsieur Paul Reynaud.

The desk-clerk offered a supercilious grin.

'Lunch is still finished, monsieur. I regret it, but there it is.'

'Perhaps you don't understand me,' Vivian suggested. 'This is the Prime Minister of Great Britain, come to confer with your own Prime Minister . . . '

'Oui, monsieur, Monsieur Paul Reynaud,' said the desk clerk helpfully.

'Surely,' said Vivian, 'if only for the honour of the Republic . . . '

'The honour of the Republic!' the man exclaimed. 'Ah, monsieur!'

He made as if to spit, in a symbolic gesture of contempt.

A man in a dark suit, with brilliantined hair and moustache, came in through a doorway behind the reception desk.

'Monsieur,' he said smiling, 'we have had those poor people outside coming in here all morning. We have been compelled by charity, monsieur, to give them every scrap of food we possess. We are depleted, monsieur. Depleted, and exhausted. My staff are exhausted, Madame is exhausted, I am exhausted. If Marshal Pétain, if the King of England, were to ask us to give him lunch, there is nothing we could do.'

He spread out his hands hopelessly.

'Perhaps you would permit Mr Churchill and his companions to wash here, after their long journey, and to rest here in your lounge until Monsieur Reynaud arrives,' Vivian suggested.

The manager knew the thin end of a wedge when it was presented to him.

'Alas no, monsieur,' he replied.

He stared away over Vivian's shoulder. His eyes widened.

'Qu'est-ce que nous – ah – donnerez-vous à manger, monsieur?' Mr Churchill's voice growled from behind Vivian.

The manager's face collapsed into an ingratiating smile.

'Forgive me, your excellency,' he said, coming round from behind the desk. 'I did not believe your excellency would do my establishment so much honour, your excellency. It is true we have very little to offer, but I can assure your excellency that my wife and the chef will do their utmost with what remains to us.'

'*C'est bon*,' Churchill told him without a smile.

General Ismay touched Vivian on the shoulder.

'Sorry, Major Hardwicke,' he said. 'But somebody's going to have to keep a look-out for the French P.M.'s arrival. Think you can manage it?'

'Of course, sir,' Vivian assured him.

He went out onto the pavement where he could see down the length of the Rue Buffon to the side of the Prefecture. Standing among the encamped refugees, he drew up the collar of his trench-coat against the drizzling rain. It had been a long time since his rather hurried breakfast, and the day was going to be a long one, of that he was sure. On the other hand, he would have felt distinctly uncomfortable had he been asked to lunch with the distinguished and not entirely happy statesmen inside the hotel. He had an uncomfortable feeling that Mr Churchill was about to hold him responsible for everything from the standard of the Grand Hotel's cuisine to the situation on what could only laughingly be called the Western Front.

Twenty minutes later, a black Cadillac pulled up outside the entrance to the hotel, and Paul Baudouin, the French Foreign Minister, climbed out, followed by Sir Edward Spears. Vivian saluted as they came up the steps. Monsieur Baudouin offered him a charming, boyish smile in return.

'At ease, my boy,' said General Spears.

He waited until Monsieur Baudouin had disappeared into the hotel foyer.

'Winston in a bit of a bate, is he?' he asked.

'Not yet, sir,' Vivian replied, 'but heading that way, in my opinion.'

'He will be by the time he's had a jaw with Baudouin,' Sir Edward told him confidentially. 'Dreadful little blighter! Dreadful!' He lowered his voice still further. 'Sort of chap we'd call a "tout" when we were at school . . . Had any tiffin yet?'

'No, sir,' Vivian replied.

'I'll see if I can forage a sandwich for you, or something,' said Sir Edward. 'Mustn't let the chaps starve, eh?'

'That's very good of you, sir,' Vivian replied.

Another twenty minutes passed before the British delegation came out of the hotel. Vivian noticed immediately that Mr Churchill's face was black with strangulated fury. Monsieur Baudouin accompanied him; his youthful smile was as rigid as if it had been applied with paint. Mr Churchill acknowledged Vivian's salute with a flourish of his cigar, to Vivian's relief. Lord Beaverbrook, General Ismay, and

Sir Alexander Cadogan trooped after, like school-prefects who knew that they were about to observe the head-man dish out the most appalling wigging. Lord Halifax gave a tolerable impression of a school chaplain whose mind was on higher things. General Spears brought up the rear.

'Here, my boy,' Spears muttered.

He drew from the flap of his own trench-coat, a half baton of bread with a thick sliver of beef in it.

'Best I could do,' he said. *'Bon appetit!'*

'Thank you very much, sir,' said Vivian.

He thrust the sandwich into the skirt pocket of his trench-coat.

He and Sir Edward brought up the rear of the procession which negotiated its way on foot through the refugees' encampment, back to the Prefecture. As they reached the entrance to the cloisters, the heavens opened. Mr Churchill turned on the steps under the dripping vines, and glared at Vivian, whom, clearly, he was about to hold responsible for this new indignity. He glanced down at Vivian's groin. Vivian followed his look. The half-baton of bread was thrusting forward obscenely under the skirt of his coat.

'What in God's name is the matter with you, man?' Mr Churchill snarled.

Vivian felt a sudden surge of mutinous anger. He felt the touch of Sir Edward's hand on his sleeve. He rearranged the sandwich in his pocket, and followed the party along the cloisters to the Prefect's office. There they found the Minister of the Interior, Georges Mandel, sitting in solitary state. He was sitting at the Prefect's heavy Second Empire desk. In front of him was a picnic hamper, a plain white plate on which stood the remains of half a cold, roast spring chicken, and a three-quarters empty bottle of Muscadet which, nevertheless, still had on it the bloom from having been recently chilled.

'You have dined well, I trust, monsieur?' said Mr Churchill, eyeing the chicken and the wine with an obvious, childish envy. Mandel rose, wiped his lips and fingers on his starched white napkin, and shook Mr Churchill by the hand.

Mr Churchill was introducing the rest of his party to Mandel, as Reynaud and his advisers arrived, accompanied by Sir Ronald Campbell. As they filed into the office, Sir Ronald paused to thank Vivian for all the trouble he had undertaken. It was a gracious gesture which Vivian appreciated. When the council was assembled, Sir Edward came to the door and whispered to him,

'I'm afraid you'll have to do stag, my boy. Nobody else available. Don't have to actually stand at the door, but make sure you have an eye on it, eh? And don't let anybody – and that does mean *anybody*, male or female, if you catch my drift – disturb us, there's a good fellow.'

347

The door closed behind him.

Vivian retired to the plushly furnished ante-room across the corridor. With the ante-room door open, he could sit in the comfort of an armchair, and still observe the door of the Prefect's office. He took out his beef sandwich and started to eat it.

He was about half-way through it, when there came into the ante-room a short, parchment-skinned, elderly man, in white kid breeches, stiffly pressed khaki uniform jacket, and carrying a képi encrusted with rings of oak-leaves. It took a moment or two for Vivian, as he stood up, to recognise General Weygand. Nevertheless, he managed to put his sandwich down and snap his heels together.

'General!' he said.

The Generalissimo had grown older, seemed to have shrunk, since Vivian had last seen him in Paris.

'Please, major,' said General Weygand, staring at him vaguely. 'Finish your lunch . . . *Je vous en prie.*'

They both sat down.

'We have met, I believe, major,' said General Weygand.

'Yes, General,' Vivian agreed. 'At the Rue St Dominique. I am aide to General Spears. I take it as a great compliment that the General recognises me.'

'Never forget a face, major, never.' He said it sadly, as if there were a great many he would like to forget.

'Is General Spears in there?' He waved in the direction of the Prefect's office.

'Yes, General,' Vivian replied.

'I am not allowed to be in there,' said General Weygand. 'I have to stand by "for consultation" – that is how they put it. "For consultation."'

He laughed. It sounded more like a grunt. He stared across at Vivian. Vivian felt certain he should say something, but he couldn't think of anything to say.

'They regard me,' said General Weygand, 'as a trouble-maker, you see.'

He smiled sadly.

'I'm sure that isn't true, General,' Vivian told him.

'Oh yes, major,' General Weygand replied, 'it is precisely true.'

'But the General's military career – reputation – is well known,' said Vivian.

General Weygand stared down at his mirror-polished black riding boots.

'You cannot appreciate, major,' he said, 'you who are young, the bitterness in what has been set before me. When I was sent as pro-Consul to Syria, I believed that it was an honour conferred upon an old soldier in recognition of his long years of service to his country. And now, major, I have been recalled; recalled to preside over the greatest debacle in the history of French arms. Yes, greater even than that of 1871. You are still young, major. You have served your country, and have been wounded in that service. You have been honoured by your country, and you still have your life to live. What will history say of me?'

His voice rose querulously.

'My successes, my victories – all will be forgotten. Only this one catastrophe will be remembered – a catastrophe which was none of my making. The names of the incompetents and traitors will all be forgotten, but the name of Maximilien Weygand will always be remembered. My father too presided over defeat, and the collapse of his followers' fortunes, but he was permitted the crown of martyrdom. I shall be allowed only a humiliating surrender. And the Freemasons and the Jews and the Communists who have brought France to this extremity – they, major, will saddle this poor old soldier with the blame for everything.'

Suddenly, there burst into the ante-room the figure of the woman whom Vivian had encountered twice at Chissay that morning.

'Oh Maxime! Maxime!' she throbbed at the old Generalissimo. 'I knew I should find at least one friend here.'

Her make-up had been carefully if lavishly put on. Her suit was expensive, even if it hugged her body too tightly for good taste. Her hair was properly pinned up. On it perched a frivolous pill-box hat, like a hotel page-boy's, with a black net veil gathered about it. The room was filled with her scent.

'Maxime, do you know they tried to stop me entering?'

She spoke with the tragic intensity of a Rejane or Duse. If she recognised Vivian, she gave no sign of it. He had no part in her current performance.

General Weygand regarded her with evident distaste.

'Who tried to stop you, Countess?' he asked.

'Paulie's *huissiers*, of course,' the woman exclaimed. 'And I'll tell you something else, Charles de Gaulle is out there. They're acting on his orders, not Paulie's – his, and that dirty Jew's, Mandel! But you'll take me in to Paulie, won't you, Maxime?'

'No, Countess,' replied General Weygand. 'I may not enter myself, until I am summoned.'

'But that is quite ridiculous, Maxime!' the woman exclaimed. 'You are the Commander-in-Chief.'

'And a soldier, Countess. As a soldier, I must obey orders.'

'Then I shall go in alone,' said the Countess de Portes.

'Madame,' said Vivian. 'I am under the strictest orders to permit nobody to enter.'

The Countess turned and regarded him with grand, operatic disdain.

'Under whose orders, monsieur?' she demanded.

'Those of my superior officer, madame,' Vivian replied.

'Your *English* superior, I presume,' she said.

'Yes, madame.'

'May I remind you, monsieur, that you are not in England?'

'I shall obey my orders just the same, madame,' Vivian told her.

'How do you propose to stop me?' she demanded.

'By force, if necessary,' Vivian replied simply.

'Absurd!' exclaimed the Countess.

She turned on her heel and flounced out into the passage. Vivian followed her across the room. He did not dare look at General Weygand. The Countess realised that Vivian was coming up behind her. Suddenly, she threw herself at the door of the Prefect's office and started banging on it.

'Paulie!' she shouted. 'Paulie! You must listen to me! Baudouin! Please, Baudouin, come to me!'

'Madame,' Vivian protested.

'Don't you touch me!' screamed the Countess. 'Baudouin! Baudouin! ... Don't touch me, Englishman!'

Vivian was appalled. The woman appeared to be in a state of complete hysteria.

The office door opened. Baudouin came out.

'Oh Paul! Paul!' she sighed. 'This Englishman was about to – molest me!'

'Just outside the door of the Allied War Council?' Baudouin asked gently.

She clutched at his arms.

'Paul?' she asked, 'are they discussing an armistice? You have to tell me.'

'Not here, Hélène,' Baudouin said softly.

'Tell Paulie he's got to persuade the English to give up. Tell him he's got to get the English to agree to an armistice.'

Baudouin stared up and down the passage.

'I can't discuss it with you here, Hélène,' he said.

'Tell Paulie we've got to give up. We must ask the Germans for an armistice before it's too late,' she implored him.

'Calm yourself, Hélène,' Baudouin tried to quieten her. 'Please.'

'The English must agree to us asking for an armistice,' she screamed. 'Tell Churchill – tell him he can't make us go on fighting when we don't want to.'

'Be quiet, Hélène,' Baudouin snapped, 'or you'll spoil everything. It'll be all right, I promise you. Now you must go away.'

'Very well, Paul,' she subsided. 'I'll be good. But you do promise to make the English agree to an armistice, don't you?'

'I promise, *chérie*,' Baudouin told her quietly.

He stood at the office door and watched as she made her way down the corridor towards the cloisters. Then he went back into the office, closing the door behind him. Vivian subsided gratefully into his armchair. General Weygand was dozing off, his chin sinking against the rim of his high collar. Now and then, he would grunt and stir. Several times, an aide came in and woke him to whisper a message into his ear. General Weygand would nod, stare in front of him for a few moments, then nod off to sleep again.

Half an hour passed.

Vivian suddenly saw the Countess de Portes at the door of the Prefect's office. She had placed her fingers on the knob. He leapt up and ran into the passage. He pushed her aside, and stood with his back to the door.

'You may not enter, madame,' he said.

She tried to shoulder him aside. The smell of her scent cloyed in his nostrils.

'Paulie! Paulie!' she began to scream, the spittle flying into his face. 'Listen to me, Paulie! . . . Get out of my way, Englishman! . . . Paulie! Paulie!'

The door behind Vivian opened, so that he almost fell backwards into the conference chamber. General Ismay was immediately behind him.

'Major Hardwicke,' said General Ismay, 'is there nothing you can do about all this racket?'

The Countess de Portes had withdrawn a few paces up the passage. She stood regarding the two English soldiers like a tigress.

'Winston's getting a bit peeved in there, you know,' said General Ismay.

The Countess de Portes hurled herself past them both, at the gap in the door. General Ismay found himself locked in a wrestling hold with her, while Vivian tried to grab at her with his one hand to pull her off his senior officer.

Paul Baudouin appeared once again in the doorway. He calmed her again, and led her off down the corridor. General Ismay glared at Vivian.

'I'm surprised you managed to let things get as far as they did, Major Hardwicke,' he said. 'To the point where the Foreign Secretary of the French Republic has to come out to act as wet-nurse to a hysterical female. You'll have to do better next time, Major, or you'll have me to answer to.'

'Yes sir,' Vivian replied stiffly.

A minute or two later, Baudouin returned. Once again, the office door closed behind him. This time, Vivian stood guard outside it.

The afternoon lengthened. General Weygand began coming out into the corridor, and sighing noisily before retiring back into the ante-room. Occasionally aides would arrive with messages and reports for the Generalissimo. General Weygand would scribble a memorandum in pencil, and hand it back to them. Roland de Margerie

351

arrived with a gentleman whom Vivian did not recognise. De Margerie gave him a warm, friendly smile as he ushered his companion into the conference room. General Weygand watched as de Margerie closed the door behind him. He sighed even more noisily than usual, and retired once again into the ante-room. Vivian longed for a drink – scotch, coffee, tea, anything – and a cigarette.

High heels came clicking up the corridor from the cloisters. Vivian's heart sank. The Countess de Portes was approaching yet again, her absurdly frivolous pill-box hat perched on the side of her head, her expensive skirt taut over her swaying hips. She had repaired her face. There was an extra layer of lipstick on her mouth.

'You will let me pass, Major,' she announced with sharp authority.

Vivian shook his head. 'I have my orders, madame,' he told her.

'I shit on your orders, Major,' she told him.

'That is your prerogative, madame,' he replied, 'but I cannot allow you to pass.'

At the far end of the passage stood two of Monsieur Reynaud's *huissiers*. They were observing the encounter with interest. The Countess de Portes put her hand on Vivian's shoulder.

'I must ask you to remove your hand, madame,' Vivian told her.

She began to scream at him, her mouth so wide, he could see down into her throat. She grabbed at the shoulder-flaps of his jacket, trying to tear him away from the door.

'*A moi!*' he bawled out. '*Huissiers! A moi!*'

To his astonishment, they came running with something like delight written on their faces. He said to them in English, 'If you don't get this bloody woman out of here, I swear I'll pick her up and throw her out into the street myself!'

They understood at least the gist of what he had said. They dragged the Countess off him, and carried her bodily away down the passage. She struggled and screamed all the way to the cloisters, her pill-box hat hanging by one grip off her head; even when she had disappeared outside, her screams echoed round the building.

A few minutes later the door to the Prefect's office opened and General Spears came out into the passage. He was stuffing tobacco into the bowl of his pipe.

'Getting stuffy in there,' he said. 'Better air the room for a bit.'

He pressed the tobacco down.

'Had a bad time of it, my boy?' he asked.

'Uneasy, sir,' Vivian replied. 'A bit noisy. I'm sorry about it.'

'But you've seen to the cause of the trouble, eh?'

'I think so, sir.'

'Good show!'

'The Generalissimo is across the way, sir,' Vivian said, lowering his voice. 'I don't think he's terribly happy about the way he is being treated.'

'That's Reynaud's pigeon,' said Sir Edward. 'Can't do anything about it.'

Vivian glanced past Sir Edward into the conference room. At the far end, the french windows were open. Beyond was a formal garden. There was a ragged, ill-kempt lawn with a small stone fountain in the centre. The rain had stopped, and steam was rising from the wet grass into the warm air. Along the gravel path at the edge of the lawn, and standing in a row with their backs to the fountain, were Mr Churchill, Lord Halifax, Lord Beaverbrook, Sir Alexander Cadogan, and Sir Ronald Campbell. All had their trousers unbuttoned, and all were pissing into the flower-bed.

'Ah,' said Sir Edward, 'the very man we've been waiting for. *Bienvenu, Charles, mon cher.*'

General de Gaulle had arrived. Vivian noticed that he was wearing the white kid breeches he had always affected to despise when he was commanding in the field.

'You remember my young friend, I daresay,' Sir Edward asked.

'Of course,' General de Gaulle replied. 'How are you, Major 'ardwicke?'

'Congratulations on your promotion, General,' Vivian replied.

'Ah!' General de Gaulle replied with an air of boredom. He stooped under the lintel of the door and went into the office. Sir Edward followed him. As he turned to close the door, he said, 'It won't be long now, my boy. Don't worry.'

The door closed. General Weygand was standing framed in the doorway of the ante-room. His cheeks were mottled purple with rage, the tendons on his neck were quivering. He bellowed at the door of the conference room, at the top of his powerful voice.

'They sit with their unwiped arses on their chairs – and they don't give a shit that all this time our brave soldiers are being butchered. Butchered,' he repeated, the spray flying from between his lips.

Almost immediately, the door of the Prefect's office opened. General Ismay came out. He closed the door behind him. Placing his hand on Vivian's stump, he drew him a short distance down the passage.

'Look here, old chap,' he said kindly. 'Eddie Spears has told me you've got quite a difficult job out here. But you really must try to do a little better than this ... '

His mild rebuke was interrupted by a stentorian bellow from General Weygand directed at the conference room door.

'Why did you recall me? Me, Weygand? Why, you *crapules*, if you don't want to listen to what an old soldier of France has to say?' His voice cracked.

'Excuse me, sir,' Vivian said to General Ismay.

General Weygand's head was bowed to his chest. Vivian went to him.

'Permit me, General,' he said gently.

He guided the old man back to the ante-room, and lowered him in to a chair. He noticed that the skin on the top of General Weygand's bald head had been flaked and yellowed by the Mesopotamian sun.

General Weygand stared up at him.

'What will the history-books say of me, Major?' he asked.

General Ismay was standing by the door. He was looking down at the tearful old Generalissimo with unconcealed contempt.

'Major Hardwicke,' he said coldly. He pointed across to where Vivian had been sitting earlier. On the arm was the wreckage of his beef sandwich. 'I would remove that, if I were you, before Winston spots it.'

'Yes, sir,' said Vivian.

He felt angrier than he had felt all day.

It was after five o'clock when the conference finally broke up. Vivian walked with General Spears, a few paces behind Mr Churchill and Monsieur Reynaud, as they went to the Prefecture car-park on the far side of the cloisters. Two gentlemen were waiting for Mr Churchill, as he stepped out into the cloisters. Monsieur Reynaud introduced them as Monsieur Herriot, veteran Speaker of the Chamber, and Monsieur Jeanneney, President of the Senate. Monsieur Reynaud then returned to the Prefect's office as Mr Churchill walked under the cloister arches with Messieurs Herriot and Jeanneney, one on either side of him. The other members of the British delegation trailed along behind them.

'Monsieur Churchill,' Monsieur Jeanneney was saying, 'we have come to implore you, and the people of Great Britain, not to abandon France. We can assure you that, whatever may have been said to you this afternoon, there are many thousands of true Frenchmen and Frenchwomen who are ready to die rather than see France making peace with the enemy.'

A third man came up, a middle-aged, military figure.

'Monsieur Churchill, may I present,' Monsieur Jeanneney continued, 'Monsieur Michel Clemenceau.'

Mr Churchill stopped.

'Son of the old Tiger?' he asked.

'Yes, monsieur,' Michel Clemenceau replied, 'I have that honour.'

Mr Churchill put his cigar into his mouth, and grasped Michel Clemenceau's outstretched hand in both his own. Then he removed the cigar from his mouth.

'We have a great deal in common, Monsieur Clemenceau,' he said.

'Yes, monsieur?'

354

'We both of us have fathers who were giants,' said Mr Churchill. 'Giants of the old world. And we both had – ah – mothers who came from America. The young blood of the new world mingling with the greatness of the old, hm?'

Michel Clemenceau smiled.

'Monsieur Churchill,' he said. 'A short time before his death, my father wrote that "nations have never cheerfully followed any leaders except those that have asked them to shed their blood". My father was such a leader . . . '

Mr Churchill nodded his agreement.

' . . . But there are none here today, I think,' Michel Clemenceau continued, 'except Monsieur Winston Churchill.'

Mr Churchill stood stock still. Vivian could see the tears on his cheeks.

'*Merci, mon brave,*' Churchill muttered. '*Merci!*'

Suddenly, he reached out and embraced Michel Clemenceau in a bear-hug. The lean face of Lord Halifax, who stood head and shoulders above the rest of the British delegation, turned away in embarrassment.

Vivian stood on the cloister steps and watched as the British ministers got into the three Cadillacs which were to return them to the air base and their journey back to London. The leading car, with Mr Churchill inside, was about to turn out into the Rue de Buffon, when Vivian saw the Countess de Portes. She was running up the pavement, determined on throwing herself in front of the Cadillac. Vivian jumped down from the step, ran the twenty yards across the sanded gravel, splashing through the puddles, and managed to catch her by the arm. As Mr Churchill's car swept past, she tore herself free and shouted in at the passenger window,

'Monsieur Churchill! Monsieur Churchill! My country is bleeding to death! You must hear my side of the story!'

The big car disappeared into the crowds of refugees encamped in the Rue Buffon. The Countess de Portes stood watching. Then she turned away, and walked back across the car park towards the cloisters. She caught sight of Vivian close by the steps leading into the Prefecture. She rushed at him, shrieking as if possessed,

'Assassin! Assassin! You want to see French soldiers die!'

Vivian struggled to hold her off as she clawed at his face with her long, scarlet nails. He was aware of a confused knot of militia and *huissiers* pulling her away, and trying to calm her. He walked up into the Prefecture. He could feel the scratches burning his cheeks. His jacket was twisted under his Sam Browne belt. He felt shaken by the violence of the scene.

He went through to the washroom to examine his wounds and to do what he could to make himself tidy. To his surprise, he found Sir Edward Spears and General de Gaulle standing at the washbasins. It was clear that they had been engaged in a confidential chat. Vivian was about to retreat.

'Come in, my boy. Come in,' called Sir Edward. He examined Vivian's face. 'You've really blotted your copy-book now,' he said.

General de Gaulle smiled a long, mournful, gothic smile.

'Alas, Major 'ardwicke,' he said, 'one expects the mistresses of important men to be beautiful, intelligent, and members of the Comédie Française. The Countess de Portes is none of these things. Nevertheless, to be physically assaulted by the mistress of a Prime Minister is to win a place in the footnotes of history.'

'Thank you, General,' Vivian replied sourly.

'Vivian, my boy,' said Sir Edward. It was the first time he had addressed Vivian by his christian name. Vivian was not at all sure that he liked it. 'While you can be of little use here, now that you have made an enemy of the Countess de Portes, you can still do us a very great service – and France.'

'Indeed, sir?' asked Vivian rather coldly.

He glanced at his face in the mirror above the washbasins. The scratch was clearly visible as a white graze, but the Countess had not drawn blood.

'General de Gaulle and I are both convinced of your courage and of your ingenuity, my boy,' Sir Edward continued.

Fine words butter no parsnips, Nanny Grey had used to say when Vivian was little.

'And of your discretion,' Sir Edward added. 'We want you to go to Paris immediately – as soon as we can commandeer you a car – you'll have to drive yourself. The General tells me you have met Victor de Bart-Mendel . . . '

'At La Berlière?' asked Vivian.

'He is now in Paris, in his home off the Avenue de Wagram – the Square de Brey to be precise . . . Do you know about the Tondeau of Chartres?'

'Yes, sir,' Vivian replied, 'the Baron showed it to me.'

'We need it, Vivian,' said Sir Edward. 'The present government cannot hold. Reynaud is talking of retreating into a Breton redoubt, but none of the military are making any plans. Reynaud would fight on if he could, but he's surrounded by defeatists, and the next administration is bound to seek an armistice. It is a matter of time. They have not told Winston, but they have decided to declare Paris an open city.'

'They'll surrender Paris without a fight?' exclaimed Vivian.

'It is true,' said General de Gaulle.

'Whatever happens, General de Gaulle here intends to continue the struggle,' Sir Edward continued. 'Perhaps in a Breton redoubt. Perhaps in North Africa. Perhaps, at the worst, from England. The point is this. If a legitimate French government were to make peace

356

with Germany – with an instrument of surrender, or peace treaty, duly signed and sealed – any Frenchman who continued the fight would legally be in a state of armed rebellion. And so would those who followed him ... What we want you to do, Vivian, is to persuade de Bart-Mendel to bring the Tondeau of Chartres to General de Gaulle. Or, if he will not come himself, to give it to you. Tell him that if a leader is to emerge from the ruins of a defeated France, he will need the insignia of St Louis to carry, like the *Oriflamme* in the olden days. It will act as the mark of his legitimacy, don't you see?'

'You will have to move quickly, Major 'ardwicke,' said General de Gaulle. 'The Germans have crossed the Seine below Rouen.'

'It is a matter of hours rather than days before Paris is invested and cut off,' said Sir Edward Spears. 'It really is a matter of going in, persuading de Bart-Mendel either to come in person, or let you have the Tondeau, and returning immediately, before you are all trapped in Paris.'

They walked into the cloisters together. The darkening air was cool and fresh, and smelt of damp leaves. On the far side, under the dripping arches, they could see the Minister of the Interior deep in conference with Herriot and Jeanneney.

'Would he be willing to join you?' Sir Edward asked quietly.

De Gaulle did not answer.

'He is a Jew,' he said, 'and a true son of France. De Bart-Mendel is, I believe, a true Frenchman. It seems one must be Jewish to be a true Frenchman, these days.' He turned to Vivian. 'De Bart-Mendel will give you the Tondeau, Major 'ardwicke,' he said gravely. 'Tell him that I, de Gaulle, need it.'

After de Gaulle had returned to the Prefecture, Sir Edward told Vivian to take the car in which he, Sir Edward, had driven up from Chissay. They were standing in the car-park together.

'Let's have no cock-ups, eh, my boy,' he said. 'If you're in any doubt whatever as to where to go, or what's going on, get the bloody thing back to London. We can decide what to do with it afterwards.'

'But ... ' Vivian was about to start.

He glanced up at the Prefecture. Sir Edward smiled.

'Orders, my boy,' he said. '"Theirs not to reason why ... ".'

'Yes, sir,' Vivian replied.

35

'Julie, it's time you were going.'

She knew before she opened her eyes that the table-lamp beside the bed had been switched on. She resented being woken up. Lying with her head and shoulders buried in the warm softness of the pillows, she was in that state of complete relaxation which comes of physical exhaustion.

Victor was standing over her. He was fully dressed. She saw that it was still dark outside.

'Going where?' she asked sleepily. 'What's the time?'

'A quarter to four,' Victor told her. 'You are leaving Paris straight away.'

She blinked and rubbed her eyes.

'Why?' she asked.

For the past day or two there had been neither the sound of gunfire nor bombing-raids. The city had seemed silent.

'I'm ready, papa.'

Julie sat up. She pulled the flounce of her nightdress onto her shoulder. Hugo was standing in the doorway, dressed in grey flannel trousers and blazer like an English prep-schoolboy. He looked wide-eyed and anxious. His hair was unbrushed.

'Wait downstairs with Severin,' Victor told him.

Julie was surprised. Victor had always referred to the butler as *Monsieur* Severin when addressing Hugo.

'Yes, Papa,' Hugo replied submissively.

'And give your face a good wash, and brush your hair.' Victor ordered sharply.

'Yes, Papa,' Hugo called back from the landing.

'Up you get,' Victor said to Julie. He drew the bedclothes from off her legs. 'I need your help more than I've ever done,' he told her. 'I'll talk to you while you dress, if I may.'

'But Victor . . . ' she began.

'Don't ask questions. You must be very grown up, now.'

Why did he have to say that? she wondered. She got off the bed and went over to the dressing-table. As she began to dress, he sat down on the bed. Julie remembered from when she had been a sixth-form girl, the headmistress's Saturday evening informal chats – how she had said that you could always tell a gentleman by the fact that, when you told him you couldn't go bathing with him, he wouldn't ask why, and that he would never sit on your bed, not even when you were ill.

'I received a phone call from the Minister of the Interior, half an hour ago,' said Victor.

'The Minister of the Interior?' she asked, suitably impressed.

She stood with her back to him as she fastened her brassière. She could see his reflection in the mirror. He looked very pale in the lamplight.

358

'He rang me to tell me that the *Conseil de Guerre* decided yesterday to declare Paris an open city. Do you know what that means?'

'Does it mean they just let the Germans walk in without a fight?' Julie asked.

'Exactly, my dear. Any time they choose. They've already crossed the Seine. The Minister believes they've reached Evreux and Bernay. If they haven't marched into Paris by tonight, they'll certainly have sealed it off. So you see, you haven't a moment to lose.'

'Are you coming?' Julie asked.

He shook his head.

'Why not, for God's sake?' she demanded.

'That is far too complicated a question for four o'clock in the morning,' Victor replied.

'What about Hugo?' Julie asked.

'I'm asking you to take him with you,' said Victor. 'It would be a very great kindness. Will you?'

'Of course,' she said. 'What do you think?'

She was feeling irritable.

'You see, I trust you, Julie,' he told her. 'You know that there have been,' he shrugged, 'women in my life; but you are the only one, except for his mother, to whom I would entrust the safety of my son.'

She had sat down on the dressing-table stool, and was fastening up her stocking.

'You don't have to say things like that, Victor,' she told him. 'I happen to be the one who's here at the right time.'

Victor sighed.

'I'm sorry, Julie,' he said.

'Where do you want me to take him?' she asked. 'To friends?'

'I've written down the name and address of some old friends,' he told her. 'They live in Oxford – at a village called Old Marston. He teaches at the University. I know they will welcome Hugo – and it's a place where a child can be happy.' He smiled. 'I'm asking you to take him with you all the way to England, you see? Do you mind, Julie?'

She saw his face in the mirror. She got up and went over to him with one stocking still rolled loosely on her knee.

'Oh Victor,' she said, 'of course I don't mind. I only wish that you were coming too.'

He kissed her cheek.

'Thank you,' he said. 'Listen – there's an envelope I'm going to give you. It contains a little money, and also a letter to Coutts' Bank in St James's, with instructions regarding funds for Hugo and money for whatever expenses you may incur. There is also a packet containing some gold coins and some jewelry – it is difficult to know how long the franc can maintain its value in times like these. They are yours to dispose of as you wish.'

Julie nodded.

'Now, you must finish getting ready,' he told her.

She went back to the dressing-table, and pulled on her slacks and sweater.

'Do you think France is really defeated?' she asked.

'The war may be continued,' he replied, 'In the south perhaps – or Brittany. But as far as we civilians are concerned, I'm afraid she is.'

Julie tied her unbrushed hair back in a ribbon. She started throwing everything which lay to hand into a suitcase. It was just as well there would be no time for her to cry, she thought.

'You know how to drive, don't you?' asked Victor.

He had stood up, and was waiting for her.

'Yes,' she told him.

She had never driven on continental roads or handled a left-hand drive.

'You can take Severin's little Renault. It'll be easier for you to handle under the conditions you might meet, and it won't be too conspicuous. Also it isn't so heavy on petrol as a bigger car. And don't go throwing cigarette ends into the back. Joseph has put in as many cans of petrol as you'll need to get you to the coast.'

Julie swept her toilet things onto the roughly folded clothes on the top of the case, and closed the lid.

'The government is on the move from Tours to Bordeaux,' Victor went on. 'I've got a Michelin tourist guide for you, and I've marked several routes. You must go west as far as Dreux, and then head south-west to Le Mans. That way you should manage to keep clear of the refugee traffic heading south, and escape the Germans moving round Paris from the north-east. After you reach Le Mans, you'll have to decide for yourself whether it'll be best to head for Bordeaux, via Angers, or to make straight for the north coast of Brittany, and the Channel Islands.'

He came over and took the case from her.

'Kiss me goodbye, Victor,' she told him. 'Now.'

He put down the case again. He took her in his arms and kissed her mouth.

'That was good,' she told him. 'I suppose that when I come back to Paris, there'll be somebody else, won't there?'

'I expect so,' he replied smiling.

He cleared his throat, and Julie did not dare say anything more, for both their sakes.

He carried her case downstairs.

'Hugo?' he called. 'Will you carry Julie's things out to the car?'

'It's a bit heavy,' Julie warned him.

Hugo tried holding it.

'I'll manage,' he said bravely.

Julie followed Victor across to the study. Glancing back across the hall, she noticed under the shadow of the stairs where the door led to the kitchen quarters, Severin taking the case from the small figure of Hugo, and taking him by the hand to lead him away.

Alain was already in the study. He was wearing off-duty check flannels and a polo-necked, diamond-patterned sweater. He was unshaven, and his hair was unbrushed. His walking-stick was suspended by its crook handle from the edge of the table.

'Everything is ready for Miss Armitage,' he told Victor.

A small dispatch-case was lying open on the table.

'Letters of credit,' he said, pointing. 'Francs. Pounds sterling. Necklace, earrings, and two bracelets. Twenty gold *louis*. Hugo's passport. Letters of introduction, for England.'

'And this,' said Victor.

Alain took the large, flat, black leather case, and placed it reverently in the dispatch-case. Julie looked across the table to the bookcases. Victor was hanging the portrait of the serene-faced beauty from the Belle Époque back on its hook.

'No!' Julie exclaimed.

'Yes,' Victor told her. 'You are now the sole custodian of the *Tondeau de Chartres*. I can give you no instructions, no orders, not even advice. You must dispose of it how you judge best.'

'No,' Julie repeated. 'You can't entrust something like that to me.'

'Why not, Julie?' asked Victor. 'I've entrusted my son to you.'

'Why can't you come with me,' she asked, 'and look after it for yourself?'

'Monsieur le Baron is very busy,' explained Alain quietly. 'There are in Paris thousands of Jewish people. Many of them are already refugees, without any means of support. When the Germans come ... '

He spread out his hands in an eloquent gesture.

'Monsieur le Baron is doing his best in the time which remains to us,' he continued, 'to ensure that funds are put into the hands of his gentile friends, so that when the Germans arrive, they will be able to do what they can for our Jewish citizens.'

'The Tondeau should be looked after by somebody who is French,' said Julie desperately.

'There's no one,' said Victor. 'You'll discover the best thing to do, Julie, in the same way as St Louis did when he was escaping through the marshes of Mansurah.'

St Louis was captured by the Saracens, thought Julie; but she nodded her consent.

'Take it,' said Victor, 'wherever there are brave Frenchmen who continue to resist the dark forces which are now overwhelming us. Give it to whoever leads them in their fight. Tell him to do that for me, Julie?'

'Yes, Victor,' she replied solemnly.

'So you see, my darling Julie,' he whispered, 'I trust you very much.'

Julie swallowed hard.

Alain snapped shut the dispatch-case. He remained in the study as Victor, carrying the little case, went out with Julie. They went under the stairs into the silent darkness of the kitchens and out through the yard into the garden. There was a slight hint of paleness in the sky behind the stars shining above the roof-tops. Julie and Victor went under the shadow of the trees, through the small door set in the garden wall, and out into the street.

The car's engine was already running; Hugo was sitting beside the driver's seat, hugging his own suitcase. Severin held the door open for Julie. Victor put the dispatch-case onto the back-seat, on top of her suitcase. Julie saw the petrol cans on the floor. She got in behind the wheel.

'You can manage the controls, mademoiselle?' asked Severin.

She nodded. She didn't want to speak.

Severin closed the door firmly. Despite the darkness, Julie could see that Hugo's eyes were brimming with tears. She found the hand-brake. She raised her hand in salute, then released the brake.

'*Bonne chance, mademoiselle,*' Severin said through the window.

Victor was standing back on the pavement. His eyes caught hers. He nodded, and smiled.

As she drove off down the street towards the Avenue de Wagram, Hugo twisted round in his seat to look back at his father. She heard him make a slight, strangulated sound, but said nothing.

Victor walked alone down the street after them, as if to see them safely on their way. He felt emotionally numb; the parting had come at the coldest, most hollow hour of the day, just before dawn. He came to the corner of the Rue Brey and the Avenue de Wagram. The Avenue stretched deserted in either direction. They had gone.

For a minute he stood shivering in the cold freshness of the very early morning, then turned to go back to a house which would feel as cold and empty as the Avenue. As he was returning up the street, he noticed a large Buick sedan parked up a side alley with its lights switched off. Peering at it, he saw that there were two men sitting in the front. Although he could see no detail of their appearance in the dark, their presence was sufficient to fill him with unease. He walked rapidly back to the garden door. Going in, he bolted the door behind him. He crossed the garden at a run. As he came out into the hall from the kitchens, Severin met him.

'Something has happened, monsieur,' he exclaimed. 'In the study.'

'Where's Alain?' Victor asked.

'He's gone, monsieur,' Severin replied.

Victor went into the study. The papers from his desk were scattered across the floor. The drawers had been wrenched out, and their contents scattered over the papers. Then he noticed the bookcases: the portrait of his mother lay face down on the carpet amid a litter of smashed glass. The door to the safe was wide open.

'Alain!' he shouted.

Nobody but the secretary and himself knew the combination.

'Severin,' he called. 'Go across the square to his apartment. See if he's gone home.'

'Very well, monsieur,' the butler replied.

He went out through the front doors.

Victor's foot brushed against something on the carpet. He bent down and picked up Alain's walking-stick from where it had been lying in the shadows under the table. The end had been snapped off two or three inches above the ferrule. Then he saw the mark dug into the edge of the table where, presumably, it had been struck by the end of the stick. Alain must have been hitting out at somebody.

At that moment, he knew that he was not alone downstairs in the house. It was as if there was evil lurking in the unlit corners. The feeling was sufficiently strong for him to run across the hall to the lounge. Quickly, he unlocked the drawer in the sideboard, took out a small, black automatic, cocked it, and laid it carefully on the top. He poured himself a stiff brandy. Putting the stopper back into the decanter, he looked up at the painting which hung immediately above the sideboard. It was the work of an anonymous Dutchman of the mid-seventeenth century. The subject was a game of cards. The players round the table were all staring out of the canvas as if the beholder had just come in and disturbed their game. All were smiling: the inveterate gentleman-sharper in mock self-reproach; the grandmother in zealous enjoyment of one of the few pleasures remaining to her; the youth in genuine delight at recognising the newcomer; a buxom maid, who was filling the glasses of the players from a jug, in coquettish knowledge that the beholder could see into the gather of her low-slung bodice.

This time, there were two unfamiliar faces smiling out of the glass: a dark-haired girl with a round, pock-marked, Spanish-looking face, and another, who had the appearance of a schoolgirl with her hair drawn back under a tortoiseshell band, except that her cheeks were hollow, and that there were crow's-feet about the eyes, as if she were

363

changing from adolescence to old age with no intervening period of maturity. And both were staring fixedly at him.

Carefully, he picked up the cocked automatic. He turned round. The room behind him was empty. He walked quickly over to the door. The hall was silent and deserted. Across it, on the other side, hung a great mirror. As Victor stepped out of the lounge, he saw in the glass the same two girls standing framed in darkness with their backs to him. They were looking at him over their shoulders. The dark, Spanish girl had her hand on the other's neck and was caressing it. Both were grinning at him as though they were children who had committed some forbidden act which he had been powerless to prevent. Just as he was about to turn to face them, they vanished in the blackness.

He ran across the hall to the open door of the dining-room. The french windows were open. The dawn breeze moved the curtains very gently. He went across to the windows, and looked out onto the garden. The dawn was only just coming; the light was as pale and cold as moonlight. The lawns were empty.

He returned to the study, closing the door behind him. He placed the automatic on the table, within easy reach, and started looking round. Nothing, as far as he could see, was actually missing. The intruders had come for one thing only.

There was a knock on the door. It was Severin.

'Monsieur Alain is not in his apartment,' he said.

'You will have to tell the staff what has happened,' Victor told him. 'I shall have to call the police.'

'Of course, monsieur.'

'You have never told anybody where we were keeping the Tondeau, have you, Severin?' asked Victor. 'Or about the safe.'

'Certainly not, monsieur!' replied Severin, shocked.

There was Julie of course. Who could Julie have talked to? Somebody down at the Gare Montparnasse? Then as he recalled showing the Tondeau to Julie, he remembered Danielle framed in the study door.

'What time do the maids come down?' he asked.

'The kitchen maid comes down at half-past five, monsieur,' Severin replied. 'The two housemaids and the chambermaid come down at a quarter-past six.'

'Tell Danielle when she comes down that I wish to see her straight away, will you?'

'Very good, monsieur.'

Victor went back to the lounge. He sat down, and telephoned the *Préfecture de Police*. He asked to be put straight through to Monsieur Langeron. As he had expected, Roger Langeron was in his office. He explained what had happened.

'Did these people find the *Tondeau de Chartres*?' asked Langeron.

'No. It's on its way to safety, I hope,' Victor told him. 'I'm much more concerned about Alain. He seems to have disappeared.'

'Do you suspect him?' asked Langeron.

'Certainly not, Roger,' Victor replied. 'In any case, he knew the Tondeau wasn't in the safe. These people I saw – they looked like kids.'

'That doesn't surprise me,' the Prefect told him. 'There's plenty of gangs of kids roaming about, taking advantage of the present situation.'

'Alain left his stick,' Victor explained. 'He can't get about without his stick.'

'If it's kids, there's nothing to worry about. He'll turn up,' said Langeron. 'They'll thieve, but they won't murder . . . To tell you the truth, Victor, I've got virtually no men. The entire uniformed force has been put at the disposal of General Hering for the defence of the city, so the *Sureté* is stretched to the limit.'

'The defence of the city?' asked Victor. 'Haven't you been told yet? Paris was declared an open city yesterday. General Hering has been told to withdraw his forces.'

'This isn't a joke is it, Victor?' asked Langeron, clearly shocked.

'Not at all, *cher ami*, I was told by Georges himself – Georges Mandel. He rang me from Azay during the night. General Hering is withdrawing the Paris garrison to the south-west. And General Dentz has been appointed Military Governor to negotiate the surrender of the city. Have you heard nothing of this?'

'Nothing at all,' the Prefect replied.

'There's no doubt about it,' Victor told him.

'I'd better try to get through to Tours or Chissay immediately,' said Langeron.

'You might be too late,' Victor replied. 'The government is moving to Bordeaux.'

He heard Langeron breathing at the other end.

'Victor?' he said at last. 'If this is true, get your man to drive you and your son out of Paris as quickly as you can.'

'I'm staying, Roger,' Victor said, 'as, I am sure, you are. Hugo has gone already. He's on his way to England.'

'I'm absolutely stunned,' said Langeron. 'They know I've twenty thousand men standing by to defend Paris street by street, and they can't bring themselves to tell me they've surrendered the city.'

'I suggest you ring General Dentz's headquarters,' said Victor.

'I'm completely stunned,' was all Langeron could say.

The brandy soothed Victor. He began to doze in his armchair while he was still holding a cigarette between his fingers. He sat forward and stubbed it out, then lay back resting his cheek against the leather wing of the back of the chair. He had been very abrupt with Hugo when he got him up. He had lacked the courage to show his affection for the boy lest he should have broken down completely. He hoped that Hugo had understood.

Memories floated through his mind: sitting in the Tuileries Gardens, or in the Bois, watching little Hugo at play under the light-filtering leaves; riding with Olivia, cantering up the grassy avenues of Rambouillet. It was wonderful how memories assuaged solitude, as if they could people the brain.

A tap on the door brought him to the present. The room was now filling with daylight.

'You wanted to see me, monsieur?'

Danielle was standing just inside the door, her hands folded in the lap of her starched apron.

'Ah yes, Danielle,' Victor replied. He pulled himself up in the chair. 'You appear to have discovered something known only to Monsieur Severin, Monsieur Alain, and myself.'

She looked as if she could not decide on the expression she should wear on her face.

'Yes, monsieur?'

Poor child, he should have seen to it, of course, that she obtained a good position in another household the moment that his brief affair with her – if it had merited the description 'affair' – was over. At the time, however, such an action would have seemed to him moral cowardice. She had always been an excellent servant as well as a very decorative one.

He stood up. 'Come with me,' he said.

He took her across to the study. He pointed to the mess. 'Thieves,' he told her. He went to the open safe. 'And they knew what they were looking for.'

Danielle fingered the stiff, detachable white cuffs which protected her sleeves.

'They also knew where to look,' he added.

'Monsieur?' she asked.

Her show of defiance was paper thin.

'I've sent for the police, Danielle,' he told her.

'It's nothing to do with me, monsieur,' she said, with a pretence of bewilderment.

'But you had found out where the Tondeau was kept, hadn't you, Danielle?' He spoke very gently.

'Yes, monsieur,' she admitted.

She was gripping one of her starched cuffs so tightly, she must surely have tugged it off.

'If monsieur has no further need of me,' she said, 'I have some work to do for Mademoiselle Armitage.'

366

'Miss Armitage has left Paris,' Victor told her. 'With Hugo.'

'But, monsieur, her clothes are still in the laundry-room.'

'They had to leave very suddenly,' he replied, absently. He was not to be diverted. 'I had to call the police, Danielle. I'm afraid the people who broke in may have done something to Monsieur Alain.'

She stood amidst the litter on the floor, unable to think of anything to say or what attitude to adopt.

'Monsieur?' she whispered.

'What is it, Danielle?' he asked.

He raised her chin to look into her face. She was crying.

'Whatever you may have done, Danielle,' he told her, 'you've nothing to fear from me.'

'I hate myself, monsieur,' she whispered.

'Why?' he asked.

He was afraid of the answer. She blinked against her tears.

'I've stolen from you, monsieur,' she said.

He smiled at her.

'But you didn't try to steal the Tondeau,' he replied.

He could see into her unhappiness – the months of jealousy he had imposed on her. The realisation of his own responsibility opened before him like a chasm.

'I didn't realise they were going to try to steal it, monsieur,' she sobbed.

He put his arm round her shoulder to comfort her.

'Let's go somewhere more comfortable, eh?' he suggested.

He took her back to the lounge, and closed the door.

'Let's sit down together for a minute or two,' he said.

He took out his cigarettes and offered her one. She shook her head.

'Tell me about it,' he said.

She buried her hand under her apron. From the pocket of her blue cotton frock, she took out a crumpled white visiting card. Victor took it from her, glanced at it, and put it into his waistcoat pocket.

'Tell me about this Monsieur Papayannis,' he asked.

36

Vivian drove through Chartres as the sun rose. He had visited Chartres on several occasions, but he had never seen it as he did then. As he approached from the south-west, the tall cathedral reared up out of the fields alone in its glory. To Vivian, wearied by the events of the previous day and a difficult night drive, it appeared like a vast stone angel with pinnacled wings, standing in the circle of the rising sun like the Angel of the Book of Revelations. It was a sight which he neither forgot nor was able to recapture.

Once through Chartres, everything seemed to him to have returned to normal, as if he had passed through the curtain of a dream. The refugees were all gone. There was no trace of military activity. As he drove through the small towns and villages towards Paris and the Porte d'Orléans, it was as though the war was over. Farmers' wives in bonnets, with wooden floats in their arms, were busying themselves in the farmyards amid the morning squawk and flutter of poultry. A man with a walnut-wrinkled face under his flat cap and old-fashioned sabots on his feet, was driving the cattle off the road into a meadow. Under the orchard trees, brilliant in the slanting sunlight, two girls in cotton dresses, their hair tied back in dusters, were giggling to one another as they hung white linen on lines stretched from branch to branch.

The early morning sunlight proved deceptive. By the time Vivian entered the Paris suburbs, the sky was clouded over, and a thin drizzle had set in. The city's Left Bank was so quiet that it seemed to have been deserted by its inhabitants. Once across the Seine, however, he found the shops opened, the striped awnings pulled out over the windows, and the white-aproned waiters unstacking the chairs at the café tables. There was no sign of any military uniforms but the uniformed police had reappeared on the pavements. He circled the almost empty Étoile and turned into the Avenue de Wagram. He turned left under the archway gate leading into the Square de Brey. He stopped at the concierge's office. The concierge's wife who had been watching from the office window, came out onto the pavement.

'Bonjour, madame,' said Vivian through the open window of the car. 'Is this the residence of the Baron de Bart-Mendel?'

'It is, monsieur,' the woman replied.

'Can you tell me, madame, if I am likely to find Monsieur le Baron at home this morning?' he asked.

'As far as I know, monsieur,' the woman answered. She glowered into the car. 'Are you in a fit condition to drive, monsieur?' she demanded.

At first, he thought she was asking whether he was drunk, and assumed that his own fatigue must have been more obvious than he had supposed.

'Your arm, monsieur,' said the woman.

'I have never driven into anybody yet, madame,' he said.

'It isn't a joking matter, monsieur,' she told him severely. 'The servants' children often play in the square.'

'I shall take care, madame,' Vivian promised.

He drove on, circled the centre garden, and stopped at the foot of the steps leading to the main entrance. The bell was answered by the butler. Vivian asked to see the Baron. He took off his cap as he entered, and put it under his stump.

'I remember you,' he said. 'Severin, isn't it? You were just about to leave the Château de la Berlière when I arrived that Sunday morning.'

Severin bowed slightly.

'I have not forgotten you, Monsieur le Commandant,' he replied.

'And I remember you, as well,' said the Baron de Bart-Mendel. He had appeared at the door of the dining-room, his napkin in his hand. He glanced down at it.

'I'm just having my breakfast, Major Hardwicke,' he said. 'You must join me.'

He shook Vivian's hand.

'I should be very glad of some breakfast,' Vivian replied. 'I haven't eaten since I left Tours in the early evening, yesterday.'

'Then you shall have an English breakfast,' announced de Bart-Mendel. 'Severin, will you ask Maryvonne to make an omelette for the Major?'

'You are very kind, Baron,' Vivian said.

De Bart-Mendel showed him into the dining-room.

'I must admit,' he said, 'that if somebody had told me that there would be a uniformed officer standing on my doorstep this morning, I should have expected a German rather than an Englishman. For your own sake, I shall not press hospitality on you.'

He offered Vivian a chair at the table.

'I presume, since you've come from Tours,' he continued, 'that you are still on de Gaulle's staff.'

Vivian sat down.

'Actually, I did speak to General de Gaulle yesterday,' he replied, 'but I am now on the staff of our own General Spears.'

De Bart-Mendel poured him a bowl of coffee.

'What does the Long Asparagus think of the present situation?' he asked.

'He hasn't told me in so many words,' replied Vivian. 'But I can tell you this – he intends to continue the struggle, whatever the government of the Third Republic may decide to do when it reaches Bordeaux.'

'And where will he continue the struggle, Major Hardwicke?' There was a distinct note of amusement in his voice.

'There's talk of a Breton redoubt,' said Vivian seriously, 'or of a final stand in the Pyrenees. Or of continuing the war from North Africa.'

'Or from Great Britain?' asked de Bart-Mendel.

'Let's hope it won't come to that,' Vivian said.

De Bart-Mendel sat back in his chair.

369

'It will, Major,' he said. 'You know that as well as I. There's no will left among our leaders. And when Charles de Gaulle has left his ministerial post, what is he? A mere General of Brigade. Who would follow him?'

'General de Gaulle has told me himself,' said Vivian, 'that he wishes you would join him.'

De Bart-Mendel laughed.

'And Georges Mandel, I suppose,' he said. 'A junior general and two Jews? In a France riddled with anti-Semitism, what a gift for Dr Goebbels, eh? No, I don't think even Charles de Gaulle would be as crazy as that.'

He dabbed his mouth with his napkin.

'The moment I saw you, Major Hardwicke,' he said, 'I knew why you had come.'

Vivian looked at him steadily.

'It is precisely because de Gaulle is only a General of Brigade, Baron . . . ' he said.

' . . . he needs the St Louis Tondeau,' said de Bart-Mendel.

'Yes,' Vivian agreed.

De Bart-Mendel thought for a moment.

'It isn't here,' he said. 'I have sent it out of Paris.'

'May I know where it is?' Vivian asked.

'I don't know myself,' de Bart-Mendel replied. 'I suspect it is on its way to your country, Major. For the past few weeks, an English lady has been staying here. During the night, I put my son Hugo – you remember Hugo? . . . '

Vivian nodded.

' . . . into her charge, to take to England. They left here by car. She is also carrying the Tondeau.'

'May I know the lady's name, Baron?' Vivian asked.

'No, Major. I'm sorry. The lady has my instructions in this matter. I would prefer to see which way Charles de Gaulle jumps before I surrender the Tondeau into his care. There are too many people who are after it. This house was broken into only last night by people who were searching for it. I do not mean to sound offensive – please understand that – but the fewer people who know of its whereabouts, the better.'

Vivian nodded.

'I understand perfectly, Baron,' he said.

He remembered an Alfred Hitchcock thriller he had seen shortly before he had left London for France. In it, there had been a retired governess, played by Dame May Whitty, who had been carrying a secret message from her erstwhile employees in central Europe to the headquarters of the British secret service in Whitehall. Was this lady something like her?

'Baron,' he said. 'I'm sure that General de Gaulle's concern for you

370

– his wish that I should bring you out of Paris – was wholly genuine. There are people who are worried about your safety if you remain here.'

'I know,' de Bart-Mendel replied, 'but I can't leave. I was told last night that the *Grand Rabbin* has left Paris. Those of my race who have the right contacts, or who are wealthy enough, have all gone. Somebody must stay for the sake of the rest. Does that sound mock-heroic to your English ears, Major?'

Vivian shook his head.

'Ah, now I remember,' said de Bart-Mendel. 'When my son drew attention to your decoration – the Military Cross? – and I rebuked him for embarrassing you, you replied that one likes to have one's virtues recognised.' He laughed. 'It's good to see you again, Major Hardwicke. And now you must eat your breakfast.'

At which moment, Severin entered carrying a small tray with a silver-covered dish.

Vivian left de Bart-Mendel and set off out of Paris as soon as he had finished breakfast. He took the quickest way through the suburbs, recommended by the Baron: by the Porte Maillot and through the Bois de Boulogne. He had just passed through the Bois when he noticed a small roadside café. Immediately in front of it a British 15 cwt. lorry had been parked against the kerb. On its freshly painted tailboard it carried the distinguishing mark of the 2nd BEF, and the insignia of the Royal Military Police. Under the awning of the café, and very much at their ease, were a sergeant and two lance-corporals.

Vivian parked his car, and got out. The military policemen had just finished a cooked meal which they had washed down with a litre of red wine. As soon as they saw Vivian approaching, they grabbed their peaked caps, and scrambled to attention.

'Sar'nt,' said Vivian, who could scarcely believe his eyes, 'what in God's name are you doing here?'

They looked smart enough: their buttons shone; their web belts and anklets were blancoed a spotless white.

'Sir,' snapped the sergeant, gazing unblinkingly over the top of Vivian's head, 'we was ordered to patrol the Pontoise–Germain-en-Laye road, if I pronounces it properly, sir. We was to intercept a convoy of a dozen – twelve – REME tank-recovery vehicles heading in a southerly direction, and to re-route them back to Cherbourg . . . Sir! We thought as we might permit ourselves the – er – luxury of a square meal, long as we kept our eyes skinned for the road-junction down there, sir.'

'At ease, sar'nt,' Vivian told him. 'At ease, lads. I don't know where you've come from. . . . '

'Lisieux, sir,' the sergeant replied less formally. 'Couple of days ago.'

'Do you know where the Germans are?' asked Vivian.

'No, sir,' the sergeant replied.

'Well, neither do I. But I know this: they'll be well on their way to Lisieux by this time, if they haven't actually taken it. As for your REME convoy – if anything comes down that road, it'll be Jerry's, not ours. And if we don't get out of here pdq, we'll either be dead or heading for a POW cage. So pay your whack, and let's get out of here.'

As the sergeant went into the café to pay the bill, Vivian asked the two lance-corporals when they had arrived in France.

'Two weeks ago, sir,' one of them replied. 'At Cherbourg, with the 2nd BEF.'

'It's our second tour in France, sir,' the other added. 'We was taken off at Malo-les-Bains, near Dunkirk, wasn't we, Rosie?'

'That's right,' said the first lance-corporal. 'Me, and Corporal Clarke, and Sergeant Micklewhite, sir. We was some of the first off the beach. A week in Blighty, and then we was off to Cherbourg.'

They looked incredibly young and fresh-faced.

'Were you given any contingency orders?' asked Vivian. 'I mean, when you were sent here to wait for the convoy.'

'No, sir,' said Lance-Corporal Rose, 'we was just told to wait for the REME vehicles, as far as I know.'

The sergeant came out of the café.

'Sergeant Micklewhite?' asked Vivian.

'Sir?'

'I think it would be best if you were to place yourselves under my command, for the time being,' Vivian told him. 'I am Major Hardwicke – Tank Regiment – and aide to General Sir Edward Spears, Mr Churchill's special envoy with the French Government. I am returning to London, and since you will be reporting back to Cherbourg, I take it, it would be best if we travelled together.'

'Yes, sir,' Sergeant Micklewhite agreed. He was clearly delighted that a superior officer had arrived to take over responsibility.

'How are we off for petrol?' asked Vivian.

'Tank's almost full sir, and ten five-gallon jerrycans in the back locker.'

'We found an abandoned fuel dump, sir,' said Lance-Corporal Rose. 'Frog, sir.'

'I just hope we don't get hit, eh, sar'nt?' said Vivian.

'That's right, sir,' Sergeant Micklewhite replied judiciously.

'I'll ride with you,' Vivian told him. 'Corporal Clarke, is it? – immobilise my car, will you.'

'You heard the major, Clarke,' snapped Sergeant Micklewhite. 'Get to it, lad!'

He was looking almost cheerful.

Vivian climbed into the cabin of the small lorry, beside the sergeant.

'What have we by way of armament, sar'nt?' he asked.

'Our service-revolvers, sir. One rifle, SMLE. Thirty rounds each, .45. Thirty rounds .303. Tried indenting for a bren, at Lisieux. Q.M.S. weren't having none of it, though.'

Vivian looked into the back of the truck. It was filled with conical red-and-white striped road-markers, and red warning-lamps.

'In case the REME convoy had to stop on the road, sir,' Sergeant Micklewhite explained.

'Good,' said Vivian. 'If we think Jerry's coming, we'll be able to stop him by putting down a few markers and warning-lamps, won't we?'

'That's the ticket, sir,' agreed Sergeant Micklewhite.

His face wore the expression of philosophical seriousness adopted by all senior NCO's on hearing yet another idiotic suggestion by a commissioned officer.

37

Cybele stood staring down at Alain who lay slumped unconscious on the chair by the window. All sentiment was numbed – disgust, pity, or any fear of the consequence either in this world or the next. Very soon her reason would become equally paralysed; even pain would cease. But she would be herself still, locked inside herself, aware of the paralysis, aware of the nothingness.

She had been seven years old when Sister Marie-Philomène had instructed her in her Good Friday exercise. She was to walk in the garden until it was time for chapel, and the veneration of the Holy Cross. While she was walking, she was to meditate on God's punishment of sin. Consider, Sister Marie-Philomène had told her, what it would be like if no one was kind or loving to you – not your *Maman* or *Papa*, or your friends, or anybody at all, for ever and ever, amen. Think what it would be like if nobody, nobody at all, would talk to you, or look after you, or give you anything, or accept anything from you, or even hurt you. At the time, Cybele had told herself that in fact it might be rather nice: there would never be penalties, or tellings-off, or disappointments like people saying they were going to give you a treat and then forgetting about it. But even then she had known that she was lying to herself. To live alone, isolated in nothingness, was the most terrible punishment of all. And, as she looked down at Alain, she knew that it had started.

She looked up at the others.

'Let's go to the sea-side,' implored dumpy little Marie-Claire. She glanced at Florence. She was afraid of Florence, as well as loving her. Cybele envied her.

'Bébé hasn't seen the sea, ever,' said Marie-Claire. 'Let's take her to the sea-side.'

Manuela lay sprawling across the top of the ormolu-decorated table. She had her flick-knife in her hand. She had scored a deep channel into the lacquered surface of the table, and was sweeping the wood-dust to the floor with the back of her hand.

'What's the point?' she asked. 'How do you know where they're going?'

'They're going to England,' said Papayannis.

His white melon face was sweating with anxiety.

'They will have to go to Arromanches or St Malo,' he said. 'They will try to reach the Channel Islands.'

Manuela reached out from the table with her foot. She pushed Alain's head with her toes.

'This lump of his mother's self-abuse said Bordeaux, perhaps,' she remarked.

'Bordeaux is at the sea-side,' said Florence.

She put her arm round Marie-Claire.

'I tell you, they won't go to Bordeaux,' said Papayannis.

His voice was rising to a falsetto. Cybele wanted to laugh. It would be far more amusing to break his arms than it had been breaking Alain's. He really would squeal for mercy. The amusement would be like a reassuring tickle through the numbness.

'The Germans will be between them and Bordeaux. They must go somewhere between Arromanches and Dinard,' he continued.

'Supposing the Germans stop us?' asked Pauline.

'I am a neutral,' said Papayannis, 'they will let us through. And you will be paid, as I said, in gold.'

'If we stay here,' said Ines, 'we can pick up whatever we want. We can take all the gold in the world without even the bother of shitting for it.'

Papayannis giggled suddenly. The girls gaped at him.

'You heard what this poor fellow said,' he told them. 'You're not going to get away with it. That's what he said. And the Baron saw two of you, didn't he? Have you heard any guns? Have you seen any soldiers?'

He looked at them, at their stupid, menacing incomprehension. Even El Chamoun and Rahman weren't as stupid as these wretched, vicious children.

'The city has been surrendered, that's why,' he told them. 'The

French army has gone. The police are remaining at their posts until the German army moves in. Even now, the gentlemen of the *Sûreté* will be at the Square de Brey, examining your fingerprints. They will check with the Police des Moeurs, and your identities will be known. There's going to be no golden age, *mes enfants*, for the likes of you. Not in Paris.'

'I'm sick of Paris,' Florence said, her arm still round Marie-Claire. 'And this place stinks of shit.'

'You're the biggest shit,' Ines told her. 'You'll take the stink with you.'

'I'm offering you gold whether we succeed or not,' said Papayannis.

He pulled out his cologne-scented handkerchief and wiped the palms of his hands.

'We'll go to the sea,' said Cybele. She turned to Pauline. 'We'll piss on these others.'

'I'll go and get Bébé ready,' said Marie-Claire.

She left Florence's side and went off to the bedroom.

Ines sat on the table. She cradled Manuela's head in her lap. 'We'll stay,' she said.

She held the crucifix which hung about her neck, between her fingers.

'That one has the evil eye,' she said, pointing it at Papayannis.

Papayannis merely smiled.

'What if the *flics* come here?' asked Pauline.

Ines shrugged.

'They'll come for us if it's time for them to come for us.'

'What about you?' Pauline asked fat Severine.

'We'll stay,' Severine replied. 'Not here. Not with that heap of shit.' She pointed to Alain's unconscious body. 'We'll go back to the old place. It was nice there. French or Boche – it doesn't make any difference to Ginette's puss.'

Ginette sniggered.

Pauline slipped her arm into Cybele's.

'Do you love me?' Cybele whispered.

'What do you think?' asked Pauline. 'Why do you think I put up with you, eh?'

For how long, Cybele wondered; for how long could Pauline put up with her whining, her drinking, her bouts of savage temper?

'Perhaps the sea will blow so fresh, it'll blow right through my head,' she said. 'They say sea air makes you sleepy.'

'We must go,' said Papayannis, 'before the Englishwoman gets too far ahead of us – and before the police come here.'

Manuela, Ines, Severine, and Ginette watched as Marie-Claire came from the bedroom hugging her doll to her, and joined the others following Papayannis down the stairs.

The two cars were parked a few yards up the street from the entrance into the Rue des Francs Bourgeois. The girls were about to get into the second car, when El Chamoun, who was to be their driver, tried to take the doll from Marie-Claire. Marie-Claire hugged it to her, and shook her head wildly.

'There's no room,' El Chamoun grunted.

He tried to tear the doll from her by one of its arms. Papayannis came over. He took the damp cigar stub from his mouth.

'We'll buy the little girl another doll when we've finished our business,' he said unctuously.

'Let her keep it!'

Cybele's voice rang out with its old authority. El Chamoun looked across at Papayannis. Papayannis nodded. El Chamoun returned to his driving seat. He was muttering to himself. Papayannis pushed his bulk into the Buick sedan, and collapsed into the leather seat at the back. He settled himself among the cushions. He glanced at Rahman's back, the black stubble on the pock-marked neck. Once he had obtained the Tondeau, he would take it straight to German Special Intelligence. Once under German protection, he would rid himself of Idris Rahman and El Chamoun, and no longer need fear Aris Liassides. The prospect of complete independence and prosperity spread without limit before him.

Up in the apartment, Manuela was watching the street through the rain-smeared window. There were tears in her eyes. She drove the point of her knife into the sill again and again.

'That Greek shit,' she said, 'has spoilt everything – everything.'

38

Victor, with two of his business colleagues, stood in the garden, in the centre of the lawn. All three had raincoats draped over their shoulders against the steady drizzle. They were watching Joseph who, disregarding the weather, was in his shirt-sleeves, digging out a neat rectangle from the well-rolled grassy turf. One of the businessmen bent down to help him as he lifted out a heavy box wrapped in oilskin, and placed it on the grass beside the small trench. As he filled the trench once again, and replaced the turf, Victor unwrapped the oilskin and opened the box. He took one of the ingots from it, and passed it to one of his companions.

'Joseph and I buried them four years ago last April,' he said, 'when the victory of the *Front Populaire* seemed inevitable.'

His companion weighed the ingot in his hand.

'I imagine most heads of the "Two Hundred Families" were doing the same,' he said.

He replaced the ingot in the box. Joseph closed it, and wrapped the oilskin round it.

'My friends,' said Victor, 'what I wish you to do for me, is to wait until the franc stabilises under the German occupation; then realise the value of this gold, and see that the money is divided up among my servants according to the percentages laid down in the letter I gave you.'

'So you have decided to leave at last, Victor?' asked one of the men.

Victor nodded.

'Please God it isn't too late,' the man said.

He hitched his raincoat up onto his shoulders.

'It will comprise a very generous sum,' said the second man.

'There will be little chance of my returning home, whether I succeed in getting away or not,' said Victor. 'I should like to be sure that those who have looked after me so well should be free of financial worry.'

'Taking into account the sums you've placed at the disposal of the *Cour de Consistoire*,' said the first man, 'are you sure you have sufficient left for yourself and your son?'

'There are securities in London and New York,' Victor replied.

Severin came through the french windows of the dining-room, and hurried across the lawn.

'*Monsieur le Préfet de Police* is on the telephone, monsieur,' he announced. 'He says it is a matter of urgency.'

Victor nodded to his colleagues.

'Thank you, Severin,' he said. 'Will you help Joseph take this box out to Monsieur Speranski's car?'

He returned to the house, and took the call in the study.

'Listen, *cher ami*,' Langeron spoke to him. 'The *Grand Rabbin* has been caught by the Germans. They've cut the Orléans road. They've sent him back to Paris to await their instructions. For God's sake, get out while you can.'

'Will you do me a favour, Roger?' asked Victor.

'If I can,' Langeron replied.

'It's simply this,' Victor told him. 'I would like the German authorities, when they arrive, to believe that the *Tondeau de Chartres* has been stolen by Paris criminals. It will give my carrier a better chance of getting it away.'

'Very well, Victor,' said Langeron. 'But get yourself away, as quickly as you can. Take the Rambouillet road.'

'Rest easy,' said Victor. 'I shall not wait for the Germans.'

'Good,' Langeron replied. 'That is good news. *Bonne chance, cher ami.*'

377

Victor hung up the phone, and returned to the garden. Joseph and Severin had carried the gold out to the car waiting in the street outside. Victor said goodbye to his colleagues and stood and watched as they drove away. Then he went back to the house. Its emptiness was all about him. Loneliness had never been very far away from him since Olivia had died; but there had always been the intimation of loneliness rather than the reality of its pain, Hugo had seen to that. He had known that he should not depend on Hugo's companionship too far, but the day when Hugo might seek his independence had seemed so very far off.

He went upstairs. The room which Julie had occupied had reverted to the clean, well-aired anonymity of a spare guest-room. He went out onto the balcony. Olivia had never really liked the Hôtel de Brey, much preferring the character and antiquity of La Berlière. Olivia had been all in all to him. She had transformed him utterly. She had taught him not only to listen to others, but to appreciate the richness in what he heard. She had taught him how to be still, to the extent that he truly believed that he had never really heard music until he had known her. She had opened his eyes, had taught him to see what was in front of him. He had wondered what it was that he ever gave her in return for the richness of her gifts to him.

Now he stood at the edge of the void; before him, a vision of purposeless suffering.

He went along the corridor to Hugo's room. It too was clean, dead and silent. Perhaps it would never again be a child's room. Toys and books lay still. Behind the white curtain, the rain had speckled the windows with motionless drops. He sat on the bed, knowing that he was torturing himself.

Danielle came to the door. She had on a blue apron over the white; it was damp in patches, and stained with polish. She was clutching a large rag and a tin of polish.

'I'm sorry, monsieur,' she said. 'I didn't realise.'

The events of the morning, and her confession, had robbed her of any chance of regaining her composure.

'Danielle?' he asked.

He reached out for her hand. She hesitated. Then wiped her palm quickly against her apron, and gave it to him. He had forgotten how rough her hand was.

'Will you indulge me, Danielle?' he asked.

'What, monsieur?' she asked, not understanding him.

He tried to smile.

'I'd like to walk out just once more with a pretty girl,' he told her, 'before the Germans come. Will you be very kind to me? Will you go up to your room and change, and come out for a walk with me?'

'Walk where, monsieur?' she asked, utterly confused.

'The Tuileries Gardens? The Bois?' he suggested.

378

'But it's raining, monsieur,' she replied.

He nodded, and released her hand.

'You're right,' he told her.

She tried to smile back at him through her confusion.

'May I go on with my work, monsieur?' she asked.

'Yes. Yes, of course,' he replied.

39

Julie and Hugo had driven about half way to Dreux. On her left, through the rain-smeared window, she could see the edges of Rambouillet Forest across the broad, rolling meadow. In fact, the drizzle had stopped as they had passed through Montfort. In front of them the countryside glistened in fresh sunlight.

Julie had let Hugo cry. After a time she asked him how he felt.

'Have you ever been sent away from home before?' she asked.

'Oh, yes,' he replied. 'I've been to the sea-side, with Joseph.'

'With Joseph?' Julie asked. 'Where did you go?'

'To Lion-sur-Mer. Joseph's sister lives in Lion-sur-Mer,' said Hugo. 'I've often been to stay with her. Well – about three times.'

'I'm terribly ignorant,' said Julie, keeping her eyes on the road ahead. 'I don't know where Lion-sur-Mer is.'

'It's not very big,' Hugo assured her. 'It's in Normandy, near Caen. Joseph's sister's husband keeps a shop there, for fishermen.'

Julie heard a heavy droning noise above the noise of the car's engine. It was growing louder, and creeping over their heads. She slowed down and peered upwards through the rain-drops which still clung to the windscreen. Like an immense shadow, a dark-grey, high-winged monoplane was flying over them, following the direction they were taking. It was so low that Julie could hear the individual strokes of the aero-engine pounding in her ears. As it drew away ahead of them, she saw with vivid clarity the black and white outlines of the Balkan Cross painted on the side of the narrow fusilage, the detail of the wing-struts, and the shape of the door-handle behind the small perspex windows of the cabin.

'It's only a spotter-plane,' said Hugo, all tears forgotten. 'It's a Fiesler Storch. It's unarmed.'

'You ought to meet my friend Elaine,' said Julie grimly. 'You'd get on well with her.'

'Who's Elaine?' asked Hugo.

'An actress, like me,' said Julie, 'but she knows all the aero-planes.'

She felt slightly sick. The droning continued, fading, then coming closer, then fading again. A narrow lane led off the main road. A short way down it was an avenue of thickly leafed oak trees. Julie turned into it, and sped for the shelter of the trees. She pulled up.

'They're probably enjoying themselves up there,' said Hugo. 'You know – scaring people. That's what the Boches are like, aren't they?'

'They're getting good at it,' said Julie. 'They've scared me.'

The noise of the aero-engine faded into the distance. When it stopped Julie started the car once more.

'I think we'll stick to the lane for a bit,' she said. 'It might be safer.'

The lane seemed to follow the same general direction as the road to Dreux. They drove on in the morning sunshine, meeting nobody for several miles. They had been driving for about twenty minutes when they came to a farm alongside the road. Three military lorries were parked up on the grass verge opposite the farm, leaving just enough room for Julie's small Renault to pass. A group of soldiers had dismounted from the lorries. Several were sitting smoking, their legs stretched out on the grass. One or two were sitting, their legs dangling, on the farm-yard wall by the gate. Two soldiers were in the farm-yard, laughing and flirting with two girls in flowered pinafores and mudstained rubber boots, while a third was crouched down pretending to make friends with a sheepdog. All the men had their sleeves rolled up, and were bareheaded. Their blond hair was cropped, and their faces and forearms were as tanned as holiday-makers'. An army motorcyclist was sitting astride his machine, talking up to the driver of the third of the lorries in his cabin. He looked up the lane, then, grinning at Julie, waved her on. Julie raised her hand as she passed, to thank him. As she drove on up the lane, between the hedgerows, Hugo asked in a tight little voice,

'Julie?'

'Yes?'

'You did know they were Germans, didn't you, Julie?'

Julie was shocked. The cheerful, young, tanned faces had seemed so normal and friendly – nothing like the goose-stepping, helmeted robots in the newsreels. But there had been the grey uniforms and the heavy, dusty jackboots. She shivered.

When they had travelled for several miles without meeting anybody save one fat, elderly village priest on his ancient bicycle, Julie began to feel calmer. The woodland closed in on either side of the road protectively. They came to the main road; a large sign on the opposite verge read, 'Dreux $7\frac{1}{2}$ kms'. Julie turned onto it. Immediately ahead was a lorry which had been drawn across the road to form a barrier. Two grey-uniformed soldiers wearing helmets, their rifles slung on their backs, advanced to meet her. They were holding up batons with red and white discs. Their eyes peered grimly from under the dusty lips of their helmets. Julie slowed down and stopped. An officer wearing a peaked cap got out of a small grey car parked against the hedge. He marched smartly across to her; she could feel her heart beating against her ribs. The two soldiers who had approached from the lorry were standing against the bonnet of the Renault, staring at her through the windscreen. The officer bent down to look through the window.

'*Où allez-vous, mademoiselle?*' he asked slowly, carefully choosing his words as if in a schoolroom.

Julie could feel Hugo's hand in her back, gripping her seat. She looked straight into the officer's face. He seemed very young.

'Argentan, monsieur,' she replied. '*Je suis une americaine. Vous parlez anglais, monsieur?*'

The officer shook his head.

'*Eh bien, alors!*' she continued, managing a smile. '*Je conduis de Paris mon petit cousin chez sa tante. Sa tante qui demeure en Argentan.*'

She took a deep breath. What idiocy had possessed her to lie like that, she wondered? Now he would ask to see their passports.

'*Ce n'est pas possible, mademoiselle,*' the young officer replied. Her heart sank. This was it.

'*Vous devez retourner à Paris, mademoiselle,*' said the officer in his painfully slow French. He smiled at her. '*Votre ambassadeur, Monsieur William Bullitt, reste en Paris encore,*' he told her, as if that would be sufficient reassurance. '*Et vous et votre petit cousin serez sans danger en Paris comme Monsieur Bullitt. Ici, c'est la guerre, vous comprenez, mademoiselle.*'

Julie turned the car round. The young officer bowed slightly and saluted as she drove off. She felt a hysterical desire to laugh as the realisation came to her that he had not been stationed there to catch fugitives, but to prevent ordinary travellers from driving into an active military area.

About half an hour later, as they were approaching once again the outskirts of Montfort, they slowed down at a crossroads. A sign-post pointing south, indicated the road to Rambouillet. Julie wondered whether to take it, and to head west once again from there. She was pulling out the Michelin road guide from the door pocket beside her, when she saw coming up the road in front of her, the distinctive shape of a small British Army 15 cwt. lorry. It slowed down at the crossroads, then came on. As it passed, she leant out of her window, and shouted across to the British officer sitting beside the sergeant driver in the cabin. The lorry drove on. She saw two British tommies sitting behind the tailboard. She scrambled out of the car, and shouted after them, waving frantically. The lorry slowed down and stopped some fifty yards up the road. Hugo got out of the car. The sergeant scrambled down from his driving-seat into the ditch. A second or two later, the officer jumped down onto the road, and the two tommies clambered out over the tailboard. As the sergeant came marching towards Julie, the other three dusted down their trousers and stretched their legs.

Hugo ran forward to meet the sergeant.

'Germans!' he said in English. 'Germans – many!' He pointed up the road. As the sergeant reached him, he added excitedly, *'Il y avait un* Fiesler Storch!'

The sergeant smiled, not understanding a word.

'There are Germans straight ahead,' Julie explained. 'Only a mile or two ahead. You'll drive straight into one of their road blocks. We've just been turned back to Paris by one of them.'

The sergeant shouted back up the road.

'Lady says as there's a Jerry road block ahead, sir.'

As the officer came running down the road, the sergeant added to Julie, 'You're English, ain't you, miss?'

Julie didn't answer. She had seen the British officer's empty sleeve.

'My God,' she said, 'it can't be!'

Vivian stopped in his tracks.

'I don't believe it,' he said.

'Hello, Vivian,' said Julie.

'Julie,' said Vivian.

The sergeant cleared his throat.

'And I remember this young man as well,' said Vivian, in French. 'Hugo de Bart-Mendel, isn't it?'

Hugo offered his hand.

'We met at La Berlière, Monsieur le Commandant,' he said gravely.

'So you're the elderly governess who is taking the Baron de Bart-Mendel's son to England,' Vivian told Julie. 'I've just left the Baron,' he explained. 'In fact, I always meet you when I've just left the Baron de Bart-Mendel.'

Julie laughed nervously.

'It's a small world,' the sergeant remarked. 'If you'll excuse me. What with Jerry just round the corner.'

'Quite right, sar'nt,' said Vivian. 'I take it that you and the boy are making for the coast,' he added to Julie. 'Will you join us? We're trying to head back for the Cherbourg peninsular, and the 2nd BEF. Safety in numbers – that sort of thing.'

He was embarrassed, Julie noticed.

'Yes, please,' she said.

'We'll go south a few miles, and then turn west,' he said. 'Maybe we'll manage to outflank Jerry's advance. Sar'nt, call one of the lads to fetch their things from the car, and have them slung into one of the lockers.'

He walked back up the road to the lorry with Julie.

'You are glad to see me, I hope?' he asked.

'What do you think?' she replied.

She glanced across to Sergeant Micklewhite.

'It's just . . . *tu me bouleverse*,' she said.

Vivian helped her up into the back of the lorry. Then he lifted Hugo in his one arm. He was showing off. He glanced back to where Lance-Corporal Clarke was bringing the suitcases. He wondered in which of them was the Tondeau. Not that it mattered to him that much; he was too happy to care.

40

There was just sufficient room in the back of the lorry for Julie and Hugo to sit comfortably with the two lance-corporals. Vivian had ordered that the road-markers and warning lamps should be taken out and left at the roadside.

'I've signed for them, sir,' Sergeant Micklewhite had protested gloomily. 'In triplicate.'

They had thrown them into the grass, in a sad heap, nonetheless.

The two lance-corporals, who had eyed Julie's figure with undisguised interest when they had been standing out in the road, had, as so often happens, become tongue-tied as soon as they found themselves sitting within groping distance of her. Finally, she took pity on them, and introduced herself. There was an immediate release of tension.

'I'm Rose, miss,' the first told her. 'Sid's the name. Sid Rose.'

He had the perky, comedian look she recognised from the road-manager in the concert party.

'An' this one here's Clarke, miss,' he continued, digging his companion with his elbow. 'Nobby Clarke. All Clarkes is Nobby, miss.'

Vivian glanced back from the front seat, then looked ahead at the road again.

'Where's you from, miss?' asked Lance-Corporal Rose, who had completely regained his social confidence.

'The Lake District,' Julie told him. 'But I live in London.'

'We're Londoners, miss,' said Lance-Corporal Rose. 'Well, I am, at any rate. Nobby here's from Wapping – foreign parts, know what I mean?'

'Why don't you shut up, Rosie?' asked Lance-Corporal Clarke.

'Language, Nobby,' said Lance-Corporal Rose. 'In front of ladies and kids.'

'Well, miss,' Lance-Corporal Clarke said to Julie, 'he don't half go on about Wapping. Gets boring when you hears the same bleeding thing day after day, don't it?'

'Where do you come from, Rosie?' asked Julie.

'Bethnal Green, miss,' said Lance-Corporal Rose.

'Yer! The posh part,' Lance-Corporal Clarke added quickly.

'There ain't no posh part of Bethnal Green, stupid,' said Lance-Corporal Rose.

'That's what I mean, don't I?' replied Lance-Corporal Clarke.

The score being equal, they lapsed into silence.

They travelled south-west, through the western edge of Rambouillet Forest, and on past Nogent-de-Roi. From Nogent, they followed the narrow country roads through the thickly wooded and hedged countryside of southern Normandy for mile after mile. Lance-Corporal Rose surveyed the pastoral scene glumly.

'All them fields,' he commented. 'Gives you the flamin' creeps.'

At least, thought Julie, it was all peaceful, with no hint of war.

They stopped in the market square of Châteauneuf-en-Thymerais. Around them, the high white gables rose above the trees.

'Miss Armitage and I will do some shopping,' Vivian announced. 'We'll buy some lunch, and something to take with us for the rest of the journey.'

He got out, and helped her down.

'Bring us some fags, will you, sir?' asked Lance-Corporal Rose.

He pulled some crumpled ten franc notes from the breast pocket of his battle-dress tunic.

'You can pay me back,' Vivian told him.

He noticed Julie's anxious glance at the locker where the suitcases had been stowed.

'Don't worry,' he told her. 'They'll look after your things. They're military policemen.'

They crossed the square to the shops on the far side, with Hugo walking between them.

'So you've been staying in Paris since our last encounter?' Vivian asked.

'Actually, yes,' Julie replied. 'Sort of holiday, I suppose you could call it. Did I tell you, I'd never been to Paris?' Her voice was just a shade too bright.

'Left your visit a bit late, didn't you?' he asked.

She laughed. 'How about you?' she asked.

'I've been in Paris. With our Embassy. I moved out to Tours with them. I just went back for what I suppose you might call a flying visit.'

384

'You left that a bit late too,' Julie suggested.

They were speaking in English. Hugo, not understanding, was staring about him.

'I met my friend here, when I was going to Paris – after our – ' she hesitated – 'encounter? It was a really awful journey. The train from Laon was stopped by the bombing and had to go back, so everybody got out and walked towards Soissons. Then the road was crowded with refugees, and a German aircarft attacked us. Fortunately, I met Hugo and his father, and they brought me to Paris. I was very lucky. They let me stay at the Hôtel de Brey.'

She wondered whether she had obfuscated the truth successfully.

They bought several loaves, cheese, and bottles of wine and Perrier water without difficulty. They went into a shop and asked for cigarettes.

'Alas, monsieur,' the motherly woman behind the counter said, 'there are none. I don't think you'll find any hereabouts. The German soldiers bought all the cigarettes they could find.'

'The Germans, madame?' asked Vivian.

'This morning, monsieur. There was a whole column of them, in lorries. They were very polite, and they paid for everything they took. In francs, too.'

'Which way were they heading, madame?' Vivian asked.

The woman smiled at the absurdity of such a question.

'Oh monsieur, how should I know?'

Vivian, Julie and Hugo ran back to the lorry.

'Let's move,' Vivian shouted to Sergeant Micklewhite, as the two lance-corporals pulled Julie and Hugo aboard.

Vivian climbed in beside the driving seat.

'We'll take the Alençon road,' he said. 'Please God, the Germans were heading south.'

All afternoon they drove along the narrow winding lanes between the deep, labyrinthine hedgerows. Vivian sat with a road-map spread on his knees, calculating how they might avoid major road junctions and towns. The journey was uneventful. It was not until early evening that they began to overtake the debris of a retreating army. The road they were on was rather larger than those they had been travelling on earlier. It was littered with discarded military packs – packs with greatcoats rolled about the tops, and tin mess-plates under the cross-straps on the backs. Rifles had been thrown down into the gutters under the hedges, with bandoliers and ammunition pouches. Several times they encountered abandoned vehicles which had been driven wildly into the hedgrows, and Sergeant Micklewhite had to negotiate the 15 cwt. carefully round them. The final one, a large pantechnicon, was on fire, the flames spilling out from under the engine-hood, catching the branches of the hedge which spat and crackled in the quivering heat.

Once they had to skirt round a bomb crater in the centre of the road. Sergeant Micklewhite inched the lorry up onto the verge. The wheels skidded. There were several bodies sprawled across the rubble and grit of the road's surface close by the crater. Julie looked at them with horrified fascination. An elderly peasant lay on his back, his blue cotton jacket and corduroy trousers fallen apart. His stomach had been ripped open so that he resembled the centre figure of Rembrandt's 'Anatomy Lesson'. A soldier was crouching on his knees. Only the small pool of blood in which he knelt showed that he was dead.

The lorry jolted forward, and they bumped down again onto the road. They were heading for the dark line of a wood in the gathering dusk, when they saw the solitary figure of a French soldier advancing towards them in the centre of the road. He was wearing his helmet and full equipment over his grimy uniform. He was clenching his rifle against his chest. One of his puttees had come unfastened and was trailing along for a yard and a half behind his boot. Sergeant Micklewhite slowed down. In a quiet, very controlled voice, Vivian said into the back of the lorry.

'Get out, into the ditch, and lie down!'

The two lance-corporals pushed Julie and Hugo over the tail-board, as Vivian and Sergeant Micklewhite scrambled out of their seats and into the back.

'Rose,' said Sergeant Micklewhite. 'Let's have the rifle, lad.'

A voice from the front of the lorry, shouted out, *'Ils ne passeront pas!'*

There was a loud shot. The bullet smashed into the windscreen and lodged in the wood of the tailboard. Julie and Hugo were already lying in the grass. The two corporals joined them, followed by Vivian.

'Ils ne passeront pas!' the voice shouted again hoarsely.

'He thinks we're Germans,' Vivian said. 'He's out of his mind.'

Another shot rang out.

'He'll hit the bloody fuel tank,' Vivian shouted across to Sergeant Micklewhite.

Sergeant Micklewhite was standing behind the rear mudguard of the lorry, holding his rifle. He eased the bolt and snapped it shut. Suddenly he stepped out into the open road, levelled the rifle at his shoulder, aimed carefully, and fired a single shot. He lowered the butt from his shoulder, knocked the bolt-handle up, released the spent cartridge into the grit of the road, and snapped the bolt to. He held the rifle out to where Lance-Corporal Rose was kneeling.

'Here you are, lad,' he said. 'Pull it through right away. No point in leaving it dirty.'

They were climbing back into the lorry, when Julie saw the body lying in a heap in the centre of the road. Sergeant Micklewhite had climbed in behind the wheel, and was removing the loose fragments about the neat bullet hole in the windscreen. Vivian was beside him.

'You're not going to leave him just lying there,' Julie exclaimed, horrified.

'We've no time . . . ' Vivian began.

'We'll drive round him, miss,' Sergeant Micklewhite reassured her gloomily.

Julie felt sick. Vivian must have seen her face in the driving mirror. He swivelled round in his seat.

'What do *you* think we should have done?' he asked quietly. 'The poor fellow was going to kill us.'

'You're behaving as if he was just an animal,' she protested, also in a low voice.

The lorry jolted forward. Vivian did not reply; he turned and faced the road ahead.

The dense green of the woodland closed around them in the dusk. The amount of debris they were encountering increased. Cars and vans had been left abandoned on the roadside with tyres punctured and ripped to shreds, radiators blackened, or fuel tanks open and dry. Family groups sat hopeless and exhausted in the ditches and under the hedges, as if they no longer had either the energy or the incentive to flee further from the homes they had abandoned. Discarded luggage lay in the sides of the road. Some suitcases had been opened and their contents lay littered about them.

The lorry began to overtake groups of wounded soldiers, some leaning on sticks plucked from the woods and hedgerows, some on crutches. A few were being carried on stretchers. A scattering of hospital equipment was spread in front of a gate leading into a field. Vivian told Sergeant Micklewhite to slow down. He called out to the French medical orderlies who were guarding the equipment asking them what had happened. Their leader, a sergeant, replied that a platoon of army deserters had seized their ambulance at gun-point, and had driven away in it. The sergeant had ordered his men to arrange the equipment – oxygen cylinders, plasma and drip equipment, white and metal dishes, dressing-chests and instrument boxes – in an orderly fashion, and was prepared to wait until he could find some transport to take them all on to the Military Hospital at Rennes.

As Sergeant Micklewhite drove on, Julie could see, beyond the confusion along the roadside, the farmers in the twilit fields gathering in the first hay-crop as if nothing were amiss.

Darkness had fallen when they drew up at a farm which stood close to the road. Everywhere was still. As they climbed down from the lorry, and went through the gate into the yard, there was no sign of light, and no dogs began to bark. Vivian had decided that though they must drive on westwards through the night, they should stretch their legs, and see whether they could buy some eggs and milk. The lance-corporals were left to fill the lorry's tank from the jerrycans in the locker. Hugo was already asleep, lying in a bed made up of army greatcoats, along the floor of the lorry. Vivian, Julie and Sergeant Micklewhite went across the dark farmyard to the front door.

As they approached it, they could see that the ground-floor windows were all smashed, and the shutters were hanging torn from their hinges. The door had been smashed in quire recently; the splintered fragments of wood were still fresh. Vivian nodded to Sergeant Micklewhite. He drew Julie back, then drew his revolver from its holster. Sergeant Micklewhite pushed open the wreckage of the door with his foot, and Vivian stepped in. The only sound was of his boots on the stone floor. Sergeant Micklewhite followed into the blackness, and then Julie. Her foot crunched onto a broken fragment of china, breaking the stillness. There was a bare table dimly visible, with a hurricane lamp standing on it. Julie went forward, ignoring Vivian's restraining hand. He whispered, 'All right.'

She took out her matches, lifted the glass of the lamp, and lit the wick. As she wound up the wick, light spilled across the parlour in which they were standing. Sergeant Micklewhite looked about him.

'Looters, sir?' he suggested to Vivian.

Broken crockery was scattered all over the floor. The cupboards, the dressers, the larder door – all had been broken into and smashed. The furniture had been broken, and the upholstery ripped up.

'There's nothing for you to take, messieurs. Nothing!'

She was sitting in a high-backed wooden chair at the cold hearth: a farmer's wife, still quite young, though her face was tired and drawn. Her flowered overall was torn where the buttons had been ripped away. One of her woollen stockings had fallen about her ankle. Her hair had matted on her white face where the sweat had dried.

'They have taken everything, messieurs,' she said.

Her voice rasped with dryness. She stared up at Vivian.

'*Vous êtes mutilé de la guerre?*' she asked.

Vivian nodded. It was confirmation of his honest intent. She began to talk rapidly with him. Julie translated quietly for Sergeant Micklewhite's benefit.

'French deserters came here. A lot of them. She tried to bolt the doors and windows but they smashed their way in. They stole everything, she says. They said she had gold hidden away. They said all farmers keep gold hidden away. So they tore up the beds and the furniture. And they – they took advantage of her – several of them. She can't remember how many.'

She went to the woman and crouched down beside her.

'Find some water if you can,' she told Vivian.

Vivian nodded, and went searching for the back kitchen.

'Where's your husband, madame?' Julie asked.

'At the war,' the woman whispered.

'Are you all by yourself?' asked Julie.

'There's the maid,' the woman replied.

'Where's she?' asked Julie.

'I sent her home at midday. There was nothing for her to do.'

She stared into Julie's face.

'You are very pretty, mademoiselle,' she said. She smiled. 'Very pretty.'

Julie smiled back. 'Thank you, madame.'

'My husband always keeps his gun locked up in the shed,' said the woman, 'otherwise I would have killed two of the pigs. Two barrels. Two pigs, eh?'

'I'm sure you were very brave, madame,' Julie told her.

Vivian brought in a cup of water. The woman took it, and drank from it greedily.

'Is there anybody we can fetch, madame?' asked Julie. 'The maid? A neighbour, perhaps? Monsieur le Curé?'

The woman shook her head. She handed the cup back to Vivian.

'Excuse me,' she said, 'but it is time for me to go to sleep now.'

Julie felt Vivian's hand on her arm. The woman looked up at him.

'Time for me to go to sleep, monsieur,' she told him.

'Of course, madame,' Vivian replied.

He drew Julie up beside him.

'We must go,' he said firmly.

'We can't just . . . ' she began once more.

'What should I do?' Vivian asked. 'Advertise our presence to the entire neighbourhood? Wait for Jerry to catch up with us? He can't be many miles away from here.'

He released her arm. He went to the table, raised the lamp and blew out the flame. The darkness descended on them like the fall of a blanket. Julie followed him and Sergeant Micklewhite out into the yard. He indicated to Sergeant Micklewhite that he should go ahead.

'Julie,' he said, 'we have one job only and that is to get you to the coast. It is no part of it to take any risks that we may avoid.'

Did he know about the Tondeau, she wondered. Then she thought, as he led her back to the lorry, how wonderful it must be to have a direct sense of duty and purpose. It must make everything seem so straightforward.

Lance-Corporal Clarke took over the wheel. Sergeant Micklewhite sat beside him. Vivian sat beside Julie in the back, with Hugo asleep at their feet. Lance-Corporal Rose kept watch over the tailboard. How Hugo could remain asleep was a mystery to Julie, as the movement of the lorry bounced her bottom on the hard shelf of the locker. No one spoke, as if out of respect for the night. Victor and Ambrose, she thought: they were like planets in a Jules Verne adventure. The one was now drifting away into the infinity of space; the other was drawing nearer, becoming more evident. She was caught up in a nomad existence.

'It was a most remarkable thing, meeting you, this morning,' said Vivian as quietly as the rattling of the lorry permitted.

She was about to agree with this anodyne sentiment, when he continued, 'Do you know, there hasn't been one single day since Laon, when you haven't been in my mind?'

'You shouldn't say things like that,' Julie replied. 'It's a bit heavy, isn't it?'

'I know,' he replied, 'but I couldn't have borne the idea of not having said it, if . . . '

'If anything happened?' she asked. 'I know.'

She sat thinking in the darkness, with the hedges rushing past on either side.

'I'm glad you did,' she told him finally. 'Really.'

His hand found hers. She let him hold it.

41

Victor heard the noise out on the Avenue at first light. He was lying in his room facing the square, on the opposite side of the house. He had been waiting for it as surely as he had been waiting for the dawn. He got out of bed, and pulled on his dressing-gown. It was strange he should have been unable to sleep; his mind was dull and heavy rather than over-active. Now he was on his feet, he felt weary.

He went to the end of the gallery, the thick pile of the carpet hushing his footsteps. No one was about yet. He turned and went down a short flight of stairs. Through a curtained alcove was the small drawing-room which had always been Olivia's sanctum. And above the English-style fireplace hung her portrait.

Victor crossed the room to the window. It looked down over the Avenue. One or two workmen were pedalling past on their bicycles. A group of cleaning-women strolled up the opposite pavement, carrying battered shopping bags, and talking volubly. Under the trees were parked four motorcycle combinations. The crews were standing nearby. They were wearing the squat, ugly, face-concealing helmets and grey tunics recalled over a gap of twenty-one years. Around their throats were the metal gorgets of the Field Gendarmerie. They were keeping watch up the street, one or two of them with cigarettes in the palms of their hands.

He left the window and went over to the mantlepiece. He took a cigarette from the box there, but instead of lighting it, stared up at the portrait. Olivia had sat for it at Tamara de Lempicka's studio near the Observatoire. On the occasions he had been to watch de Lempicka at work in the surroundings which, with its chrome fittings and beige upholstery, resembled the cocktail-bar of a fashionably luxurious cruise-liner, he had felt distinctly jealous. The willowy, blonde Polish artist postured with as much calculation as she posed her model. The gestures she used in her brushwork suggested that the act of applying colour was a sensual one. To emphasise this, she painted with her mouth slightly open, the wet gleaming on her bright scarlet lip-rouge. At first, he had found the completed portrait an impertinence. Olivia's pure heart-shaped face had been endowed on the canvas with an odalisque mingling of sexual appetite and sadness.

While she was still alive, he had found it difficult to understand the painting. Nor had he been put at ease by her defence of de Lempicka as an artist: 'She knows how to explore very deeply.' It sounded too much like the admission of having yielded to a seduction. After he had passed through the agony of bereavement, however, he had recognised, Orpheus-like, that the portrait was indeed that of Olivia, and he had gone to it as he might have gone to someone who had loved her also – to the only person who could share his own sense of loss.

He lit his cigarette, and returned to the window. The sun was on the roof-tops opposite: a wet, clear light which could not last. There was the noise of heavy vehicles approaching. The motorcyclists were mounting their machines, and riding out from under the trees. Behind them, the first of a column of lorries, painted steel grey and stippled with black came into view. Victor watched as the column passed underneath in the direction of the Étoile. Each lorry contained a cargo of four ranks of steel-helmeted, field-grey infantry sitting stiffly erect, their rifles gripped upright between their knees.

When the last of the column had passed underneath, he drew the curtains. He went out of the small drawing-room, closing and locking the door behind him. He would never return to it. He went back to his rooms, had a bath, shaved and dressed carefully. Feeling more refreshed, he went downstairs to the study to smoke a second cigarette and to make a final arrangement of his papers.

Optimistically, he rang the bell. A few minutes later came a timid knock on the study door. He opened it.

'Monsieur rang? I'm the only one up, Monsieur.'

She was no more than a child, wiping her hands on her apron, and in black stockinged feet with her little toe sticking through a hole in the foot of her stocking.

She glanced down quickly.

'Please excuse me, monsieur. I was outside in my pattens. I didn't have time to put my shoes on.'

He smiled at her.

'You are Claudine, aren't you?'

'Yes, monsieur.'

'Claudine? Do you think you could make me a pot of coffee?'

'Of course, monsieur.'

She was a child. The way she spoke filled him with sadness.

'Thank you, Claudine,' he said.

He closed the door after her. Almost immediately, there was a harsh ringing at the front door. He went out into the hall. Claudine was already struggling with the bolts and the great brass handle. She swung it open. In the sunlight on the step stood the dapper figure of a young German officer in black tunic and breeches, and polished belt and riding-boots. He was holding his cap under his arm.

'I wish to see Monsieur le Baron,' he said stiffly.

Claudine looked round. Her eyes were startled.

'It's all right, Claudine,' Victor told her. 'You may return to the kitchen. Perhaps you will bring two bowls for coffee?'

'Yes, monsieur,' Claudine managed to whisper.

'And now,' said Victor in German. 'To whom do I owe the pleasure . . . ?'

'I'm sorry, Baron. It is very early.'

'I believe that calls at this hour are not uncommon in the Germany of today,' said Victor.

The German visibly stiffened. Out in the square, at the foot of the steps, stood one of the tinny-looking yet powerful little cars used by the German army. There was a machine gun mounted between the front seats. Three soldiers were standing beside it, on the pavement, smoking.

'And I, as you see, am up,' Victor added.

He held open the door. As the officer walked in, Victor observed his insignia.

'I hope you will take coffee with me, Rittmeister,' he said.

The officer clicked his heels.

'Dieter von Leonarte, 1st Cavalry,' he introduced himself.

Victor led him to the lounge.

'Please sit down, Rittmeister,' he said. 'Make yourself comfortable. Smoke if you wish.'

'You are most kind, Baron,' von Leonarte replied. 'And you speak German. That is very helpful for me!'

'The language of Mozart and of Heine is a language worth knowing,' Victor replied.

'Did you study in Germany?' von Leonarte asked.

'Yes, Rittmeister, I did. I was your prisoner for more months than I care to remember. I was wounded during the Nivelle offensive of '17. I expect I owe my life to German doctors.'

'Jews fought bravely for both France and Germany during the last war,' von Leonarte blurted out. He blushed.

'Thank you, Rittmeister. Would you care to tell me why you have come to my house?' he asked.

'It is my duty, Baron,' said von Leonarte, 'to ask you if you would be so good as to hand over to me a certain – *objet?* – which my superiors believe is in your possession.'

'The *objet* in question being the *Tondeau de Chartres?*' asked Victor.

Von Leonarte swallowed.

'Why yes, Baron,' he replied. He hesitated. 'I'm sorry, Baron. I am under orders,' he insisted.

Victor allowed the young man to remain embarrassed for a moment or two. He glanced at the Knight's Cross at his throat.

'You, of course, are a gentleman – a man of honour?' he said gently.

'I hope I may be considered so, Baron,' von Leonarte replied.

'Is there anything else?' asked Victor.

'No, Baron, except that I should like to say that my superiors intend to return this – ah – Tondeau to France at the earliest opportunity.'

'They do not intend to hold it as the booty of war?' asked Victor.

'No, Baron. As soon as the military situation permits, it will be returned to a citizen of your country held in high respect and esteem by his fellow citizens.'

'In a word, Rittmeister, a very distinguished traitor?'

Von Leonarte winced.

'Or to a man so old and feeble in his wits that he cannot understand the implications of what is happening?' asked Victor.

'I do not know who my superiors have in mind, Baron,' von Leonarte replied. 'I know only my orders.'

'I suspect, Rittmeister, that you, as a man of honour and a Prussian officer of some distinction, will be quite relieved to know that I do not possess the Tondeau.'

He laughed.

'You don't believe me? You think the Jew is lying?' he asked.

He waited for the gibe to sink in.

'Two nights ago, the Tondeau was stolen out of this house,' he went on. 'You will appreciate that our police are operating under great difficulties. The life of the criminal has been relatively easy these past few days.'

'Baron,' said von Leonarte carefully, 'if I were in your position and you in mine, I should lie. I should consider it my patriotic duty – nothing to do with being a Jew.'

'But I am not lying, Rittmeister.'

He could have liked the man despite his very pale eyes. He had the prematurely-lined look on his healthy tanned face of the very young

393

man who has had to accept the responsibility of commanding under fire.

Claudine pushed open the door. As she came across to where they were sitting, and put the tray down on the table beside Victor, she couldn't help staring at von Leonarte's uniform.

'Thank you, Claudine,' Victor told her pointedly.

When she had gone he said, 'I'm sorry, Rittmeister. She is still very young. And I'm afraid she hasn't had time to become used to German uniforms yet.'

He poured out the coffee.

'Yes,' he continued, 'not only am I telling you the truth, but I am in a position to help you with your quest. I am certain I know who is responsible for its disappearance, and I can put you on his trail. The leading criminal was assisted, you see, by somebody inside the house – one of my servants. She has since confessed. She gave me this.'

He drew from his waistcoat pocket the creased, rather dirty pasteboard card which had been given to him by Danielle. Von Leonarte took it and stared at it. Victor saw the surprise registered on his face.

Von Leonarte looked up.

'I believe you, Baron. I believe you absolutely,' he said.

Thank God! thought Victor. It would buy a few extra hours for Julie and Hugo to escape.

As von Leonarte left, putting on his cap and drawing on his leather gloves, he said, 'Why don't you leave Paris, Baron? Immediately. Before General von Bock makes his entry? The Rambouillet-Maintenon road was left open last night to permit General Hering to withdraw his rearguard.'

'Thank you, Rittmeister,' Victor replied. 'It is most kind of you.'

Von Leonarte clicked his heels, saluted, and returned to the *kübelwagen*. He heard the door close behind him.

'On board, lads!' he ordered. He handed the crumpled visiting card to Helm. 'Can you guess who that is?' he asked.

'The Greek?' asked Helm.

'Yes, Helm. The fat Greek at La Berlière. He bribed a servant here. He got away with what we're after, two nights ago. So we'll go to that address.'

Helm opened his Paris street guide.

'That fat white turd, Herr Rittmeister?' asked Radinski from the back.

'Save us a spot of bother if he's holding the medallion for us,' said Graser. 'We'll be able to have a weekend in Paris.'

Radinski's laugh was painfully predictable.

'That man will be saving it for nobody but himself,' said von Leonarte. 'I expect he'll be heading for the coast as fast as he can go.'

'Perhaps we'll catch him, Herr Rittmeister,' said Radinski. 'Perhaps we'll have to persuade him to hand over the medallion the same way he persuaded that poor old woman at La Berlière!'

Von Leonarte said nothing. His encounter with the Baron de Bart-Mendel had filled him with an unexpected sense of guilt. Far from being a Jewish fraud, de Bart-Mendel had personified the values and courtesy he had been brought up to expect; while both La Berlière and the Hôtel de Brey had revealed none of the vulgar ostentation of wealth which was said to be the distinguishing mark of the rich Semite everywhere. At the same time, the pursuit of the Tondeau had become entirely purposeless. It was obvious that the war was almost finished, and that General von Bock's triumphant army could march to the Church of St Eustache and sing lustily, 'Now Thank We All Our God!' as von Moltke's had done after the Battle of Sedan. The days of heroism, of the high singing of the blood, were done. The days of the guttersnipes, as Uncle Alfred had called them, were coming.

The clear, early-morning sun disappeared behind a great flat lid of grey cloud as Helm drove them up towards Montmartre. Over the northern and eastern suburbs hung even lower the dense layer of smoke from the army supply depots set alight by General Hering's retreating rearguard. The few people who were already out on the street glanced quickly at the *kübelwagen* as it rattled past over the cobbles, most of them hardly aware that they were looking at Germans. Those that did realise glanced a second time with a startled look in their eyes.

They parked at the top of the Becquerel Steps. Von Leonarte left Helm with the *kübelwagen*, and took Graser and Radinski with him down into the Passage de Pantois. He stood back as Radinski knocked at the door. There was no reply at first; it was so quiet that he wondered whether it was occupied at all. Above his head, a shutter banged against a wall, and a child's voice shouted, *'Maman! Maman!* Come and see!'

A woman's voice shouted stridently, 'How many times have I told you not to lean out of the window?'

'But *Maman!'* shouted the child.

A man and a woman, both elderly, came out into the passage. The man was coughing. The woman stared. Somebody inside one of the houses was shouting, 'The Boches are here!'

The woman who had shouted at the child now shouted, 'Gaby, stay away from the window. Do you hear me?'

Radinski knocked on the door again. In the first floor window, a curtain was twitched aside.

'Shall we break in, Herr Rittmeister?' asked Radinski.

Von Leonarte shook his head. 'We'll wait a moment,' he ordered.

A minute or two later, the door was opened. Von Leonarte glanced up at the windows behind him. A number of faces quickly vanished. He turned back and saluted.

'Forgive me, madame,' he said. 'Is Monsieur Papayannis within?'

He tried to sound pleasant, but his stilted *gymnasium* French was against him.

'Mademoiselle,' the woman corrected him sharply.

The lady had the face of a mademoiselle – the sort of mademoiselle who taught French grammar, ruler in hand, and had a spine which put a Prussian grenadier drill-master to shame. She was dressed like a mademoiselle, in a severe black two-piece. Her skirt was twisted, however, and several of the blouse-buttons under her frilled jabot were undone.

'I'm sorry, mademoiselle,' he said.

'Monsieur Papayannis is away from Paris, monsieur,' she told him stiffly.

'It is important that I should find him,' said von Leonarte. 'Perhaps you will tell me where I may find him?'

'I am not permitted to divulge that information, monsieur,' the woman replied.

'I am compelled to insist,' said von Leonarte. 'May we go inside?'

'Monsieur Papayannis is a neutral; he holds an Egyptian passport,' the woman protested.

'But you are French?' he asked.

'Of course, monsieur. But this is Monsieur Papayannis's house.'

'It is not an Embassy, mademoiselle.'

He pushed the door open, forcing the woman to step backwards.

'Graser,' he ordered, 'you will remain outside.'

The woman went in through the office door just inside the front door. At the far end of the hall, at the foot of a flight of stairs, a young girl was standing. She was dressed as a boy, with a pair of man's flannel trousers tied with an artificial-silk scarf about the waist, and a man's white flannel shirt which, in her haste, she had buttoned wrongly. With her short cropped hair, she would have looked like a boy but for the small mounds of her breasts and the black spit-curl on her forehead.

'Lina? What's happened?' she called.

'Nothing, *ma petite*,' the woman called back. 'They just want to talk to Monsieur Chris.'

'I want a cigarette,' the girl said.

She came down the hall.

'Go upstairs,' the woman ordered.

The girl pouted. Von Leonarte pulled out his cigarette-case and held it towards her.

'Go on,' he invited.

'Go upstairs!' the woman shouted.

'But Lina,' the girl protested.

'Take two or three,' von Leonarte suggested.

'Natalie!' shouted the woman.

The girl took three cigarettes. She smiled coyly.

'Radinski,' von Leonarte ordered, 'take the old hen into that room, and ask her about the Greek – where he's got to.'

He waited until Radinski had pushed the woman into the office. She was still shouting. He closed the door.

'The trouble is that the neighbours will think that we. . . . ' He tried to select the right words. ' . . . that we are doing bad things,' he said. 'Is she your mother?' he asked.

The girl laughed. 'Oh no,' she said.

There was something in her face which shocked von Leonarte. When he had been a little boy with his mother, visiting Berlin, they had been returning through the wet, lamplit streets from a cinema to their hotel, much later than he was usually out of bed. There had been girls with the same short, lacquered hair, smirking from the doorways of the *cabarets*. Their smiles had frightened him – had followed him into his dreams.

'Have you a light?' he asked.

'Upstairs,' she replied.

'I'll light one for you now, shall I?' he asked.

He flicked on his lighter. She lit her cigarette.

'What do you think of Monsieur Papayannis?' he asked.

'Monsieur Chris?' she replied.

'Yes, Monsieur Chris.'

'He is a pig, monsieur. Both Lina and I think he is a pig. Only Lina works for Monsieur Liassides, and Monsieur Chris works for Monsieur Liassides.'

'Do you know where Monsieur Chris might be?' asked von Leonarte.

'Not telling, monsieur,' the girl said.

She smiled up at him.

'Lina will beat me if I tell you,' she said. 'She likes beating me – only I don't like being beaten.'

She sniggered.

'Monsieur Chris and his friends are bad men,' said von Leonarte. 'The *Sûreté* want them as well as we. If you, or Lina, don't tell us where he has gone, we shall have to take Lina to the Prefecture for questioning. Monsieur Chris has murdered somebody, you see.'

Obviously, the news did not surprise the girl.

'Lina isn't a criminal,' she grinned.

'But we must ask her questions to find out where Monsieur Chris is,' said von Leonarte.

The girl was a degenerate. The fact that she was pretty concealed from the first glance that she was mentally defective.

He opened the office door.

'Radinski,' he called, 'take the woman out. We'll hand her over to the *Préfet de Police*.'

'Come,' Radinski said to her. 'Come, quick!'

When she didn't budge, he grabbed her by the arm. He was enjoying himself.

The girl watched as Radinski dragged the woman protesting and shouting at them, to the door. Graser went to help him.

'Don't!' the girl shouted. 'Don't! Dirty pigs!'

Von Leonarte stood in her way.

'We can't let murderers go free,' he told her.

The girl stared at him. She tried to get past him. He stopped her. He could feel the desire to use unnecessary strength rising in the midst of his disgust at her. He gripped the front of her shirt as if to shake her. Her small breasts were bare inside the white flannel.

'Tell us where Monsieur Chris has gone,' said von Leonarte.

'To the seaside,' said the girl.

'Natalie!' shrieked the woman.

Radinski and Graser had got her as far as the front door.

'Where, at the seaside?' asked von Leonarte.

'Natalie! No!' the woman shouted.

'But they'll take you away,' the girl shouted back.

'Where has Monsieur Chris gone?' asked von Leonarte. 'What part of the seaside? Has he gone to Bordeaux?'

'No,' the girl replied.

She struggled again to push past him. Radinski and Graser had pulled the woman out into the street. The girl was wild-eyed with fear.

'What shall I do without you?' she cried out to the woman.

'Don't tell the pigs,' the woman shouted back.

'Herr Rittmeister,' Graser shouted in through the front door, 'there's a lot of people coming out.'

'You haven't anything to be afraid of, *mon enfant*,' von Leonarte told the girl. 'You'll be able to visit your friend in Le Fresne Prison.'

The girl looked even more terrified, as he had intended she should be.

'No, monsieur! No!' she appealed to him.

'Very well,' he said reasonably.

He wondered whether she was too simple actually to know where on the coast Papayannis had gone. Perhaps the roles should be reversed. Perhaps they should take the child for questioning. He would try one more gambit.

'Have you heard of the Gestapo, *mon enfant*?' he asked.

The girl nodded.

'The Gestapo will arrive in Paris tomorrow. We shall have to hand over your friend to the Gestapo. I'm sorry.'

The girl stared at him. Tears poured from her eyes. Her mouth quivered.

'St Malo, monsieur,' she whispered. 'Or Dinard. I don't know.'

'You're a good little girl,' von Leonarte told her. 'It's good to be loyal to your friend.'

He turned.

'Release the woman,' he called.

Graser and Radinski let go of the woman. She came back into the hall. She and the girl stood staring at each other. The girl was trying to control her shuddering.

'I didn't know what would become of me,' she said in a voice hoarse with tears.

Von Leonarte went into the office. He glanced at the bric-à-brac around him.

'All stolen goods?' he asked.

There was no reply. Out in the hall, the woman reached out her arms for the girl. The girl clung to her, sobbing. The woman said, 'There, there. There's nothing to be afraid of.'

She repeated it over and over again, caressing the girl as she did so. She lifted the girl's face and kissed her mouth.

Von Leonarte saw the picture hanging above Papayannis's desk: the drawing by Felicien Rops, with the demure stiffness of the model's posture, the austere respectability of her dress, and the slack-mouthed fatigue in the face, and the pouched eyes.

'Do they call this art, do you think?' he asked.

Graser had come into the room.

'With the Herr Rittmeister's permission,' he said, 'I'd call it disgusting.'

Von Leonarte took the drawing down carefully from the wall.

'With the Herr Rittmeister's permission,' Graser said, 'there are a number of people come out onto the street. Perhaps it would be better – I mean, since we have not yet officially taken over the city. . . . '

'Quite right, Graser,' von Leonarte told him.

He laid the picture down on the floor, and smashed the heel of his boot into it. He stamped on it several times.

'Come,' he said to Graser.

They returned to the narrow street outside. Small groups of people were standing watching. As von Leonarte, Graser and Radinski marched back to where Helm was waiting for them at the top of the steps, a woman came up to him.

'Why didn't you take them, monsieur?' she asked. 'We can do without those sort here – and the Greek.'

'You must speak to your own police, madame,' von Leonarte told her.

He saluted, touching the peak of his cap with his gloves.

42

Victor returned to the lounge and finished a second bowl of coffee after von Leonarte had taken his leave. He was shivering slightly. Perhaps he should have something to eat; but he had no appetite. He waited a few minutes, and then rang the bell. Severin appeared, having only just pulled on his black jacket.

The time had come.

'Severin,' he said, 'I have made up my mind to leave you all.'

He paused. Then, relaxing a little he said, 'The German officer who was here just now was good enough to tell me that his army has left one road open out of Paris, and to suggest that I should take it.'

'I'm sure that everybody will be very relieved to hear it, monsieur,' Severin told him gravely. 'We have all been very concerned at your staying on, if you'll forgive me saying so.'

'Thank you, Severin,' Victor replied. 'I shall be leaving immediately – just as I am, I'm afraid. I want no farewells. I am informing you because I think that one member of the household should know. You shall not tell the others until this evening, please.'

'Very good, monsieur,' Severin said.

'You shall thank everybody on my behalf for the way they have looked after me – and for their friendship . . . You shall tell them that I have made certain arrangements to ensure that each one of them will be looked after until she can obtain another position in which she – or he – will be as happy as I believe she has been here.'

'Thank you, monsieur,' said Severin.

There must be something more to add, thought Victor. He spread his hands helplessly.

'Perhaps, monsieur,' Severin began, 'when the Germans have gone again . . . ?'

Victor nodded.

'Yes, *cher ami*,' he replied. 'Of course.'

He held out his hand. Severin took it in both of his own.

'God bless you, monsieur, and keep you safe,' he said.

'He will,' replied Victor. 'God bless you, *cher ami*. And, once more, thank you.'

He withdrew his hand from Severin's grasp. Severin followed him out into the hall.

'Your coat, monsieur?' he asked.

He helped Victor to put on the coat as he had always done, then handed him his hat, gloves, and stick.

'Thank you, Severin,' Victor said, 'and *au revoir*, eh?'

'*Au revoir*, monsieur,' said Severin.

As he set off down the pavement, Victor heard the front door being closed behind him. The drizzle had started again. It was still quite early in the morning. Out on the Avenue de Wagram, there was a scattering of workmen and shop-girls on their way to work. Outside the flower-shop near the Étoile, a pale-faced girl in a coloured cotton smock was arranging the flowers in the painted barrows in front of the window display. Boots scraped on the gratings behind the iron screen of the *pissoir*. On the outside, a faded poster for *La Grande Illusion* was peeling away in the damp.

Two young women and a grey-haired older woman were pushing a wooden handcart piled with their belongings across the Étoile. They were being assisted by two laughing German *landsers* whose grey tunic sleeves were rolled up despite the rain, and whose forage-caps were folded under their shoulder-tabs. The first of the refugees were finding their way home.

Along the Avenue Bosquet, the waiters were opening up the cafés. A small group of German Field Gendarmes were standing by their truck, staring up at the Eiffel Tower. One of them was taking snap-shots of his companions as they stared. A band was playing in the distance – not the dancing rhythm of 'Marche Lorraine' or 'Sambre-et-Meuse', but the thud-thud-thud of a Brandenburger march with its monotonous jangle of Turkish bells.

He caught a bus on the Boulevard Garibaldi. For the first time in many years, he stood on the platform, letting the damp breeze cool his face. Inside, there were few passengers: a handful of matronly women with creased shopping-bags; a small, elderly man, with a rectangle of plate-glass between his knees. It was hard to believe that anything unusual was happening in Paris, except that the streets through which they were rattling were unwontedly quiet, and that one of the matronly women and the elderly man were holding handkerchiefs to their eyes.

Victor got off at the bottom of the Avenue du Maine. He had only a five minute walk to Maurice Levasseur's apartment opposite the Hospital of St Anne, of which Dr Levasseur was Director. He went up in the lift to the fourth floor. He rang, and Levasseur himself opened the apartment door.

'Victor!' he exclaimed. Then he said, 'You've been walking in the rain.'

'I've walked part of the way,' Victor agreed.

Dr Levasseur was in his shirt-sleeves. He had not shaved. His breath smelt of brandy.

401

'Come in, *mon vieux*,' he said, holding open the door.

Victor went inside.

'Maurice,' he said, 'when I asked you what you would do when the Germans approached Paris, you said something about going on a journey.'

Dr Levasseur laughed.

'Ah yes,' he replied. 'A little further than England, eh?'

He opened the living-room door.

'Come in! Come in!' he said.

Victor went through into the room.

'And has your attractive young friend gone to England?' he asked.

'I hope so,' Victor replied. 'She has Hugo with her.'

'Good,' said Dr Levasseur. 'Good.'

The room was half study, half doctor's consulting-room. Glass-fronted cupboards and a dazzlingly white sink-unit were ranged on the opposite side to the wide window overlooking the hospital. Bookcases were set against the other two walls.

'A glass of Armagnac, *mon vieux*?' he asked.

'If you please,' said Victor.

He was finding it increasingly hard to speak.

'Would you accept the company of a friend on your journey?' he asked.

His throat was very dry. Dr Levasseur turned, the brandy-glass in his hand.

'Are you sure that you wish to accompany me on the journey I'm taking?' he asked.

He held out the glass. Victor took it.

'Entirely sure,' he replied.

They drank slowly.

'The hospital?' asked Victor, gazing out of the window.

'Arrangements have been made,' said Dr Levasseur. 'The Board knew that the Germans would not allow me to remain at my post. They were prepared for my letter of resignation. And you?'

'I have put my affairs in order,' Victor replied. 'All arrangements have been made.'

Dr Levasseur put down his glass.

'Embrace me, *mon vieux*,' he said.

They embraced one another.

'Are you ready to set out?' asked Dr Levasseur.

'Quite ready,' Victor whispered.

He sat down in one of the deep leather armchairs by the window. Dr Levasseur went over to one of the glass-fronted cupboards. From an enamel dish inside, he took out a hypodermic syringe. He charged it from a small bottle, and examined the tip of the needle, ejecting a tiny spurt of liquid.

402

'There,' he said.

'What ... ?' asked Victor.

His voice dried up.

'Morphia,' Dr Levasseur replied. 'Nothing to worry about. Its effects are quite – benevolent. Very gentle.'

Victor took off his jacket, unfastened his cuff-link and rolled up his sleeve.

'You must understand something, Victor,' Dr Levasseur told him, 'I cannot administer the injection.'

Victor looked up at him.

'I am bound by my Hippocratic Oath,' said Dr Levasseur. 'I can't absolve myself from it. I can tell you what to do. I can guide you, but I can't actually administer the injection.'

'I've always hated injections,' said Victor.

But he reached out for the syringe.

'Help me,' he said.

Dr Levassuer put his forefinger on Victor's bared arm, just below the inside of his elbow. Victor laid the tip of the needle on his skin. He looked up again.

'Quite shallow,' said Dr Levasseur. 'And gently. Nothing to be afraid of.'

Victor inserted the needle under the skin.

'That's it,' said Dr Levasseur.

Victor injected a few drops of the colourless liquid. There was no discomfort.

'Enough,' said Dr Levasseur.

Victor withdrew the needle. He returned the syringe to Dr Levasseur, and sat back in the chair.

Dr Levasseur wiped the needle with a piece of cotton-wool.

'Old habits die hard,' he said.

He sat down in the armchair facing Victor. He stretched out his arm and clenched his fist. Bending his arm a little, he administered the injection, then put down the syringe on the window-ledge beside him. He smiled to Victor.

It could have been his imagination, but Victor felt that he was beginning to float backwards into space. He heard his own voice speaking in the depths of his brain. He heard each word quite distinctly, and saw Maurice Levasseur nodding encouragement to him.

'*Shema Yisroel....* !'

It took him by surprise, but Maurice was nodding even more emphatically.

'Hear O Israel, our God, our Creator is One!'

And Maurice was smiling, and whispering across the void,

'Yes, Victor. Yes!'

He was falling now, faster and faster. As he fell, he was calling, despite the buzzing in his head, and the terrible dryness of his mouth, 'Thou shalt love the Lord God with all thy heart, and with all thy mind. . . .'

And Maurice's face was floating further and further away, still smiling, still nodding encouragement.

43

They all felt increasingly safe as they drove on through the morning. Lance-Corporal Clarke had been relieved at the wheel by Lance-Corporal Rose. He now sat at the tail-board, whistling between his teeth as they plunged deeper and deeper into the Cotentin *bocage*, with its densely wooded valleys and deep sunken roads. It was inconceivable that they could ever be spotted travelling between those toweringly high hedges and through the twilit woods.

Vivian had decided that they should head northwards. That way, they would avoid the retreat of the demoralised French army while maintaining the possibility of catching up with the rearguard of the 2nd BEF. He wanted to reach the coast as close to Jersey as possible, in the hope of persuading a skipper to give them passage across to St Helier. He insisted that they should press on, stopping only to refuel, to stretch their legs, and to answer the calls of nature. All sat patiently, even Hugo, as they passed through village after village, through an ever changing landscape.

For many hours everywhere had seemed at peace. It was surprising, therefore, when they came across a sign stuck in the hedge which read, 'BEF/CRASC Bretteville.'

'Sight for sore eyes, eh, miss?' said Sergeant Micklewhite, who was sitting beside Julie.

'Think we've made it, sir?' asked Lance-Corporal Rose from behind the wheel.

Vivian sat with the map stretched across his knees. 'Let's hope so,' he said.

They turned down the lane indicated by the sign, and bumped along over an unmade road for about half a mile. They reached a second sign, which read, '3/4 Coy. RASC'. Rose pulled up, and switched off the motor. There was silence. The air was heavy with the smell of burning rubber. They jumped down from the lorry, and went over to the gate leading into the field.

'Looks like the municipal dump,' said Sergeant Micklewhite.

Close to the gate was a broad, standing pond, its edges churned by thick-tyred wheels into a mire. Two lines of camouflaged bell-tents stood intact but deserted. Not far from them was a burning massive pile of blackened and twisted machinery, engines, chassis and upholstery, and tyres. Army Bedford lorries were scattered about the field, either burnt-out or still smoking.

'Had to get out quick, if you asks me,' Clarke observed.

'Right,' said Vivian, 'we've all had a good look. Let's get moving.'

They climbed back into the 15 cwt., and turned round. As they jolted back down the track towards the road, Hugo asked, 'Have the English left us behind?'

'It seems like it,' Julie told him.

Vivian turned round in the front seat.

'We'll make for the coast road to Cherbourg,' he said. 'We can't be more than a mile or two from the coast.'

They drove down a steep hill into a small town. As they passed along the street leading to the market-place, the stall-holders on the pavements and their customers regarded the presence of a British army lorry with no more than casual interest.

'We'll buy some lunch,' Vivian said.

They parked in the small market-place, and got down. The houses all about were steeply gabled, reminding Julie of the Shambles in York. The sunlit air was very clear. Gulls were circling above the roofs.

The shops were full of food, and on the stalls were straw punnets filled with the year's first crop of strawberries. Julie bought five punnets, and asked Rose, who had already burdened himself with a pack of two hundred American cigarettes, to take them back to the lorry. Vivian took her arm and drew her over to where a crate was standing on the cobbles beside one of the stalls. Julie could see through the slats that it contained tomatoes.

'Look at the label,' Vivian told her.

An oval-shaped label had been pasted over the slats. It read 'St Saviour, Île de Jersey.'

'Well?' asked Julie.

'I'm fairly sure the Channel Islands don't sell tomatoes in bulk to France,' Vivian replied. 'The French don't need them. So this must be a local trade with Jersey. These people are probably buying direct from a Jersey grower. Don't you see? It means that somebody not too far away is bringing them over. . . . Look, it's worth a shot. You ask the woman there if she gets them fresh, and from whom. See if you can find out where they're landed. Make it seem as if you're just a woman who's interested in her shopping.'

Julie nodded. Hugo went with Vivian back to the lorry and the strawberries. Julie caught the attention of the woman behind the stall.

'Excuse me, madame,' she asked. 'Are the tomatoes really fresh?'

'Of course, mademoiselle,' the woman replied.

Julie picked up one and examined it.

'Are they grown in this part of the country, madame?' she asked.

'They are brought over from Jersey, mademoiselle,' the woman replied.

'I'll have a kilo,' said Julie.

As the woman weighed them, Julie asked, 'Does someone round here bring them over from Jersey?'

'There's a fellow down in St Pelagie, sails his boat across twice a week,' the woman replied. 'Makes a living at it.'

'Carrying tomatoes?' asked Julie.

The woman looked at her. 'And other things, mademoiselle,' she replied with a hint of a smile.

She held out the bag of tomatoes.

'Here, mademoiselle.'

Julie took them. She returned towards the lorry, pushing her way through the crowd of women with their broad shopping baskets, haggling about the stalls. Her shoulder was jolted so sharply that she very nearly dropped her tomatoes. She turned. As she did so, the girl who had struck her turned also. Julie found herself staring into the plump, half-recognised face. The girl tried to smile, unsure of herself, then turned and hurried into the throng of shoppers. As soon as she had disappeared, Julie remembered her, and the journey to Soissons, and the sad, dirty little baby. She stepped out into the street to see if she could catch sight of her again. At the far end of the market-place stood an old, black Buick sedan. There were four girls standing by it, one of them the now remembered figure of the girl who had just pushed past her; she was clutching what she took at first to be the baby, but then saw was a life-size doll. Three of the girls were dominated by the fourth – a slender giantess in black, with red hair framing her pallid face. All four were staring down the square at Julie. And between them, peering round the curtain over the Buick's rear window, was the smooth-faced, albino-white head smiling at her, so that she could smell the cologne like a palpable sick-sweet smell of death.

The face disappeared into the darkness behind the curtained window. The girls were climbing into the car. One of them smiled over her shoulder, back at Julie, before the door was shut. Julie saw that half the face was scarred.

'Julie,' Vivian called to her.

'Did you see?' she asked him. 'That car?'

'What car?' he asked.

'The big, black one over there. The Greek is in it. The Greek I told you about.'

But that had been so long ago.

406

'Not the one who tried to rape you on the road to Montcornet?' Vivian asked.

'Yes,' she said.

'Are you sure you're not imagining things?' he asked.

'He saw me one Sunday morning, on the Parvis de Notre Dame,' she told him. 'Only a couple of weeks ago. He's following me – I'm sure of it.'

'Come on,' said Vivian, 'we'd better be going.'

Clearly he didn't believe her, but he wasn't going to say so.

'I found out something,' she managed to tell him.

'What?'

'There's a man with a boat. He sails to Jersey from somewhere called St Pelagie. Twice a week.'

'Good girl,' Vivian told her. 'So let's find out where St Pelagie is.'

'And Vivian?' said Julie.

'Yes?'

She swallowed.

'About the Greek. He's got a bunch of women with him. And they're freaks – all of them. I've met one of them, Vivian. I'm not making it up. They scare me.'

'I'm sure they don't,' Vivian replied, 'but you must be utterly exhausted. Let's get to this place – St Pelagie – as quickly as we can. If we don't have any luck there, we'll still be near the main coast road to Cherbourg.'

The two lance-corporals were already sitting in the back of the lorry. They were eating large crusty sandwiches, and sharing a bottle of red wine between them. Hugo was sitting opposite them. One of the soldiers had bought him a large, sticky gâteau. Sergeant Micklewhite was already in the driving-seat.

'We're looking for a place called St Pelagie,' Vivian told him. 'On the coast. Can't be very far away. Have a look on the map.'

'When I told Victor about the man – the Greek, I mean,' Julie said, 'he believed me.'

'Victor?' asked Vivian.

Oh God, thought Julie; he was right. She was tired – very tired.

'Victor de Bart-Mendel,' she said.

Vivian nodded, giving away nothing.

'When I told him,' said Julie, 'he told me that the demons always came crawling out of chaos.'

She laughed. She sounded a bit hysterical, she decided.

'"*Vexilla regis prodeunt inferni*"', said Vivian.

'What's that?' asked Julie.

'Latin,' replied Vivian.

'I know that, cuckoo,' said Julie.

She realised she shouldn't call him names in front of his men. But he was smiling.

'It's Dante,' he said. '"The banners of the King of Hell go forth".'

Clarke leaned over and helped her into the lorry. Vivian pushed her up by her bottom. The impertinence made her feel a lot better.

They drove up another steep hill out of the town. As they reached the top, they saw fields stretching away on either side in the brilliantly clear afternoon light. Men and women were scything and gathering in the bleached hay. Above them, seagulls circled and cried. They drove on towards a dark pine wood. On one side of the road, a severe grey château reared its sloping roofs above the trees. The walls were unornamented, and built very thick.

They passed through the pine wood. On either side were hay-fields once more, sloping downwards and then rising again towards the bright, empty sky.

'I bet it's the sea on the other side of that ridge,' said Julie.

'The main Coutances-Cherbourg road runs along the top there,' said Vivian. 'We'll turn left, and follow it for half a mile or so. There should be a lane that will take us down to St Pelagie, between the cliffs. It looks a tiny place.'

There was the drone of an aircraft somewhere above them.

'Hallo, hallo, hallo!' said Sergeant Micklewhite.

He peered upwards over the wheel.

'There we are,' said Vivian, pointing.

They all followed his finger, staring above the bullet-smashed windscreen. The aircraft seemed to be hovering high above the ridge ahead of them.

'Could be one of ours, sir,' Sergeant Micklewhite said. 'There's an RAF base on Jersey.'

The seemingly motionless aircraft was growing perceptibly bigger. The haymakers in the fields were dropping their scythes and rakes, and were running away from the road. Julie recalled standing in the middle of the road to Soissons. It had been the same then.

'Out!' Vivian shouted. 'Into the hedge!'

The tailboard crashed down. Clarke was lowering Hugo into the road. Julie jumped, hitting the road-surface with the soles of her feet so that they stung on the rough stones. She grabbed Hugo's hand. Rose was throwing the rifle down to Clarke. Above the roar of the aero-engines, Julie heard Vivian shouting, 'Don't shoot, sar'nt. It's ours.'

She could feel the vibration of the propellers. She heard the ear-splitting, tearing noise of machine-guns, and wondered who was firing. She threw herself down, dragging Hugo with her, and tried to crawl on top of him, the twigs of the hedge tearing at the front of her blouse and at her sleeves, as she did so. So great was the violence of the explosion, that it seemed to enclose her. Fire seemed to burn at her ears. Pebbles and black dirt were falling like rain over her. She was aware of the wings of the aircraft having passed over her like a cloud.

She heard screaming as the noise of the engines diminished. She sat up. Hugo put his arms round her, and buried his head against her. The screaming went on. Dust and smoke obscured the road. She could see the outline of the lorry, and could see the flames flickering over the canopy. Vivian had staggered to his feet in front of her.

'Are you all right?' he asked.

She could hardly hear his voice. For a moment she thought she had gone deaf, then realised it was because of the noise of the screaming. Suddenly, she remembered. She staggered up.

'My suitcase!' she cried. She tried to push past Vivian to the lorry. 'My things. In the locker.'

Vivian realised what she was referring to. He ran out into the road himself, to the back of the lorry. He reached into the back, and dragged the case out of the locker. He threw it down into the road. Julie ran out to fetch it. At the same moment, she saw Sergeant Micklewhite sprawled motionless in the roadside grit. Then she saw Lance-Corporal Clarke. He was crouching out on the road, writhing in pain. The rifle was lying a foot away from his clenching and unclenching fist. His was the voice that was screaming.

'Down!' shouted Vivian.

He threw himself away from the back of the lorry onto the road, and covered his head with his hands. Julie was aware of Lance-Corporal Rose leaping onto her, and bearing her backwards into the grass. She heard the rushing sound, like a furnace door being opened. Orange burned through her eyelids. The heat was on her arms. She tried to call for Hugo.

Hugo was lying beside her. Rose got up.

'Stupid fucking bastards!' he shouted in a dry, cracked voice. 'Stupid rotten cunts!'

'Rose!' Vivian called.

His voice was hoarse.

He was standing up, his uniform covered in dust from the road. His hand was bleeding. He limped towards them. Julie's case was still lying in the middle of the road. The lorry was a skeleton in the heart of the subsiding blaze. In the quiver of the heat Clarke was lying spreadeagled on the ground. His head was blackened and charred.

'The bastard was one of ours,' Rose shouted. 'It was a fucking Blenheim!'

'Be quiet, Rose!' Vivian shouted at him.

'Bastard killed my mates, sir,' Rose tried to shout.

He had lost his voice. Blood dripped from Vivian's hand onto the ground.

Julie put her arm round Hugo. He was crying.

'They thought we were Jerry,' Vivian said.

He went over to the remains of Lance-Corporal Clarke, and removed the two identity tags from about his neck. He then went to the side of the road, and did the same for Sergeant Micklewhite. He put his hand into the breast-pocket of Micklewhite's b.d. blouse, and drew out his AB 64. He put both sets of tags and the paybook into his own breast pocket. Blood was dribbling down his wrist.

'They thought we were Jerry,' he said, 'because they expected to find Jerry here.'

'Let's see your hand,' said Julie.

'It's just a graze,' he told her. 'I scratched it when I fell. Better go and fetch your case.'

She went out into the road, and picked it up. She tried not to look at Clarke. As she returned to the grass, Vivian asked her, 'Do you have a clean handkerchief?'

'I think so,' Julie replied.

She knelt down and opened the case. She took out a handkerchief and gave it to him.

'It's a bit ladylike,' she said. 'Hadn't you better have two?'

'All right,' Vivian said.

'Here,' said Julie. 'Let me do it!'

She made a pad of one handkerchief, placed it on the cut on the heel of his palm, and tied it in place with the other.

'There,' she said.

She got up.

'We'd better see if these people can help us,' said Vivian.

They walked a little way up the road to a gate into one of the fields. A neat looking old man was hurrying over the parallel ridges of cut hay, towards them. As he approached, Julie saw that he was white-haired, with a trim, nicotine-stained moustache. He was wearing tweed plus-fours, a Norfolk jacket, and carried a shooting-stick under his arm. The cut of his clothes was too exact for an English squire.

'My dear friends! My dear friends!' he exclaimed. 'You are not harmed, mademoiselle? Gentlemen? I was just coming through the plantation up there, when I heard what had happened.'

'We are just a little shaken, thank you, monsieur,' Vivian replied. 'But two of our companions have been killed, I'm afraid.'

'What a terrible thing!' exclaimed the man. 'War is such a terrible thing. And what an experience, mademoiselle, for you, and the little man, here.'

He had dropped the point of his shooting-stick, and was leaning resting on its folded handle.

'You were trying to reach the coast, of course,' he went on. 'Let me introduce myself. My name is de Fremonde. My home is that stone pile you must have seen as you passed through the woods. What hospitality it has to offer, is yours, my friends.'

'We are trying to reach the coast,' Vivian admitted. 'A village called St Pelagie?'

'Alas, Major . . . ?' asked de Fremonde.

'Hardwicke,' replied Vivian.

'Alas, Major Hardwicke, St Pelagie is scarcely a village. A gap in the cliffs, and a few hovels. Mademoiselle . . . ?'

'Armitage, monsieur,' Julie told him.

'*Enchanté*, Mademoiselle Armitage,' de Fremonde went on. 'Mademoiselle Armitage and the little man must be totally exhausted by their experiences. *Comment appelles-toi, mon enfant?*' he asked Hugo suddenly, reaching out to take his chin in his hand.

'*Je m'appelle Hugo, monsieur,*' Hugo replied. 'Hugo de Bart-Mendel.'

'Good gracious!' de Fremonde exclaimed. 'Your papa isn't Victor de Bart-Mendel, is he?'

'Yes, monsieur.'

'What a surprise!' exclaimed de Fremonde. 'Who would have believed it! I remember your mother well, a most beautiful woman, and a very gracious hostess!'

'She is dead, monsieur. She has been dead these four years.'

'*Oh, mon pauvre petit.*'

De Fremonde turned to Julie and Vivian.

'I have not moved in Paris society for the past five years,' he explained. 'I am one of those dull, country gentlemen, I fear.'

'We were hoping to find a skipper who would give us passage to Jersey, monsieur,' Vivian persisted.

'At St Pelagie, Major?' de Fremonde laughed.

Julie was about to say that they had heard of somebody, but the fact that Vivian had said nothing warned her to keep quiet.

'We hoped somewhere along the coast,' said Vivian finally.

'There is always hope, Major,' said de Fremonde. 'Though not in St Pelagie, I fear. To the north, perhaps. Allow me to make a suggestion. Let the boy and his governess – you *are* the boy's governess, I take it, mademoiselle?' he asked.

Without giving herself time for thought, Julie replied, 'Yes, monsieur.'

She squeezed Hugo's hand, signalling that he should not deny it.

'Let them come with me, Major, and take shelter in my home, while you and your man reconnoitre the coast for a ferryman to take you to the *Îles Anglo-Normandes*. It would give me the greatest pleasure, as a friend of the Baron de Bart-Mendel from the old days.

411

They will be safe with me for as long as is necessary. In any case, you won't be able to cross before the morning tide.'

Julie did not want to be separated from Vivian again. She was about to decline the invitation, when Vivian said, 'You are very kind, monsieur.'

There was the faint hum of an aircraft in the distant sky.

'Julie, I think you and Hugo should go with Monsieur . . . ' Vivian went on.

'*Comte,* major. Le Comte de Fremonde. Titles are old-fashioned in these Republican days, I know; but my family have borne theirs honourably down the centuries, and as last of the line, I should like to carry it to my grave.'

'Of course, Monsieur le Comte,' Vivian told him. 'And Corporal Rose and I will come to the château when we have made the necessary arrangements.'

'You need not concern yourself with those poor, brave men,' said de Fremonde, pointing to the road. 'My people will see that they receive a Christian burial.'

'Thank you,' said Vivian. 'I'm sure their families will appreciate your kindness.'

He glanced at Julie. She wished she could have talked with him alone. She was uneasy about separating.

She caught his eyes – the slight smile of reassurance.

'May I keep your handkerchiefs?' he asked.

She nodded, not trusting herself to speak.

'Goodbye, miss,' said Lance-Corporal Rose.

His face was still white with shock, but his voice was steady.

'Come back quickly,' she said to him.

'Of course, miss,' he replied.

Vivian and he strode off across the hay-stubble. De Fremonde led Julie and Hugo up the field towards the woods.

'*Tu parles français, ma chère?*' he asked.

He addressed her as if she were a child, or a servant, thought Julie. But she had said that she was Hugo's governess, so she supposed it was her own fault.

'*Mademoiselle Julie parle français impeccablement,*' Hugo replied instantly on her behalf.

'Julie,' de Fremonde replied, 'such a charming name. A French name!'

Julie glanced across the field. Vivian and Rose were increasing the distance which separated her from them, as if they were walking up the opposite arm of a capital V. Vivian looked round, and waved to her.

44

Julie went to the connecting door between her own room and that of Hugo. She finished buttoning down the front of her frock, and stood erect. Hugo yawned deeply. The poor little thing should be going straight to bed, she decided; but de Fremonde had invited him to go down to have dinner with them, and French boys were expected to comply with such invitations.

'Have you washed your face?' she asked.

The peak of his hair was damp over his forehead. It was sufficient; she didn't feel she had the energy to enquire more deeply. She buttoned the cuffs of her dress over her wrists.

'Put on a clean shirt,' she ordered.

'You're not really my governess,' grumbled Hugo.

'I'm more important than a governess,' Julie told him.

She half-expected him to reply,

'Yes – you're my father's mistress.'

She said, 'So hurry up!'

'When will Major Hardwicke be coming for us?' he asked.

'I don't know any more than you do,' she told him.

She went back into her own room, went to the dressing-table mirror, and flicked open her compact. As she powdered her face, she realised that the situation was almost wholly out of her control; there was no way in which she could draw Vivian back to her. She felt frightened.

She didn't like the château. She told herself that it was because it was so medieval, with its thick stone walls, its stone staircases, and black wrought-iron lamp standards. It was just like the set of Basil Rathbone's castle in the Errol Flynn picture of *Robin Hood*. But it wasn't only that. She remembered what Victor had said about people making places holy by the spirit they brought to them. Perhaps people could also make a place unholy. And yet de Fremonde had given her no cause for such an uncharitable thought.

She snapped shut her compact and went over to the chair by the four-poster bed. Her handbag was hanging over the back of the chair. She dropped her compact into it. She was standing at the casement-window. She leaned across the thickness of the stone sill, and looked down at the twilit garden below. There was a sheer drop of fifty or sixty feet into the moat. The moat was dry, and grassed-over. Flowerbeds and alpine rills had been dug and arranged up the opposite bank.

'Ready, Hugo?' she called.

She went back to the dressing-table and carefully arranged her newly washed and brushed hair over her shoulders. Hugo came in through the connecting door.

'I'm glad your room is next to mine,' he said. 'I'd be scared if I was all by myself.'

She took his hands.

'Will you come up to bed when I do?' he asked.

'Yes,' she replied. 'I promise.'

They went down to the main hall. Julie gripped the rail firmly as she went down the uneven stone steps in her high heels. The dining-table stood on a square of carpet: a candle-lit island in the centre of the wide expanse of stone-flagged floor. The lofty stone walls hung with tapestries and ancient weapons were in shadow. When she had sat down at the table, the draught lapped round Julie's ankles as if she were dangling her feet in a fell-side stream. The food, however, and the wine were both excellent.

'It is a pleasure to have guests with so hearty an appetite,' de Fremonde assured her.

Hugo had eaten well. He was struggling to keep awake, Julie noticed.

'I never travel up to Paris, now,' de Fremonde continued. 'Like Hugo's father, I used to keep a grand Paris home, but no longer. Here one may still live in the way to which one was born. The people here have not entirely lost their sense of order, of self-discipline.' He gave her a wise sort of smile. 'Perhaps we country people are still able to hear the voice of God from time to time,' he suggested, 'like the shepherds of the Bible. For many years now – since the foundation of the Third Republic – our poor France has been ruled by venal politicians who have boasted that they were opportunists. We have even had an Opportunist Party. What do you think of that, eh?'

Julie didn't really have an opinion on the matter. In a vague sort of way she had always assumed that organised political parties were opportunist.

'There are few people in government,' de Fremonde was continuing 'who love France. It's hard to find any organised section of the people who care about anything save their own interest. The workers make demands, and if their demands aren't met, they take to the streets. The industrialists and financiers take vastly more than their share of profits, then buy gold instead of re-investing their capital. Neither side has the welfare of France at heart.

'I hope you will not think me anti-Semite, Miss Armitage. I have told you of the great respect in which I hold this young man's father. It is quite disgraceful to regard the race of our blessed Saviour and his holy Mother as being less than human – I mean, as do the National Socialists in Germany; but one cannot deny that, in this unhappy

414

country, both Capital and Labour have been demoralised and corrupted by the acquisitiveness which they have learnt from the Jewish character. The Jew is, of course, among the most gifted and brilliant of the human species; but because of their traditions and beliefs, which have cut them off from the historical and cultural traditions of the most civilised of the European peoples, Jews can never become, whole-heartedly, citizens of a great nation-state. They lack any true patriotism, and will take from the nation whatever is to their personal advantage. It is stupid to look for a Jewish conspiracy. The international power of the House of Rothschild is not the result of a conspiracy; the influence of Karl Marx and his Jewish disciples is not a world conspiracy. It is no more than the natural effect of the development of the Jewish character, a character which could never grasp the sense of patriotism.'

De Fremonde reached over, and refilled Julie's wine glass. Julie tried to keep her eyes on his face, so as to appear as if she was paying attention to his monologue. He was an old man, living alone. Old men have a habit of talking to people as if they are talking to themselves. The candlelight emphasised the narrowness of his face. If he had had long, pointed whiskers instead of his small military moustache, he would have looked like a rat.

'I'm old enough to remember *l'Affaire Dreyfus*, Miss Armitage,' he told her. 'You have heard of *l'Affaire Dreyfus?*'

'Of course,' Julie replied. Paul Muni had played the part of Emile Zola in the picture, and Joseph Schildkraut that of Alfred Dreyfus.

'I lived in Paris then, with my dear mother,' de Fremonde continued. 'My dear mother is dead – long since dead.'

He cleared his throat.

'There have been no other women in my life, Miss Armitage. It is my deeply held belief that God grants us sufficient fidelity for only one person in our life. And that one person for me, was my dear mother. So I have never married. I have never had a *liaison – une étroite amitié*. My dear mother was very beautiful. As beautiful as the mother of our sleepy young friend here.'

He smiled at Hugo.

'I have kept no photographs, no portraits. They are empty shadows to torment one. They are devoid of substance, like the mirrors in which damned souls can see no reflection. But her beauty remains with me – here.'

He pressed the ends of his fingers against his temple. The gesture reminded Julie of a man pointing a pistol at his brain.

'My dear mother had no doubt whatever of Dreyfus's innocence. She never believed the charges laid against him – never. And I will never forget her nobility, the calm of her beauty and dignity, like a light in the darkest days of the *Affaire*. Her friends deserted her. She was no longer invited to the best *salons*. Her lovers forsook her – oh yes, she had many lovers. In fact, she used to say that the reason why I was her only true lover was because I never made love to her.'

He laughed. Julie tried to smile understandingly.

'She was the true image of France. She had courage; the clarity of true reason; the generosity to give of herself without losing a shred of her natural dignity. But she suffered. She suffered deeply, Miss Armitage. She was a gregarious person. Ostracism tormented her in a way it could never torment me. And I was privileged to remain her sole friend in those days.

'You can imagine how I felt when one was forced to watch how the Jew-inspired Radical movement and Jewish financial interests began to manipulate the fact of Dreyfus's innocence to their own advantage. How they exploited it to undermine the Army, and the Church – institutions which may have been tragically mistaken in the position they adopted over the *Affaire,* but which represented the best in selfless dedication to the noblest traditions of France. Make no mistake, Miss Armitage, since the end of the *Affaire* France has been ruled by Jewish and Protestant Freemasons and atheistic leftists. It is my opinion – and you may laugh at an old man's opinions if you wish ... '

'No,' cried Julie in the nick of time. 'No!'

'It is my opinion that this terrible war is God's lesson, warning us that His followers should at last seize control of the destinies of France from the apostates who have ruled too long. Only when men and women of virtue assert their natural-born right to lead the French people – men and women who are the spiritual children of Jeanne d'Arc, of Charles VII, of the Bastard of Orléans ... '

'My father says,' Hugo announced suddenly to Julie, 'that the Bastard of Orléans wore the Tondeau when he fought beside Jeanne d'Arc.'

'You know you shouldn't interrupt when a grown-up is speaking,' Julie rebuked him quickly. 'I'm sorry, Monsieur le Comte,' she added to de Fremonde. 'It's because he's so tired.'

For a moment she thought she might have deflected de Fremonde's interest in what Hugo had said.

'Not at all, Miss Armitage,' de Fremonde told her. 'If we invite him to the grown-up meal of the day, we should expect him to want to take part in the grown-ups' conversation.'

He turned to Hugo.

'You mean the *Tondeau de Chartres,* of course, eh, Hugo?' he asked. 'It would have been worn by Jacques Dunois when he became Charles's *Connétable,* after the coronation at Reims.'

'Oh no,' Hugo replied, 'my father said that Dunois wore it at the Tourelles. At the siege of Orléans.'

'That is most interesting,' said de Fremonde. 'I have never heard that before. Tell me, young man. Has your father ever shown you the *Tondeau de Chartres*?'

'Yes, monsieur,' Hugo replied.

'Then you are very fortunate,' said de Fremonde. 'I have never seen it.'

Hugo had at last caught Julie's eye.

'Papa keeps it very carefully,' he told de Fremonde.

'I'm sure he does,' said de Fremonde. 'France has no more sacred a possession in private hands. Have you seen it, Miss Armitage?'

Julie hesitated before replying, 'It is very beautiful. I've never seen anything quite like it.'

'Not even in your Victoria and Albert Museum?' asked de Fremonde. 'There are many beautiful things in your Victoria and Albert Museum.'

'Nothing quite like that,' said Julie. 'Nothing that is so beautiful and has so much history.'

'It is a great responsibility,' said de Fremonde, 'as well as a great privilege to guard the *Tondeau of Chartres*. To some, it might seem an almost intolerable burden.'

Julie realised that she would certainly have sacrificed the Tondeau to secure Hugo's safety – and even Vivian's and her own. No object on earth was more important than people, she decided.

'I suppose it could seem so, to some,' she replied.

De Fremonde laughed, 'Ah, Miss Armitage, but then you are neither a Frenchwoman, nor a Catholic, are you?'

'I'm afraid not, Monsieur le Comte,' she replied.

De Fremonde smiled roguishly at her.

45

'Julie,' Hugo called, 'what are you doing?'

'You should be asleep,' Julie called back.

She was standing beside her bed. She had taken the Tondeau from its black, embossed leather case, and had placed it on the counterpane. The trouble was that she had no real plan of what to do. She looked around her. Without anything inside the case it would be too light. And whatever she put in, in place of the Tondeau, it must not shake or feel loose.

She saw a small crystal ashtray on the mantlepiece.

'I thought you'd gone downstairs again,' Hugo called.

'I promised I'd stay up here,' Julie replied. 'I keep my promises. Now go to sleep.'

She slipped the Tondeau between her pillow and the bolster. She took the ashtray from the mantlepiece and placed it in the depression in the lining of the case. It was very slightly too large, so she pressed it down. The lining gave. She closed the two wings of the lid and relocked it. Then she went to the window, leaned over the stone sill, and opened it. For a moment, there was the absurd hope that she would see Vivian and Rose crossing the lawn, but garden and lawn were empty. She threw the small key from the case down into the moat – it was too small ever to be found. She closed the window again, and lay down on the bed, sitting up against the pillow and bolster. She took needle and thread from the suitcase open beside her.

'What are you doing now?' Hugo called.

'Sewing,' Julie replied.

'What are you sewing?' asked Hugo.

'Never you mind,' Julie replied.

'Your *culottes*?' asked Hugo.

'Don't be so rude,' Julie told him. 'Go to sleep.'

What on earth were they going to do if Vivian didn't come back, she wondered. Supposing he still hadn't returned by morning? Should she stay where she was, and risk the Germans catching up with them? Or should she try to find her own way back to England with Hugo?

She finished her sewing and fell asleep; but the question stayed in her mind, unresolved.

She was woken up by a gentle knock on the door. She sat up. Her light was still on, and she was still fully dressed, but she was certain she had slept for a long time.

'Who is it?' she called.

'It is I – de Fremonde,' came the reply.

She picked up her wrist-watch from the bedside table. It was almost four o'clock.

'Come in,' she called.

The door opened, and de Fremonde came in. He was wearing a black satin dressing-gown. A white silk scarf was about his neck.

'You remained dressed, Miss Armitage,' he said. 'A wise precaution.'

'Has Major Hardwicke arrived?' Julie asked.

'Alas no,' said de Fremonde, 'but I'm afraid you will have to leave immediately. I've had word by telephone, only a few minutes ago: the Germans are in Barneville to the north, and Coutances to the south. They are moving to seal off the coast. They will be here in a matter of hours. The only chance for the boy is for you to reach the coast immediately and try to arrange passage for the two of you. If Major Hardwicke comes here, I'll tell him what has happened.'

Julie got down off the bed. She reached for her high-heeled shoes and threw them into the case. She laced on her brogues. 'You're very kind,' she remembered to say.

'Not at all, not at all. I wish there was more I could do, if only for the boy's sake.'

Julie went through to Hugo's room. He whimpered on being roused.

'Dress quickly,' she said, 'we're leaving.'

He rubbed his eyes.

'Has Major Hardwicke come back?' he asked.

'No,' said Julie.

'Then why . . . ?' he began.

'The Germans are coming. They'll be here very soon. You must hurry.'

She went back into her own room. De Fremonde was standing by her bed. He had been looking into her suitcase, she was sure of it. He turned his head as she came in.

She walked round the bed. She folded the slacks and blouse she had been wearing the day before, and put them in the suitcase. She took out her cardigan and pulled it on over her frock.

'Miss Armitage,' de Fremonde spoke in a low voice. 'You will forgive me, I am sure. I know that, as the boy's governess, you will have his welfare at heart before all else.'

'Naturally, Monsieur le Comte,' Julie replied.

'I think you may have something with you – something even more precious to France than the son of the Baron de Bart-Mendel.'

'What do you mean monsieur?'

She had been expecting this. She looked directly at him, challenging him to speak openly.

'I must insist you give it to me before it is too late,' he said. He paused. 'The de Fremondes are to be trusted with it,' he said. 'We have served France honourably for many centuries. The Tondeau de Chartres belongs to those who love France. At best, Miss Armitage, you will take it out of the country; at worst it will fall into the hands of the Germans. I cannot allow either of those things to happen.'

She stared at him without replying.

'I know you have it there, hidden under your garments,' he pointed at the suitcase.

A token resistence would be best, thought Julie.

'Monsieur le Comte, I promised the Baron de Bart-Mendel that I would take it to England for him,' she said. 'I have to keep my word.'

'I deeply regret to have to say this, Miss Armitage,' said de Fremonde, 'but I cannot let either of you leave my house with it.'

'Very well,' she said in what she hoped sounded a sulky voice. She reached into the suitcase, and drew out the black, embossed leather case.

'I do not have the key,' she said, 'but I don't suppose you'll have any trouble forcing it open.'

He weighed it in his hands. He looked at the lock.

'It only requires a pin,' he remarked.

'A hairpin?' asked Julie. 'I can give you one.'

She held a kirby-grip out to him.

'There's no need, Miss Armitage,' he smiled.

'Will you put away the case, Monsieur le Comte,' said Julie, 'before Hugo sees what I have done.'

There was a look of solicitous understanding on de Fremonde's face.

'Of course, Miss Armitage,' he said.

He slipped the case into his dressing-gown, under his arm.

'Let your conscience be at rest, my dear,' he said. 'No harm or dishonour will come to it. It will be where it truly belongs.'

'That is no concern of mine,' said Julie. 'As you pointed out, Hugo is my concern.'

Hugo appeared in the doorway. He was untidily dressed, with his shirt buttoned the wrong way, and hanging half-out. He was still dazed with sleep. Julie closed her suitcase and picked up her handbag. De Fremonde led them downstairs, with Julie tugging Hugo along by the hand. They went out of the main entrance, and across the dew-covered lawn to a gravel causeway which led into the pine wood.

'Go straight along,' said de Fremonde, 'and you'll come out onto open ground. If you keep straight on, you'll come to the main Cherbourg road. The cliffs, and the path down to the shore, are to the left along the road.'

They set off down the causeway drive. Strange stone animals loomed up on either side against the early dawn sky – gryphons, lions, huge lean greyhounds with coronets about their necks. Julie glanced back. De Fremonde was gone. Against the pale emptiness reared the spires and mansard turrets of the château.

At the end of the causeway, they entered the long black tunnel through the pine wood, their feet padding softly on the damp, scented carpet of last year's needles. They reached the grey light at the other end and hurried out onto the grass turf of the heath, between thick clumps of broom and gorse. Clutching her suitcase in one hand, and dragging Hugo along with the other, Julie pushed between the gorse-bushes towards the point where she could see no more land against the sky.

A rough path wound between boulders and outcrops of rock. It was dotted with sheep's droppings. At one point the path stopped altogether, confronting them with a large broken rock. They climbed up it, and scrambled over, Julie dragging her suitcase behind her. On the other side, the path descended steeply to a hedgerow, and a wide

420

main road. As Julie stood looking down, she saw, on the other side of the hedge, figures moving, and caught a glimpse of a grey steel helmet.

She crouched down.

'Quick! Back!' she whispered.

They crawled back over the rock, and dropped down the other side. As Julie slithered down, her skirt caught about her knees, and she had to struggle to release it. She wished she had been wearing her slacks.

'What is it?' asked Hugo.

'Germans,' said Julie. She gave his hand a squeeze.

She leaned her back against the rock to catch her breath. Raising her skirt, she examined her stockings. By some miracle, they weren't laddered.

'What are we going to do?' asked Hugo. 'Will we find Major Hardwicke?'

Voices could be heard quite distinctly on the fresh morning air. The soldiers were staying down on the road. Hugo tugged at Julie's arm. She grabbed her suitcase, and they both plunged into the bracken, dropping down behind a clump of broom. They were only just in time. A file of German *landsers* appeared between the granite outcrops a little way up the path, and came strolling down towards the road, talking noisily and laughing. They were wearing full equipment buckled on their T belts, and carried rifles. One of them was carrying a long barrelled machine-gun across his shoulder in the manner of an old-fashioned musketeer. He and his immediate companion were festooned in ammunition belts. Another was carrying a battered pewter milk-can, and was slopping the contents onto the path as he jolted down the slope. All appeared to be at their ease; several had taken off their helmets and were carrying them in their hands. One of them was smoking a pipe.

Julie held her breath as they went by. A frond of bracken was touching her eye, but she dared not move. It was a nightmare; yet the German soldiers were young, open-faced, and happy. They would surely have treated her kindly. Probably they were more to be trusted than the Comte de Fremonde.

The soldiers scrambled over the broken rock, shouting, laughing, and spilling more of the milk. Their voices faded down the hillside. Julie waited five minutes. Leaving her suitcase with Hugo, she crawled out of the broom. She climbed up the rock once more, and looked over. The Germans were still waiting on the far side of the hedge, but this time there were two standing out on the road, rifles in hand, and another two on the nearside of the hedge keeping watch up the hill.

For a minute or two, Julie crouched on the rock. She tried to come to terms with her own misery. They were cut off from the shore, and they had lost Vivian. She felt utterly lonely, and weighed down with responsibilities she had never sought.

Hugo whispered up to her, 'What are we going to do, Julie?'

Go back to the château. What else? There was just the vaguest possibility that Vivian might have returned. She took Hugo by the hand, and led him, half-running, back to the cover of the pine wood.

'Don't ask questions,' she snapped.

They stumbled along the dark avenue to the lines of carved stone beasts. Before them, separated from them by the dew-glistening garden, stood the château, its lofty, sloping roofs tinged with pink in the morning light.

They stopped. Julie was gasping for breath. Putting down her case, she went to the moss-covered balustrade, and peered across the lawn to the house from between the moss-stained talons of an up-rearing gryphon. There were lights being switched on and off inside the house as if people were running from room to room. Women's voices were shouting. Shadows moved against the windows.

'Julie, what – ?' Hugo tried to ask.

'Sh!' Julie whispered.

There was a shriek of pain, and then another. It had the note of somebody pleading. Julie gripped the cold stone edge of the balustrade. There was another shriek, and then another. Then it stopped. A few minutes later there came the sound of a car's engine revving up. There were voices calling outside, and the slamming of car doors. Wheels crunched on the gravel. The car came sweeping round the front of the house at full speed, gravel chips spinning up from behind the rear wheels. From across the lawn, Julie recognised the bulbous shape of the dust-smeared Buick, the curtained rear windows, and the swarthy, Mediterranean profile of the man at the wheel.

She stood behind the cover of the gryphon, sick with fear, as she listened to the car tearing away down the drive. Why not go back to the road? she thought. Why not simply give themselves up to the soldiers? They looked like honest, straightforward young men. As de Fremonde had said, they would almost certainly treat her in a chivalrous fashion, and they surely would not ill-treat a child. The idea of surrendering all responsibility was very tempting.

'Come on,' she said to Hugo. 'We'd better see what has happened.'

She took his hand once more, and led him across the grass to the main entrance to the château. The doors were open at the top of the steps. They went inside. The elderly servants were either not yet awake, or preferred not to be about. The place could have been totally deserted. Julie led Hugo up the short flight of stone stairs to the lower gallery. They went along to de Fremonde's drawing-room. Once again, the door was ajar. They went inside. De Fremonde was staring straight at them. He had been tied to his chair. The moment Julie saw the empty sockets, and the state of his face, she dropped her suitcase and grabbed at Hugo, pressing his head against her breasts.

'Don't look,' she whispered. 'Don't look, darling.'

The scent of cologne still hung on the air.

'I saw,' Hugo whispered, his lips moving against her frock.

He was shivering.

All about the room, books, furniture, ornaments and bric-à-brac lay in confusion about the floor. Julie knew what the intruders had come for. They had been following her. And she knew why they had been following her. She remembered now quite vividly; that day she had ridden in the Buick, the Greek had been travelling to La Berlière.

She drew Hugo out of the room and closed the door behind her. Whatever happened, they must not be caught up in an investigation into de Fremonde's death. They must leave again immediately. She had left the suitcase in the drawing-room. She was wondering how to find the courage to go back for it when she heard voices downstairs at the front entrance. She pulled Hugo down the gallery and pushed him into a doorway hidden behind an alcove curtain.

Boots rang on the stone flags below the gallery. Men's voices were speaking quite loudly, but she could not distinguish either words or language. She put her arms round Hugo, and hugged him close to her. She could hear footsteps coming up the stairs. If the voices turned out to be German, she decided, they would give themselves up. She was too shocked, too tired, to take any more.

The footsteps came up the gallery and stopped outside the drawing-room door.

'My God!' It was Vivian's voice. 'Take a look at this!'

'Jesus fucking wept!' cried Lance-Corporal Rose.

Julie pushed her way through the alcove curtains.

'Vivian, where the bloody hell have you been?' she demanded.

Then she burst into tears.

46

'Gold,' Papayannis repeated. 'Gold is the only international passport. It doesn't matter whether Germans rule, or the Two Hundred Families, eh? Gold opens all doors.'

As if to confirm what he was saying, he put his hand on Pauline's thigh, and squeezed it through the tight-fitting crêpe-de-chine skirt.

He could feel the top of her stocking. He ran the edge of his hand between her thighs, and rested it against the hardness of her lap. He could feel no undergarment there.

He preferred Pauline to the other girls. He found something perversely attractive about plump, childish little Marie-Claire, not least because of the dirtiness of her appearance; but she smelt of sweat. There was no doubt that Cybele was a striking-looking woman; it wasn't so much her height that put him off as a dislike of any woman who assumed authority. Florence was a most attractive girl when she managed to conceal her dreadful disfigurement; but her unpredictable savagery had a psychopathic quality like that of Aris Liassides.

Pauline stirred his lust beyond containment; her quiet good sense and self-control, her ability to manage Cybele and Florence, combined with a shamelessness in the heat of sex, reminded him of the woman in the drawing by Felicien Rops hanging above his desk in Paris.

She was smiling, pressing her mount against the pressure of his fist – but without turning to look at him.

'Want to go inside, darling?' she asked softly.

'When we have made our arrangements,' he replied, demonstrating that he, too, was capable of iron self-discipline.

He released her thigh, and took a green baize bag from the attaché-case beside him. He spilled the old, gold napoleons onto the white of the table-cloth. The girls laughed as they watched, breathlessly, as if in orgasm. Even Rahman and Chamoun stared.

They were sitting in the enclosed courtyard-restaurant of the Bouilloire d'Or, in Bretteville. It was still quite early in the morning; the *patron*, even when he had seen the roll of coloured notes held by a rubber band, which Papayannis had pushed under his nose, had not been sure whether the establishment was open or not. He had, however, let them in. There had been two women sitting at one of the tables set out on the cobbles under the roof of trellised vines. They had been in black skirts and blouses, but their white aprons had been folded on the table beside them as they drank their breakfast coffee. One was middle-aged, the other adolescent. Neither was pleased to have to start work. The young girl took the order for coffee, brioches and a bottle of cognac. She had been scowling as she stood at the table, but Papayannis had smiled at her, and had thrust a note behind the crumpled handkerchief in her apron pocket. Her expression changed immediately.

The girls must have been utterly fatigued after the journey and the night's exertions, but success and the prospect of gold had put them in holiday mood. Florence and Marie-Claire had been attempting to seduce El Chamoun and Rahman in the most blatant, disgusting way. It would be amusing to watch them all when they really went to it –

particularly in the company of Pauline. The good humour had begun
the previous afternoon when, first, Marie-Claire had recognised the
English girl in the market-place, and then when they had all seen her
with de Bart-Mendel's little son. It had been a shame they had fled
the Château de Fremonde; Papayannis would have enjoyed a second
encounter with the English girl, but it was not to be. Now, the
sunlight was filtering between the vine-leaves over their heads, and
the heavy, embossed, black leather medallion case was in front of him.
There was no mistake about it, even without the key to unlock it; in
the corners, in thin gold tooling, was the florid monogram of the de
Bart-Mendels. There would be time enough to force it – and an
enchanted pleasure in gratification deferred. 'I think perhaps that
Mademoiselle Cybele should distribute the reward,' he suggested.

He pushed the gold coins over to her with the back of his thick
hand. She had been sitting aloof, preoccupied. He took the lid from
his *café filtre*, and looked inside.

'*C'est bien, ça,*' he exclaimed, relishing one of the small pleasures
of life.

He lifted the filter from off the cup, allowed the last of the
percolated coffee to drip through, and placed it on the tray beside
him. He dropped two sugar-lumps into his cup, then put a fresh cigar
into his mouth and let Pauline light it for him.

It was while Monsieur Chris was preoccupied with drawing on his
cigar to keep it alight, that Marie-Claire, who was facing the street
entrance, saw the Germans come in. There was an officer and three
men. They were armed; one man had a small machine-gun slung over
his shoulder, the other two were carrying rifles, and the officer had
a pistol at his belt. They were wearing their helmets slung on their
arms, and were smoking.

'Those men are Germans,' Marie-Claire whispered to the doll
which was sitting on her knee.

Poor Bébé had been up all night. She had watched how Aunt
Florence had punished the stupid man in the château; it was
important she should learn what happened to naughty people who
didn't do what Aunt Florence told them to do.

The Germans settled themselves round a table in one of the vine
covered alcoves at the other end of the courtyard. The older waitress
went over to them. Maire-Claire suddenly noticed the expression on
Monsieur Chris's pallid, fat face. He had seen the Germans and he
was terrified. He was wiping the sweat from his face just like that
stupid, shrunken little old man in the château when they had been
asking him about the medallion. There was something very wrong;
the others did not seem to notice, but Marie-Claire felt unease
crawling all over her. El Chamoun had his large hand under her dress;
he was being very naughty indeed, coaxing the damp into her pants,

425

and trying to make her all excited. She pushed his hand away, and got to her feet. She cradled Bébé in her arms to reassure the others.

'Where are you off to?' Florence demanded suspiciously.

The cruelty was still in her voice. It scared Marie-Claire.

'Bébé wants to do *pi-pi*,' she said in a silly little voice which sometimes excited Florence and sometimes irritated her.

Florence shrugged. Cybele was concentrating on her arrangment of the gold coins in small piles. Monsieur Chris tried to smile up at her. She crossed the cobbles to the kitchen entrance, and asked the middle-aged waitress to show her the way. As soon as she was enclosed within the narrow stone cell of the *cabinet*, she pulled her pants down to her ankles, afraid that someone would spy on her, and see that it was only her fear which had brought her there. She waited with the doll on the bunched skirt in her lap, her thighs and legs bare, crouched like a twitching, cowering mouse in its hole.

A moment after Marie-Claire had disappeared into the kitchens, von Leonarte got up and went over to where Papayannis was sitting. He was grimly amused by the way the man's florid mouth quivered as he watched him coming across the yard. He was aware of the others, particularly of the tall, hectic-faced redhead sitting beside the Greek. He did not bow.

'Monsieur Papayannis?' he said.

'You have a good memory, Captain,' Papayannis giggled.

The sweat was standing on his forehead.

'We have followed you from Paris, monsieur,' von Leonarte said. 'Your route was observed by our people. You undertook a task for us. I hope you have been successful.'

He put his hands on the shoulders of Rahman and Florence who were sitting between himself and the table with their backs to him. He pushed them aside and placed his fingers on the black leather medallion case.

'This is it?' he asked.

Papayannis nodded.

'Very good,' said von Leonarte.

He picked it up. Papayannis reminded him of the fat, grease-shining, obsequious faces of Jewish entrepreneurs in the Ministry of National Enlightenment's film, '*Der Ewige Jude*'. He was revolted by the spectacle.

'The key,' said Papayannis, 'is missing.'

Von Leonarte put the case under his arm. He smiled.

'I don't suppose we shall have difficulty in opening it,' he said. 'And you still have your cognac to finish.'

He returned across the courtyard. Helm looked up from the table.

'Congratulations, Herr Rittmeister,' he exclaimed on seeing the case.

426

Radinski and Graser offered their congratulations enthusiastically. Von Leonarte put the case down on the table.

'Get it open,' he said to Helm.

Helm pulled it to him. He took his clasp-knife from his pocket.

In the old days, when von Leonarte had been a small boy, there had been a beggar. This beggar had not been one of the army of ex-servicemen, pitiful in their respectability, but a filthy, verminous, drunken old tramp – one who, even in years of plenty, would never have worked for a living. Every month or so, he would appear at the back door of the Bishop's house. He would bow, grovel, and whine for a hand-out. In the words of the Bishop's groom, he would have eaten horse-shit for the price of a drink. Once or twice he had met little Dieter out on the road, or on some woodland path. He would wave to him, smile and beckon to him as if they were social equals, and had appalling secrets to share. Such claims to intimacy had given Dieter nightmares. Papayannis's sweaty obsequiousness had brought the nightmares back to von Leonarte's weary brain.

'Give me the Schmeisser,' he said to Helm.

Helm looked up in surprise from the lock on the medallion case. He handed over the Schmeisser. Von Leonarte snapped back the firing mechanism and switched to automatic fire.

'Radinski! Graser!' he ordered.

He realised that he could not trust Klaus Helm for this sort of work.

'These *gangsters*,' he used the English expression, 'must not be allowed to murder again.'

Radinski and Graser brought their rifles. Von Leonarte led them out of the alcove. The young waitress was in the yard, the middle-aged one and the *patron* were standing in the kitchen doorway. Papayannis struggled to rise as he saw von Leonarte and his men approaching. Because of his bulk, the buttons of his waistcoat caught under the edge of the table, and he had to bend double to release them. He struggled to pull out his passport from his inside pocket.

'You are guilty of murder and of looting,' von Leonarte announced. 'As an officer of the occupying power, it is my duty under military law to make an example of you.'

The long-haired girl was on her feet. She tried to move out of the way.

'Monsieur,' she whined, 'I haven't done anything.'

Radinski pushed her back to her seat. She sat down whimpering. It was astounding, thought von Leonarte, that anybody so dreadfully disfigured should be so anxious to live – particularly a young woman.

'May I remind the captain,' said Papayannis, 'that I am under the protection of a neutral power?'

Von Leonarte did not bother to reply.

Only the tall, red-haired woman remained completely unmoved. She smiled. She unbuttoned her black jacket and opened it. She was so painfully thin that von Leonarte could see the outline of her ribs through her blouse and petticoat. She held her jacket open, turning her small breasts towards him.

'*Consummatum est,*' she said in a matter-of-fact voice.

One of the frizzy-haired Levantines suddenly swung round on his chair, his lead-coloured automatic half out of his jacket. Von Leonarte squeezed the trigger of his Schmeisser. Bullets smashed through the man's jacket. The automatic clattered on the ground, and Graser kicked it away. As the Levantine fell sideways off his chair, von Leonarte fired his second burst, this time into the fat belly of the Greek. He stumbled and fell backwards, crashing down over his chair and splintering the trellis behind him. The girls were screaming. Radinski and Graser were firing as well. The noise in the enclosed courtyard was deafening. The second Levantine tore the tablecloth down to the ground with him, covering himself in coffee from the filters. He was hit in an artery. Blood pumped over the cobbles, amid the spent shells rolling into the crevices between the stones. There was a stench of cordite. The tall girl waited for death, then jack-knifed on the ground as she was hit, like a shot rabbit. The dark-haired girl in the tight crêpe-de-chine skirt managed to run, hobbling, a little way. Von Leonarte let her go, then fired a burst into her back. She fell across a second table. Radinski dropped to his knee, aimed his rifle, and shot her. She went on moaning and twitching as the sound of shooting stopped and died away against the walls of the courtyard. The magazine of the Schmeisser was empty. Von Leonarte handed the gun to Graser. He drew the pistol from his holster. He crouched down and dragged the wounded girl from under the table. He put the muzzle of his pistol to the back of her neck. She was still trying to struggle, moaning all the time. He held her firm, and shot her straight through the neck. Her head slumped as if it would fall off. As the reverberations of the pistol shot died away, there was silence.

Von Leonarte rose to his feet. He put the pistol back in his holster. He felt unpleasantly shaken. He turned to Radinski. 'Cover them,' he ordered. 'Use the tablecloths.'

He went across to the kitchen door, kicking aside spent shells as he did so. The *patron* and the elder waitress came out to meet him. The young girl stood just inside the door, shaking and sobbing in terror. She was cramming the knuckles of her hand into her mouth to stop herself screaming.

'Please accept my apologies,' von Leonarte began stiffly. 'It is distressing, I understand that. These were criminals. They have committed murder.'

The *patron* and the waitresses stared at him in blank incomprehension.

428

'They were enemies of the French people,' von Leonarte tried to explain. 'Their victims were not the enemies of France, but honest French men and women.'

The *patron* and the waitresses continued to stare at him.

'They were scum,' said von Leonarte. 'They do not deserve pity.'

He became quite hard.

'You will fetch coffee and cognac for my men and myself if you please.'

He clicked his heels, turned, and went back to the table in the alcove. He took out his cigarette-case. His hands were shaking as he put a cigarette between his lips and lit it.

Helm had forced the lock of the medallion case. He pushed the empty case and the crystal ashtray across the white cloth. He stared up into von Leonarte's face. Von Leonarte sat down. He turned his head away from Helm and dared not look at him.

Marie-Claire waited for five minutes after the last shot was fired. She drew her pants up over her bottom, straightened her dress, and left the tiny *cabinet*. She went through to the kitchen. She was careful to carry the doll under her arm; it was Bébé no longer. The motherly waitress rushed over to her.

'They're still there – the murderers,' she whispered. 'Don't go out there.'

'What shall I do?' said Marie-Claire with just a hint of a whimper in her voice.

'Jean,' the waitress called to the *patron*, 'take the poor child up to the parlour.'

The *patron* hesitated.

'Do you want her to be murdered by those butchers, as well?' demanded the waitress.

The *patron* shrugged fatalistically.

'All right,' he said to Marie-Claire. 'Come.'

He led her up the whitewashed-walled staircase which led to the living-quarters. He left her sitting dumbly on the sofa by the potted fern, in the parlour. As the waitress came up to see how she was, she began to cry.

The waitress said, 'Don't worry, my darling. You can stay here until they're gone. There's no rush.'

'I don't know who those people were,' Marie-Claire sobbed. 'The fat man offered me a lift to Cherbourg. I was taking the doll to my little niece in Cherbourg. She lives with my Aunt Elise, and I was going to stay with her. I'm a nurse, really ... Well, not a hospital nurse – a receptionist.'

The waitress sat down and put her arm round her.

'There,' she said.

'I was working in Laon, for a Dr Vauthier – ever such a nice man. Only the Germans came, and Dr Vauthier sent me back to Paris. I'm an orphan, you see. I was brought up by the Little Friends of Jesus at their convent in Paris. And then the Germans came to Paris, and the Good Sisters said I should go to my Aunt Elise in Cherbourg. So I brought the doll to give to my little niece . . . Now I don't know what to do.'

'Things will settle down, my darling,' said the motherly waitress. 'You'll see.'

The *patron* came in. The waitress looked up at him.

'The poor child is absolutely exhausted,' she said. 'She needs to rest. And she can't go while those pigs down there are still around.'

'Madame,' Marie-Claire exclaimed, 'you're so kind!'

She looked at the *patron*.

'I can work, monsieur,' she said. 'I'm not afraid of hard work.'

'I'm sure that no girl who has been brought up by the Sisters of the Little Friends of Jesus is afraid of hard work,' the waitress confirmed.

She went over to the window and looked out between the lace curtains.

'Assassins!' she said loudly.

'Thérèse!' exclaimed the horrified *patron*. '*Tais-toi!*'

Marie-Claire decided she had better remain tearful for a little longer.

47

'We found what we were looking for,' said Vivian. 'A skipper named Jardeheu. He owns his own boat – and he does live in St Pelagie. We went to his cottage, but he wasn't at home. One of the neighbours told us he always sails to Jersey on this morning's tide, though whether he will today is another matter.'

They had returned up the path through the pine wood. Vivian led them off down a rabbit-track between the trees.

They were a weary, bedraggled little bunch now. The two men's uniforms were creased and stained. Hugo still had his shirt buttoned up wrongly and one shoe-lace trailing behind him on the ground. Julie's matinee frock was as shabby as a relic in a church jumble sale. She was clutching her handbag still, but she had left her suitcase behind her; nobody seemed to have noticed. She wished Vivian and Rose would throw away their revolvers: they represented nothing but danger.

'When we got back to Bretteville,' Vivian went on, 'we found it full of Germans. That's why we were so long getting to you.'

'No bloody joke getting across all them fields and ditches in the dark,' said Rose. 'Know what I mean?'

'And we were worried as hell about you and Hugo,' said Vivian. 'The chap who told us about this skipper, Jardeheu, also told us about le Comte de Fremonde. Apparently, back in 1931 or so, when his mother was still alive and mistress in the château, he was a member of the *Camelots du Roi* in Paris.'

'What were they?' asked Julie.

'Same as Mosley's Black Shirts,' Vivian replied. 'Fascist street-fighters.'

'He looked a bit small for that sort of thing,' said Julie.

'Like Dr Goebbels,' suggested Vivian. 'What does *camelot* actually mean?' he asked.

'I thought it meant "stable-boy" or something,' Julie replied.

'Somebody who sells songs or pamphlets on the street,' Hugo told them unexpectedly.

'A broadsheet seller,' Vivian translated into English. 'Very good, Hugo. Thank you.'

'He tried to make me give him the Tondeau,' said Julie.

'Did he succeed?' asked Vivian.

'He thought so,' said Julie.

'We saw your friends, by the way,' said Vivian. 'They came hurtling out of the drive in a big black car. That was the most frightening thing of all.'

They were walking out onto the heathland.

'That's what happened,' Julie said. 'I'm sure, they were after the Tondeau.'

'Beg pardon, sir,' said Rose. 'Wouldn't it be better if we took off our jackets and carried them folded, sir? I mean, it would make us less conspicuous and that.'

And throw away those revolvers, Julie felt like suggesting. She helped Vivian to unbuckle his Sam Browne. Draping it, weighted with its revolver holster, over her arm, she insisted on unbuttoning his jacket, and helping him to take it off. It was the only thing she had done in days which afforded her any real satisfaction.

They went on down through the bracken, climbing between outcrops of rock. They crossed several fields to reach the road. As they approached it, they heard the steady roar of traffic, and could see the grey and stippled black camouflage on the canopies of the lorries.

'We'll get down to the hedge,' Vivian said. 'As soon as this convoy is past, we'll nip across the road.'

They crouched behind the hedge, resting against the steep, grassy bank. Through the thorns and the hovering mist of dust, they watched the steady stream of lorries packed with grey-uniformed infantry, escorted by motorcycle units, service trucks, field-kitchens, ambulances, and columns of 88 guns trailing behind their limbers and draped in camouflage nets. An entire division was on the move, heading up the peninsular towards the 2nd BEF's final beachhead round Cherbourg.

A small *kübelwagen* drove past, a black pennant fluttering from the wing-mast. Behind it there was nothing but the drifting, settling dust.

'Let's go,' said Vivian.

Rose helped him to force a hole in the hedge; the thorns clutched at their shirt-sleeves. Julie and Hugo crawled through. They were just scrambling to their feet when they heard the sound of motorcycles coming up the road. For a second, Vivian thought of telling them to dive back into the hedge, but it was too late. A motorcycle combination with a machine-gun mounted on the side-car, followed by a four-seater *kübelwagen* flying a red pennant, came towards them. Behind them, a long column of lorries was approaching.

Julie took Hugo by the hand. She stood on the verge as boldly as if she was waiting for a bus to arrive. Vivian and Rose followed her example. The motorcycle drew up. The rider lifted his gauntleted hand, signalling the convoy to halt. To Julie's astonishment, instead of dismounting, and coming over to question them, the motorcyclist waved at them to cross as if he were a London traffic policeman. As they stepped out onto the road, Julie gave the soldier a slight wave and what she hoped was a dazzlingly actressy smile. As she passed in front of him, the German's face under his dusty goggles cracked into a grin.

They went down a steep, pebble strewn path into a gorge between high, grassy hills. Scarcely able to believe their good fortune, they dared not hurry until they were out of sight of the road. At the bottom of the hill, they went through a gate and along a path which led them to the village of St Pelagie. It consisted of a single row of stone cottages nestling under the steepness of the hill, and looking out over a single stone quay. Another steep-sided hill, rearing up out of the sea-washed rocks to a craggy skyline, formed the other side of the harbour. Against the quay were moored three fishing-smacks. Nets and boxes littered the stone pavement beside them. There was a heavy smell of fish. Gulls swooped and circled, crying between the hills. At the harbour mouth end of the quay, where the sea entered between a gap in the cliffs, was moored a black, rusty motor vessel, dirty and sea-stained. It reminded Julie of the small coastal tramps she had seen in Cumbrian ports like Whitehaven and Maryport.

'That is Jardeheu's boat,' said Vivian.

They followed him to the last cottage of the row.

'Keep a look-out,' Vivian told Rose.

Rose turned to watch the path by which they had come. Julie noticed to her horror that he reached under his folded battledress blouse and unfastened the cover over the butt of his revolver.

Vivian knocked on the cottage door. It was opened by an immensely fat man in a torn and dirty seaman's sweater. He had several days' growth of beard on his broad, jewelled cheeks. He looked at Vivian and Julie with suspicion.

'Monsieur Jardeheu?' asked Vivian.

The man coughed the brochial cough of the heavy smoker.

'What do you want?' he growled in a thick voice.

'Are you sailing to Jersey on this tide?' asked Vivian.

'Guernsey, monsieur,' the man replied. 'What of it?'

'In spite of the Germans?' Vivian asked pleasantly.

'Why not?' asked Jardeheu. 'The Boche's quarrel is with the government, not with honest traders.'

'Will you take three passengers and a child to Guernsey?' asked Vivian.

'Ah, monsieur!' Jardeheu said, as if he had realised only that moment what Vivian was after.

He coughed again, and cleared his throat.

'No, monsieur,' he replied.

'Why not?' asked Vivian. 'We can pay.'

'In gold if you wish, monsieur,' said Julie.

She opened her handbag, and let Jardeheu look inside. He peered into it, thought for a moment, then shook his head.

'No,' he repeated. 'I have a living to make. The Germans may take away my licence if they find I have been carrying English people across to the *Îles Anglo-Normandes*.'

He stepped back inside the cottage. He tried to close the door, but Julie suddenly wedged her foot in it. Jardeheu looked down at her toe.

'Excuse me, mademoiselle,' he said.

'Julie!' Vivian tried to persuade her.

He was afraid that Jardeheu would stamp on her foot if she persisted.

'Monsieur, I wish to speak to you alone,' said Julie. 'Inside, if you please. It is very important.'

Jardeheu stared at her in surprise.

'What are you going to do?' asked Vivian in English.

'Appeal to his better nature,' Julie replied. 'I'm taking a long shot.'

'I'm not carrying you or any English people to Guernsey,' said Jardeheu, 'but you can come in if you wish.'

He held open the door, and wiped the fingers of his other hand on his sweater.

'Julie,' Vivian protested, 'you can't.'

'I'm going to, Vivian,' she replied, and went into the evil-smelling darkness of the cottage.

The door was closed firmly on Vivian. He stood and stared at it, then at the dirty, ragged net curtains which were hung across the broken pane of the window. He walked back down the quay, to where Hugo and Rose were waiting.

An aircraft droned high above the circling gulls. All three of them looked up into the brightness of the sky. It was no more than a silver speck moving lazily inland.

'What's she doing, sir?' asked Rose.

'Trying to persuade the man to take us,' said Vivian.

'Will she do it, do you think, sir?' asked Rose.

'I know no better than you do, Rose,' Vivian replied.

'I wish we had some bread,' said Hugo in French, 'to feed the seagulls.'

'It would be nice,' Vivian said.

'I expect,' said Hugo, 'she's showing him the Tondeau.'

Vivian paid no attention, and Rose couldn't understand French.

'I expect you can see the Channel Islands from the top of them cliffs, sir,' said Rose.

'Oh do be quiet,' said Vivian, 'there's a good chap.'

A minute or two later, Rose offered him a cigarette. He took it, and even managed a smile.

It was a long ten minutes after that when Julie reappeared. She came out of the cottage door, handbag in hand as if she was just about to go shopping. Jardeheu came lumbering after her. He was wearing sea-boots, and had an oilskin coat draped over his arm. He went to another of the cottages, knocked at the door, and then on to another.

'He's going to take us,' said Julie.

She repeated it in French for Hugo's benefit. Hugo clapped his hands. Rose congratulated her warmly.

'It's great news,' Vivian told her.

He could hardly justify even to himself the sulkiness in his voice. Jardeheu, followed by two equally disreputable-looking men, walked down the quay to the motor-vessel. Julie led the others after them. They all went up the gritty, rotten-looking wooden gang-plank. They remained on deck as the engines were started. The stench of diesel fumes rose between every plank of the deck. With surprising agility one of the men jumped down over the rail to the quay, cast the mooring ropes off from the bollards, and clambered back on board as the boat moved off.

They chugged out of the harbour, between the towering cliffs, into the open swell of the sea. The spray struck their faces, needle-point cold and clean. The black diesel smoke drifted away across the choppy little waves. Seagulls came following after, as the deck began to roll

434

above the steady vibration from the engines. Julie stood beside Vivian at the rail. Some stubbornness within her made her refuse to offer an explanation as to how she had prevailed with Jardeheu. Vivian was filled with resentment and the restlessness of utter fatigue. His lost arm was aching like hell. At this moment, when they might be successful, he felt most wretched.

Hugo had disappeared into the wheelhouse, and had been made welcome there. Rose was leaning over the rail on the opposite side, being sick.

Vivian looked back. He could see the road running along the ridge above the cliff-top. German vehicles were travelling nose to tail northwards, through a high curtain of dust. The division was advancing at such a speed that it had no time to occupy out of the way villages like St Pelagie, or to check on small vessels putting out to sea. And the sky was quite empty.

He could stand it no longer.

'How did you manage it?' he asked, knowing that he was making a fool of himself.

'Not like *Boule de Suif* at any rate,' Julie replied. She did not sound pleasant.

Julie turned, leaning against the rail, and stared directly at him. She looked quite beautiful with her tousled hair blowing across her face, and her dress flapping against her legs.

'I thought I'd persuaded you to trust me, Vivian,' she said. 'Quite a long time ago, in fact.'

It was the first time since they had met once again, on the road to Dreux, that she had referred directly to that night they had spent in the hotel at Laon. He reached out for her hand. She let him take it.

'I'm sorry, Julie,' he told her.

She looked him straight in the face.

'If I hadn't been properly brought up, Vivian,' she said, 'I'd say you were a bit of a shit.'

It was mid-afternoon, and Jersey was a thin outline of land on the horizon to starboard, when they saw the grey shape of a Royal Navy minesweeper approaching. They saw the flash of the Aldis lamp from its bridge which kept appearing and disappearing like a bright but fitful star. The throb of the engines underneath their feet suddenly ceased, and they were floating aimlessly on the swell.

The minesweeper plunged towards them, cutting the darkness of the sea into shreds of white lace on either side of the prow. As it stood off, shutting down its engines fifty yards from the motor vessel, they could see the White Ensign fluttering from the stern. To Vivian and Julie it was wonderfully reassuring.

Rose hardly noticed. He sat on the forward hatch-cover, hugging his stomach and groaning.

Vivian led Julie to the wheelhouse. A voice rang out across the water through a bull-horn on the minesweeper's bridge. It demanded in heavily accented French to know the boat's destination.

'St Pierre-Port!' Jardeheu bawled back through a dented voice-trumpet.

'Do you have any English aboard?' the bull-horn sounded across the water.

'Four,' shouted Jardeheu.

The big grey hull of the minesweeper, rising and falling in the swell, looked as stained and rusted as that of the motor-vessel.

'We wish to take them aboard,' called the English voice. 'Please come alongside. We will lower the campanion-way.'

'Your sailors give me orders,' Jardeheu growled to Vivian through the open window of the wheelhouse.

It was no more than a token grumble. Hugo was standing smiling behind him. The engines began to vibrate once again. The motor-vessel plunged forward into the swell, then began to swing round in a wide U. It drew up alongside the minesweeper, bumping and scraping against the rivets on the armour-plating. Julie drew Hugo out of the dirty little wheelhouse. He was even grubbier than he had been when they came aboard. Vivian put his arm under that of Rose.

'Come on, lad,' he said.

Sergeant Micklewhite would have approved his nice balance between firmness and kindness, he thought.

'Sorry, sir,' groaned Rose.

A dribble of yellow bile hung from his lower lip.

'Can't be helped, lad,' Vivian assured him, 'but the Navy's here. We're on our way home.'

As Julie went with Hugo to the foot of the canvas-sheeted companion-way, the wind caught the fullness of her skirt and whipped it up. She clutched at it, and pressed it down against her legs. A wolf-whistle sounded from the minesweeper's rail above. English faces grinned down at her. They were waiting for the wind to lift her skirt again; but they represented home for all that. She walked up the companion-way with her arm round Hugo's shoulder.

'Welcome aboard, miss,' said a young sub-lieutenant.

Julie looked back. Vivian was thanking Jardeheu. He was holding out a roll of French money to him. Jardeheu was protesting at the idea of being offered money. Vivian was about to put the notes away again, when Jardeheu snatched them from him, and stuffed them into his belt. Vivian led Lance-Corporal Rose up the companion-way.

'Robinson, sir,' said the sub-lieutenant. 'I'm the Number One. Welcome aboard.'

Two seamen came forward and took Rose away to the sick-bay.

'You're bloody lucky, actually,' said the sub-lieutenant. 'If you'd

436

gone on to Peter Port, you'd probably have found Jerry there. We completed the evacuation yesterday – HMG has decided the Channel Isles can't be defended. We've been sent to fish for stragglers out of Dinard and St Malo who might be trying to make it across to St Helier. We were just about to head back for Pompey when we saw you.'

They stood at the rail, and watched Jardeheu's dirty little tramp grind away. Vivian waved, but received no response.

'Come up onto the bridge and say hello to our old man,' said the sub-lieutenant.

The sound of English voices all round them was quite wonderful, thought Julie. Poor Hugo must be feeling very strange and foreign. She gave him a big hug.

Later, they were sitting alone in the tiny wardroom, drinking huge mugs of tea which tasted of cabbage-water. Hugo had been put to bed in the First Lieutenant's cabin, and was fast asleep.

'I'll tell you what happened,' Julie said, in answer to the question which Vivian had not dared to ask a second time. 'I spoke to him about the Tondeau. I explained what it was, and why I was taking it to England. In fact, I told him just what – ' she hesitated, ' – Victor told me. Have you a knife – a pen-knife?' she asked.

'I think so,' Vivian replied.

He took out the schoolboy's knife he always carried with him, drew open one of the blades with his teeth, and handed it to her.

'See that nobody comes in,' she said.

He stood obediently, at the door, though he had little idea of what he would do should one of the ship's officers want to come in.

Julie turned her back on him. She lifted her skirt and petticoat, and held them under her chin. She cut the Tondeau from where she had stitched it onto the wide centre panel of her suspender-belt.

'There,' she said, 'I couldn't think of anywhere else where it wouldn't show.'

She opened her handbag, folded the medallion into one of her handkerchiefs, and put it inside.

'Did Jardeheu want to see it?' asked Vivian.

'Naturally,' Julie replied.

'What happened?' Vivian asked.

'He was very embarrassed,' Julie replied. 'To tell you the truth, I don't think he's ever had very much to do with women.'

EPILOGUE – July 13, 1940.

'How much time have we got?', Julie asked

Vivian reached over to the bedside table. He held up his wrist-watch.

'About half an hour, before General Spears comes round here,' he said.

The afternoon was hot. They were lying together on top of the counterpane. The window was wide open, but no breath of wind disturbed the white gauze curtains. Outside, the sun glared on the summer leaves of Belsize Lane. Someone on the opposite side of the street was practising the first movement of Mozart's A major piano sonata, and making the same mistake over and over again.

Julie turned her head on the pillow to look at Vivian's face.

'You are beautiful, you know,' she said.

'You have very odd standards of beauty,' he told her.

He rolled over and put his arm round her to draw her to him.

'Go away,' she told him. 'You're not to excite me any more. You'll wreck my hair, and it cost the earth.'

Twenty-four hours earlier, she had had it waved and set at a dreadfully expensive place in the Burlington Arcade. Until this afternoon, she had treated herself like a porcelain doll for fear of disarranging it; but she had needed Vivian to reassure her, she felt so ridiculously nervous.

She got off the bed. Her underwear and stockings were lying on top of the dressing-table. Ducking down so as not to be seen through the open window, she crossed the room.

'Wouldn't it have been better if somebody important had been asked to give it to him?' she asked as she started dressing. 'I mean, they could have done it tomorrow, in front of all his men.'

Tomorrow was Bastille Day; General de Gaulle, with Admiral Murelier, would be leading two thousand men of the French Volunteer Legion on a march from the Cenotaph in Whitehall to lay a wreath at the statue of Marshal Foch at Victoria.

'Nervous?' asked Vivian.

'It isn't that,' she replied untruthfully. 'I just think it ought to be done by somebody important.'

'Such as?' asked Vivian.

He was pulling on his shirt.

'In this country there isn't a Frenchmen important enough, and we can't have an Englishman investing a renegade French general with the insignia of the Constable of France. I'm sure General Spears will explain it all to you.'

'I wish we could walk up there – just you and me,' she said. 'It seems silly having to get into a car to go to Frognal Gardens, hardly worth it.'

She would have liked to have told Vivian how, earlier in the week, she had taken a taxi round to Ambrose's flat to tell him she could not return to him. But this afternoon had been usurped by the task she had to perform, as if there was nothing else which could be talked about seriously.

'General Spears will be bringing his car round,' said Vivian. 'I don't suppose he'd fancy the idea of walking up Rosslyn Hill.'

Julie tucked her blouse into her skirt. She went over to the window.

'I wish whoever it is would get that piece right,' she said.

Vivian came and stood behind her so that he was touching her.

'There's no need to be nervous,' he said. 'I'm sure General de Gaulle feels nothing but gratitude towards you.'

'I know that,' Julie replied.

She leant against him.

'It's just that one thinks of him now as *being* France,' she explained. 'It makes him rather awe-inspiring, doesn't it?'

'I'm sure General de Gaulle feels exactly the same way himself,' Vivian told her. 'You two ought to get on like a house on fire.'

'Oh Viv! You are an idiot!' Julie laughed.

Vivian melted: it had been so long since anybody had said that, with that particular tone of affection.

She had just finished helping Vivian to buckle on his Sam Browne belt, and was pinning on her small trilby hat at a fashionably rakish angle, when the doorbell rang. As Vivian went to answer it, she glanced out of the window. Through the branches of the trees, she could see the big, camouflaged Wolseley saloon parked against the kerb. A woman of about her own age – a sergeant in the ATS, wearing a man's battledress trousers and a khaki blouse with the sleeves rolled up – was standing beside it. She was holding a lighted cigarette half-concealed in the palm of her hand.

Vivian brought in Sir Edward Spears.

'This is Juliet Armitage, Sir Edward,' he said.

'Ah yes! The young lady who brought the Tondeau of Chartres from Paris. I'm very pleased to make your acquaintance, Miss Armitage.'

She held out her hand to him. He took it, giving it a slight squeeze.

'All ready for the great occasion, eh?' he asked.

'Very nervous, Sir Edward,' she replied.

He smiled, with the flattering, fatherly attention men of a certain age pay to attractive young women who know they have nothing to fear from them.

'No need to feel nervous, my dear. No need at all. General de Gaulle will be very pleased to see you, and to thank you in person.'

He glanced down into Belsize Lane. He took out his cigarette-case and offered it to Julie and to Vivian.

'We'll give Auxiliary-Sergeant Jennings time to finish her gasper, shall we?' he suggested. 'There's no hurry.'

Vivian offered Julie a light.

'You haven't spoken to anybody about the Tondeau, of course?' asked Sir Edward. 'The gentlemen of the press – or anybody else?'

'Major Hardwicke warned me not to talk about it, before we got off the boat in Portsmouth, Sir Edward,' Julie told him.

'Good show,' said Sir Edward. 'Wouldn't do at all if Jerry were to find out that the British had anything to do with it.'

Julie glanced at Vivian.

'As far as you're concerned, my dear,' Sir Edward continued, 'it's just as the Good Book says: you must do your good deeds in secret, and your Father who is in Heaven will reward you in secret ... The MoI,' he added to Vivian, 'will circulate a highly unconfirmed report about the Cardinal Archbishop of Paris granting a faculty allowing Lebrun, when he was President of the Republic, to invest the commander of the French land forces with a sacred relic of St. Louis. Lebrun will have to deny it, of course, but everybody will think that the Germans and Pétain have been putting pressure on him.'

As they were going down in the lift to the front door, General Spears asked Vivian,

'Any news about your future, Hardwicke?'

'I've received a posting, sir,' Vivian replied.

He hadn't told Julie anything about it.

'Home, or overseas?' asked Sir Edward.

'Home,' said Vivian. 'Scotland.'

Sir Edward laughed.

'Had a word with that fellow Parchment, did you?' he asked.

It was evident that he knew all about it.

'Yes, sir,' Vivian replied. 'Colonel Parchment.'

Julie felt the pang go right through her. She told herself that she hadn't said anything about her visit to Ambrose: one was so afraid of spoiling happiness these days.

Vivian gave her a quick look as they stepped out of the front door into the sunlight. He wanted reassurance; she gave him a smile she did not feel.

The heat was beating off the pavement. The ATS sergeant was standing to attention, holding open the rear door of the Wolseley. She had an attractive face, with a clear complexion, Julie noticed, but her expression, under the stiff peak of her unbecoming khaki cap, was as set and impassive as that of a Buckingham Palace sentry – as if she were trying very hard to be an army sergeant.

General Spears climbed onto the rear seat beside Julie. Vivian got in the front, beside the driving-seat.

'Do you think General de Gaulle will offer us tea?' Julie asked, as they set off.

'Very unlikely, my dear,' General Spears laughed. 'I was telling Major Hardwicke the other day: when we landed – de Gaulle and myself – after flying from Bordeaux, we went straight to the canteen ... It was an RAF base, you know. Somebody produced a hot cup of something for de Gaulle, and by God, the poor fellow couldn't tell whether it was coffee, tea, or soup! His face was enough to remind one of Joan of Arc at the stake!'

At the top of Haverstock Hill, an Evening Star poster was wired to a billboard fixed against the brick wall of Hampstead underground station. The lettering was slightly faded but clearly legible. It read:

'France defeated. Cup Final – Great Britain v. Germany.'

They drove up the narrow, twisting lanes of upper Hampstead, and over the hill into Frognal. They drew up outside a large house in Frognal Gardens. The ATS sergeant came round and opened the rear door. As she got out onto the pavement, Julie felt herself sweating under her blouse.

'I bet my nose needs a spot of powder,' she said to Vivian.

She looked round at the ATS sergeant, but the sergeant was standing to attention, holding the car door open for Sir Edward Spears, and staring into the middle distance. Julie took her compact from her bag, opened it, and dabbed quickly at her nose. She put the compact away again, and twisted round to inspect the seams of her stockings.

Vivian and General Spears moved, one on either side of her. General Spears took her arm.

'*Courage*, my dear,' he said to her firmly. '*Le diable est mort.*'

The two men led her up the steep garden steps to the house. One of them might at least have told her that she was looking good, thought Julie.

When it was all over, General Spears remained in the house to confer with General de Gaulle about the arrangements for the next day's parade and Bastille Day ceremonies. Julie and Vivian decided to walk up to the Heath. Arm in arm, they strolled up to Whitestone Pond and Jack Straw's Castle. Julie felt an overwhelming sense of relief.

'Victor would have been pleased with me, wouldn't he?' she asked.

It was a tactless, possibly even unkind thing to say, but she felt she had to – it was important.

'He would have been very pleased with you,' Vivian confirmed. 'You were perfect – didn't put a foot wrong.'

'You are good!' said Julie.

They crossed the road to look out over the Heath. Over the trees, and the roofs of the houses tucked into the Vale of Health, all London was spread before them; even the Surrey hills were dimly visible in the early evening light. Children rushed from bush to bush along the edge of the Heath, rat-tat-tatting with crudely-made wooden toy guns.

Julie said:

'I suppose nothing is ever like you expect it to be. I mean, I was so scared when I told him about Victor wanting to give it to a real Constable of France – it sounded so presumptuous. And then I saw his eyes were full of tears! Oh, I don't know!'

'Anybody would have been moved by it,' Vivian told her.

Julie laughed.

'He was the wrong shape, somehow,' she said. Then she said, 'I was terribly moved too. I thought I wasn't going to get the words out.'

They walked along the top of the Heath in silence, towards The Spaniards Inn.

'I went and told Ambrose about us,' she said suddenly. 'Two days ago.'

Vivian thought for a moment.

'Was it bad?' he asked.

'Not really. He was the perfect gentleman, as always.'

She changed her mind.

'Actually,' she said, 'it was pretty awful . . . I didn't really tell him about you. I just said I'm met somebody – somebody I'd become very fond of.'

She put her hand under his arm.

'Am I allowed to say that I'm glad?' Vivian asked.

'Yes. Of course,' Julie replied. 'I thought, at first, I'd just tell him I'd decided to go on staying with Cousin Ginny – at her flat. It's the truth, after all. And then I thought perhaps it would be kinder really to tell him that . . . well, I'd fallen in love, I suppose.'

The children burst out of the bushes in front of them and ferociously machine-gunned a passing taxi.

'Are you in love with me?' Vivian asked.

'What do you think?' asked Julie.

'You never told me,' he said.

'You never told me you were going to be posted to Scotland,' said Julie.

'I didn't want to spoil your great day, Julie,' he replied quietly.

He had expected, when they had returned to London after landing at Portsmouth, that he would be kept waiting for orders for months on end, hanging about the bars of West End hotels like so many of his fellow officers who were awaiting postings. Instead, less than three weeks after his return from France, he had received a telegram ordering him to report to the St Pancras Railway Hotel, room 177c.

On arriving, he had found an RAOC corporal waiting for him in the lobby. The corporal had taken him up in the lift to the fourth floor, and had directed him down a long corridor, the entry to which was signposted 'Women's Armed Services – Supply (underwear)'.

As far as the management of the hotel was concerned, it was a disused wing. The carpets had been taken up, leaving only faded, cracked linoleum. There had been a smell of stale damp and cat's urine. Vivian had made his way down the corridor until finally he had reached room 177c. At the far end of the corridor there had been a square window; through the grime, he had been able to see the pigeons flying over the long roof-tops of King's Cross station.

He had knocked on the door.

'Come!' a voice called.

Vivian went in.

'Major Hardwicke!' exclaimed the solitary occupant of the room, rising from his chair.

He wore the insignia of a lieutenant-colonel on the shoulder-tabs of his ill-fitting battledress blouse, and the flashes of the RAOC on his sleeve.

'Glad to have you aboard, Major.'

He held out his hand. Vivian saluted and took it.

'Parchment's the name, old chap. Colonel – 2nd Battalion, Royal Marines.'

There was an army-issue office table in the centre of the bare floor, on which were a few sheets of note-paper and some buff-coloured envelopes; and there were two uncomfortable-looking upright chairs. Otherwise the room was unfurnished. There wasn't even a bulb in the light socket hanging from the dusty, cobwebbed ceiling.

As Colonel Parchment motioned Vivian to sit down on the second chair, he noticed him glancing at his RAOC flashes.

'I know, old chap,' he said. 'Camouflage. To put Fifth Columnists off the scent, don't you know. We're all terribly hush-hush these days .... And you're just back from France, eh? Jolly good show! Anyway, to get to the point – er – Hardwicke: I've been appointed to take over no. 13 Commando. You've heard of the Commandos, have you? Terribly secret, of course.'

'I have, actually, sir,' said Vivian.

Who hadn't? he reflected. There wasn't a cocktail bar between Green Park and the Lower Haymarket which didn't have two or three fellows confiding into their cups that they expected to be posted to the Highlands and Islands any day now, for special training.

'Leopards, Winston calls us,' Colonel Parchment explained. 'We're to pounce on Jerry when he's least expecting it, and chew off his balls, eh? 13 Commando is assembling up on the west coast of Scotland – God-forsaken spot between Portnacraish and Ballachulish, on Loch Linnhe. Your job will be to form and take charge of the Independent Troop attached to 13 Commando. Special purposes troops.'

'What sort of special purposes, sir?' asked Vivian.

'Aha!' Colonel Parchment wagged a finger at him. 'You know better than that, Hardwicke . . . When you get there, old chap . . . Here you are. First class rail warrant from Euston to Oban, for Tuesday 16th July.'

Vivian had taken the folded warrant, and had buttoned it into his tunic pocket. Colonel Parchment had accompanied him down the long, bleak corridor. Vivian had supposed that he was being seen to the lift, but when they had reached it, Colonel Parchment had turned to the corporal who was still standing there, on guard.

'Bring that with you, Coleman, there's a good fellow,' he had said, pointing to the notice on the wall.

The corporal had removed the notice and had tucked it under his arm before joining Vivian and Colonel Parchment in the lift. As they went down, Vivian had said,

'The powers that be do realise . . . ' and he had indicated his empty sleeve.

'Absolutely, old chap,' Colonel Parchment had assured him. 'Your name was recommended to me . . . '

He had lowered his voice as though Corporal Coleman was not standing a mere few inches away from them.

' . . . by Number 10. It seems you particularly impressed Winston by riding a motorcycle all over northern France – in spite of your – er – disability.'

Vivian had been on the point of explaining how Mr Churchill had got the whole story completely wrong, when he realised that it would imperil his chances of taking up his new command. He had held his peace.

'Winston likes chaps to have a bit of the Nelson touch,' Colonel Parchment had said, as they stepped out of the lift.

'All the same, you should have told me,' said Julie.

The trouble had been his own satisfaction at finding himself still of use. It had made him feel guilty, as if he was planning to be unfaithful to her. Now, he found it impossible to repeat his excuse about not wanting to spoil her day, though he had believed it himself, the first time.

'So you're off to Scotland?' she asked.

'On Tuesday night. I've booked a sleeper from Euston to Glasgow.'

'It isn't a desk job, I suppose?' she asked.

'The label says, secondment to the RAOC: Women's Services, Supply, underwear in brackets. I'm not lying,' he added.

To his relief, Julie giggled.

'You aren't lying,' she said. 'I bet somebody is, though.'

Then she said,

'And I'll have another bloody week after that before we go off on tour. I'm not even sure I want to go on tour!'

She thought of the vacuous, unfunny black-out sketch, the feed-lines for the equally unfunny East End comedian, and the whole cast of eight, the girls in satin shorts, tapdancing and singing, to accordian, piano and drums, *When you're up to your neck in hot water, Be like the kettle and sing.* She had been spoiled by her experiences, as if she had come to need excitement. It was unfair that Vivian should go off to whatever awaited him in Scotland, while she could only look forward to prancing about on works-canteen stages in tapdancing shoes and satin shorts.

'I think I'll dress up as a soldier – a real soldier,' she said, 'like Cicely Courtneidge in "Me and Marlborough", and come up to Scotland to look for you.'

'I'd like that,' he assured her.

The children dashed round them, and plunged down the slope, rat-tatting into the bushes. The noise of their play hung in the warm air.

'Do you know?' said Julie. 'When I left Ambrose's flat, the other night, I felt so bloody happy, I wanted to ring you up straight away. I wanted you to take me out on the town and get me absolutely sloshed.'

'Why didn't you?' asked Vivian.

'I couldn't,' she said. 'It wouldn't have been right, somehow.'

'Will you come back with me tonight?' he asked. 'Stay the night?'

'I don't know,' Julie replied. 'Cousin Ginny is bound to write to my mother if I don't go back there. She's done it before, you know.'

'I'd like you to stay with me until I go on Tuesday,' said Vivian.

'Oh Viv!' said Julie. 'You're really raising the ante, aren't you! ... I wish you'd get yourself a nice quiet desk job. But you wouldn't like that, would you?'

'No,' he admitted. 'I wouldn't.'

'My period is just about due,' she told him. 'That's what's going to happen from now on, you know. Every time we get a chance to be together, it's going to be my period!'

She had raised her voice slightly, in her sense of the unfairness of life. An elderly man riding past on a bicycle, his gas-mask tied by a string on his back, wobbled and swerved before regaining his balance, and pedalling on.

'Oh to hell with Cousin Ginny!' said Julie. 'Of course I'm going to stay with you. I'll even come and see you off at Euston on Tuesday, and cry all over you most likely.'

Vivian put his arm round her and kissed her. They stood together, gazing out through the trees to the panorama of the city spread before them. Barrage balloons gleamed silver in the long evening light as they hung motionless over the domes and spires of the City churches.

'It's so beautiful,' Vivian said. 'And you make me very happy.'

She turned to him, and put her arms round his neck. She stared at the knot of his tie, as if she was too shy to look into his face.

'I'm very happy too,' she told him. 'And scared about what's going to happen, at the same time. Do you think that sounds ungrateful?'

'Not at all,' he told her. 'I love you, Julie.'

'I love you, Viv,' she said. 'But I think you're going to have to take me along to The Spaniards and buy me a very large drink.'

ACKNOWLEDGEMENTS

Obviously, in writing a book of this sort, I am deeply indebted to a number of authors, especially Charles de Gaulle, for *Call to Honour*, Volume I of his memoirs (London 1955), General Sir Edward Spears, for *Assignment to Catastrophe*, Volumes I and II (London 1954), and Alistair Horne, for *To Lose a Battle: France 1940* (London 1969).

Other authors on whom I have depended include:

Beaufre, Gen. André – *Le Drame de 1940* (Paris 1965)

Beauvoir, Simone de – *The Prime of Life* (London 1963)

Chapman, Guy – *Why France Collapsed* (London 1969)

Churchill, Winston S. – *The Second World War*. Vol I: *The Gathering Storm* (London 1948), Vol II: *Their Finest Hour* (London 1949)

Colville, Sir John R. – *Man of Valour: Field Marshal Lord Gort VC* (London 1969)

Cooper, Matthew, and Lucas, James – *Panzer: The Armoured Force of the Third Reich* (London 1976)

Fest, Joachim C. – *The Face of the Third Reich* (London 1970)

Glaser, Hermann – *The Cultural Roots of National Socialism* (London 1978)

Grove, Eric – *The Mechanics of War: German Armour, Poland and France, 1939-1940* (London 1976)

Grunberger, Richard – *A Social History of the Third Reich* (London 1971)

Guderian, Gen. Heinz – *Panzer Leader* (London 1952)

Jackson, Robert – *The Fall of France, May-June 1940* (London 1975)

Liddle Hart, B.L. – *The German Generals Talk* (New York 1948)

Shirer, William L. – *Collapse of the Third Republic* (London 1970)

Weygand, Gen. Maxime – *Recalled to Service* (London 1952)

Len Deighton's excellent *Blitzkreig* came out too late (September 1979) to affect the actual writing of the story – otherwise it would certainly have had a place on my list. As it was, it proved invaluable as a source of reference during the revision of the manuscript.

I also owe a debt of gratitude to my friends Peter C. Dawson and Peter Smith, both of them ex-tankmen, who during the course of many conversations provided me with insights into the individual experience of tank warfare.

I am also indebted to my son Stephen whose knowledge of militaria of the Second World War far exceeds that possessed by those of us who lived through the period.